STROGANOFF IN THE BALLET

G000117367

CARYL BRAHMS & S. J. SIMON

Stroganoff in the Ballet

An omnibus volume comprising
A Bullet in the Ballet, Casino for Sale
&
Six Curtains for Stroganova

London
MICHAEL JOSEPH

First published in Great Britain by
MICHAEL JOSEPH LTD
52 Bedford Square
London WC1B 3EF
1975

ISBN 0 7181 1387 X

Printed in Great Britain by
Hollen Street Press Limited at Slough, Berkshire
and bound by James Burn at Esher, Surrey

STROGANOFF IN THE BALLET

When we wrote these books we made the following dedications:

A Bullet in the Ballet

*Overcome by sudden affection due to not having to
meet for the next six months, the authors
dedicate this book to one another*

Also to
HELGA, CHARLES and HAROLD
who are convinced that but for them . . .

Casino for Sale

*The authors having once again parted forever
their solicitors dedicate this book to*
DEE

Six Curtains for Stroganova

To
NINA TARAKANOVA, *Ballerina*
and
JUDY CAMPBELL, *Nightingale*

*Now that the three books are under one cover,
these dedications stand, but I would like to dedicate
the total gesture to the memory of*
S. J. SIMON *who wrote them with me and who
never failed to laugh.*

CARYL BRAHMS

A Bullet
in the Ballet

CHAPTER I

SINCE it is probable that any book flying a bullet in its title is going to produce a corpse sooner or later—here it is.

Dressed somewhat extravagantly in trousers of red and yellow check. Its white jumper is scalloped with scarlet and jade. It wears a yellow bouffon wig, a Russian clown's hat and undertaker's gloves. It is bending over the top of a booth, its arms swinging limply over the sides. There is a neat little bullet hole in the centre of its forehead.

It died magnificently in the presence of two thousand people, most of whom had paid for their seats.

Petroushka! And on this occasion none other than that famous dancer Anton Palook.

Palook had danced energetically and must have been very annoyed when that bullet robbed him of his curtain calls—six under contract. At any rate Vladimir Stroganoff, though still alive, was definitely furious. For the past two years he had jerked his company safely if hysterically through Australia, Harbin, the Gold Coast and Chicago, and here, on the opening night of his London season, they had gone and bumped off his leading dancer. It was not that he felt any particular affection for Palook, in fact privately he was inclined to think that Palook had been asking for it for years—but good Petroushkas were scarce. If it had been Ernest Smithsky now, who mimed his way so conscientiously through *Lac des Cygnes*, or that English girl with the impeccable technique and the impregnable mother, or Stanley Simpson, his indispensable secretary.

But they had picked on Anton. And *Petroushka* was in the bill again on Wednesday week. And it could not be taken out on Wednesday week for that was to be a gala performance in honour of Benois' birthday. And even though the veteran had declared that nothing would induce him to come over to see

9

Palook (he who had seen Nijinsky, Bolm, Woizikovsky!), this
had been suppressed and all society had promised to be present.

Stroganoff scowled furiously at the clustering stage hands.
"Move the body," he commanded. "*Et vite!* Take it away.
Forget it. Prepare the next scene."

Fortunately the audience had no idea of what had occurred.
The stage manager had rung down the curtain with commendable promptitude and what's more, kept it down. The more
determined of the company, unaware of the disaster, cursed
him in a variety of languages and pushed their way to the front
of the curtain. The gallery clamoured for Petroushka.
Stroganoff, with what he afterwards insisted on describing as
great presence of mind, tripped over the tassels to announce
that Palook had suddenly been taken ill. Gradually the clamour
subsided to a sympathetic murmur and the audience trickled
out into the foyer.

*   *   *   *   *

The first interval on the opening night of a ballet season is
always an animated affair. The dominant note is one of shrill
ecstasy, but the impartial observer may also discern an undercurrent of hysteria, jealousy, fashionable display, posturing,
thrusting upon and drawing back. There is a curdling of
mothers explaining why other mothers' daughters have got the
roles, a preening of other mothers accepting congratulations, a
hesitancy of fathers, an edging away of critics, all society, all
the intelligentsia and any odd dancer who can stake a claim on
the company's hospitality. And not a single strong silent man
among the lot.

To-night the hubbub was much as usual, but it was moving
definitely towards the doors and concentrating on one topic.

*   *   *   *   *

"I'm simply frantic about Anton," said a man with a flaccid
mouth. "Simply frantic, my dear. He must be frightfully ill to
miss his curtains."

"Dying, I should imagine," observed his companion drily.

A critic standing nearby endorsed the verdict. He had known Anton for eleven years, he said, and the nearest the latter had ever come to missing a curtain call was when the theatre had caught fire in Santiago and he had had to make do with three.

"A poor performance, I thought," observed a second critic, who did not feel that his august paper could in any way be concerned with what had happened after the curtain came down. "The death scene was singularly unconvincing."

"And his passion for the Doll distinctly lukewarm." said a girl who knew everybody.

"It is," announced a man who knew everything.

Outside, the stage-doorkeeper was fast losing his patience. The clamouring mob around him did not seem to understand plain English.

"No," he said for the hundred and fifth time. "You cannot see Mr. Palook."

"But he's expecting me."

"I've got an appointment."

"I always see Anton after a performance."

"I'm Petunia Patch of the *Daily Distraught* and I want to ask him . . ."

"Mr. Stroganoff said that . . ."

"The press agent told me to . . ."

"We want to know how dear Anton is . . ."

"He's dead," said the stage-doorkeeper, his patience evaporating. He regretted it immediately, as half a dozen determined critics, their copy already in the office, pushed their way past him and started fighting for his telephone.

*   *   *   *   *

But the show must go on. This is unfortunate as the next ballet is by that advanced choreographer Nevajno, and depicts Ajax laboriously wrestling with the lightning to Tschaikovsky's "1812." So though poor Anton is in his dressing-room together with a balleto-medico (who for once has found no difficulty in diagnosing the cause of death), Mr. Saintly the manager, Stroganoff and his secretary Stanley Simpson, the audience are back in their seats and the curtain has been rung up on a miscellaneous collection of rocks.

But though the critics must stay and watch, we are under no such obligation.

CHAPTER II

THE Flying Squad tourer pulled up outside the Collodium stage door, tactlessly omitting to make that fascinating noise that accompanies police cars on the screen, and with adequate rapidity disgorged its occupants. These consisted of two police photographers, a police surgeon, Detective-Sergeant Banner and Detective-Inspector Adam Quill.

Detective-Inspector Adam Quill is due to loom largely throughout this narrative, so it might be as well to pause and look at him now.

Detective-Inspector Adam Quill is a serious young man who has joined the police force as a careerist. The first thing you notice about him is his height, which is six foot three, the second his good looks, which are those of the *matinée* idol stamp, lacking only the practised profile that distinguishes the latter. Fair hair, a good-humoured mouth, large capable hands and an unemotional manner. Not supernaturally intelligent but not naturally stupid, he started life as one of Lord Trenchard's young men and has only just managed to live this down, mainly by calling everybody in sight "Sir." He is not altogether without experience, this is his second big case since his Inspectorship (in the first he arrested the wrong man) and this time he is determined to be more careful. He is not a man much given to advance speculation, but judging from the cold precise message received over the 'phone from the theatre manager, Mr. Saintly, it does not seem to him that this case will present many difficulties. From what little he knew of the stage, actors were a jumpy crowd and it should be a matter of mere routine to discover a suspect to fill the three cardinal clauses in the Detective's Handbook—"Means, Motive, Opportunity." As likely as not, he reflected, he would be greeted by some hysterical young woman already in the throes of repentance.

But he was, in fact, greeted by the stage-doorkeeper, who refused to let him in.

Fortunately Stroganoff appeared in time.

After the preliminary greetings, Quill expressed a wish to examine the scene of the crime. The request seemed to puzzle Stroganoff.

"Poor Anton," he said. "He is in his dressing-room for the last time."

Quill looked up sharply. "I thought he was shot on the stage."

"*Mais naturellement*," agreed Stroganoff. "On the roof. It was lucky," he added, "that it was the end of the ballet, so the audience they know nothing and are happy."

"Then you've moved the body?"

"*Mais naturellement*," said Stroganoff, appearing even more puzzled than before. "You cannot have a body in *Ajax* and anyway the *décor*, it is different."

"Am I to understand," asked the persevering Quill, "that you have moved the body and calmly gone on with the performance?"

"*Mais certainement*," said Stroganoff with evident self-satisfaction. "We are well-organised, yes?"

"But were you not aware," asked Quill coldly, "that in a serious matter like a shooting, nothing should be touched until the police have arrived?"

"Sure!" Stroganoff nodded so affably that Quill felt certain he had not understood a word.

"In England the police like to see everything as it was at the time of the event. And now this is no longer possible."

"*Mais oui*," beamed Stroganoff. "*Pour nous tout est possible.* All will be put back on Wednesday week."

This was too much for Quill. "Wednesday week?"

"Sure—we give *Petroushka* again then. For Benois himself. Though who shall dance Petroushka now that Anton is dead I cannot decide. Pavel Bunia, perhaps, but then maybe he is too young—no?"

"No," agreed Quill involuntarily. The patter was catching and it was Stroganoff himself who switched the conversation back to the main subject.

"But you wish to see poor Anton—yes? I will take you. He is in his dressing-room. The star's dressing-room. It was in his contract. I will give it now to Pavel, and if Rubinska's mother, she is angry—poof—that does not matter."

Accompanied by his photographers, the Police Surgeon, and Sergeant Banner—the latter reluctantly detached from his fascinated study of Ajax's defiance—Quill followed Stroganoff up the stairs into the dressing-room. This, at first sight, appeared to combine the functions of the sorting department of a post office with the salient features of the Chelsea Flower Show. There was a smother of photographs of Palook's old dancing masters, his dancing partners, his dancing pupils, the whole culminating in a large and slightly repulsive oil painting of Palook himself in the last act of *Giselle*. The dressing-table was railed off by a curtain, drawn to reveal the usual assortment of dirty towels, cold creams, mascara, rouge and false eyelashes. The golden *Sylphides* wig, due to be worn at tomorrow's performance, was already laid out awaiting the wig-groomer's attention. But readers are asked to suppress the gulps in their throats. They did not see Palook's *Sylphides*— it was horrible.

On the sofa, nonchalantly covered by a Spanish shawl (*Tricorne*), lay the body of the dancer. The fair-haired young man, who had been sitting on the chair beside it, sprang to his feet as the procession entered.

"Stanley," said Stroganoff sharply. "Why are you not in the box watching the performance for me? Go away. You must not interfere with the Inspector who has come to arrange an assassin for us."

Quill quite liked this novel angle on his duties, but as his staff seemed to be enjoying it too, he suppressed his smile and walked over to the sofa.

"Where," he enquired, "is the doctor who examined the body?"

"Gone back to see the ballet," volunteered Stanley Simpson. "Stalls—eleventh row—side. I made a point of enquiring in case you wanted him," he added with evident pride.

"Call him," said Quill.

Stroganoff was delighted to see Stanley go. He was always delighted to see Stanley go. Stanley had no vision—only a head for figures—and figures were easily the most unpleasant factor in Stroganoff's life. Sunnily he turned to the Inspector.

"You have everything—yes? Then I go to rub up my speech."

"Just a moment," said Quill. He turned to the Police-Surgeon who had by this time completed his examination.

"Perfectly straightforward," said the latter. "Shot at a range of about ten yards or over. Death instantaneous. I suppose you'll want the bullet, so let's take the body away and get on with it."

Quill nodded and the body was duly carried out, though not without a howl of protest from Stroganoff, who argued that he needed the corpse's costume for the next presentation.

By this time Quill had an uneasy feeling that the proceedings were not going to be as straightforward as he had supposed. As yet he had but the vaguest idea of the setting of the crime. He knew that it had taken place on the stage, towards the end of a ballet called *Petroushka*, and that the victim was on some sort of roof—why or how he had yet to ascertain. Palook, he understood, was an important person, which meant presumably that he had his fair quota of enemies. He had been shot in full view of the audience, but the range of the shot eliminated the further parts of the house and it seemed unlikely that anyone in the stalls or circles could pull a gun and get away with it. There remained the boxes, the orchestra, the wings and possibly the stage itself, assuming the scenic structure permitted. He would get that scene reset sometime, and before Wednesday week at that!

Manfully he set himself to discover further details. This took rather a long time for at first Stroganoff flatly refused to believe that Quill did not know *Petroushka* intimately, and when finally convinced, showed a strong tendency to take him through the ballet step by step. In this he was energetically assisted by the balleto-medico who had arrived with a heated criticism of *Ajax* on his lips and appeared only too eager to lay his forty years of ballet-going experience at the detective's feet. At the end of twenty minutes Quill began to collect a hazy impression that Palook had thoroughly deserved to be murdered if only because he was no Nijinsky.

Somehow he managed to gather that Palook had died at the moment when Petroushka dies in the ballet. He had been standing on some sort of a roof. The stage, save for some sort of a magician, was deserted, but a few minutes previously it had been overflowing with the entire cast plus a large number of extras. Palook had been standing centre stage in full view of the audience. No shot had been heard, which argued a silencer, and as the position stood, any one of about two hundred people might have done it.

"But," finished Stroganoff, "you will see for yourself what a good work it is. You lucky, lucky man—what an ecstasy there is coming to you. It is arranged then, that you come to my box on Wednesday week. And afterwards," he added as one conferring a great honour, "I introduce you to Rubinska."

"I am afraid," said Quill apologetically, "I shall have to see it before Wednesday week. In fact I would like you to re-enact the scene for me at once. Just as it was at the time of the performance, with everybody who was on the stage then, on the stage now."

"*Pardon?*" said Stroganoff, startled at last.

Quill, in a slow, clear voice, repeated his request. At the fourth time Stroganoff understood.

"*Impossible*," he said in triumph. "First there is Palook. He is dead."

"One of my men will substitute for him."

"But it is a role *bien compliqué*," protested Stroganoff. "No policeman will be able to dance it, even if he could learn quick enough."

At this point the balleto-medico, recovering his sanity, explained to Stroganoff that what Quill wanted was not so much a dancing performance as a reconstruction of the crime. He wanted to see the stage as it was at the time of the shooting.

"But my company is tired," said Stroganoff. "Come to-morrow and all shall be prepared. *Mais moi—je ne vois pas la nécessité.*"

"It is very necessary," said Quill. "And I would prefer to have it now."

"To-morrow at twelve," said Stroganoff firmly. "And even so it is a great favour I do you, for we should at that moment rehearse *Giselle*." He regarded Quill with a new ray of hope. "You would not come to *Giselle* instead—no? It is very beautiful."

But Quill was spared the embarrassment of an answer by the appearance of Stanley, who announced that *Ajax* was over and that the audience, while not exactly clamouring for Stroganoff, were nevertheless making sufficient noise to warrant his appearance before the curtain.

"I come," said Stroganoff. "I have a speech to make," he explained to Quill. "Stanley he wrote it. It is bad. I think I make another. You come and listen."

And, linking his arm affectionately through Quill's, he propelled that resistant figure down the stairs and planted him firmly in the wings. Though why, he asked himself in astonishment, he should take so much trouble over a man who had never seen *Petroushka.* . . . *Tout de même c'était un beau garçon.*

The fascinated Sergeant Banner edged his way through and ranged himself beside his superior. This was life.

*   *   *   *   *

As he listened to Stroganoff's lyrical improvisations, from which the only fact to emerge clearly was that this night was the greatest night ballet had ever known and would ever know —until Wednesday week, Quill found himself wondering uneasily where his next step in this mad world would lead him.

CHAPTER III

IT was perhaps as well that Palook could not remain alive to read his own obituaries, for he would not have been at all pleased with the manner in which these were framed. By an unfortunate coincidence Hitler had selected the day of his death to threaten the world with peace, collaring the greater part of the front pages and every first leader in the country. This left a mere double column for Palook's sensational end, and much of this had been used up by the sob-sisters with graphic descriptions of everybody's reactions to the event, except, of course, Palook's. There were also obituaries which meanly dragged up the matter of his three unsuccessful marriages, that disastrous season with Balieff, his broken contracts, and the seven times he had walked out on, and crawled back to, Stroganoff. Not an *entrechat*, not a *cabriole*, not so much as one of his six magnificent turns mentioned. Here and there came a grudging admission that his line was good, but this was invariably followed up by a slur on his elevation.

Neither did Palook fare much better on the posters. The morning papers ranged from "Mystery Death of Dancer" to "Well-known Dancer Dead," while in the sporting editions he was entirely obliterated by the gloatings of sundry racing correspondents. (Hector napped Hippopotamus. Won 7-2.)

But even though the world at large did not seem unduly perturbed by its shattering loss, in Palook's own world the reaction was highly satisfactory. Up in the classrooms of the Collodium theatre everybody was in tears. Twenty-six dancers in the *corps de ballet*, fifteen mothers, three fathers, twelve small-part dancers, six *danseuses etoile* and six ballerinas were all refusing to lend each other handkerchiefs. Two ballerinas, who, owing to Stroganoff's beaming vagueness, both claimed to be *assoluta*, were exchanging tears with the pianist, who was herself too upset to utilise the occasion to suggest a small loan. Two bright young journalists—not allowed to be bright this morning—a distraught sugar daddy, absently fondling the wrong pair of shoulders, The Only Man Who Knew About Ballet, and The Only Woman Who Flatly Disagreed With Him, had made their way early to the scene of lamentation. There was Stroganoff edging away from Stanley but bumping into Mr. Saintly, who kept asking his views on the probable box-office reactions. And finally there was Arenskaya, ex-ballerina to the Maryinsky theatre (ex-mistress to Anton Palook), director of classes to the Stroganoff ballet and sole dictator to her husband P. Puthyk. Shrivelled but arrogant she is sitting upright in a gilded chair (*Good Humoured Ladies*) presiding over the mourners. One hand is using Stanley's handkerchief to wipe her eyes, the other eluding the sympathetic pats her husband is endeavouring to administer.

"*Laisse-moi,*" she says. "I am inconsolable. I want nothing. Go and fetch my bag that in my distress I left on Stroganoff's table, my cigarettes which are in my dressing-room, and my shawl which I left at home. I am freezing."

P. Puthyk, *Premier Danseur* to the Maryinsky theatre, 1895, *maître de ballet* to every European house in somewhat convulsive rotation, and principal walker-on to the Stroganoff Company, ambled happily off. "Her shawl," he mumbled. "Her cigarettes. And something else which I will remember later."

"*Vite!*" shouted Arenskaya through force of habit.

"*Vite, moia krassavitsa,*" agreed the old man, slowing down to exchange greetings with a new member of the company who still thought he was someone important. He was not nearly so affable to Pavel Bunia who bumped into him in the doorway. That Pavel did not like women was his misfortune; that he had liked Palook no longer mattered; but that he should claim to dance *Le Train Bleu* better than Dolin—that was intolerable. The conceit of it. The impertinence. The young man must be put in his place. He, Puthyk, would do it.

"*Pardon,*" he said coldly, and scuttled off.

Pavel was not noticeably damped. He presented a languid cheek to Stroganoff and the backing Stanley, and sauntered towards Arenskaya.

"Poor Anton," he sighed. "Terrible. I assure you I did not shut my eyes all night. Little did I think when we came to London that it should be I who would dance Petroushka."

Half a dozen heads jerked up sharply at this statement, among them Kasha Ranevsky, a newcomer to the company, who had hoped vaguely that he might secure this distinction. Noticing his depression, Arenskaya beckoned him over, but not, as it transpired, to offer consolation.

"Where," she asked, "is Rubinska this morning? What have you done with her?"

Kasha protested ignorance.

"Nonsense. Bring her at once," commanded Arenskaya.

"She is a bad girl. Last night in *Petroushka* she was four beats late with her entrance. And for why?"

"Er—I'm afraid that was my fault."

"Of course it is your fault. That is what I am saying."

"You whisper in the wings," interposed Stroganoff, "and—poof—she is late. Do not do it no more." He dismissed the young man airily and bent over Arenskaya.

"*Ma belle*," he said, "presently there comes here a young man who has never seen *Petroushka*. But a good boy *quand même*. He is from the police and will catch our assassin. We must help him all we can. It is for him that we do the last act of *Petroushka* this morning."

"Why only the last act?" asked Arenskaya really hurt. "Is the rest not good enough for him?"

"It is not for the dance that he comes to see," explained Stroganoff. "It is because, because . . ." In vain he tried to remember just why it was Quill had insisted on the reconstruction. "Still that is not important. What I wish to say is that this young man will surely ask you many questions."

"The police they always ask questions," nodded Arenskaya from a vast store of mixed experience. "But this time I am not afraid. My passport it is perfect."

"You must be careful what you tell him."

"Me—I am discreet."

"Of course, darling," said Stroganoff, "but you like to talk—no? So do not tell him our secrets—that Rubinska, she is over seventeen, nor that I have not yet signed the contract with America, that I am almost obligated to Cochran to dance at the Trocadero, and that Anton want to leave us to form his own company with that man with the newspapers who takes my ballerinas out to supper and lends me money."

"Excuse me, sir," interposed Stanley, "but I think you have got the wrong idea of the sort of questions the police are likely to ask."

Stroganoff looked at him with deep annoyance.

"You can tell them if you like that Stanley will be leaving us soon."

Stanley laughed heartily in his English way at what he supposed was a joke, and continued:

"They will be more interested in the mechanics of the crime. I shall be able to give them a lot of help there. I have been working out some calculations on muzzle velocity this morning. And then, of course, they will be looking for a motive. That means they will want to probe into Anton's life, his friends, his enemies, his affairs. That is where you will be able to give them information."

"But of course," agreed Arenskaya. "Me—I will tell them how cleverly I seduce Anton ten years ago."

"Poof," said Stroganoff, "they will not be interested."

"*Mais c'était très intéressant*," protested Arenskaya. "Palook, he did not want. He *mauvais sujet*. Havelock Ellis he have chapter about it."

Stanley blushed. He could never quite get accustomed to these franknesses though he came up against them on an average of fifty times a day.

"I would suggest," he began.

"You are always suggesting," said Stroganoff. "Go away."

"It is time we start the class," agreed Arenskaya. She rose and clapped her hands imperiously.

It would be an exaggeration to say that an instantaneous silence settled on the room. In fact nobody took any notice. However, with the aid of much thumping with her stick, some energetic shooing by Stroganoff, and a bleat or so from Stanley, the handkerchiefs were at last abandoned and there was the usual scuffle as to who should lead the *barre*. The young Rubinska, who had only just entered, came off badly in the contest. She looked pale and tired as she made her way listlessly to an inconspicuous position by the mantelpiece.

"Stop," said Arenskaya to her. "You are late. But I excuse you. In fact I forgive you. You will lead the class. And you," she turned to the fat girl, who had planted herself firmly at the head of the *barre*, "go back. Right back," she added and glared defiantly at the fat girl's mother.

There are two types of teachers. The first give the class their *battements* early in the lesson, thus reducing them to pulp and leaving them no energy for the remainder; the second give their class hell all the way through, reserving *battements* as the final torture. Arenskaya belonged to either according to her mood. To-day she gazed long at the ceiling in search of inspiration while the class got peacefully through their *pliés*.

"*Battements*," she said evilly. "First *des petits* and then *des grands*."

The pianist struck a weary chord and the scufflings started.

That Palook was dead was no longer important.

*   *   *   *   *

Meanwhile Quill at his breakfast table gazed with revulsion at a plate of cold cereals and wondered why he, who faced cut-throats, blackmailers and con. men unflinchingly should lack the courage to give in his notice to Miss Treackle. In front of him was spread the accumulated data of the crime, acquired with superhuman pertinacity. He had obstinately remained in the theatre till 4 a.m., relentlessly turning down Stroganoff's suggestions of a bite of supper somewhere, and ignoring the many flattering glances that fell his way from all and sundry. He had set out on what seemed to him the fairly simple task of collecting the names and addresses of the company who had been around the stage at the time of Palook's death. But many of the company had left the theatre, and though everybody knew with whom everybody else was living, they were all very vague as to where they were doing it. On top of this there had been an undeniable tendency to regard him as an emotional outlet and also a heaven-sent ally in their private fights with Stroganoff. Altogether an exhausting evening.

Still he had made some progress. He had the cast of *Petroushka* and their addresses. The full medical report would be to hand shortly, and he was due to witness the reconstruction of the last act this morning. After that it ought to be a straightforward matter of docketing the data and sifting the evidence.

Grimly he rose to his feet, buckled on his raincoat, and strode out. An eager Sergeant Banner was waiting for him at the stage door.

"They're upstairs," said the sergeant, "little bits of things most of them."

They arrived in the classroom to find the company ranged expectantly in the centre of the room in rows, waiting while Arenskaya had it out with the pianist.

"When I say 'ta-ra-ra,'" she was screaming, "I mean 'ta-ra-ra' and not 'to-ro-ro.' You—you play 'tootle-ootle-oo' all the time. Now then once more."

The girls went miserably back to their series of predicaments, while Quill, and the slightly less fascinated Sergeant Banner, took in the practise costumes, which included many-coloured pullovers—mostly in a state of disrepair—worn over scant tunics and whatever coloured tights happened to be to hand. The hair was worn back from the ears and kept in place by nets and bandeaux. Ubiquitous thighs were encased in knitted pullovers. Feet, that looked so dainty on the stage, appeared long and bony in darned pink satin ballet shoes. Save possibly in the bosom of a mother, ecstasy is not one of the emotions that is evoked by the spectacle of a dancer working in class.

Feeling uncommonly clumsy in the face of so much precarious balance, Quill edged his way over to Stroganoff and tapped him on the shoulder.

"Go away," said Stroganoff absently. He thought it was Stanley.

But Arenskaya, catching sight of the good-looking young

man, stopped the class and came towards him with a slow but very determined gait.

"I am Arenskaya," she announced. "Meet me."

"Ah," beamed Stroganoff into whose consciousness the aura of the detective had at last penetrated. "It is our nice young man who has never seen *Petroushka*. You have slept well—no?"

"I did not close an eye," declared Arenskaya. "First there was poor Anton and then there was my husband who would keep on talking. Here he comes—the villain," she added as Puthyk came hurrying up with a cushion, a small valise and a footstool. "And this you bring—what is it? I did not ask for these things."

"Poof," said Stroganoff. "They will do just as well. And if not, we send Stanley."

He glanced incredulously at his elbow. But for once Stanley was not there. He was at the moment measuring up the stage with a foot rule thoughtfully purchased for that purpose at Woolworth's this morning.

"Never mind Stanley," said Arenskaya. "It is not him that M'sieu have come to see. It is me. He and I we have business together. We go to my dressing-room while my husband take the class."

"*Enchanté*," said Puthyk with alacrity and happily started shouting a number of muddled orders.

"He is a good teacher," smiled Arenskaya as she propelled Quill through the door. "Not as good as me, but still good. He knows my method." She threw open the door of her room. "Now we have a nice little chat while Stroganoff he go down and prepare the stage."

But Stroganoff, into whose plans the idea of a *tête-à-tête* between Quill and the loquacious Arenskaya had definitely not entered, seemed unwilling to relieve the pair of his tactful chaperonage.

"I," he began.

"You," said Arenskaya, drawing herself up and screaming,

"You are impossible. I have worked for Mordkin, Reinhardt, Ziegfeld and all, and you are more lazy than any of them. *Petroushka* yesterday was a disgust. Not only did you allow poor Anton to die, but the bear he come on like a fox terrier. Here is a young man who will see *Petroushka* for the first time, and you—are you interested? No. You care nothing. You are not an artist. Only a man of business."

Though he realised that this was intended as a crushing insult, Stroganoff felt vaguely proud. It was the first time anybody had called him a business man. Off he trotted to boast about it to Stanley.

Alone with Arenskaya, Quill began to feel more normal.

He was about to interrogate a witness, which, as every reader of detection is aware, is the groundwork of any murder case. True this particular witness was not exactly the normal type. Yet, separated from her chaotic companions, it should still be possible to handle her along the lines laid down in the Detective's Handbook.

The first rule was to put the witness at ease, but it was early evident that this would not be necessary. Already Arenskaya was seated in a chair and was waving him to another. (By rights he ought to have been asking her to sit down.) She was offering him an evil-scented cigarette. (By rights he ought to have been asking her if she cared to smoke.)

"Now," she said comfortably, "you tell me all about it."

Quill remembered the second rule: let the witness talk. This witness needed very little encouragement. Already she had expressed an admiration for the appearance of the London Police and was well on the way to expressing her lack of admiration for passport officials, who had been very unreasonable over a matter of an unnotified change of address, caused by an awful landlady, who could not make coffee, who stole her underclothes, and who still expected to be paid. Now she always stayed at an hotel—a good hotel—the Savoy she believed it was called.

Quill jerked hopelessly at the only thread that might turn the conversation into the channel he desired.

"Was Palook living at the Savoy?"

"No," said Arenskaya. "He lived with Pavel. It is disgusting that he still like men after I go to all that trouble to seduce him."

Quill pricked up his ears.

"You were in love with him?"

"Me?" said the astonished Arenskaya. "But no. We sleep a little that is all—me, I love only my husband."

"And did your husband know of this—er—liaison."

"*Pardon*," said Arenskaya. "But of course he know. Everybody know. My husband tell me himself it would be no good, but I do not listen."

But perhaps this husband was not as *complaisant* as Arenskaya made him out. Had he stumbled on a possible motive?

"And when did this happen?"

"Oh—it is now ten years. You must understand I am now old. I do not have many lovers now. But at your age it was different. I must tell you the time when the Grand Duke he . . ."

With difficulty Quill managed to ward off the reminiscence. (Rule 5. Keep the witness to the point.)

"Where," he asked firmly, "were you at the time of the murder?"

"In my box," said Arenskaya. "With Stroganoff—no, Stroganoff he leave before the end."

"Then you saw Palook die?"

"Yes, and for once he die beautifully—right in the middle of the beat."

"Did his death strike you as in any way unusual?"

"But very unusual. As a rule Palook he die two beats too late. But me, I thought it was a fluke. It was only afterwards I realise that somebody shoot him in good time."

"Who told you?"

Arenskaya reflected. "It was Rubinska, I think, yes, I am sure. She was crying when I go to her room to tell her how bad she dance, so *naturellement* I ask what is the matter. I am soft-hearted—*moi*. And she tell me that Palook was shot."

"And how did she know?"

Arenskaya shrugged. "I do not ask. Maybe she shoot him. Oo knows?"

"Would she have any reason to shoot him?"

"We Russians we do not need a reason," declared Arenskaya. "She loved him. That is plenty. And Palook, he no longer love her. That is more than too much."

Quill could almost feel the text book nodding approvingly at him.

"He had left her for another woman?"

"*Pas exactement*. But he left her."

"And you think she shot him to revenge herself?"

"I think nothing," declared Arenskaya. "Maybe she do—maybe she don't. There are others that did not like Palook. Nobody like Palook except Pavel, and even Pavel jealous of his dance. Anyway," she waved an arm, "he is dead, so let us not talk of him any more. It depresses me."

Quill too felt that he had stood all he could digest from this witness for the moment and was relieved when Stanley's eager face popped round the door to announce that the stage was ready.

CAAPTER IV

STROGANOFF was shocked to hear that Quill had never seen *Petroushka;* we feel uneasily that most of our readers will never even have heard of it. If, then, they are to go on with the story (and frankly we see no reason why they shouldn't) they must, for a clearer understanding, hear about it now. Quill has only to sit through the third act, but we must take you through all the scenes as they are danced. Anyway, it is Art.

The stage is set for a Russian Fair in the Admiralty Square, St. Petersburg, 1830. The square is flanked, to the left and right of the stage, with the curtained façades of booths. These have ample balconies, from which merry-makers wave and shout at the crowd below.

The back of the stage is almost entirely taken up by a long, low booth beyond which the snow-covered roofs of the city can be seen. When the ballet begins, bright curtains are drawn across the booth, but later they will be drawn aside to reveal the rooms that house the three puppets. Petroushka, a tradi-tional Russian clown, the Moor, his richly attired rival, and the Doll, for whose affections they compete—these are the tragic triangle than an old showman—the Charlatan, he is coldly called on the programme—has, by means of his enchant-ments, brought to life. The magician is old and swarthy—an oriental Pygmalion whose puppets have got strangely out of hand, and blames him for their misdemeanours.

When the curtain rises the stage is filled with a shifting gesticulating crowd—the boisterous merry-makers of a Russian fair-ground. The roystering on the stage is swollen and heightened by the roystering in the music. Robust and reeling bursts of sound make the icy air feel the keener to ruby cheeks and vulnerable toes and fingers, by contrast.

Maids and moujiks, women and children, coachmen, nurses, gipsies and merchants fill the booth-fringed square, drifting enquiringly about the stage, now breaking into a spurt of some traditional dance, now stopping to crowd over to some other point of interest. Then breaking up again, and again that enquiring shifting and drifting.

An organ-grinder churns out a tune from a wheezy hurdy-gurdy. It has a romantic treble and an unpunctual bass. Two street-dancers go through their routine with a practised spontaneity, and the crowd gapes. From the balcony the gipsies and their clientele throw down coins. Presently the dancers pack up. The shifting and the drifting starts all over again—until a sudden roll of drums divides the crowd and holds them agog either side of the stage.

From behind the curtains of the puppets' booth emerges Pygmalion. He pipes a wily tune on a reed, swaying to left and right as the phrases rise and fall, and eyeing the crowd between the passages like a suspicious virtuoso who has presented a rival with a complimentary stall and is now bent on making quite sure that he is still sitting in it.

The curtains of the booth are parted, and lo! three puppets loll inanimate in their separate cells. The Charlatan pipes a perky phrase—a puppet springs magically to life. Another phrase—up pops a puppet. A last perky pip-pip, and all three puppets are eyeing the musical director anxiously. The baton swoops—the puppets, the entire orchestra, and half a hundred balletomanes, who have been waiting for this moment for some seven months or more, plunge into a dance.

Sound crescendos into a stressed stridency. Rhythm quickens. The puppets burst from the cells and take the centre of the stage. Petroushka, white-faced—agonised—nimble as quicksilver. The Moor, horridly affable. The Doll, wide-eyed, scarlet-cheeked, with the fine airs of a gay lady imported to this snowy scene from the warm walls of Paris. The puppets have a child-like directness, and their jerked movements are more convincing than many a naturalistic presentation.

They dance with jerky velocity, compelled by some wild force outside themselves. A vitality born of the crashing spells of the magician. They dance until the fierce cogs of the orchestra seize up.

Comes the black-out.

Comes, as well, a curtain—extremely worn—depicting the Magician taking his ease on a number of comfortable-looking clouds, the emblems of his trade—(you want the finest spells—

we paint them). The initiate hail this faded masterpiece with an ecstatic: "Ah, *le rideau!*" The novice will no doubt fumble with an obstinate match and the obsolete programme notes.

Meanwhile, a roll of drums conducts the audience to the second scene of the ballet—a close-up of Petroushka's cell. Here he is, imprisoned in his black hell. The three dark walls are broken sharply by a white door, a shark's-tooth frieze of icy mountain crags. A picture of the Magician is painted implacably upon the wall—a constant reminder of servitude.

Petroushka is more nearly human than the other puppets, more keenly aware of the division between himself and the meanest of mankind. His arms move—but only by favour of the Magician. His heart pays homage—but in a stuffed frame. His words of love are the miserable slaverings of an idiot. His smile is a pathetic scarlet gash, slipping sideways into self-pity. In his inability to express himself, he is the most articulate figure that the Ballet knows.

While he is screaming his blame at his immediate God—the old Charlatan—the Doll enters. She advances to him on the point, calmly poised, and conscientiously devastating. But the wildness of his welcome terrifies her and "Poof—she run away," as Stroganoff told the fascinated Sergeant Banner. After her startled exit, Petroushka, in an ultimate frenzy, tears down the walls of his cell.

Again the roll of the drums, that is inserted to catch the imagination of the audience and waft it, charged with expectation, to the Moor's cell.

A luxurious apartment, this, walled richly in orange and jade and pomegranate. There is an exotic air of palm and pineapple about the place, and when the curtain rises the Moor is reclining upon a velvet divan, tossing a coconut into the air with his toes, and failing to catch it in his hands.

"But accidents, not always they can happen—though Pavel is toffee-fingers," explained Stroganoff to these receptive lobes, the sergeant's ears. And on this occasion we will take it that the Moor has successfully tossed and caught his toy.

The Moor is richly clothed. Moreover he appears to be steeped in a rather tallowy sex appeal. His name, you could swear, is Pedro.

He catches the coconut, shakes it, rolls his great eyes at it, crouches in homage before it.

Enter the Doll, a tasselled trumpet to her lips. She dances gaily round the stage while a trumpet in the orchestra emits a series of hoots and bubbles on her behalf.[1] This utterly captivates the Moor—or perhaps it is her mixture of sophistication and naïveté. Together they go clumsily through the movements of a *pas-de-deux*. Together they retire to the divan. Together they . . . but what is that shrill sworl of sound?

It is Petroushka.

The Doll faints. The Moor takes to his heels, Petroushka after him. There is a wild fight. The Moor emerges from it first, and flings Petroushka out.

And now we come to the fourth tableau—"The Tableau of Death," as Stroganoff said eerily to the goosey Sergeant Banner.

The Fair is at its height. Egged on by the heightened rhythms in the orchestra, the pink footlights, and possibly the assistant stage-manager, who has been at pains to tear up a large number of paper strips, a rich merchant descends from the balcony to scatter largesse among the merry-makers. He is accompanied by a pair of gipsies who inevitably have a sister act that they feel the urge to put across. A band of nursemaids enter. They dance in the square—one of those traditional dances that flutter with gay inadequate handkerchiefs. A bear lumbers soberly across the stage, chained to a begging-cup. Some coachmen get together. They squat on their heels and throw out their legs, and the audience shouts *"Bis! bis!"* A party of masqueraders, the giant-headed carnival revellers, whip the

---

[1] "My orchestra—it is perfect": Stroganoff.

gambols to a frenzy. Snowflakes fall softly upon the whirling crowd.

Suddenly the curtains of the puppets' booth are shaken. The shrilling of the puppets is heard. They burst from their booth in a wild death rout. The Moor strikes Petroushka with his scimitar, and, surrounded by the crowd, he dies most piteously in the snow. The crowd gather about the limp body to stare at Petroushka, "And also," Stroganoff explained, "so that Anton, he could crawl away, and the audience, they should not see him."

A watchman is sent for the Charlatan, and soon Pygmalion arrives, summoned from some nice warm tavern where he has been going over those dear old days when he used to show tame bears, instead of temperamental puppets, while the barmaid yawns and pushes across the vodka bottle.

Out in the square it is icy. He is an old man. His public are looking reproachful. They threaten him. It looks like the beginning of a Russian roughhouse. But the old man calms the crowd.

"See," he tells them, "Petroushka is only a puppet. He has no existence outside my art. See . . ." and pushing his way to the back of the crowd, he holds up a limp sawdust puppet.

The crowd laughs. In twos and threes they drift into the gathering shadows. The Charlatan is left alone on the darkening stage, trailing his sawdust puppet.

Then the wild voice of Petroushka screams out above the booth. High on the roof his spirit is seen mocking the magician, until with a last tormented writhe, it, too, collapses as limp as the puppet below in the Charlatan's horrified grasp.

* * * * *

But a ballet without an audience is like a cherry orchard after Tchekov has finished with it. The fruit hangs wearily and nobody seems to care how it tastes. The dancers are saving themselves for the evening performance. They go through their movements conscientiously, but on the flat. The scenery has a dead look because the lighting has not been adjusted. The conductor is unleashing all those nasty comments he would have liked to have made the evening before. The oboist is looking hurt, the harpist has a cold and the leader of the third violins hasn't turned up at all. Out in the house, the stalls under their dust covers stretch wearily across the auditorium like the dead waves of a white sea. It is almost a shock in the middle of this vast emptiness to see Stroganoff's amiable dome, bald and shining, and bobbing about as if it were in its own office. Beside him Arenskaya is nothing but a loud voice from a twisted shadow. Quill and the fascinated Sergeant Banner, the latter firmly planted in the front row, complete the effect. The curtain has just gone up on the noise and bustle of the last act.

"*Voilà*," said Stroganoff proudly. "Just as Benois designed it in 1910 in Paris. Even some of the costumes they are the same."

Quill nodded vaguely. He had the strained expression of a man who is trying to absorb everything at once. This was awful. Not a square inch of the stage but had its gyrating occupant, and none of them seemed to gyrate in one place for long. From the balconies gipsies waved and mouthed, handsome Russian women cavorted gaily, the crowd pushed and jostled. Now three energetic coachmen produced an inspired rough and tumble, but only to give way to Carnival figures with great heads and beaks, who leapt about the stage getting in everybody's way. Snow began to fall and the curtains of the puppet booth, running almost the length of the stage, were agitated as though by a hurricane. From them burst the affrighted Doll, the Moor, scimitar raised on high, and a wizened Petroushka ambling furiously round the stage like a bumble bee in a hurry.

"*Mon Dieu!*" Arenskaya's shrill voice almost drowned the miscellaneous noises in the orchestra. "It is my 'usband! Why?"

Stroganoff, holding her forcibly in her seat with one hand, explained with the other that this was at Puthyk's own request.

"The good old one is always asking me to allow him to dance Petroushka and to-day it cost nothing to give him that pleasure."

Meanwhile, the Moor, unable to postpone catching this rather laggard Petroushka any longer, had killed him several bars too early and had now advanced to the footlights to reason with the conductor.

"You," he said, "you never look at the stage, and if you did it would make no difference."

"You," retorted the conductor, "cannot count nine in a bar when you hear them."

The Moor burst into what sounded to Quill like Arabic. Actually it was Russian. The conductor, an unsubtle soul, called the Moor a bastard. Stanley's anxious head appeared round the wings. It was the last straw. Like a billiard ball Stroganoff shot from his seat, gathered momentum down the gangway, and grasped the conductor ungently by his hair.

"You shall not annoy many more of my dancers," he bellowed. "Through you I was estranged from poor Anton, and now you wish to lose me my Pavel. You watch your stage and you take your time from them. You hear me. And afterwards you are sacked."

"You cannot sack him," hissed Stanley in an agitated undertone. "His contract is watertight."

"Poof," said Stroganoff. "My advocate he soon alter that." He waved his arms furiously at everybody. "Now go on. Proceed. *Continuez*. I have a man here who has never seen *Petroushka* and this is the effect you show him."

Meanwhile, the dead Petroushka had risen, unseen behind the crowd that clustered in front of him, and was being helped up a ladder back stage that led to the top of the booth, where his spirit was due to appear.

"*Ostorojno!* Be careful, my darling," shouted Arenskaya who could not see him but knew well what must be happening.

"It is all right," the old man shouted back cheerfully, "I am almost up."

The ballet went on. To a quieter rhythm the stage was cleared of its multitudes till there was only the magician dragging the lifeless effigy of the stock Petroushka across the sawdust. The squeal of the oboe shot through the air, mouthing Petroushka's death agony for him. Immediately Puthyk bobbed up on the roof, waved his arms furiously at Quill, twisted his head frantically in all directions, and finally collapsed in mock death.

"Excuse me," Quill asked Stroganoff, "but did Palook move his head like that in the part?"

"Not like that," said Stroganoff, shocked. "Much better."

This was disappointing, as a twisting head meant that it would be difficult to fix the direction from which the shot had been fired with any certainty. Nevertheless, the reconstruction had served its purpose. There were not many places around the stage where the murderer could have concealed himself to fire unseen at his target. The balconies on each side of the stage were the most probable of them. They had been crowded with performers during most of the ballet and if one of them had elected to stay behind? He had better examine the balconies at closer quarters.

*   *   *   *   *

He arrived on the stage just in time to prevent the stage hands from dismantling it, and began climbing up the stairs that led to the balcony.

"What for you climb up there?" asked the interested Stroganoff. "The ballet it is finished." As Quill did not answer, he followed him, babbling excitely, up the steps to the balcony where he stumbled over a figure crouched in the shadows.

"Stanley," he said in disgust. "Go away. It is impossible," he complained to Quill, "either he follow me or else he get there first."

But Stanley was far too excited to be squashed.

"Look," he gloated and stretched out his palm dramatically.

"Poof," said Stroganoff unimpressed. "It is a button. I can find you tousands like it."

Stanley withered him with a look and passed his capture— a small pearl button that might be worn by any member of the cast—up to Quill.

"Don't you think," he pressed, "that this was dropped by the murderer?"

Quill smiled at him. He liked this youngster's enthusiasm, which joyously ignored the fact that the scene had been struck and set before the reconstruction.

"It might," he said gently, "but it might also belong to any of the dozen people that have occupied the balcony this morning."

"Shall I check up on the dresses?"

"Don't bother," said Quill. He had an idea. "Tell you what —if you really want to be helpful you might make me a list of all the people who mount this structure during the last scene."

Stanley was clearly delighted. He darted off.

"That," said Stroganoff awed, "was an idea. I will remember him."

The inspection of the balcony was soon completed. As Quill expected, the ledge offered an excellent hiding-place for a murderer. Crouched behind it a person was completely concealed from the wings and stage. He tested this for himself. (Detective's Handbook, Rule 27.)

"Can you see me?" he shouted to Banner.

"No," Banner shouted back.

"Try me from another angle."

Banner took a walk and reported that from one or two places the dim outline of Quill could just be made out.

"You are *drôle*," said Stroganoff amused. "In the performance the lighting it is different or the snow it would not show. If you stay like this down on the floor no one can see you. Anyway no one would want to look while Petroushka die."

Quill felt inclined to agree. If the murderer had indeed selected this spot, the chances were that he had remained unobserved. Probably the conditions on the balcony opposite were much the same. Still, he had better look at them.

The balconies proved to be identical.

"You have finished?" asked Stroganoff hopefully as they descended. "Then we set the stage for *Copélia*. You have seen *Copélia*—no?"

But it appeared that this unnatural person was still not satisfied. He was climbing up on to the roof where Petroushka had stood. Here Stroganoff firmly refused to accompany him. He was too old to climb up ladders, he said, and soil expensive new suits from Savile Row, which Stanley insisted on ordering, and which fitted in all the wrong places.

Quill completed his inspection alone. But beyond a few blood-stains there was nothing to learn.

"Loonch?" asked Stroganoff hungrily as he descended.

Quill excused himself. He wanted a rest from Stroganoff. He was planning a quiet hour of recuperation at a neighbouring pub.

CHAPTER V

BUT Quill was not allowed to recuperate. No sooner had he got outside the theatre than he was joined by a bowler-hatted Stanley, glancing furtively around him.

"Gave old Stroganoff the slip," he announced joyously. "You see I have one or two theories on this case you might like to hear."

Quill accepted the offer and invited him to lunch—on Scotland Yard. Not that he had much confidence in the theories, but there were several questions about the company he wanted to ask, and after all Stanley was English. He steered him to the pub.

"Now," said Stanley comfortably as the waitress departed with the order, "I realise, of course, that everybody connected with the crime is under suspicion. As I'm anxious to help you, it is necessary that I should be eliminated at once from the list. I will therefore give you my alibi."

The astute reader at this point will immediately jump to the conclusion that Stanley must be the criminal and that this ingeniousness is merely low cunning designed to mislead. Even Quill had read enough detective stories to feel vaguely suspicious. However, he merely nodded to Stanley to proceed.

"At the opening of the fourth act," said Stanley, "I was in Stroganoff's box. Presently I said something and he told me to go away. He is always telling me to go away," he added a little sadly. "So I went back stage to have a word with Shura."

"Shura who?"

"Shurra you've been troubled!" said Stanley, succumbing to the temptation. He repented his lapse instantly and became serious. "Her full name is Shura Lubova. She is one of the most promising of our younger dancers and I'm frightfully sorry for her. You see the poor chick has fallen for that bounder Pavel. It's almost a tragedy. So as I knew she was not due on till *Ajax*, I thought it would be a good moment to go to her dressing-room and offer her some advice."

"How did she take it?" asked Quill, waiving his professional duties for the fascinating picture thus conjured up. If this Shura was a younger edition of Arenskaya. . . .

But it appeared that Shura had not been in her dressing-room. Shura, in fact, had generously offered to deputise for one of the gipsy walkers-on in *Petroushka*, and Stanley had arrived in the wings in time to see her mounting the balcony.

He did not speak to her but had stationed himself where he could congratulate Rubinska on her performance when she came off the stage.

Quill consulted his programme. "That's the girl who dances the doll?"

"So you've noticed her," said Stanley delighted. "Of course you can't help noticing her. She's a wonderful person." He coughed modestly. "She's—er—my girl, you know?"

This did not tally with Arenskaya's version.

"I thought she was in love with Anton Palook?"

Stanley said that wasn't serious. Just a passing infatuation she would have got over in any case even if Anton hadn't been murdered. She was just a normal healthy English girl and, after the fascination of being admired by pseudo-celebrities, or Lesbians like Tania Ospova, had worn off, would no doubt fall into his arms. He was positive about it.

Quill hurried to agree.

"So your alibi," he suggested, "is that you were talking to Rubinska when the shot was fired?"

"Not altogether," said Stanley. "As a matter of fact she went straight past without seeing me and young Kasha Ranevsky collared her, he's hopelessly in love with her, poor devil, and they went off whispering. I didn't like to butt in, so I stayed where I was and watched Anton. Curiously enough I was just thinking what a wonderful target he made up there on the roof, when somebody shot him. Rather a coincidence—wasn't it?"

"What made you think of targets?"

"Well," Stanley hesitated, "there's no point in trying to conceal it, Inspector, as you're bound to find out sooner or later anyway—but I'm rather a dab with a revolver. As a matter of fact I practise at the Leicester shooting galleries every week."

"Oh, you do," said Quill amused. "Of course that puts you very high in the list of suspects at once." He smiled. "Now if you'd only tell me that there was nobody standing near you at the time. . . ."

"But there was," said Stanley. "The wings were full of people waiting to take their curtains. I was standing next to the stage carpenter, he's bound to remember it, and beside me were . . ." He enumerated a list of Russian names too quickly for Quill to follow. "Good Lord, if you really suspect me I can bring you . . ."

Quill hastened to reassure him. He pointed out that he had to make certain of everybody's movements and offered Stanley another drink. But by the time he had finished it, Stanley was himself again, and telling Quill proudly that while he had not actually heard the plop of the revolver, he had been one of the first persons to realise that something was wrong, and dash round to the roof. He had also, he said, told Stroganoff not to disturb anything till the police arrived, but the latter had, as usual, told him to go away. So he had accompanied the body to the dressing-room and kept guard over it till Quill had arrived.

Having thus, as he felt, firmly established his innocence he went on to offer his theories of the crime. Quill let him talk, feeling that this was as quick a way of gathering information as any other.

Stanley began by saying that the solution of every murder case lay in the concentration upon the three cardinal clauses: Means, Motive, Opportunity. Quill allowed this infringement of the Detective's Handbook to pass without protest. The means they knew—a revolver with a silencer. Routine work would establish the opportunity, and as for motive, said Stanley, he could think off-hand of a dozen persons with sufficient inducement. Despite *de mortuis nil nisi* and all that it was no use blinking the fact that the late Anton Palook had been a bit of a bounder, in fact a thoroughly nasty bit of work. He had no scruples, no sense of honour, and had never been to a public school. He was both a sex maniac and—er—a homosexual. He quarrelled with everybody and double crossed everyone.

Quill begged him to be more specific.

"Well," said Stanley. "Take Palook and Stroganoff. Stroganoff made Palook. When Stroganoff found him, Palook was a nobody. But was Palook ever grateful? No! He was always making trouble, always demanding more salary, always threatening to leave at critical moments. He did in fact leave him several times, but he always came back. Never did any good alone. But he never learnt his lesson. In fact, this is confidential of course—he had been planning to leave Stroganoff again—this time in a big way—to form his own company and take most of Stroganoff's best dancers with him. As a matter of fact old Stroganoff was quite worried about it. You see, there was a rumour that Palook had persuaded Lord Buttonhooke to back him, and with his money he would, of course, have been able to offer far higher salaries than Stroganoff could afford. So in a way Palook's death is quite a good thing for Stroganoff. Not, of course, that I think for a moment that the old boy did it."

Quill was inclined to agree, but decided to keep an open mind on the matter. It was not that he could not visualise that effervescent Russian letting off a gun at Palook, but he could not see him hitting him.

"Then," said Stanley, "there's Volti-Subito—the conductor. You saw an exhibition of his temper this morning. He and Palook were deadly enemies. They had a row after every performance and rehearsal. Of course you could put it down to artistic temperament, but it always seemed to me that there is something more behind it than that. You might probe into it. And I happen to know that Volti is a first-class shot."

Quill nodded. "Any other suspects?"

There were plenty. It was unpleasant talking about it, but there was no doubt that there was a lot of what Stanley blushingly called "unnatural sex" in the company, and that the passions it aroused seemed far stronger than that produced by its natural counterpart among ordinary healthy Englishmen.

Palook had lately started an intimacy with Pavel—the man who had kicked up that row with the conductor this morning —and the intimacy had reduced Pavel's dresser—a fellow called Serge Appelsinne—to the depths of despondency. Appelsinne was a homosexual who had been superseded by Palook in Pavel's intimacy. Since then he had been going about, muttering gloomily, speaking to nobody, and hardly being able to bring himself to look at Palook. He had even stopped watching him dance. And then there was Pavel himself, who, although a man, seemed more jealous than any woman. Palook recently had been showing some friendliness towards young Kasha Ranevsky and every time Pavel saw them together he threw a fit of hysteria and threatened to kill Palook if he were ever untrue to him. In fact they had had a furious row about it just before the fatal act. Of course, Stanley had not thought anything of it at the time and had not watched Pavel when he came off the stage after dancing the Moor. Had he known that he would find himself assisting Scotland Yard in a murder case he would, of course, have kept his eyes skinned.

Quill did not contradict this self-appointed partnership. The information he was getting was far too valuable. There remained the feminine element. Here in view of his confession, Stanley was likely to be more reticent, so Quill resolved to try to startle him into candour.

"Then," he said, "there is your girl friend—Rubinska. Palook had thrown her over."

The effect was instantaneous. Stanley sat up stiffly and glared at him.

"Absurd," he said coldly. "And anyway it's not what she told me. She said she had decided to cut him out."

"Arenskaya thinks she might be capable of it."

"Arenskaya is an ass," said Stanley firmly. "You might as well suspect Arenskaya herself or that doddering old idiot her husband."

"I do," said Quill. He was satisfied that Stanley's indignation was genuine and that whatever share Rubinska may or may not have had in the murder, there had been no collusion between the two. . . . "I suspect everybody," he explained, "and I suspect nobody for the moment. All I want is facts. Rubinska has a motive of sorts—she may have had opportunity. She was not with you at the time of the shot. I shall examine her in the course of ordinary routine, just as I must see everybody. You understand that surely."

The appeal was successful. Stanley apologised rather sheepishly for his outburst. Quill must understand that he loved the girl. Quill reassured him that he understood.

Stanley now produced a list of the players who had mounted the balcony during the fatal scene, which he assured Quill was complete, and Quill's congratulations on his efficiency in acquiring it more than sufficed to restore him to his usual mood of bright efficiency.

After Stanley had departed, Quill sat over his coffee trying to sort the miscellany of information that had been thrust upon him into some sort of order. All Stanley's statements would have to be checked, of course, but assuming his facts to be correct the situation, as recorded in his note-book, now stood as follows :

Palook had been killed by a revolver shot fired at a range of not less than ten yards, and not more than fifty yards, at the climax of the ballet when all eyes would be on the performers. The shot might have been fired from wings, orchestra pit, circles or stage boxes, but the most likely place was one of the two balconies on the left and right of stage. These were occupied by several members of the cast almost till the moment of the murder. It was possible for the murderer to linger on there after the others had left and make his descent after the final curtain when all eyes were elsewhere. Enquire whether anybody saw person or persons descending from balcony after shot was fired.

List to hand, provided by Stanley, probably not complete, of all persons entitled by the script of the ballet to mount balcony in scene. Check up list and if possible obtain evidence of time of descent of occupants.

If Palook was shot from wings, murderer would need secluded spot. Is there such a place before a final curtain? Investigate. Find out who, in the company, own revolvers.

Motive for murder. According to Stanley there is an abundance of motives. Palook appears to have been the best hated man in the company. Investigate the following:

Stroganoff. Palook was about to form rival company under auspices of Lord Buttonhooke, taking Stroganoff's best dancers. This presumably would mean ruin, therefore ample motive. Check S's movements at time. If in box, find out if in stage box.

Rubinska. Jilted by Palook. Danced doll in *Petroushka*. Found by Arenskaya shortly after murder in dressing-room, very distressed and with full knowledge of events. How did she know? Seen previously by Stanley walking away with Kasha Ranevsky, after first stage death of Petroushka.

Kasha Ranevsky. In love with Rubinska and growing intimacy with Palook (possibly assumed). Danced coachman in *Petroushka*. Seen by Stanley with Rubinska as above.

Pavel. Pervert. Danced Moor in *Petroushka*. Apparently second best hated man in company. Intimate with Palook, but objects to growing friendship between Palook and Kasha. Leaves stage after first death of Petroushka before the end of ballet. Subsequent movements unknown. Find out.

Serge Appelsinne. Dresser and intimate of Pavel. Thrown over by Pavel in favour of Palook. Furiously jealous. Movements at time of crime unknown. Enquire.

Arenskaya. Former mistress of Palook. Claims her husband did not mind. Probably correct but——

P. Puthyk. Husband of Arenskaya. Once famous dancer. Walker-on in *Petroushka* and on Stanley's list as one of the people on left-hand balcony in scene. Question on subject of wife's infidelity and try to gather real feelings.

Shura Lubova. In love with Pavel. Palook would be obstacle to bliss. Has no part in *Petroushka*, but deputised for one of walkers-on. Surely this is unusual. Observed by Stanley mounting left balcony.

Volti-Subito. Conductor. Bad terms with Palook. Motive hardly adequate, but Stanley hints may be other and better grievances. First-class shot. Opportunity to shoot unobserved unlikely, but just possible as all eyes are on stage.

On the whole Quill was fairly satisfied with the morning's work. From a vast babble of sound, the ballet world was beginning to sort itself into a number of well-tabbed cogs, and his next few steps were at any rate reasonably clear. He had to interview the people on his list and confirm and expand the information in his possession.

He called for his bill, paid it, noted the amount on his expenses sheet, and, feeling considerably fortified, walked back to the Yard.

There he learnt that the inquest on Palook was fixed for Friday. Armed with a sheaf of subpœnas he made his way back to the theatre. When this case was over, he promised himself, he would definitely give his notice to Miss Treackle.

CHAPTER VI

BACK at the theatre Quill asked for Pavel and was directed to his dressing-room. The call boy, who had escorted him, retreated a few steps and took up an expectant attitude at the end of the corridor. Quill knocked. There was no answer. Quill knocked again. Nothing happened. Quill thumped. This time the door did open, but only a few inches, and an old ballet shoe whizzed past his ear. It was neatly fielded by the call boy.

Quill began to feel dimly that his presence was not wanted. Nevertheless he knocked for the fourth time.

"In the name of the law," he tried.

It worked. The door was flung open.

"Ah, Mr. Inspector, it is nice of you to call. Why did you not say sooner it was you?" Pavel, revolting in a resplendent dressing gown, gushed a welcome. Behind him a tall bullet-headed man with slanting eyes and high cheek bones, stood in a non-committal silence. This, thought Quill, must be Serge Appelsinne, the jealous dresser.

"Make yourself comfortable," fawned Pavel. "Wiskyan-soda?"

"There is no soda," said Serge grimly, "or whisky."

"Never mind," said Pavel. "We will make you Russian tea instead. Serge—the kettle."

Quill glanced round. The room, though slightly smaller than the dressing room he had seen the previous evening, had much the same atmosphere. There were the same curtains drawn to reveal the same kind of dressing-table, loaded with the same kinds of grease paints. There were the same photographs on the wall, the same wreaths, but smaller, and the same telegrams. There was as yet no repulsive oil painting of Pavel in *Giselle*, but this, one felt, was merely a matter of time.

They drank tea while Pavel sighed over Palook's death.

"He was my best friend," he sighed. "But do not let him hear." He pointed to Appelsinne who had retreated to the wardrobe. "He is jealous—that one."

"Quite," said Quill.

"What an artist!" said Pavel. "What a dancer! His death it is a loss irreparable to the company. It is true that I shall dance Petroushka as well as he—maybe a little better—but who now shall dance the Moor?"

What would Stroganoff say to this, Quill found himself thinking? There was only one answer.

"Poof," he said experimentally.

The effect was electrical. In an instant all Pavel's amiability had departed. He leapt to his feet, livid and quivering, while Appelsinne leapt and quivered beside him.

"The Moor," said Pavel, "it is the most difficult role in the ballet."

"Every educated person knows that," said Serge.

"He is symbolic."

"He has a scene all to himself."

"And a *pas-de-deux*."

"He is subtle. He must depict passion. There is no one in the company except Pavel subtle enough to take him."

"No one," said Pavel with evident satisfaction. He bowed to Appelsinne and sat down.

Quill remembered something.

"What about Kasha Ranevsky?"

Once again Pavel leapt to his feet. Kasha, it appeared, was impossible, a clumsy elephant, no dancer, an artistic calamity, and altogether quite beyond the admittedly broad-minded pale of the Stroganoff company.

"Further," said Pavel, "it is a mistake to suppose that Palook admired him. He was only being kind, and anyway he was no judge of a dancer."

"And yet," said Quill, dropping another stone into the pool of rather savage sorrow that seemed to surround Palook's death, "I was informed that Palook was engaging him to dance leading roles in the new company under Lord Buttonhooke."

Appelsinne laughed derisively. "The new company! That is funny. Very funny. The leading roles. I do not think."

"Now that Anton is dead," explained Pavel, "it is assuredly I who will form the Ballet Buttonhooke, and Kasha will not be in the company at all."

"You think that Lord Buttonhooke will approach you?"

"*Assurément*—he approach me first and while we dispute the contract, Anton he come and offer the double cross."

"*Schwolotz*,"[1] said Appelsinne.

"'That is not kind," said Pavel, reprovingly. "He was not a *schwolotz* only a *merzavitz*.[2] Anyway he is dead and can grab no more contracts. How he grab all the good contracts that man! A genius. Only Stroganoff too much for him."

That seemed to be that. Quill offered his cigarettes, but his gaspers were scornfully waved to one side.

"I would like," said Quill, "to ask you a few questions about the time Palook died."

The two men glanced at each other.

"Alas," they said in unison, "we know nothing."

Quill assured them it was a matter of mere routine. In the case of murder he had to question everybody.

"When you left the stage yesterday," he asked Pavel, "where did you go?"

Pavel pondered. "I stand in the wings to take my curtain."

"Curtains," corrected Appelsinne.

"The left or the right wing?"

"The right."

"And did you take your curtains?"

Pavel pondered again and to Quill he seemed a little uneasy. "*Certainement*," he said at last.

"Then presumably you did not hear that Palook had been shot till later?"

"Much later," agreed Pavel.

"As a matter of form," said Quill, "did anybody see you standing in the wings?"

"*Mais oui*," said Appelsinne. "I was with him. I wait for him with the dressing-gown."

"This dressing-gown," said Pavel, proudly.

"Who else was near you?"

Neither of them could remember. There were many people

---

[1] Schwolotz—Swine.   [2] Merzavitz—Scoundrel.

in the wings at the end of *Petroushka*, but they were of no interest. Quill persisted. Surely they must have noticed somebody specific. But neither Pavel nor Appelsinne could remember. They were, they said, far too interested in each other to notice. It was an unsatisfactory statement and, as he rose to go, Quill resolved to have this alibi confirmed by independent witnesses before he accepted it.

The pair ushered him out with solicitude, but to Quill there seemed a certain amount of relief in their bearing at his departure.

*   *   *   *   *

Quill's next call was on Stroganoff. He found the latter in his office talking explosively at a pair of tortoiseshell spectacles and a large cigar.

"Ah," he broke off to beam at Quill. "The man who has never seen *Petroushka*. Meet my press agent—M'sieur Saussisson."

"Sausage," corrected the cigar wearily. "Hiram B. Sausage."

"Saussisson," said Stroganoff proudly, "he hot dog. Very hot dog. But he have no heart. Does he weep for Anton? No. 'Poof,' he says, 'it is good publicity.' He must use. And he say that we give another performance of *Petroushka* damn quick while the iron it is warm. Me I hesitate till Stanley say it is no good—the British public would not like—then I realise that Saussisson is right. So we give extra performance of *Petroushka* on Thursday, and Saussisson he make the publicity."

"Leave it to me," said Sausage. "Handled right the story will stay on the front page of every tabloid for a week." And off he went, presumably to handle it.

"Wiskyansoda?" asked Stroganoff.

But there was no whisky—only Russian tea. This Quill refused firmly. Stroganoff was sorry and poured himself out an enormous glass.

"And our assassin," he asked cosily. "You have found him—no?"

"We are doing our best," said Quill. "The inquest is on Friday." He handed Stroganoff the subpœna. Stroganoff examined this with interest.

"What is that?"

Quill explained. "It is an official enquiry into the cause of death."

"But," Stroganoff objected, "for what purpose? We know already that Anton is shot."

"In spite of that your presence will be necessary."

"*Mais, mon ami, ca ne m'amuse pas,*" said Stroganoff. "And besides this I am too busy. Every Friday morning I work with Stanley on my autobiography."

"I will buy a copy," Quill promised.

"I give you one for nothing. Signed."

"Thanks " said Quill. "But I'm afraid you must attend the inquest just the same. It won't take long and anyway they will pay you for it."

"Poof," said Stroganoff, "the money it interests me not. I am an artist. How much?"

Quill temporised and succeeded in leaving Stroganoff under the impression that he was coming into a small fortune.

"Me," he beamed affluently at Quill, "I have the theory. I tell you. To-day when I lunch I begin suddenly to think. Who, I ask myself, would want to kill Palook? Everybody, I answer. But who would want to kill him especially, I continue. Well, there is still many people. There is even myself. I do all for Palook. I make him star, I gave him best dressing-room, I lend him money, and all he say is contract, contract, contract. But me, I do not suspect myself, so I knew it must be somebody else."

Quill suppressed a smile. "I follow your reasoning," he said gravely.

"It is clear—no?" said Stroganoff delighted. "Then I ask myself—is it M'sieur Saintly? No. Arenskaya? No. Puthyk? No. Kasha, Pavel, Nevajno? No. The *corps de ballet?* No. They work too hard. Stanley—per'aps, but I think he is too stupid. He would miss. The little Rubinska? No. But the mother of Rubinska! Ah, I tell myself, here is a different colour of a cow."

"Horse," corrected Quill.

"Horse," agreed Stroganoff affably. "That mother I put nothing past her. She is awful woman—the daughter of a dog, *une femme formidable*. First she want a contract for seven years for her daughter, then she want no contract, only more money. Then she want all the best roles, and then to please her I must sack my Shura who dance so nice. Our assassin—*assurément* she is him."

"And your reasons for this view?"

"You English you always want reasons," said Stroganoff irritably. "For me it is enough that I suspect."

"But what makes you suspect?" Quill persevered. So far the story sounded like mere personal animosity, but there might be something behind it.

Stroganoff sought a sulky refuge in his tea. Then suddenly he brightened as one to whom light has been vouchsafed.

"Yesterday," he said, "she came to me before the performance and ask to borrow my revolver. She always ask for something, so I lent it her and think nothing of it."

This was altogether incredible. Quill said as much. Stroganoff persisted weakly, but eventually gave way.

"Oh, all right," he admitted cheerfully. "That I invent. But now I tell you the truth."

"And mind it is the truth," said Quill. With another man he would have delivered a severe censure on the enormity of attempting to mislead Scotland Yard, but with this particular witness it would clearly be a waste of time.

"The truth," said Stroganoff solemnly. "It is you will understand *la scandale*, so you must not repeat. You will be discreet— no?" And with many gestures he launched into the story.

"Until last year," he began, "the little Rubinska she dance the Swan Queen *comme une petite vierge*. No good. Often I tell

her so. My child, I tell her, *mais gentilment*, you must take for
yourself a lover. And I select for her many estimable young
men. But always she refuse. These English girls they are so
respectable. And then suddenly I notice she dance right. So
I enquire. And to my disgust it is Anton. Alas, I say, that is
bad. *Une mauvaise affaire*. Anton will tire soon and—poof—
off he go."

So, Stroganoff went on, he had gone to warn her mother.
Quill gathered that it had been a difficult interview. Stroganoff
in his innocence had assumed that the mother knew all about
the affair and, unaware of Palook's true character, probably
approved of it as likely to help her daughter's career. It had
taken a long time to convince the mother that her daughter was
no longer a virgin, and then she muddled the issue by insisting
upon marriage. Stroganoff had not been able to move her from
that view. If the villain would not marry her daughter, she
said, she would strangle him with her own hands.

"But she shoot him instead," said Stroganoff happily and
leant back in his chair with an air of triumph.

But this man who had never seen *Petroushka* seemed singularly hard to convince. He kept on worrying about the
mother's opportunity to fire. Was she anywhere near the stage,
he asked, which was stupid, as everybody knew that woman
was always near the stage when her daughter danced. "Other
mothers they obey, but this one never. Besides she have a part
in *Petroushka* and stand on the balcony to wave a scarf. Only
this time," he ended triumphantly, "she wave a pistol."

"Then she was on the balcony that night."

"*Mais naturellement*," said Stroganoff, "I tell you . . ."

What he was about to tell remained a mystery for at that
moment the door was flung open and a large disgruntled
tornado burst into the room. A smaller tornado followed.

The large tornado circled the room and came furiously to
rest in front of Stroganoff's desk, where it solidified into the
formidable outlines of Madame Rubinska and demanded:

"Is it correct that you have decided to give Anton's dressing-room to that man?"

"Which man?" said Stroganoff playing for time.

"Pavel," put in the small tornado who in repose appeared as a dark, tired wisp of a girl. She had the soft voice of a dancer and a dancer's large expressive eyes. Her mouth was also large, but this she inherited from her mother.

"Pavel," echoed the large tornado. "Pavel!" And the concrete walls quivered beneath the noxious syllables.

"I do not give him," said Stroganoff craftily, "I only lend him."

"That's a lie," said the tornado briskly, "and you know it. They're nailing up his mascots there now."

Stroganoff looked at Quill, and found his expression a mixture of sympathy and awe, but no admiration. It seemed to give him courage.

"All right," he said defiantly. "It is a lie. I give it to Pavel. So what you do now?"

"I'll tell you what I'll do," said the tornado. "I'll tell you what I'll do . . ." she thought furiously.

"Maybe," asked the ever-hopeful Stroganoff, "you like your contract back—no?"

"Exactly," said the tornado. "Unless that flying fish goes out of the dressing-room to-night, I go to Buttonhooke to-morrow."

"Alone?" asked the optimist.

"With my daughter. She shall not dance for you again."

"Poof!"

"Further, she shall not dance for you to-night."

This shook Stroganoff, but not nearly as badly as it shook Rubinska. It was to be her first London appearance in *Lac des Cygnes* since her celebrated deflowering, her first chance to confound the critics who last year had markedly admired nothing but her technique. And here was Momma getting impulsive again.

"Aren't we being rather hasty, Mother," she put in.

A hurt and dazed tornado flopped into an armchair. Quill felt that had she but known the expression, she would have said "*Et tu Brute.*"

"After all," continued Rubinska, "Pavel is a star and we don't want to upset him. Besides, his lifts are magnificent."

"*Epatant*," agreed Stroganoff, rallying to this unexpected ally.

"Lifts," soughed the tornado. "You have been ignored, insulted, pushed aside for the benefit of a man who looks like a lounge lizard, and dances like a policeman, and all you can do is rant about his lifts."

"They are important," said Stroganoff critically. "Not so important as elevation. . . ."

"And not so important as that matter of the dressing-room."

"A good elevation," pursued Stroganoff, wrapped in his own eloquence, "it is a quarter of the combat. The other three-quarters it is the management." He bowed tactlessly at the tornado. "A good management," he added quickly, "it is like a mother to a dancer. It pushes, it praises, and it is always by her side."

"If," said the tornado grimly, "you imagine you can flatter me into forgetting my daughter's interests for a moment, you are wrong. That dressing-room. . . ."

"We do not discuss that now," said Stroganoff magnificently, if a trifle late. "It is not important. What is important is that my company are good comrades, that we work together, that we turn over every stone, that we all one happy family—until Wednesday week. Your daughter then must dance the doll before Benois himself—if he comes. And if he do not come we do not tell the papers, so the effect it is the same. So how can you think of dressing-rooms at such moments? Besides," he added, "I just decided not to give it to anybody. I give it to our friend here to help him find our assassin." He waved a baleful hand at Quill. "He is from the police and very quick to catch assassins," he said meaningly. "Soon he will ask you many questions *bien embarrassant*."

"I will not have my daughter worried on the evening of a performance," declared the tornado glaring at Quill defiantly. "She must have calm and rest. After the show we'll have to put up with you, but not now. Come, darling."

She flounced out of her chair, easily evaded Stroganoff's gallant attempt to kiss her hand, and sailed out. The daughter followed obediently.

*   *   *   *   *

"Poof," said Stroganoff, uneasily.

"Poof," agreed Quill.

"Now that you have seen her," said Stroganoff, "you are convinced that she is the assassin—no?"

Quill regretted that he was, as yet, not persuaded and resumed the discussion that the mother had interrupted.

"You said she was on the balcony that night."

"Sure," said Stroganoff, "I see her myself."

"Then you were in the wings?"

Stroganoff shrugged. "Sometimes in the wings, sometimes in the box, sometimes I talk to the critics. Me I am everywhere."

"But where exactly were you at the time of the murder?"

Stroganoff shifted uneasily.

"Poof," he said, "that does not matter."

Quill said it did matter. Stroganoff pleaded that it was personal business and nothing to do with the crime. Quill insisted. It was merely a matter of routine, he stressed, but he had to get these things right.

Thus pressed, Stroganoff admitted reluctantly that he had been involved in some slight unpleasantness. He was in his box during the fatal act watching the performance, when suddenly he noticed someone on the right-hand balcony who had no right to be there.

"An impostor," he said indignantly. "An impersonator. So me I run to the wings, borrow the Arabian dressing-gown and climb up to catch him blue-handed. But I am too slow and when I arrive he already invisible. So I come down and then Anton is dead and I am too busy since to tick him off. But I do it now." He rang a bell. Nothing happened.

"Did you see anybody on the balcony when you were up there?" asked Quill.

"But there were many people," said Stroganoff. "Only they all coming down—but I push and look only for one man. But it is evident that he come down before I arrive."

"And this man you were looking for—who is he?"

"That," said Stroganoff, "is a matter for the Ballets Stroganoff only."

"In a case of murder it is also the business of the police. I must insist on his name."

"Me—I forget it," said Stroganoff evasively. "It is difficult to remember all these long Russian names—no?" he added hopefully.

However, Quill was not to be put off. For five minutes Stroganoff wriggled, prevaricated, dived into and was jerked back from many fascinating byways. After which time, exhausted, his memory returned. Reluctantly he yielded the name.

It was that of Pavel's dresser—Serge Appelsinne.

CHAPTER VII

IT was just after 4 p.m. that Quill left Stroganoff's office and made his way to the stage-doorkeeper's room, where instinct told him he would find his assistant, Sergeant Banner. The sergeant, he felt, could well relieve him of the next step in the case—the checking up of the contradictory statements made by Stroganoff and Serge Appelsinne. Stroganoff claimed to have seen Appelsinne on the balcony. Appelsinne's statement was that he had been standing in the wings with Pavel's dressing-gown and subsequently talked to Pavel. With the numerous witnesses available for interrogation, Quill felt that it ought not to be difficult for the sergeant to discover which of these statements was correct. If it could be proved that Appelsinne had been on that balcony—well, the latter would have to do a lot of explaining.

His instinct had not misled him. The sergeant was sitting in front of the fire, drinking tea—English tea—listening enraptured to the stage-doorkeeper's lurid, and in most cases slanderous, recollections of life behind the scenes.

" 'Noel,' I says to him, 'Noel,' I says, 'you're wasting your time,' " the latter was orating. " 'She won't look at you.' But would he listen to me?"

Quill would not have minded listening himself, but the dignity of the Yard would hardly permit it. He beckoned the reluctant sergeant outside, presented him with Stanley's list of the occupants of the balconies and gave his instructions.

"Leave it to me," said Sergeant Banner importantly. "I'll make them talk."

"They'll talk all right," smiled Quill. "Your trouble will be to make them keep to the point."

Curiously complacent at having thus neatly saddled Banner with part of his own sufferings, and pondering happily whether the reactions of the sergeant to the company would be stronger than the reactions of the company to the sergeant, Quill took a taxi to the hotel to interview the Puthyks. In spite of the exciting contradictions which Banner was now perspiringly investigating, he had no intention of neglecting any alternative avenues, however remote. Both Appelsinne and Stroganoff might turn out to be lying, but it did not follow from this that either was necessarily guilty of the murder. (To travel cautiously is better than to fall down—Detective's Handbook,

Rule 27.) To remind him of this there was the awful example
of his last case; a small matter of destruction by fire of a block
of service flats, a restaurant and bridge club, the owner of
which not only possessed a heavy overdraft, no tenants, and
an insurance policy due to lapse the following week, but had
been observed just before the outbreak, fondling a tin of
petrol. In spite of the fellow's protests that his car had run dry
some quarter of a mile away, he was arrested, only to prove
at the trial—in a defence meanly reserved—that he had been
speaking the truth and that the fire was caused by a common-
place gas leak. Subsequently he sued the police for wrongful
arrest and cleaned up a packet—all of which made things no
easier for Quill. So he was jumping to no conclusions now,
however tempting they might be.

The Puthyks occupied a double bedroom on the fifth floor.
Quill's luck was in for Arenskaya was out. Amid the wildly
congested acreage of five cabin trunks, seven hat-boxes, a
fleet of attache cases and Puthyk's cabinet, the old man
was enjoying a doze. He yawned vaguely at Quill's entry.

"We pay the bill next week," he promised and turned over.
It seemed almost a shame to disturb him, but Quill patted
him on the back and thrust his official card into his hand. It
blinked Puthyk into wakefulness. He jumped from the bed and
exuded hospitality.

"Wiskyansoda?" he asked.

But there was none.

"Cigar?"

The cabinet was empty.

Quill offered his cigarette case. Puthyk accepted happily.

Quill followed with his subpœna. The old man, not understanding, seemed delighted.

"I will make you tea," he promised. "Russian tea with
lemon." Before Quill could stop him, he had bustled to a
trunk, thrown out a dusty file, a number of ballet shoes and an
old pair of corsets, and triumphantly produced a dilapidated

kettle, a rickety spirit stove, and an evil-looking lemon. Then he busied himself with the sheer mechanics of the problem. After this Quill could not very well refuse the yellow concoction that was beamingly handed to him.

While the kettle had been boiling, Puthyk had kept up a continuous stream of babble, drifting from subject to subject, but concentrating mainly on a eulogy of his own performance in *Petroushka* that morning. The ritual of tea-drinking, however, while not reducing him to silence, at least made him pause long enough to swallow, which enabled Quill to get in his little speech about a routine interrogation.

"I understand," he said, "that you were among those that occupied the right-hand balcony during the performance."

The old man blushed and bowed his head. "It is true," he admitted. "I—Puthyk—premier ballerin of the Maryinsky, who have danced before the Tsar, the Kaiser and many presidents, and received their congratulations, now walk on to the balcony. But what would you? One must live—and they say I am too old to dance. But they are wrong," he said more loudly. "My legs are a little tired, maybe, but my technique and my *caractère*, they are still unequalled. Did I not prove it to them this morning?"

"You certainly did," Quill consoled him.

"Ah," said Puthyk sorrowfully, "you understand. You are an artist. But the others, they are not convinced. Nevertheless, I will convince them. You will see."

"Of course you will," Quill agreed. "But when you were on the balcony did you notice anybody or anything that struck you as in any way unusual?"

The old man pondered.

"I notice that Anton he dance disgusting. But that is not unusual. He always dance disgusting. When I remember the Petroushkas that have been—Nijinsky, Bolm, Woizikovsky—myself—and then Anton Palook—well—my blood it simmer like a samovar."

With some difficulty Quill managed to dislodge him from the subject of Palook's inferior technique.

"I have been informed," he said, "that you and Palook were not on the best of terms."

"It is a lie," said the old man indignantly. "We never speak to each other."

"And why was that?"

Puthyk shrugged. "*Il est peu intéressant.* He was just what you say—a conceiter. We have nothing in common."

"Your wife found him interesting."

"My wife," said Puthyk, "think as I do. She always afraid he drop the ballerina. But he only do it once—in *Aurore.* It was Durakova and the things she say to him afterwards!" The old man slapped his knee and laughed heartily at the memory. "Anton explain later that he was sozzled, but for a dancer that is no excuse."

Once again Quill felt that they were drifting from the point.

"Still," he said, "your wife thought more of him as a man than as a dancer."

"But no," he said. "It is ten years since she slept with him."

"And you have forgotten and forgiven?"

"Forgotten?" said Puthyk. "No. I never forget that."

Quill waited.

"My wife and I," said Puthyk, "we often laugh at it still. You see," he added confidentially, "Anton very bad in bed. Now when I was a young man I . . ."

Quill staunched the reminiscence just in time. He was beginning to realise that as a jealous husband Puthyk hardly came up to scratch. He turned the conversation to Puthyk's movements on the balcony, but here the old man was vagueness itself, and even showed a tendency to get huffy at what he clearly considered Quill's tactlessness in concentrating on his present lowly status as a dancer. He was just reminding Quill of his triumph in Paris, when the door opened to admit a large cabbage, a bouquet of roses, a box of Turkish delight, a portable gramophone and a shrill stream of Russian. Behind them was Arénskaya.

"Ah," she beamed at Quill. "M'sieu le detective. Wiskyan-soda?"

This was too much for Quill. He collapsed weakly in a chair.

"There is no whisky," explained Puthyk.

"Then we make him Russian tea."

"I have done so," said Puthyk with dignity.

"It matters nothing," said Arenskaya. "We make some more." She grinned wickedly at Quill. "So you come to see me already? You are, what they call, a quick worker!"

"You make the mistake," said Puthyk. "He come to see me and soon I give him my autograph."

"But no," contradicted Arenskaya, pityingly. "He does not come to see you. You just here. It is evident he come for me. He try to make the *rendezvous* this morning. So now you must go away and leave us."

Quill rose hurriedly. He could not be really certain that Arenskaya meant what she seemed to be meaning, but he was taking no chances.

"I will see you at the theatre to-night," he said and fled.

"He is in a hurry that one—no?" said Puthyk wonderingly.

* * * * *

Back to the theatre to find a purple-faced Sergeant Banner clamouring for the arrest of a young exquisite who had amiably mistaken the Sergeant's shy approach for a suggestion of quite a different character. To the pub, to repair the Sergeant's self-respect and send him back to an enquiry he threatened to abandon. Back to Earl's Court, to evade Miss Treackle and find a boiled shirt, a tepid meal, and the theatre again. Straight into Stroganoff's welcoming arms.

"You have never seen *Lac des Cygnes*—no?" beamed the latter, grasped him by the arm, planted him inescapably in his box, and told him to keep quiet.

The curtain was going up.

CHAPTER VIII

As to the presentation of *Lac des Cygnes*, there are two schools of thought.

School One presents the ballet in four irrelevant acts. In addition it supplies a fleet of cardboard ducks and trails them triumphantly across the painted waters of the back-cloth, to well-timed gasps of admiration. School Two abolishes the birds and admiration, and stops short only of abolishing the entire ballet, condensing it into a single act, which sends the unseasoned ballet-goer away with the unfortunate impression that the hero has been left alive after all.

Stroganoff, with great resource, combined both methods. He gave the ballet in one act, but inserted all the more formidable features of the other three. He reduced the pictured lake to the dimensions of a puddle, but rolled on a couple of tipsy-looking turkeys. Puthyk proudly collected these masterpieces of carpentry as they arrived in the wings and trundled them round the back, ready for despatch upon another voyage at the end of the ballet.

To-night the birds were tired and stopped half way across.

A body of pudding-faces, wearing bi-coloured leotards and Glyndebourne hats came hurrying on to the stage. The birds ignored them. The huntsmen strode about, making tallyho gestures with their wooden hunting bows and cursing the turkeys under their breath. They were led by a fair, slim dancer, alert and really interested in what he was doing. Quill recognized Kasha Ranevsky.

To them, revolting in purple and primrose, Pavel, the Prince. He paused to receive some scattered applause. Not so the conductor. Volti-Subito had no intention of allowing his " boys " to lose their places while that purple petunia stood and smirked at the gallery. He worked up a smart *accelerando* that sent the huntsmen hareing off and brought on the Swan Queen at the double. Now, however, he relented, for he liked the little Rubinska.

Dressed in the foam of a white tu-tu, a crown of brilliants upon her sleek hair, her slender legs taut, and tapering to a pink satin ballet-shoe, and all about her a shimmer of brilliants —drops of clear water that she had not shaken from her plumes—the Swan Queen preened herself. Changed by the enchantments of a wizard into a swan, she could emerge only in this hour of blue limes, white spots, surprise pinks and no amber. What the Emperor Concerto is to the pianist, what Juliet is to the actress, what the triple squeeze position is to the bridge player, is the Swan Queen to the dancer.

Rubinska's Swan Queen was more bird than ballerina. There was something very tentative about this swan. The tough and tried old Swans in the *corps de ballet* made this fledgling seem the more touching for their air of rather tired experience.

Pavel was a raddled prince. The lines of his role had, as it were, grown on him. He stalked the stage with a certain weary grace, and though, in the *pas-de-deux* that followed, his eyes were on the ballerina, his hands ready to catch and lift her, it was all a matter of habit.

To see Pavel was not, as a rule, to love him. In fact their first meeting had had the very reverse effect upon Quill. But here, in the ballet, everything was different. The Swan Queen saw him—loved him.

There follows a passage of expressive mime, in which Rubinska flaps her arms to show that she is a swan—besides she is dressed in feathers. Pavel looks sadly at his wooden bow and carefully shakes his head. Together they wander off presumably for some more of this animated conversation. On troop the swans. They run about flapping their arms and arching their necks. No doubt they mean well. Lines, never the strong point of the Ballets Stroganoff, were always at their most wavering in *Lac des Cygnes*.

"My company they are artists—they wish always to express themselves, and you cannot," explained Stroganoff urgently, "express yourself in a straight line. Arenskaya, she curses, but me I say 'Poof,' and afterwards I fine them."

At the end of the dance the swans wedge themselves neatly in the corner of the stage, while the pudding-faces wander back, and aim their wooden bows at them. To them Pavel. He was about to reason with them and beg them to spare the swans with a great deal of romantic arm work, when the insubordinate turkeys, heretofore sentient, began bucking like bronchos. Rubinska, running on to stand in front of the *corps de ballet*, protecting them with her own slim arms, bit back her laughter. This was her big chance to show all London, and her mother, what she could do with the role. She caught sight of Kasha, and took heart.

Kasha Ranevsky wore his role with a difference. Here, you felt, would one day be a Prince to match the wondering quality of Rubinska's Swan. Indeed, the ballet reached the high point of its achievement in the difficult lift in the grand *adageo* that followed, when the ballerina, having danced with her Prince, is caught, as she falls to the stage, and lies tautly across the arm of the second cavalier. Kasha looked down at Rubinska. Rubinska looked up at Kasha. Even Quill felt at that moment that something had been born.

After this the *pas-de-quatre* for the cygnets. A certain amount of hooting and tooting from Volti-Subito's "boys" heralded on the four shortest, but not necessarily youngest, members of the company.

"My orchestra, it plays well, no?" observed Stroganoff complacently.

The cygnets linked arms and began one of the most famous dances in the ballet.

"*Magnifique*," said Stroganoff.

C

But the tough appearance of the four seasoned ducks that made up the *pas-de-quatre* in the Ballets Stroganoff was altogether too much for Quill. . . . He excused himself.

"The door at the bottom of the passage," waved Stroganoff absently, wrapt in his contemplation of the stage.

In the wings the confusion was reasonable. This means that it was not so bad as it might have been, but still worse than anything that Quill had visualized. Since the entire *corps de ballet* was at this moment disporting itself on the stage, in a patch of undisciplined beauty that was at once the delight of Stroganoff and despair of Arenskaya, only the principals were in the wings. There was, of course, the usual whiskered foam of generals that surround even the minor activities of ballet. There were also several vigilant dressers, several even more vigilant mothers, several hampered stage hands, a livid stage manager and his fumble-fisted assistant. There was Arenskaya making rude remarks about the fat girl, and the fat girl's mother carefully failing to hear them. There was Puthyk, bent double over the contraption of pulleys that worked the turkeys, imperiously waving off the stage carpenter whose job it was, and Stanley, to whom anything mechanical held an irresistible appeal. There was Sergeant Banner, once again fascinated, sitting on a piece of scenery that would shortly be required, and there was Rubinska.

She was tapping a satin shoe, testing the block before the cascade of *échappés* that she was due to perform with the ease of an angel and the toes of a martyr, while beside her, on guard, stood the mother dragon, her eyes defying young Kasha Ranevsky, standing hopefully a few yards away, to come any nearer. Quill, who fancied himself as a psychologist, strolled over and congratulated her on her performance.

"It was better?" asked Rubinska. "Warmer?"

"Great," said Quill. "Even greater than your doll this morning."

"Ah, this morning, I could not dance," sighed Rubinska. "I was sad."

Quill nodded. "You were very friendly with Palook."

"I was his mistress," said Rubinska simply.

But the mother rushed in to defend her child's honour.

"Of course," she said, "they were engaged."

"That is a lie," said Rubinska wearily. "We were not engaged. In fact our affair was over, as everybody in the company has no doubt already informed the Inspector."

"Well!" gasped the mother. It was a new experience to have her daughter defying her, and one she felt curiously incapable of handling. She backed away like a defeated steam-roller. "You will find me in your dressing-room when you have recovered your senses," she snapped.

Rubinska smiled at Quill. "Poor mother, she can't get used to it." Then suddenly, as though jerked by a string, she left Quill's side and sped on to the stage.

The fascinated Sergeant Banner rose and crossed over to Quill.

"I'm getting on better," he confided. "Have all you want by the morning. An' it seems to me that most of the blokes you saw this morning was liars."

Quill was interested. "You've found out something?"

"Plenty," said the Sergeant. "But I'm not through yet. Several other people I gotter see. As a matter of fact," said the Sergeant unexpectedly, "I'm taking one of them to supper. That one." He pointed to the fat girl.

"Sergeant!" said Quill, shocked.

"It's only in the course of my duty," said Sergeant Banner solemnly. "You told me to ask questions, didn't you? And all women talk better over steak and chips." He strolled importantly away and then ruined his effect by turning round and winking.

Rubinska was back in the wings. Then she was on the stage again taking curtain after curtain. Now she was surrounded by a crowd babbling congratulations. It was some time before Quill could get at her.

"I'm having supper with Kasha," she told him in response to his request for an interview, "but if you like, you can come and talk to me in my dressing-room while I'm changing."

"Your mother?" said Quill.

"I'll get rid of mother," promised Rubinska. "I'm sick of mother."

She was as good as her word. Quill, waiting in the corridor, heard an explosion of angry sentences and then the dragon emerged, slammed the door, blasted Quill with a look, and trundled dazedly off.

Quill knocked and entered. Rubinska, at her dressing-table, looked at him mischievously.

"That's the first time I've ever stood up to mother," she confided, "and it's surprising how easy it is once you start." She paused. "Now, what is it you would like to know?"

Quill delivered his usual speech. Rubinska nodded.

"You are hoping that, as Anton's mistress, I might have something interesting to tell you. But I'm afraid you'll be disappointed. I doubt if I can tell you anything you haven't already heard from the others. And I was in my dressing-room at the time of the shot, so I didn't even see anything that might prove useful."

"Does that mean," asked Quill, "that you didn't take your curtains?" He had been revolving in the ballet world long enough by now to realize that this was almost incredible. But Rubinska nodded.

"It's unheard of, I know, but I went straight to my dressing-room after leaving the stage. Kasha Ranevsky escorted me, so he can bear me out. And then Arenskaya came and found me."

Quill remembered something "She found you crying."

"So she's told you," said Rubinska. "Yes, I was crying."

"Because Palook was dead?"

"I didn't know he was dead," said Rubinska, and for no reason that he could discover, Quill believed her. "No—I was crying because something that happened during the performance upset me. That's why I didn't stop for my curtains."

Quill smoked thoughtfully.

"I don't want to seem tactless," he said at length, "but could you tell me what it was that upset you?"

"It was nothing to do with the murder."

"Very probably not," Quill admitted. "But one never knows in these cases—and I can't afford to take any chances. Should it prove irrelevant I promise you that anything you say will be treated as strictly confidential."

"But it was nothing," said Rubinska. "Just that Anton and I had a quarrel during the performance."

"During?"

"You know the booths that house the puppets at the back of the stage. Well, my booth is next to Anton's and the walls are very thin." She swallowed. "Well—I know a girl is supposed to have her pride and all that but," she swallowed again, "it was the first time that I've found myself anything like alone with Anton for over a month—he's taken care of that—and I couldn't resist an appeal to him. I started it in the first scene and he wasn't too unkind. Not that he said anything definite but he called me *malenkaia dyrotchka*—that means 'little fool'—and that was always his favourite form of endearment."

"One moment," interposed Quill. "The booth on the other side of you, if I remember rightly, is occupied by Pavel. Do you think he could overhear your conversation?"

Rubinska actually laughed. "He could and did. But—believe it or not—I'd forgotten all about him and his jealousy until I saw his eyes in the middle of our *pas-de-deux*. The hate in them was positively terrifying. It's no wonder Arenskaya says I danced badly last night. I defy anyone to dance well with a partner they feel wants to murder them. I've heard since that Anton and Pavel had a terrific row in the interval."

"About you?"

"About me. But I didn't hear about it till much later. That's why, when I was back in the booth in the last act, I spoke to Anton again. And this time he wasn't so kind. In fact he was just beastly." And to Quill's horror and embarrassment, her eyes filled with tears.

Palook, she went on to tell him, had exploded at her first words. He had said that he was sick to death of being pestered by jealous women—or men for that matter—that when he was through he was through. An artist who lived on his emotions never went back to an old love—of either sex— and to-night he was going to accept the invitation of a society woman, who would be too scared of her reputation to make a fuss when he had tired. Couldn't Pavel and she console each other and leave him alone? And he had not bothered to lower his voice throughout—Rubinska thought he wanted to make certain that Pavel should hear him.

"But it wasn't only Pavel who heard. Kasha Ranevsky, I think, heard too, though he never said anything. But he was waiting for me when I came off and he escorted me to my dressing-room without making any comment, and left me alone to cry. He's a dear boy," added Rubinska irrelevantly.

There was just one other point to be cleared up.

"And when did you learn that Palook had been shot?"

Rubinska said it was shortly after Arenskaya had left her. Her mother had told her.

"It's curious," said Quill bluntly. "Arenskaya said you told her."

Rubinska seemed surprised. "We hardly spoke at all. She came bursting into the room, I imagine to curse me for my dancing, and found me crying. She asked me what was up, and I said, 'Anton.' And she gave a yelp and literally raced out of the room." She turned to Quill. "Do you think I looked so tragic that she thought I meant Anton was dead?"

"Anything is possible with these Russians," said Quill tactfully.

As a matter of precaution he had a few words with Arenskaya before leaving the theatre. Her version tallied with Rubinska's.

"Naturally," she said, "I know something happen to Anton when he do not take his curtains. And then I find Rubinska cry and shout his name. And I know at once that something terrible has happen. He is dead, I think, and I go to see. And was I not right?"

She also added that she had witnessed the quarrel between Pavel and Palook, but such things were *trop ordinaire* to interest her.

CHAPTER IX

A HIGHLY complacent Sergeant Banner greeted Quill on his arrival at the Yard the following morning. Listening to his exploits, Quill had to admit that this complacency was to a large extent justified. The Sergeant might not, as he proudly claimed, have solved the mystery, but his researches had certainly revealed some startling facts. His report, which he insisted on elaborating with some quite interesting but entirely irrelevant personal adventures, may, in its essentials, be summarized as follows:

Stroganoff had told the truth. Several people had seen him going up on the balcony, several people had seen him on it, and a carpenter and two members of the *corps de ballet* had noticed him coming down a few seconds before Palook was shot. Stroganoff, therefore, was not the murderer.

Appelsinne had lied. He was on the balcony, dressed in

a peasant's costume, exactly as Stroganoff had stated. Several of the cast had noticed him. However, he had descended before Stroganoff had arrived (this also was vouched for) and was standing in the wings when Palook was shot. (Vouched for again.) Therefore, he, too, was not the murderer. Nevertheless he had thought it necessary to lie to Quill. Why?

The answer, it emerged, was Pavel. Pavel and Appelsinne had provided each other with an alibi. But Pavel had not been in the wings as he claimed. He had been on the balcony. The same three witnesses who had seen Stroganoff had seen Pavel, on leaving the stage, sprint round and climb up on the balcony, arriving as the cast on the balcony were preparing to go down, and standing in the rear, near the doorway, where he could not be seen from the front. Several of the cast had noticed him in his Moor's costume as they brushed past. One of them had even noticed Pavel beckoning urgently to Appelsinne, who had come over and after a few words handed over something—they could not say what. Curiously enough no one had seen Pavel come down, though the carpenter thought he had caught a glimpse of him at the bottom of the balcony stairs and making for the curtain a few seconds after it had been rung down—that is, a few seconds after Palook had been shot. He had appeared in front of the curtain to make his bow to the audience, as he had stated. He had, however, been one of the last players to do so.

Thinking over the evidence, Quill decided that it was quite possible for Pavel to have done the murder. He had the motive—jealousy—and now it was proved that he also had the opportunity. As shown in the statement he was on the balcony at the critical moment and the time between the shot and Pavel's appearance in front of the audience was just about long enough for Pavel to leave the balcony and dash round before the curtain. This was also consistent with his rather belated appearance.

As for means, it had only to be proved that Pavel possessed, or had access to, a revolver—and the case was almost complete.

A sudden thought struck Quill. Stroganoff. Stroganoff had gone up to that balcony to look for Appelsinne. He had not found Appelsinne. But he must in that case have seen Pavel. Why had he not mentioned it? He could not have overlooked him. A lesser member Stroganoff might not have noticed—but Pavel in the Moor's make-up and costume must have leapt to the eye—especially as he had no right to be there. And Stroganoff had already amply demonstrated his capacity for spotting people who were where they had no right to be.

Quill determined to tackle Stroganoff about this and found himself wondering how the wily Russian would explain it away. That he would not be at a loss for an explanation Quill was certain.

With three liars to interview, Quill was in some doubt as to which liar to approach first. Eventually he decided that he would start with Appelsinne, if only because he seemed a little less glib than the other two. Realizing that it was essential to see Appelsinne alone, Quill arrived at the theatre at eleven o'clock, when Pavel was pretty certain to be in class. To make sure, he looked in at the practise room on his way up.

"When I say ta-ra-ra," Arenskaya was shrilling, "why do you play ti-ta-ta-tum?" The pianist snorted and banged down the loud pedal.

Everything was evidently quite normal. Quill noted Pavel in a corner doing the *barre* a favour and, satisfied, went on his way.

But a pop-eyed Stanley materialized in the corner and grasped him urgently by the arm.

"I've found something frightfully important," he panted.

"Later," said Quill, only just resisting borrowing the Stroganoff formula of "Go away."

"You'll never guess what it is," said Stanley, oblivious.

"Another button?"

"Better than that." Stanley glanced round mysteriously. "I've found it."

"What?"

"This." Stanley delved into his pockets and produced a bulky shape rolled in a handkerchief. Quill unrolled it. It was a revolver.

Quill experienced the emotion felt by the celebrated Inspector French at least a dozen times in every volume. That is to say he was delighted. He examined his capture gloatingly while Stanley stood by awaiting the applause.

It was an ordinary service revolver—of the same calibre that had killed Palook. One bullet had been fired from the chamber. It was doubtless the murderer's gun.

"Good boy," said Quill approvingly. "You remembered not to touch it."

"Well—I did touch it at first in my excitement at finding it," admitted Stanley reluctantly. "But I only touched it a little."

"And where did you find it?" asked Quill. If only he had found it in Pavel's quarters.

He had. In the waste-paper basket—of all places.

"After everybody had gone yesterday," explained Stanley, "I decided to search all the rooms."

"Why?" asked Quill. "The police searched the place pretty thoroughly on the night of the murder."

"You never know," said Stanley. "Thought I might find something useful. And didn't I?"

This was undeniable.

"I found a lot of queer things," said Stanley, blushing slightly at the recollection, "but none of them seemed relevant. And then I came to Pavel's old dressing-room. He moved to Palook's room last night, you know. Well, I said to myself, people often leave valuable evidence behind when they move."

But hardly, thought Quill, a gun with which they have committed a murder.

"Well," said Stanley, "the place was a mess. But I went over it thoroughly. And then I noticed the waste-paper basket which was full of telegrams, letters, empty tins, dead flowers and so on. So I thought I might as well look through that. And there half-way down was the revolver. And now," he finished eagerly, "I suppose you're going to arrest Pavel."

Quill laughed. "It isn't as simple as that. There is no evidence at all that it is Pavel's revolver or that he put it there. And in any case it could not have been there when the police searched. It may have been planted there later. I suppose quite a lot of people go in and out of Pavel's quarters during the day?"

"Plenty," said Stanley downcast. But soon he brightened again. "Shall I get you a list of all the people that have been in Pavel's rooms since the murder?"

Quill imagined the list would comprise the entire company, but it was as good a method of getting rid of Stanley as any other.

"Do," he said cordially.

With an important nod, Stanley went off on his task and Quill reached Pavel's dressing-room without further interruption.

Appelsinne, in his new quarters, was busily ironing a costume in which, in due course, Pavel would no doubt appear revolting. He did not look at all pleased to see Quill. He did not even offer him Russian tea.

"My master is in class," he said curtly, and went on ironing.

"Direct attack is best with sulky suspects." (Detective's Handbook, Rule 57.)

Quill came to the point at once.

"Why," he asked, "did you lie to me yesterday?"

Appelsinne regarded him warily, but said nothing.

"You told me that at the end of *Petroushka* you were waiting in the wings."

"Yes."

"With Pavel."

"Yes."

"Actually," said Quill, "you were up on the right-hand balcony wearing a peasant's costume."

"It is a lie."

"I have half a dozen people who saw you."

Appelsinne put down his iron, picked up the dress and hung it carefully in the wardrobe. Then he returned and faced Quill.

"It is true I was up there," he admitted. "What of that?"

"Only," said Quill gently, "that this is a case of murder. There may be nothing wrong in your being on the balcony, but it is very serious when you lie to me about it."

Appelsinne sulked.

"I was up there to get a better view of the dancing."

"Why did you not tell me this before?"

Appelsinne smiled. "That is simple. It is against the rules that I go up, also I had to borrow the costume, and I feared that you would tell all this to Stroganoff and then he fire me."

"But some of the company who saw you might have told Stroganoff."

"No."

"Actually, Stroganoff himself saw you."

"I know," said Appelsinne wearily. "He told me."

"But why," asked Quill, "run such risks merely for a better view of *Petroushka?*"

"It is my favourite ballet," said Appelsinne defiantly.

"I suggest," said Quill, "that you were on the balcony for an entirely different reason."

"No."

"You were up there to shoot Palook." And quite suddenly

Quill felt that he had hit on the truth. Appelsinne was furiously jealous of Palook. He had gone up on the balcony to shoot him. Stroganoff had seen him there. So had Pavel. Stroganoff had gone round to curse. Pavel, divining his intention, to stop him. Pavel had got there first, taken his gun (here was the object that was seen being passed) and sent Appelsinne away. And then Pavel, who'd just had a row with Palook, had yielded to sudden opportunity and shot him. It was all pure theory, of course, but it fitted the facts.

Appelsinne's reactions, too, confirmed it. As far as it was possible for such a swarthy skin, he had turned pale.

"No," he said.

"You were jealous of Palook."

"No. Yes. I was jealous. All the world know I am jealous." Appelsinne was rapidly losing control. "Many times I could shoot with pleasure." He recovered himself. "But nevertheless I did not shoot him. I was not on the balcony when Palook die. I was in the wings. There will be people who see me."

"That's all right," said Quill. "I never said you shot him. I know you were not on the balcony by that time. I only said you went up there to shoot him. And you admit that—don't you?"

"I admit nothing," said Appelsinne stubbornly. "Anyway, it is no crime to want to kill Palook."

"I am not accusing you of any crime," said Quill patiently. "I am only trying to get at the facts. We know," he bluffed, "that when you went up on the balcony you had a revolver with you."

It worked. "You know that?"

"We do."

"Then I deceive you no longer," said Appelsinne graciously. "It is true I went to kill Palook. But you cannot do anything to me for that."

"And what made you change your mind?"

Appelsinne shrugged. "I just change. I think—maybe Pavel come back to me anyway—so I decide to let Palook live."

"It was not," said Quill gently, "because Pavel came and stopped you?"

Appelsinne threw up his arms in despair. "You police, you know everything."

"Almost everything," corrected Quill. "So much, that you cannot help yourself or Pavel by hiding anything now. We are bound to find out anyway and it will be better if you tell us yourself."

Appelsinne hesitated. "You suspect Pavel?"

"We suspect nobody," said Quill. "All we want is facts. If Pavel is guilty your silence will not help. If he is innocent you will only harm him by not speaking."

Appelsinne considered again. "All right," he said, "I tell you everything. But remember that Pavel did not do it."

Gradually the story emerged. It was identical with Quill's theory. Pavel, dancing on the stage, had noticed Appelsinne on the roof. Appelsinne had often told Pavel that he would kill his rival and Pavel, seeing him on the balcony, had guessed his intention. Immediately on his exit, when Petroushka lay dead on the stage, Pavel had dashed round and standing on the balcony had called Appelsinne over. He had taken away the gun and ordered him down. Which was just as well, said Appelsinne, for no sooner was he down than he saw Stroganoff hurrying up. Another moment and he'd have been caught and in the heat of the moment that would have meant the sack. As it was, forty-eight hours later, Stroganoff had cooled down sufficiently to let him off with a fine.

"So you see," he added, "I did not do it. And Pavel did not do it either, for he has to come down quick to take his curtains."

Quill nodded. "We have witnesses that he took his curtains."

"Ah," said Appelsinne relieved.

Quill noted the relief with satisfaction. He did not want Appelsinne to know how gravely Pavel was suspected until the case against him was almost complete. And it was almost complete. He handed Appelsinne both his own and Pavel's subpœnas to the inquest to-morrow and carefully explained their meaning. Appelsinne nodded gravely. He was the first man in the company who did not seem to regard the summons as a privileged invitation to a special form of entertainment.

The matter disposed of, Quill returned to his cross-examination.

"By the way," he said almost casually, "has Pavel still got the revolver?"

"Most certainly."

"May I see it?"

"But why not?" Appelsinne produced a dressing-case, unlocked it and passed over a neat, little silver-plated gun. It was obvious that this had not been fired for some time. It meant nothing of course, one way or another—Pavel might easily have had two revolvers, but Quill pretended to be satisfied.

"Not been fired I notice."

"Naturally," said Appelsinne. "I tell you we did not do it."

"Is this the only revolver your master possesses?"

"That is so," Appelsinne nodded. "He buy bigger revolver the last time we were in London, but it got lost long ago."

This being as satisfactory as anything he was likely to hear, there was no need to prolong the interview. Quill thanked Appelsinne for his information and turned to leave.

"Please," said Appelsinne suddenly. "You do me a favour?"

"Yes?"

"You do not speak to my master of this to-day."

Quill had had no intention of approaching Pavel until, and if the time came for his arrest, but this request was so unexpected that he pretended reluctance.

"I say nothing to him myself," said Appelsinne, "and please you say nothing, too, to-day. You see," he explained, "my master must dance *Petroushka* to-night and the audience will be critical. He must dance his best. And if he knows he has been suspect—it will upset him—he will be excited. And that is bad for dancing. So please you say nothing till after the programme."

This suited Quill's plans beautifully. He pretended to hesitate and then consented. Appelsinne shook him warmly by the hand.

For no reason at all Quill suddenly felt a cad.

CHAPTER X

QUILL lunched alone. The revolver Stanley had found was at Scotland Yard, with one of those experts that can hang you on a scratch, bending double over it. Another sleuth, armed with Pavel's photographs, was visiting the gunsmith's where the revolver had been purchased. Stanley was in his seventh heaven, frightfully busy, checking irrelevant details of quite three-quarters of the company. Arenskaya had been shaken off and Stroganoff had shown no signs of wanting to come. Quill enjoyed his momentary solitude. His mind was almost made up. If the revolver should prove to be the one that killed Palook and its owner identified as Pavel, he would risk its unusual repository and arrest Pavel. After all, an overflowing waste-paper basket was not such a bad hiding place; as a rule the contents would be transferred to the dustbin in one vast heave. Pavel mig. t thus have relied on the revolver getting carried away with the other refuse.

It was not very satisfactory but the rest of the evidence was very strong.

However, he still had to find out why Stroganoff had omitted to tell him that he had seen Pavel on the balcony.

So that afternoon he made his way back to the Collodium and found it in the throes of an audition.

*   *   *   *   *

There are two sorts of audition. The more remunerative is presided over by a large cigar, beaming approvingly at every blonde head that bobs beseechingly at it, noting—why, nobody has yet discovered—the names and addresses of hard-working brunettes, refreshing itself distastefully from a large glass of water, and reminding everybody in sight that it has been in the business for twenty years. The other kind of audition is a test of dancing.

The Ballets Stroganoff as usual had its own variant. Arenskaya stood at the side of the stage frightening the girls out of their wits, while Stroganoff sat importantly in the centre chair and promptly turned down anybody of whom Stanley approved. This method, as a rough working rule, was sound enough.

The present audition was held to engage dancers for his winter season at the Casino de la Bazouche. To Stroganoff's continued amazement, few dancers who had survived a season at la Bazouche ever expressed the desire to go through another. Always he had to bribe—some with offers of small parts, others with infinitesimal rises in salary—and still many departed always, and always he had to search for fresh talent. The search was always arduous.

He glared his disgust at a girl from Streatham who was doing her best to register Spanish Passion.

"Your address," he said. "Your name," he added as an afterthought.

He sat engulfed in a sea of gloom, wearily submitting to a Russian Gipsy, a Columbine, a fiendish Tarantella (with not a bell missing from its conscientious tambourine) and even withstood a classical soloist, aloof in pale pink. But at the trickle of certain well-known limpid notes from the piano, he stirred ominously. Soon his worst fears were realized. Came a pair of threshing arms, a wobbling *pas-de-bourrée*, the whole surmounted by a tufted ballet frock.

"*Non!*" groaned Stroganoff. "*Non. Assez de Pavlova. Arretez! Arretez tout de suite!* Go away." He flapped his irate hands at the terrified swan. "Get you out. You shall not even leave your address."

"I go now," he said to Arenskaya. "I have suffered enough. You finish—and send to me the girls that are least bad. I arrange the contracts. Goodbye." He waved an escaping hand and disappeared quickly. Quill followed and caught up with him outside his office.

"Go away," said Stroganoff, not too hopefully. "I am in conference with myself."

"Shan't keep you a moment," said Quill easily and followed him in. Stroganoff with Russian resignation accepted his entry.

"Wiskyansoda," he murmured absently.

"There isn't any," said the experienced Quill.

"No," said Stroganoff. "All right—then we have Russian tea." He pressed a bell. Nothing happened.

"Please don't trouble," Quill assured him. "I don't want any."

"But *moi*—I want it," said Stroganoff. "I want it very much." He put his finger on the bell-push and kept it there for fully half a minute.

"Poof," he said suddenly, "I remember now—it is out of order. *N'importe*—we use the telephone."

Quill waited patiently while he wrestled with the obnoxious instrument.

"I want," he enunciated carefully, "three spoonfuls of the best Souchon. You will add *des citrons* cut *mais très mince*—some sugar—*de l'eau bien bouillante* and . . ."

"Russian tea," said a curt voice. "Oke!"

This weighty matter satisfactorily settled, Stroganoff sank back in his chair and beamed at Quill. He was himself again.

"Good mornings," he said. "You have come to thank me for my *Lac des Cygnes*, no? All right—I listen while you tell me how much you like."

"I'm afraid," said Quill, "I'm here to investigate Palook's death."

"Still?" said Stroganoff, astonished. "Me—I hardly recall it. It is regrettable," he conceded, "but the ballet it must go on."

"You told me yesterday," said Quill, "that you went up on the balcony in the last act."

Stroganoff pondered. "Doubtless you are right," he agreed, "but me I do not remember."

Quill jogged his memory. "You had seen Appelsinne up there."

"Ah, *oui*," said Stroganoff. "I recollect now. I see him. And yesterday I fine him five hundred francs. But alas! I owe him three *mille*, so it do not help me mooch."

"When you reached the balcony, Appelsinne had already left it?"

"He was lucky. Otherwise—maybe I lose the temper and then I am terrible."

"Who was on the balcony when you arrived?"

Any doubts that Quill felt that Stroganoff might not have seen Pavel up there, vanished with the question. It took the impresario fully two seconds to answer and then he said that he did not remember.

"But you remember seeing Appelsinne from the front?"
"*Oui*."

"And you remember going up on the balcony?"
"*Certainement*."

"And Appelsinne was not there?"
"*Non*."

"But who was there?"

"Me," said Stroganoff cleverly.

"And who else?"

There was a knock at the door.

"Ah," said Stroganoff, "the tea."

But it was Stanley. For the first time in this record Stroganoff was pleased to see him.

"Ah," he beamed, "I give you now to Stanley. Stanley he very clever boy. He show you everything. Good-bye."

Quill could deal with that easily. He winked at Stanley.

"Go away," he said. And Stanley, delighted, made stealthily for the door.

"Now," he turned back to his task grimly, "will you tell me who you saw on the balcony?"

"*Mais, personne.*"

"Then I will tell you."

Stroganoff crumpled—but only slightly.

"If you know," he said defiantly, "why you ask?"

There was a knock at the door.

"Ah," said Stroganoff, "the tea."

But it was Puthyk, come to complain that Pavel was dancing Petroushka that night.

"When I dance Petroushka so magnificent yesterday," he explained, "I say to myself—I am superb. Surely our wise director, Stroganoff, will now see that I must dance the part. But you are still blind. You have give him to Pavel, who dance even worse than Anton."

To Quill's surprise Stroganoff did not seem annoyed. With extraordinary gentleness he put an arm round the old man's shoulders, led him to the door, and pushed him out in Russian.

"That one—he was a great dancer, a great artist," he began hopefully. "If you like I tell you his history."

But even as Quill tried to prevent the launching, the door opened again.

The new arrival was well built but not well dressed. He

had magnificent shoulders and a yellow polo sweater, the physique of a Greek god and old flannel trousers, the pale cast of thought of a Gielgud, with the beaming spiritual spectacles of a J. B. Priestley, a shock of black hair and one sock coming down. He was already talking.

"I have been inspired with the most colossal idea that ever happened to anybody," he announced to the unintroduced Quill.

"Come in and propound it," said Stroganoff gratefully. "Sit down. Have a cigarette. You are not in a hurry—no?"

The intellectual relaxing, slightly dazed, into an arm-chair, remarked that he was in no hurry at all.

"I present you," burbled Stroganoff, "to M'sieu Quill. He is a great lover of the ballet and also a policeman. For you M'sieu Quill," he said in ringing tones, "you have the pleasure to meet the choreographer of the future—Nicholas Nevajno— whose work you must learn to love though—alas! it take time and much money. We will now listen to his new idea."

"It is superb," said the choreographer of the future, modestly. "I tell you. But first you schange me small scheque?"

"No," said Stroganoff.

"Olright," said Nevajno, not noticeably disappointed, "I still tell you. This morning I find a paper in the bus so I read it. It was a long journey," he explained apologetically, "and I had no book. And I notice that the red shirts they are angry—and the black shirts they are angry too. The brown shirts they are making speeches, the yellow shirts, they are insulted, and the green shirts, they may not wear it. All the nations, all the politics, all the armies—it is shirts. Very well, I decide, we will make the symbolic ballet with many shirts."

"How many shirts?" asked Stroganoff apprehensively.

"Not many," said Nevajno. "Say—four dozen."

"Two dozen," bartered Stroganoff. "Silk—it is expensive."

"These, they will not be in silk," said Nevajno grandly.

"Silk is not modern. They shall be of aluminium. That is settled. The first scene," he went on, "it is New York in a hundred years. The skyscrapers, they are twice as high. We have one on the back-cloth. The setting it is constructivist. Upstairs a big aeroplane with machine gun. Downstairs a prison. That, too, is symbolic. Then we see the Dictator in orange shirt."

"Pavel," said Stroganoff.

"It is possible. He dance an oration to the *corps de ballet*, who wear the bandages round the mouth. That, too, is symbolic. The next scene . . ."

"Another scene," said Stroganoff. "You ruin me!"

"*Mais oui*," Nevajno was not at all put out. "There will be seven scenes and an apotheosis. Each shall have its shirt and a back-cloth that is unique."

Stroganoff groaned.

"All the best composers they shall write the score. Stravinsky, Ravel, Prokofiev, Honegger, Poulenc and maybe Constant Lambert. Picasso shall do the *décor* and Peter Arno the *rideau*. Never will the world see a ballet like it."

"Never shall they see it," agreed Stroganoff, recovering his senses.

"But it is colossal."

"It ruin me."

There was a pause.

"Olright," said Nevajno. He did not seem unduly downcast by the repudiation of his child. Almost one might have said he had expected it. "In that case, I ask you a favour. Now that you save the expense of production—you schange me small scheque till Wednesday?"

"No."

"Olright," said Nevajno philosophically. He turned to Quill. "Per'aps you schange it?"

"No," said Quill.

"Olright," said Nevajno—and went.

"That one," said the ever-hopeful Stroganoff, "is a great artist, too. If you like I tell you his story."

But Quill had had quite enough of this.

"On the contrary," he said, "you will tell me that you saw Pavel on the balcony."

Stroganoff leapt to his histrionic feet. "The scoundrel—he was there? Then I fine him too. I cannot think," he added, "how I come to overlook him."

"Neither can I," said Quill, "particularly as he was in the Moor's make-up."

"The balcony it was dark."

"On the contrary, it was well lit."

"I did not have my glasses."

"I have never seen you use them yet."

"I was looking at the conductor."

"Have a heart," said Quill. "There is no point in keeping this up. You will save us both time if you admit that you saw Pavel on the balcony. You are not even helping Pavel by lying. I have several witnesses who saw him up there."

Stroganoff abandoned his amateur theatricals and looked annoyed.

"Inspective Detector," he snapped, "you should have tell me this before. Then I not try to lead you round the gooseberry bush."

"It was not a very wise thing to attempt anyway," said Quill. Somehow he could never get cross with this man. "Why did you try it?"

"But it is simple," said Stroganoff. "If I tell you that I see Pavel on the balcony with a gun, you think that Pavel shoot Anton and then, maybe, you arrest him—no? And who then shall dance *Petroushka* on Wednesday week before Benois himself—if he come? You say, poof! that is not important. You are the policeman. All you desire is someone to hang. But me, I am an artist and business man. And if Pavel cannot dance there is none to take his place."

"But if Pavel murdered Palook?"

"What does it matter to me who killed Anton?" asked Stroganoff not unreasonably. "He is dead and we must find other dancer for *Petroushka*. And that is Pavel. So we cannot afford that the police they interfere. I tell Saussisson that I see Pavel on balcony," he confided, "and he tell me to guard my hair. So I decide I tell nothing till Wednesday week. After that, I say, I hide nothing no longer. Even though it mean I have to find new dancer, I tell police everything."

Expressed like that, Quill felt that this was really rather handsome of him.

"But," said Stroganoff, "you find out and everything is lost. Please," he looked at Quill appealingly, "you do me favour—no? You do not arrest Pavel till after Wednesday week?"

"It is not yet certain that we shall arrest him at all," said Quill, "and if you are wise you will not mention the matter to Pavel. It might," he added cunningly, "upset his dancing."

To this Stroganoff nodded judiciously.

"You are right, *mon cher*," he agreed. "He is not as calm as I."

*   *   *   *   *

At the Yard, Quill was informed that his chief wanted to see him. Quill was not amused. His chief, he thought, ought to have been a ballet critic, for he had now reached the enviable position from which he had nothing to do but criticize the efforts of others. This duty he performed with the detachment of a Constant Lambert and the invective of a James Agate—though unfortunately not in French. Still, thought Quill, even his chief could not grumble at an arrest within forty-eight hours. That is, if he could make the arrest.

He interviewed the gun expert who produced a series of photographic plates, all of them identical to the casual eye, which, he assured Quill, proved conclusively that the revolver Stanley had found was the one that killed Palook. So far so good.

Better still, the sleuth who had been to the gunsmith returned with the news that the gunsmith—an awfully decent fellow who had only missed the sleuth at Marlborough by some fifteen years—had picked out Pavel immediately from the bunch of photographs handed to him. His books recorded that the revolver had been sold two years ago, the exact date being August 17, 1935. He recalled the transaction distinctly as the purchasers were not the sort of clients who generally came to his shop—or indeed, ever. Pavel had been accompanied by an amiable bald-headed gentleman who said "Poof" and would try to test the gun before they reached the shooting gallery. The latter had also been fascinated by an old cannon which he had tried his hardest to persuade the gunsmith to fire, promising to buy it—by instalments—if he liked the noise.

Fortified with this information, which he felt clinched the case, Quill entered the chief's sanctum hopefully.

"Sit down," said a cold voice behind the desk. It did not say "wiskyansoda." It did not enquire "you have slept well —no?" But at least it did not expect him to drink Russian tea.

"I've been reading over your scanty reports," said the Snarl, "and it seems to me that it ought to be a fairly simple case. And I almost envy you working amid that fascinating background. It reminds me," said the Snarl, suddenly human, "of the St. Petersburg pearls case, when I took the divine Arenskaya out to supper."

"Who?" said Quill, startled.

"It was before your time," said the Snarl condescendingly. "She was a famous dancer and, very, very beautiful. Mind you, she had a will of her own."

"She still has," said Quill.

"So beautiful," went on the Snarl, oblivious, "that I could

not find it in my heart to be cross with her when the stolen pearls turned out to be a stunt for the papers—the first of its kind, I believe. Ah, she was beautiful, beautiful," he sighed. "And what is more, she like me."

"She likes me too," said Quill. "But alas, she is no longer so beautiful. She's with the Stroganoff company now," he explained.

The Snarl was suddenly interested. It had half a mind to run down to the theatre and renew old acquaintances.

"They are giving *Petroushka* to-night," said Quill. "You have seen *Petroushka*—no?"

The Snarl looked startled. It was not customary for its subordinates to use such curious English.

"Not for ages," it admitted boyishly. "Book me two seats for to-night. No—one seat," it amended.

Quill, who by this time had lost all sense of caution, asked if he should ring up a florist as well. But this, though clearly a good idea, savoured too much of levity to please the Snarl. It scribbled a hasty memo and returned to its official displeasure.

"What have you to report—if anything?"

"Sir," said Quill, "I would like to apply for a warrant for the arrest of Pavel Bunia of the Stroganoff company. . . ."

*   *   *   *   *

"*Mais, mon cher,*" said Stroganoff for the fifteenth time. "*Soyez raisonable.* There is no one else to dance Petroushka."

"Very sorry," said Quill for the sixteenth time.

Stroganoff was in despair. He paced the office like a fogbound captain on an uninsured deck, waving his arms and letting his Russian tea get cold on the table. You felt that if he'd had any hair, he'd have been tearing it.

"But you promise me that you do not make the arrest till after Wednesday week!"

"Sorry," said Quill.

"And now you will not even wait till after the performance to-night."

"Sorry," said Quill.

"The tickets they are sold, the dancers they are ready, the audience it comes dam' quick and—poof—there is no *Petroushka*."

"Sorry."

"I have to return all the moneys and again I am broke. You do not wish that—no?"

"Sorry," said Quill inexorably.

"But," said Stroganoff, trying a different tack, "what for you is the difference? You wish to arrest Pavel now—I consent that you arrest him at *minuit moins quart*, so now we are agreed. Let us," he suggested, "forget our quarrel. Wiskyansoda?"

"There isn't any," said Quill.

"*Mais, si*," said Stroganoff, opening and shutting drawers with an air of an absent-minded conjurer who has forgotten where he put the vanished lady. "*Voilà!*" Proudly he deposited a bottle on the table.

"Say why?" he said, squirting the soda experimentally.

"I'm sorry," said Quill, "but your request is impossible. It is entirely without precedent to postpone an arrest for the sake of a performance."

"It is entirely without precedent," retorted Stroganoff with dignity, "to take away a Petroushka before he even start."

"Sorry."

"You refuse."

"I refuse."

"You are frighten that he escape. But that," said Stroganoff, "is stupid. *Imbécile*. He is on stage all the time—he will not go till he take his curtains and when he come off—poof—you catch him. That is agreed then? But," and fresh despair overcame him, "who shall dance *Petroushka* on Wednesday week, I really cannot think."

Quill began to feel sorry for the old boy. After all, he reasoned, what did it really matter if he postponed the arrest. And he was certainly likely to get Pavel away with less fuss and trouble if he waited till after the performance.

"All right," he said, "I agree. After the performance."

In his relief Stroganoff drank the whisky and soda.

CHAPTER XI

As usual, that uncanny psychologist Hiram B. Sausage, had been right. The Great British Public did not, as Stanley prophesied, refuse to stand for a second performance of *Petroushka* so close on the heels of the tragedy. Indeed, they stood for hours, in talkative serried ranks. By eight-fifteen the house was almost packed. There was a curdling of mothers, a hesitancy of fathers, an edging away of critics, all society, all the intelligentsia—but we dealt with this in the opening chapter. The only notable addition this evening was Quill's chief, the Snarl, miraculously transformed into a blush behind a bunch of orchids.

"Ah," shrilled a voice, as he puffed his way laboriously across the foyer, "it is my ol' friend Jellybags."

It was Arenskaya, resplendent in a Spanish shawl (*Good Humoured Ladies*), a Russian tiara (*Oiseau de Feu*), and an ostrich egg pearl necklace (*Scheherazade*), and a red silk evening dress (her own). The Snarl blushed deeper and, old Continental memories stirring, bent gallantly to kiss her hand. It only just managed it.

"You 'ave got fat," said Arenskaya frankly.

"You, Madame, are more fascinating than ever," announced the Snarl, getting into its stride and presenting the orchids with a portly flourish. Arenskaya pounced on them with shrill cries of ecstasy.

Her pleasure gratified the blush. It was not so gratified, however, to observe Quill standing a few yards away and looking every bit as pleased. It became definitely annoyed when Arenskaya beckoned Quill over, and it was the last straw when she introduced them.

"This," she said proudly, "is M'sieur Jellybags. His other name I forget."

"I know it," said Quill.

"He and I were very great friends," began Arenskaya with unusual delicacy. "But that long time ago. I do not think he so good in bed now," she finished, making up for it.

"Not at all," declared the blush, too confused to know exactly what it was it wanted to deny.

Quill could not remember when he had last enjoyed himself so much. Gallantly he resisted the temptation of digging his chief in the ribs and calling him a gay old dog.

"Well, well," he said jovially, "I must not intrude on this providential reunion," and he bolted, blissfully unaware that by so doing, he missed overhearing what must surely have been the most unusual invitation ever handed out to an elderly Scotland Yard official.

"Next autumn," said Arenskaya, "I am forty-one."

At this outrageous statement the blush was almost transformed back to the Official Snarl with a passion for facts and an uncomfortable memory for figures, but it stopped itself just in time.

"Impossible," it said ambiguously.

"*Pas de blague,*" said Arenskaya delighted. "It is true. And to celebrate it I give a little dinner in Vienna. *Trente deux couverts.* The only woman there, it is me, and the only men it is my lovers. My 'usband he preside. You make me the compliment of coming? You are the favourite of all my lovers." She took his acceptance for granted and linked her arm fondly through his. "And now you come with me to my box and you will see that no ballerina to-day can dance like I dance once."

The Snarl came quietly.

*　　*　　*　　*　　*

Already the house lights were fading. The curtains, thick folded shadows, veiled the stage. Soon the opening chords of a Chopin Prelude filled the theatre with a sweet sad nostalgia.

"'Ush," said Arenskaya unnecessarily. The Snarl looked hurt.

The shadows parted gently to reveal a group of Sylphs in a moonlit glade. Wearing the long white ballet skirts of a Taglioni, her small brittle wings, stood Rubinska, her *corps de ballet* grouped lovingly around her, and to the sound of the Nocturne the old print stirred to life.

Les Sylphides is a ballet of mood rather than of movement. It is the visible animation of a sigh. Its dances are the coveted prizes of the company. By her *Sylphides* shall ye know her, can be said of the Ballerina.

The lovely line of the *arabesque*, the aerial flight of the *jeté*, the perpetual surprise of the *developpé*—lightness, neatness, and a sense of abstract role, all are called for in *Les Sylphides*.

With the first bars of the Nocturne, the group dissolves into two lines. Now the first line is moving deftly forward on the point. Now they kneel. Now the second line advances on the point between the kneeling figures. Now they crystallize into groups once more.

Soon Kasha will be dancing with his two ballerinas, Rubinska, dark and brilliant, and Lubova, with a divine *developpé*, and the determined air of an Elizabeth Bergner sharing a close-up with a Marlene Dietrich.

"Lovely, lovely," sighed the Snarl.

"In *Les Sylphides*," said Arenskaya, "all that matters is the make-up—*mais Giselle, c'est autre chose*. I remember when I dance 'er at the Maryinsky. . . ."

But the Snarl's eyes were on the stage where the Girl with the Impeccable Technique and the Implacable Mother was studiously putting over the first valse.

And since this seems as good a moment as any, let us look at her by no means unique career.

The Girl with the Impeccable Technique is first to be seen, aged about five, an anxious expression surmounting an unsteady pose in the window of the local photographer. By the time she is ten she will have won every competition in sight.

So far nothing has been called for from The Implacable Mother, save possibly an enigmatic expression, and the modest disclaimer, "Anna always wins." This basilisk gaze is, however, merely the portent of the calm before the storm. Some pretty strenuous years lie ahead of Momma.

Soon Anna finds herself being ferried from one expostulating management to the other, leaving a trail of broken contracts in her wake. She is levered from the *corps de ballet*, trailed through *demi-caractère*, and hoisted into a species of *Matinée* performance Ballerinadom. She has been with Stroganoff for seven weeks, and already Momma is getting a little restive.

And so by this time is the audience, for, though her background is the tranced *corps de ballet*, and though her dancing is meticulously neat, her points twin rocks that no amount of blundering breakers can displace, her arms now taut, now curving, but always with an academic correctitude, her *relevés* relentlessly on the beat, somehow her performance seems uninspired.

"To-morrow, I give 'er 'ell," observed Arenskaya with relish, "and 'er Mother she take 'er off to Buttonhooke."

Now the *corps de ballet* frames the stage, as Rubinska comes flying on in the first Mazurka. The long white ballet skirts and the tiny wings, and her manner of turning her sleek little head as she rises from the stage, turn the proscenium arch once more into the frame for a print of Taglioni. She rises on wings, and her points cut the air. Or she travels across the stage on the tapering pink satin ballet shoe, and all is poetry.

It was almost a pity that the Snarl had no moustachio. Undoubtedly he would have twirled it here.

Kasha Ranevsky was dancing the man in *Sylphides* to-night. He invested the simple role with a sense of style that argued well for his future. In a fair wig and the black coat and flowing white sleeves of the Benois design, he took the stage like a veteran. The knowing in the audience turned approvingly to one another.

Arenskaya said: "'is coat it is too tight," and left it at that.

Now Rubinska returns to dance the *pas-de-deux* valse with him. She floats in his arms on to the stage, a white petal, tossed upon a summer's breeze. Presently she will fly from him, a white moth taken by the candle-flame of the footlights, and he will gently, caressingly, draw her back to safety by her two tiny wings.

Together they depart, and Shura Lubova enters to dance the prelude. Shura was a young St. Joan, her questing dictated by her "voices." She danced as one dedicated to some compelling purpose. The tenderness, the lightness, and the disarming eagerness, that is so implicit in the accepted reading of the wistful little role, was missing from this performance. Shura's was the expression of a single-minded saint—the passage of a fanatic.

"She is pale to-night, Shurushka," Arenskaya observed. "I t'ink it is for love of Pavel—what a pity—she is a girl of good sense—plenty courage—but with 'im she be'ave like a little virgin."

And now the mood that Shura had created was dissipated by the entrance of the sylphs in the moonlit finale. The curtain descended upon a tableau of frozen loveliness. Rubinska with her head on Kasha's shoulder. Shura beside him,[1] and around her, grouped lovingly, the immobility of the *corps de ballet*.

The slow swish of the descending curtain summed up the ballet with its whispered sigh.

*   *   *   *   *

Up in the star's dressing-room Pavel was giving a display of that temperament that had endeared him to so many of his enemies. He cursed the solicitous Appelsinne, he cursed his wig-maker, he cursed the London weather, and, just for luck, he cursed Stroganoff. Here he was, in his first really important role in London, and he had had to pay for his own wreath.

"When you have had the success," Appelsinne assured him, "we ask for more salary."

"And we not get," said Pavel, struggling furiously into his clown's costume. "Already that *succinsin*[2] owes me a fortune."

The *succinsin* bustled in just in time to overhear the last sentence.

"Who owe you money?" he enquired indignantly. "You tell me and I stop it from their salary. Unless, of course," he amended hastily, "you have schanged scheque for Nevajno. There I can do nothing. Already he owe me moneys."

Nervous as he was Pavel still found time to wonder how Nevajno had achieved this miracle. Eventually he enquired. But Stroganoff, who had been caught once, was giving away no secrets.

"I go now," he said, and stumbled over Shura Lubova, who, fresh from her triumph in *Sylphides*, was entering in a dressing-gown. He wagged a roguish finger at her.

"Not before the performance," he said.

[1] In the Ballets Stroganoff it is the custom for the Prelude Ballerina to pair with the Ballerina of the *Pas-de-deux*. The Ballerina of the Valse reclines impartially at their feet.
[2] Russian expression implying illegitimate birth.

D

"I will see to that," said Appelsinne grimly, transfixing Shura with a look that would have scared anybody except a ballet dancer out of the room at once.

But Shura was long inured to a certain amount of unpopularity from Pavel's friends. She advanced unwaveringly.

"You look magnificent," she said to Pavel, who, owing to the heavy clown's make-up, did, as a matter of fact, look slightly less revolting than usual. "It should be I who dance the doll with you to-night."

"That was impossible," said Pavel curtly.

"Did you ask Stroganoff as you promise me?"

"Pavel promise you nothing," broke in Appelsinne roughly. "And anyhow Stroganoff would laugh at the idea. And me I laugh too—ha! ha! As a dancer you do not compare with Rubinska."

Shura's lips tightened. "Do you think so too?" she asked Pavel.

Pavel hesitated. He looked helplessly from Appelsinne to Shura and from Shura to Appelsinne.

"Yes," he said, weakly.

"You skunk," said Shura, "you low, crawling, abject worm. You are frightened of your dresser. You are terrified to go near a woman because of him. You've been terrified ever since Anton was shot—and what's more I shouldn't be surprised if you knew who shot him and why."

"Me, I suppose," said Appelsinne. "I laugh. Ha! Ha!"

"Yes—you."

"You shall not insult my Serge," said Pavel, whitely.

"Oh, you needn't worry," said Shura. "I shan't tell the police. I do not need the police to look after me."

"You go away," said Appelsinne. "You are upsetting my master."

"I will upset him a lot more before I've done."

"Another threat," said Appelsinne, "always she threaten and always I laugh. Ha-ha! And she never do nothing."

"Never," agreed Shura more gently, "until one day you'll drive me just a little too far and that day," she eyed Pavel, "I'll kill you."

The call boy put an end to the irregular triangle. With a whisk of her dressing-gown Shura vanished. Pavel applied the finishing touches to his face and made his way down to the stage. The curtain would be up in a few minutes. Rubinska was already in her booth and Nevajno, who had secured the role of the Moor, was entering his. Pavel scowled at them both impartially, entered his booth, and settled into his arm rest to await his cue.

Judge then of the crack in his perilous calm caused by the strong smell of brilliantine and Volti-Subito. The conductor's face smiled evilly at him round the canvas edges of the puppet booth.

"Hello, big boy," said Volti, every inch the villain. "So this is your great chance—eh? Only not while I'm conducting."

*   *   *   *   *

A new Petroushka will always draw your connoisseur, though judging from their noncommittal attitude, the connoisseurs to-night were not expecting too much. The balleto-medico, in fact, went so far as to declare that he had only turned up for the sake of his collection. He collected dancers as other men collected stamps; all the choicer specimens of Petroushka were already affixed in his album and he only needed Pavel for a swop. The rest of the audience seemed to be in much the same frame of mind and, as the orchestra broke into the opening bars, even Stroganoff sensed that this evening, though financially a good thing, was unlikely to prove an artistic success.

"My orchestra it play well—no?" he said, but without much conviction. And was plunged deeper into gloom when Stanley agreed with him.

"Go away," he said, and, as Stanley lingered: "Bring me a list."

"What list, sir?"

"Any list," said Stroganoff, turning wearily back to the stage where maids, moujiks, women, children, coachmen, nurses, merchants and gipsies were drifting conscientiously about the booth-ringed square. The audience seemed but vaguely aware of them. So, too, but less pardonably, did the conductor.

"That one—I sack him," muttered Stroganoff as Volti-Subito passed a hand over his hair, straightened his tie, and flicked a wrist vaguely in the direction of the big drum, who had already entered two beats ago and was audibly trying to make up his mind whether to start all over again or ignore the episode entirely.

"This is like old times," said the Snarl fondly to the stupefied Arenskaya. He was not particularly musical.

On the stage the organ grinder churned out his tune. The street dancers went slickly through their routine. From the balcony, the gipsies threw coins at them. In the wings, Sergeant Banner felt uneasily in his pockets.

From behind the curtains, steps the magician. He pipes a wily tune on a reed, the flautist, oblivious, two bars behind him. The curtains part and—lo!—the puppets loll inanimate in their cells. Rubinska—eager in her stillness. The Moor —Nevajno—obviously thinking of something else. And Petroushka, his face so quiet it might have been a mask.

"Pip-pip" goes the flute, and the Moor, abandoning the problem he is working on, springs jerkily into life.

"Pip-pip" Rubinska is on her points.

"Pip-pip" but Petroushka still lolls inanimate.

"What did I tell you?" said the balleto-medico with satisfaction, "he's missed his cue."

"Pip-pip" went the flute again a trifle impatiently.

But Petroushka took no notice of his master. He was

huddled in his cell. A dark stain was beginning to appear on the side of his white clown's tunic.

The magician took a step forward, touched him gingerly, and withdrew gazing fascinated at a hand that was red and wet.

The crowd swept forward.

"Curtain," screamed Arenskaya from her box.

*   *   *   *   *

Pavel was dead. He had been shot through the back in line with his heart. Death, whenever it had been administered, must have been instantaneous.

Quill looked at the body. The company, silent, stood about in small groups. The Snarl came hurrying over, behind him Arenskaya and Stroganoff. Speechlessly they ranged themselves beside Quill.

It was Stroganoff who broke the silence.

"What a pity," he said. "Just as you were going to arrest him, too."

CHAPTER XII

THOUGH Palook went to his grave with a grouch at the scant notice taken by the world of his quitting it, Pavel had no such grievance. His was definitely a front page story. The murder of two dancers—in the same ballet, in the same role, at the same theatre, within four days of each other, roused the Press to a height of enthusiasm that had never been reached by their performances in it. The regular ballet critics were gently brushed aside and Ace Crime reporters rushed out to take their places. They did their job well. From the masterly scare lines (A Bullet in the Ballet. Another Clown Dances to Death.) through pulsating paragraphs (. . . still, lifeless, with a slow red patch seeping through his blouse, the clown lay dead. . . . Pavel Bunia would dance no more. . . .), past the stricken comments of the company ("I loved him," says Arenskaya),[1] to a highly imaginative picture of a vengeful Stroganoff vowing to give up vodka till he had laid the murderer by his *entrechats*. . . . It was a lovely story. If Pavel had any complaint it could only have been that his dancing abilities were not noticeably stressed.

Even the Fleet Street News Editors seemed satisfied and one of them, happily relegating Liberia's appeal to the League of Nations to the gossip columns, was actually overheard to remark that it made good reading. Dazed by their success, the reporters staggered out to consolidate their position. They interviewed Hiram B. Sausage, who with a fine impartiality distributed photos, not only of Pavel but of the rest of the company. They interviewed Appelsinne, who refused to talk. They interviewed Puthyk, who refused to stop. They interviewed Rubinska, Shura, and the Implacable Mother. They interviewed Stanley and got tired first. They chased Stroganoff all over the theatre till he sought refuge in the orchestra pit, only to give himself away by picking out "Otchi Tchernia" with one finger on the piano. They made whoopee with Sergeant Banner, and mocked at Quill's guarded statements. And then, their appetites still unappeased, they all turned up at the inquest on Anton Palook.

The Coroner, Mr. A. Zzugg, whose only distinction up to date was that his was the last name in the telephone book, welcomed them with gusto. This time, he felt, he had definitely put one over on a certain colleague. Had that colleague, he thought, but foreseen the second murder, doubtless he would have wangled Palook's corpse into his own district —if necessary with his own hands. But he had carelessly failed to anticipate it and now he, Zzugg, had the opportunity to get some of his own observations on the front page.

[1] Actually she said: "I loathed him," but a tactful sub-editor altered this.

The court was packed. Fifty happy reporters and a complacent coroner did much to dissipate the formal atmosphere that is so much in evidence on those occasions. While it could not be called a fashionable inquest—"eccentric" describes it admirably. The front seats in the spectators' sections had been pinched by a whiskered froth of Russian generals, the mothers, well to the fore from force of habit, were just behind them, while the company, the orchestra and those balletomanes who were not already queueing up outside the Collodium, took up the remaining seats. Poor Mr. Jones[1] of Muswell Hill, who never missed an inquest, found himself, to his annoyance, pushed against a wall next to a young man sporting a perfume that even his wife would not dream of using.

In the well of the court an ostrich feather waved magnificently.

"It is 'ot," said Arenskaya, and Puthyk, taking over the fan, waved eloquently.

"This reminds me," he said, "of Salome."

It was a fascinating theme. "When I dance 'er in Monte Carlo," began Arenskaya to Stroganoff.

But Stroganoff was oblivious. He had many other things to think about. His finances seemed to be improving. The house would be packed to-night and the night after. But who would dance *Petroushka* on Wednesday week to Benois himself, if he come? He had not had time to have his lemon tea this morning. And why would they not wait for him to put on his admiral's uniform before they take his photo yesterday? How they lie these papers. They called Stanley his right-hand man.

"It is not true," his anguish burst out.

"*Mais si c'est vrai*," corrected Arenskaya, "when I was at the sixth veil the Prince he could stand the suspense no longer."

"Poof!" said Stroganoff, and went back to his broodings.

[1] Not the one you know.

Ernest Smithsky would now demand to dance *Petroushka*. Beads of horror broke out at the presentiment.

Nevajno was looking round the court hopefully. These people who had been so obliging yesterday, here they all were. He must talk to them gain. Happily he fingered his diminished cheque book.

A frantic usher was telling Quill that he had been quite unable to keep the witnesses out of the courtroom. In spite of his protests they had swept magnificently past him, announcing that the management had presented them with complimentary seats.[1] Quill gave Banner his instructions and watched grimly while he dealt with the expostulating Stroganoff, Kasha and the affable Puthyk. He was too fed up to extract any amusement from the Sergeant's battle.

He felt heavily responsible for Pavel's death. If he had not yielded to Stroganoff's blandishments, Pavel would still have been alive. On the other hand it looked now as though he would once again have been arresting the wrong man, and yet the evidence against Pavel had been convincing enough. The revolver, the motive and the time lag—all fitted in. Even his murder could not absolve him entirely of suspicion, but it certainly shook Quill's faith in his guilt.

Last night had not been pleasant. The Snarl had been far from sympathetic. Keeping the company in the theatre till the early hours of the morning had not been easy. The routine interrogations had been laborious and almost profitless. This was one of those ridiculously simple murders that it was impossible to get down to. Somebody—one of the many people that had passed behind the booth—had parked a gun against it, shot Pavel, and left the gun beside it. The gun had been promptly identified by Stanley as his own— he had missed it yesterday but had gleefully decided not to present the police with his own clues—Blast him! No mystery at all as to how the murder was done—only who did it.

[1] "They do this for me because I too am impresario," Stroganoff.

Almost, felt Quill, he would have preferred one of those cases where all the doors and windows were locked and nobody had been near the house; one of those cases where you had only to discover how it was done and the murderer fell into your handcuffs automatically.

Once again his note-book was bristling with names but the Detective's Handbook (Eliminate your suspects with caution) was singularly unhelpful. Quite frankly he had not the remotest idea who had killed either of them. Perhaps when he had had a few quiet hours to think, some theory might present itself. In the meantime he would not stress his suspicions of Pavel to the coroner.

The jury were looking intelligent. In the witness-box the balleto-medico was telling his story. He showed a slight tendency to dwell on artistic details and the coroner, in blissful ignorance of what was coming to him later, was under the impression that he was faced with a difficult witness and was handling him extremely well. He was shocked to learn that the body had been moved at Stroganoff's orders before the police arrived, and made up his mind to deal faithfully with that witness when he came up. He plied the balleto-medico with questions. How did he come to be summoned to the corpse? No public appeal for a doctor had been made to the audience.

"I was called by Mr. Stroganoff's secretary."

"How did he know you were present?"

"Everybody knew," said the balleto-medico with pride. "I am always present at a ballet *première*. I have been present at every ballet *première*—bar one—for the past fifteen years."

"Which one?" asked the coroner, interested in spite of himself.

"*Gare du Nord.*"

"And why was that?"

Nevajno, too, was on his feet hotly demanding an explanation. It was his ballet.

"I was down with 'flu."

"Olright," Nevajno, obviously relieved, subsided into his seat. "For just a moment I fear it was because you do not admire my work."

"I don't," said the balleto-medico.

Nevajno leapt to his feet again.

Order was restored with difficulty.

The police-surgeon who followed struck a more formal note. His evidence was a model of what evidence should be. Cold, curt and precise—nobody listened to it. Following him, Quill confined his evidence to an outline of fact and refused to allow the coroner to lure him into theorizing of any kind. A dull witness, thought the disappointed coroner.

He brightened slightly as Stroganoff took the stand. This one looked much more promising.

"You are," he said, speaking very distinctly as one must when speaking to someone who probably does not understand English very well, "Vladimir Alexander Stroganoff?"

"But of course," said Stroganoff surprised.

"You are the proprietor of the Stroganoff Ballet at present performing at the Collodium theatre?"

"We try to get Covent Garden," explained Stroganoff, a little shamefaced, "but de Basil he get there first. His not bad ballet," he conceded magnanimously, "maybe some day we go into partnership."

"On the night of the sixth," said the coroner firmly, "you gave a performance of a ballet called *Petroushka*. In this ballet Anton Palook was found shot."

"This I know already," said Stroganoff, wearily.

"I understand that it was at your orders that the body was moved from the stage before the police arrived?"

"Of course," beamed Stroganoff, "I give all the orders in my company."

"*Quelle blague*," said Arenskaya loudly.

"Silence," said the usher.

"What made you do this thing?"

Stroganoff looked perplexed. "But what else can I do? Would you wish that I leave poor Anton in the middle of the Ajax *décor*—a ballet that he could never support?"

"He had no taste," shouted Nevajno defiantly, "it is well known."

"Silence," said the usher.

"But were you not aware," pursued the coroner, still sweetly reasonable, "that the police would wish to find everything undisturbed?"

"But the audience very disturbed if they find dead body on stage in my theatre," retorted Stroganoff, "the police, they do not pay for seats. The audience they do—some of them, *au moins*."

"But was it essential to continue the performance that night? With your dancer shot?"

"We do not continue the performance yesterday after Pavel die," said Stroganoff, "and look what happen? Many people they try to get their moneys back. That they fail is caused only by our admirable Mr. Saintly. Ah! *Bonjour, mon ami*," he waved a cordial hand in the direction of a blushing pincenez.

"So," said the coroner less affably, "your box office meant more to you than the death of your leading dancer. You did not care that your action might be helping a murderer to escape."

"The ballet it must go on," said Arenskaya.

"Silence," said the usher.

"*Mais, mon cher*, I put it to you as one artist to another," burbled Stroganoff, "where would my ballet be, if for every little accident we make a stop? We must continue always. In Bled there are riots—but my company it perform every night. Some town in Mexico they kill the president in the *entr'acte* but the Ballet Stroganoff it ignore, and we give the last act to new president. They shoot him too next week —it was sad. In Salonika the orchestra they strike—but we

buy good gramophone. And then there was Paris—big night
—fashionable audience—all seats paid for—Pilaff was with us
then—he dance Petroushka—it was in the bill that night.
And then, half-hour before the performance, I go to his
dressing-room—and—poof—he is suicided. But do I lose
my head? No. We give instead that old favourite *Casse
Noisette*—in its entirety. A little under-rehearsed perhaps,
but the audience they are pleased. And later I give the role
of Petroushka to Anton." He stopped suddenly. "*Tiens!*" he
said, "that is curious. My three Petroushkas—they are all dead!"

During the scuffle at the Press table that followed, Quill
passed a note to the coroner. The coroner nodded.

"This Mr.—er—Pilaff," he asked, "you say he committed
suicide? What form of suicide?"

"He shoot himself."

"What was his reason for suicide?"

"Who can tell why an artist kill himself?" asked Stroganoff.
"May be he love someone who do not love him. We all
very excited about it at time—but it is soon over and we
go back to work. Our work," said Stroganoff, "it is to us
everything. We eat, we drink, we love, we kill—but first of
all we dance. A dancer," he went on, warming to his theme. . . .

Quill began to feel a certain sympathy for the coroner.
He had been through it himself.

Stroganoff was now well in his stride. Words cascaded
from him in a mingled stream of French, Russian, and
occasionally, English. The coroner bleated at him pathetically,
the clerk rallied to him with a series of shocked "hushes,"
but they might as well have tried to stop a sports car at an
amber light.

They were sympathetic, these English. They listened.
Clearly they were impressed by his theory that *Pagliacci*
would have been more convincing as a ballet. . . .

It was a naturalized juryman who rescued the court. He
shouted something in Russian. The uncouth adjective jerked

Stroganoff out of his stride, he abandoned his discourse and began to reply in kind. Both subsided. The coroner, taking no further chances, dismissed the witness hurriedly. This was not the curtain Stroganoff had expected, but after waiting hopefully for a round of applause which did not materialize, he allowed himself to be led away.

But his evidence, extricated from its froth, was the stone that started a great many rings of activity.

Three dead Petroushkas were a lovely gift to the Press. They linked the two London murders, sensational enough in themselves, to the eerie chain of the supernatural—the theme that always fascinates—paving the way to superstition and panic. Already members of the company in court were whispering to each other, speculating, with delightful shivers, upon who would be offered the role next. For Quill the news meant a new factor in his enquiry, the despatch of telegrams to Paris, a possible reshuffle of all his ideas.

Stanley was now in the box, efficiently furnishing details of his name, education and career, and almost explaining how it was that he had so mysteriously failed his Smalls. His description of his own indispensability to the ballet nearly brought Stroganoff back hot foot to deny it, while his version of the assistance he had given the police tempted Quill to do the same. Why, said Stanley, it was he who by sheer deduction had found the revolver with which Palook had been shot.

This was the first the court had heard of any revolver and the coroner turned a reproachful eye on Quill. Quill quickly passed up a note stating that the police were not yet ready for this aspect of the case to come out. But Mr. Zzugg was not to be browbeaten. He dismissed Stanley and recalled Quill.

"Did you," he asked, "have the revolver given to you as stated by the last witness?"

"Yes."

"Has it been established as the revolver that killed the deceased?"

"Yes."

The coroner paused before putting the vital question. He was aware that Quill did not want it asked, but he was not going to let the police bully him into suppressing all the more interesting evidence.

"Has the owner of the gun been traced?"

Quill was furious. "Yes."

"What is his name?"

"The police would prefer not to disclose it at the moment."

"Is that so? Curiously enough," said the coroner mildly, "I was under the impression that I was conducting this inquest—not the police."

He was asking for it, thought Quill. All right, he would get it.

"His name was Pavel Bunia."

The effect was extraordinary. For the first time in the history of the Ballet Stroganoff, you could have heard a pin drop.

"The man who was killed last night?" said the coroner hollowly.

"Exactly," said Quill. "Are there any further questions you would like to ask?"

"No—no."

There was another scuffle at the Press table.

Quill stepped down leaving the coroner a prey to conflicting emotions. By his own insistence he had unearthed a sensational piece of evidence, but if he followed it up, it was likely to result in a verdict of murder against a person who had himself been murdered. Could he risk this anomaly? Mr. Zzugg decided he could not.

Proceedings now took on a quieter note. There was nothing in the demeanour of Shura Lubova to suggest the vixen of the dressing-room last night. She gave her evidence with composure and spoke of the dead man without rancour or warmth. She admitted to having been on the balcony on the night of his death—where she had no right to be. One of the company had a migraine and Shura, out of pure kindness of heart, had allowed her to lie down in her dressing-room and had taken her place.

"Eight or nine girls in a dressing-room, it is not good for migraine."

Who was the girl? Her name was Anna Szonnova and she was still unwell. Certainly the coroner and the police could have her address. Doubtless the management would know it.

"Is it not unusual for a star dancer to deputize for a walker-on?"

"I did not think about it. The girl was unwell."

"Were you on the balcony when deceased was shot?"

"I left it with other dancers a few moments previously."

"You did not while on the balcony notice anything that might help the court?"

"Nothing."

"You did not like the dead man?" said the wily Mr. Zzugg.

"Nobody liked him," Shura answered. There was still no rancour in her voice.

The coroner dismissed her and called the next witness. This was Puthyk. Quill, himself, was vaguely uncertain why he had caused the old man to be subpoenaed but Puthyk took his importance for granted. He beamed affably at the coroner, the jury and the Press. He beamed at Arenskaya and Quill. He beamed at Stroganoff. He even beamed a trifle absently at Nevajno.

"Your name," said the coroner, "is P. Puthyk?"

"*Oui.*"

"You are a dancer in the Ballet Stroganoff?"

"Assuredly. My legs they get a little tired but my elevation it is perfect."

"Quite."

Puthyk turned triumphantly in the direction of Stroganoff. "You see. That one he understands."

"You are a small part dancer?" said the coroner tactlessly.

"Who say that?" Puthyk swung round again while Stroganoff tiptoed guiltily towards the doorway.

"It is true," Puthyk explained to the court, "that now I dance only small parts, but it was not always so. At the Maryinsky . . ." and before the coroner could stop him he had plunged into a recital of his triumphs.

". . . and to-night I dance *Coppélia*," he finished. "And after that," he looked hopefully to where Stroganoff had crept in again, "it is agreed that I dance *Petroushka*."

"*Oui, oui*," said Stroganoff, winking heavily at the coroner.

"*Bon*," said Puthyk, all affability again. "You shall see then that I am superb. You come too?" he invited the coroner. "You nice man. I give you box."

The coroner intimated that he would like to ask Puthyk a few questions. Puthyk graciously permitted it. His answers were a little vague. He may have been on the balcony that night, but next week he was dancing the main role. Had they not heard? He was anxious to help the court but his role it must come first. He and Woizikovsky. . . .

It was a very tired and disgruntled coroner who eventually addressed the jury. The inquest had not proceeded on the lines he had visualized. Instead of holding the centre of the stage as he had intended, he had been thrust firmly off it by the powerful personalities of the various witnesses. Instead of handling the witnesses, the witnesses had, for the most part, handled him. And as for investigating the cause of death, the only time he had come across anything promising he was brought to a full stop by the murder of the suspected person. In fact, he was robbed of everything save the prosaic direction to the jury to bring in a verdict of wilful murder against person or persons unknown. This he did, skating carefully over the thin ice of the discovery of the revolver.

The jury duly obliged.

CHAPTER XIII

THAT evening Quill sat in his rooms covering page after page of foolscap with schoolboy handwriting.

"When in doubt," counsels the Detective's Handbook, "document your facts and stare them in the face." Quill had followed this counsel. After some work he found himself looking at the following: *Petroushka*. Three dancers who danced, or were due to dance, this role have died within the past two months.

Feb. 2. Marius Pilaff found shot in dressing-room of theatre in Paris. Verdict—suicide.

April 6. Anton Palook shot on top of booth in last scene of *Petroushka* at the Collodium theatre. Verdict—murder by person or persons unknown.

April 8. Pavel Bunia found shot in booth in first scene of *Petroushka*. Inquest not yet fixed.

The following facts have been established concerning each of the deaths:

Death of Pilaff.

Pilaff was found dead in his dressing-room just before a performance of *Petroushka*, the ballet in which he was dancing the main role, was due to start. Revolver in hand. Verdict of suicide but no good reason for suicide ever discovered. Further particulars may be to hand from Paris Police shortly.

Death of Anton Palook.

The shot was not fired at close quarters and it has not been found possible to fix the exact range or direction. Might have been fired from any part of the house—except gallery and upper circle. Most probable positions for firing unobserved, however, are (*a*) the balconies flanking the sides of the stage, (*b*) the stage boxes.

A revolver, subsequently proved to be the weapon that killed Palook, produced by Stanley Simpson, who claims to have found it in waste-paper basket in Pavel Bunia's old dressing-room. Revolver identified by gunsmith as one purchased by Pavel in his shop on August 17, 1935.

The following are known to have motives of sorts for the murder:

Rubinska. In love with Palook but discarded. Had made an attempt at reconciliation while in the booth during the performance, which had been roughly repulsed. State of mind probably suitable for murder. Evidence, however, shows that she was in her dressing-room at the time of the shot. (Confirmed by her mother, Kasha Ranevsky, and Arenskaya.)

Shura Lubova. In love with Pavel Bunia who had come under the influence of Palook. Had deputized for one of the company on balcony, but claims to have left latter before the shot. No witnesses positive enough to confirm this.

P. Puthyk. Wife unfaithful with Palook. Ancient history now. Further Puthyk, when matter was mentioned, exhibited none of the reactions of a jealous husband nurturing a grudge. On balcony during the performance. Time of descent unestablishable. Puthyk vague and nobody noticed his coming down.

Stroganoff. Fear that Palook would leave him for Lord Buttonhooke. Doubtful if such fear would prompt him to murder, while his accounts of movements, fully checked, left little time over for unobserved shooting practice.

Volti-Subito. Known to dislike Palook. May have more definite grievance. Opportunity to fire unobserved from orchestra pit just possible. First-class shot. (Evidence of Stanley Simpson.)

Stanley Simpson. In love with Rubinska. In wings at time of shooting. Chance of shooting unobserved extremely remote.

Pavel Bunia. A very strong case of circumstantial evidence surrounds this suspect. Was furiously jealous of Palook's association with Rubinska. Had quarrelled over it with Palook in interval. Had gone up on balcony after leaving stage to stop Appelsinne, who admits he was there with intent to murder, from shooting Palook. Had taken Appelsinne's revolver, sent Appelsinne away, and stayed behind himself. Seen by Stroganoff. Means, motive, opportunity—all complete.

Appelsinne had produced a revolver, unfired and not fitted with a silencer, which he says is the gun Pavel took from him. Questioned as to possession of second revolver Appelsinne stated that Pavel had bought one two years back but that this had been lost some time ago. This is in all probability a lie. On the other hand there is only Stanley's word for it that he found revolver in waste-paper basket.

Evidence considered strong enough to secure warrant for Pavel's arrest. Arrest postponed at Stroganoff's request till after performance of *Petroushka*. During performance Pavel found shot in booth.

Death of Pavel Bunia.

Pavel found shot in booth at 10.45. Seen entering booth at 10.30 approximately.

Volti-Subito last person to speak to deceased. Observed talking to Pavel in his booth just before rise of curtain on *Petroushka*. Time approximately 10.33. Subito admits coming on stage for express purpose of making a gibe at Pavel, but says that Pavel did not answer his remark. It must, therefore, not be taken for granted that Pavel was still alive when Subito spoke to him.

It was undeniably possible for Subito to have shot Pavel while talking to him. There is, however, no shred of evidence to confirm this suggestion.

Numerous persons passed behind booth during performance, but it has been found impossible to find any of the company who will admit to having done so, or to have seen other people passing. This, however, is clearly accounted for by (*a*) fear of suspicion, (*b*) screening of comrades, (*c*) general lack of observation always prevalent during a stage performance.

Revolver with one chamber fired and fitted with silencer found behind booth. Revolver identified by Stanley as his property which he claims to have missed for the first time that afternoon.

The following have motives—of a kind—for the murder of Pavel:

Shura Lubova. In love with and spurned by Pavel. Uttered threats in dressing-room prior to performance.

Volti-Subito. General dislike—or more as in case of Palook. Had opportunity for the murder—see above.

Kasha Ranevsky. Only man in company with whom Palook was on friendly terms. Nothing to show, however, that Kasha felt particularly friendly to Palook, especially as Kasha is in love with Rubinska, notoriously deflowered by Palook. Claims to have been in dressing-room from rise of curtain till discovery of body, but no external evidence to confirm this. A very far-fetched theory, suggested by the jealous Stanley Simpson, is that Kasha suspected Pavel murdered Palook, and murdered Pavel in revenge.

Stanley Simpson. Sympathy for Shura and public school principles would make Pavel obvious villain in Stanley's eyes. His revolver fired the shot. Did Stanley kill Pavel in mistaken sense of chivalry to save Shura from herself? Then did he also kill Palook to protect Rubinska, with whom he is in love, and then claim to have found revolver in waste-paper basket? Extremely improbable.

But then everything about these murders is improbable.

Theories concerning the murders.

There are two distinct theories.

The first assumes that the two murders and the suicide,

which may have been murder, are inter-related. This assumption is made on the fact that the three dead men were dancing or about to dance the title role in the ballet *Petroushka*.

The second theory is to treat the two murders as independent entities, admitting only that the first may have influenced, or prompted, the second. Into this theory the Paris suicide does not enter and is, in fact, entirely irrelevant.

The second is the more probable of these theories if only because it permits Pavel to remain suspect for the murder of Palook. The first theory automatically acquits Pavel by reason of his death and reduces the circumstantial evidence against him to mere coincidence. But it is an astonishing coincidence that Pavel should find himself in a position with the opportunity, the means, and possibly the desire to kill, while the real murderer was crouching elsewhere.

Assuming that Pavel killed Palook, Pavel's death might now be the revenge of a friend. Snag is that Palook cannot be found to have had any friends with possible exception of Kasha. A more probable theory is that Pavel was killed by an enemy (he had plenty of these), who had got the idea from the murder of Palook.

Theory that the three deaths are related.

Three dancers in the role of Petroushka have died. Pilaff (dressing-room, Paris); Palook (shot at end of third scene in *Petroushka*); Pavel Bunia (shot in booth at beginning of first scene). If there is no connection between the cases it is certainly curious that death should have overtaken the three, while dancing or about to dance *Petroushka*. If there is a connection it argues the presence of a person in the company with an antipathy for all *Petroushkas*. For this antipathy to extend to homicide argues a madman.

Detective's Handbook not helpful in this respect. "Watch carefully for indications of an unbalanced mind." But the entire Stroganoff company showed strong indications of unbalanced minds a dozen times daily.

Reticence is not one of the qualities of Russian dancers, but so far have not encountered any persons revealing a dislike of *Petroushka* in their speech. It seems to be a favourite part and much coveted by dancers. Even old Puthyk, in spite of his age, still hankers after it.

Assuming there is a *Petroushka* hater in the company, would he or she not give themselves away every time they spoke of the ballet. There can be no harm in discussing the ballet with various members of the company and noting the reactions.

*   *   *   *   *

As he looked at the last entry it struck Quill that it was a pity that the murders had not taken place during a ballet by Nevajno. By all accounts the place was bristling with people who did not like Nevajno's ballets. Quill smiled at the idea. From there his thoughts passed to Nevajno himself.

Immediately Quill felt slightly excited. Not that Nevajno was any madder than the rest, but his mania lay in a passion for the modern, combined with an extreme sensitiveness of any disparagement of his own work. A ballet like *Petroushka*, though created as late as 1910, might easily appear to Nevajno as old and absurd—and its obstinate success might easily breed a hatred of it, which in turn might translate itself into a hatred of the performers in it.

On the more prosaic question of opportunity, Nevajno had not been dancing in the ballet when Palook was killed. As there was then no possible reason to rank him among the suspects, his statement that he had been in the wings had not been closely checked. When Pavel was murdered Nevajno was dancing the Moor and occupied the next booth but one to Pavel. This offered an opportunity of slipping out for a moment, shooting Pavel, and slipping back again.

If this was the crime of a lunatic there could be no better suspect. However, psycho-analysis was not one of his strongest points and it might be as well to have an expert opinion when tackling Nevajno.

Reasonably satisfied with the night's work, Quill put away his notes and went to bed.

CHAPTER XIV

SCOTLAND YARD was not the only body to get in touch with Paris over the matter of Marius Pilaff's suicide; the whole of Fleet Street had had the same idea. But while the connection between the three dead Petroushkas was only one of alternative theories to Quill; to the Press, unhandicapped by the need of making an arrest, it had become a burning faith. In some mysterious way the dead clowns seemed to have altered the face of London. Every small tobacconist-and-sweet shop had its bulgy window propped up with some such inviting tit-bit as "Death Stalks the Ballet." "Three Clowns No Longer Laugh." In trains, bobbing eyes focused on "The Ballet with the Trail of Blood." At home, dressing-gowned wives shuddered delightfully over composite pictures of the three Petroushkas hunched upon the stage, and strongly suspected Stroganoff of being the bluebeard, mainly on account of his foreign name. Newsboys, the latest details strapped to their persons, ambled blissfully through the streets, and the head waiter at the Hotel des Gourmets so far forgot himself as to swop a theory with a customer who had asked for sausage and mash.

The *Night Despatch* hurriedly abandoned its series of "Latter-Day Landrus" in favour of "Tragedies in Sawdust" (Petroushka, Pierrot, Pagliacci, etc.).

"Three Crumpled Clowns," flaunted the *Daily Distraught* posters.

"The Clown With The Cloud of Death," achieved the *Evening Scoop*.

"They Danced Petroushka and Died," announced the *Evening Yelp* pathetically.

"Is There a Hoodoo on This Ballet?" asked the *Mystical Times*.

"Abandon This Ballet," demanded *Fascism for All*.

"Ballets, Bullets, Blood . . ." promised a popular weekly.

And then there were long articles, hurriedly commissioned from prominent writers of detective fiction, not one of which omitted to point out that truth was stranger than fiction.

The *Daily Distraught* ran a special by their ace sob-sister, Petunia Patch.

"The terrible fate of the three crumpled clowns cries to the world for vindication. . . . What is this role that brings with it a heritage of doom?

The trail of death is set in Paris—City of Laughter—City of Love! There, huddled in his dressing-gown, his sightless eyes raised to the powerless ceiling, his pitiful hands forever still, crouched the first fated clown, Marius Pilaff (who was, of course, first cousin to the well-known diplomat, Prince Andrey Andreyev). Known to balletomanes the wide world over, for the brilliance of his *tours en l'air en seconde*.

In London, Anton Palook (whose Petroushka ranked second only to that of Nijinsky, Bolm, Woizikovsky, Massine, Lichine, Shabelevsky and Wilzak) met his death in full view of a brilliant first-night audience.

Petroushka, the comic figure of a thousand Russian fairings, Petroushka, the tragic hero of a ballet weighted with tears. Petroushka—No man and Everyman. Petroushka, high on the roof of the blue-fringed booth, his mimed agony turning suddenly to the pangs of a terrible death . . . the second clown is a crumpled shape against the deep shadows of a painted world.

And still the grisly tally has not been concluded. . . .

Behind the curtains of the puppet's booth—hiding what dreadful secret? Screening what cunning hand? The finest dancer of them all[1] lurches against the canvas walls. His features are still, beneath the running grease paint. His mouth has sagged horribly. Pavel Bunia has met a death more secret, perhaps more terrible, than any of those fated clowns.

Public opinion may question the propriety of giving *Petroushka* at the Gala Stroganoff, which has been promised for April 14th, but the determination of the management remains unshaken. All London will be gathered to do honour to the Grand Old Man of Russian Ballet—Benois himself.[2] 'It is inconceivable,' said the manager of the theatre, Mr. Montague Saintly, 'that *Petroushka*, his greatest work, should not be given.'

The ballet of the world would be the poorer for the banning of *Petroushka*, and the ballet of the world, it must go on![3] But who will be willing to dance Petroushka—who will flout the chain of death?

Perhaps it will be only in the hearts of those who have known and loved the ballet that Petroushka's voice will be heard screaming its dumb indictment to the silent sky. For all Russians are grown-up children—laughter-loving children —with a child's love of make-believe and a child's fear of darker things. And what could be darker, more eerie, and more pitiful than the memory of those three dead clowns, strung on that mysterious, that tragic chain?

'Who is to be the next Petroushka?' the dancers ask each other, 'and what will happen to him?'

In what familiar guise does death stalk the Ballet, these children of superstition cry? And who will be foolhardy enough to take the role on Wednesday week?

[1] Poet's licence.
[2] "If 'e come"—Stroganoff.
[3] Pardonable lapse due to constant button-holing of Stroganoff.

Who brave enough?

WHO ?"

Stroganoff was sick of the question. The waiter who brought his chocolate in the morning. The commissionaire who called his taxi. The stage-doorkeeper at his theatre. Sundry members of his company lingering about the stairs. Mr. Saintly with his enquiring pince-nez bobbing outside his office door. Hiram B. Sausage with Fleet Street at the other end of the line. And finally, the unescapable Stanley, arriving early and clamouring for his answer.

To make it worse he had not the faintest idea who *was* going to dance Petroushka.

*   *   *   *   *

Ernest Smithsky was his most experienced dancer now, but it was impossible to visualize Smithsky as Petroushka. Or rather only too easy to visualize that grim conscientiousness, pirouetting as faultlessly and as unemotionally as a whirling top. Still, Smithsky was a coward, he would probably be only too relieved not to be offered the part. But his other dancers were almost as unsuitable. The only one of his younger members who showed any signs of talent was Kasha Ranevsky.

Stroganoff remembered suddenly that he had promised the part to P. Puthyk to keep him quiet at the inquest. Puthyk must be told at once not to take the promise too seriously— at any moment he might go and make the announcement to some reporter. It would not be pleasant breaking the news to the old man. Bright idea—he would tell Stanley to do it!

"But you be tactful—no?" he finished.

What was that clever English axiom about breaking off two glass houses with one stone, reflected Stroganoff happily as Stanley departed. Certainly he had achieved it this time. Life perhaps was not so complicated after all. His ballet was a sensation as never before; all seats sold weeks ahead and the management actually asking him to extend his season. For the first time for many years he saw himself solvent. What with his profits and those gold shares he had bought last week that would soon be double, he would be rich and prosperous; and his broker, he would at last be polite. "I ring him up now," he promised himself, "and find out how they are feeling."

But here was M'sieur Quill, doubtless in a very good humour over the new assassin that he must find. Stroganoff pushed away the receiver and produced his usual welcome.

Quill replied shortly that he had not slept at all.

" Me, when I cannot sleep," said Stroganoff irrepressibly, "I hum to myself 'Otchi Tchernia.' It go like this. . . ."

Quill stopped him. "Not now. I've come to ask you some questions."

Stroganoff was instantly depressed.

"Useless to come to me and ask who dance Petroushka next. It is a problem *bien difficile*. First we have none who can dance it good, and second, if we should find such a one he would be afraid. All my dancers think that when they dance Petroushka next they die. It is your newspapers that have done this thing to me." Indignantly he picked up the *Daily Distraught*, brandished it and threw it into the waste-paper basket, only to rescue it the next moment. "My shares, they are in that!"

"I would like a few details about Pilaff's suicide," said Quill, and Stroganoff sighed.

"If he were only alive my problem it would not exist. He was superb as Petroushka. Not as superb as Woizikovsky, but better much than Anton Palook."

The 'phone bell rang.

"*J'écoute*," said Stroganoff. "I am dancing him myself," he finished fiercely.

"I would like to hear your own account of Pilaff's death."

Stroganoff shrugged. "It was strange. Pilaff very nice man. He laugh, he joke, the girls they all like him and never he ask me for the advance. And then . . . poof! he suicided. It is the mystery insoluble."

"Did he, to your knowledge, have any enemies?"

"*Mais non!* We all love him—except maybe Nevajno. Nevajno a little cross because Pilaff he never consent to dance in his ballets. Pilaff old-fashioned and would never dance anything later than Fokine."

"And that upset Nevajno?"

"What would you? Nevajno is an artist. He lives only for his work. To ignore it, to dismiss it as Pilaff did—that is the insult. Nevajno so hurt with Pilaff he never even ask him to schange him scheque."

After Quill's speculations about the modernist, this was distinctly interesting.

"Was Nevajno in the theatre on the night of the suicide?"

"*Mais pourquoi pas!* All the company it was there. Anton and Pavel they share a dressing-room then," he remembered, "but it was not a success."

"Was the personnel of your company the same in Paris as in London?"

"*Absolument,*" said Stroganoff with pride. "My company they never leave me—I am to them like a father. Sometimes," he admitted reluctantly, "there is a little exception—but then, children they sometimes quarrel and leave their fathers too. But my principals they never go—not even to Button'ooke. Especially," he added naively, "now that I shall be able to pay them. And that remind me." He dialled.

"I desire," he said, " M'sieu Johns. Is this M'sieu Johns? Good mornings. I am Stroganoff. You remember me without doubt. My shares they feel well—no?"

"No!" he repeated, startled. "*Tiens! c'est curieux!* Still, it can't be serious. Doubtless they will get up soon, Maybe it is good idea to buy some more? . . . No! but, *mon ami*, you are too cautious. Do you not realise that to make money you must risk something?"

But the broker appeared to be adamant and after some further protests Stroganoff hung up.

"He advise me to sell," he confided indignantly. "What you think of that? If I sell to-day I lose already fifty pouns."

"You do not consider," said Quill, trying hard to bring him back to the point, "that Pilaff did not commit suicide? That he was murdered?"

Stroganoff did not seem interested. "Per'aps, but that was long time ago and in Paris. So why you worry? Me, I must worry first for a Petroushka for Wednesday week. That it will not be Ernest Smithsky I am determined. I go now to frighten him good." And carefully folding the *Daily Distraught* at Petunia Patch's Crumpled Clown article, he strode off to drop it carelessly in Smithsky's dressing-room.

Quill let him go. There was no help to be got out of Stroganoff this morning. Only one person in the company could be relied upon to remember the details of a three-months'-old death, and that was Stanley. Quill set off to find him.

Stanley, found, had forgotten nothing. There was not a single detail of his sojourn in Paris that he did not remember and attempt to retail, including an irrelevant story of an expensive adventure of incredible purity in the foyer of the Folies Bergeres. As to the death of Pilaff, Stanley's chief emotion seemed to be one of irritation at the Surete, who had not allowed him to help. He himself had never been satisfied with the suicide verdict. Not that he particularly suspected anyone, but he had been given no chance to investigate.

"I tell you what," said Stanley, tapping Quill's chest impressively, "I've come to a conclusion. There is a murderer in this company."

"No!" said Quill.

"There's something fishy about three dead clowns."

Stanley, too, had read Petunia Patch. "Seems to me most likely that one person did in all three. And what's more I have a theory as to who it is. Don't ask me about it," he went on quickly. "I don't want to talk about it till I've got proof—and I hope to have proof soon."

"Oh," said Quill.

"It's dangerous, of course, but I'm used to danger. And directly I've got the evidence I'll let you know."

"But," began Quill.

"Don't thank me," said Stanley, "I'm only doing my duty as a citizen."

Quill left him to his researches, in which curiously enough he felt no great confidence, and went out to lunch.

*   *   *   *   *

Quill returned to the Collodium that afternoon to find the foyer besieged by Balletomanes—rather small Balletomanes with rather smart Mammas. Saturday afternoons were scholars' afternoons at the Ballets Stroganoff.

On the whole the gathering was more sedate than those that were wont to muster on grown-up occasions.

True, the corridors were awhirl with socked and coated ballerinas rotating imitatively, but the Collodium is by no means unique in harbouring this touching sight. How often has the foyer at Covent Garden itself offered the pleasing spectacle of a boiled-shirted balletomane, pink but persevering, poised winsomely on one toe while the other descries all manner of involved sequences? True, the younger set came armed with a battery of cushions, but again the Collodium Juvenilia is by no means unique in this respect, for how many baffled balletomanes have, in their day, perched upon the pursed-up ledge of their seat at Covent Garden—a ledge that wheezes and whangs and collapses at the most embarrassing junctures.

Quill, making his way through the bobbing sea of curls,

spotted Stroganoff beamingly at anchor by the box office. Evidently the balletomane of the future was more to his taste than the balletomane of the past. Besides, he had just succeeded in shunting a local Mamma, who would be forced now to show her sheaf of pictures to the pinned-down Stanley. In a burst of well-being Stroganoff turned to the nearest unknown in the bobbing sea and patted its disgusted head.

"So you came to see the *Casse-Noisette* Stroganoff?"

"Worse luck!" The unknown hunched his shoulders.

"What!" said the impresario astounded. "You do not like the *Casse-Noisette* Stroganoff?"

"No."

Light began to dawn. "It is perhaps that you prefer the *ballet sérieux? Sylphides—Oiseau de Feu—Petrou*—that is to say, *Lac des Cygnes?*"

"No," said the unknown firmly.

Stroganoff tried again. "You clasp me by the leg. Next you will be telling me that you prefer *le Cinéma!*"

The unknown nodded eagerly.

"*Le* Meeckymouse?" enquired Stroganoff. But this, it appeared was "Cissie." What the unknown yearned for was something modern, something that had a relation to life as it was lived in the Bowery. Tough-guy stuff

"Then," said Stroganoff sagely, "you will like well the choreography Nevajno. *Très* Tough-guy. *Bien* bump-off. I give you ticket if you like for *Gare-du-Nord.* It is a masterpiece you tell me—and I will not contradict."

He produced a white slip, but the unknown waved it scornfully aside. Defeated, Stroganoff wandered away to bestow his affability elsewhere. Quill went off to the auditorium. It was now merely a matter of time before Stroganoff would be saying: "You have seen *Casse-Noisette*—no?" and it would be gratifying to startle him with an affirmative. Besides this, he was beginning to acquire a sneaking liking for ballet.

He made his way to Stroganoff's box[1] which was occupied by the balleto-medico, gazing sulkily at the fat girl on the stage—surely the largest Little Clara on record. He looked at Quill without seeing him and burst into a torrent of denunciation. Quill received the invective with a nod and settled beside him. He would have been glad to escape elsewhere, but he had remembered his speculations about Nevajno and wanted the opinion of the balleto-medico concerning them.

Eventually the curtain came down to much juvenile applause.

"Appalling," said the balleto-medico.

"Cheer up," said Quill, "it might have been by Nevajno."

"In which case I wouldn't be here."

"You don't like Nevajno?"

"He's mad." The balleto-medico dismissed him from the conversation. But Quill brought him back.

"Mad enough to be certified?"

"Absolutely. If only," said the balleto-medico wistfully, "I had a ballet-loving colleague, I'd see to it myself. Anything to stop the fellow."

"But who, then, would dance the Moor on Wednesday week before Benois himself if he come?" quoted Quill glibly.

The Stroganoff touch awoke the balleto-medico to Quill's presence.

"Oh, it's you," he said in some relief. "I thought it was Stanley."

Quill laughed. "He's busy finding the murderer for me."

"Talking of the murderer," said the balleto-medico with interest, "I've come to the conclusion that I rather admire the fellow. He hasn't killed a good dancer yet. The man has taste. I wish he'd exercise it more often."

"He very likely will."

"Hope so," said the balleto-medico blandly. "You know,"

[1] "Come to my box when you will. I charge you nothing."—Stroganoff.

he confided, "I sympathize with him to some extent. I've often felt like murdering Anton Palook myself after one of his triumphal appearances, and as for killing Pavel before he could lay his hands on Petroushka, why, it was nothing but the action of a public benefactor."

"Am I to take it," asked Quill, "that you believe the Petroushkas were killed because they danced badly?"

The balleto-medico sighed. "I wish I could believe it. It's the sort of censorship the Ballet Stroganoff needs."

Quill took the plunge. "It is one of the police theories that these murders might be the work of a madman."

The balleto-medico saw the point. "You mean there is somebody whom the sight of a Petroushka prompts to homicide?"

"Perhaps."

"Might be something in it," said the balleto-medico thoughtfully. "I had a patient once who felt that way about crooners. But then, his wife had eloped with one."

Quill remembered the Puthyks. "A ballet dancer would hardly mind that."

"Agreed," said the balleto-medico. "On the other hand they can work themselves into passions over matters that, to the tennis club mind, are utterly without importance."

"I've noticed that," said Quill.

"Take Nevajno, for instance. You can't insult the fellow in a normal manner. Call him every name under the sun, sleep with his mistress or slap his face, and the chances are that he won't even notice it. But any slight—real or imaginary—on his work brings him foaming to his feet."

"He must be pretty active when you're about." Quill laughed and proceeded to take advantage of the opening. He explained his suspicions, said he was planning to interview Nevajno the next morning and, pointing out that while the police-surgeon knew a lot about insanity, he knew nothing about ballet dancers and might easily be confused by the some-

E

what similar symptoms, begged the balleto-medico to accompany him. The latter jibbed a bit, protesting that he had an appointment, that he was not speaking to Nevajno and that anyway Nevajno lacked the taste to have done the murders. But Quill insisted. They wrangled through two acts and it was not the final curtain of *Casse-Noisette* that the balleto-medico capitulated.

They fixed a *rendezvous* for the following morning. Then Quill went off to see Stroganoff.

*   *   *   *   *

Stroganoff stood in an impressive posture in front of the fireplace, his right hand sawing short cuts through the air to register determination and defiance. In front of him, sleekly brilliantined and lolling in an arm-chair, sat Volti-Subito, smiling meaningly at a morning coat that had done its best to look as though it had been cut in Savile Row.

"*Inutile* to argue," Stroganoff was saying as Quill entered. "I am resolute. On the morning after Wednesday week you are sack."

The unruffled Volti selected a fresh cigarette. The morning coat only just refrained from rubbing its hands, and took up a sheet of paper. Quill sat down to watch the entertainment.

"According to clause 7 (*c*) of my client's contract," gabbled the morning coat smoothly, "if the employer shall at any time hereafter commit or endeavour to commit a breach of any kind whatsoever of clause 3 (*d*) hereof, and or/if the conductor shall at any time hereafter commit any such breach as aforesaid of any of the provisions of clause 5 (*e*) hereof and/or if either of them, the employer or the conductor, shall commit any such breach as aforesaid of any term or condition herein contained, other than any term or condition contained in either or both of the said clauses 3 (*d*) and 5 (*e*), then and in any such case the employer shall pay to the conductor, or the conductor to the employer as the case may be, as liquidated damages, the sum of five hundred pounds or its equivalent in whatever currency shall be most expedient, together with interest at the rate of £5 per centum per annum from the date of such breach or from the date when such breach is first discovered, whichever is the earlier, until such time as payment has been made."

"Poof!" said Stroganoff.

"An expensive poof," said Volti nastily.

"I care nothing for the expense," said Stroganoff. "Me—I am an artist. Because my orchestra it is perfect I am glad. But I weep because my conductor he is rotten."

"Slander!" said the morning coat.

"Therefore I say I dismiss my conductor. A bad musician it is a pain in the ear."

"On what grounds," asked the morning coat, still smooth, "do you base your assertion of my client's alleged inefficiency?"

"He do not watch the stage."

"Who would," asked Volti, "when the Stroganoff Ballet is dancing on it?"

Stroganoff drew himself up to his full height.

"You insult my ballet. That," he said, a gleam of hope in his eye, "is the libel. I take the action and get much damages. I, too, have an advocate," he added.

The morning coat smiled quietly.

"You laugh," said Stroganoff infuriated. "You think that you have me in hollow stick—no? You think that I, Vladimir Stroganoff, am helpless with your contracts? That I will pay quietly all that you ask?"

"Not quietly," said Volti.

"But soon you will laugh the other side of your cheek. For I am decided. I pay nothing. Not one *centime*. And if you take me to the Court you will be overcome with sorrow at the things about you that I tell the coroner."

"Judge," said the morning coat, shocked.

"Both," said Stroganoff. "I tell everybody That on Tuesday

you double the pace of *Sylphides* and my dancers they are compelled to run. That on Wednesday you forget the cuts in *Lac des Cygnes*. That on Thursday you kill Pavel. . . ."

"What!" said Volti, shaken at last out of his perilous calm.

"It is decided that you kill him," said Stroganoff blandly. "My friend here—M'sieu Quill—just tell me that he arrest you soon." He winked heavily. "*N'est-ce pas?*"

The morning coat slid nearer to the agitated Volti and whispered to him not to worry. "Damages for wrongful arrest," it said, "were worth a fortune."

But Quill was making no arrest that afternoon. He said so. Stroganoff seemed disappointed.

"The police they still have an eye on you," he threatened Volti. "And on Thursday mornings you go."

The morning coat seemed about to start reading again, but changed its mind.

"In view of the special circumstances," it said, " and taking into consideration the fact that my client is almost as anxious to leave your employment as you are to dispense with his services, he has intimated to me his willingness to consider an amicable settlement for a sum considerably less than that stipulated in the contract."

"*Pardon*," said Stroganoff.

"It means we'll take two hundred," said the morning coat suddenly human. "And between you and me and the lamp-post. . . ."

"Lamp-post?"

The morning coat became formal again. "That is our final offer. You would be well advised to accept it. If the matter gets to Court it will cost you considerably more than that in costs alone."

Stroganoff reflected. "You watch the stage on Wednesday week," he said to Volti, "and then maybe I think about it."

The interview seemed to have reached as satisfactory a stage as it ever would. Volti nodded and got up.

"Come, Mr. Shapiro," he said to the morning coat. They left, and Stroganoff, relieved, sank back into his arm-chair. He sprang up again the next moment for Stanley had entered.

"Go away," he said.

But it appeared that this was what Stanley wanted. He had come to ask for the evening off.

"*Impossible*," said Stroganoff promptly. "Who then will lead the applause in the Upper Circle?"

"Doesn't the Upper Circle applaud for itself," asked Quill. This seemed a new angle on stage life.

"For the Ballets Nevajno—no," said Stroganoff. "And to-night we give *Gare du Nord* and Nevajno he is sensitive to *le silence*."

"But," said Stanley, "I've promised to help the police and I want time off to follow up a most important clue."

Stroganoff looked at Quill incredulously. "You have asked Stanley to help?"

"He's offered," said Quill tactfully.

Stroganoff shrugged. "*Mais mon ami, c'est votre affaire*. In that case I give Stanley the permit, and Appelsinne he can go up and shout '*bis*' instead."

"Not Appelsinne," said Stanley panic-stricken.

Quill suppressed a smile. So Stanley's suspect was the dour Appelsinne. Stanley had got his cast a bit muddled. Appelsinne might have wanted to kill Palook, but he could never have wanted to kill Pavel.

Stroganoff, too, had divined the situation. "You come here to tell me that you suspect my Appelsinne?"

"I am revealing nothing for the moment," said Stanley, the sphinx.

"But you have revealed, *déja*, and the thing it is *rigolo*. Appelsinne to murder Pavel—poof!"

"Stranger things have been known," said Stanley darkly.

"When?" asked the interested Stroganoff.

Quill came to Stanley's rescue. "Have you any proof?"

"Not yet," said Stanley gratefully. "But I'll get that to-night with any luck. I have a plan."

"All right," said Stroganoff. He had tired of this un-profitable discussion. "And meanwhile, you get out—no?"

Stanley got out, and after a discreet interval, Quill followed.

CHAPTER XV

QUILL sat in his room, reading, with a certain amount of jealousy, about an obnoxiously successful French detective, and avoiding night starvation on the rather un-satisfactory gas-cooker provided by Miss Treackle. It was past midnight and Quill was pleasantly tired. The evening at the theatre had been as uneventful as any evening containing a performance of Nevajno's *Gare du Nord* could be. Quill himself had been completely bewildered by the snarling locomotive that sprawled right across the backcloth, the weirdly dressed and unusually agile porters, the boiling of noises in the orchestra pit, and the station master (the choreographer himself) who spent all his time dancing with the more attractive passengers. The action was explained in the programme, but it did not help Quill much to be told that the station was the Universe, the train Fate, and the passengers the nobler emotions of the human soul, such as hatred, jealousy, vanity and greed.

Nevertheless, a part of the audience had seemed to like the ballet. Many of them were on their feet shouting "brava," "superb" and even "Nevajno." But another faction, led by the balleto-medico, sat back in their seats and talked con-temptuously of design, dynamic rhythm, plastic values, grouping and line. Nevajno had made a speech containing a number of gibes at Petipas, and some dark allusions to a new and even more revolutionary work on which he was at present engaged. Listening to him, Quill had found himself anticipating to-morrow's interview with a certain amount of apprehension.

The French detective in Quill's book was just expatiating on psychology to an audience born to be admiring, when a knock on the door, which somehow managed to combine fury and prudery in equal proportions, brought him to his feet.

Miss Treackle, her flannel dressing-gown—a raw pink—tasselled firmly round her waist, her hair braided for the night, gave tongue.

"A lady to see you." The brevity of the sentence was more than compensated for by her expression.

A horrid vision of Arenskaya, an abandoned Russian gipsy, dropping feverish cigarette ends on Miss Treackle's carpet, floated before Quill's eyes.

"Show her up," he said resigned.

"That I won't do," said Miss Treackle firmly. "Really, Mr. Quill, I'm surprised at you. My house has always been respectable. You will see her downstairs in the drawing-room. The fire has gone out but I can't help that."

A week ago Quill would have descended meekly to shiver in front of Miss Treackle's sister's wedding group, a photograph which, in addition to the rather dazed-looking relatives, also included a picture-hatted Miss Treackle, gazing enviously at the not very prepossessing capture of the bride. But now he had been infected with some of the buoyancy of the Ballet Stroganoff. He was damned if he was going to catch cold to please Miss Treackle's furious sense of propriety.

"You will show her up here," he said firmly.

Miss Treackle tightened the tassel of her dressing-gown. "Never under my roof."

"In that case," said Quill affably, "there will be a spare room under it next week. This room," he elaborated.

"Are you giving me notice to vacate?"

"Yes."

Miss Treackle seemed about to snap an acceptance but stopped short. Never late with the rent. Never quibbles about extras. Never questions the laundry bill. Hardly ever in. And anyone else would certainly insist on having the room re-papered.

"Is the lady a relative?" she asked charitably offering a loophole.

"My grandmother," said Quill.

"That," said Miss Treackle, allowing no trace of incredulity to appear on her features, "is different." She stalked out and returned to usher in Rubinska.

"Thank you, Miss Treackle," said Quill.

"Not at all, Mr. Quill." The door snapped to, but not before a scornful "grandmother " had floated through it.

Rubinska was clearly labouring under some emotion. She crossed impulsively to Quill, snatched at his hands, and gazed at him with large pleading eyes. She was altogether adorable.

"You must promise me something."

"Of course," said Quill. In his relief that she was not Arenskaya, he was willing to promise anything.

"You must arrest Kasha Ranevsky at once."

Quill began to revise his views about promises. "Why?"

"To save his life."

"How?"

"Don't you understand," said Rubinska impatiently. "Nothing short of an arrest will stop him dancing Petroushka and then he'll be killed."

"Has Stroganoff offered him the part?"

"Not yet—but he's going to. I know he's going to—everybody says so."

"But surely," said Quill, "if you feel that way you can persuade him to refuse."

"I've tried," said Rubinska. "I've been trying all evening.

But Kasha's too ambitious. He laughs at the danger. He even says there is no danger. And there is—isn't there?"

"There may be," Quill was forced to admit.

" Then you must arrest him."

Quill led her to a chair and fed her a cigarette.

"Take it calmly," he said. "You must realise for yourself that I can't take Kasha into protective custody on the strength of a superstition."

"Then you must order Stroganoff to give another ballet."

Quill explained patiently that Scotland Yard could hardly order the cancellation of a ballet on the grounds that somebody might be murdered in it. They could not afford to advertise their incapacity in this manner.

"Then you will do nothing?"

Quill said every precaution would be taken. Plain clothes men would surround the stage; he was even toying with the idea of introducing some of his men into the crowd scenes. The killer, even assuming he would be at work again, would undoubtedly be caught afterwards.

"But first," said Rubinska, " he will kill my Kasha."

Quill sighed. "Your Kasha. Alas! poor Stanley."

"Poor Stanley," agreed Rubinska. "Should I marry Kasha, he will be inconsolable for at least a day. Already because he saw me kiss Kasha before the performance to-night he has gone drinking with Appelsinne."

Quill laughed. "It wasn't a broken heart that made him do that."

"No?"

"No. He suspects Appelsinne of having murdered Pavel and I suppose the alcohol is to loosen Appelsinne's tongue. But Appelsinne will drink him under the table."

A quaking hand knocked at the door and an agitated finger drew Quill into the passage.

"There's a young man downstairs," hissed Miss Treackle. "He's followed her. This is terrible. What shall we do?"

"Show him up," said Quill.

"No," said Miss Treackle. "I will not have bloodshed in my house. Confide in me, Mr. Quill. Is he her husband?"

"He's going to be," said Quill comfortingly.

"I knew it," wailed Miss Treacle. "Look-out," she added as the beaming face of Kasha came running upstairs.

"She has not left yet?" Kasha enquired.

"She's gone," lied Miss Treackle, game to the last.

"Gone?"

"She's here," said Quill. "It's quite all right," he explained to Miss Treackle. "We're not going to kill each other. This," he could not help adding, "is my grandfather."

Panic left Miss Treackle. She tightened her tassel and bade them an acid good night.

Kasha followed Quill into the room and embraced Rubinska affectionately.

"So she hasn't persuaded you to arrest me," he grinned.

"Not quite," said Quill. "All the same," he added, "why don't you do what she asks and refuse the role?"

"It hasn't been offered to me yet," said Kasha. "If it is I shall certainly take it. I've always longed to dance Petroushka."

Rubinska moaned. "But you'll be killed."

"Why should I be killed? This girl here," he explained to Quill, "seems to think there's some lunatic at large killing off every Petroushka in sight."

"She might even be right," said Quill gravely.

"Even if she is," said Kasha obstinately, "I'm still taking the role if I get the chance. I'd be a fool to miss the opportunity."

"An opportunity you would never had had but for the murders," Quill pointed out.

Kasha nodded. "From that point of view I'm grateful to the murderer. I'd almost commit murder myself to dance that role."

Rubinska shrugged. "You see, he's hopeless."

"Absolutely hopeless," agreed Kasha. "But don't worry.

If I get the role Mr. Quill here will see to it that I'm not killed."

"I'll do my best," said Quill. "My reputation won't stand a third murder."

"You see," Kasha picked up Rubinska's coat and helped her into it. "So now we'll go home and let my guardian get some sleep. Besides I have a taxi waiting."

"Spendthrift," said Rubinska.

"Not at all," said Kasha. "Stanley is going to pay for it."

"Why Stanley?"

"Because he is in it. Tight as a lord."

Rubinska was not at all pleased. "Why did you bring him?"

"Someone had to look after him and get him home," said Kasha. "Only it was rather late and I came here first."

Quill escorted them into the street. From the cab Stanley peered owlishly at him.

"Awfully sorry," he said thickly. "He wouldn't talk."

CHAPTER XVI

FOR the London season Nevajno had installed himself in a semi-detached studio in Bloomsbury—an insufficiency of isolation which appeared to cause the neighbours occasion for complaint. Quill and the balleto-medico, reaching the mews at eleven o'clock on Sunday morning, had no difficulty in finding it. A scowling garage proprietor led them to a door through which an alarming fanfaronade of discords was penetrating, and callously left them to their fate.

"Prokofiev," said the balleto-medico.

Quill knocked, but, realising immediately that this was a mere waste of time, entered.

Deep in an arm-chair, screened by a cloud of smoke, Nevajno was listening entranced to his portable gramophone.

He was wearing a high-necked Russian blouse of luxurious plum velvet, flannel bags and camel-hair bedroom slippers. He waved a vague welcome at his visitors.

"Sit down," he said. "Listen."

The balleto-medico made himself comfortable on a wicker basket that had once belonged to Stroganoff. Quill selected the collected works of Proust. They listened while the record screeched itself to a close, and it was not until Nevajno showed every sign of putting on the other side that Quill intervened.

"Er," he began.

"Later," said Nevajno. "First we must listen to this. It is by Polyshumudshedshi."

"Prokofiev," contradicted the balleto-medico in his forth-right English way.

"Prokofiev pale compared to Polyshumudshedshi," said Nevajno. "Listen and you will be convinced." He attacked the handle. "It is to this music," he announced, "that I have the idea magnificent for a ballet."

The balleto-medico moved restlessly.

"It is called," said Nevajno oblivious, *Table d'hote*. He started the record. "The action it take place in a restaurant. The backcloth it is a bill of fare. I compose it later—it is decided only that it will be symbolic. On the left is painted the black jacket of the *maitre d'hotel*, on the right, one asparagus."

"And that," said Quill ingratiatingly, as a succession of crunching sounds ruined the morning sunshine, "is the heavy-footed waiters shuffling."

"On the contrary," said Nevajno. "That, it is the celery."

Quill subsided but the balleto-medico took action. He crossed to the gramophone and stopped it. Nevajno looked at him like a hurt child.

"Why you do that?" he asked.

"I've heard enough," said the balleto-medico, "I'm sick of your Universal eaters."

"But they are symbolic." Absently Nevajno picked up

Quill's cigarette, lit his own, and tossed the detective's carelessly into the waste-paper basket.

"Appetites," he explained, "are universal. Man he is hungry for food. The nations they are hungry for territory."

"Appetites," said balleto-medico, "are not balletic."

Nevajno turned to Quill. "Take no notice of that one. The way I do it, you have not to fret. Everything I do is balletic. I could take the *sujet* of the Royal Academy," he boasted, "and in my hands it would become beautiful. And symbolic. And balletic."

"You have never been to the Royal Academy," accused the balleto-medico.

"*Naturellement*," said Nevajno. "It is not necessary. Diaghilev did not go to Persia to commission *Sheherazade*. Balanchine went not to ancient Greece for his *Apollon-Musaguets*. Massine did not visit Hamley's for *La Boutique Fantasque*. And I myself was led blindfolded through the *Gare du Nord*, lest what I might see should influence my ballet."

"That," said the balleto-medico, "is obvious."

"You liked it," said Nevajno pleased. "It is unshackled—*n'est-ce pas?* Untrammelled. *Libre*. Nothing there of the *petit bourgeois* with his season ticket."

"And nothing there of Ballet, either," said the balleto-medico.

The yell of rage that Nevajno let forth told Quill that it was time for him to intervene. He had come here to discover if the genius was mad—not to goad him into it.

"I enjoyed it very much," he said placatingly.

"You enjoyed it," said Nevajno, livid. "This ballet that should shake you to the very soul, this ballet that is an abyss of all suffering, that is black with the despair of the world and the futility of endeavour—you enjoy it."

"Very much," said Quill.

"No doubt," said Nevajno cuttingly, "you enjoy also *Sylphides* and *Petroushka*."

"They are real ballets," said the balleto-medico gloatingly. "Though not, of course," he added, "as performed by the Stroganoff company."

Another scream of rage came from the doorway. It was Stroganoff, almost dropping the package he was carrying in his fury.

"That," he said, "is the libel. It is also not true."

The balleto-medico was amused. "Privileged occasion," he said.

"It is the last privilege you shall have of me," retorted Stroganoff. "From now on you pay for your seat and I see to it myself that they put you behind pillar."

"I would prefer that he do not come to the theatre at all," said Nevajno. "He is Philistine."

"Without a doubt," agreed Stroganoff. He paused for a moment. "Still," he resumed, "it is not to debate with the quacks that I have come to you this morning."

Nevajno was immediately on the defensive. "If it concerns that scheque you schange for me . . ."

"*Mais non, mon cher,*" said Stroganoff. "That is all right."

"Olright?" echoed Nevajno incredulously. "The bank they have pay it?"

"Doubtless they will do so shortly," said Stroganoff consolingly. "And if not—poof—it matters nothing. We are artists—you and me—not doctors."

But Nevajno still looked puzzled.

"Look," said Stroganoff, getting busy with his parcels, "I bring you little present. *Foie-gras.*" He deposited a package on the table. "Champagne." He produced two magnums. "And a little caviare to tempt the appetite."

Nevajno circled the display warily. "Why you bring me all this?"

"It is the compliment from one artist to another."

Nevajno brooded. To Quill it seemed that something was preying on his mind.

"You schange me small scheque?" he asked in his grimmest voice.

Stroganoff gulped a little but rallied. "*Assurément*," he said. Nevajno struck the table with his fist.

"*Assassin!*" he roared.

"*Mais non*," said Stroganoff.

"*Mais si*," bellowed Nevajno. "All is now clear. I understand everything. All this champagne—all this artist to artist— it is to murder me. Do you deny that it is to ask me to dance Petroushka that you have come here?"

Stroganoff sat down on a pile of suitcases. It was clear from his expression that Nevajno had guessed correctly.

"There is no danger," he said coaxingly, "and as Petroushka you will be superb."

"I shall not be superb," said Nevajno. "It is a role I do not covet. The ballet it is old fashioned and the symbolism it is for the children."

Stroganoff still pleaded. "If you dance this for me I produce for you the ballet of a million shirts."

"Not the shirts," said Nevajno petulantly. "That was last week. Now I work on new idea. *Table d'hote*. It is magnificent. I will play the music now."

"Er," said Quill.

"Not again," said the balleto-medico.

"Later," said Stroganoff. "You dance Petroushka, and I produce that too."

"What will it benefit me if I am dead?" asked Nevajno.

Stroganoff switched his attack to a new angle. "To die for your art it is the greatest thing of all."

Nevajno nodded. "There I agree. To die for *Gare du Nord* —that is the death glorious. Willingly would I sacrifice myself. But to die for *Petroushka* that is merely silly. I will not take the risk. The ballet of the future it need me too much."

"You obstinate yourself," said Stroganoff.

Nevajno in a few piercing sentences confirmed this suspicion. Stroganoff gave up the struggle.

"In that case," he said nastily, "I take out the scheque from your salary. Also I take back this caviare to give to Kasha."

"You can take your champagne too," said Nevajno defiantly. "And all your friends with you. I desire to work."

But before Stroganoff could collect his bottles, there was an ecstatic shrill from the door.

"Champagne!!!" Arenskaya hurried in. "What is it that we celebrate?"

Puthyk too had reached the table and was examining the bottles lovingly.

"Moet-Chandon," he announced happily. "It is my favourite. I drink to you, my darling."

"Where are the glasses?" demanded Arenskaya, always practical.

"There aren't any," Quill prophesied.

He was right, but the balleto-medico came forward with a quantity of cups. Puthyk opened a bottle.

"To what," repeated Arenskaya, passing up her cup for a second helping, "to what is it you said we drink?"

"We drink to nozzing," exploded Stroganoff, who had been watching the performance with growing irritation. "We just drink, that is all. And now I have no champagne left to take to Kasha."

"It is his birthday?" asked Arenskaya interested.

"No," said the balleto-medico rushing in. "It is the Stroganoff idea of a Petroushka."

"He will not need coaxing that one," said Stroganoff, looking meaningly at Nevajno. He put his art before everything."

Puthyk looked depressed. "He is very young to die," he said sadly.

This bland assumption by everybody that the next Petroushka would die as a matter of course, wounded Quill's professional pride.

"The Police have the situation well under control," he said.

"He will die," stated Puthyk unimpressed. "The poor young man."

Arenskaya crossed to Quill. "He must not die," she said earnestly. "He is a dancer of great promise. And when I have taught him that he shall not bend the knee when he do the arabesque, nor pinch the arms for the *tour en l'air*, and some dozen other little trifles, he will be the dancer complete. So you must guard him with your life or else the little Rubinska she will claw your eyes out."

The waste-paper basket burst into flames.

They were all mad, decided Quill drearily. One as mad as the other.

CHAPTER XVII

ON Monday Kasha had caviare for breakfast.

He was not very fond of caviare for breakfast and he did not grudge the three reporters who kept him company their share.

The Ballet Stroganoff was still in the headlines. Kasha's acceptance of the role of Petroushka had kept them there. The Sunday news sheets perforce had had to be content with speculations as to whether the ballet boasted any dancer brave enough to take the risk—the Monday Press had found its hero. Kasha Ranevsky was news.

"New Star to Dance Petroushka," said the early editions.

"Kasha Ranevsky to challenge Death."

"Young Dancer in Fatal Role."

"*Il Dance pour l'Amour*," said Paris.

"Aryan Dancer Defies Jewish Killer," gloated Berlin.

"Ballet Dancer to Brave Bumper-off," announced New York.

By lunch time Kasha was startled to find that he had given a special interview to the *Daily Distraught*.

"My art," he had apparently told Petunia Patch, " is to me everything. The Ballet Stroganoff it is like a father. Vladimir Stroganoff is a wonderful man."

The source of this message was easy for Quill to divine. When he ran into Stroganoff during his barren plodding round the theatre that afternoon, the latter not only admitted it, but went so far as to complain of the cutting. "They do not print my picture," he said peevishly.

Evening found Kasha under contract to write the story of his life, loves and art—with a prudent clause appointing an experienced executor to complete the work in the event of premature death. Kasha's feeble protests that he would have no time even to start it, were overruled. The experienced executor, it appeared, could look after that as well.

On Tuesday morning Rubinska joined Kasha in the head-lines. Reporters had discovered the friendship between them, forcibly affianced them, and now from every column came floods of information concerning the happy pair. How they had loved each other at first sight. How Rubinska had begged him to renounce the role. And how he had quoted Lovelace at her.[1]

Quill too, as the detective in charge of the case, came in for a certain amount of belated biography. That unfortunate matter of the wrongful arrest was dragged up again, jeers (thinly disguised as sympathy) were levelled at him for permitting Pavel to be murdered under his nose, and it was hinted that, though Kasha might be showing courage in facing death for his art, it was sheer foolhardiness not to insist on a more experienced detective before doing it. Quill bore it all with commendable fortitude, until the self-complacent Hiram B. Sausage complimented him on the publicity he was getting.

[1] " I could not love thee, dear, so much . . ."

"Cash in on it, my boy," he counselled.

"Your management they give you rise for this, no?" asked the interested Stroganoff.

But Quill had stopped thinking about promotion. The continued terror campaign in the Press was fast reducing him to its own level of panic. He had not at first seriously believed in the possibility of a third murder, but now, though his common sense still rebelled, he could think of nothing else. If Kasha were killed his career was finished. But even that worried him less than the responsibility of one human being for another. He was dreading to-morrow's gala. The Snarl was dreading it too. All Scotland Yard was jumpy.

It was ridiculous, this helplessness to prevent a murder before an audience of a couple of thousand people. But it happened twice. And there was nothing to do to prevent it happening a third time, except to have as many men in the theatre as possible and to watch . . . and to wait . . .

The Late Night Finals, hard-up for a fresh angle, starred Madame Rubinska as " Anxious Mother."

"If Kasha is killed," she said, "the effect on my daughter's dancing will be deplorable. My daughter is the greatest dancer since Pavlova. I love Kasha like my own son," she added as an afterthought.

Efforts were made to induce Mr. Rubinska to make a statement. The only fact that emerged, however, was that he was né Rabinovitch. Tactfully the Press refrained from printing this.

Wednesday might have been the morning of an execution, except that Kasha was not permitted to choose his own breakfast. This had to be fixed in time for the country editions. Every step he took during that day was fully reported.

On the whole Kasha stood up manfully to his ordeal. He dealt smilingly with the reporters. He shoved his enormously increased mail on to Stanley. He made friends with the plain clothes men who surrounded his rehearsals. But even he blenched slightly at the nudgings and whisperings that arose

from the queue that had waited all night, as he entered the stage
door on the afternoon of the final rehearsal for the gala
performance that night.

*   *   *   *   *

In the theatre all was frenzy. The foam of whiskered
Generals had been pushed firmly into the dress circle and their
places in the wings usurped by cameramen and a director,
recently fired from Elstree and snapped up by the Next-Minute
News Reel Company. He was there to get a picture of Kasha
at rehearsal—ready for his News Reel Obituary. On-the-dot
Evans prided himself on his far-sightedness. Provided the
murderer did not let him down, this picture would be the
scoop of the year. Ecstatically be heard the commentary:
"The Next-Minute News Reel Company posthumously
presents to you the Dance of Death. This is positively the
only action picture of that gallant young dancer, Kasha
Ranevsky, whose tragic death we all . . ."

Crash! One of the balconies had collapsed. It had never
been designed for ten stalwart policemen and as many of the
cast as could crowd themselves into this exciting vicinity.

Sergeant Banner disentangled himself from the wreckage,
adjusted a Russian beard, and ambled embarrassed over to
Quill.

"How do I look?" he demanded with diffident pride.

"Awful," said Quill candidly and wandered off to be
collared by Arenskaya.

"It is 'opeless," she shrilled. "You take them away
immediately. Your policemen they ruin my ballet—they will
not mingle."

Quill protested. "But they only have to walk about."

"*Mais, mon Dieu*," said Arenskaya, " 'ow they walk! 'Ave
you see them?"

"Well—of course, they're not trained dancers."

"That I realise," said Arenskaya. "The audience they will

realise it too. They march like soldiers. It is a sight to break the heart. Better far that Kasha should die than that Benois should see such atrocity."

The balcony had been bolstered up again and such of the company as could be cajoled were clambering on to it. Many refused, doubtless feeling that on such an occasion the privilege of nerves need not be confined to the principals and mothers alone. Storms were brewing everywhere. Always temperamental, the Stroganoff Company had reached the pitch of nervous frenzy. The plain clothes men stood dazed, helpless breakwaters in a sea of emotion. Only Kasha was calm—"the fatalistic calm of the Slav," as Petunia Patch was at the moment 'phoning her office.

Engulfed in his magician's robe, Puthyk sat in the wings, practising his flute. He need only pretend to play it at the performance but he was by nature thorough.

"They have permitted me to dance the Magician," he told Quill with pride. "It is a small role but important. And after Kasha die, doubtless I dance Petroushka."

Volti swung his baton. The breakwaters came to life, marched on to the stage, took up their positions, and almost saluted. The rest of the cast went on jabbering.

In the stalls a cub reporter laughed. They had carelessly forgotten to tell him that this was Art. Now half a dozen mothers did so simultaneously.

Down the centre aisle stalked tragedy. Bald-headed tragedy, face masked in gloom, every gesture a fresh despair. Alarmed, Quill hastened to its side.

"What's up?"

"Ssh!" said Stroganoff and led him out of earshot of the reporters.

"I am desolate," he confided. "Benois he does not come."

"Hard luck," said Quill. "Still, the house will be packed."

"You misunderstand me," said Stroganoff. "It is not for finance that I weep. The finance it is beautiful. It is the blow at my prestige that burn me up. Where there is a gala there must be *un invité d'honneur*. It is too late now to get Chaliapine. It will have to be Lord Button'ooke and he is no artist. Always he ring the telephone."

"Still," said Quill, "the audience comes to see the ballets and not Buttonhooke." Privately he was of the opinion that they were queueing up to see a murder, but this did not seem to be the moment for saying it.

Fresh despair seized Stroganoff.

"And what has the Ballet Stroganoff to show them? Policemen!"

"They are very good policemen," said Quill, a little hurt.

"Do not console me, *mon ami*," said Stroganoff. "I am resigned." He looked at the stage where an intellectual Moor (Nevajno) was condescending to chase Petroushka and brightened slightly.

"Kasha he dance well—no?"

"He is superb." Arenskaya joined the party. "He will be the best Petroushka the Ballet Stroganoff has seen."

Stroganoff was impressed. It was seldom that Arenskaya praised. "That is your opinion?"

"Have I not said so?"

The prospect of at last possessing a first-class dancer banished everything else from Stroganoff's mind. Immediately he became immersed in ambitious plans for the future, which included triumphant seasons at the Paris Opera—The Scala, Milan—and the New York Metropolitan—with a series of specially commissioned ballets by Fokine, Balanchine, La Ninjinska, Massine (triumphantly snatched from a broken-hearted de Basil) and, of course, Nevajno.

"There are not enough police on the stage," he finished abruptly. "My Kasha he must be well protected. Bring plenty more."

"*Mais non!*" countermanded Arenskaya. "You will remove half of these. I, myself, shall go on the stage to watch over

Kasha. I think," she said ruminatively, "I dance the Gipsy."

"*Oie!*" said Stroganoff. "It will tire you," he corrected himself hastily, "and I cannot have my beautiful tire herself."

Arenskaya's face set in familiar lines. "I insist."

Quill fled.

Outside the theatre a newsboy waved a paper at him. Petunia Patch was at it again :

POLICE FOR PETROUSHKA
Detectives Guard Ballet's Tragic Triangle

This afternoon, the last rehearsal of *Petroushka*, the Death Ballet, was held behind locked doors at the Collodium theatre. Only Stroganoff and a few close friends assisted at a *répétition* that must surely be unique in the annals of the Dance, performed by a company stricken with terror.

The Ballet's tragic triangle were mute—the little Rubinska (the Doll) her small pale face and great tragic eyes pleading with death. The Moor, that intelligent young choreographer, Nevajno, almost unnaturally composed, and Kasha Ranevsky, the apex of attention—Petroushka, Calamity's Clown— calm with the fortitude of the true artist, looking death unflinchingly in the face, and daring it to strike.

The calmest figure of all was that of Vladimir Stroganoff. He moved reassuringly among his company—his great family of Russian children—taking with him a message of quiet encouragement.

"Kasha," he told me, "has always been to me a son. If he die, I am desolated!"

Detective Inspector Quill was well in evidence. The tall Adonis of Scotland Yard had turned up to station a detachment of eager young constables, recalled from our Pedestrian Crossings, to guard over Kasha on the famous set.

Arenskaya, *maitresse-de-ballet*, and mother-confessor to the Stroganoff company, turned to me with tears in her eyes. "Kasha is to me as a son—a god-son."

In the stalls I was fortunate enough to snatch a word with Rubinska's mother. This is her message to you :

"Kasha will pull through, never fear. This is his big chance and he means to seize it with both hands. Besides, my daughter will be dancing with him. It is her greatest role. It is not true that la Rubinska is to sacrifice her art to marriage. She will be leaving Stroganoff shortly to form a company of her own, where no doubt Kasha will dance as well. He is a dear boy and looks upon me as a mother."

It is rumoured that a Very Important Person Indeed will be present at the Gala Stroganoff to-night.

Quill thrust the paper into his pocket impatiently. He looked incuriously at the waiting queues. Then he looked again. Somewhere he had seen those faces before—that despondency lit by a hungry gleam. Suddenly he remembered. It was outside the Old Bailey.

They were here to see a murder!

*   *   *   *   *

There was an ugly undercurrent in the house that night. It whispered through the stalls, murmured through the dress circle, and broke into open speculation in the gallery. There were many in the audience who had never seen a ballet before, but then neither had they ever seen anybody murdered, and they were cheerfully willing to submit to the first in the hope of the second. Their eagerness contrasted sharply with the anxiety of the regular balletomanes. The latter all had the air of having been drawn to the theatre almost against their will. There was none of the frantic discussion, the keen dissension, and the brittle cooing of friendly enemies, that characterises the more normal evenings of ballet. They looked uneasily at each other or shuddered their mutual disgust as some sensation-lover found temporary diversion in gazing at them. .

Even the programme girls were in a state of tension. Nobody bought chocolates.

At eight-twenty, Lord Buttonhooke arrived, alighting from his Rolls Royce, an Ermine on one arm, a Sable on the other, behind him a secretary. He was the sort of man who offers you caviare and is mildly surprised if you eat it all. They swept grandly past the welcoming Stanley and established themselves in the Royal Box. A moment later the secretary was 'phoning the office on the apparatus that had been specially installed that afternoon. He was telling them that nothing had happened yet.

Stroganoff wandered in, made a vague speech of welcome[1] and wandered out again.

"What a sweet old man," said the Ermine.

"Poof!" said the Sable in unconscious plagiarism.

Meanwhile, the Old Bailey portion of the audience had found to their disgust that *Petroushka* was not the only item on the programme. Before the murderer could reasonably be expected to get busy, they would have to sit through two ballets. Mournfully they studied their programmes.

"*Les Sylphides*. A choreographic poem in the form of a Reverie."

What was all this?

The lights were lowered. Volti rapped sharply with his baton on the conductor's desk. The curtain was a dark stain screening the stage. The reassuring notes of Chopin floated out to the house. The ballet-goers relaxed. Nothing could be really wrong with a world where they still danced *Sylphides*.

"Pretty," said an Old Baileyite approvingly as the curtain went up.

But half-way through he got restless.

It was not a good performance of *Sylphides*. The movements were jerked, the soft lines turned to angles. It was danced

[1] "It is a great honour that you come, but Benois he would have been better."

by a cast that was afraid. The moonlit glade was oppressed with a general anxiety.

Nobody was really sorry when the curtain swished down to the usual polite applause.

Buttonhooke's secretary was on the 'phone. The news editor was sharp. Would they kindly refrain from disturbing him until something had happened. The alternative story was already set up, anyway.

To Quill, the interval seemed endless. He wandered unhappily back-stage, smiled wanly at Nevajno's frantic directions to the scene-shifters, evaded Arenskaya with a practised neatness, exchanged a few reassuring words with his men, and wandered back into the auditorium.

"*Ajax*. An allegoric fantasy in one act. Choreography by Nevajno."

The Old Baileyites suffered patiently as Ajax leapt his defiance over the miscellaneous collection of rocks. There seemed a sporting chance that he might stumble over one of then and break his neck.

In his dressing-room Kasha sat talking to Rubinska. The sympathetic Sergeant Banner, on guard, pretended not to listen.

Kasha was making an effort to appear light-hearted. Rubinska had given up pleading. She, too, was calling on her courage.

They were arguing about their wedding. Kasha was stating firmly that nothing would induce him to invite Petunia Patch. Rubinska said nothing would persuade her mother not to.

Stroganoff's shining dome bobbed round the door.

"You are ready—no?"

Together Stroganoff and his two children wandered arm in arm down the corridor.

CHAPTER XVIII

FOR once Volti-Subito was watching the stage. The music fell keenly on the ear. The noises of the fair bore an added message of excitement to-night. The shifting and drifting of the crowd began. As they passed they eyed each other warily. So many extras on the stage to-night. So many possible killers.

The street dancers went through their routine. They were keyed up. The crowd caught something of their excitement. Against their will the ballet-goers were infected by their emotion. This was a real performance of *Petroushka* that the Ballet Stroganoff was giving.

The Old Bailey-goers shifted restlessly. "Is that him?" they asked, every time a fresh dancer appeared in the centre of the stage.

Engulfed in his robe, Puthyk bobbed out between the curtains of the Puppet's booth.

"The Magician," explained an assiduous programme reader in the Upper Circle.

The Magician piped his wily tune. The curtains parted. The puppets lolled inanimate in their cells. The Doll, eager in her stillness, the Moor lackadaisical, and Petroushka, his face so quiet it might have been a mask.

"They're all dead!" The all-night wait had proved too much for someone in the gallery.

"Pip-pip." The Moor came jerkily to life.

"Pip-pip." The Doll was on her points.

"Pip-pip." The malevolent magic twitched Petroushka to his feet.

A sigh of relief came from Quill. The Old Baileyites on the other hand felt mildly cheated to find Petroushka still alive.

However, there was plenty of time yet, they reflected. Three more scenes. Three more chances.

"God! He's dancing well," murmured the balleto-medico, peering round his pillar.

Kasha was inspired. He was dancing with the wild abandon of the dupe who is not master of himself, who twitched to order in a dictated frenzy he had no power to subdue. Through him the Doll became something more than the controlled mistress of her feet, and even the Moor lost his detachment and acquired something of the clownish savagery of Fokine's conception.

The applause as the curtain came down was terrific. The house had almost been trapped into forgetting the impending murder.

*   *   *   *   *

" Ah!—*le rideau!*"

*   *   *   *   *

A dominant hand pushed Petroushka into his cell. He was quivering, but still alive.

He hammered the walls of his personal hell, mouthing his misery at the image of the magician above him. His arms move, but they are only sawdust. His legs support him, but they are not real. His feet are but two black rag blobs. His heart loves the Doll, but it does not beat.

Kasha was a poignant as well as a passionate Petroushka. The lines of his agony were painted on his face. The feeling of his agony weighed every gesture. His hysterical welcome of the Doll startled even Lord Buttonhooke into a shudder.

Terrified, the Doll fled from Petroushka's clumsy embrace.

*   *   *   *   *

"*Epatant*," said Arenskaya.
"*Terrifique*," said Stroganoff.

*   *   *   *   *

The scene between the Moor and the Doll was almost a relief. The Old Baileyites laughed at the Moor's antics with his coco-nut. By dint of persuading himself that this was symbolic, Nevajno was putting up quite a creditable performance.

The humours of the *pas-de-deux* went across with a bang. Here were two characters straight out of a comic strip. But into their laughter cut the scream of Petroushka.

"He can conduct that one—when he wants," said Stroganoff approvingly.

In a white rage of jealousy Petroushka leapt at the pair on the sofa. The Moor sprang up. The rivals clinched in a rough and tumble.

The Doll fainted ballet-wise on the sofa—one leg in the air.

*   *   *   *   *

In the wings stood the magician. He was almost in tears.

*   *   *   *   *

Back to the fair. The rhythm in the orchestra heightened, the rhythm on the stage quickened. The music lashed at the excited crowd. A pair of dancing gipsies took the centre of the stage. Neither of them was Arenskaya. (For once she had lost an argument). They danced. A band of nursemaids fluttered their handkerchiefs. The bear lurched ominously across the stage. The coachmen flung themselves wildly into a Russian dance. And everywhere carnival figures jerked their grotesque heads. Snowflakes fell softly on the whirling crowds.

The audience was deadly still.

At the back of each balcony stood a cluster of policemen. Watching.

A tremor passed through the curtains of the puppet booth. Their folds blew open. The orchestra screamed. The puppets leapt on to the stage. Round and round leapt Petroushka. Faster, faster came the Moor, scimitar in hand. Faster, faster, until at last the scimitar cut through the air and Petroushka lay stretched on the ground. Horrified, the crowd edged close. The piping voice of Petroushka mouthed its pathetic farewell.

"Dead?" asked a man in the Upper Circle as the crowd screened the figure from sight.

They sent for the magician. He came to lift a sawdust effigy from the spot where Petroushka had died. Reassured, the crowd drifted off, leaving the old man trailing his rag puppet across the ground.

High on its booth the spirit of Petroushka arose, screaming defiance at the tortured world.

Now! A dozen backs straightened in their seats.

Something was wrong with the magician. His mouth was working. He reeled as though the strength had gone from his legs. Something fell from his hand and clattered on to the stage.

"It is no use," said Puthyk pathetically. "I cannot shoot him. He dance too well."

*   *   *   *   *

Lord Buttonhooke strode from the theatre, a disappointed man.

EPILOGUE

LETTER from Vladimir Stroganoff to Detective-Inspector Adam Quill.

Grand Hotel de la Bazouche,
May. . . .

Mon cher Monsieur Quill,

How are you? This is to tell that the Ballet Stroganoff will soon be in your lovely England once more, doubtless for a season even more triumphant than the last. Alas, that we could not secure Covent Garden. But that is for another year.

With us all is well. Kasha and Rubinska they are long time married—they dance better every day. But me I do not tell them this lest their mother ask for bigger contracts. Volti he is the reformed character—he always watch the stage now. No one is dead since London.

We are bringing with us a big new ballet by Nevajno. It is called *Civilisation*. It is symbolic. There is a scene where the *corps de ballet* is shot with a machine-gun. London will be shaken.

And now, *mon cher*, I want to ask of you one big favour. It concerns my poor Puthyk. I know, *mon cher*, that you do not feel so warm towards the old one as I do. I know that he give you lots of trouble and much anxiety. But remember, M'sieu Quill, he is not *le vrai assassin*—he kill for his art. Petroushka, it was to him his life. He was with Fokine when he invent it. To see it dance bad was more than he could bear. And then he had the delusion. Always he saw himself young, his wife beautiful—it was natural that he should come to think that he alone in the Ballets Stroganoff could bring to the role all that it demanded. We, in the Stroganoff company, knew this well—never were we unkind to the old man when he asked for the part.

(They might have told me, reflected Quill, a trifle bitterly).

Often I reproach myself that I did not do as he ask. But no it was impossible. And poor Puthyk he think that I am blind—obdurate. So he decide that all who dance Petroushka shall die until in the end only he is left to take the role. It is a situation *bien ridicule*, but poor Puthyk he reason that to kill for his art it is not crime.

First he kill Pilaff in Paris, but we all think it suicide. Then he stay up on the opposite balcony and shoot Anton. And still we do not suspect him. Even you, Mr. Quill, who are trained to catch assassins, did not suspect. And still the old one he do not get his role. So he say to himself—this Pavel—he is a dancer mediocre, good to support the ballerina, but he has not the fire for Petroushka. It is a crime against art that he dance it. Poof! I kill him before he can begin. And that, M'sieu Quill, is why he shoot Pavel in his booth.

And then he decide to kill my Kasha. Petroushka it is not for the inexperienced. Petroushka he bear the whole philosophy of life. But when the time come Kasha has danced the role well. The old man is a connoisseur. He sees the role is safe in the ballet while Kasha he is with us. For himself he cares no more. And so he does not shoot.

You will understand now *mon cher* Quill, that it is not an assassin, but an artist, that you have put in that pretty home in Sussex. They tell me he is happy. He write often to Arenskaya. All the time the ballet it goes on in his mind, and often he dance Petroushka to the other guests.

You will do me the favour, M'sieu Quill, if you go down to prepare my Puthyk for our coming. He will no doubt give you the welcome royal. Always he speak kindly of you in his letters. Tell him that we will come and see him often and that the Ballet Stroganoff still go on.

Mille remerciements,
Gardez-vous bien,
V. STROGANOFF.

Rubinska send her love.

With a sigh Quill put away the letter and returned to his notes on the case on which he was engaged. Somehow it was difficult to work up a real enthusiasm over the fate of a vanished laundry van.

F

Casino for Sale

'The Provinces exceed anything that could be put into a novel. Never will a novelist invent the incident of the wife of a Major of *Gendarmerie* putting into verses the Vicar's sermons.'

The Goncourt Journals.

CHAPTER I

CASINO À VENDRE. Occasion Unique.

CASINO FOR SALE. Original Opportunity.

Apply at once

Baron Sam de Rabinovitch,

89 Boulevard Sens Unique,

La Bazouche, A.M.

'Tiens!' said Vladimir Stroganoff, slapping his bald dome with an inspired hand. 'Ça c'est une idée.'

A casino, he explained to the startled stranger in the *Club des Imprésarios*, was a certain source of wealth. With the fabulous profits that would roll in from the roulette and baccarat he would at last be able to endow the Ballet Stroganoff with the magnificence that had always been his dream. He was off to buy it at once, before somebody forestalled him. Had the stranger by chance a time-table to lend him?

*　　*　　*

'Sign here,' said Baron Sam de Rabinovitch with a strong sense of astonished frustration. Delighted as he was to get rid of his old Casino so easily, he could not avoid an undercurrent of bitterness that it had been achieved without the aid of the convincing sales talk he had spent so many hours in preparing. But the bald-headed gentleman who had rushed into his office without knocking had given him no chance to get going.

'You received my telegram—no?' he panted.

The Baron had indeed received a rather breathless telegram that morning. It read:

'DO NOTHING TILL I COME. WAIT. STROGANOFF.'

'You are M'sieur Stroganoff?'

The bald dome nodded happily. 'It is I. You have heard of me—no?'

'No.'

'You have not heard of the Ballet Stroganoff?'

The bald dome shook off an obvious bewilderment. 'Poof,' he said, 'it matters nothing, for now I buy the Casino. My lawyer he come to-morrow but we do not wait. How mooch?'

Baron de Rabinovitch had not yet grasped the full possibilities of the situation but he had grasped them sufficiently to approve the last sentence. Taking a lightning decision he passed over his best cigars. Stroganoff absently stuffed one in his pocket.

'This I smoke later,' he announced. 'But now I buy the Casino. How mooch?'

Cautiously the Count named his first figure.

'It is cheap,' said Stroganoff to his horror, 'but I buy just the same.'

Ten minutes later he was signing document after document with lightning speed. Baron de Rabinovitch watched him broodingly. He could not decide whether he was elated or depressed.

*   *   *

'Voilà!' said Stroganoff with a last triumphant flourish of his pen. 'The Casino it is mine. I go to look at it immediate.'

And leaving the Baron de Rabinovitch suspended between two breaths, he strode from the room, darted across the boulevard and halted in rapture before a pendulum of workmen dangling in front of a festoon of windows. Gloatingly he advanced upon the chromium plated door and grasped the handle only to ricochet into the arms of the Baron who had followed him out.

'The key,' said Stroganoff eagerly.

The Baron was slightly anxious, but the feel of Stroganoff's pink slip in his pocket gave him courage.

'This,' he said, 'is the Casino Buttonhooke.'

Stroganoff goggled at him. Somewhere he had heard that name before. Suddenly he remembered. It was the man who borrowed his ballerinas. A grim foreboding began to steal over him.

'But where,' he asked weakly, 'is my Casino?'

'Taxi,' said Baron de Rabinovitch triumphantly.

CHAPTER II

THE collection of pained-looking palms, tiled turrets, and
Lotissements à Vendre notices known as La Bazouche A.M.
might have served for the décor of a ballet—Plage Fleurie. A
décor, set by an absentminded *Régisseur*, who had forgotten
to send out for the flowers, and was making do with property
orange trees.

Designed as a background for loitering fashion, Le Bazouche
hopefully borders a stretch of the Mediterranean, as blue, as
rock-threaded, and as inaccessible as any other Edwardian
fashion resort. But the laggard call-boy must have forgotten to
round up the more exclusive players, for only egg-faced
walkers-on, in guise of the petite bourgeoisie, are to be seen
trailing stoically about the bijou harbour and the promenade[1]
obviously wishing that the sun would come out. That *Régisseur*
again! For though each night he was at pains to cover the
cyclorama with as neat a design in pin-point stars as is to be
found anywhere between San Remo and Hyères, he frequently
appears to mislay the warm amber orb beneath which the
visitor to the French Riviera expensively browns. In addition
to the stark promenade, the tiny port, and the orgy of effervescent architecture which is the *Ville*—tram-riddled and
narrowly paved—there is the *paysage*. Those stairs-for-giants,
by means of which thrifty peasants have cultivated the surrounding mountains. These are mostly given over to grey-green
carnations, still in the leaf, or green-grey olive trees.

Add to these natural advantages the *Hôtel Moins-Magnifique*
—500 *chambres en face de la mer*.

On a sunny day the terrace bears a luxuriant crop of multi-

[1] *des Anglais*, of course.

coloured mushrooms, beneath which the star players in this fascinating production are wont to sit and wait for their drinks. This afternoon it was not raining.

The Beard on the hotel terrace looked sympathetic. Not that it would have mattered if it had looked formidable, for Stroganoff was in no mood to notice shades of expression. He flung himself furiously into the chair opposite.

'I have been swindle,' he announced.

'Assurément,' agreed the Beard courteously.

'I buy a Casino and—poof!—it is the wrong one.'

Somewhat miraculously the Beard seemed to follow this sketchy scenario.

'You mean that Baron de Rabinovitch has sold you his Casino by the sea.'

'I do not believe that he is Baron,' said Stroganoff violently. 'But I buy the Casino—yes. I am the innocent. I do not know that Buttonhooke have the Casino here already. I do not discover until I sign everything.'

'But you must have noticed the new Casino as you drove from the station?' said the Beard. 'You can't avoid noticing it.'

'I notice it,' agreed Stroganoff, 'but, naturellement, I think it is this Casino that I buy. And the price seem so little that I sign at once before the Baron he ask more.'

It took a few minutes more for the Beard to digest this tale of high finance while the author of it waved his hands furiously at an oblivious waiter. 'Pourcentage' Citrolo, journalist, ballet critic, cynic, blackmailer, and potential corpse, was used to dealing with fools and eccentrics. This one seemed to be both. Furthermore his face was familiar.

'This,' exploded the familiar face, 'is insupportable. First there is the slow journey. Then the stationmaster who do not believe I lose my ticket. Then I am swindle. And now the waiter he take no notice. Never, since Arenskaya decide she want to dance "Giselle," has there been such a day.'

The card index which served as Citrolo's memory clicked over and stopped at the right place.

'You are then Vladimir Stroganoff?' it indicated.

Stroganoff was pleased. 'You know my ballet?'

'Of course.'

'You attended my season in London?' asked Stroganoff hopefully.

'Alas, no!'

'It was superb,' said Stroganoff. 'You were in Paris maybe?'

'Unfortunately, no.'

'In Vienna, Belgrade, Sofia?'

'I was in Marseilles last week.'

'Oh,' said Stroganoff, dimmed. 'You realize,' he explained hastily, 'that we were not at the strength complete?'

'I realize,' said Citrolo tactfully, 'that you have a dancer there of great promise.'

'The little Ostorojno? She is my discovery. It was,' said Stroganoff, 'the flaire magnificent. When first I see her, she is in class in Holland Park. No fouetté—no développé—only a mother. I interest myself in the child. I send her to Paris. I get her best teachers. I even listen while the mother she talks. And how that child develop. Blum he is astonished. De Basil enchanted. Even Massine remark her. But it is I who have the contract.' A shade of gloom crossed his face. 'But her mother she now say that she break because in Marseilles the press it is not sympathetic. Maybe,' said the broadminded Stroganoff, 'it is possible that our performance there left a little to be desired, but is that, I demand you, a reason why the critics they write as though my ballet it always dance like that?'

But to Stroganoff's surprise Citrolo did not appear to agree.

'A critic,' he said, 'is concerned only with that performance which is taking place before his eyes.'

'Poof,' said Stroganoff, 'the critics write what the owner of the paper tell them.'

'But not Citrolo,' said the critic majestically. 'It is well known that Pavlo Citrolo has never written a line that was not his sincere opinion.'

The name seemed to impress Stroganoff more than the credo. He delved into his pocket to produce a newspaper cutting.

'It is you, then, the criminal who has written this?'

Citrolo bowed.

Stroganoff did not bow back. Instead he drew himself to his full height and tried to quell Citrolo with a look. Unfortunately, Citrolo wasn't playing. His eyes had wandered down the terrace where a neat ankle, a jaunty hat, and a portable typewriter were hurrying towards him. Coming closer, the ingredients consolidated into anxious blue eyes under a froth of curls. Stroganoff looked at them in some annoyance.

'Go away, Galybchik,'[1] he said.

Galybchik took no notice. After three months as Stroganoff's secretary, August Greene was used to being told to go away.

'Am I in time?' she asked eagerly.

'Too early,' said Stroganoff, 'much!'

'We mustn't buy the Casino,' said Galybchik. 'That beastly Buttonhooke has built a better one almost next to it.'

Stroganoff glared. 'Why do you not tell me this before I buy?'

'You've bought it?' wailed Galybchik.

'Naturellement, I bought it,' said Stroganoff, 'it is the ruin absolute. Unless,' he added, always hopeful, 'I find someone to take it from me.' He looked at Citrolo. Citrolo shook his head.

'Oh, dear,' said Galybchik, and sat down suddenly. She was crying. Citrolo, loath to miss an opportunity, patted her sympathetically—not quite on the shoulder. Absently she tried to slap his face, missed by a mile, and went on crying.

Stroganoff watched the scene in some confusion. He did not quite know what to do next.

Down the vista came Nicolas Nevajno, choreographer of the future, wrapt in his latest creation. He saw the group, brooded his way to their table, sat down, gulped Stroganoff's Cinzano and continued his meditations.

'Garçon,' said Stroganoff urgently.

'Ssssh,' pleaded Galybchik, 'Nicolas is thinking.'

'Stop him,' said Stroganoff, 'else he will have the idea superb

[1] Russian for 'Little Darling.'

for new ballet, and whenever Nicolas he have the idea superb it cost money.'

But it was too late. Genius was visibly working.

'This place,' he said, 'fills me with a depression profound. The tasteless building. The little stifling streets, the sea that is like a picture postcard—it is worse than a Golovin. There is no rhythm, no Gesamtkunstwerk. It is not symbolic of anything.'

'But it has two Casinos,' said Stroganoff, 'and I have bought the wrong one.'

Nevajno brushed this trifle aside.

'Never has dejection grasped me so firmly. But I suffer it gladly. It is in my depressions that I work best. It was from just such a womb that "Boutique Infame" was born. Who knows but out of this morass of gloom will be born an even greater masterpiece.' He paused for his effect. ' "Plage Bourgeoise." '

'Wonderful,' cried Galybchik.

'It will be the success superb and make for Stroganoff much money. So,' said Nevajno, suddenly practical, 'you schange me small scheque?'

'No,' said Stroganoff.

'Per'aps,' said Nevajno, noticing Citrolo for the first time, 'you do me this favour?'

Citrolo did not trouble to reply.

'Do I not tell you,' said Stroganoff, 'that we are the ruin? We buy the Casino, and Buttonhooke he have a better.'

'Then why we buy it?' asked Nevajno, rather confused.

Galybchik explained the situation patiently but Nevajno was still puzzled. In what way, he enquired, was the Casino Buttonhooke superior to the other? He had passed by both and didn't like either.

Citrolo went into some practical details which in their cumulative effect reduced Stroganoff to the verge of tears, but the genius was not even listening.

'You forget,' he said, 'that there is one asset Stroganoff possess that Buttonhooke has not.'

'What?' asked Galybchik agog.

'Me,' said Nevajno.

With a clatter the table fell to the floor. Stroganoff was on his feet, his eyes shining, all his depression forgotten.

'But you are right,' he cried, 'I am stupid. What matters it to me that Buttonhooke has the buildings, the publicity, the millions? It is I who have the Ballet Stroganoff.'

'So what?' said Citrolo.

'It is not the millions that make the success. It is the artistic directions. Buttonhooke—poof! Casino Buttonhooke—poof!'

He paused on the eve of a portentous announcement.

'I bring to Bazouchka my ballet!'

'Bravo!' cried Galybchik.

CHAPTER III

THREE months have sped energetically on their way since the waiter cleared the empty glasses that had been confidently raised to the new management.

Though it must be admitted that during this period of intense activity the Casino Buttonhooke prospered, it can also be claimed that the Casino Stroganoff has not yet failed.

For every six sables that sweep their accompanied path through the portals of Casino Buttonhooke, a dyed squirrel finds its way to the Casino by the sea. Stakes at the Casino Stroganoff are smaller than those wagered '*au Cercle Button'ooke*,' but they were just as passionately pledged. Buttonhooke, it is true, has the world of fashion reclining about his roulette wheel—a soupçon of royalty suspended above the flick of a card. But the Casino by the sea opened out a number of fascinating vistas for Stroganoff to play with.

His pet innovation was his school for Croupiers. Every morning at half-past eleven, while Arenskaya was giving his Ballerinas hell at her classe de perfectionnement, a waxed moustache surmounted by a glassy eye gave languid lessons in throwing and raking to a prentice personnel. This proved to be quite a good scheme until Buttonhooke meanly riposted with a glib manual 'POINTS FOR PUNTERS' and immediately the attendance fell off.

As a slogan: 'TOUT LE MONDE GAGNE CHEZ STROGANOFF' was hard put to it to compete with the calculated propaganda emanating from the Buttonhooke Press with its tentacles spreading to Paris, New York and Berlin.

Each night the horizon blushed under the cherry-coloured

Neon assertions of the Direction Buttonhooke, while the single ejaculation 'NEVAJNO' flashing defiantly from the Casino by the sea kept only the ballet-lover away.

Each morning saw a notice posted back stage on the board of the Stroganoff theatre. *Casino Call* 15 *heures*.

Members of the company, who could be snatched from whatever rehearsal was furiously being waged at the hour in question, were pressed into service as walkers-on during the slack session in the rooms, and though this involved the management in some elaborate book-keeping, the net effect was good.

Kurt Kukumber, as befitted a methodical gambler, always arrived at the rooms early. He would take up his seat within easy vision of the wheel, open his notebook, and pass the next forty minutes in annotating and recording, until, statistics collected, he was ready to start his infallible system. At five o'clock he would leave—broke—and wander off in search of a prospect to supply him with funds for to-morrow.

To-day his luck was rather better. It was already a quarter past five and he still had ten francs left. Hopefully he pushed a *jeton* on twenty-five. A lean hand reached over and removed it.

'It is foolish what you do,' said Nevajno to the switched round glare, 'I cannot bear to see you lose your money any longer on a method so devoid of line. The roulette wheel it has a rhythm dynamic: the numbers they like to emerge in the plasticity irrevocable. Never would fate be so unbalanced in design as to allow twenty-five to follow fourteen.'

'Vingt cinq,' said the croupier.

'Excuse me,' said Nevajno, 'an appointment.'

Twenty-five had brought luck to Stroganoff's star dancer, Olga Ostorojno. She gathered in her counters, and turned her sleek dark head to flash a grateful smile at that dubious rake, Citrolo, standing behind her. She even thought for a moment what a nice man he was.

Citrolo, who had been thinking for quite a long time what a nice girl she was, smiled back at her and suggested a cocktail. Experience should have made him wary of ballerinas; he had known many and actually married one, the famous Dyra Dyrakova, who had divorced him even before he had had time to be unfaithful. But ballerinas still fascinated him, and this one, so young, so eager, and probably so easy, attracted him strongly. Besides he had not yet met her mother. He was, however, destined to meet her very shortly.

No sooner had Ostorojno accepted his invitation to a glass of champagne than the fat woman beside her turned round and forbade it. Olga did not argue. Neither, after one look, did Citrolo. Obstinacy was visible in every feature of Madame Ostorojno. It showed, too, in her gambling. Relentlessly she had been backing her daughter's age until even the kindhearted Dutchman next to her was moved to plead with her.

'Please, madame, try another number.'

Madame Ostorojno glared and pushed a further *jeton* on eighteen.

The croupier regarded her wonderingly. Almost he felt tempted to put the lady's stake in his pocket and stand the loss himself if a miracle occurred. Dino Vanilla had a contempt for all punters. He had a contempt for everybody who was willing to gamble the wrong side of a percentage, and more especially for the system-mongers who tried to cajole the laws of mathematics into getting the sum wrong. He himself had no objection to an investment with the market rigged, the horse doped, or the pack stacked; but until somebody invented a method of regulating a roulette wheel, the game held no appeal for him. In happier days, before an incautious description of Mussolini as a Socialist had run him out of Italy, he had served his apprenticeship under that Prince of Manipulators, 'Banco' Dacarpo, and though he had not had time to finish the course, he was efficient enough at any rate for the clientele of La Bazouche, unsuspicious souls who attached no special significance to the angle at which the tie tilted at an accomplice, and did not even comment on his elaborate shuffling of the packs that were placed in the Baccarat Shoe. How they amused him— the suckers!

'Dix-huit,' he said evilly. 'Pardon—trente cinq.'

'Let us,' said Citrolo, 'escape to the bar while your maman is engaged in the discourse so amiable with the croupier?'

Olga Ostorojno nodded. They crept unobserved through the gamblers, round the table and reached the door only to find the way blocked by a small but commanding figure in vivid red. It was Arenskaya, Ballet Mistress to the company.

'I am very angry,' she announced, waving an accusing finger, in time with the famous red feather in her hat. 'I who have had Pavlova, Kchesinska, Spessitsiva and Karsavina, all come to me that I might give them hell—I, Arenskaya, have to tramp through the rooms that I may give hell to a little nobody. Do you not know, my precious one, that your batterie is of the most revolting, that your turns they would not pass in a cabaret, and that your fouetté, it practically does not exist? It is half an hour since you should be in class. Transfer yourself.'

'As for you, M'sieur,' she looked at Citrolo, 'you will come with me. I am thirsty.'

She beckoned, and Citrolo followed obediently. People always followed when Arenskaya beckoned—except possibly Stroganoff. He was used to her. They went into the American Bar.

'Blue Whizzbang?' asked Hank, the barman, hopefully. It was his specialty.

'Champagne,' said Arenskaya. 'You charge it to the Direction.'

'Now,' said Arenskaya, as they settled in their chairs, 'I tell you why I devote to you my time. It is for two reasons. The first—you must cease to be unkind to my friend Stroganoff in your writings.'

Citrolo was annoyed. Criticism of his work always annoyed him.

'My notice was quite fair.'

'Bien sûr—it was fair. But why you write it?'

'Madame,' said Citrolo in tones of a refrigerator salesman referring to a rival make, 'it is as well that we should understand each other on this subject. I am a critic.'

'Entendu!'

'I do not aspire to be called an honest man.'

'Ça c'est évident.'

'I have done many things in my life of which other men might be ashamed. I expect to do many more. Of decency—what the English call le public school—I have, thank God, not a trace. I will cheat when there is a reasonable certainty that I will not be caught. I will steal provided it is safe. I will seduce any attractive wife whose husband possesses neither a revolver nor a solicitor. I will blackmail anyone foolish enough to pay. There is only one thing in the world of which I am proud. It is my artistic integrity. There is no money in the world that could make me write one word I do not believe.'

'Mais, c'est pas logique, ça,' protested Arenskaya, 'if you would be a villain you must be a villain toujours.'

Citrolo nodded. 'I agree. But there it is. Often this conscience of mine has annoyed me extremely—it has spoiled for me many opportunities that I might have turned to profit either in bank or bed. Sometimes I've tried to be nice to some young artist who might be nice to me, but it was always useless. The moment I sit down to write, my pen is steeped in vitriol. Au fond, I would not have it otherwise. You complain that I have given the Ballet Stroganoff a bad notice. Have I given the Buttonhooke Ballet a better?'

'Non.'

'If the Stroganoff Ballet wants a good notice from me it must give me a good performance—croyez-moi, madame, there is no other way.'

Realizing that she was fighting a losing battle, Arenskaya changed the subject.

'The second reason I bring you here is more simple. It is to tell you that you shall not sleep with the little Ostorojno.'

'Why?' asked Citrolo, puzzled.

'I do not consider you good influence. Ostorojno is still vierge and her lover he should play a part in the artistic development. I have for her already a mate. His elevation it is wonderful. I perceive him when he lift her in class and I see them at once together in *Sylphides*.'

Citrolo was genuinely shocked.

'You can't mean the Englishman who danced with her yesterday. Madame, I am ashamed of you.'

'Mais, non—it is not Ernest Smithsky,' said Arenskaya, 'he is fairy anyway. Me, I talk of D. Dovolno—he is with Button-hooke. So now you understand why it is essential that they sleep together. Not only will Ostorojno be contented, but it will bring Dovolno back to us.'

Citrolo bowed. 'Your scheme is admirable. My one regret is that I cannot connive at it. The girl appeals to me. I have always had a weakness for ballerinas.'

'You have slept with many?' asked Arenskaya, interested.

'I have had my successes.'

'That is enough then,' declared Arenskaya. 'Now you oblige me and live on your memories.'

'It is just my memories that trouble,' said Citrolo. 'When I watched her in *Lac des Cygnes*, I was reminded of another dancer—a greater dancer.'

'Dyrakova,' said Arenskaya. 'Bien sûr, there is a resemblance. She is a great artist that one. But a silly woman. It is well known. And her taste in men—'orrible.'

'Thank you,' said Citrolo, 'she was my wife once.'

'Sans blague?' enquired Arenskaya dumbfounded. 'But she leave you, of course?'

'Of course. But not before she had taught me all I know of the technique of dancing.'

'What does she know of technique that one?' snapped Arenskaya.

Galybchik trailed in, looking round vaguely.

'Go away,' said Arenskaya.

Galybchik was furious. Only Stroganoff was allowed to tell her to go away.

'I am looking for Nicolas,' she told the barman.

'No use looking for him here,' said Hank. 'I schanged him a scheque yesterday.'

Galybchik nodded sadly and trailed away to the gaming rooms. But Nevajno was not there either. He was sitting on the beach, watching a bather who had got into difficulties, and meditating a new symbolic work to be called *Défense de Nager*.

*   *   *

In London ex-Inspector Detective Adam Quill was startled to receive the following letter:

Casino de La Bazouche.

Monsieur

The three suits you make for me are a disgust. I am glad you remind me I have not paid you. Whistle.

Stroganoff

Directeur du Casino de La Bazouche.

Quill sent the letter back to La Bazouche and three days later the right one arrived:

Mon cher M'sieur Quill (it read)

I invite you urgently to come and pass your vacances at my Casino. Casino—you exclaim in surprise! Mais, oui—c'est vrai! I, Vladimir Stroganoff, have bought a Casino here in La Bazouche. It was the bargain immense.

You have doubtless read of La Bazouche in the paper of my enemy, Lord Buttonhooke. Buttonhooke he has the Casino too, so he make the publicity enormous that will bring the visitors hot hand to Bazouchka. He is mean man—all the space he devotes to his Casino which is large and ugly. Never by chance does he mention the cosy maison that is mine. But, poof, it matters nothing. It is but the inartistic that will go to Buttonhooke—the connoisseur he will come to me. I have for him the attraction irresistible.

You demand what it is? Can you not guess? You are right, mon cher. It is the Ballet Stroganoff. I have transported here all my company. Arenskaya, Nevajno, Ernest Smithsky and a new dancer of great promise whom you will glow to meet. The little Olga Ostorojno, though her mother you will not like too much. Our opening night it was the succès fou. The theatre it was nearly full, and the critics in the ecstasy of delight. All save one, but him I will deal with soon.

Buttonhooke he have the ballet at his Casino too. It is so bad that to improve he must always try to steal from me my dancers. But my children they are loyal. Save for Dovolno, Shasslyk, Cashcavar, and Yaghout, no one has listened to his blandishments. And anyways I have the plan that will reduce him to drink the dust.

You have doubtless heard of the great Dyra Dyrakova— the most enchanting Sugar Plum since Trefilova. She is coming to us. It is practically arranged. Already I have find her address and written the letter eloquent. She has not danced in France for two years—ever since Anton Palook he drop her in Aurore. Never, she swear, will she appear in France again—it is to her not lucky. So she take a studio in Paris, and les petites Anglaises from your so draughty Sadler's Wells, they flee to her for lesson. But time it soften the memory—even that the accident happen in my company— and it is with confidence that I predict she will not resist the magnificent offer that I make her. The sensation of her appearance will be immense, and all le monde will desire to see and come to me. Buttonhooke will be broken man.

So you see M. Quill, it is the holiday intéressant that I offer you. You will find the Casino irresistible. We have the American Bar, the restaurant, and the Baccarat. Our clientele it is regular. They are becoming to me a second family. Often I desire to restrain them when they play too heavy but my croupier principal, the good Vanilla, he reason with me. The more they lose, he point out, the quicker we shall be rich, and I realize that he is right. He is a man remarkable that one, and loyal. Already he refuse to go to the Casino Buttonhooke. A man with vision.

Nevajno he is working on new ballet. The première is in two weeks. So hasten to us, M. Quill, that you may arrive in good time. I send you fare, for I am rich since my London Season when my Petroushkas so sensationally perish. Though already my stockbroker, he make the demands exorbitant, and my Casino it borrow from time to time. Bring with you your good friend, the Sergeant Banner, and any other

*policemen that you may love. We give them all the welcome
royal.*

Amicalement.

*Stroganoff
Directeur du Casino Stroganoff*

*P.S. Last night a gambler in temper suicide—my Casino
it is now complete.*

Quill spent the rest of the morning trying to visualize
Stroganoff running a Casino. His imagination not being up to
it, he decided to go and see for himself. He had the leisure. A
legacy from an aunt, who had never seen *Petroushka* either,[1]
had enabled him to retire from Scotland Yard, and the
Detective Agency that he had started on the strength of it did
not as yet take up much of his time. So far he had had only one
client—a fascinating lady of fashion with a mislaid husband
and a lover whom she suspected of trying to find him.

Quill caught the Blue Train, was made to alight from it in
the middle of the night at Toulon, waited four hours for the
local, and eventually arrived at La Bazouche in time for lunch
at the *Hôtel Moins-Magnifique*. It was revolting.

The restaurant was crowded and he was forced to share a
table with a bow tie, detachable cuffs, and a hopeful expression.
Kurt Kukumber welcomed Quill with the enthusiasm of a
Montmartre guide sighting an American tourist, praised the
climate, expatiated on the view, and recommended the hors
d'œuvres. Quill thanked him.

'De rien,' said Kukumber and proceeded to further
courtesies. In spite of frequent disappointment, Kukumber
still clung to a child-like faith that such pleasantries could
never fail to promote unfaltering confidence in the recipient
and turn the trick that followed into a mere matter of routine.
What trick he would use on Quill, he had not yet decided.

Neither had Quill, though by this time he was quite certain
that one was about to break. He waited for it, but it gradually
became apparent that Kukumber did not believe in hurrying

[1] Special joke for readers of *A Bullet in the Ballet*.

his victim and that this lunch was due to terminate with no mention of the gold brick, the fabulous legacy, or even the Spanish prisoner. Quill found himself looking forward to the moment when they would certainly make their appearance, and got quite a kick out of allowing the insistent Kukumber to pay for his lunch. But he began to feel mildly irritated when Kukumber followed him out of the hotel, hailed a *fiacre*, justled Quill into it and drove furiously to the Casino, not even slowing down as they passed a fascinating glimpse of Stroganoff watering the geraniums. At the Casino, Kurt alighted hurriedly, leaving Quill to pay the cabman. He could not stop, he shouted over his shoulder. He must be there for the start. His system demanded it.

An avuncular commissionnaire directed Quill to Stroganoff's office. 'Do not hope for too much,' he advised, 'Monsieur le Directeur he rarely buy from travellers.'

Quill plodded his way up a faded carpet, past a yellowing statue, through dingy curtains, along a threadbare oilcloth and came to a sudden stop outside a newly painted door. The inscription in chromium letters stood out:

VLADIMIR STROGANOFF
Défense d'entrer.

Quill knocked and went in.

Galybchik was sitting at the typewriter attacking in a spirited manner a letter to the *Conseil Municipal*, which complained bitterly of the noise made by clients leaving the Casino Button-hooke. It purported to come from a body of sleepless rate-payers who, somewhat unaccountably, had elected Stroganoff as their spokesman. Just an item in the Stroganoff campaign against Buttonhooke, as Galybchik in a burst of confidence explained to Quill.

'He's full of plans,' she said, admiringly, 'though, of course, not all of them are practical. But to-night we are playing our ace.' She paused. 'Nicolas,' she said.

But Quill, it seemed, had never heard of Nicolas.

'Nevajno,' explained Galybchik.

Quill remembered. 'Schange small scheque,' he said reminiscently.

The major part of the instinctive liking that Galybchik had taken to the handsome profile that had walked into her life, dwindled away.

'Geniuses are different,' she said firmly. 'Ordinary people have no right to grudge the little extra it costs to support them. Nicolas says so.'

Quill changed the subject. 'So Nevajno is going to save the day?'

'It's a wonderful ballet,' breathed Galybchik, 'Nicolas has never done anything better. I can hardly understand it myself,' she added in awe.

Stroganoff bustled in, proudly deposited a solitary tulip in a large vase, stood before it, gloated, caught sight of Quill, turned round, and before the ex-detective could do anything about it, kissed him warmly on both cheeks.

'And the good Sergeant Banner?' he enquired, clearly prepared to greet him in like fashion.

Quill explained that he had come alone.

'No matter,' said Stroganoff, 'I introduce you to my new secretary. Her name I forget, so you shall call her "Galybchik" like everybody else.'

'We have already met,' said Galybchik, smiling brightly.

'She is as stupid as Stanley, explained Stroganoff, 'but somehow she annoy me less.'

The smile died.

'But why we linger here?' demanded Stroganoff of himself. 'You have not yet seen my Casino. Come.'

Along the frayed oilcloth, through the dingy curtains, past the yellowing statue, down the threadbare carpet, went the bald dome and the profile. An amateur photographer eyed them lovingly as they passed. A picture of the pair, he felt, would easily sell to *Esquire* under the caption, ' . . . so she ran off with my best friend.'

In the restaurant they were preparing for the seven o'clock rush. To them, Emilio—Prince of Waiters. Sacked from the

Ritz, the Carlton and the Buttonhooke Casino, he was hopeful of holding down his present job for at least six weeks.

But Stroganoff waved him away. Emilio had been engaged on the strength of his assurance that most of the customers of the Casino Buttonhooke would follow his napkin, but already a succession of soup-stained clients had shaken much of Stroganoff's confidence in this statement.

'Plus tard,' he said, and hurried Quill into the American Bar. 'Wiskyansoda?' he suggested.

But Hank was already busy with a couple of Blue Whizzbangs.

Citrolo came hopefully up but Stroganoff bowed coldly.

'He's a critic,' he explained to Quill. 'One without taste.' And Quill made the correct deduction without difficulty.

*   *   *

'This,' said Stroganoff, with the pride of an Archbishop officiating at a Royal wedding, 'IS MY ROULETTE. Let us approach.'

Advancing to the edge of the crowd Stroganoff balanced himself precariously on tiptoe. Quill's superior height enabled him to see more easily.

'Everybody seems to be backing five,' he said to the over-balanced Stroganoff.

'Poof,' said Stroganoff, picking himself up. 'At roulette the direction it cannot lose. There is the pourcentage,' he explained.

'Cinq,' said the croupier. A hum went round the table. It was the third time in succession that the number had come up. The croupiers distributed lavishly.

'Do not fret yourself for me,' said Stroganoff, who had managed to edge nearer the table. 'One losing coup it is nothing. See they are backing five again and we get it all back.'

'Cinq,' said the croupier.

As always when the bank is losing, a wave of excitement went through the crowd. It was a miracle, but miracles have a knack of repeating themselves. An avalanche of counters fell on five.

Stroganoff came to a decision. 'Stop,' he said to Vanilla, 'you are not in the vein to throw. I myself will do it.'

He pushed Vanilla off and mounted the rostrum. Acting on impulse, Quill staked fifty francs on number five.

Stroganoff beamed avuncularly at his audience.

'Rien ne va plus, mes enfants,' he announced and threw.

'Cinq,' he said, despairingly, a moment later.

Into the night strode a disconsolate figure. It was Kurt Kukumber. He was the only player who had lost that afternoon.

*   *   *

It was a beautiful evening. The *Régisseur* in charge of the ballet, *Soirée en Bazouche*, had let himself go in the matter of sunsets. The sky was a picture postcard labelled 'Evening with the Fishing Fleet.' The trees were dark, squat silhouettes against the streaked crimson and gold. The Casino Buttonhooke had been pleasantly reduced to a square shadow dotted with lights, while the sea was a soft and distant shimmer. In the bay, Lord Buttonhooke's yacht, *Ziegfeld Girlie*, rode the shimmer. She had a lovely line. Almost the *Régisseur* felt tempted to turn the moon on her, but remembering that the cast must have time to change for dinner, he concentrated on the sunset. You felt that it would never rain again.

It was a beautiful evening, but for once 'Pourcentage' Citrolo was unresponsive to the perfumed breeze. He, who always prided himself on avoiding show-downs, had been trapped into one. Grateful that for once he could reconcile conscience with his desires, he had praised the dancing of Olga Ostorojno, but had added incautiously that it would never blossom to full maturity until it had escaped the *bourgeois* tentacles that were encircling it. The reference to Madame Ostorojno was unmistakable and Madame had made no mistake about it.

Energetic darting from room to room had enabled Citrolo to avoid her for two days. But that careless cocktail hour stroll in the garden had proved his undoing. With a suddenness that suggested she had been crouching there, Madame Ostorojno materialized from behind a rose bush and attached herself firmly to his arm.

'Why do you dislike me, M'sieur?' she began.

There were a number of reasons but it did not seem politic to dwell on them. Citrolo contented himself with a polite disclaimer.

'Then why,' demanded Madame Ostorojno, 'do you call me an octopus?'

Citrolo winced and tried to shake himself free. The resemblance was striking.

'You misunderstood me,' he pleaded. 'What I meant was that young art should be given a chance to develop on its own lines. I do not approve of stifling the impulse.'

'Neither do I,' agreed Madame Ostorojno. 'You must not think of me like you do of other mothers in the ballet. I am not like them. I never attempt to interfere with Olga. I advise her, of course, and guide her, and push her a little sometimes— but influence her? Never!'

'You wish to tell me,' said the sarcastic Citrolo, 'that you are not like mother and daughter.'

'How right you are,' cooed Madame Ostorojno. 'Olga looks on me as a friend. Her best friend.'

They were in sight of the terrace where Citrolo observed with some annoyance that Olga Ostorojno was sharing a far too intimate cocktail with a far too good-looking young man. Madame Ostorojno saw them too.

'I'll soon put a stop to that,' she said, with a comforting assurance, and taking a firmer clutch of Citrolo's arm led him away again.

'I'm glad,' she said, 'that our little chat is helping us to understand one another.'

'Completely, Madame,' Citrolo assured her, 'but I must hasten to dress.'

'Just one little matter,' the octopus pressed. 'Should Lord Buttonhooke ask your views on Olga you will recommend her—of course.'

Citrolo was fast losing patience.

'On the contrary,' he snapped, 'I shall tell him that she is as yet too young.' It did not suit him at all to have this bud transplanted to a company where she would be in constant proximity to the handsome young sprig on the terrace.

*   *   *

The young sprig in question was at the moment warmly pressing Olga's hand under the table.

Olga looked at him in mock reproach. 'I do not believe that you love me. No man who loved me could stand idly by, while Ernest Smithsky partnered me in Swan Lake.'

Dovolno laughed. 'Do not let us go all over that again. What future was there for me with Stroganoff?'

'As much as with Buttonhooke. More—for with Stroganoff you could have danced with me!'

'You should have come to Buttonhooke too.'

'But I don't want to go to Buttonhooke,' sighed the little Ostorojno.

*   *   *

'But I don't want to go to Buttonhooke,' sighed the tearful Galybchik a few tables away.

'My art demands that you should come,' said Nevajno grandly. 'You are necessary to my concentration.'

Flattered, Galybchik sighed again.

'But can't I help you to concentrate with Stroganoff?'

'Stroganoff is limited,' explained Nevajno. 'He lacks the capital. Par example—my name outside it is not in the neon—only in the electric light.'

'I'll speak to Stroganoff,' promised Galybchik weakly.

*   *   *

'I'll speak to mother,' promised Ostorojno. 'But it will not be any use. Mother does not permit me to go out after the theatre.'

'She was quite willing for you to have supper with that rake Citrolo.'

'That's different. He's a critic. Besides I never told mother.'

Dovolno sulked. 'That sounds as if you wanted to go out with him.'

'I did. I had to. I mean,' said Ostorojno, 'there were reasons.'

'Reasons of publicity.'

'And others. He's a beast,' added Ostorojno violently, and Dovolno was instantly mollified. He was a placid person and now that it was established that the reason was not the obvious one that could matter to him, he was utterly incurious about its actual origin.

'If you went out with Citrolo without telling mother, you can go out with me the same way.'

'She'd find out. Just as she found out about Citrolo.'

'Buttonhooke,' said Dovolno approvingly, 'stands no nonsense from mothers. You'd be much better off with him.'

'Shut up,' said Ostorojno. 'Anyway, he hasn't asked me yet.'

* * *

'Anyway,' said Galybchik, 'he hasn't asked you yet.'

Nevajno looked his contempt at this quibble.

'Nevajno does not wait for things to happen. He plans them in advance. When Buttonhooke has seen my *Sleeping Princess* it is certain he will clamour for my services.'

'Perhaps he won't like it,' suggested Galybchik and was instantly repentant.

But it was too late. Deeply offended Nevajno had already stalked away.

With a sigh Galybchik paid the waiter.

* * *

On his yacht Lord Buttonhooke was gazing indulgently at a yard or so of tulle helped out with a few expensive spangles. Of all his hobbies, Sadie Souse easily cost him most. One could generally forecast the running expenses of a yacht while one could never quite guess what whim might seize Sadie next.

At the moment she was being comparatively reasonable. All she wanted was some refined adornment for the tulle—say a large diamond tiara—somep'n that Prince Alexis Artishok would admire.

'I'm nuts about that guy,' she added with a dazzling smile.

Lord Buttonhooke had noticed this already. It did not worry him unduly. Like so many exiled Russians, Prince Alexis had more charm than money, so Lord Buttonhooke, with more money than charm, quite liked the fellow. The man was a sportsman, even if he was a foreigner. Anyone who could win at pinochle so seldom and laugh at his jokes so often must be a sportsman. Together he felt they made a good team. And even if his Japanese valet did spend hours over the Prince's trousers, that was merely a trifle.

'The Prince,' said Sadie, clamping a spray of orchids to her corsage, 'has been telling me about the snow-white stallions he used to keep in Russia. I think I'd like a snow-white stallion— only a little one.'

Lord Buttonhooke agreed peevishly, making a mental note to have a word with the Prince. If the fellow was to remain a guest on his yacht he must really be warned to make his reminiscences less expensive.

The Expensive Memoirs just then made their appearance. Prince Alexis Artishok looked uncannily like exiled Russian Royalty is expected to look. Making way for him on the *Promenade des Anglais* one searched instinctively for the lines of resigned suffering under his eyes. They were there. As he passed on his way it was almost impossible to refrain from some comment on the horrors of the Russian revolution.

The Prince came forward and buried his bearded dignity in Sadie's hand.

'So,' he said, 'we all go to see the new ballet by Nevajno?'

'Not me,' said Sadie quickly. She had started life with Ziegfeld, and wished to be allowed to forget it.

'You are right, Madame,' declared the Prince. 'I myself am not overfond of the Ballet Moderne. Give me the Maryinsky with its spacious spectacle and the glamour of the great ballerinas. Would that there were to-day some vast theatre where illusion might be permitted to reign as then it did.'

'Say, that's an idea,' said Sadie.

'Oie,' said Lord Buttonhooke, forgetting his refinement.

Sadie and the Prince exchanged a mutual shudder.

*   *   *

'Good-bye, Madame,' Citrolo made his exit from the terrace with deep relief.

'Good-bye,' said Madame Ostorojno. 'See you to-night at the performance. Your seat is next to mine.'

CHAPTER IV

In its inessentials the first night of a new ballet is the same the whole world over, whether this event happens to be taking place at Covent Garden or in Kansas City.

Or even at La Bazouche.

Expectancy is in the air, not unmixed with a certain amount of dread. There is sure to be something to look forward to in the casting—something to regret. Some ballerina is certain to have hurt her foot, another is equally certain to have remained obstinately healthy. There will be the usual strong rumour that the dress-rehearsal was a flop, that the ballerina loathes her *variations*, and that the costumes have not yet all arrived. The novelty digested, it will be discovered that the first ballet—probably by Fokine—is to serve the purpose of a sort of public limbering up, and the last work, a divertissement ballet—*amende honorable* to those of the company with no rôle in the new work—through which the company will trundle with a formal, switched-on radiance.

There will be a number of hurt balletomanes who feel entitled to free seats and have not got them; and a number of hard-pressed Philistines with free seats thrust upon them by their persuading wives and sisters-in-law. There will be a sprinkling of ecstatic intellectuals and a churning of dancers from some other company. And, of course, the usual whiskered foam of Russian generals. In this case many of them have sat up in the train all night in order to get here.

The amateur photographer enthusiastically focussed his camera on Lord Buttonhooke's astrakhan collar, which had just come striding through the entrance, and pressed a flash-light.

'Blast!' he said. Somebody had jogged his elbow and all he got was a picture of Arenskaya talking to Quill.

Lord Buttonhooke strode to the vestibule. Behind him, a rather plumper, a rather shorter shadow, in a slightly smaller astrakhan collar, bounced. A little late in life, the Baron Sam de Rabinovitch had developed a violent bout of hero-worship. Lord Buttonhooke had contrived to be in a big way all those things that the Baron had always aimed at in a small way. A Brain! A Colossus among men!

The Colossus, at the moment, was getting distinctly the worst of it with an usher who was adamant that the seventeenth row side was the right seat. Horrified, the attendant Baron fought his way back to a bustling Stroganoff and launched his protest. Stroganoff shared his horror.

'My box it is at your disposal,' he said courteously. 'It is almost empty.'

It was, in fact, occupied by Arenskaya, her pianist,[1] Galybchik, Quill, and a fidgety Nevajno.

'To-night,' Arenskaya was prophesying comfortably, 'will be the flop terrifique.'

'Hush,' said Galybchik, 'Nicolas is nervous.'

'I am not nervous,' flared Nevajno, 'only high strung.'

'Me, I suffer badly with nerves always,' announced Arenskaya firmly. 'To me the ballet it is an ordeal. I suffer double—first I suffer for my children and then I suffer for myself when I was young and danced the rôle. Always I remember the moment when I was first to dance *Raimonda* before the Tsar—and also the night I dance *La Péri* privately for Rasputin, who had eye on me.'

At the mere recollection the lights modestly went out. The curtain rose on *Carnaval*. One look at Florestan, and Citrolo went out, too.

*   *   *

Save for Vanilla, moodily stacking a pack of cards, the Baccarat room was empty. He did not appear to welcome Citrolo with any particular enthusiasm.

[1] Their permanent feud temporarily in abeyance.

G

'Bon soir,' said Citrolo, 'I have been reflecting, and it seems to me that you are cheating a little on your returns, n'est-ce-pas?'

Vanilla glowered.

'That, mon cher,' said Citrolo, 'is not prudent. I have been very reasonable with you. Many blackmailers of my acquaintance would not have been content with a mere twelve and a half per cent of the profits you make from your so skilful manipulations of the cards. It is my principle never to be greedy nor to press my collaborators too hard. But really, mon ami, I have to insist that you must, as our English so elegantly put it, play fair.'

A torrent of words broke from Vanilla's outraged mouth. It was evident that he did not regard Citrolo's twelve and a half per cent as reasonable. He pointed out that 'Banco' Dacarpo, who had taught him his trade, took only five per cent—and this by courtesy. Not under compulsion.

'Dacarpo taught you,' Citrolo said smoothly, 'but I found you out. That is always more expensive.'

Vanilla looked at him in grudging admiration, and changed his tactics.

'Business has been bad,' he pleaded, 'one of my pupils mistook a signal and went Banco at the wrong time. My returns are accurate—only the profits are small.'

'It was on those small profits that you present Arenskaya with a bracelet?'

'It was stolen, that one,' Vanilla said defiantly.

Citrolo nodded. 'Eh, bien, mon ami—this time I will overlook it. But only this time. Should your profits be small again, our friend Stroganoff will have a shock coming to him.'

'It would give me much pleasure,' said Vanilla lovingly, 'to put poison in your fish.'

'Assuredly,' agreed Citrolo.

'I often ask myself how it is I have not done this thing before.'

'I will explain,' Citrolo was kindness itself. 'I select my collaborators with much forethought. Blackmailees are divided into many classes—of which only two are dangerous. The very desperate and the very clever. With these I do not collaborate. You, my friend, are neither.'

Vanilla's vanity was wounded. He seethed with rage.

'That I am not desperate is not your fault. But that I am clever, everybody admits. Dacarpo himself has always claimed me as his best pupil. There is only one reason why I do not kill you.'

'Precisely,' said Citrolo, 'C'est question de courage. You are frightened of the guillotine.'

'It is not true.'

'But emphatically it is true. You might have the courage to knife me on an impulse—in the back—and against that I can protect myself. But you would never commit a premeditated murder—you would see the shadow of the knife hanging over you, even as you planned. So you see, mon ami, I am quite, quite safe.' He put out his cigarette and turned towards the door. 'Au revoir,' he said, and don't forget, 'twelve and a half per cent to the last centime.'

He went.

Vanilla seized a pack of cards and relieved his feelings by tearing them across.

'Wish I could do that,' said a wistful monocle, materializing at his elbow. 'But,' it added, 'I know an awfully good trick with a couple of goldfish. I'd like to show it to you.' It looked round helplessly.

*   *   *

In leaving the auditorium so early Citrolo had been even wiser than he guessed. No sooner was he clear than Ernest Smithsky came on breathing heavily as Eusebius.

'Who's that?' said Lord Buttonhooke, startled.

'He is a dancer superb,' said Arenskya, with a certain low cunning. 'Your company it need him badly. Why you not bribe him to go?'

But Buttonhooke, though no balletomane, knew better than that. He took refuge behind his inscrutable smile, a sheer waste of concealment, for by this time Arenskaya's eyes were fixed in some horror on the fat girl—half a beat behind the rest of the corps de ballet. Presently she began to express herself freely on this subject. From force of habit, the pianist looked affronted.

The ballet straggled on. The only person who seemed to enjoy it at all was Galybchik. She gasped her pleasure as Ostorojno tapped her pointed way across the stage as Columbine. In her cherry-sprigged flounces, with cherry-coloured flowers in her hair, Olga Ostorojno took her audience as surely as she took her stage. Her dark beauty warmed the wan little rôle, and suddenly, with her entrance, a period came to life.

'That's the girl I want,' said Buttonhooke.

'You try and I scratch your eyes out,' announced Arenskaya affably.

Nevajno was sulking. Even the fact that Harlequin was at this moment energetically muffing his *brisés*, failed to mollify him. He had always thought of Buttonhooke as the patron—almost the father—of Progress, and here he was, enjoying Fokine.

Gazing at the poke bonnets, the mittens, the crinolines, Quill found himself homesick for the Tiller girls.

At last *Carnaval* came to a crowded end. Arenskaya dismissed it in a sentence. 'Pas d'une gaieté folle,' she pronounced.

Nevajno got up. 'At last,' he said, and hustled importantly out, Galybchik at his heels.

*   *   *

Backstage all was confusion. A vital piece of scenery—the aluminium escalator—had not arrived. Nevajno was protesting that on no account would he allow the curtain to go up on a property staircase left over from last season's performance of *La Bohème*.

*   *   *

To the born balletomane, the most important part of any ballet is its interval. Here he is free to describe his emotions to an audience far too busy describing its own to contradict.

Buttonhooke, though officially established as a patron of the art, never felt himself a really happy bubble in this artistic kettle. Particularly as this was the moment when mothers and others with ambushed ambitions bore down upon him to establish contact with a view to contract.

To escape the onrush he wandered into the roulette-room and threw the maximum on seventeen. Seventeen duly turned up.

'We celebrate,' said Arenskaya behind him.

*   *   *

'It is a very generous offer that Lord Buttonhooke has empowered me to make you,' said the Baron de Rabinovitch for the eleventh time.

'Non,' said Stroganoff firmly.

The Baron wiped his brow. While not exactly a menace, the Casino Stroganoff was still a thorn in the side of the Buttonhooke policy, and the Baron had been told off to buy out the impresario. He was still trying. His arguments were eloquent and irrefutable. Even a child could grasp that behind Lord Buttonhooke's offer lay only the desire to do his old friend Stroganoff a good turn.

'Non,' said Stroganoff, again, 'I will not be the swindle twice.'

'But you don't understand,' began the Baron all over again. . . .

'Mon cher,' said Stroganoff, 'I follow everything that you say. Your arguments they are superb. But me, I argue to myself like this: the good Baron—he is the swindle. The good lord— he is the swindle even bigger. If they desire that I sell my Casino, then it is clear that I must keep.'

'You do not trust us,' said the Baron, hurt.

'Assurément non,' agreed Stroganoff blandly, 'I would not trust you with the pole of a barge.' He turned suddenly, delved into a drawer and produced an opulent-looking box of cigars, which he held out to the Baron. 'But we have not the hard feelings—no?'

'No.' The Baron, mollified, stretched out his hand.

But the box was empty.

'Big joke,' explained Stroganoff, laughing consumedly, 'I catch everybody.'

The Baron controlled himself. 'About the Casino. . . .'

'But I have tell you already,' said Stroganoff, still slightly puzzled that the Baron did not seem amused, 'I do not sell. That you wish to buy assures me that my Casino will soon be the success immense. The prestige of my ballet it will resound round the world and millions will rush to congratulate me. Tiens—here is one already,' he added, as a wrathful figure pushed its way towards their corner of the foyer.

The Balleto-Medico had not seen Stroganoff for several weeks, but he was in no mood for polite greetings. It was evident at once that his all-night journey with the whiskered foam of Russian generals had done little to mellow his judgment.

'Your *Carnaval*,' he opened, 'should be taken down, dusted and not put back again. It is the worst since last season at the Wells.'

'Impossible,' said Stroganoff, horrified.

'Never,' said the Balleto-Medico with some justification, 'have I seen a Eusebius like Smithsky.'

'It was in his contract that he dance the rôle,' groaned Stroganoff.

'Console yourself, my unknown friend.' Ambassador de Rabinovitch, wishing to stand well with the foreign power to which he had been sent, attempted to pour oil on the troubled waters. 'Your all night vigil is soon to be rewarded with the new ballet by the genius Nevajno. . . .'

'Nevajno!' said the Balleto-Medico scornfully.

'Nevajno,' said Stroganoff royally, 'and that reminds me,' he asked, 'how you get in?'

'Press,' said the Balleto-Medico, not without pride, 'I am covering this for *Rhythm To-morrow*.'

Instantly Stroganoff was affability itself. 'You will write glowingly—n'est ce pas?'

'I hope to give it hell,' said the Balleto-Medico.

The affability vanished. 'You are the ingrate. The son prodigal. After all the seats I have given you in Opera Houses the world over.'

'Behind pillars,' put in the Balleto-Medico.

'That was the coincidence regrettable. To bear the malice, it is not kind. Recollect the many favours that I have done you. Who taught you first to love the ballet?'

'Diaghilev,' said the Balleto-Medico.

'Who made clear to you the inner beauty of *Le Cotillon?*'

'De Basil.'

'Who was it allowed you the acquaintance of my so beautiful ballerinas?'

'Arenskaya,' said the Balleto-Medico.

'Poof,' said Stroganoff, avoiding defeat. 'Nobody read your paper anyway.' He turned to resume his skirmish with Rabino-vitch, but the Baron, his mission a failure, had departed to make his report to Lord Buttonhooke.

Buttonhooke was at the bar with Arenskaya drinking champagne. Rabinovitch whispered in his ear while Arenskaya finished the bottle.

'Stroganoff cannot hold out much longer,' he surmized. 'If we can only fix a really good scandal it would finish him.'

' 'Ank,' ordered Arenskaya, 'Encore de champagne.'

*   *   *

Citrolo had wandered backstage through the pass door, and into Ostorojno's dressing-room. Assuring himself that her mother was not present, he walked in, planted himself on the arm of her chair and teased her gently.

'I have been talking to Buttonhooke,' he said, untruthfully.

Olga swung round. 'Did he like my *Carnaval?* Was it good?'

'He adored it,' said Citrolo glibly. 'He wanted to offer you a contract, but remembering how unkind you were to me last night I managed to persuade him that you were as yet too young.'

'Oh—you didn't!'

'But I assure you, Mademoiselle,' said Citrolo, 'I did this thing. And I assure you I shall continue to do it until . . .'

Olga applied heated wax smoothly to her eyelashes. 'But this is old-fashioned melodrama,' she said, unwilling to believe that Citrolo could be serious.

'I am the old-fashioned villain,' said Citrolo, rolling his eyes horribly.

'Old-fashioned villains are always killed in the end,' laughed Olga.

'And who shall kill me?' demanded Citrolo, grabbing her hand while he had the chance. 'Not that little wrist.'

'This little wrist has a mother, and a boy friend. Either will kill you quite cheerfully.'

But the mother who bustled in did not seem to be meditating murder at the moment.

'Your shoes?' she said. 'Are they comfortable? Is your hair secure? Your shoulder-straps—let me test them. How do you feel? Where's your shawl?'

Citrolo fled.

* * *

'So I give her hell,' Arenskaya was saying, 'and the next time she dance perfect.'

A bemused Buttonhooke looked at her.

'There is no doubt I am the greatest teacher of all time.'

Champagne had lent a sparkle to the lights, a richness to the dim plush hangings, and a glamour about Arenskaya's services. Art, thought Lord Buttonhooke with a clarity of perception that belongs to the slightly drunk alone, is art. His class, he decided, could do with discipline.

'I will give you a contract,' he said jovially.

Arenskaya drew herself up to her full height. She was still not very tall. 'Is it,' she cooed, 'that you are making me an offer for my services?'

'Why not?'

'I will tell you why not,' screamed Arenskaya suddenly. 'You are the serpent—the serpent in the bosom—not mine!

You creep here, you crawl there, you force me to drink the champagne, and then when you think I am sou you try to rob poor Stroganoff of me, though you are well aware that without me the Ballet Stroganoff it could not go on one day.'

'Hush,' pleaded Lord Buttonhooke.

'I will not 'ush,' Arenskaya assured the relieved spectators. 'He is a crétin, a crook, a robber. He rob us of Dovolno—that poor boy who is too young to know what he does—and leaves us Smithsky to dance with Ostorojno. You who have seen Smithsky to-night will understand the crime he has committed.'

A murmur of approval ran through the audience. Inspired, Arenskaya rose to greater heights of oratory. Lord Button-hooke felt himself becoming unpopular. Slightly red behind the ears he turned to the bar.

Hank took this opportunity to present him with the bill.

* * *

In the baccarat-room the Baron de Rabinovitch, oblivious of Vanilla's tilted tie, incautiously went banco. He did not win.

'You are reckless, my friend,' said Citrolo, who had the knack of appearing at awkward moments.

'A trifle,' said the Baron airily, 'a mere two thousand francs.'

'Business is good chez Buttonhooke.'

Champagne had rendered the Baron foolhardy. 'Wonderful,' he said. 'A gold-mine.'

'I thought so,' Citrolo mused, 'I have been thinking so for some time. It is beginning to appear to me, that the small sum you pay me monthly for the collaboration of my silence con-cerning a certain incident at Avignon in your so adventurous life is no longer sufficient.'

'My overheads,' began the Baron much too late.

'My friend,' said Citrolo, 'I am not one to turn the screw. Many blackmailers of my acquaintance would seize on your prosperity to double or treble their demands. I am content with a modest increase of fifty per cent. This you can afford easily especially if you refrain from going banco when Vanilla is croupier.'

A deflated Baron nodded meekly and dwindled away towards the bar. Citrolo edged towards the table. Almost he felt like a small flutter himself, but after one glance at the angle of Vanilla's tie he changed his mind.

'Banco,' said Prince Alexis Artishok, beside him.

Citrolo studied with interest the long elegant fingers that reached out for the cards and flicked them carelessly over on the table to expose a Queen and a Nine. He looked at the Prince again and sighed both his recognition and regret.

Vanilla had evidently been taken by surprise. He shovelled over the counters in a daze, his eyes glued on the magician who had achieved the impossible with a stacked pack. The magician smiled—very slightly. Into Vanilla's eyes crept a look of reverence.

'Maître,' he muttered under his breath.

*   *   *

'And so,' said the pianist, 'I told Arenskaya exactly what I thought of her.'

'Did she listen?' asked Quill.

'No,' said the pianist.

*   *   *

Kurt Kukumber, elegant in a tight-waisted dinner-jacket and a ready-made tie, looked at Citrolo pleadingly:

'Business has been bad,' he explained. 'The public to-day reads too much. Every time I begin a story my prospect has read it already.'

Citrolo was merciless. Annoyance with himself at his caution in not tackling the higher game had made him impatient with the smaller fry.

'You must alter your methods.'

'I will do so,' said Kurt eagerly. 'Always I am studying my trade, learning all the latest tricks. It is unfortunate that all the good swindles I discover need capital, and my system it is for the moment unlucky.'

Citrolo yawned. 'It is hardly worth collaborating with you my friend. Almost would it be of more profit to myself to collect the small reward that the police at Nantes still offer.'

'Give me time,' pleaded Kukumber. 'I have to-day found a prospect very promising. An Englishman of the most gullible. We met at lunch and already I have him interested. . . .'

*   *   *

The Promising Prospect and the pianist wandered wearily down the corridor that led to the auditorium. She was telling Quill how she had nearly won the Premier Prix au Concervatoire de Bruxelles.

*   *   *

'Nicolas,' gasped Galybchik, 'is being temperamental.'

There was only one solution.

'Send him here,' said Stroganoff resigned, 'and I schange him small scheque.'

*   *   *

The sonnette went off like a fire-alarm. Slowly, almost reluctantly, the players left their tables and drifted back to the auditorium. Stroganoff entered his box, found no vacant chair, and wandered off to lean sulkily against a pillar. From his comfortable seat in the stalls the Balleto-Medico waved to him.

With a smirk the conductor took his bow. The spotlight focused maliciously on the double bass and unwaveringly held its ground. The conductor gave up and swung his baton.

The Balleto-Medico leant back and closed his eyes as a fitting prelude to the strains of Tschaikovsky. He opened them indignantly a moment later. Tschaikovsky had certainly not written this. The curtain rose to reveal a chromium-plated palace.

In the box Quill determined to be intelligent. A diligent re-reading of the argument in the programme had enabled him to grasp that this amazing mass of metal was the scene of the christening of the Princess Aurora.

King Impecunious has invited six fairies to stand God-mother to the Infant Princess: They are:

> Fairy Film-face
> Fairy Yumph
> Fairy Stock-Exchange
> Fairy Gold-digger
> Fairy Sugar-Daddy
> and
> Fairy Malthusia.

Each arrives at the party to bestow her own particular quality on the Princess. There is also a Fairy Godfather, but the poor wretch is far too busy partnering the ballerinas to have time to deliver his present.

Relentlessly the fairies dance. In turn they are supported, relinquished, regained, and lifted—but not dropped.

The guests—in spun glass and zip-fasteners—circle the royal cradle, obviously checking up on the window space accorded to their gifts. The cradle bears a distinct resemblance to a model battleship, while the baby looks exactly like Winston Churchill.

Suddenly a perfectly furious fairy comes shooting down the escalator. King Impecunious has carelessly omitted to invite the Most Important Fairy of All—her name is Publicity. Piqued, she looks round and dances a hideous curse: 'Never shall any one of you make the Front Page until . . .'

With a final furious series of pas de chats she vanishes. Queen Impecunious takes up the pas de chats. She is telling her husband what she thinks of him.

Tableau 2. Dawn. The gaiety is at its height. Several of the guests have remembered to bring their toe shoes, and several others are showing every sign of breaking into a traditional Russian dance—traditional, that is, to the Ballet Nevajno. Mercifully, the early editions arrive before they get started.

Not a headline. Not a photograph. Not a gossip item.

Furious, the guests turn on King Impecunious.

*   *   *

Furious the Balleto-Medico turned on Stroganoff.

*   *   *

Tableau 3. King Impecunious goes to war. Nobody believes his intentions are peaceful, and he's got to convince them some way. He is unable to mobilize an army as he cannot obtain publicity for his recruiting campaign.

Tableau 4. Peace Celebrations. The Princess Aurora, a well-equipped eighteen-year-old, sends to the chemist for a sleeping draught. All her natural qualities have led inevitably to a certain lassitude. 'I should like,' she says, turning a yawn into an *arabesque*, 'to sleep for a hundred years.'

Tableau 5. She does so.

Tableau 6. The awakening. Prince Foie-gras enters to awaken the Princess with a kiss. In his hand he carries a detonator. (This, Quill was given to understand, was Symbolic.)

Tableau 7. The wedding of the Princess Aurora. A quiet affair almost without Bridesmaids and practically without a Prince.[1] Vulgarity is out of fashion. Everybody is tremendously refined.

Suddenly the Fairy Publicity, swearing horribly, comes shooting down a light ray. She brandishes a newspaper placard at the well-bred guests. It reads:

IMPECUNIOUS PRINCESS MARRIES MONIED
MONARCH

*   *   *

The curtain came down but before the audience had time to recover it went up again. The company bowed their acknowledgments to a stunned silence.

A shock of black hair strode furiously on to the stage.

'Speech,' called the pianist, taking her cue.

[1] Prince Foie-gras is being danced by Ernest Smithsky, which may account for this.

Oblivious to the fact that it prevailed already, Nevajno raised a majestic hand for silence.

'Imbéciles,' he began, 'why you not boo?'

'Boo,' said the Balleto-Medico obligingly.

'That you like my ballet I do not expect. But that you should not greet it with turbulence I cannot understand. Almost might I be Petipa. Where are the whistles, the hisses, the hoots that the Nevajno tradition demands on its first night?'

This time the house responded. Nevajno stood beaming amid the cat-calls. Now he was in his element.

Buttonhooke, an unaccustomed pang of sympathy reaching his heart, hurried over to Stroganoff. Calamity had made them brothers.

'C'est terrible,' shouted Stroganoff above the din. 'Worse even than the première of *Gare du Nord*.'

Citrolo, passing by, stopped to hurl a casual thunderbolt.

'How many "r's," ' he enquired smoothly, 'in horrible?'

'Gag him,' advised Buttonhooke earnestly. 'Gag him before he gets his notice off to the papers.'

'Oui,' said Stroganoff mournfully, 'mais comment?'

He pondered, stroking his bald dome. Inspiration came suddenly. 'I have the idea magnificent,' he confided, and bustled off.

*   *   *

Prince Alexis Artishok had not bothered to watch the performance. He had remained in the baccarat-room to the growing indignation of Vanilla. It was nice and social of the Master to come here to demonstrate his skill, but there was no need for him to win quite so much money doing it. And it was almost unethical on his part to lend his aid to the assortment of tulle and sequins playing beside him.

Sadie Souse on the other hand, was delighted. She never lost at baccarat while Lord Buttonhooke was within call, but she seldom won.

'If I was always as lucky as this,' she confided to the Prince, 'I could lose the old walrus altogether.'

The Prince took a look at Vanilla's scowl and decided that he had tormented the croupier enough for one evening. He helped Sadie scoop in her winnings and led her, protesting slightly, away from the table.

'That is the feed for the chickens, Madame,' he reproved her. 'One of your accomplishments should not be interested in a few milles.'

'No?' said Sadie.

They settled at a table and the Prince passed his cigarette-case.

'Just now,' said the Prince, making play with his mon-grammed onyx lighter, 'you spoke of your dependence on a walrus. Almost you seemed to imply that you were not in love with our good host.'

'Cheese it,' said Sadie.

Prince Artishok smiled. 'In that case you will permit me the liberty of suggesting, Madame, that you are not making the most of your opportunity.'

Sadie was hurt. 'I'm not doing so badly.'

'You are content with trifles,' contradicted the Prince. 'Furs, bagatelles of jewelry, nothing of real value. Should Button-hooke cease to admire you, you would be forced to find another protector almost at once.'

This was a new viewpoint to Sadie. It had never occurred to her that her demands were too small.

'You mean I should soak him for something really big?'

'Imperatively,' said the Prince.

'A settlement?'

'If you can manage it.'

Sadie shook her head. 'I couldn't. Not now. Not a really handsome settlement that is.'

'Exactly,' the Prince nodded. 'It is both too late to discuss settlements and too early. A Protector may be induced to make a settlement before—when he is eager—or later—when he has tired—but not during.'

'I was a mutt,' Sadie sighed.

'We all make mistakes,' the Prince comforted. 'Besides, there is still time. You may not be able to persuade Buttonhooke to give you large sums of money for there is in that, to him, no glory—only disbursement. But you can still persuade him to spend it for your benefit.'

'You mean some really expensive present?'

'I mean an exceptional present,' said the Prince. 'A sensational present. Something that Buttonhooke could boast of giving.'

'The Kohinoor,' said Sadie inspired.

The Prince was amused. 'Alas, it is not on the market. Neither for the moment is any other notorious jewel.'

'Oh.'

'However there is still the famous Otchi-Chernia diamonds. They are not on the market officially, but I might persuade them to become so.'

'How much are they worth?' demanded Sadie the practical.

'Five million francs perhaps.'

'And you can get them?'

'Possibly. They are in the possession of the famous Russian dancer, Dyra Dyrakova.'

Sadie was interested. 'The same that Percy was talking about getting to dance for his company?'

'The same. It was my suggestion,' said the Prince, smoothly, 'that he should engage her.'

Sadie looked at him in admiration. 'Got it all planned—haven't you?'

'Almost,' the Prince agreed. 'With Dyrakova here I think I can persuade her to sell. She has always declared that the necklace is her most valued possession, it was given her by the Grand Duke and made a lovely scandal at the time—but, well, I happen to know that she has not so much money now. But she's as proud as the devil, and it will need great tact.'

'You got that!'

'I've got that. Anyway, I think that I can persuade her to sell. But,' the Prince asked, 'can you persuade Buttonhooke that he wishes to buy?'

'Leave it to me,' said Sadie, with assurance.

CHAPTER V

'MAIS, mon cher,' said Stroganoff. 'Soyez raisonnable. You ruin me.'

'You exaggerate the power of my pen,' said Citrolo, dryly.

'Mais non,' said Stroganoff. 'It is well known that for the *Ballet Sérieux* there is only one critic.'

'Haskell!' suggested Citrolo.

'Haskell—poof!' said Stroganoff. 'Everybody they read Haskell. But for the real criticism, for the seasoned judgment, for the higher understanding and for that kindliness of vision that warms the heart of the balletomane, there is none that can approach Pavlo Citrolo. Whenever there is a new ballet, the connoisseur he rushes for your column in *Paris Soir*.'

'*Le Matin Populaire*,' corrected Citrolo, not at all pleased. 'You are not logical, my friend. You praise my work and at the same time ask me to betray it.'

'Not betray,' urged Stroganoff, 'just disguise a little.'

'For Nicolas' sake,' put in Galybchik, pleadingly.

There was a knock at the office door. Vanilla entered.

'Chips,' he said abruptly.

'Encore,' said Stroganoff, appalled.

Vanilla nodded. Stroganoff opened a box and counted elaborately, while Galybchik made complicated entries in two ledgers.

'My system—it is perfect,' explained Stroganoff with pride as Vanilla took his departure. 'Every franc we lose, I can find him.'

'Admirable,' Citrolo agreed. 'I wish you good night.' He rose.

Stroganoff pushed him playfully back into his chair.

'Mais non,' he protested. 'We are not agreed. We have not yet had the little talk, the little smoke.' Hurriedly he reached for the opulent box on the table and passed it to Citrolo. 'Cigar?'

The box was empty.

'Big joke,' explained Stroganoff into the silence. 'Galybchik, les cigares véritables.'

Citrolo lit a cigarette.

'My friend, there is nothing for us to discuss.'

There was a knock at the door.

'Go away,' said Stroganoff.

But it was Madame Ostorojno. Clearly she was finding it difficult to decide whether to bawl out Stroganoff or beam at Citrolo. Stroganoff settled the question by attacking first.

'What you want?' he snapped. 'I cannot do it.'

Madame Ostorojno glared. 'I've come to tell you we're leaving. After to-night's fiasco we cannot stay any longer. We have our future to consider.'

Stroganoff winked at Citrolo. 'Big bluff,' he explained in an audible aside, 'to raise the salary.'

'Oh, no it isn't,' said Madame Ostorojno. 'To-morrow we go to Buttonhooke.'

'I have your contract,' said Stroganoff comfortably.

Like a tank, Madame Ostorojno buffeted her way to the desk, rummaged in the drawers and emerged triumphantly brandishing a document. The resourceful Galybchik pounced and snatched it from her. Stroganoff in turn snatched it from Galybchik and walked to the safe.

'This,' he said, twiddling furiously, 'I put in here where only I know the combination.' He muttered, 'S. Y. L. P. H. . . .' He straightened himself and rubbed his hands. 'Now you may depart to Buttonhooke and my advocate he get me big damages.'

Undaunted Madame Ostorojno swept to the doorway. 'You've not heard the last of this,' she snapped. 'Come, Mr. Citrolo.'

But Citrolo settled himself more comfortably in his arm-chair. Of the two he preferred the frying-pan.

'You realize now,' said Stroganoff, as the door slammed,

'the trouble that I have to overcome. I have to think for my whole family and prevent them when they would be foolish. They look on me as father—it is on me they depend in everything. That is why I plead with you so hard not to write unkind. You would not have it on your conscience that you took their mouths away from the bread.'

Citrolo shrugged.

'Would you condemn the little Ostorojno on the threshold of her career?'

'She danced efficiently,' said Citrolo, 'I shall say so. The blame lies with the choreographer.'

'You do not understand Nicolas,' said Galybchik hotly. 'His conception is above your head. He is a genius.'

There was a knock at the door. Genius strode in. Ignoring Stroganoff he went straight over to Galybchik.

'We celebrate,' he said, 'Come.'

'Celebrate what?' asked Citrolo puzzled.

Stroganoff explained. 'It is a system. Nevajno he always celebrate the reception disastrous.'

'I suppose he books a table in advance,' said Citrolo.

Galybchik stepped into the breach. 'Leave us, Nicolas. We are talking business.'

'Business!' said Nevajno disdainfully, 'Ollright—I wait for you in the cabaret.' He went.

'You weaken, no?' Stroganoff asked Citrolo hopefully.

Citrolo stood up. 'I'm sorry,' he said with finality. 'You are wasting your time. Nothing can induce me to write what I do not feel.'

'The conscience artistic,' said Stroganoff despairingly. He had met with this before.

'I regret.'

'Maybe,' suggested Stroganoff brightening, 'if I should write it for you? I am the writer eloquent. Already I begin my memoirs.'

There was a knock at the door. It was Lord Buttonhooke and the Baron de Rabinovitch. Oozing tact the Colossus and his shadow advanced on Citrolo.

'We have come to congratulate Stroganoff,' said Buttonhooke, 'but we see that you are before us.'

'He has not congratulated us yet,' said Galybchik meaningly.

'Nor has he any such intention,' put in Citrolo.

'Tut-tut,' Lord Buttonhooke reproved. 'Surely among men of the world such matters can be adjusted.' Instinctively his hand stole to his pocket.

Light dawned on Stroganoff. He beckoned Buttonhooke to a corner and started to whisper frantically. The words ' 'Ow mooch?' floated clearly across the room, causing Galybchik to blush and bang her typewriter. Citrolo smoked on imperturbably.

'Five thousand,' whispered Buttonhooke.

'C'est terrible,' whispered Stroganoff. 'Never have I paid more than two.'

'Five thousand,' whispered Buttonhooke firmly.

'Three,' whispered Stroganoff.

The whispering became bitter and impassioned and ended only when the Baron joined in to point out that Stroganoff was bargaining with the wrong person.

'You are right,' said Stroganoff, escorting them to the door. 'It is foolish,' he said cryptically, 'to spoil the liner for a pennyworth of paint,' and turned to face his Cunarder.

'M'sieur,' he said coldly, 'you will not listen to my pleadings—you will not listen to my heart. I must recourse to the only thing that you appreciate. 'Ow mooch?'

Somewhat surprisingly Citrolo put back his head and laughed.

'You appeal to me,' he said, 'you do really. I'm almost sorry to have to refuse you.'

'Two thousand francs,' said Stroganoff the tempter.

'Not enough.'

'Three thousand,' said Stroganoff. 'We have the little drink and we seal the bargain. Galybchik—the glasses.'

'I'll have the drink,' agreed Citrolo, 'but not the bargain. And then really I must say good night. I go to press in forty-five minutes.'

'Five thousand,' said Stroganoff.

'No.'

'Six,' said Stroganoff despairingly.

'No.'

This was unbelievable. Possibly, reflected Stroganoff, the sight of ready money might influence this sea-green incorruptible. He had not, of course, anything like the ready money available but perhaps a cheque? His hand went to his chequebook pocket but encountered instead a small glass bottle. His sleeping draught. Instantly an entirely new train of thought began to bubble in that fertile dome. He glanced at the whisky bottle and the glasses that Galybchik had produced and got busy.

'We drink first,' he said, 'and we talk more business later.'

The unsuspicious Citrolo drank.

*   *   *

' . . . impossible to contradict that the new Nevajno choreography bears the signs of the genius irrefutable.' Stroganoff was saying: 'Full stop.'

Galybchik's pencil flew.

'The faultless technique of Ernest Smithsky,' he resumed, shuddering slightly at the memory, 'once again awoke the acclaim of the immense audience enthusiastic. Full stop. Of the corps de ballet, it can be exclaimed: "Never has a band of artistes so on-the-beat been seen!" They truly proved themselves to be the pupils of their famous teacher—Arenskaya.'[1]

Galybchik scribbled conscientiously. In his armchair, the august critic of the *Matin Populaire* slept blissfully on. Four tablets from a bottle sternly marked 'ONE ONLY—*to be taken at bedtime*'—had been sufficient to safeguard his complacency for some hours to come. His subconscious must have been pretty indignant over the eulogies his self-appointed literary ghost was hacking out for him, but it was in no position to do anything about it.

'A décor,' Stroganoff was fervently dictating, 'both costly and modern. . . .'

[1] 'It is kind to give the old one the poof.'—VLADIMIR STROGANOFF.

'And symbolic,' suggested Galybchik.

'And symbolic,' Stroganoff agreed. 'A Tchaikovsky-Stravinsky score, added to, and orchestrated by the brilliant young composer, Polyshumedshedshi. Dancing of a virtuosity unrivalled in a conception of the most ravishing—all combined to make the evening memorable for the ballet-goer. The work was rapturously received. Full stop.'

'Had we better?' asked Galybchik nervously.

'Certainement,' said Stroganoff, 'I myself heard a voice cry "bis!" '

'That was me,' said Galybchik.

The door opened. A wisp of tulle came quickly into the room. It was followed by a beard.

'Pardon me,' fluted Sadie Souse, 'is Percy anywhere around?'

'Lord Buttonhooke,' explained Prince Alexis Artishok.

'He is gone,' said Stroganoff shortly. 'You go too, no?'

But Sadie was examining the sleeping Citrolo with some interest.

'Passed out?' she enquired. Here was a condition that aroused her sympathy.

'Oui, oui,' Stroganoff nodded energetically. 'The good Citrolo he has drink too much. We leave him here to sleep it off.'

The Prince obligingly collected the tulle, apologized smoothly for the derangement, and departed.

'We ought to have locked that door,' said Galybchik.

'Why you not think of it?' Stroganoff snapped. He crossed to the door just in time to push out the Balleto-Medico.

Soberly they went back to work. But soon Stroganoff was himself again.

'And what,' he was demanding, 'shall we write of the Man Behind the Ballet? Of the heart that found the courage to present, the brain that had the vision to perceive, and the patience that withstood the many shocks of the artistic impasses that are part and parcel of a conception so immense—What, in short, shall we say of Vladimir Stroganoff?'

'What?' asked Galybchik.

CHAPTER VI

Ex-Detective-Inspector Adam Quill woke thankfully from a dream in which Arenskaya—in a scarlet nightgown—was gazing at him with much the kind of expression Marlene Dietrich had turned on Herbert Marshall in a Lubitsch film, and with about as much success. He stretched out his hand and reassured himself about the empty pillow beside him. A luxurious yawn linked him to the present. He was on holiday. He was in the South of France. He was in the sunshine. He was in the company of easily the most amusing people in the world, and this time he had no corpse to worry him.

He stretched out his other hand to throw back the shutters. The room was small but it had its comforts. Rain slanted in. Quill shut the window and rang the bell.

Some twenty minutes later an old man came trundling in with a tray. Beamingly he removed the lid to reveal a few greasy strands of bacon and the hard fried remains of a very small egg.

'Voilà!' he said triumphantly, 'Le h'english breakfast.'

Quill was not impressed. 'Bring me some tea and toast.'

'Café,' said the waiter reproachfully.

'Tea,' said Quill firmly.[1]

The waiter shrugged and shuffled out.

The telephone rang. A cascade of words burst into Quill's eardrums. It was Stroganoff burbling about bodies and police.

'Please,' pleaded Quill. 'A little slower and a little softer.'

But slowness, it appeared, was out of the question.

'Mais mon cher, do you not understand? The body it is in my office, it is dead entirely, and me I am almost in the prison.

---

[1] On subsequent mornings he drank coffee.

So you come at once and tell the gendarme that it is not I who kill him.'

'Kill who?' asked Quill, struggling hard to find some handle to this slippery stick.

'Absolument,' agreed Stroganoff. 'He is dead. So you come at once.'

Quill gave it up and started to dress. Presently the 'phone rang again.

It was Galybchik.

'Mr. Quill,' she gasped. 'Something terrible has happened. They have arrested Stroganoff.'

Quill groaned. It seemed hard that this thing had to happen to him on the first day of his holiday.

'Hurry,' begged Galybchik. 'Don't bother to shave.'

Quill promised to go right over. 'Don't touch anything,' he added entirely through force of habit.

As he was leaving the 'phone rang for the third time. Guessing correctly that this would be Arenskaya he did not trouble to answer.

*   *   *

'Bonjour,' said the Commissionaire, hailing Quill as an old friend. 'Useless to call to-day. The director has been arrested.'

'Why?' Possibly, thought Quill, this man might know something.

The commissionaire shrugged. 'Sais-pas. It is easy to get arrested in Bazouche. Our Gustave is very excitable. All his life he has arrested first and asked the questions after.'

'Really?' said Quill.

'But do not mistake me,' said the commissionaire, worried that Quill might think he was casting aspersions on Bazouche's Chief of Police. 'Gustave is the man honourable. Never will he take a bribe—practically. He respects and honours the profession that is his, as every man should. He is not,' he said with unexpected indignation, 'like the critic Citrolo, who was doubtless well paid to write this.' He picked up a copy of *Le Matin Populaire* and pointed with a quivering hand to a

column. 'It is infamous that anyone should stoop to write this.
Read it, M'sieur, and you will share my indignation. I love the
ballet,' said Anatole, the Commissionaire, with deep emotion,
'I have loved it all my life. But last night I did not love. I would,
if I could, warn every balletomane in the land of this outrage
on beauty. But, alas, I have no paper. Citrolo has the paper
and always till now I have respected him for his judgment and
fairness. But now I see that he is like the others—only worse.
Balletomanes have learnt to trust Citrolo—to believe what he
writes. In writing this,' he pointed to the column again, 'he has
betrayed their trust.'

As Quill was glancing incredulously on the glowing eulogies
Stroganoff had dictated last night, Galybchik came rushing out
and grasped him urgently by the arm.

'Police,' gasped Galybchik. 'They're up in the office. Hurry
or they'll move the body.'

'Whose body?' asked Quill petulantly. 'Won't anybody tell
me who's dead?'

Galybchik considered the request and appeared to find it
reasonable.

'Citrolo,' she said.

Quill remembered a vague meeting in the cocktail bar
yesterday.

'The critic?'

Galybchik nodded.

'Bon,' said the commissionaire with deep satisfaction.

* * *

Up in Stroganoff's office, the scene might have been taken
direct from a sleuth's nightmare. There was the body, lolling
against the armchair, its features horribly contorted. Beside it
lay a revolver, an empty bottle of iodine marked 'poison,' and
a glass of milk—untouched. There was a bullet hole. It was
not in the corpse. It was, in fact, as Quill was to note later, on
the wall opposite. There was a noose dangling from the ceiling.
There was an armchair, overturned as though for luck, a half-
smoked cigar on the mantelpiece and some promising-looking

ash on the carpet. The safe was open. The bureau had obviously been ransacked. On the desk lay the prospectus of an appetizing gold mine.

A plump little man in a soiled blue uniform was sitting at the desk studying what was obviously a clue-riddled letter, It read:

All is discovered, so—poof—I kill myself. Pavlo Citrolo.

He scowled forbiddingly at Quill and Galybchik.

Quill introduced himself. Instantly the little man was all smiles.

'It is an honour to meet you, M'sieur. I read about you in the case of the dead Petroushkas. You permit me to present myself. I am Gustave Clemenceau. No relation. Always I have been the admirer of your Scotland Yard. It will be an honour, cher collègue, to work with you.'

Quill made suitable noises.

'It is a pity, of course,' said Gustave, 'that the case is so simple. Already I have arrested one murderer and I hope soon to have the second.'

Quill examined this high-speed worker with a certain amount of grudging admiration. He himself would never have the confidence to make an arrest within two seconds of seeing the victim. Of course, Gustave had mistaken his suspect. Inevitably he found himself wondering if, when the mistake was discovered, the comments of the Sûreté to Gustave would, in their essentials, equal the comments made to him by Scotland Yard when, after some three weeks of hesitation, he had arrested the wrong man. But, of course, it was possible that the Sûreté encouraged Gustave to work on the inverted principle of arresting everybody in sight, arguing mathematically that the greater the number of arrests, the better the chance of the murderer being among them.

'This morning,' began Gustave. 'I am in my garden with my marrows. They are beautiful. Madame Bonfemme arrives to tell me the telephone rings in the police-station. I do not expect a call this morning, so I know at once something unusual has happened. I hurry. It is the director of the Casino. There is a dead man in his office. A famous dead man—a figure well known to us all. The critic Citrolo. He is dead—suicided I am led to believe. But Gustave believes nothing. Only his trained eye sees, his trained brain notes.'

'You've had a lot of experience,' said Quill.

'Of big crime—no,' said Gustave candidly. 'It is my first murder. But I have read and I assure M'sieur that I am capable.'

'Evidently,' said Quill.

'I tell the director to touch nothing till I come. I cover my marrows and I hurry to the scene.'

With the narrative approaching its climax Gustave paused for effect. With studied casualness he passed over an opulent box of cigars.

It was empty.

'Big joke,' said Galybchik tearfully.

Quill passed his cigarette-case.

'So,' resumed Gustave only slightly disconcerted, 'I arrive, and what is the scene that greets my eye? This!' He stretched out an accusing hand. 'And in the middle of it a large bald man. It is Stroganoff. He talks all the time. He tells me Citrolo is suicided. But I wave him aside and I look for myself.'

'I examine the body. It is clear at once that the man Stroganoff lies. It is not suicide. The victim has been strangled. See the bruises are on his throat.

'I question the man Stroganoff. I ask him how comes the body into the office? And, believe it or not, M'sieur, he confesses that he leaves it here last night. He admits, if you please, that Citrolo was with him till a late hour drinking. Then he drank too much and fell asleep. And then, if you please, the man Stroganoff tried to make me believe that, with his victim reduced to insensibility, he went home and left him to sleep it off.'

'So he did,' said Galybchik defiantly.

'You are still here,' said Gustave coldly. 'You go.'

Galybchik remained rooted. Only Stroganoff could tell her to go away.

'Next,' said Gustave complacently, 'I examine the room. At

once I see that the suicide theory is not logical. Citrolo has chosen for himself too many ways of death.' He counted them over on his chubby fingers. 'The poison, the pistol and the armchair overturned, which is the most foolish of all. For your suicide,' he pointed out, 'does not tussle with himself. Neither does he strangle himself with his own hands.'

'Relentlessly I reason. This scene has been arranged to deceive me. Me—Gustave Clemenceau. No relation. Who, I ask myself, has set this trap? The answer is easy. It is the man Stroganoff.'

Quill ran a perturbed hand through his hair. The exuberance of the props fitted in only too well with his knowledge of the Stroganoff mentality. He was reasonably certain that Stroganoff had not committed the murder but there seemed no doubt that the old boy was deeply involved.

'I pounce on the man Stroganoff,' cried Gustave, 'I riddle him with questions. He turns, he twists, he telephones, but like the bullets of a machine-gun my logic it pursues him. It is the test of endurance. Which will exhaust the other first?'

Quill found himself wondering. It must have been a great battle.

'But the trained mind wins,' said Gustave triumphantly. 'At last the man Stroganoff ceases to struggle and admits all.'

'All?' said Quill.

'Almost all,' amended Gustave. 'He denies only that he killed Citrolo.'

Quill suppressed a smile.

'He admits that he set the scene, and arranged the many ways of suicide. But he still swears that Citrolo was asleep when he left last night and that he arrived this morning to find him dead. It was the fright, he says, that turned him *Régisseur*. So I arrest him. As you see, cher collègue, it is a case peu compliqué.'

'You are making a big mistake,' said Galybchik loyally.

'Taisez-vous,' snapped Gustave, 'or I arrest you too.'

Quill remembered something. 'Talking of arrests, you spoke of a second murderer.'

Gustave nodded wisely. 'That is so. It is a murderer that one would hardly suspect.' He paused. 'It is the man Lord Button-hooke.'

Galybchik gasped while a tremor of unholy glee ran through Quill. This last sounded much too good to be true.

'You are astonished,' said Gustave, 'I am astonished too that a lord so prosperous should be so debased. But there is little doubt. In his terror of arrest the man Stroganoff try to save himself by exposing his accomplice.'

A shock of black hair strode into the room. It looked for Stroganoff, failed to find him, looked blandly round, failed to notice anything unusual, saw Quill, recognized him, assumed its most amiable expression and made straight for him.

'You schange me small scheque,' said Nevajno winningly.

In her corner Galybchik quietly fainted.

*   *   *

'Mais, mon cher,' said Stroganoff, 'soyez raisonnable. Could I foretell that the good Citrolo would make for himself the bump-off?'

The gaol at La Bazouche had not kept pace with modern ideas and Stroganoff's cell lacked many of the amenities to which the comfort-loving impresario was accustomed. There was no roll-top desk, no easy chair, no opulent box of cigars and no carpet to spill ashes on. Instead there was a truckle bed, a bench, and an iron grille that gave out on an empty cell opposite. Stroganoff was stretched on the first, cosily sipping an inexplicably produced glass of Russian tea, while Quill, uncomfortable on the second, was manfully trying to extract from him the salient facts of the case.

Not for the first time that morning Quill found himself sighing for one of those retentive-minded witnesses, so obligingly doled out to other detectives, who could be relied on to relate the circumstances in chronological order, leaving out no detail however small. Gustave, who had insisted on accompanying him in his study of the scene of the crime, had been far too busy audibly fitting clues to his own theory to be of much use. Galybchik, recovered from her faint, obviously knew something but stubbornly refused to divulge it. While Nevajno, having at last been made to realize what had occurred, was concerned only with a new idea for a ballet to be called 'Vacances Sanguinaires.' The corpse had been removed for an autopsy and the contents of its pockets collared by Gustave and put under seal. So Quill was reduced to relying on Stroganoff.

The latter, at first, had persisted in sticking to the version he had supplied to Gustave, and it was only after much pressure that Quill could induce him to admit that he and Citrolo were not sufficiently buddies to get drunk together. From there it was but a step to obtain from him a confession of the enthusiastic notice he had written for himself.

'It was good—no?' asked Stroganoff, pulling out a cutting and lingering gloatingly over the best phrases.

Quill was gloomy. 'It seems to me that you are in a bad jam. You admit that you drugged Citrolo—that you wrote the notice. . . .'

'Mais non,' said Stroganoff quickly. 'I do not admit that. It is big secret and I tell only to you.'

'A secret anyone who reads the notice can discover.'

The journalist was hurt. 'Pensez-vous! But it is very efficient.'

'It contains the Stroganoff signature in every sentence.'

'I forget that.' Stroganoff nodded pontifically. 'My style it is distinctive.'

'Exactly.'

'But why you worry?' Stroganoff demanded. 'Since I tell you that it is not I who do the bump-off it is then some other. So cease to pester me, mon cher, and hurry to find this criminal, for I am eager to be at my Casino to-night.'

Patiently Quill explained for the third time that before he could reasonably be expected to find the criminal he must know more about the victim and the curious scene of his death. He would like to know how much of the mischief in the study Stroganoff was responsible for and how much had been contributed by others.

'Try and remember,' he pleaded, 'and tell me exactly what you did this morning.'

Stroganoff's brow puckered in a tremendous frown of concentration.

'First,' he said brilliantly, 'I awake. At once I send a boy for *Le Maton Populaire*. My notice it is there. My best sentence—the one that concerns myself—it has been cut. Then I am furious. Almost I telephone the paper to reason with them, but I remember in time that it is not I who is suppose to have write it. So instead I ring for my breakfast. I shave, I dress, I go to the Casino. I reach my door. I unlock it.'

'You always keep the door locked?'

'Certainement,' said Stroganoff with dignity, 'except when I forget. You must understand, mon cher, that in the room are many things of the most valuable.'

'Such as?'

'First, there are the records of the Ballet Stroganoff. Then there are the contracts. There are the chips for the Casino and the account books for the losses. It is curious,' he mused, 'why there is always more chips in the book than in the drawer.'

'Never mind that,' said Quill.

'But I mind enormous,' said Stroganoff. 'Comme ça my roulette it is the ruin. That is why I am glad when you write that you come here for your holiday. M'sieur Quill, I say, will assurément solve for me this little mystery.'

'Is that why you asked me?'

'Mais non,' said Stroganoff quickly and changed the subject. 'Also in my office there are the two chapters of my auto-biography. They are very valuable; there are many who would give much to look at them. So you understand it is essential that the door it is locked so that nobody can get into.'

It did not seem to Quill that so much emphasis on the impregnability of the room was at all wise in Stroganoff's predicament.

'You are certain that the door was locked?'

'Certainement.'

'Is there any other entrance to your office?'

'Non. The window it is locked and the wall it is sheer.'

Quill sighed. Here he was at last presented with one of those cases with all doors and windows locked which every hard-pushed author resorts to sooner or later. Of course, it had to come on his holiday.

'Is there more than one key to the door?'

'Si,' Stroganoff nodded. 'Galybchik—she have one.'

'Anyone else?'

'Non. But certainly,' Stroganoff argued, 'a little lock it is not difficult for the cunning assassin.'

'Of course anyone who had wanted to could have had an impression made.'

Stroganoff nodded. 'So you see you have the many clues and . . .'

'I shall want the many more,' finished Quill. 'Let us continue. You unlocked the door. . . .'

'I unlock the door,' resumed Stroganoff resigned. 'I enter. You understand that I am prepare to find Citrolo much awake and cross so I am ready with the speech tactful. But Citrolo he is still sleeping. I am worried. Maybe I give him too many tablets. I approach closer and I see that he is bump-off. Strangle.'

'Now,' said Stroganoff, 'I am much upset. I realize I am in the danger. I have fall from the fire into the soup. The circumstances they are of a suspicion formidable. I too have read the detective stories. So I reason with myself. To call the police tout de suite it is not wise. They will ask the question, they will learn that it is I who see Citrolo last and then I will be in prison. At all costs, I say, I must prevent that. The Ballet Stroganoff it need me too much.'

Quill looked round the cell but said nothing.

'So I arrange the décor that it look like the suicide.'

'Like several suicides.'

'Alas,' said Stroganoff simply, 'it is the impresario in me.'

'Of course,' said Quill, 'it never occurred to you that you were doing your best to destroy any clues the murderer might have left.'

'Pas vrai,' snapped Stroganoff. 'I destroy nothing. I only add.'

This was a slight improvement. Quill produced his note-book and took a deep breath.

'Can you remember exactly what you added and exactly what you found?'

'Certainement,' said data-Stroganoff with dignity.

'Very well. Then, first—was it you who put the bottle of iodine beside the corpse?'

'It was I,' said Stroganoff. 'We get it when Arenskaya she run the sword in the Prince[1] when she rehearse Giselle. The Ballet Stroganoff it waste nothing. It was not the poison of the most convincing,' he apologized, 'but I can find no other bottle that bear the symbol.'

'The rope?'

'I fix that,' said Stroganoff. 'At first I plan to put in it the body but I shudder too much.'

'The overturned armchair?'

'I stumble after I fix the rope. But I think it good idea so I leave it comme ça.'

'The revolver?'

'It is mine,' said Stroganoff sublimely. 'But again I lack the courage to fire into the body. So I select a place on the wall where even the policement he could not miss it.'

'The gold-mine prospectus?'

'That I did not have time to read,' said Stroganoff regretfully.

'The glass of milk?'

'It is the mystery complete. Me I never drink the milk.'

'The cigar?'

'It is the kind that Button'ooke smoke. I put it there,' said Stroganoff, 'for loock. Also the ash, which I notice in my reading gives all the detectives mooch pleasure.'

'Why did you accuse Buttonhooke?' asked Quill, abandoning the list for a moment.

Stroganoff looked very pleased with himself. 'That was the coup d'état. I realize that with all my precautions I am still in the danger of arrest. Gustave he do not appear convinced. And

[1] Smithsky.

I ask myself if I am arrest what then will happen to the Casino Stroganoff? With me in prison the Casino Button'ooke it will have the walk-over. The only chance it is to put Button'ooke in the prison also. So I make the accusations against Button'ooke and the police they mistake me and think we are the accomplice. That, mon cher, is imbécile but it suits me well for the moment, so I do not contradict.'

'Your accusations, of course,' said Quill, 'were entirely without foundation.'

'Pas du tout,' said Stroganoff hurt. 'It is bien possible that Lord Button'ooke he is the assassin. It was he who advise me to muzzle Citrolo. Also Button'ooke he have the ballet too, and maybe he worry what Citrolo will write about it. Il a bien raison, aussi, mon cher. Citrolo did not wish to write well even of the Ballet Stroganoff. Picture you what he would write of the Ballet Button'ooke!'

Quill returned to his note-book. 'The open safe? The ransacked bureau?'

Stroganoff shrugged. 'Of that I know nothing. It is thus I find them. Doubtless the assassin he search for something.'

'Have you missed anything?'

Stroganoff clasped an anguished forehead. 'Mon Dieu, I have forgot to look!' He sat up. 'You go at once,' he said urgently, 'and fetch me here the two chapters of my memoirs, the mortgage papers of my Casino, my address book and the contracts Ostorojno, Lubova, but not Smithsky. Also . . .'

'Presently,' Quill promised. Only a few more questions and he would be ready to start work. Stroganoff was a fair-minded man. He groaned slightly and leant back on his couch.

Having reduced Stroganoff to passivity Quill set about his task. He explained that in every murder there were three basic facts on which the detective had to concentrate. Means, Motive, Opportunity. The passive one sprang to life to point out that there would be plenty of scope for enquiries along the motive lines. One with so little taste must have plenty of enemies. For example, Buttonhooke. . . . With some difficulty Quill got him to lie down and resumed his argument.

It was clear, he managed to convince Stroganoff, that this could not have been a premeditated murder. No murderer could have relied on Stroganoff drugging Citrolo and leaving him tempting and isolated throughout the night. It was therefore the murder of someone who saw an opportunity and was quick to act on it. This narrowed the circle from which the murderer sprang to the people who might reasonably be supposed to know of Citrolo's presence in his office. So would Stroganoff tell him the names of all the people who . . .

He questioned Stroganoff and bit by bit extracted from him an unbelievably large list of people who had been hovering around and butting in upon his private sanctum last evening. These he jotted down in his note-book for private pondering.

'You get busy soon,' urged Stroganoff. 'It is of importance the utmost. . . .' He broke off and with a triumphant exclamation pounded eagerly across to the grille.

'Bon jour, mon ami,' he greeted the manacled astrakhan that was being trundled down the passage.

Lord Buttonhooke glared.

*   *   *

Leaving Stroganoff and Buttonhooke to their amiable discourse Quill took shelter among the collection of disconsolate marble tops that called itself a bar.

Though it was raining, trade at the *Dernier Douzaine* was anything but brisk. At the desk Madame Dupont was saying so to an elderly but sympathetic waiter.

'Courage, Madame,' he said, 'Il en reste toujours les anglais,' and ambled up to overcharge Quill for the modest bock he ordered.

'Il a raison, il faut en avoir du courage,' nodded seventeen Madame Duponts in the green reflections of the mirrors that lined the walls.

Quill settled down to a good ponder. The more he pondered the more he disliked the case, and the less he felt inclined to blame Gustave for his precipitate arrest of Stroganoff. All the evidence pointed to Stroganoff. The means, the opportunity—

even a motive that was typically Stroganoff. It was only his knowledge of the latter that induced his belief in his innocence. But it was going to be a devil of a job to prove it.

To get down to it he would have to ferret out many more facts than he had at present. First, there was the dead man. All he knew about Citrolo at the moment was that he was a dramatic critic with a habit of expressing himself candidly. His first step, therefore, must be to find out something of his private life. Interviews with people who knew him were indicated and a visit to his rooms might be helpful.

Quill got up, paid his bill, and left the café. Almost immediately he was in it again. With him was Arenskaya. She had collared him outside.

'Champagne,' she ordered.

'What did I tell you?' signed the waiter to the seventeen sea-green Madame Duponts.

'Me, I always drink the champagne when my nerves they are tricky.'

Quill nodded. 'You are upset this morning?'

'But it is natural that I am upset,' said Arenskaya. 'My new friend—Citrolo—is dead, and Stroganoff is the idiot.'

'But,' said Quill to cheer her up, 'Lord Buttonhooke is the idiot too. He's in gaol as well,' he explained.

'Tiens!' Arenskaya was interested. 'You are sure?' she asked.

'Positive,' said Quill. 'When I left he was enjoying a quiet little chat with Stroganoff.'

'Bien.' Arenskaya gulped down her champagne. 'It is then the moment for me to get back Dovolno to the Ballet Stroganoff.' She arose. 'You will understand,' she said, 'that with Stroganoff absent it is I who deputize.'

Quill nodded.

'In Lyons there is the crisis effrayant. The fat girl she wish to dance "Blue Bird." Me I am all for it since it is Smithsky who will have to lift her and it gives me pleasure to see that one work. But my personal enjoyment I put aside and I forbid.'

'Who,' interrupted Quill, the detective, 'is Dovolno?'

Arenskaya looked at him saucer-eyed. 'But you do not

know? He is the dancer the most promising since Kasha Renevsky. His terre-à-terre has the most style since Massine, his turns leave Lichine standing, and Idzikovsky never jumped higher.' She broke off impatiently. 'I forget always that you are the ignoramus complete and know nothing of ballet. So I tell you something that interest you more. Dovolno—he want to sleep with the little Ostorojno.'

Quill blushed. 'I am interested in Citrolo.'

'He want to sleep with her too,' said Arenskaya. 'It is curious how experience turns to youth.' She ogled Quill invitingly.

'Then Ostorojno is the person to tell me most about Citrolo?' Past practice enabled Quill to ignore the ogle.

'Du tout.' The flamboyant feather in Arenskaya's hat quivered with the strength of her denial. 'She has a mother that one. And I too help to put the spoke in the wheel of Citrolo. Who is he to interfere with my choice of mates for my ballerinas?'

'Do you supervise all the love affairs in this ballet?' asked Quill startled.

'I help a little,' said Arenskaya modestly. 'And sometimes I stop it. Always the benefit of my experience I put at their disposal.' She simpered. 'But interfere—no? Have I not said that to one of my nature it is impossible. Never do I repeat to the ballerinas what they tell me about each other—only once when I tell Dyrakova. . . .' She stopped. 'Tiens,' she said, 'there is one who will be sorrowful this morning. Even she cry a little per'aps.'

'Who,' asked Quill, 'is Dyrakova and why will she cry?'

'Mais c'est incroyable!' cried Arenskaya. 'Not to know the great Dyrakova—the greatest of all ballerinas—who live in Paris like a Queen and refuse to dance for anyone.'

'But why will she cry this morning?'

'The death of an 'usband it is always sad,' said Arenskaya solemnly. 'Even one that is many divorces away.'

'Was Citrolo one of her husbands?'

Arenskaya nodded. 'Always she marry her lovers. She is a stupid woman. It is well known. Also she is not always the dancer that the critics claim. In Vienna . . .'

Quill listened patiently as Arenskaya plunged into a recital of Dyrakova's worst performances interspersed with highly improbable accounts of her own successes, and then tactfully steered the conversation in the direction of Citrolo's murder. But here Arenskaya had no definite theories to offer. Citrolo, she claimed, was the typical smooth type of villain whom almost anybody might have a reason for murdering.

'Also,' she said, a personal grievance rising to the foreground, 'he was the meanness itself. He order champagne and leave me to pay for it.'

Quill paid the waiter hurriedly.

'Meanness,' said Arenskaya, 'it is the one thing that I cannot tolerate. Meanness and mothers. To those that have neither I can forgive much. That is why, M'sieur, I bear with the approaches of that poor Vanilla who have eye on me. He do not earn very much, but always he find the money to spend and give me presents which I would accept from one many times richer. Regardez!' She thrust an arm proudly in front of Quill to dangle three large emeralds in an embossed band of gold. Quill looked at it.

'An expensive present?'

Arenskaya nodded. 'Bien sûr. Vanilla he give me all I ask. But all the same I do not trust him. We are friends, but I watch him closely.' She gathered her wraps. 'But, really, M'sieur Quill, I cannot linger here and listen to your talking. I have the business serieux to do. I go to deal with young Dovolno while he is still too sleepy to argue much.'

*   *   *

The Garçonnière rented by Citrolo for his enjoyment of the winter sunshine at Bazouche was situated high on the slopes, named in a burst of inspiration, '*Beau Soleil*.' It was raining. A perspiring Talbot-Darracq deposited Quill at the entrance. In the passage a scrubbing concierge splashed water indifferently about his feet. She shook a gloomy head at Quill's enquiry and pointed vaguely towards the sky.

'Cinquième étage,' she said. 'L'ascenseur ne marche pas.'

She detached from her wrapped round person a large key and, muttering something about a faulty bathroom tap, a m'sieur who detested getting out of bed to answer the front door, and her rheumatism, thrust it upon Quill and returned to her scrubbing.

Quill examined the notice that for the past two days had been hanging outside the lift gates. It read '*Arrêt Momentaire*.' Cursing his luck he started to climb the stairs. In a vile temper he reached the top.

Unaccustomed to the inauspicious entrances that French landlords, as a class, delight in supplying, Quill was surprised to find the apartment itself distinctly comfortable. The room was predominantly grey with pearly walls and ceiling. Deep armchairs beckoned Quill to rest from his arduous climb. On the wall hung an exquisite print of the *Pas-de-quatre*. The desk boasted a signed photo of Diaghilev and the mantelpiece an Arabesque signed 'Dyrakova.' A bijou piano almost tempted Quill to try out his five-finger exercises. It was the room of a cultured man who could afford to gratify his tastes. The battered typewriter was the only professional note in the restful amateur symphony.

Quill would have liked to potter happily among the books which progressed in an orderly manner from politics to pornography. He had indeed started at the latter end when his eye fell on a bulky volume entitled *L'Etude Complet De Chantage* 1810-1907. Quill picked it out. It appeared to be a neat analysis of the methods of all the brighter blackmailers of the past century, and though outwardly the author seemed to write with reproof the undertone was one of sterling admiration. It was inscribed 'To my son Pavlo—from his affectionate father. Saint-Sulphice. 1908.'

With reluctance Quill tore himself away from the fascinating pages and walked over to the desk. Meticulously he began his inspection. Soon he was engrossed in his task. It was a funny thing, he mused, the way you could bring a dead man to life by the objects that surrounded him. With every moment a clearer image of Citrolo was forming in his mind. His cigar and wine bills indicated the Bon Viveur, his invitations showed him to be one who was sought after—possibly even a man of charm. His pasted-up press book and the files of dancers' photographs indicated pride in his profession. The lack of love letters pointed to his discretion and his moustache-curlers to his vanity with a hint of pomposity. Quill glowed with pleasure at his own shrewd psychology. Come to think of it that was all that detection meant. Applied psychology and (here the Scotland Yard in him reared its official head), of course, endless routine work. Thank the Lord he was finished with that. It was Gustave's baby now.

Humming he returned to his research. Really it was quite a pleasure to work for such a corpse. Everything was in its place, tidily arranged and beautifully accessible. With every move the feeling grew in Quill that though the witnesses in this case left much to be desired the dead man could not possibly have been more thoughtful. It was almost as though, foreseeing his own death, he had determined to make the detective's job as easy as possible.

Where would such a man keep his valuable documents? Quill reflected. The answer was easy. Obviously he was due to find a safe delicately concealed behind some not too callisthenic cache.

He tried the strikingly modern clock, set in the mantelpiece. He was right first time. The clock face swung open and there was the secret treasure. It consisted of a small faded note-book. Quill took it. At first sight it seemed to be a record of a number of people who owed Citrolo money and were paying it back by instalments. Quill took it to the window where the light was better. One look at the street and the note-book was in his pocket and he was crossing back to slip the clock face into its original position. A perspiring bicycle (with an expiring motor attachment) had come thankfully to rest outside the house. From it leapt Gustave.

He pounced on the concierge. The concierge called off an Alsatian that had pounced on him. It was old, lean, and very friendly.

'Conquième étage,' she answered Gustave's order. 'L'ascenseur marche,' she added with considerable pride. 'Profitez de l'occasion.'

Some few minutes later Quill was considerably annoyed to hear the lift groaning its way up. He would have a few words with that concierge when he left.

'You!' cried Gustave, bouncing into the room and nearly bouncing back again as he recognized Quill. 'What for do you tell the concierge that you have come to mend the bathroom?'

'What?' said Quill.

'It was not the act of a friend,' Gustave shook his head reproachfully. 'If you wished to see this room there was no need to do it in secret. You had but to come to me. Would I not fling open every door to assist you?'

Most of them leading nowhere, thought Quill, and offered his apologies.

Gustave waved them away. 'It is not important. The appartement it is not interesting. It is only a matter of routine that brings me here.' He looked round the room with disapproval. No trellised wallpaper, no statuettes, no naughty pictures, and nothing of Louis Quinze. 'He had not much taste—the dead man—hein?' He turned to business. 'You have searched the room?'

'Yes,' said Quill.

'Bon,' said Gustave relieved. 'Then I go home now to prune my pear. Almost I fear I would not have time to attend to it to-day. I offer you a lift?'

Standing on the spoke projecting from the back wheel of the bicycle the unresisting Quill found himself being coasted back to the Casino. But he hardly noticed the journey. He was busy thinking out excuses for not lunching with Gustave.

CHAPTER VII

Safe in his hotel Quill retired to the lounge and opened the note-book he had captured from Citrolo's safe. Closer inspection showed that the book was not confined to figures of financial transactions alone but contained some elucidating sidelights on the Citrolo philosophy. The first page was headed '*Apologia*,' and read as follows:

'If this book should ever fall into hands other than mine it would be displeasing to me that the possessor should think of me merely as a blackmailer. He must understand that I am as proud of my "blackmail" as I am of my essays on the ballet and everyone who has met me knows how much I value the latter.

'This, then, is not an attempt at vindication. It is an attempt to open the eyes of the unreflecting; to show them how strongly my despised profession, cleverly disguised under some happier name, has embedded its roots in modern civilization.

'Blackmail is an unfortunate word, ugly and unmelodious. It conjures up visions of pale-faced clerks driven to falsifying ledgers and ultimately to suicide; or trembling spinsters with lost virginities and church-going fiancés. And, of course, somewhere in the background an evil chuckle.

'But such scenes are only the minor manifestations of a great industry. Blackmail—real blackmail—works on a much larger canvas.

'Blackmail in its highest form is found in Politics. There it is called "Diplomacy."

'Governments balance their budgets with it. Here it is called "Income Tax"—a quarter of your earnings or . . .

'The working-man finds it impossible to get a job unless he belongs to a trade union—Subscription? . . .

'What is the difference between a trade union and an employer, and a blackmailer and his victim?

'How did France get its vacances payées?

'How did Lord Dash get his peerage?

'When does a gold-digger get the most out of her sugar daddy?

'Have I not proved my case? Is it not blackmail that makes the world go round?

'The world does not condemn what I have described. It shrugs its shoulders and accepts it. C'est la vie! Why then should it condemn the blackmailer, simple and undisguised, who in straightforward manner demands money with menaces?

'Try as I may I cannot see any difference.

'It was early in my youth that I discovered nature had endowed me with one undisputable asset—an ability to stumble on secrets others did not wish to share. Wherever I went it was never very long before the facts of any guilty endeavour in the neighbourhood, past, present and future, were in my hands. My luck was uncanny. My memory and my ability to interpret apparently insignificant details in the correct light did much to help. Had I been stupid or conventional I would have become a detective. Instead I became a blackmailer.

'I studied my profession as closely as a confidence trickster studies his victim. I was determined to avoid the mistakes of some of my brothers. Why end up with a cut throat, or in dock with a Mr. A. giving evidence against me? Presently I evolved for myself the following three golden rules:

'1. Never do business with the weak, the desperate, or the ruthless.

'2. Never be too greedy.

'3. Always make it clear to your sucker that he is paying for being found out and not for his guilt. This makes him more careful in future and occasionally even grateful.

'It was soon evident to me that my most profitable sphere was to be the underworld. Crooks are delightful people to work with—they seldom bear malice. There is no need to explain to them my third golden rule. They understand it only too well. Some of them are almost my best friends, and whenever I can do so without danger I am only too willing to put what business in their way I can. Of course, in such cases I charge a small percentage, but that is only reasonable. I make a habit of talking of "commission" rather than payment: they call me "Pourcentage" Citrolo. I am proud of the name.

'A proof of my efficiency is that most of my customers pay promptly—practically without complaint. Occasionally one lags—then I threaten gently. If the threats fail I close the account with a cordial letter, in which it is made quite clear that the ex-customer has nothing to fear from me. I never have any intention of carrying out my menaces—there is no profit in exposure, only unpleasantness. As in diplomacy I rely entirely on my menaces. If the bluff is called I retire with grace. But it is called seldom.

'If I have any faults as a blackmailer it is perhaps that I am a little timid in going after the really big commissions. I have in my possession information against some half-dozen "big shots," who, if they paid, would pay well. But would they pay? It is dangerous to try. With the big people externals are deceptive and it is difficult to be certain that you have got their pyschology. I made an attempt on such a one early in my career—it nearly cost me my life. It is possible that I am over-cautious now.

'But then I am anxious to die in my bed.'

*   *   *

Quill smiled as he finished reading. Poor Citrolo. With all his precautions he had still failed to allow for a distracted impresario with a box of sleeping tablets.

His thoughts now switched to a gloomier direction. Stroganoff had been shrewder than he knew when he hinted that there would be plenty of scope for enquiries along the 'Motive' lines. Probably every one of the many people who had been in the room that night had one. The same one. Quill was inclined to doubt Citrolo's boast of his excellent relations with his clients.

He turned the pages to the accounts section. This was exactly like a money-lender's ledger. There were the names of the customers in the left-hand column, each accompanied with the amounts of their payments and the dates. Some of the figures were underlined, which showed that the next instalment was overdue. There was also a column for comments. Here and there, Quill noted, a customer was marked as doing well and able to pay more, while in other cases a decrease was contemplated. It was all very businesslike. Only in the case of Kurt Kukumber, whose payments seemed practically non-existent, was there any evidence of the dead man's slightly malicious sense of humour. Here the comment read: 'For Amusement Only.'

Some of the names came as a distinct shock to Quill. Others occasioned less surprise. From his point of view the most interesting were those of people at present in La Bazouche and hovering around the fatal room last night. Two names in particular stood out. Vanilla, the croupier, and Baron Sam de Rabinovitch.

Vanilla, Quill saw, was a fairly recent customer. His payments dated back little under two years. This, Quill assumed, was probably around the date when he had first taken service in the Casino, then run by Baron de Rabinovitch. It was reasonable to assume that his racket, upon which Citrolo with his flair had stumbled, was in some way connected with the gaming rooms. Quill marked down Vanilla for early questioning and passed on to the Baron.

Baron Sam de Rabinovitch must have been practically Citrolo's oldest customer. The payments began in 1925, and formed a clear reflex of the rises and falls in the Baron's prosperity. Starting with a comparatively low figure they rose steadily till 1927, fell in 1928 and ceased altogether from

1929-31. (In gaol, thought Quill.) In 1932 they started again at
an even lower level than in 1925, but they rose very quickly.
In 1935, the year that the Baron had opened the Casino, the
payments soared abruptly and from then on showed a slight
yearly increase. That the Baron was still flourishing was shown
in the comment, which revealed that yet another substantial
increase was contemplated. Quill made a rapid calculation and
worked out that if the Baron agreed to the latest demand he
would be paying Citrolo over 10,000 francs a month.

There was yet a third section in the book. It was headed
pathetically:

'Alas—No Courage.'

It contained a list, presumably the 'Big Shots' mentioned in
the *Apologia*, that Citrolo lacked the pluck to tackle. Reading
through the names Quill began to understand why Citrolo
lacked the nerve. Some of the names were almost household
words. There was a European Dictator, who apparently did
not compose his own speeches. An International Financier
only recently found out. Lord Buttonhooke. And a learned
judge who thought the American régime had much to com-
mend it.

The remaining names were all well-known to a wistful police.
It was almost a Debrett to the evasive peerage of the underworld. There was 'Gold Tongue' Gene, who had once almost
persuaded Mongolia to start a navy with the contents of a
decrepit shipyard. There was 'Banco' Dacarpo, who having
put it across the simple-minded Greek Syndicate at Deauville
had vanished into the blue. And there was Dimitri Dmitrius,
who had lived on credit for twenty years, suing himself under
various names for fortunes he never possessed. And others
equally fascinating.

To think that here was a blighter walking about with
information about half the crooks in Europe—information
that the police would give their large-sized ears to possess—
and he had been careless enough to let the man die under his
nose before he (Quill) could bully, cajole, or bribe it out of him.

With a regretful sigh Quill laid aside Citrolo's note-book and produced his own. It was time to tabulate the information he had acquired.

His best friends had never called Quill a brilliant detective. But he was conscientious and capable. His reports of a case were invariably masterpieces of lucid presentation, hailed as such by Scotland Yard and passed on to abler detectives for solution. But there was only Gustave to help him here. Quill felt a twinge of guilt at withholding the note-book from Gustave, but he suppressed it firmly. With that note-book in Gustave's possession there would not be a citizen in Bazouche left at large.

Methodically Quill went to work. Whenever it was possible he liked to set out the crime in the form of a time-table, and he did it here.

11.15 p.m. Citrolo, Stroganoff and Galybchik in office.

11.30 p.m. Vanilla enters to ask for chips.

11.40 p.m. Madame Ostorojno arrives to demand daughter's contract. Stroganoff opens safe and puts contract in it.

11.50 p.m. Nevajno arrives and departs.

Midnight approx. Lord Buttonhooke and Baron de Rabino-vitch visit the office.

12.10 a.m. Citrolo drinks drugged whisky.

12.20 a.m. Stroganoff begins dictating notice.

12.30 a.m. Prince Artishok and Sadie Souse arrive looking for Buttonhooke. Told by Stroganoff that the sleeping critic is drunk.

12.35 a.m. My friend, the Balleto-Medico, tries to enter office. Pushed out by Stroganoff.

1.00 a.m. Stroganoff finishes notice and departs. Claims to have locked door.

1.00 a.m.—9.00 a.m. Citrolo is strangled.

9.15 a.m. Stroganoff arrives to find Citrolo dead.

9.15 a.m. Stroganoff arranges scene.

9.30 a.m. Stroganoff telephones Gustave.

10.00 a.m. Stroganoff telephones me.

Plenty of material here, thought Quill, though of course as yet no information at all of those critical hours during which Citrolo met his death. Still there was an abundance of suspects —the note-book probably contained a complete list of the dead man's enemies, several of whom were about the premises. Both Vanilla and the Baron de Rabinovitch had actually seen Citrolo in Stroganoff's office and assuming that they felt any interest in the matter, could have been in a position to note than he had not left it.

Pondering thus Quill became aware of a short, wasp-waisted figure, striding up and down in anxious concentration, pausing irresolutely in front of his desk, clasping its forehead, audibly changing its mind and striding up and down again. At last Quill decided he could stand it no longer. He looked up severely. The figure started elaborately and hastened to his side.

'What's the matter?' Quill asked.

Kurt Kukumber shook his head dramatically, turned away and recommenced his striding. But not for long. Presently he was back again at Quill's side.

'M'sieur Quill,' he said, 'can I trust you?'

'Why not?' said Quill.

Kukumber stooped and sent a searching beam into Quill's eyes. What he saw seemed to satisfy him. He nodded emphatically twice and drew up a chair.

'M'sieur,' he said, 'on me a heavy responsibility has fallen.'

Where had Quill heard that opening before.

'My uncle,' began Kukumber.

'In Australia,' supplied Quill.

'In Toronto,' said Kukumber in all seriousness. 'He has died. Suddenly.'

'Leaving a will?' asked Quill.

'An amazing will,' said Kukumber, dazed but persevering. 'An astonishing will. A will that is typical of his eccentric but generous nature.' He sighed. 'A wonderful man, my uncle.'

'Lovable,' suggested Quill.

'His will,' said Kukumber, 'has left me the chief beneficiary but . . .'

'There are many bequests to charity to which you have to attend first.'

'It is a clause,' said Kukumber solemnly.

'You have to distribute—how much is it?'

'Pardon?'

'And you want a trustworthy person to help you do it.'

'M'sieur,' said Kukumber.

'If I can produce—say twenty thousand francs to show that I am a man of substance. . . .'

'Er,' said Kukumber.

'And leave them with you for half an hour to show I trust you...'

'Enough,' pleaded Kukumber. 'M'sieur, I apologize. But how was I to tell that you too were one of our profession?'

Quill passed one of his visiting cards.

Kukumber blushed deeply and apologized even more profusely. He also remembered a pressing engagement. But Quill would not let him keep it.

'Sit down,' he said firmly.

Kukumber sat down.

'About Pavlo Citrolo,' said Quill.

Kukumber sprang to his feet.

'It is a lie,' he said. 'I did not kill him.'

Quill pushed him back into his chair again. 'How did you know he was dead?'

'All Bazouche knows.' Kukumber sighed. 'Alas—poor Pavlo.'

'You knew him well?'

'I was his best friend,' declared Kukumber stoutly.

'Yet he blackmailed you!' Quill threw his bombshell.

It failed to explode. 'I paid for his silence,' said Kukumber. 'It was only fair,' he added ungrudgingly.

It was this remark that started the high esteem which Quill was eventually to feel for the Blackmailer's *Apologia*.

'He was a fair man,' said Kurt kindly. 'He did not charge me as much as the others and would not reproach me too much if I fell behind with my payments. You see,' he said with the assurance of the artist born, 'I show great promise—it needs only time for me to be the big shot. So Citrolo was content to wait.'

Quill toyed with the idea of showing him the comment in Citrolo's note-book but decided that the moment was not yet.

'How's business?' he asked chattily.

'Bad,' said Kurt. 'The luck is against me. My infallible system has broken down again.'

'And your rackets?'

'One disappointment after another,' said Kurt, man to man. 'First I think I find an English sucker—and he is you. Then I start to sell a gold-mine and what happens? It is my prospect who gets sent to gaol.'

Light dawned on Quill. 'The gold prospectus in Stroganoff's office—you put it there?'

'Yes,' said the unwary Kukumber.

'When,' snapped Quill.

Kukumber hesitated. 'I gave it to him downstairs.'

Quill lit a cigarette wearily. Here he was back on the dear old familiar ground. The lying witness who in all probability had nothing important to conceal.

But Kurt clung stoutly to his denial. He had posted the prospectus. He had given it to the commissionaire. He had dictated it across the telephone. He had never seen it in his life. But he had not put it there! Finally Quill changed the subject and asked Kukumber to describe his movements during the last night.

'You suspect me?' asked Kukumber alarmed.

'Purely a matter of routine,' said Quill from force of habit. Kukumber reflected. 'I have the perfect alibi,' he said triumphantly. 'I watch the new ballet. It was beautiful,' he said wistfully.

Clearly this could not be true. 'You never went near it,' Quill diagnosed.

'Useless to attempt to deceive you,' said Kukumber. 'If you know that, then you know also that Citrolo and I had a little disagreement last night.'

Quill nodded. 'I know.'

'It was not a disagreement exactly,' said Kukumber. 'Just such a cloud as comes sometimes between friends. Citrolo was a little put out as he left the baccarat room. Doubtless Vanilla

had been difficult again. I am not fond of Vanilla,' said Kurt
Kukumber a trifle irrelevantly.

'Was Vanilla fond of Citrolo?'

Kukumber was quick to catch the inference. 'It is curious
that he is the one man who never spoke well of poor Pavlo. It
is he who did it,' said Kukumber inspired, and grasped Quill
affectionately by the arm. 'Prove it, M'sieur, and you will earn
the gratitude of many.'

Quill was surprised. 'Is Vanilla so unpopular?'

But it was not that. Under the easy-going direction of
Stroganoff, the Casino, it appeared, had become the little
crook's Paradise. Petty swindles flourished in every corner and
even the croupiers could occasionally be cajoled into paying
out over the wrong numbers. With Stroganoff in gaol the
danger of Buttonhooke buying the Casino and reinstating the
eagle-eyed Baron de Rabinovitch loomed only too imminent.
It was not, Quill was given to understand, Vanilla's immediate
arrest that mattered so much as Stroganoff's immediate
extradition.

Quill extricated himself from the babble of words and
returned to the business in hand.

'What happened during the interview between you and
Citrolo?'

'It was nothing,' Kurt assured him. 'He wanted a little money
on account, but I persuaded him to be patient.'

'How did you spend the rest of the evening?'

'I played my system. No luck. So I went home to sleep.'

'Did you know that Citrolo was in Stroganoff's office?'

'No.'

'Did you go near it?'

'No.'

'Then how did the Gold Mine Prospectus get there?'

'What prospectus?' asked Kurt blandly.

*   *   *

'It's a scandal,' Madame Ostorojno was saying. 'My
daughter dancing for a murderer!'

'I don't believe Stroganoff is a murderer,' said her daughter.

'Murderer or not,' snapped the mother, 'you're not going to work for a gaol-bird. We're going straight to Buttonhooke.'

'He's in gaol, too,' put in Quill helpfully.

'It's a scandal,' said Madame Ostorojno again. 'I'm going straight to that policeman to tell him what I think of him.'

'Presently,' Quill sighed. Already he regretted the foolhardiness that had prompted him to place Madame Ostorojno's name at the top of his interview list for no better reason than that she was staying at his hotel. He ought to have known what to expect from a dancer's mother. 'Go where you like, but please answer a few questions first.'

'It's a scandal!' repeated Madame Ostorojno obstinately.

*   *   *

'Rien ne va plus,' said the new croupier. His name was Samson and a distracted Galybchik had handed him his diploma that morning. 'Rien ne va plus,' he repeated a shade apprehensively. To his astonishment everyone obeyed him. The new croupier relaxed. This was going to be easy.

It was five o'clock at the Casino Stroganoff. As Quill arrived Kurt Kukumber left. Quill put it down to guilty conscience, but he was wrong. Five o'clock was the hour when Kukumber always left—broke.

The green cloth tempted Quill. He had come in search of Vanilla, but he might as well allow himself the luxury of losing a few francs. He flung a counter on seventeen. A lean hand stretched over and removed it.

'It is foolish what you do,' said Nevajno to the switched round glare. 'I cannot bear to see you lose your money on a method so devoid of line.'

'Vingt-cinq,' said the croupier.

'Voila!' said Nevajno triumphantly. 'Now we put it on number seven.' He did so.

'Zero,' said the croupier.

'N'importe,' said Nevajno. 'You have another louis?'

Quill felt it was time to dissolve this superimposed partnership. He got up and pushed Nevajno into his seat. Nevajno accepted the situation philosophically and reached out a lean hand to move his neighbour's stake into better alignment.

'Excuse me,' said a breathless stranger to Quill, 'but would you introduce me to your friend—the great Nevajno?'

Quill looked curiously at this hunter of unusual lions.

'Have you got a cheque-book?'

'Why—yes?' The lion-hunter seemed surprised.

'Just show it to him,' said Quill, 'he will be delighted to meet you.'

In the *Salle de Baccarat* Vanilla was presiding over a moderate assemblage. His tie was tilting happily all over the place. The afternoon sessions showed Vanilla his greatest profit. Afternoon players were all small punters, far too absorbed in their own speculations to notice anything else. Quill's experienced eye picked out Vanilla's two accomplices almost immediately. The first might have been Kurt Kukumber all over again—a little wasp-waisted man across whose face eagerness and anxiety continually clashed. There was a seediness about the second. His suit was debonair, if dog-eared. Nicotine stained his fingers. There was a droop about his eyelids. A man, Quill decided, who had seen better days— probably aboard a Cunarder. He would have been willing to bet that Vanilla underpaid them both for their assistance.

'Banco,' cried the eager one.

'Idiot,' hissed the other.

But it was too late. Glaring, Vanilla pushed across the counters to a palooka in a pince-nez.

Thanks to Citrolo, Quill found little difficulty in following the rigours of the game. Abashed by his mistake, anxiety was now uppermost on the little man's face. He muffed three 'bancos' in succession. The thin veneer of immobility that masked over Vanilla's rage was a delight to Quill. Clearly he would have loved to strangle his accomplice. Quill looked at the hands that moved with precision and efficiency and noted the strength in the lean deft fingers. 'The perfect strangler,' he thought professionally.

Presently the syndicate scored a triumph. The eager one got a signal right. Determined to take no more chances Vanilla glanced at the clock and declared the session over. The players disbanded. Quill went over to Vanilla and introduced himself.

Vanilla was inclined to be curt. It was clear that he was eager to get away for a few words with his syndicate. But the official visiting card awed him.

'I know nothing,' he insured himself, before Quill had a chance to fire a single question.

Quill looked closely at the ferrety face and decided that a bludgeon would be best.

'You know a lot about Citrolo,' he said coldly. 'How much you know about his murder, we will discover presently.'

The ferrety face twitched.

'What is there to know about the murder?' he asked. 'The guilty one is already under arrest.'

'Citrolo had too many enemies to be certain of that,' said Quill. He paused. 'You were one of them,' he accused.

Vanilla was hurt. 'I was his best friend.'

'Shut up,' said Quill, 'you have been paying him blackmail for years.'

'You know that!' Vanilla was staggered.

'I know nearly everything about you—including your baccaret racket with your rather childish cheats.'

'They are childish,' agreed Vanilla, natural indignation rising above fear. 'Never will I be able to teach them.'

'Still,' said Quill smoothly, 'their mistakes do not matter much so long as you can rectify them by helping yourself from Stroganoff's box of chips.'

It was a bow at venture but it succeeded.

'You have found that out!'

Quill nodded. 'I also know that the emerald bracelet you gave Arenskaya is stolen property.'

'Even my private life,' muttered Vanilla, helpless.

Quill smiled to himself. These Latins were easy. He could never have pinned a Russian down like this.

'You can see that you are in a tough spot,' he resumed relentlessly. 'If I wanted I could make things very unpleasant for you.'

Vanilla nodded. He saw.

'But the law-breakers of France are not my concern. I am working for Stroganoff. Answer my questions and I won't make any trouble.'

Vanilla took up a pack of cards and absently tore them across.

'What is it you wish to know?' he surrendered.

'First,' said Quill, 'you went into Stroganoff's office last night.'

Vanilla nodded. 'That was to get some chips.'

'Tell me what you saw.'

'There was M'sieur le Directeur in argument with the critic Citrolo. With him was his *poule*.'

'His what?'

'His secretary,' amended Vanilla. 'I do not like her,' he added irrelevantly. 'She us not my type.'

Quill remembered Arenskaya. He nodded.

'I take my chips and I go. That is all.'

'Did you come back again?'

'No.'

'How did you spend the rest of the evening?'

'I am in the baccarat room till five. Then I go home.'

'The baccarat game broke up at five a.m.?'

'Yes.'

'There were many players?'

'Just the one table.'

Quill reflected. 'Can you give me the names of the late players at your table?'

But on this point Vanilla appeared to have lost his memory. Quill had not attached any importance to the late players so far, but Vanilla's reluctance to divulge their names made them suddenly significant. After all, the murderer would need some pretext to remain at the Casino and the baccarat table provided an admirable excuse. He would only have to leave it for a few minutes. Quill pressed the matter and gradually Vanilla began to remember. Eventually he produced the following list:

Lord Buttonhooke.

Prince Alexis Artishok.

Sadie Souse.

M'sieur André Dupont, Mayor of La Bazouche.

The Baron de Rabovitch.

Herr Van de West, and, of course, Vanilla's two accomplices, who, said Vanilla, had been quite outclassed by the formidable company. Had it not been for the Mayor and Lord Buttonhooke the evening would have been utter ruin.

Quill wondered why Vanilla should have been so reluctant to give this list. The names were interesting enough—one name in particular—but he could see no reason why Vanilla should want to hold them back. However he did not press the point.

'The Baron de Rabinovitch,' he asked, 'he used to be your employer?'

'He did,' said Vanilla, 'the cochon.'

'He wouldn't let you get at the chips?' Quill guessed.

'He kept them in the safe.'

Quill nodded sympathetically. 'It is harder to guess a combination than to pick a lock.'

Vanilla stared at him.

'Perhaps I am underestimating you,' said Quill; 'no doubt you have had a duplicate key to the office door made long ago.'

For some odd reason Vanilla looked relieved. 'I have no key. M'sieur le Directeur forgets to lock the door so often there is no need.'

'Did he leave it open last night?'

Vanilla shook his head. 'Last night it was locked.'

'How do you know?' Quill snapped.

Vanilla floundered helplessly. 'Did I say last night? I am confused. I refer to the night before.'

'So you did go to the office last night?'

'It was the night before,' insisted Vanilla. 'Last night I go to the office only once when I ask for the chips. After the game I go straight home. I have a witness,' he added proudly.

'Who?' asked Quill.

'A witness of quality—of integrity unimpeachable—the Prince Alexis Artishok,' said Vanilla. 'He gave me a lift.'

'What on earth did he want to get out of you?'

Vanilla fidgeted slightly. 'He is a great gentleman. It was raining. Doubtless he did not wish me to get wet.'

For the time being Quill let it go at that.

*   *   *

Remembering Stroganoff's request for 'possessions of the most valuable' left in the office, and thinking that he could, without offending Gustave, combine this small act of courtesy with a quiet prowl round of his own, Quill made his way upstairs. In the alcove by the broken statue he came upon two figures. Nevajno and his public. For once Nevajno was not talking. He was listening speculatively while the lion-hunter propounded the theme he had been waiting to unloose for many years. The perfect ballet.

'We will call it,' he finished on a note of ecstasy, 'NEPTUNE AGONISTES.'

Nevajno pondered for a long time.

'You schange me large scheque?' he demanded ambitiously.

Reluctantly detaching himself from this artistic collaboration Quill went up to Stroganoff's office. From inside came the pounding of a typewriter. Quill entered. Galybchik looked up eagerly from her machine but her face fell as she recognized Quill.

'Oh, it's you,' she said. 'Haven't you got him out yet?'

'We will soon,' Quill assured her. He glanced round and noted that the office had been restored to an apple-pie order it had certainly never possessed while its owner was about.

'Who tidied the room?' he asked.

Galybchik pleaded guilty. 'Was it wrong?' she asked apprehensively.

'Very,' said Quill.

'But the police had taken away everything they wanted,' pleaded Galybchik. 'And they've had the nerve to go through our ledgers.'

'How do you know?'

'They didn't put them back,' explained Galybchik. 'I found them on the shelf we use for our kettle and we always keep them locked in the drawer.'

Quill remembered those ledgers. They had been on the shelf that morning so it was not the police who had put them there. He docketed the information for further pondering and produced his list of the things Stroganoff wanted.

Together they crossed to the safe.

'Here's the biography,' said Galybchik, producing a formidable sheaf of foolscap. 'It's marvellous,' she breathed. 'The whole Ballet Stroganoff seems to come to life as you read. And nobody has ever been so right about Nicolas. Listen,' she began to turn the pages feverishly.

'Er,' said Quill.

'After that memorable performance the Tsar he say to me, "Vladimir Stroganoff you are astonishing." No—that's not it.' Galybchik turned a few more pages. 'Vladimir you are superb. . . . No. Vladimir you are a genius. . . . No. Vladimir . . .'

'Find it later,' Quill pleaded.

With a sigh Galybchik laid aside the memoirs and delved into the safe again. She produced the mortgage papers and the contracts marked 'Lubova' and 'Smithsky,' rummaged some more and emerged with a puzzled expression.

'The Ostorojno contract is missing.'

'Really,' said Quill, on whom the magnitude of the disaster had not yet penetrated.

'But this is terrible,' wailed Galybchik, 'our best dancer gone. How shall I tell Stroganoff?'

'I'll tell him,' Quill promised.

'It's that woman,' flared Galybchik. 'She tried to sneak it last night.'

'What woman?'

'The Ostorojno creature. The mother. She saw Stroganoff put it in the safe and came back for it.'

'Does she know the combination?'

'*Sylphides?*' asked Galybchik. 'Why, yes, I should think so.

Even if she didn't know she could guess it. Mr. Stroganoff is much too confiding. He tells everybody that it is always the name of a ballet and there aren't so many of them with nine letters.'

Quill became practical. 'But even assuming she could work the combination how did she manage to get into the room? She, or her daughter?'

'Oh—it wouldn't be Olga,' said Galybchik quickly. 'I like Olga.'

That seemed to settle that.

'Then how did the mother get in?'

Galybchik had no constructive suggestions to offer. She walked to the window, gazed down the flat wall and shook a puzzled head. Her own key had never left her—she never lent it to anybody—not even Nicolas.

Quill interrupted. 'So you have a key?'

'Of course,' said Galybchik, 'Stroganoff trusts me implicitly.'

'Which makes you a very suspicious person from my point of view,' Quill smiled.

Galybchik began to tremble visibly.

'Tell me,' Quill coaxed, 'you did go back to this room last night—didn't you?'

'No,' said Galybchik tautly. 'That is—no.'

Quill knew she was lying. It did not worry him unduly. Whatever felony Galybchik had compounded it was certainly not murder and in any case it would not be long before she would be telling him all about it.

Bestowing a paternal pat on her indignant curls he left her to her conscience.

*   *   *

The restaurant was crowded. This is explained, not by the excellence of the cuisine, which was appalling, but by the lavish system of credit that prevailed. Remembering the hungry days of his ballet, Stroganoff could never bring himself to refuse a ravenous customer food. Even Nevajno was allowed to sign a bill for his dinner. But it had to be signed. Every franc lost had to be accounted for in the books.

Quill had come to the restaurant on the track of the glass of milk found beside the dead man. But at his entry Emilio bustled forward with the smile of welcome reserved for cash customers, and before he realized what was happening Quill was seated at a table under the orchestra, allowing himself to order caviare, bortsch and pirojki, sole Stroganoff, Kiev cutlets, and Bombe Arenskaya, washed down with vodka and (a belated attack of firmness, this) vin du pays. It seemed an expensive way of cajoling a witness into a good temper.

'There are a few questions,' Quill began.

'M'sieur need have no fear,' said Emilio, 'the fish it comes fresh every day from St. Tropez,' and vanished.

He reappeared some ten minutes later carrying a dish of sardines. Caviare, it appeared, was off.

Quill smiled pleasantly. 'No matter,' he said, 'tell me—were you on duty last night?'

'Every night,' said Emilio, with a distinct sense of grievance. 'Always I am the last to go.'

'Then perhaps you can tell me. . . .'

'Un petit moment,' Emilio darted off and neatly fielded a bowl of soup trembling on a waiter's tray.

'Gaston est enervé ce soir,' he told Quill confidentially. 'He has discovered that his wife is faithful after all.'

'About last night,' interposed Quill.

The orchestra struck up *Madame Butterfly*. It struck, too, a reminiscent chord in Emilio's breast.

'I sing that once,' he said, wistfully, 'in Milan. Not the Scala.'

'Quite,' said Quill. 'But . . .'

'Ssssh,' said Emilio, reproachfully, and wandered off.

Quill pushed away the sardines and waited for the bortsch. When it arrived it was tomato soup. The orchestra played *Tosca*. Emilio was too sad to talk. It was the favourite aria of the girl who had almost married him.

The sole Stroganoff arrived next. It was smoked haddock.

'Pardon,' said Emilio, 'a little mistake. Le chef est enervé ce soir.'

'His wife?' asked Quill sympathetically.

'Sa maîtresse.' Emilio shook his head. 'Elle est extravagante.'

'About last night,' said Quill. 'Do you remember a glass of milk? . . .'

'Tout de suite,' said Emilio, and ran.

He reappeared a moment later apologetically carrying a beaker. Kiev cutlets were 'off,' but here was the milk M'sieur demanded.

Quill nearly threw it at him.

'It is curious,' mused Emilio, 'how much you English like the milk. Last night par example . . .'

The orchestra attacked *Tannhauser*. It was the trumpet's big moment.

'And so,' finished Emilio, the rest of the story buried beneath the tramping feet of the pilgrims, 'I understand too late that it is really the milk she wants. So I give it.' And he darted away to supervise the coffee-tray underling—doubtless *enervé* also.

The Bombe Arenskaya lived up to its name. It exploded the moment Quill touched it.

'C'est bon?' demanded Emilio, determined that someone should enthuse over the chef's masterpiece.

Quill wiped himself energetically. 'Who was it you said asked for the milk last night?'

'Mais la petite Anglaise,' said Emilio. 'Elle est gamine celle-la. Mais froide,' he added regretfully.

'Who?'

'Mais Mademoiselle Galybchik. It was after one o'clock when she came to me with her big eyes to ask for milk. Naturally, I do not suppose that at that hour anyone can really desire milk. But what do you suppose, M'sieur?'

'She wanted milk.'

Emilio nodded sadly. 'She wanted milk. Only milk. Moi—I am enervé to-day,' he added, and dashed off.

The orchestra burst into 'On with the Motley.'

* * *

The Ballet—it must go on!

Arenskaya was assuring everybody within screaming distance that a mere imprisoned impresario meant nothing to her. To-night *Oiseau de Feu* would be danced as scheduled, and no worse than usual. Nerve storms, sundry crises, and private quarrels must be put off until the old man came back to cope with them.

The curtain was going up in half an hour. Where was Ostorojno? Where was her mother? Where was the *Régisseur?* Where was everybody? Smithsky hurried over to reassure her that he, at least, was there, but she did not seem to notice him.

'You,' she grasped a soloiste roughly by the shoulder. 'Look at your hair—it is a disgust!'

A tired urchin lurched wearily over. He carried a note of frantic instructions from Stroganoff. It was the fifteenth note he had brought her since tea-time.

'Pas de répose,' snapped Arenskaya, stuffing the note with the fourteen others in her handbag to be read later.

The tired urchin lurched blankly away. No doubt this meant another journey.

CHAPTER VIII

THE Ballet of La Bazouche by night is played against a spangled backcloth. With any luck the *Régisseur* will have cleared away all traces of rain, and there will be some fascinating *entrées* for the corps-de-ballet. Take, for instance, the stream of waiters going off duty, whizzing past another stream of waiters crawling on duty. Take the hopeful trickle of gamblers making their way to one or other of the Casinos. Take a vivacious sprinkling of ballerinas, making for opposition shows on one of the rare nights when they happen not to be needed in any ballet on the programme, or when injuries to arms, ankles, or feelings, have temporarily intervened between their ambitions and their careers. Their hopeful faces will be framed in the unemotional orbit of the box-office window. 'Two, please.' The embarrassed expression dodging behind them of the boy-friend.

Take the residents—but there are none. In season La Bazouche is given over strictly to its visitors—clients who come to play at the Casino. The good Bazouchian who is neither hôtelier nor croupier has the decency to go right away— probably to try his luck at Monte Carlo.

Take the restaurants, they are just beginning to empty, as their clients make their way to café or casino. Take the cabarets. They are still the sleep-bound hide-holes for makers of synthetic whoopee.

Take Quill. He has made his way down a twisting hill, along a promenade, and has paused for a moment before entering an erection of ferro-concrete with an Astorian frontage and an Odeon lighting scheme. The lordly commissionaire, every shining button in place, has obviously decided that the Casino

Button'ooke is the perfect *décor* for his treacle-coloured moustachios. He is right about this.

Up those milky marble stairs, through those chromium-plated swing-doors. Past the lines of needlessly superior flunkeys such as Press Barons require to help them forget their ancestral homes. Past the beaky scrutineer, enthroned in a chaste signal-box. Into the gilded halls of the gambling hell strode Quill.

Here he paused, a little bilious. The interior of the Casino Buttonhooke had clearly been salved from plans jettisoned by Maison Lyons on the grounds of gaudiness. Never can more spurious alabaster have been found suspended from one ceiling. Never was there so much pseudo-marble. Silken carpets positively pushed the patron's foot from its soft resting-place. Settees were opulent. Service was prompt and impersonal. The lifts were in working order.

Quill took one.

A flunkey, in the discreet tones of an usher at a fashionable wedding, had told him that the Baron would doubtless be found in his Lordship's private office.

In Lord Buttonhooke's sanctum the need for tinted glasses became increasingly evident. A large boiled shirt bulging from an oil painting challenged the eye of the caller and created, from the outset, the proper feelings of reverence. Beneath it, also bulging, but rather more actual, posed another, smaller boiled shirt. Baron Sam de Rabinovitch, deaf to Quill's punctilious knock, was practising that look of well-fed benevolence that had persuaded so many investors to plunge heavily in the Buttonhooke concerns.

It seemed a shame to disturb this touching tableau, but duty was duty. Quill coughed. The Baron, startled out of his pose, looked first sheepish and then angry.

'Well?' he snapped.

'The Baron de Rabinovitch?' asked Quill.

'Yes. What do you want?'

Quill produced his card and explained that he was conducting an enquiry into Citrolo's death. The Baron did not appear impressed.

'Well?'

'If you would answer a few questions?'

'But why should I answer any questions?' asked the Baron coldly. 'You appear to have no official status whatever.'

Quill tried an appeal to better nature. 'An innocent man has been arrested.'

'Two innocent men,' interrupted the Baron, 'and when Lord Buttonhooke gets out, Gustave is going to wish he had never been born.'

'The French are inclined to be impetuous,' said Quill, tactfully.

'I am a Frenchman,' said Baron Sam de Rabinovitch.

Quill decided not to waste any more time on tact. He crossed the carpet, sank into an armchair and lit a cigarette.

'Making yourself at home?' jeered the Baron.

'Definitely,' said Quill, 'you and I have a lot of things to discuss.'

'I've already told you I won't answer questions.'

'You might answer this one,' said Quill. 'What were you doing from 1929 to 1931?'

The Baron said nothing but a gleam of apprehension in his eye told Quill that the shaft had got home. Mentally he blessed Citrolo's note-book.

'I wonder,' he mused, 'whether Lord Buttonhooke knows that his trusted assistant is an ex-convict.'

'I was innocent,' said the Baron from force of habit.

'Of course. Still,' said Quill, 'why bring up these unpleasant memories? I only want to ask a few simple questions.'

There was a pause.

'Very well,' said the Baron, resigned.

Quill produced his note-book. 'It was about one o'clock when you left Stroganoff's office on the night of the murder?'

'About that. I went to play baccarat,' said the Baron. 'I played till the game broke up. Then I went home.'

'You did not return to Stroganoff's office during the evening?'

'Certainly not,' said the Baron quickly.

I

'Have you a key to the office door?'

'No. I gave both keys to Stroganoff when he took over the Casino.'

'You did not keep a third key for yourself?'

'No.'

'Is there anyone else you know who might have a key to the door?'

'No.'

Quill glanced round the office, pondering his next angle of attack. He found it unexpectedly as his eye fell on two large ledgers on a shelf immediately behind the desk. It was the exact position in which the ledgers in Stroganoff's office had been found that morning, moved there, according to Galybchik, by intruders. But if Rabinovitch always kept his ledgers in this position he had doubtless kept them like that in his days at the old Casino. And if it was Rabinovitch who had examined Stroganoff's ledgers last night might he not unthinkingly have put them back in what was, to him, their usual repository. At any rate it was worth trying.

'Why are you so interested in Stroganoff's ledgers?'

The question took the Baron by surprise. It took him several moments to compose his features into an expression of injured innocence. Satisfied that he was on the right track, Quill changed the subject.

'You knew the dead man well?'

The Baron shrugged. 'I knew him only as a critic. We were never intimate.'

'Had he, to your knowledge, any enemies?'

'Every critic has his enemies. Your client had as good a reason as any to fear him.'

'As good a reason as yourself?'

'What reason could I have?' asked the Baron blandly. 'We did not have one single interest in common.'

Quill nodded and put away his notes. The Baron had already said quite enough to prove himself a liar and there was no object in inducing him to repeat himself. The moment was not yet ripe for confronting him with Citrolo's memoirs.

'I shall want to see you again,' he promised, and rose to leave.

There was a knock at the door. A pair of aristocratic eyebrows arched at them impartially from the doorway.

The Baron remembered the conventions.

'Er—Prince Alexis Artishok,' he said.

Quill bowed briefly. 'Delighted,' he said, and left.

The Prince and the Baron circled each other warily.

*   *   *

The cocktail bar at the Casino Buttonhooke was a symphony of red leather and stainless steel.

Quill pushed his way to a vacant stool and ordered a double Scotch. The barman nodded and dived under the counter.

'Make him show you the bottle,' said a voice beside Quill. 'They've got some of their own stuff they unload on you if you're not looking.'

Quill obeyed orders and then turned from the discomfited barman to thank the pale green Schiaparelli from which the voice came.

'Not at all,' said Sadie Souse. 'I hate to see an Englishman soaked by foreigners. I adore Englishmen,' she added, dazzlingly.

Not exactly his taste, Quill reflected, but undeniably more attractive than Arenskaya. He smiled back.

'You're English—aren't you?' demanded Sadie.

'Certainly.'

Sadie studied the handsome profile with interest. 'How d'you get here, anyway? You look more the huntin', shootin', fishin' type to me.'

Quill explained that he was here on holiday at Stroganoff's invitation.

'And he gets into gaol just as you arrive,' Sadie commented. 'Inhospitable I call it.'

'Worse,' said Quill. 'I've got to spend all my time getting him out again.'

Sadie was thrilled. 'Are you a busy?'

'I used to work at Scotland Yard.'

'Gee!' Quill found his arm seized enthusiastically. 'Can you get Percy out too?'

'Percy?'

'Lord Buttonhooke,' explained Sadie.

'Are you interested in Buttonhooke?'

'Am I interested? Gosh!' Sadie looked at Quill incredulously. 'Don't you know?'

'Know what?'

'I'm his girl-friend.'

'Congratulations.'

'No foolin',' said Sadie. 'I'm serious. What use is Percy to me in gaol? What sort of a temper do you think he'll be in?'

'Foul—I imagine.'

'Exactly,' said Sadie, 'and I particularly want him sweet and generous just now. So you gotta get him out.'

'We'll try,' Quill promised.

'That's dandy. You know,' announced Sadie, gazing at Quill over her glass. 'I like you.'

Quill bowed.

'This English reserve of yours gets me every time. Thank heavens Percy hasn't got any of it.'

'No?'

'No. Gee! I'd never dare to try and persuade you to buy me the Otchi Tchernia diamonds.'

'What sort of diamonds?'

'It's a necklace,' said Sadie. 'A hell of a necklace. Belongs to a Russian dancer—Duraska or something.'

'Dyrakova?' said Quill, startled.

'That's it. Anyway, I've decided that I want Percy to buy it for me.'

'And will he?'

'You bet he will. Of course, he doesn't know about it yet. You see,' she explained, 'Percy is getting this Dyrakova down here to dance and the Prince says he can persuade her to sell it. Well, I mean I can't miss an opportunity like that—can I?'

'Would that be Prince Alexis Artishok?'

'Isn't he grand?' demanded Sadie. 'I thrill all over every time he touches me. Why is it,' she demanded petulantly, 'that anybody I really like never has any money? Have you any money?'

'Very little,' said Quill quickly.

'I thought so.' Disappointed Sadie ordered another cocktail. 'Guess I'll have to stick to Percy. He's not such a bad old stick,' she added philosophically, 'and he's so busy that a girl gets lots of time to herself.'

'Alas,' said Quill, 'what with getting Stroganoff and your Percy out of gaol like I look being a very busy man.'

Sadie laughed.

'Instead of flirting with you I've got to ask you questions.'

'Questions?'

'Nasty official questions. For instance I understand you went into Stroganoff's office with the Prince last night.'

'Sure.'

'And was Citrolo sleeping it off?'

'He wasn't sleeping it off,' declared Sadie unexpectedly. 'I've seen too many people sozzled to make any mistake about it. As I told the Prince, that guy had been drugged.'

Quill controlled his alarm at this disturbing insight into Stroganoff's big secret.

'Did the Prince agree with your impression?'

'He hadn't noticed.'

'Where did you go after that?'

'We looked for Percy and found him playing baccarat, so I played too. I won a packet,' she said proudly.

'You won!' Quill was surprised. What on earth had Vanilla been thinking about.

'The Prince brought me luck,' said Sadie. 'He won a packet too. Poor Percy lost though,' she added.

'Did you play late?'

'Darn late.'

'I wonder if you noticed whether any of the players left the room for any space of time.'

Sadie nodded. 'Most of them went out for a bit some time

or another. All except Percy. Percy played all the time without stopping and still wanted to play when the game finished. Maybe it was because he was losing.'

'It's asking a lot, I know,' said Quill, 'but can you by any chance remember the approximate times at which various players left the room and how long they were absent?'

'Have a heart,' pleaded Sadie.

'Please try.'

Sadie gazed at him intently. 'I get you. You think one of them may have slipped upstairs to bump off the critic guy.'

'I don't think anything,' said Quill, 'I'm just trying to assemble my facts.'

'Sure.' Sadie was not to be side-tracked. 'But you never told me you were looking for the murderer.'

'I told you I was trying to get Stroganoff out of gaol.'

'Sure,' said Sadie again. 'He's your client. I suppose you've got to try and pin it on somebody else.'

Quill was mildly annoyed. 'You sound as if you thought Stroganoff guilty.'

'He doped his drink—didn't he?'

Quill brought the conversation hurriedly back to the baccarat room and spent the next half hour in jogging Sadie's memory. On the whole, considering that she had not been concentrating on the players' movements, it proved remarkably good. She could vouch for the following:

Prince Alexis Artishok had gone out to get some air around two-thirty. He was away about twenty minutes. She was certain about this because her luck had mysteriously changed the moment he left, and changed back again when he returned.

The Mayor of La Bazouche had left the room about five times for intervals of about three minutes.

Around three-thirty the Baron de Rabinovitch had excused himself. Sadie did not notice how long he had been gone, but it did occur to her that the Baron seemed slightly distraught on his return and played without much concentration or success.

She herself had gone to the ladies' cloakroom about two o'clock. She mentioned this because she found it occupied by a grim old lady gloating over a sheet of paper. On seeing Sadie the old girl had hurriedly stuffed the paper into her bosom, glared, and waddled out. From the description it was not difficult to recognize Madame Ostorojno.

Quill enquired after Vanilla. Sadie remembered that at one period the croupier had left the game, leaving an assistant in charge. The time? It was just after the Prince had won a large bank against a funny-looking, wasp-waisted little man. It must have been about two-twenty.

'At any rate,' said Sadie, 'it was just before the Prince went for his walk. I remember the Prince left the moment the new croupier took over.'

'The Prince also gave Vanilla a lift home—didn't he?'

Sadie laughed, 'He did that. In Percy's car. Percy was quite annoyed about it.'

'But didn't he ask for permission?'

'Of course,' said Sadie. 'In that regal manner he's got which implies that a refusal never even occurs to him. Anyway, Percy was tired and wanted to get to bed, but he hadn't got the guts to say no.'

Just then the regal manner appeared at the top of the marble stairs and began a royal descent. A smile here, a bow there, even an occasional kindly word somewhere else. The court obediently made way for his progress.

'You're darn late,' said the plebian Sadie.

'A million excuses,' the Prince apologized. 'The Baron and I were discussing a matter of some importance.' He bowed coldly to Quill.

'The Otchi Tchernia diamonds?' asked Sadie.

The Prince frowned warningly. 'A matter of business.'

'But of course,' said Sadie, 'I'm silly. There's no need for the Baron to know anything about it. He doesn't like me so much, anyway.'

'Shall we proceed to the prison,' the Prince suggested.

'Sure.' Sadie jumped up. 'Must say good night to Percy. And I think,' she mused, 'I'll just drop him a teeny-weeny hint about the diamonds.'

The Prince frowned again.

'Mind if I walk with you?' asked Quill. 'I ought to say good night to Stroganoff.'

'How is your enquiry progressing?' asked the Prince courteously. 'Favourably I trust.'

'He's been asking me all sorts of questions,' put in Sadie. 'He's actually trying to find another murderer. He won't believe Stroggy did it.'

The Prince nodded. 'Personally, I, too, am sceptical of his guilt. He has not the temperament of the strangler.'

Quill was in no mood to swap theories. 'Shall we go?'

'But assuredly,' said the Prince.

They started off.

'You know,' mused Sadie as they left the Casino, 'I don't think I shall mention the diamonds to Percy to-night. I don't feel it's the right moment.'

The Prince sighed deeply.

*   *   *

'Mais mon cher,' Stroganoff was saying, 'soyez raisonnable. Fifteen francs for a small cigar it is too much!'

'Fifteen francs.' Gustave was adamant. 'I have to live. If it is too dear there are the cigarettes Celtique I can supply for ten.'

'It is the swindle,' sighed Stroganoff. 'Ten francs for the Russian tea, fifty francs for the chicken that was tough, two hundred for the champagne. You make the fortune from my misery.'

'I have to live,' said Gustave relentless.

Stroganoff sighed and extracted a note from a rapidly diminishing wallet. Gustave pocketed it without a change of expression, nodded affably to Quill, unlocked the cell door for him, and went off to escort the rest of the party to Lord Buttonhooke's quarters.

'Gustave he is the thief,' Stroganoff greeted Quill. 'He should be here instead of me. But without this.'

He pummelled a downy pillow, tucked in a lavish quilt, and peevishly tested a hot-water bottle. Incredulously Quill took in the Persian rug, the reading-lamp, the large bouquet of orchids (a present from Arenskaya) and passed on to the table laden with asparagus, wine, cold chicken, and hot-house grapes.

'No caviare,' said Stroganoff pathetically. 'Nobody they think of me.'

From the opposite cell came a roar of rage. It was Button-hooke telling Gustave what he thought of the prison skilly. Prince Artishok and Sadie listened in dismay.

'Allow me,' said Prince Artishok, producing from his wallet the sprat destined to catch the Otchi Tchernia mackerel.

'You'll do nothing of the kind,' said Buttonhooke sharply. 'I'm determined this scoundrel won't make a penny out of me.'

'Comme vous voulez,' said Gustave the philosopher, and left them. 'If M'sieur should desire the English breakfast,' he said, through the grille, 'it will be thirty-five francs only.'

An unintelligible roar followed.

'Otherwise,' said Gustave, 'there is cocoa.'

'He is mean that one,' explained Stroganoff to Quill. 'He will not consent to pay Gustave's prices. But a man must live—even a policeman.'

'Thanks,' said Quill.

'Pas de quoi,' said Stroganoff magnificently. 'Why,' he enquired, 'have you English the expression "To live like a lord"? Never yet have I seen an English lord who knew how to live.'

The one in the adjoining cell was now shouting to Gustave about the nasty time his leader-writers were going to give him the day after to-morrow.

'He has the language inspired,' said Stroganoff approvingly, 'but,' he added, with a shake of his head, 'the vision of a little man. With all his money his ballet it is a joke. He has not the vision nor the daring of Vladimir Stroganoff.' He purred complacently. Never could he have had the courage, like I have had, to induce the great Dyrakova to dance for him.'

The Dyrakova motive again, thought Quill. It kept on recurring.

'All,' said Stroganoff magnificently, 'is arranged. This day I get from her a telegram. Look.' He passed it to Quill.

It read: 'Vladimir stop pestering me. Love. Dyra.'

'See,' pointed out Stroganoff, 'how she weaken.'

Quill felt that he ought to tell the old boy that Buttonhooke too was negotiating for Dyrakova, but weakly decided not to complicate life any further at the moment.

'Eh bien,' asked Stroganoff, putting the telegram away. 'Our assassin you have found him?'

'We're trying,' said Quill.

'Hurry, mon cher,' pleaded Stroganoff, 'I am worried by my ballet. The performance to-night it was all right—yes?'

'I didn't see it,' said Quill.

'I have the worry about Arenskaya,' confided Stroganoff, 'I fear what she might do without me. All day I write to her but she do not answer. M'sieur Quill—I beg you—keep the eye on Arenskaya for me.'

'Eh,' said Quill, startled.

'Restrain her if she would be impetuous. Paint the picture pitiful of how I fret in here. Make her feel for me the sorrow. It is as well that she should be well disposed towards me.' He cogitated and appeared to reach a decision. 'Yes—I will do it.'

'Do what?' asked Quill.

'Make her the present,' said Stroganoff. 'The present expensive. It is in third drawer of my bureau. I bought it for . . . but no matter. You will give it to her, Mr. Quill, and you tell her that I bought it for her birthday—no—she is sensitive— just tell that I buy it expressly for her.'

Quill promised.

'There is one other little matter,' said Stroganoff. 'It is the chips. Again to-day a large number is missing. You attend to that and find me the thief tout de suite for if it continue I am the ruin.'

'How do you know about the shortage?'

'Galybchik she send message. She will be here presently and you can ask her the questions.' He glanced at his watch. 'She should be here it is a long time,' he said irritably.

A lavender tie strode gloriously into the gaol, raised an eyebrow at the furnishings of Stroganoff's cell, passed on to hand Lord Buttonhooke his English mail and drifted back again.

'Mr. Galybchik,' appealed Stroganoff.

The lavender tie stopped dead. 'My name,' it reminded Stroganoff stiffly, 'is Hugh Bedford.'

'Mr. Galybchik,' said Stroganoff, waving the unnecessary English name aside, 'I ask you, have you in your duties come across my Galybchik?'

'Are you speaking of Miss August Greene?' asked the lavender tie.

'Mais non,' said Stroganoff, 'I speak of Galybchik—the little one with the head of curls. She should be here it is an hour.'

There was a scuffle in the passage. A tattered Galybchik darted down the corridor and finding the cell door unlocked sought Stroganoff's protection. Behind her lumbered a sheepish Gustave.

'He tried to kiss me,' pointed Galybchik accusingly.

'Everyone try to kiss her,' said Stroganoff to Quill with pride. 'Always I have to protect. Lord Buttonhooke he have not this trouble.' He added mischievously, 'nobody I think try to kiss Mr. Galybchik.'

The lavender tie made an icy departure, Gustave confusedly following in its wake.

Stroganoff became businesslike.

'You are late,' he said. 'Have I not taught you that punctuality it is the virtue of the Tsars? Me—I am never late.'

'Oh,' said Galybchik.

'Explain yourself,' said Stroganoff, 'and be certain that you have the alibi convincing or else——'

'Or else what?' asked Quill meanly.

'Poof,' said Stroganoff, 'just—or else——'

'I was searching the office,' said Galybchik. 'I looked everywhere—I couldn't find it. . . .'

'You have lost something?' asked Stroganoff, all sympathy.

'In the desk, under the carpet, in the armchairs—even the towel cupboard. But it had vanished.'

'Poof,' said Stroganoff, 'it turn up. And if not I buy you another. What is it, anyway?'

'I daren't tell you,' Galybchik trembled.

'Mais si—my little one. Do not be frightened.'

Stroganoff found no difficulty in leaping to conclusions of his own about the missing object. 'The young they must be young, and Nicolas he is careless—it is well known. So tell me.'

'It's too awful!'

'Mais non,' soothed Stroganoff, 'even if the worst it already happen, there is always Switzerland. I take you there myself. So do not fret any more, mon brave, but give me my Ostorojno contract.'

'But you don't understand,' wailed Galybchik, 'it is the Ostorojno contract that is missing.'

Stroganoff leapt to his feet. 'Comment!'

'I knew you'd be angry,' said Galybchik, 'but it wasn't my fault.'

'But this is the ruin. You are certain it has vanished?'

Galybchik nodded.

'You have looked everywhere?'

'Yes.'

'The desk, the armchair, the carpets.'

'You put it in the safe,' Quill reminded him, 'and it was certainly not there when we opened it.'

Stroganoff paced his cell pouring a stream of Russian invective at a fascinated Quill who would gladly have paid much for a literal translation.

'It's that woman,' said Galybchik, 'I know it is!'

Stroganoff stopped pacing and let out a howl of fury.

'The thief—the bandit—the pirate! You are right. She saw me put it in the safe.' He ran to the grille. 'Gustave,' he hollered, 'à moi.'

Gustave came rushing in with a revolver, but stowed it away on seeing that Stroganoff was not being attacked by Quill.

'What is it now?' he asked, querulously.

'You arrest for me immediately that woman,' demanded Stroganoff. 'She is the thief.'

Gustave looked incredulously at Galynchik.

'Pas celle-la,' screamed Stroganoff, beside himself. 'The fat one—the mountain—the mother!'

Light dawned on Gustave. 'The one that pester me all day?'

'Si, si,' Stroganoff mopped his brow.

'It will be a pleasure to oblige you,' said Gustave, licking his lips in anticipation. 'I arrest her the next time she calls.'

'You go to search for her,' pleaded Stroganoff.

'There is no need,' said Gustave, 'she will be here soon. Of what is it,' he asked, 'that you accuse her?'

'She has burgled my safe.'

Gustave looked slightly downcast. 'You have the evidence?'

'But what for you want the evidence?' demanded Stroganoff. 'Did you wait for the evidence to arrest me?'

Gustave was on his dignity. 'Without the evidence there can be no arrest.'

'Poof!' said Stroganoff. 'We invent some.' He turned. 'My friend here has much experience in manufacturing the evidence for his English Scotland Yard. Give Gustave your assistance so he goes quick to collect our mountain.'

There was a sound of distant pounding. Unfalteringly the mountain bore down on Mahomet.

Madame Ostorojno's gait contained determination and fallen arches in equal quantities.

'Once again,' she said, 'I demand that you release Lord Buttonhooke.'

'You have demanded it ten times,' said Gustave, 'and I tell you no. No one shall be released till M'sieu le Préfet he come to-morrow.'

'I shall come here every hour till you release him.'

Puzzled, Gustave turned to Stroganoff for information.

'What is there between the English lord and this woman? Why is she so eager for him? It is inconceivable that she should be his petite amie.'

'C'est un voleur,' said Stroganoff hotly. 'You arrest her.'

'Volontiers,' said Gustave, 'but for what?'

'She has stolen the Ostorojno contract.'

The mountain crossed to the grille.

'So you have lost it,' she jeered. 'Isn't that a shame! But now I can take my daughter to Buttonhooke.'

'Thief,' howled Stroganoff, shaking his fist. 'Give me my contract or else we put you in the manacles.'

'You allow that man to insult me?' cried outraged woman-hood.

'Certainly I offer the insult,' said man, the brute. 'I offer it with much pleasure,' he embroidered amiably, 'and if you do not give me my contract I complain to the Consul and poof! you are exported.'

A great light dawned on Gustave.

'Votre carte d'identité, Madame?' he pounced.

Madame Ostorojno fumbled in her purse and presented it defiantly.

'It is two days out of date,' said Gustave with relish. 'The penalty it is the fine or the prison.'

'Not the fine,' said Stroganoff urgently, awful visions of having to pay it himself floating before him.

'Have no fear,' said Gustave, 'for this one, it is the prison. Shoo!'

The gaol was becoming quite full.

From his cell the local pickpocket launched a weary protest. Was he never going to get any sleep that night?

*   *   *

Every night, some three-quarters of an hour after the dancers in the rival ballet companies had acknowledged their polite curtains with weary radiance, the seventeen grey-green mirrors in the café-bar, *Dernier Douzaine*, abandoned their reflections of the fat Madame Dupont and her hopeful satellite[1] in favour of an assemblage of impertinent little hats perched upon tired, but eager little heads. The companies came here to eat after their shows. And not only to eat, but to work lovingly on every shred of scandal that could be produced, until a large-sized tapestry had been woven from the doings of the day. Even in

[1] 'Courage, Madame—il nous en reste toujours les Ballets Russes!'

uneventful times the sessions lasted long into the night. Someone had always fallen foul of Arenskaya, and—in this midnight
version—neatly imparted a crushing blow. Someone else had
just walked out of, and into, one or other of the companies.
Someone had had words with a principal. Someone had had
words with her mother. Someone had been 'relieved' of a rôle.
Someone had never had the luck to be given one.

Whatever the scandal, the verdict never varied—it was a
shame!

By the time Quill arrived in the wake of the hurrying
Galybchik, the session was in full swing. No single mirror
reflected the same collection of hats for more than a few
minutes at a stretch. As each fresh arrival burst in with a new
scareline, she was passed from table to table, where friends
from both companies were detailing, embellishing, drinking in,
and suggesting. Feuds were sunk, petty enmities forgotten, in
the common quest for sensation.

'Have you heard the latest—they're hanging Stroganoff at
dawn!'

'But surely, guillotining,' corrected a purist.[1]

'Hanging,' firmly. 'It is true—I was told so.'

'Without a trial?'

'This is France, my dear!' The saucy little hat shook sagely
and darted away to another table.

In a corner, Ostorojno was smiling mysteriously at Dovolno.
Gossip washed around them as the sea washes the Eddystone—
and with just about as much effect.

'I've got a surprise,' she was telling him, 'I great surprise.
But you mustn't ask me about it till after to-morrow night.'

'Have you heard the latest?' A gay little hat burst
triumphantly into the bar. 'Buttonhooke has . . .' a dramatic
pause ' . . . hanged himself!'

'Impossible!'

'It's quite true—with his silk braces—someone told me.'
After which irrefutable evidence the hat passed on with its
important trivia.

[1] Ernest Smithsky.

But Dovolno and the little Ostorojno paid no heed. They meant to make the most of their time before her mother appeared to cut it short. They looked so happy that Quill hated interrupting them.

'Your mother,' he told the girl gently, 'has decided to spend the night with a friend.'

Olga opened astonished eyes.

'Two friends to be exact,' Quill amended. But before he could break the news, a whirlwind interrupted him.

'They've found another,' it screamed, 'a body, I mean— dead! They say it's the English policeman—Quirk! . . .'

At a table by a screen Arenskaya was sitting drinking Russian tea with her pianist.

'But the Grand Duchess, she do not believe that I am going on for *Giselle*, and it is for this reason that my 'air it is down, and my gown défait,' Arenskaya was saying. 'And me, I do not blame 'er,' she added fairly, 'for you do not dance *Giselle* in the peignoire séduisante. . . .' She paused for the laugh. The pianist yawned.

'Have you heard the latest?' This time it was a pale young man who was playing the Greek Messenger. 'They have discovered the assassin.' He turned confidentially to Quill. 'The Englishman from Scotland Yard,' he hissed.

At their table in the corner Ostorojno received the news of her mother's incarceration with fortitude (Dovolno received it with gratitude). Almost, you might have thought, she was relieved. Soon she returned to the fascinating subject of her secret.

'You'll be awfully surprised,' she told Dovolno, 'and perhaps a little—just a very little—happy.'

He squeezed her hand expectantly. 'I too have a surprise up my sleeve,' he boasted. 'It's for you, darling, and you're going to be mad about it—only you mustn't ask anything till after to-morrow night.' They drank to one another in orange juice.

'Have you heard the latest? Stroganoff has confessed!' The words flew round the room. 'He killed Citrolo with a knife from *Thamar*.'

'A rope from *Tricorne*.'

'A pistol from *Jardin Public*. . . .'

'Come and join us,' sang out the warmhearted Galybchik, taking compassion on Quill's solitude, 'Nicolas is nervy,' she added.

On his way to Nevajno's table Quill stopped short at a nook near the buffet. Two middle-aged men were arguing hotly the points of the dancer, Dyrakova.

'I say it is her artistry that is unrivalled,' the Balleto-Medico was insisting.

'And me, I say it is her arabesque,' persisted Anatole, Stroganoff's commissionaire.

At an adjoining table a further argument was in progress. Kurt Kukumber was hotly debating the ethics of the gaming-room suicide with Vanilla, who had taken the late session off.

'A man has no right to call himself a gambler,' he insisted, 'if he behaves in a manner so indiscreet. He scares away the suckers from the luckier players.' The syndicate, also on furlough from a late session, nodded in weighty agreement.

'Good evening,' said Quill.

They did not seem particularly pleased to see him. Kurt Kukumber, however, made an effort at cordiality and invited Quill's opinion on the subject under discussion.

'It is not—what you call—sporting,' he argued. 'A man may kill himself if he likes—but he should not cause discomfort to others.'

'Even a well-organized suicide holds up the game for quite a few minutes,' said the eldest of the syndicate reprovingly, 'and it takes quite some time after that for the stakes to become normal again.'

'Well organized?' said Quill.

'But, yes,' explained Kukumber, 'the organization for the suicide is excellent here. Like in Monte Carlo.'

Quill turned to Vanilla. 'What happens exactly?'

Vanilla scowled uneasily. 'But nothing,' he said. 'We put the screen round and we take the body away—quick.'

'There is a secret door in the panel,' said Kukumber. 'They take it through that.'

'A secret passage?' Quill was interested.

'Of course,' said Vanilla nonchalantly. 'It leads into the garden. All casinos have such passages.'

Quill nodded and left.

'Dolt,' hissed Vanilla to Kukumber, 'must you talk of our secret passages to a detective?'

Galybchik smiled brightly at Quill as he joined her table. The gloomy Nevajno acknowledged his arrival with his left eyebrow.

'Champagne, M'sieur?' suggested the waiter, materializing hopefully by Quill's side.

'Oui,' said Nevajno, brightening slightly.

'Champagne,' Quill agreed, 'and,' he added maliciously, 'a glass of milk for Mademoiselle.'

'Milk, M'sieur?'

'Milk,' said Quill firmly.

Galybchik was visibly nervous. She essayed a smile. 'What makes you think I want milk?'

'But don't you?' asked Quill. 'I had an idea you always drank milk at this hour of the morning.'

'You are clearly insane.' Nevajno had no patience with faulty logic. 'How could such a thing be possible? Would I, Nevajno, tolerate as a companion a drinker of milk? Milk it does not stimulate either the mind or the senses.'

'Sorry,' said Quill, 'but that's the impression I got after chatting with Emilio.'

'Oh,' said Galybchik, 'so you've found out?'

'I've found out.'

'There wasn't any harm in it,' pleaded Galybchik. 'I only thought how awful that poor man would feel when he woke up after all that drug—alone and hungry. So I asked Emilio to get me a glass.'

'Is it of Citrolo that you are speaking?' demanded Nevajno.

'Yes,' said Quill.

'Do I understand that you carried milk to Citrolo last night?'

Galybchik nodded again.

'But why the mystery?' asked Quill. 'Why couldn't you tell me this before?'

'Naturellement, she did not tell you,' broke in Nevajno furiously. 'She does not even tell me. And I understand well why. A girl does not take refreshment to strange men in the middle of the night unless . . .' He turned his back and sulked.

'Nicolas,' appealed Galybchik.

'He'll get over it,' urged Quill. 'What time was it you brought the milk?'

'About half-past one,' said Galybchik. 'But you don't know Nicolas. He'll sulk for days.'

'Let him,' said Quill. 'You got in with your key?'

'Yes.'

'How was Citrolo?'

'Snoring.'

'You wish me to believe that?' said Nevajno. 'Ha!'

'But he was.'

'And you put the milk beside him and left?' asked Quill.

'I pottered about a little tidying up.'

'A little,' said Nevajno. 'Ha! And me I sit and wait for you in the cabaret and suspect nothing.'

Quill ignored him. 'Did you see or meet anybody on your voyage?'

'Well—no,' said Galybchik. 'It did seem to me once when I was in the room that I heard footsteps, so I looked out, but there was no one in sight. I suppose I imagined it.'

'The guilty conscience,' jeered Nevajno.

'You're an ass,' said Quill.

'Oh,' Galybchik wailed, 'now you've made it worse by insulting him.'

Fortunately the champagne arrived to cover the insult. Nevajno drank it with his back turned, easily resisting all Galybchik's efforts to mollify him. Wearying of the scene Quill paid the waiter and left them to it.

On his way out he stopped to interrupt Arenskaya in the middle of a reminiscence the pianist had heard three times already, and delivered Stroganoff's message.

'A present!' Arenskaya was thoughtful. 'It is many years since the old one he give me a present. What is it that he desires?'

'Read his letters,' Quill suggested, 'you might find a clue. Good night.'

'Oh—you not go yet,' Arenskaya grasped his arm. 'Wait the few minutes and we go home together.'

Quill fled.

*   *   *

Back in his hotel bedroom Quill settled down to tabulate the data he had accumulated. To think that only last night he had gone to bed with the happy prospect of a fortnight's joyous loafing ahead, and here he was, up to his ears in as eccentric a murder case as had ever happened. An abundance of suspects was presumably fairly normal in the murder of a blackmailer, but this one was positively lavish with them. In addition there were all sorts of people with guilty secrets, probably entirely irrelevant, wandering among the clues. Like Galybchik and her milk, for instance.

Quill wondered whether Stroganoff had told him the whole truth. It was quite possible that the wily Russian had committed some further imbecility he had not yet confided. Quill decided a little reluctantly that he must, for the moment, accept the Stroganoff version as the complete truth and build his case from that.

Stroganoff had left Citrolo sleeping in his office. At some time during the night somebody had come in and strangled him.

There were only two known keys to the office door. Stroganoff had one. Galybchik the other. There might be further keys. There was every indication of other people in the office during the night.

Assuming a means of admission the following were around the Casino last night and had every opportunity of paying a visit.

> The Baron de Rabinovitch
> Dino Vanilla

Lord Buttonhooke
Kurt Kukumber
Prince Alexis Artishok
Sadie Souse
Madame Ostorojno
or even the Mayor of La Bazouche.

All of them, except the mayor and possibly Kurt, knew that Citrolo was in Stroganoff's office and, if interested, could have observed that he had failed to leave.

Quill produced his note-book and conscientiously wrote down the case against each suspect. The result read:

Baron Sam de Rabinovitch

The nobility is doubtful—the career obviously chequered. Has been in gaol and has probably committed several minor swindles for which he was paying blackmail to Citrolo. Knew of Citrolo's presence in office. Left baccarat game at three-thirty—returned agitated. As previous owner of Casino, likely to have key to office. Interesting to note that ledgers in office were moved from usual place and put on shelf behind desk— the position in which Buttonhooke ledgers are kept. As emissary of Buttonhooke, who is anxious to buy back Casino, Rabinovitch would be interested in the Stroganoff finances. Quite a workable theory is that Rabinovitch had gone to the office to examine books, found his blackmailer drugged, and took his opportunity. He then, from force of habit, replaced the ledgers in the position where he was used to finding them.

In cross-examination this afternoon the Baron lied like hell, claiming only slight acquaintance with the deceased. This does not necessarily make him the murderer—naturally he would not wish to admit to being blackmailed.

Dino Vanilla

Croupier. Crook. Runs baccarat game with rather clumsy accomplices. Pays blackmail to Citrolo—probably for this. The solution of the Stroganoff missing chips mystery. Practically admitted this in cross-examination. Left baccarat game at two-fifteen for short interval. Large sum in chips taken from office during night.

This makes it almost certain that Vanilla entered office during night. Has he a key? Finding Citrolo asleep Vanilla might easily have taken his chance. He has the hands of a strangler—can tear a pack of cards across quite easily.

Apprehensive when questioned upon night's activities, but curiously enough rather relieved when it was suggested that he possessed key to office door.

Prince Alexis Artishok

Something very peculiar about this Prince. Appears to be lucky at baccarat—is intermediary in big Otchi Tchernia diamond deal pending between Lord Buttonhooke and the dancer Dyra Dyrakova. It might be merely a matter of a straight commission, but it would bear watching.

Prince left room (breath of air) at two-thirty while Vanilla was absent. Subsequently gave Vanilla lift home in Buttonhooke's car, risking the latter's displeasure. Why? Did the two men meet outside the rooms when something transpired that made a further interview advisable?

Note: Prince knew Citrolo was not sleeping but drugged.
Memo: Investigate Prince's antecedents.

Madame Ostorojno

Saw Stroganoff put contract in safe. Was anxious to get contract back so as to transfer daughter to Buttonhooke ballet. Discovered in cloakroom by Sadie Souse gloating over piece of paper. Ostorojno contract missing this morning. Madame Ostorojno almost certainly the thief. Mystery—the means of entry.

Lord Buttonhooke and Sadie Souse

Not seriously considered.

Kurt Kukumber

Small time confidence trickster and roulette fan. On Citrolo's list—as joke. Unlikely murderer—sounded almost fond of dead man. Chief point of interest—Gold-Mining Prospectus found in Stroganoff's office. Obviously put there by Kurt. Kurt denies this vigorously. But why should he bother unless he had put it there some time during the fatal night? Makes no secret of his profession. Rather proud of it. But how did Kurt get in?

And that was that, thought Quill. Everywhere there was ample evidence to suggest numerous entries, but how had they been effected? Not all these people could have had keys.

Suddenly Quill remembered the suicide carried through a secret passage into the garden. There might be another secret passage in the Casino. Perhaps that was the solution.

Quill remembered how Vanilla had frowned while Kukumber talked of the secret passage and felt certain he was on the right track. A passage to Stroganoff's office would explain everything. With it all his suspects could have spent the night popping in and out of the place. Quill decided to go up to the office first thing next morning to try and find it. He was not very expert in looking for secret passages, but he had a firm conviction that if one prodded and pushed long enough something slid open.

Of course a secret passage would not solve the mystery, he had too many suspects for that, but it might help.

CHAPTER IX

QUILL pushed back the shutters. It was raining.

'Du thé,' announced the waiter proudly, trundling in with a tray.

'Coffee,' said Quill.

'Du thé,' corrected the waiter, 'et bien chaude.'

'Coffee,' said Quill.

'Always M'sieur change his mind.' The waiter shook his head sadly and went.

Quill shaved apprehensively, expecting a telephone call at any minute. It came when he was in his bath. Gustave.

'I am worried, mon cher,' he confided. 'Is it possible that the man Stroganoff is innocent?'

'It is,' said Quill comfortingly.

'He does not behave like a guilty person, that one,' expatiated Gustave. 'He eat, he drink, and all the time he grumble. This morning when I take him the omelette that I have made myself, almost he throw it at me—the toast, it appears, it was not Melba!'

'Why don't you release him?' asked Quill.

'M'sieur le Préfet arrives this afternoon, and I must have for him an assassin to justify his journey,' explained the hard-pressed Gustave.

'What about Buttonhooke?'

'There the evidence is not so irrefutable. Maybe I was hasty there—what you English call "trop de zèle." '

'But,' began Quill . . .

'But, you ask me, why then do I trouble you at this so early hour, on a morning when the rain refreshes à merveille our dusty oliviers? It is in case M'sieur le Préfet releases my two prisoners. Where do I look for my new assassin?'

'Where?' agreed Quill.

'M'sieur, I implore your assistance. All yesterday you were busy with the research—have you no theory yet?'

'Have you none?' countered Quill.

But it appeared that Gustave was baffled. Yesterday he had been unable to sift the evidence. First there had been his gardening, and then, even before the light began to fade, there had been Stroganoff. Every time he sat down to make a tabulation, the man Stroganoff wanted something. And his assistant—who, Quill must understand, was *bon gosse* and incidentally his godson—was still *en Vacances*.

Quill regretted that he had no concrete suggestions as yet. But the case was developing in an interesting manner—he would keep Gustave advised.

'Ah, bon!' said Gustave. 'I leave it in your hands, cher collègue. I go now to talk business with the woman Ostorojno.'

Quill completed his toilet and sauntered out into the street. He went back again to get his mackintosh.

'Useless to call to-day,' remarked Anatole, helpfully, when Quill arrived at the Casino. 'M'sieur le Directeur is still in prison. But do not lose heart,' added that kindly soul, 'next week, when he is released, you will doubtless get the order for whatever it is you sell.'

Quill was a trifle tired of the commercial traveller gambit. He handed Anatole his card.

'They sacked you?' asked Anatole, interested in the 'late of.'

'I resigned,' replied Quill, with dignity.

'Bien entendu,' said Anatole, with a buddie's smile to make it quite clear that he was not meant to believe a word of this. 'The resignation, it is fashionable. Signor Vanilla would have resigned too, had not the Baron himself removed to the other casino, and I resigned from the Moulin Mort after M'sieur le Patron find me with his petite amie. What was it that they catch you at, when you resigned from Scotland Yard?'

'Buying drinks after hours,' said Quill good-humouredly and made his way upstairs.

With his mind dwelling on secret passages Quill entered the office.

He rapped on a promising-looking panel. A barometer nearly brained him. He tugged at some ornamental moulding—it came away in his hands. He tried a bookcase—*The Ballet in Western Europe* missed him by inches.

Flushed with success he sought repose in an armchair. Almost immediately he found a knitting needle. Galybchik had been seeking it for weeks. There was still a certain amount of jumper on it.

A picture of the croupier's annual dinner—enlarged and coloured—looked promising. Quill peered behind it, and drew a dusty blank.

He washed his hands and went to work systematically. Conscientiously he rapped, tapped, and prodded every panel in the room. He slid immobile mouldings, pressed obdurate buttons and picked up splinters from perfectly innocent floor-boards.

Exhausted he leant against the filing cabinet. The next moment he was on the floor. The cabinet had swung inwards and here was his secret passage. It looked cold and damp and took most of the elation out of him. But manfully he pulled out his torch, stooped and entered.

It was evident at once that the passage had not been designed for comfort. The concrete was rough and the cracks, as Quill discovered almost immediately, were many. The ceiling was low, the walls mildewy, and there was no electric light. No house-proud charwoman had swept it for years—in fact, no charwoman of any kind had been near it since it had been built.

But there was every indication that the passage was in frequent use—mainly by chain smokers. Cigarette ends were all over the place. Quill stooped and conscientiously scooped up an assortment of samples for future inspection. He also collected the butt end of a cigar. His torch raked the surface as he progressed searching for further clues. A distant gleam lit his heart. A diamond! He stooped. Only a sequin. He picked it up and sighed for a Sergeant Banner to rifle innumerable wardrobes in search of sequin dresses. Women wore these things on scarves he remembered, and he had a vague idea that bull-fighters wore them too—doubtless to dazzle the bull. It would not surprise him in the slightest to find a bull-fighter embedded somewhere in the maze of this fantastic murder.

Further research showed that the mildew had been disturbed shoulder high in streaks along the passage, and in a crack he found the regulation shred of cloth. In his Scotland Yard days the shred would have been sent meticulously round to every cloth manufacturer in the country for identification, but Quill was damned if he was going to bother.

The passage turned abruptly to the left. Quill had not observed this. The exciting crimson dab on the wall came from his own nose. But on the floor beneath it was a piece of lace. Quill examined it and decided at once that it belonged to no ballerina. No tender breast ever rose and fell under it. It was much too coarse. No laundry, try as it might, could do a thing to it. Either the maid had struggled uncommonly hard or the seducer had been an octopus. Quill thought of Vanilla's strong fingers, but Arenskaya would never struggle—neither would she wear such lace. On the other hand, not only would Madame Ostorojno wear it with pride, but boast of the bargain she had picked up at the sales! The floor sloped upwards at this point and no doubt she had trodden on the lace-trimmed edge of her underskirt.

Quill went on with a vague sense of something missing. These discoveries were all very well, but there was something else he ought to have found. Something one always found. Presently realization dawned on him. There was no button. No sign of a button. He grew quite angry about this as he went on with his search. Why was there no button? He had never handled a crime yet without its exasperating, unclaimed, unassignable, and usually entirely irrelevant button. He could not feel normal until he had found one.

Instinct had not misled him. Back at the point where he had bumped his nose lay the missing clue. Quill purred with satisfaction as he stowed it lovingly away in his pocket. That it was ordinary black ebony and might belong to any suit was only to be expected.[1]

The passage came to an end at an impassable wall. Quill pushed it. Nothing happened. He prodded, pressed, slid, coaxed, reinvestigated and started all over again. No use. Finally he gave up and retraced his steps. But the other end had swung back too and presented difficulties. Quill swore softly.

Quill swore.

Quill swore loudly.

Quill stopped swearing and decided to chain-smoke too. Striking a match against the wall his hand came into contact with a bump in the plaster. Without much hope he pressed. The wall swung inwards. . . . He dodged it just in time.

*   *   *

Quill stumbled into the office and with a sigh of relief sat down to recuperate. He was tired and dusty, but on the whole not displeased. The mystery of the murderer's entry into the office was a mystery no longer. All he had to do was to check up on the numerous people who appeared to have used the passage and decide which one of them was the murderer.

He spread the evidence collected in the passage on the table in front of him and contrasted it with his own list of suspects. It fitted well enough, in fact there was almost too much of it. The cigarette ends were mainly of coarse French tobacco such as Vanilla might smoke, but there were also the remnants of expensive-looking Egyptian which Quill for the moment could not place. And there was a cardboard holdpiece from a Russian cigarette of the kind Stroganoff ought to smoke but did not. Quill had the impression that only recently he had seen someone with this kind of cigarette and racked his memory to remember. But the latter refused to function. Making a mental note to keep his eye open for the smoker, Quill passed on to the cigar-stub. It was the end of a Henry Clay. The Baron de Rabinovitch smoked Henry Clays—Quill remembered the box in Buttonhooke's office.

[1] Later he was to discover that it belonged to his own waistcoat.

'Ha!' thought Quill.

The lace was easy. It almost certainly belonged to Madame Ostorojno, and in any case it should be simple to check up on it. The sequin and the shreds of cloth were different. He would need some luck to identify them.

Quill collected his evidence and stowed it away. He would have to interview all his suspects all over again—confront them with his discoveries and get their reactions. Tentatively Quill sketched out his programme. First he would say good morning to Stroganoff and tell him about the passage. It was just possible that the old boy knew about it already, but for some vague reason of his own had omitted to tell him. Then he would have a few words with Rabinovitch and Vanilla. And it might also be as well to see little Kurt Kukumber, whose reticence about the Gold Prospectus in the office was now fairly clear. Almost certainly Kurt had used the passage to deposit his bait, had seen the sleeping Citrolo—might even have murdered him—or, as was quite possible, he might have arrived after the murder. Quill was confident in his ability to make Kurt tell all he knew—he only hoped he knew something interesting.

It might also be worth while to have a few words with Prince Alexis Artishok and get him to explain his sudden passion for giving croupiers lifts home.

*   *   *

Quill left the office and went downstairs. At the bottom of them was Arenskaya, tapping her heel impatiently for the pianist who was late for class. The fact that Arenskaya was twenty minutes early made no difference to her wrath. She would tell that woman what she thought of her when she came. Lovingly she curled her tongue round the preliminary sentences.

'Hallo,' said Quill.

'Ah!' Arenskaya beamed. 'My present!'

Quill had forgotten all about it. 'It's in the office. I'll get it.'

'We go together,' said Arenskaya.

Quill stepped back to allow her to precede him.

'Not the stairs,' said Arenskaya surprisingly. 'The stairs they tire me. I know a better way. Come.'

She put her arm through Quill's and led him into a corridor. Here she stopped in front of three sulky Cupids ignoring a *prima donna* bosom. It was a faded oil painting in the Rubens manner—but only just. Arenskaya stepped unflinchingly up to it, punched an unsuspecting Cupid in the eye, and the framework swung inwards to reveal the now familiar mildew stains.

'Entrez,' said Arenskaya hospitably.

Quill was distinctly annoyed. To think of the blood vessels he had nearly strained looking for it.

'How long have you known about this passage?' he demanded.

'Mais tout le monde know it,' said Arenskaya, astonished. 'Vanilla he show it me many weeks ago. I think,' she mused, 'it was because he could find no other way to get me in the dark.'

'Does Stroganoff know of this passage?'

'Mais non,' said Arenskaya, 'we take care not to tell him.'

'Why?'

'It is clear you do not understand our Vladimir,' said Arenskaya indulgently. 'He has the mind of a child. If we show him the passage he would play there for hours, he would install the electric light and the carpets. He would boast of it to everyone, and it would be a secret no longer. Also, my poor Vanilla he would not get his chips.'

'Good God,' said Quill, 'are you in on that too?'

'Mais bien sûr,' said Arenskaya. 'Anyways,' she added righteously, 'I make him promise not to borrow too much.'

'But your loyalty to Stroganoff?' asked Quill amazed. He had always thought that there was real affection between these two eternal combatants.

'Of what is it that you accuse me?' shrilled Arenskaya, indignant. 'My devotion to the ballet it is without questions. I have sacrificed all to its interests. Have I not stayed with

Stroganoff fifteen years—on and off? Have I not turned down the offers fabulous from Berlin, Vienna and even 'Ollywood? It is the impertinence what you suggest.'

'Hush!' pleaded Quill.

'I will not 'ush,' said Arenskaya. 'You apologize for your insinuation monstrous.'

'But,' pleaded Quill, 'don't you see what you're doing? You're helping Vanilla to rob the Casino.'

'The Casino it is not my concern,' declared Arenskaya. 'It is bad joke, anyway. And the gambling it interfere with the performance. The sooner Stroganoff tire of it the better, and besides this, for the moment he is rich.'

'He will not stay rich if everybody takes his chips.'

'He will not stay rich in any case,' declared Arenskaya. 'Mon ami, you do not know Stroganoff. Why should not my poor Vanilla get his share while the going it is good? Especially,' she added, 'when he spend so much of it on me.'

The rather peculiar moral code was altogether beyond Quill. He decided not to meddle with it any further.

'Come on,' said Arenskaya, and pushed him in.

They reached the study without accident. Quill opened the third drawer of the desk. Two brown-paper parcels loomed up at him. He selected the bigger.

'For me?' cooed Arenskaya from force of habit. 'Open it quick for I am impatient.'

Quill obliged. Several pairs of ballet shoes fell out.

Arenskaya screamed.

'But he has turned imbécile, the old one.' She picked up a shoe. 'They are not even my size.'

It dawned on Quill that he had made a bloomer. He extracted the other parcel. It was square and thin.

Arenskaya smiled again. 'Doubtless a first edition for my library. Open it—quick.'

Quill opened it. Weak with laughter he deposited the gift on the table and sat down to enjoy Arenskaya's expression as she crossed to gaze at it. It was a full-sized photograph of Stroganoff in his Admiral's uniform.

'The insult,' screamed Arenskaya. 'The slight unforgivable. The libel. That is how the miserable old gaol-bird repay me for all my loyalty. It is for this that I refuse Rheinhardt and walk out on René Clair. Pah!' she said, more calmly, 'it is foolish to be angry. He is in his dotage. A baby.'

Quill had a good idea. He opened quite another drawer. A jeweller's case was enshrined cosily in it. Quill took it out and extracted a large diamond 'D' in a cumbersome gold setting.

'The darling,' said Arenskaya. 'I run to kiss him. It is such a sweet thought. The "D," ' she explained, 'it stands for Dyshenka which is Russian for little darling.'

Remembering the words in which Stroganoff had instructed him about the gift, Quill thought it more likely that it stood for Dyrakova, but said nothing.

'I fly,' said Arenskaya, settling more comfortably in her armchair. 'I hasten to his side to offer him the embrace.' She lit a cigarette—an Egyptian, Quill noted. But that could hardly be called a discovery now.

'Shall I telephone a cab?' he asked.

'We stroll,' said Arenskaya. 'But first we drink a little champagne to celebrate. Come.'

'But your class?' said Quill.

'Mon Dieu!' said Arenskaya. 'I forget.'

She rushed out.

*   *   *

The prison was a hive of industry. Quill arrived to find both impresarios in the throes of composition. From his bench Lord Buttonhooke dictated laboriously to an upright lavender tie, whose shorthand was in no way strained to keep up with the output. Galybchik's task, though more luxuriously housed, was less easy. Her shorthand, for all practical purposes, did not exist and her typewriter galloped to keep pace with the peculiarly formed flowers of rhetoric that cascaded from Stroganoff's golden-hued memory.

'Vladimir, this is incredible!' dictated Stroganoff. 'Your Highness, I reply, it is nozzing. Wait till you see the dress rehearsal.' He broke off to greet Quill. 'Bon jour, mon ami. Sit down. We are busy.'

Quill sank into the most comfortable armchair and looked round in admiration. All the luxuries of yesterday were here, but in addition room had been found for a divan, a Flemish tapestry, and the roll-top desk at which Galybchik was working. The table had gained a magnum of champagne,[1] a porcelain monument of caviare, and a colossal water-melon. There was also a bottle of French Scotch and a syphon.

'Wiskyansoda,' said Stroganoff, interrupting himself. 'See how I remember you.'

From the adjoining cell the voice of Buttonhooke rose. It was apparent that he, too, was engaged on his memoirs.

'It was in the spring of 1933 that I first met that effervescent, eccentric, Vladimir Stroganoff.'

'What it mean—effervescent?' Stroganoff asked Quill suspiciously.

'Bubbling,' suggested Quill.

'Bon,' nodded Stroganoff. 'It was in London,' he dictated loudly, 'that I first met the bubble Buttonhooke.'

'Wassat?' Buttonhooke pounded across to the grille.

'I describe you in my book,' said Stroganoff, bouncing to meet him. 'I am very kind.'

'You called me a bubble,' accused Buttonhooke. 'I heard you.'

'But it is well known that you are the bubble,' explained Stroganoff sweetly. 'All the financiers they explode in good time.'

An inexpressibly shocked lavender tie rushed to his chief's aid.'

'Is that an assertion?'

'Read my book,' said Striganoff. 'We publish at eighteen and six, and that to you is nozzing.'

'You've found a publisher?' asked Quill, surprised.

'I have not yet selected,' announced Stroganoff magnificently. He turned patronizingly to Buttonhooke. 'You have chosen yours?'

[1] I work better when I am not thirsty.—STROGANOFF.

K

'Blurbson,' said the lavender tie crushingly.

'Me I do not care for Blurbson,' observed Stroganoff, and one could almost see them reeling under the blow. 'I think I send to my old friend, Michael Joseph—it is good he should read something which is not about cats![1] It will be for him the surprise stunning when he find it in his spring list.'

'Pah!' said Buttonhooke, and returned to his bench.

'Poof!' said Stroganoff and cut himself a large slice of water-melon.

'Presently,' he said munching, 'we return to work. Pour le moment I repose myself.' He stretched himself on the divan and closed his eyes.

'Hey!' said Quill.

'Sssh,' objected Stroganoff. 'Do you not see that I compose myself? You lucky policeman have no idea how the literary composition it exhausts. I am prostrate,' he said correctly.

Quill refused to sympathize. 'You're much more comfortable here than I've been this morning.'

Stroganoff sat bolt upright and beamed.

'I have made it cosy—no? And when they bring me the portraits of my ballerinas, my samovar, and my stamp collection, I shall be well enough here. Though I would not recommend it to you, mon ami. The cooking it is awful, and the tariff it is the ruin.'

'Do you know Prince Alexis Artishok?' asked Quill.

'Assuredly I know him,' said Stroganoff absently. 'All the Russian nobility they come to my box. What was the name you said?'

'Alexis Artishok.'

Stroganoff pondered. 'There is no such family. Arapoff, yes. Yusupoff, yes. But Artishok—no. You have made the mistake.'

'Don't be an ass,' said Quill. 'He's here in Bazouche. With Buttonhooke. He came into your office while you were composing Citrolo's notice.'

'Ah,' Stroganoff remembered. 'The big man with the beard. I like him,' he added. 'He is very polite.'

[1] Special joke to keep publisher in good humour.

'He calls himself Prince Alexis Artishok and . . .'

'Mais pourquoi pas?' Stroganoff shrugged. 'Doubtless he finds it useful to pretend to the aristocracy. And at least he has invented the name—he is not like some others that claim real titles.'

That was all Quill wanted to know for the moment. He changed the subject.

'Were you aware that there is a secret passage leading from your office into the corridor?'

'Comment!' Stroganoff was instantly alert. 'The passage secret?'

'The secret passage.'

'Like in the haunted house?'

Quill nodded.

'Bon.' Stroganoff rubbed his hands. 'Now I understand why the swindle Baron Rabinovitch wish to buy back the Casino. Clearly there is in it the hidden treasure.' He turned on Quill. 'Maybe you find it already and come hot-hand with the good news?'

Quill suppressed a smile. 'Sorry,' he said. 'No treasure.'

'No treasure!' Stroganoff was dumbfounded. 'Poof—you have no idea how to look.'

Quill was a little hurt. He pointed out that he had found the passage in a couple of hours while Stroganoff, in all his weeks at the Casino, had not even found an alcove.

But Stroganoff was already immersed in his dreams.

'There is always treasure,' he informed Quill. 'But it is hidden well. Always one must dig.'

'Dig where?'

'There is a spot. It is marked on the plan.'

'What plan?'

'But the plan secret. It will not,' he said judicially, 'be easy to read. It will be in the cipher—but this, M'sieur Quill, is where you will be so useful. You solve for me this cipher which you will find on your return, and I give you large share of fortune.'

'Thanks,' said Quill.

'De rien,' said Stroganoff.

There was a sound of heavy breathing and Gustave appeared

carrying a gosling which he held out to Stroganoff for inspection.

'Too old,' said Stroganoff, prodding it. 'Take away.'

'But it is perfect,' protested Gustave. 'I went to the Marché to choose it myself.'

'You were the swindle,' said Stroganoff. 'But no matter. I desire now a strong garden spade. I wish to dig,' he explained.

Gustave blanched. 'Not that! My garden implements they are not for sale. Never will I lend the rake, the hoe, or the lawn mower.'

'Mais,' protested Stroganoff, 'it is necessary that we dig for the treasure that M'sieur Quill has found.'

Gustave was impressed. 'You have found treasure?'

'No,' said Quill. 'What I have found is a secret passage that leads into the Casino office. The passage,' he pointed, 'through which the murderer of Citrolo gained admission.'

'Ha,' said Gustave. 'I knew it. Always I felt that the assassin he did not penetrate by the door.' He mused. 'It seems to me that somewhere I have heard of this passage before.'

'It seems to me,' said Quill, 'that you might have thought of that before you arrested two other people.'

'It is not kind to remind one of mistakes,' said Gustave reprovingly. 'Do I remind you of the time you arrested the innocent man in England?'

How on earth did he know that, Quill wondered? Out of the corner of his eye he caught a glimpse of a red-faced Stroganoff signalling furiously. All was now quite clear.

'Anyways,' said Gustave, 'if I have made the mistake M'sieur le Préfet comes this afternoon to rectify it. As for the passage I hurry myself to inspect it as soon I have finished pruning the roses.'

'Roses,' said Stroganoff eagerly. 'You grow the roses?'

'My roses,' boasted Gustave, 'are the finest in the *Midi*.'

'It is a small place the *Midi*,' said Stroganoff unimpressed. 'Now at the flower show in St. Petersburg every year I win . . .'

Galybchik seated herself at the typewriter.

Quill left them to it.

CHAPTER X

BACK at the *Hôtel Moins-Magnifique* Quill enquired for Kurt Kukumber's room. The reception clerk, new to Quill, regarded him hopefully.

'M'sieur is a relative of M'sieur Kukumber?'

'No,' said Quill hastily.

The hotel clerk was disappointed. 'M'sieur Kukumber is expecting a visit from his rich uncle. We, too, are anxious that he should arrive.'

Quill nodded understandingly and made his way to the back of the entresol. He knocked at a door. It opened a cautious two inches and Kurt Kukumber's head peered round the corner. He seemed almost relieved to see Quill.

'I regret,' he pointed round the tiny bedroom, 'to receive you in surroundings so unimpressive, but you understand it is only for the moment. Soon it will be the Royal Suite.'

Quill sat down on the edge of the bed.

'You will pardon my attire,' babbled Kurt. 'For the moment it is flannel but soon I shall wear pyjamas of silk. The dressing-gown I have already.' He crossed to the wardrobe and proudly encased himself in three golden dragons on a purple background.

'Chinese,' he explained. 'Robert Taylor has one just like it. The Armenian on the Promenade des Anglais assured me of that.'

'Beautiful,' admired Quill tactfully.

'Dubonnet?' offered the delighted Kurt.

Quill accepted. 'Soon no doubt it will be Napoleon Brandy.'

'No doubt,' agreed Kurt wistfully. 'If only I had a little capital. But my system it is for the moment not lucky.'

'Hard lines.'

'No matter,' said Kurt sunnily. 'I have put my finger on the weak spot and my system is now infallible. This afternoon you shall see.'

Quill nodded gravely.

'But,' said Kurt, remembering that his funds were too low to give the system a thorough try-out. 'I have this afternoon also an infallible horse at Deauville. In the last race.' He looked hopefully at Quill.

Quill said nothing.

'It has been arranged for many months,' urged Kurt. 'The horse is doped and the judges are bribed.'

'You think of everything,' said Quill.

'Mais non,' said Kurt. 'It is only by accident that I hear of it. It will start at long odds. A modest fifty francs will return a thousand.'

Quill laughed.

'You do not believe me?'

'No,' said Quill.

'You think it is a trick?'

'A very old one.'

'You are too shrewd,' said Kurt. 'But this time I do not mean to take—only to borrow. See I make you an IOU.'

Quill explained that he was short of ready money himself. Perhaps Kurt's rich uncle . . .

'You do not give me away?' asked Kurt alarmed.

Quill shook his head. 'Why should I interfere as long as you answer my questions? . . .'

'More questions. But I tell you everything yesterday.'

'Everything,' agreed Quill, 'except how that Gold Mine Prospectus got into the office.'

'Alas,' said Kurt, 'I cannot remember.'

'You took it there during the night.'

'Mais non.'

'Mais oui,' said Quill brilliantly. 'Through the secret passage.'

The bombshell went down well.

'But you are a real detective,' said Kurt admiringly. 'How comes it they sack you from Scotland Yard?'

'I resigned,' said Quill. 'Anyway, let's stick to the point. You used that passage the night Citrolo was murdered.'

'That night I did not go near it. I did not use it anyway. I have no reason.'

Quill took an envelope from his pocket and extracted a few shreds of cloth. He crossed to the wardrobe and pulled out Kurt's blue serge suit. They matched perfectly.

'I surrender,' said Kukumber, the philosopher. 'It is quite true I used the passage that night.'

'I thought so.'

'You understand why I am so reluctant to tell you. I do not wish to be mixed up in the murder.'

Quill nodded. 'Quite. But now that you are mixed up in it, the best thing you can do is to tell me the whole story.'

Kurt Kukumber sat down. 'What can I say?'

'Begin with the time.'

'It was late,' said Kurt. 'Almost two o'clock. My infallible system had failed me again. It seemed to me the moment to begin my plan on Stroganoff. For weeks I had been pondering his psychology, he seemed to me one to whom the gold mine would have much appeal. It said in the stars that this day was good to start a new enterprise, so I say to myself: "Kurt . . ." '

'Yes, yes,' said Quill. 'You decided to leave the prospectus in his office.'

Kukumber looked hurt at being robbed of his climax.

'If you interrupt,' he said, 'how can I remember? But you are right. I reach the painting. I peer round. There is no one in sight.'

'One moment,' said Quill. 'How long have you known about the passage?'

'But many months,' said Kurt. 'It is no secret. Everybody knows there is a passage. One year during the crise, they even show it to tourists for five francs—and then for three.'

Quill's pride in his discovery ebbed away. Kurt resumed his story.

'I turn to press the Cupid's eye. I jump back quick and stand in the shadow. There comes out the old lady.'

'What old lady?'

'The old lady with the pretty daughter. She looks very pleased as she goes down the passage. I wonder what it is she gets from the office. But it is not my business. It is my rule,' said Kukumber, 'to attend only to that which concerns me. Neither do I like to be questioned.'

'Quite,' said Quill. 'Continue.'

Kurt Kukumber sighed.

'In the office it is dark. But I have my electric pencil that I always carry. See!' He produced it proudly.

'Soon you will have one in gold,' said the exasperated Quill.

'Why not?' agreed Kurt. 'I lay the bait on the desk where Stroganoff will find it and prepare to retreat. Suddenly someone snores. Figure to yourself how I jump! I switch round my pencil. It is my good friend Citrolo sleeping it off. I wonder why he has selected this place but decide that doubtless he had some good reason of his own. Mr. Citrolo always had a reason for everything. Possibly, I think, he has caught Stroganoff in some little mistake. So I tiptoe away, not to disturb his rest.'

'Is that all?' asked Quill.

'That is all.'

Quill thanked him and rose to leave.

'See you at the Casino,' waved Kurt affably. 'You will see this afternoon, I shall win.'

* * *

The receptionist waved as Quill descended the stairs.

'Pardon, M'sieur,' he entreated, 'but did by chance M'sieur Kukumber mention his uncle?'

'He mentioned him,' said Quill non-committally.

'He did not specify when he was due to arrive?'

'Well—no.'

'The management becomes impatient,' confided the clerk. 'Already we wait three weeks to open the chest.'

'Chest?' asked Quill.

'But it is an interesting story,' said the clerk. 'It appears that the uncle of M'sieur Kukumber is eccentric. He desires to test the will-power of his heir who is M'sieur Kukumber. He gets a small chest of iron and he fills it with money. And he says to his nephew, "Kurt, I desire to test you. I give you no money—no allowance—you must support yourself for five years. But I give you this iron chest which you shall carry with you wherever you go. It is full of money but however great your need you are not to touch it. If at the end of five years I arrive and the seals are still intact the contents are yours. The five years,' said the clerk, 'were up last week—and now we all wait for the uncle to arrive.'

'Wonderful,' said Quill. 'Where is this chest?'

'It is in the hotel safe. It is nothing to look at, just old iron, almost rusty. Never would one imagine that it contained maybe a million francs.'

'Never,' agreed Quill.

'C'est la vie,' announced the clerk. 'To have a fortune in your charge, and to haggle for centimes with unpleasant old ladies who desire a deduction from the pension for nights that they spend in prison. But I am firm with her.'

'Hallo,' said Quill. 'That sounds like Madame Ostorojno.'

The clerk nodded, and wiped his brow. The scars of battle still showed.

Quill was interested to hear that Madame Ostorojno had been released. Come to think of it she must have been released just before he arrived at the gaol, for he had not heard her arguing during his visit. He enquired her room number.

'You wish to see her?' said the clerk, incredulous. 'Bien, that is your affair. The number is 214.'

'Why is it?' asked Quill, 'that no French hotel has a room number under two hundred?'

'I will explain,' said the clerk willingly.

'Later,' said Quill and left him.

*   *   *

'So,' repeated Mme. Ostorojno grimly, 'this is the way you take advantage of my absence.'

'Yes, Mamma,' agreed Olga.

'While your mother languishes in gaol you gallivant around the town till four in the morning.'

'Not till four, Mamma.'

'It's no use denying it. I got the time you came in from the hall porter.'

'Blast,' said Olga.

'What's more, you were with that small-time dancer, Dovolno.'

'He's not a small-time dancer.'

'Don't argue, child. Small time or not he's no use to you.'

'But I adore him.'

'Not while I can stop it.'

'Look here, Mother,' said Olga in level tones. 'Why don't you accept the inevitable? I'm no longer a child. I've a right to lead my own life.'

It was an open challenge—the first Olga had ever dared to throw. Madame Ostorojno did not quite know how to cope with it.

It was at this electric moment that Quill knocked on the door.

'I'll see who it is,' said Olga quickly and darted towards it.

'Morning,' said Quill.

'Morning,' smiled the young Ostorojno and flew down the stairs.

Quill's first impression of the room was a mass of photographs. There was an arabesque. It was the little Ostorojno aged three. There was a fourth position. Olga was five when she achieved this feat. A block shoe had been put on when Olga was seven. At nine her first dancing partner made his appearance. He did not stay long. At thirteen she was dancing with Anton Palook himself. (Madame Ostorojno practically financed the company to achieve this feat.) At fifteen she was alone again, posing on the diving-board at Eden Roc. At seventeen she was shown signing a contract with Stroganoff.

In the darkest corner of the room was a strong arabesque

perfectly placed. It belonged to Baronova. Mother Ostorojno displayed it to prove that she was not like other mothers in the ballet. She was unbiassed—she thought Baronova showed promise. But she kept her in the darkest corner because Olga's arabesque was not so well turned out.

'Morning,' said Quill brightly.

'What do you want, young man?' demanded Madame Ostorojno forbiddingly. 'More questions?'

'Just a few.'

'I won't answer them.'

'You might,' said Quill. 'You must be reasonable. After all, you have committed a criminal offence by stealing the Stroganoff contract.'

'Nonsense,' said Madame Ostorojno sharply. 'Anyway, I defy you to prove it.'

'It won't be difficult,' said Quill sweetly. 'I've got witnesses who saw you coming out of the secret passage and purring over the contract in the cloakroom.'

'Oh, you have, have you? So what?'

Quill was a bit baffled about this himself.

'All right, I stole the contract,' Madame Ostorojno pursued her advantage. 'It was an unfair contract. We signed it in a weak moment.'

'But you did sign it.'

'Exactly. That's why I had to steal it back.'

'Supposing I demand that you hand it over?'

'Demand away.'

'We might prosecute.'

'Don't be an ass,' said Madame Ostorojno contemptuously. 'You know Stroganoff wouldn't dare make himself a laughing-stock.'

Quill tried a new line. 'Doesn't it occur to you that it's very unfair to Stroganoff to take away his best dancer? Particularly at this moment.'

'What do I care about Stroganoff,' said Madame Ostorojno. 'What do I care about anything except Olga's career? In twenty years' time Stroganoff will still be putting on ballets.

But Olga will be finished then, she'll be teaching sniffy little girls in a Kensington studio.'

'Is that so inevitable?' Quill asked.

'Sit down, young man,' said Madame Ostorojno, more kindly. 'Smoke if you like, but listen to me.'

Quill did all three.

'I know,' began Madame Ostorojno, 'that it is the fashion to laugh at mothers in the ballet. I know that we are not liked. They accuse us of pushing, sneering, and eye-catching in useful quarters. They say we stir up mischief. All the unrest in the company they put down to us. They say we are the biggest nuisance the management has to contend with.' She paused. 'And they are quite right. We are.

'You see we have to be. A dancer's life is short. Twenty years, fifteen years, sometimes less, and she is finished. Even at the peak of her career her earnings are mighty small. There is no old-age pension in the ballet, only pupils, and they are hard to get. Look at Dyrakova, the greatest dancer of her day. She is in Paris now, teaching. An impoverished Queen ruling an apathetic little court. Her pianist is a Russian Countess, her manager a retired General from the Cossacks. And Dyrakova is lucky for she has a constant stream of English girls who come and who pay.

'Look at the free list of any ballet company. The faded brightness, the tired charms. All the tricks of the one-time favourites to look prosperous on nothing. Once they, too, had their opportunities but perhaps they had no mother to see that they did not waste them.'

'I see,' said Quill.

'You don't see,' said Madame Ostorojno with grim humour. 'But no matter. The young never see. My daughter never sees. So it falls on us to do the worrying and fussing, to praise them when the spirit is flagging, to smile in the right places, and to snap up the best offers.

'You cannot get your daughters to take any interest in these things. They are young and there is a young man. Or if there is no young man there is a rival. They are beginning to get the rôles they covet and old age is something that does not happen. Take my own Olga.'

'I thought we would soon,' said Quill.

'Oh, all right,' said Madame Ostorojno, taken out of her stride. 'I don't know why I bother to tell you all this, anyway.'

'I'm glad you did,' said Quill and meant it.

'Anyway,' said Madame Ostorojno, 'perhaps you understand now why I won't give you back your contract.'

'Fight it out with Stroganoff,' said Quill. 'It wasn't what I came about, anyway.' He produced the piece of lace. 'Does this belong to you?'

Madame Ostorojno inspected it. 'It must have happened when I heard the stitches go.'

'Just two questions,' said Quill. 'How did you know about the secret passage?'

'How did you know I knew about it?'

'It's where I found the lace.'

'If you must know,' said Madame Ostorojno, 'it was an accident. I wanted a word with Arenskaya.'

'About your daughter?'

'Who else,' said Madame Ostorojno. 'Arenskaya was in the corridor with that croupier, Vanilla. They saw me coming and ran away. A lot of people run away when they see me coming,' she added, almost with pride, 'but I'm used to that. I followed them round the corner and saw them disappearing into the picture. And that's how I found it.'

'The other point,' said Quill, 'concerns Citrolo. Did you see him while you were in the office?'

Madame Ostorojno shuddered. 'I was terrified he would wake up the whole time I was at the safe. But he just went on snoring. The drunkard,' she said indignantly. 'I'd never have thought it of him. And to think that I actually encouraged Olga to go out with him. . . .'

*　　　*　　　*

Quill's next call was on Vanilla. The apartment house on the sea front in which the croupier lived might well have been (and probably was) constructed by the same architect who had designed the residence of the late Mr. Citrolo on *Beau Soleil*. There was the same grimy exterior, the same lift (out of order) and an almost identical scrubbing concierge. There was, however, no Alsatian—only a rather seedy Pekinese.

Of course Vanilla had to live on the fifth floor.

The croupier was on the point of leaving when Quill arrived. He had on what was obviously a new suit and the knot of his red silk tie had a precision that suggested many minutes spent before the mirror. He did not seem at all pleased to see Quill.

'What is it?' he asked. 'I am in a hurry. I have the lunch engagement.'

Quill thought lovingly about lunch himself.

'It's not very much,' he said. 'Only that I have found out all about your secret passage and the chips you stole on the night of Citrolo's murder.'

'Oh.' Careless of the crease in his new trousers, Vanilla sank into a chair.

'It was that idiot Kukumber with his talk who put you on the track.'

'Possibly,' agreed Quill. 'But whatever it was it seems to me that your one chance now is to tell me the whole truth about that night.'

'It is a lie,' said Vanilla. 'I did not kill him.'

'I didn't say you did,' said Quill. 'But a jury might not be so easy to convince. You had every reason for killing Citrolo and now it appears you had every opportunity.'

Vanilla shrugged. 'What is it you want of me? I am at your mercy.'

'Only the truth.'

'What use is that? The circumstances are against me. I cannot prove my innocence, only repeat it. There is nothing I can do to convince you unless,' he looked at Quill thoughtfully. 'Who knows of your visit to me?'

Quill glanced at those strong fingers. 'The concierge,' he said, 'Arenskaya. Gustave.'

'Enough,' said Vanilla. He pondered. 'I understand you were dismissed from Scotland Yard.'

'I resigned,' said Quill.

Vanilla nodded. 'Perhaps you would be willing to do business. I am not a rich man but . . .'

'Stop trying to bribe me,' said Quill. 'I haven't accused you of anything yet, anyway. Suppose you tell me your story.'

'But there is nothing to tell,' said Vanilla. 'That night, as always when the syndicate does not do too well, I go to the office for chips.'

'What time was that?'

'I do not remember,' said Vanilla. 'A little past two maybe. As always I use the passage. In the office Citrolo is asleep. I look and I see that he is drugged.'

'It must have been a great temptation,' said Quill.

'I do not deny it,' agreed Vanilla. 'I had little friendship for Citrolo.'

'Not unnatural as he blackmailed you.'

'As you say. And it would have been easy to kill him. But as the dead man himself told me, I have too much imagination for murder. Always I see the consequences. I do not deny,' said Vanilla candidly, 'that if I had been certain of safety I might not have taken my opportunity. But it was too risky, I decided. So I took my chips and left.'

Quill nodded. 'If you didn't strangle him someone else did. The best way of clearing yourself is to help me find the murderer.'

Vanilla started to pace the room. 'How can I do that? I am not a detective.'

'You can answer my questions. Did you hear or see anything while you were in the office or the passage?'

'No.'

'Did you meet anybody on your way back to the baccarat room?'

Vanilla reflected. 'I cannot see how it can in any way concern the crime, but Prince Alexis Artishok was on his way out to the garden.'

'Did you speak to each other?'

'The Prince,' said Vanilla with heavy sarcasm, 'was kind enough to point out that it was a lovely evening.'

'Is that all?'

'That is all.'

'Was this the first evening you had met the Prince?'

'Yes.'

'And yet,' said Quill, 'on the strength of this lively conversation the Prince went out of his way to give you a lift home?'

'Why not? It was raining by then.'

'So you told me before,' said Quill. 'Come on. Out with it. What was it that you and the Prince had to discuss?'

'A purely personal matter.'

'What? My patience has its limits.'

Vanilla thought frantically. 'You will not repeat this?'

'It depends what it is.'

Vanilla thought again. 'It concerns the baccarat. The Prince has a very shrewd eye and it did not take him long to spot my accomplices. He is the soul of kindness. On the journey he devoted himself to discussing their inefficiency and made many valuable suggestions for their improvement.'

'The Prince won that evening, didn't he?'

'He is a great player.'

'How comes a Prince to know so much about the finer aspects of the game?'

Vanilla shrugged. 'M'sieur, I do not ask such questions. Possibly you will ask him for yourself.'

'So,' said Quill, 'the Prince gave you a lift purely to teach you to cheat better. Do you expect me to believe that?'

'It is true,' said Vanilla. 'And I am grateful. Last night the profits were already bigger.'

'Is the Prince getting a rake-off?'

Vanilla started to look affronted but changed his mind. He said that he managed to persuade the Prince to take his share.

'But you will not tell him I told you this?' he said anxiously. 'The Prince would be angry.'

'I'll say nothing for the moment.'

'And the rest?'

'The rest,' said Quill, 'remains to be seen. I shall do nothing for the moment. Now run along to your lunch.'

'I am late,' said Vanilla and flew.

Quill descended the stairs thoughtfully. When he reached the street Vanilla was already out of sight.

Quill had intended to lunch at the café with the grey-green mirrors, but on nearing it he found Arenskaya telling a still puffing Vanilla what she thought of him for keeping her waiting. Taking no chances, Quill bowed, bought a packet of cigarettes, and went to the *Hôtel Moins-Magnifique*. The lunch was even worse than yesterday, but at least he had it alone. Kurt Kukumber, lunching in another corner of the room, did not come near him. He appeared to be explaining something to a saucer-eyed Dutchman.

Quill reflected ruefully that the case was not getting much clearer. It looked singularly as though he would end up with his multitude of suspects all prancing round the sleeping Citrolo, and he would have to decide for himself which one had done the strangling. Quill sighed. Psychology had never been his strong point.

Meanwhile there was the Baron de Rabinovitch to be interviewed. Quill finished his coffee, waved away the cigar trolley hopefully wheeled up, and went to the Casino Buttonhooke.

The Baron was in his usual position under the Buttonhooke portrait. He had almost concluded his day's practice in well-fed benevolence when Quill arrived.

'You again,' he said. 'What is it this time?'

'Plenty,' said Quill, switching on his most formidable expression. He had penetrated the craven heart beneath the astrakhan exterior and deliberately decided to run this interview on a bullying note.

'I have found out,' he began smoothly, 'that you are a liar, a crook, an ex-gaol-bird, and possibly a murderer.'

'Sir.' The Baron, outraged, rose to his feet.

'Shut up,' said Quill. 'Yesterday I let you tell me a string of lies. To-day you're going to answer a bit more accurately.'

The astrakhan began to moult curl by curl but it made one last gesture at affronted dignity.

'This is an outrage.'

'Shut up,' said Quill. 'Sit down. Listen. First so as not to waste time I'm going to tell you what I know about you and then you will tell me what I want to know.'

The Baron sat down.

'You claimed,' said Quill, 'that you only knew Citrolo slightly.'

'That is so,' said the Baron without much hope.

'So slightly that for a number of years you have been paying him blackmail to keep his mouth shut.'

'It is not true,' said the Baron.

'We'll get on much quicker if you'll stop denying the obvious,' said Quill. 'I'm in possession of Citrolo's account book. From it I gather that he has followed your ups and downs with a loving accuracy and charged you according to your success.'

The Baron made no further attempt at denial. He nodded. 'It could not be avoided.'

'You had therefore every reason to hate Citrolo.'

The Baron sprang to his feet. 'I did hate him. What then? Does that make me his murderer?'

'Probably,' snapped Quill.

'There were others who hated him too. Many of them are in Bazouche now. Why do you not accuse them?'

'One at a time,' said Quill. 'Sit down.'

The Baron sat down.

'Next,' said Quill, 'you told me you no longer had a key to Stroganoff's office. I have reason to believe that this was true.'

'A de Rabinovitch does not lie,' said the Baron, cheering up a little.

'But only because you know the way up through the secret passage.'

The Baron mopped his brow.

'At three on the night of the murder,' resumed Quill relentlessly, 'you left the baccarat room and made your way through the passage into the office. You stayed in it some ten minutes. You examined the ledgers, perhaps you also occupied yourself in some other way. Whatever it was you did, you were sufficiently agitated to put the ledgers back, not where you found them, but where you used to keep them. When you returned to the baccarat your agitation was clearly visible to the onlookers.'

'There's not a word of truth in all this,' declared the Baron.

'No?' said Quill. 'Then how came this cigar stub in the passage?' He held it up. 'Henry Clay. You smoke Henry Clay, do you not?'

'Never,' said the Baron, trying to screen the box on the desk by leaning forward.

'Stand up,' said Quill.

The Baron leapt to it.

Quill collected the box. 'Sit down.'

The Baron collapsed.

'Now,' said Quill, as the Baron once again mopped his brow, 'do you admit the truth of what I have been saying or must we go over the ground once more?'

'It is quite true,' said the Baron. 'Only I did not kill him. He was already dead when I entered.'

Quill nodded. 'Tell me about it in detail.'

Rabinovitch tried to pull himself to something resembling his former dignity.

'You are aware,' he began, 'that Lord Buttonhooke wishes to buy back the Casino Stroganoff?'

'I know,' said Quill. 'Why?'

'It is a nuisance,' declared the Baron. 'It detracts from the dignity of our Casino. Also too many people go to it.'

'You ought to have thought of that when you swindled Stroganoff into buying it.'

'I could not tell he would bring his ballet,' said the Baron. 'It is that which has upset our plans.'

'Go on,' said Quill.

'But Stroganoff will not sell. Buttonhooke wanted to increase his offer but I'm against it. I do not think Stroganoff can hold out much longer. So as I am on the premises it seems to me a good idea to have a look at his books, then I will be able to judge the position accurately.'

'You are a specimen, aren't you?' said Quill contemptuously. 'First you swindle Stroganoff and now you want to swindle him again. I suppose,' he hazarded, 'the idea was to see if you could persuade him to take a bit less than you'd tell Lord Buttonhooke and keep the difference for yourself?'

The Baron leapt to his feet. 'It is a lie. Buttonhooke is my friend.'

'Quite,' said Quill. He had a sudden inspiration. 'I suppose the big diamond necklace you and Prince Alexis are going to swing on him is merely a legitimate piece of business.'

The Baron looked puzzled. 'What's this about diamonds?'

'The Otchi Tchernia diamonds that belong to Dyrakova and that the Prince is going to persuade Buttonhooke to buy for Sadie Souse. Don't pretend you knew nothing about it.'

'But of this I have heard nothing,' said the Baron. 'It is outrageous!'

'Then what was it the Prince and you were discussing when I left yesterday?'

The Baron hesitated. 'Nothing. Just a friendly discussion, that is all.'

'What about?'

'But nothing. We must,' said the Baron, looking peculiarly determined, 'have another friendly discussion soon.'

'You seem somehow to be involved with the Prince.'

'But no,' said Rabinovitch. 'Not at all.'

'Oh, all right,' Quill gave up. 'To return to the passage. You entered the office . . .'

'I entered it,' said Rabinovitch. 'I switched on the light over the desk and got busy with the books. The position of Stroganoff is even worse than I thought. He cannot last out much longer.'

'What about Citrolo?'

'I did not notice him at first. It was only when I got up that I noticed a form in the chair on the other side of the room. I crossed to it and . . .'

'Go on,' said Quill.

'I realized that the man is dead. You can imagine how I felt.'

'Yes,' said Quill, without sympathy.

'I realized I must not be caught, for my legal position would not be good. So I replaced the ledgers . . .'

'In the wrong place.'

'As you say, in the wrong place, and hurried out. And that is all. Naturally I am agitated on my return.'

Quill pondered. 'So on your own admission you were alone with Citrolo in that room. There is only your word that you found him dead.'

'It is bad,' agreed the Baron dismally. 'But it is true.' He looked at Quill anxiously. 'You believe me?'

'I'm keeping an open mind.'

'What are you going to do?'

'Investigate further.' Quill got up. 'If your story is true you have nothing to fear. If it is not . . .' He made for the door.

The Baron produced a second handkerchief.

* * *

In a corner of the Casino lounge, Royalty was enjoying its after-lunch cigarette. In front of him a minute portion of Napoleon glowed warmly from its large glass. An admiring waiter stood at a respectful distance hanging on the slightest lift of a finger.

Not in the best of tempers after his interview with Rabinovitch, Quill thought he might as well have a few words with the Prince and strode over. The Prince raised a Royal elbow in greeting. The waiter jumped to it.

'Brandy,' said the Prince. The waiter darted away.

'The cellar here,' said the Prince condescendingly, 'is almost tolerable. Pray be seated.'

Quill already was.

The Prince passed his cigarette-case. Russian, Quill noted, and started to fill his pipe. To his fury the Prince lit a match for him.

Quill decided to cut short the civilized preliminaries. They took up too much time.

'You know that I am investigating the murder of Citrolo.'

The Prince nodded. 'I trust success will crown your efforts.' His left eyebrow implied that he doubted it.

'I'm checking up on the movements of everybody that night. Several of them call for explanation.'

'Meaning mine?' enquired the Prince.

'Meaning yours.'

The Prince sipped his brandy. 'If one can be of any assist-ance?'

'You can begin by telling me when last you saw the dead man.'

'But surely,' said the Prince, 'several people must have told you that already.'

'I'd like you to confirm it.'

'Très bien. It was about one o'clock. Mademoiselle Sadie and I went in search of Lord Buttonhooke. Our search took us to the office of our friend Stroganoff.'

'Your friend?'

'A form of expression. He was at work, doubtless on his biography, and Citrolo was apparently resting from his labours.'

'Apparently?'

'He was drugged. Mademoiselle Sadie told me that. A shrewd woman. She pleases me.'

'Did it please you to hear that Citrolo was drugged?'

The Prince raised a reproving eyebrow. 'How could it concern me in any manner?'

'All right,' said Quill. 'How did you spend the rest of the evening?'

'I played baccarat.'

'You were lucky?'

'What, M'sieur, has that to do with your enquiry?' All the traditional hauteur of the Artishoks was to the fore.

'You left the baccarat room at some time after two?'

'That is correct.'

'Where did you go?'

'I walked in the gardens.'

'You met Dino Vanilla in your walk?'

'Who is that?' The memory of the Artishoks was doubtless short. Quill said as much.

'You mean the dark croupier,' the Prince remembered. 'I believe now that we did pass each other in the passage.'

'You gave him a lift home.'

'Possibly, possibly.'

'In Buttonhooke's car?'

'Green is a vulgar colour,' said the Prince. 'But it runs well.'

'Why should you give a croupier a lift?'

A shade of annoyance crossed the regal face.

'M'sieur,' he said, 'I submit to your questions just so long as they can possibly concern your enquiry. Already I have allowed you considerable latitude. But when your questioning becomes impertinent it annoys us.'

'Is that so?'

'That is so.'

Quill tried another track. 'How,' he enquired, 'are "we" getting on with the Otchi Tchernia racket?'

The Prince raised both eyebrows. It was his strongest form of reproof. Quill practically wilted..

'I do not see how that can possibly concern you.'

'These swindles are in my line,' said Quill. 'I used to collect them.' He passed his card.

The Prince did not forget to adjust his monocle before reading it.

'I trust,' he said courteously, 'that the bribe for which you were dismissed was sufficiently large to compensate you.'

CHAPTER XI

A FAMILIAR figure hailed Quill as he emerged from the Casino. It was his old friend, the Balleto-Medico. After his utter rout by Prince Artishok, Quill was quite pleased to see someone unconnected with the crime.

Unlike the Prince the Balleto-Medico wasted no time on preliminary courtesies.

'Have you heard?' he demanded. 'What do you think of it? Isn't it shattering?'

Several features in Quill's mental landscape, including a pair of imprisoned impresarios, qualified under this description. But before he could single out the particular peak which was being mourned, the Balleto-Medico broke out again.

'The finest promise since Baronova. And her mother takes her to Buttonhooke. Buttonhooke! There ought to be a law against it.'

'There is,' said Quill, deducing correctly that his friend was babbling about Mademoiselle Ostorojno. 'But why should you be so upset about it? In what way is the Ballet Buttonhooke worse than the Ballet Stroganoff?'

'Pah!' said the Balleto-Medico, 'it is not a ballet at all.'

'You've always given me the impression that you considered the Ballet Stroganoff the worst ever.'

'So it is,' said the Balleto-Medico. 'But at least it has tradition behind it. Arenskaya passed through the Maryinsky— she is her pupils' link with the ballerinas of the past. They may not be able to dance their rôles but at least they approach them in the proper attitude. But the Ballet Buttonhooke—pah!—it is almost a revue.'

'Of course,' said Quill, 'I don't understand these things but . . .'

'Hush,' said the Balleto-Medico shocked. He looked round. It was all right. No one had heard.

'Still, doesn't Buttonhooke pay better than Stroganoff?'

'That's exactly what I'm complaining about,' said the Balleto-Medico. 'He bribes the few dancers Stroganoff does manage to get hold of, and sets them to work in pantomime transformations. Ivanoff at his worst couldn't touch the sort of stuff he puts on. I'm writing an article about it in my paper. I hope he sues me for libel.'

'But,' said Quill, 'at least there's no Nevajno in the Buttonhooke Ballet.'

'Don't misunderstand me,' said the Balleto-Medico. 'I roar and rave at Nevajno because the fellow is one mass of stupid conceit, but I have never denied he has something. It infuriates me to see him wasting his talent on Modernist nonsense. Did you ever see his *Bed Time Story?*'

'Nevajno's?' asked Quill, startled.

'Delicious,' said the Balleto-Medico. 'It was one of his very early works. It had all the simplicity of Fokine with the contortion of Massine on top.'

'It doesn't sound very like Nevajno.'

'It isn't now,' said the Balleto-Medico. 'He has been spoilt. It's partly Stroganoff's fault and partly the Press. Stroganoff praises too much and the Press too little. As a result Nevajno sees himself as Misunderstood Genius and his work gets more and more defiant—and more and more impossible.'

At the hotel over their tea, Quill explained that though he had come to Bazouche on a holiday, he found himself plunged into an infuriating murder case. He outlined the details and presented the Balleto-Medico with a synopsis of his investigations to date. As a Watson the Balleto-Medico was a distinct failure. He interrupted far too often and he did not say 'wonderful' once. But he grasped the essentials of the case very quickly if not exactly from the police angle. He seemed particularly interested in Citrolo's *Apologia* which Quill showed him.

'Typical,' he chuckled. 'Typical! You know I'm quite sorry the man's dead. I shall miss his critiques.'

'You knew him well?' Quill enquired.

'We both served the same mistress.'

'Not Dyrakova?'

'Not, as you say, Dyrakova—not Dyrakova alone, that is—nor yet Spessitsiva, nor Lopokova, nor Karsavina. Not even the gracious Riabouchinska, the dark Toumanova, the charming Baronova—the ethereal Markova—not any one dancer, but every dancer. Our Mistress,' continued the Balleto-Medico, waving aside Quill's interruption, 'is the Ballet.'

'Quite,' said Quill.

'And this is a love that puzzles you no doubt.'

'Well—I wouldn't say that,' said Quill, floundering. 'Though I must admit that I am a bit surprised at finding this single-minded love in the dead man.'

'Why?'

'Citrolo was a bad lot,' said Quill, 'a blackmailer who drove his victims just as far as his common sense showed him it was remunerative to go. He had no clemency. He lived the meanest way a man could choose—on the forgotten mistakes of others. Yet from all accounts this man refused to accept a bribe—or—er—a ballerina, when it came to revising his opinion of a ballet.'

'And that seems strange to you, my friend?'

'It does.'

The Balleto-Medico waved a forgiving hand at Quill. 'To me it is perfectly logical. Bribe or bed—what do these count against the accumulating passion of a lifetime—a passion that has had time to spread its deep roots in your heart? Citrolo had this enduring passion.'

'Yet he was very critical.'

'Not "yet," ' corrected the Balleto-Medico, ' "Of course." '

Quill felt that he was beginning to understand.

'Critics are of two kinds,' explained the Balleto-Medico. 'There is the man who owing to the particular key in which his temperament is set responds readily to the stimulus of his chosen art, and there is the man who may be equally discerning but less engaged with his own sensation. The first type of critic wishes only to express what he feels when he sees a work. If he can convey and spread even the smallest part of his own response to his beloved stimulus, he has achieved his aim.'

So far Quill could follow the Balleto-Medico perfectly. There had been nights when he himself on his way back from one of those films that somehow contrive to get you . . .

But the Balleto-Medico was off again.

'But there is the other type of critic. He leaves his heart on his desk, and takes only his eye, his memory, and his Oxford Dictionary. He takes his memory because the art of the ballet is repetitive. You must understand that the literature of the dance is small and that the ballerinas inherit their rôles as a miser inherits his fortune. The ballet critic will remember many a vanished grace while he is watching a new performer. He weighs her in the scales of a fine tradition. He knows that this tradition is in his keeping. A promise too early acclaimed—a gift too long ignored—a work too easily assimilated—these are the critic's pitfalls. His knowledge of technique guides him to the less apparent aspects of a promise. He in turn directs the attention of the ballet-goer. A dancer appears from the rut. For this he needs his eye. His experience of the ballet that cloys, the ballet that keeps its freshness, the ballet that dates, or that continues to amuse—for this he needs his memory. For what, in a new work, will endure, what is perishable, for the just distribution of praise or blame among the dancers, choreographer, composer—for this he needs his eye, his memory, and his flair. Then, when he has written his notice, he can go back to his desk and exercise, in the privacy of his own memory, the forgiving functions of the heart. The performance he has just witnessed will become another signpost on the path towards impeccability.'

'And Citrolo?' asked Quill.

'Citrolo was a man in whom self-control was a trade as well as a virtue. He would not so far forget his own fallibility as to take his heart either to ballet or bed—and certainly never to business. His unswerving sense of the balletic and his unwavering defence of his flair in face of any bribe—any kindness, is in keeping with his mode of conducting his life.'

'I see,' said Quill. 'What do you make the chances of an enraged ballerina—or her partner—finding him drugged, and strangling him?'

'Ballerinas,' said the Balleto-Medico. 'No. Their partners—never. But a really enraged mother, with the strong conviction that her daughter is being systematically libelled, given the necessary strength—and how strong our ballet mothers look. . . .'

'I see,' said Quill.

'But in the case of Citrolo I think we can count the ballet mother out. There is only one really formidable mother and she has too much faith in her daughter's gifts to bother to kill a critic in defence of them.'

'Madame Ostorojno?'

The Balleto-Medico nodded.

'I'm inclined to agree with you there,' said Quill. 'But if mothers and daughters are exonerated what do you feel about croupiers? Croupiers with strong wrists and ferrety eyes.'

The Balleto-Medico lit another cigarette. 'My hobby,' he began, 'has led me into, and out of, more casinos than I can count.'

'And—er—your practice?'

'You must understand I have no regular practice any longer. I only took my degree to please the old man. After he died,' the Balleto-Medico waved an extenuating hand in the direction of filial memory, 'well, it was no longer necessary that I should starve the rich and cosset the poor. But my study of dietetics has stood me in good stead in my chosen sphere. Not a dancer but shivers in her shoes at the awful word "Thickening." And these little ones, they bring their ankles, their backs, and even their husbands, and put them in my charge.'

'Must be very interesting,' said Quill.

'Where there is a ballet, there will I be found. And where there is a casino, sooner or later some hard-pressed impresario trying to save his company from those dreaded one-night stands—those stands that bring the big money with them—but also the thickened legs, the weakened muscles and the untidy technique—those one-night stands that sap the pride and the vitality of a company as surely as a blackmailer saps the pride and bank balance of his victims, those . . . Where was I?'

'At the Casino,' said Quill firmly.

'Ah, yes,' said the Balleto-Medico, 'Casinos. Take for instance that one at Monte Carlo. . . .'

'I refuse,' said Quill.

The Balleto-Medico looked startled and then smiled. 'Of course, I had forgotten. This is a murder enquiry. You were asking about croupiers.'

'Exactly. And you told me all about thickening muscles.'

'Sorry,' said the Balleto-Medico. 'About croupiers then. I've known croupiers all over the world. It may seem curious to you but most of them are absolutely honest. They are surrounded by bribery and an atmosphere of easy money, but they are well paid. Their job is comparatively cushy, and they know that if once they get dismissed from a casino, even on suspicion, they can never get a job in another—except possibly in a private gambling house. So they train themselves to develop a sort of protective armour, like bank clerks who deal in other people's thousands, and do not allow themselves to translate the counters into money. They like the heavy winners. They look on their pourboires as an investment built on other people's risks.'

'And the dishonest croupier?'

'He's a rare bird but he's dangerous. Once a croupier starts on the downward path there is nothing he is not capable of. You see his opportunities are so many, and the man who drugs his conscience every day will be its master in an emergency. If the murder was unpremeditated your dishonest croupier might well have done it.' He paused. 'Yes—Dino Vanilla is certainly a possibility.' ·

'He had every opportunity, at any rate,' said Quill. 'He was alone with the drugged man whom he hated. He's easily excitable, and he has the strongest wrists I've seen on any man.

I swear he would have used them on me this morning if I hadn't pointed out the number of people who would know for a certainty that he had done it. And yet,' he mused, 'I'm not convinced he's guilty.'

'Got a better suspect?' asked the Balleto-Medico brightly.

'The Baron de Rabinovitch.'

'Splendid,' the Balleto-Medico approved. 'I never did like him. Just tell me what you've got against him.'

Quill repeated the evidence against the Baron. Once again there was the opportunity and an even stronger motive than in the case of Vanilla, for the Baron paid far larger sums in blackmail than the croupier, a further increase was mooted, and as his prosperity under Buttonhooke's patronage increased so would the payments. A blackmailer was far more menacing to a man on the verge of big success than to the petty thief. Quill ended up with the details of his interview with the Baron that afternoon.

'I've scared him stiff,' said Quill. 'He admitted everything to me except the murder—he claimed that Citrolo was already dead when he entered the office.'

The Balleto-Medico nodded. 'There's only one point in the Baron's favour. He's hardly the type to strangle a man. A cautious knife in the back is more his mark.'

'Citrolo was drugged,' Quill pointed out. 'That makes strangling quite safe.'

'You may be on the right track,' agreed the Balleto-Medico.

'I'm almost sure I am,' said Quill. 'But I think I'll have to act quickly to get him. He's scared stiff and may do a bunk at any moment.'

'I've known the Baron off and on for years,' mused the Balleto-Medico. 'I should think he's been run out of more small casinos than any other man on the Continent. But I've never known him to attempt anything really dangerous—yet. And somehow I can't visualize those podgy hands really meaning business on a man's throat.'

'In that case,' said Quill, 'what of bogus Russian nobility?'

'Prince Artishok?' said the Balleto-Medico. 'Is he bogus? Of course, that would explain it.'

'Explain what?'

'His extraordinary ignorance of the ballet. Mind you he knows enough to keep up a superficial patter, but I hadn't been talking to him a few minutes before I realized that the man was fundamentally unsound. It puzzled me a bit at the time to find this pretence in a Russian nobleman, but of course if he's phoney that explains it.'

Quill let it go at that.

But the Balleto-Medico was not willing to leave so promising a thread. Before Quill got rid of him he had weighed the Spaniard's love of the dance against that of the Russian, found it wanting, and assessed England as a good second and catching up fast. Towards the end, Quill was hardly listening. He was wondering if it would be possible to coax Gustave into yet another arrest before there was a vacuum beneath Lord Buttonhooke's portrait.

*   *   *

'Mais mon ami,' Stroganoff was saying, 'c'est bien intéressant ce que vous me racontez. You are certain of your facts, no?'

'Positive,' said Kurt Kukumber, with assurance. The few hundred francs in his wallet that the goggle-eyed Dutchman had handed over to invest on his infallible horse, had given him fresh confidence. 'This mine that has been derelict so long—these shares that have been worthless—soon they will hit the sky.'

'Naturellement,' said Stroganoff, 'if they have found gold—then it must be so.'

'The richest vein of gold in California,' stressed Kurt.

Stroganoff was suddenly cautious. 'This engineer who makes you the secret report—you are certain that he is not the swindle?'

But it appeared that Kurt had never been more certain of anyone's probity. The engineer who had double-crossed the company by giving Kurt advance information of his discovery, was quite the most honest man Kurt had ever known.

'He is my sister's husband,' said Kurt, clinching the matter.

'Entendu.' The man of affairs was satisfied. But the psychologist still had his doubts.

'If these shares make the fortune,' he demanded, 'why do you come to me?'

'There is plenty for both,' said Kurt quickly. 'If I were not so broke,' he added with a great show of candour, 'I would keep this good thing to myself. But I need money. My infallible system at the roulette is for the moment not lucky. So I make you this offer, my friend, because I like you.'

'Also you like my ballet?' said Stroganoff hopefully.

'I adore it,' said Kurt. 'The Sylphides. And—er—the Sylphides.'

'Superb,' agreed Stroganoff. 'Bon. We do business. I buy all your shares. 'Ow mooch?'

But here Kurt rose to his greatest heights of plausibility. He could not, he declared, sell all. He had to keep a few for himself.

'All,' insisted Stroganoff, back to big business. 'All or nozzing.'

Kurt pretended to weaken.

It was at this moment that Quill chose to walk in.

Kurt could have killed him.

*   *   *

'Mais, mon cher, M'sieur Quill,' said Stroganoff, 'Ce n'est pas raisonnable. It is the fortune that you prevent me buying.'

'Like the gold shares you bought in London?'

'That,' agreed Stroganoff, 'was the swindle. Mais cela n'est pas du tout le même chose. M'sieur Kukumber has the information confidential.'

'Hence the term "Confidence Man,"' said Quill.

'I have in him the confidence implicit,' said Stroganoff. 'He look me straight in the eye when he talk and honesty it is written on his face. I fear now only that you have offended him and that he sell to Button'ooke.'

'Good heavens!' said Quill, 'don't you know a swindler when you see one.'

But Stroganoff was not convinced. 'You suspect too much. Everything to you it is the fish. Doubtless it is the policeman in you. But I, Vladimir Stroganoff, have the mind broad —the vision. Also I am the business man. I do not buy the pig in the bush. I have read the prospectus and it is most glowing.'

Quill sighed.

'Besides,' said Stroganoff, 'I have the insurance. This is an investment where I cannot lose.'

'Even if the mine is dud?'

'I do not contemplate such a possibility. But even if you should be right in your view so pessimist then I shall come out the quits.'

'How's that?'

Stroganoff chuckled.

'The good Kukumber, he have the system infallible at roulette. So the moneys I pay for the shares it come back to me, anyway.' He winked at Quill. 'Is it not droll how people always believe they can get quick rich?'

Quill gave it up. But he decided to have a word with Kurt in private and dissuade him from further enterprise.

Gustave made an agitated appearance.

'Prepare yourselves,' he hissed urgently. 'M'sieur le Préfet arrives.'

'What must I do?' asked Stroganoff worried.

'Stand to attention,' said Quill. 'Speak when you're spoken to. And don't invite him to your box for the performance.'

Stroganoff crossed to the mirror, patted his bald dome, adjusted his tie, took a second look at it, tore it off, selected another from the wardrobe, and passed it to Quill for his approval.

'What you think?' he asked.

It was at this moment that the *Préfet* came in. Stroganoff

rushed hurriedly to the mirror, his back firmly turned, his fingers busy with his tie.

'This,' said Gustave embarrassed, 'is the man Stroganoff.'

'Stroganoff,' said the frail white moustache in some surprise, 'Vladimir Stroganoff?'

Stroganoff turned round defensively. One look and the apprehension vanished.

'Mon vieux!' An ecstatic rush followed. Bald dome and white moustache embraced one another. Eventually the moustache disentangled itself to point an accusing finger at Gustave.

'Imbécile—what made you arrest him?'

'The evidence,' babbled Gustave. 'Could I guess? . . . Could I tell . . .?'

'Poof!' said Stroganoff forgivingly, 'it is no matter. The good Gustave he try to do his duty. That he is stupid, it is not his fault.' He dismissed the subject. 'But let us sit down—no—not here—the divan, it is more comfortable. Have some brandy— some caviare—a cigar.' He passed the opulent-looking box. 'Big joke.'

The white moustache and the bald dome sat down contentedly side by side.

Gustave and Quill gazed at each other.

'Ah, it is good to see you,' said the moustache, sipping contentedly. 'You ballet is with you?'

'Mais toujours,' said Stroganoff. 'You come to my box,' he added, shooting a triumphant look at Quill.

'What is it you are giving?' asked M'sieur le Préfet.

'Sylphides,' said Stroganoff, 'Boutique Fantasque and Les Matelots.'

'You tempt me,' said the Préfet. 'Excuse while I telephone my wife.'

Gustave intervened. 'M'sieur le Préfet, the man Lord Buttonhooke waits to be seen.'

'Plus tard, plus tard,' said the Préfet. 'But first, the telephone.' He trotted off happily in Gustave's outraged wake, while Stroganoff explained to Quill that the Préfet was an old balletomane—one who had a real appreciation of the art—not like that Citrolo, who so carelessly got himself killed and disturbed the routine of busy impresarios.

'I suppose,' Quill hazarded, 'that this old friend will release you and Buttonhooke.'

'Me—yes,' said Stroganoff sunnily. 'Button'ooke I think I ask him to keep.'

Buttonhooke was at the grille taking a deep interest in the conversation.

'Help me out of here,' he wheedled, 'and I'll let you have Dovolno back.'

'And Shashlyk,' said Stroganoff, 'and Kashkavar?'

'Certainly.'

'Bon,' said Stroganoff, 'it is the bargain. I give you Smithsky in exchange.'

The *Préfet* returned regretfully. It appeared that his wife had guests.

'Bring them all,' invited the hospitable Stroganoff. 'My box it is big. No? Olright—then you come to-morrow?'

'Entendu,' agreed the *Préfet*. He seated himself. 'Now my friend you and I have a little business to discuss.'

'What is that?' Stroganoff was interested.

'Concerning Pavlo Citrolo.'

'Ah ça!' said Stroganoff, 'Alors?'

'Did you kill him?'

'Non,' said Stroganoff forcibly.

'Of course. The idea was absurd.' The *Préfet* turned on Gustave reproachfully. 'Quick arrests after a murder are very useful—they keep away the Sûreté—but one must always arrest with discrimination.' He remembered Buttonhooke. 'What of the other prisoner?'

'He is innocent,' said Stroganoff. 'He runs a ballet, too.'

'You are certain?' asked the *Préfet* keenly. He was a conscientious man.

'Absolument.'

'Bon! Then we must release him.' He turned on Gustave. 'Does not that leave us without an arrest?'

'It does,' said Gustave mournfully.

'Then hurry,' said the *Préfet*, 'and clear up the little mystery. Else the Sûreté will be down on us.'

Gustave shuddered.

'The Sûreté,' explained the *Préfet* to Stroganoff, 'is to us what the dancer's mother is to you. They come in, and they meddle, and they spoil all the arrangements we have made. That is why we must make every effort to solve this murder quickly.'

Stroganoff decided it was time to introduce Quill.

'M'sieur Quill,' he explained, 'has promised to find for us the assassin. He is the great detective. Once he was with Scotland Yard.'

'Was?' said the *Préfet* keenly.

'I resigned,' said Quill.

The *Préfet* looked his disapproval. 'And what was it, M'sieur, that made it necessary?'

*   *   *

'Doucement! Doucement!' The man with the turned-up shirt-sleeves reproved his companion.

'Alors, faites passer vous même.' The sweater flung his cigarette stub on the floor and stamped on it temperamentally.

Stroganoff and Buttonhooke had made a hasty departure, and now the furniture men were removing the last traces of their sojourn. They had been at it for an hour under Gustave's anxious supervision. Quill chafed impatiently. He badly wanted a few words with Gustave concerning the wisdom of arresting Baron de Rabinovitch, but until the removal was over Gustave would be in no mood to concentrate.

At last the van trundled away. Gustave saw them off, turned on his tracks, ruefully inspected a large flake fallen from the stony wall of Stroganoff's cell and went clucking back to Quill.

'Now, mon vieux,' he said, relapsing on to a chair. 'What is it you want of me?'

'I think,' said Quill, 'that I've got your man.'

If he expected to startle Gustave he was disappointed.

'Bon,' said the gendarme placidly. 'We arrest him to-morrow.'

'To-morrow may be too late. You see,' Quill explained, 'I've frightened him, rather.'

'Méchant,' said Gustave reprovingly. 'Who is this assassin?'

'The Baron de Rabinovitch.'

Again Gustave exhibited no surprise. 'Celui-ci? Ah, bon! You have the proof?' he enquired as an afterthought.

'There is a certain amount.'

'Recount it to me,' said Gustave. 'This time I must be careful to be correct or else the Sûreté they will surely get vexed.'

Quill suppressed a smile. Scotland Yard, he felt, would have started to get waxy long ago. Soberly he outlined the evidence against the Baron, dwelling on his unquestionable opportunity and his indisputable motive. He produced Citrolo's note-book with its record of payments by the Baron. Gustave promptly collared it.

'This,' he announced happily, 'I read later—but you are right, mon cher. There is enough to hold him on suspicion,' he declared. 'We take him to-morrow.'

'At once,' insisted Quill.

'Pas ce soir,' Gustave shook his head firmly. 'Aujord-hui c'est mardi. Mardi je m'amuse.'

'That's all right,' said Quill. 'Arrest him first and amuse yourself afterwards.'

'Non,' said Gustave. 'J'ai mes habitudes et mes heures. I am too old to change.'

'Look here,' said Quill, 'if you don't take him to-night he may be gone to-morrow. And then the Sûreté will be very cross indeed.'

Gustave began to waver. 'Perhaps I come afterwards.'

'What time will that be?'

'Ça dépend,' said Gustave. 'Eleven may be.'

'Better come at once.'

'Non.' Gustave reached for his overcoat. 'It is already time for my appointment. Do not distress yourself. The Baron will not fly so soon.'

Still arguing, Quill followed him into the street.

'Vous venez avec moi?' observed Gustave. 'Ah—bon!'

He strode off vigorously. Quill followed. If he stuck close enough and nagged sufficiently he might succeed in dragging this zealous policeman away half-way through whatever party it was he was making for.

They turned down a side-street and stopped before some shuttered windows. Gustave pushed open the door. A bell tinkled down the back. A violent crimson carpet burst on Quill. So a moment later did Madame.

'Vous êtes en retard,' she rebuked Gustave. 'Mademoiselle Fifi vous attend dans la salle Chinoise depuis dix minutes.'

'Pardon,' said Gustave, making for the stairs. He paused to wave a vague hand at Quill. 'Vous vous occupez de mon ami. Il est Anglais.' He darted off.

Madame was affability itself. Had M'sieur any preference?'

'Er?' said Quill.

'J'ai une petite Russe charmante.'

Quill gulped and tried to explain.

'Je suis trompé,' he began laboriously.

Madame was a philosopher. 'Ça arrive à tout le monde. Ici on oublie. Peut-être une mignonne Japonaise?'

Quill shook his head desperately.

'Alors,' said Madame, 'vous préférez choisir.' She clapped her hands.

A confusion of shuffle, giggle, and perfume, trooped in.

Quill gave up any further efforts at explanation. He ran for his life.

CHAPTER XII

THE restaurant at the Casino Buttonhooke presented an animated appearance. News of the magnate's release from gaol had spread quickly and every inch of sable, every swell of starch, had gathered from miles around for a glimpse of the extricated Daniel.

The floor of the restaurant was packed solid with diners-out unanimously leaving their lukewarm *consommé*.

But clients expecting to see the Press Lord haggard and exhausted after his gruelling ordeal in the local gaol were doomed to disappointment. Incarceration had not affected Lord Buttonhooke outwardly in any material manner. Plump and jovial, he sat at the head of a table bestrewn with sheafs of lilac and showers of roses, beaming seraphically at one and all.

On his right, Sadie Souse emerged from a confection of pink chiffon, pale orchids, and no shoulder straps. On his left, Prince Alexis Artishok's monocle was clearly disclaiming all responsibility for the table's flower scheme. At the far end of the table the lavender tie was waiting to be spoken to before it answered. And beside the Prince, Baron Sam de Rabinovitch absently crumbed his roll.

The Baron was not himself to-night. There was no carnation in his buttonhole. He was not even making a dab at the Buttonhooke benevolence. When he smiled it was in a sickly fashion. He took no interest in his food. Frequently he leant forward as though about to speak, but each time he changed his mind. Lord Buttonhooke was eating Homard à l'Americaine. His digestion was due to pay for it later, but he felt that his palate was entitled to it now.

'Encore,' he instructed the waiter recklessly.

The Prince raised an eyebrow.

'Is it wise?' cautioned Sadie Souse. 'Had you better?' Visions of having to coax diamonds from an indigestion-racked Daddy floated before her saucer eyes.

'You're very beautiful to-night,' said Buttonhooke between mouthfuls. 'Pretty as a picture.' He placed a podgy hand on her knee. Sadie slid a practised little paw on top of it.

'I'd look a darn sight more beautiful in the Otchi Tchernia diamonds. I suit diamonds,' said Sadie modestly.

'Have you missed me?' pursued Buttonhooke, without much hope.

'Sure,' said Sadie, 'I got kinda lonely with only the Prince to look after me, and no Otchi Tchernia's to try out.'

'Poor little girl,' sighed Buttonhooke, 'never mind—I'll make it up to you, now I'm back again.'

'Darling,' the pressure increased with a practised percepti-bility. 'Prince, Prince,' added Sadie urgently, 'Percy's just promised me my Otchi Tchernia's.'

Rabinovitch edged uneasily towards his idol's eye-level, but Lord Buttonhooke did not observe him. He was bawling for brandy.

But the magnate's brandy was due to be delayed, for as his waiter moved smoothly away in search of it, a bald dome bobbed at him.

'Et mes framboises?' it demanded impatiently. 'J'attends toujours.'

'Pas de framboises,' explained the waiter slowly, loudly, and for the third time. But Stroganoff still looked hopeful.

'Pas de framboises,' repeated the waiter, 'ni de fraises, ni même de cerises.'

Shocked, Stroganoff voiced his complaint to the rest of his party. The audience reacted in their accustomed ways: Galybchik said it was a shame, Nevajno absently finished Arenskaya's champagne. Arenskaya boxed his ears. Order was restored with difficulty.

'Doubtless,' began Quill, the memory of his dinner at the Casino Stroganoff still vivid, 'doubtless, the greengrocer is enervé.'

Stroganoff looked about him distastefully.

'To eat at this place,' he said, 'it was the big mistake.'

'Then why we do it?' asked Arenskaya.

'It is the finance,' explained Stroganoff. 'Emilio he tell me the free list it must be reduced. But had I for a moment suspected that there would be no framboises. . . .' With sudden resolution he pushed aside his chair and strode over to Buttonhooke.

'Your publicité,' he complained, 'it makes the lie unpardonable.'

Buttonhooke goggled.

So, but less believingly, did the Baron.

So did Sadie.

So did the lavender tie.

Even the Prince raised an eyebrow.

'You announce us that your cuisine it is unrivalled, and poof!—there are no framboises!'

The lavender tie was the first to recover.

'In March,' it began crushingly. . . .

'Mistaire Galybchik,' appealed Stroganoff, 'what matters to me the calendar? It is the framboises that I command, and not the diary.'

'And if you wanted oysters in July?' argued the logical lavender tie.

'Oysters,' said Stroganoff with a sigh, 'do not agree with me.'

'Too bad,' said the Baron, absently.

'The dinner,' continued Stroganoff, outraged, 'was a disgust. The hors d'œuvres, the sole délice, the Caneton Sauvage, and the omelette surprise—poof!—it was not fit to offer a journalist.'

'Look here,' began Buttonhooke hotly. . . .

Stroganoff waved a magnanimous hand. 'Do not distress yourself,' he said forgivingly, 'we Russians are used to suffer.' An evil glitter lit his eye. 'Tiens!' he exclaimed. 'We prove it— we all stay to see your *Lac des Cygnes* to-night. Big joke,' he explained to Sadie, who was the only one who seemed to find his quip at all amusing.

'The house is sold out,' said the lavender tie.

'No matter,' said Arenskaya, materializing at Stroganoff's

elbow. 'Do not apologize. Not always can the stall hospitable be found. Instead,' she finished sweetly, 'we come to your box.'

'Enchanté, Madame,' murmured Prince Artishok into the stunned silence.

*   *   *

Al Fineberg hit his drum a disconsolate whang. 'Let's give 'em something hot?' he pleaded.

Bennie Schweitzer took up his saxophone and lovingly scaled to the highest note in his compass. Not content with that he slid down again like an avalanche in a silly symphony.

'A rumba,' said Moishe. He played the concertina.

'High, Wide, and Handsome,' suggested Abe Abelson, picking up his trumpet.

Isadore at the piano settled the dispute by striking up a hotted version of 'Two Guitars.'

By hiring Abe Abelson and his American College Boys for the Casino Ballroom Lord Buttonhooke had unwittingly done a keen stroke of business for his baccarat. Only in the gambling rooms could you escape their strains. Merciless amplifiers festooned the walls in every other place.

The hotted up version of 'Two Guitars,' which blared out as Stroganoff's party emerged from the restaurant, stirred the gipsy in Arenskaya.

'We dance,' she announced. Brooking no opposition, she clutched the weakest (Galybchik) and made off towards a table on the illuminated floor. Perforce the others followed.

'Consommation Obligatoire,' said Stroganoff, eyeing the notice on the wall with considerable disapproval. 'Me—I will not drink the orangeade. We go.'

'The first ballet it is *Les Sylphides*,' said Arenskaya cunningly. 'You will no doubt enjoy *Les Sylphides* Button'ooke. As for me—j'y reste.'

Stroganoff shuddered and sat down.

Arenskaya gazed invitingly at Quill. Quill looked the other way. Arenskaya advanced towards him, the gipsy very much in evidence.

A ferrety shadow loomed up in time to save Quill. It was Dino Vanilla.

'Carissima,' he muttered and wafted her away.

'He has the nerve that one,' muttered Stroganoff. 'It is but two hours since I give him the sack and déjà he dances with my maîtresse de ballet.'

'We dance?' suggested Galybchik to Nevajno.

'Quelle drôle d'idée,' said the intellectual, amused.

'We dance,' said Quill. Galybchik leapt to it.

Nevajno glared at the couple, his lean fingers drumming nervously on the table.

'But you dance beautifully,' said Galybchik, surprised.

'Long practice in night clubs disguised as a gentleman,' explained Quill.

'You dance wonderfully,' said Vanilla to Arenskaya, 'but it is only as I expected.'

'Foolish boy,' said Arenskaya, well pleased. 'Tell me why are you not at work?'

Vanilla looked pathetic. 'I have been sacked.'

'Vladimir dare to do that?' Arenskaya's shrill indignation almost drowned the trumpeter's solo passage. 'We go back and I arrange everything.'

But it appeared that tact would be needed. The English policeman had meanly told Stroganoff all about the chips and the latter had now conceived the darkest doubts concerning Vanilla's honesty.

'So now you throw the ball here?' asked Arenskaya. 'Poor boy, but no matter,' she consoled him, 'we still have your night off.'

But it appeared that every night was off. That pig Rabino-vitch, who by a curious coincidence was harbouring much the same sort of doubts as Stroganoff, would see to that.

'I attend to everything,' Arenskaya assured him. 'I threaten Vladimir that I go to Hollywood and he take you back double quick. Without me Vladimir is an empty "O." It is well known.'

The empty 'O' was at the moment homesick for a real tzigane orchestra.

'In Moscow,' he was remembering, 'there was a little

kabachok where we dance, we drink, we sing far into the night. My baritone it was much admired then.' He cleared his throat.

Unfeelingly the American College Boys plunged into the 'Big Apple.'

                    *   *   *

In her dressing-room the young Ostorojno was dabbing powder on an agitated nose.

'You know,' she said, 'we haven't been too clever this time.'

'Nonsense,' said the old Ostorojno, 'there was no future with Stroganoff. I thought I'd made you see that.'

'Not Stroganoff,' sighed the young Ostorojno. 'I was thinking about David. Maybe we ought to have had a rehearsal.'

'Nonsense,' said the old Ostorojno, looking slightly guilty. 'You know your Swan Lake backwards. And you wanted to surprise Dovolno to-night, didn't you? Anyway, I thought you danced very well with that young understudy.'

'The orchestra!' groaned young Ostorojno, showing that she was growing up fast.

Mother and daughter settled down to a nice companionable grumble about the musical director.

'Still,' old Ostorojno concluded, 'you have danced with worse orchestras before now. Remember La Bourboule.'

'And Carlsbad,' said the young Ostorojno.

'And the pier at Eastbourne.'

Young Ostorojno brightened. 'It could be worse. And it will be nice to dance with David again.'

'Won't he be surprised to see you come on,' said the old Ostorojno encouragingly.

'I hope he won't dry up,' said the young Ostorojno, all nerves again.

'Now look here,' said old Ostorojno, 'don't bring that up again. After the way you had to persuade me to persuade the régisseur to let you dance with an understudy solely so that you could surprise Dovolno to-night, I won't stand for it.'

The call-boy knocked on the door.

'Your shoes?' flurried Madame Ostorojno. 'Your hair? Stand up. Let me look at you.'

The Ballerina was on her way.

*   *   *

Lord Buttonhooke's box was feeling the strain. Arenskaya, with difficulty detached from her Vanilla, had seated herself firmly in the front row with Buttonhooke on one side and Stroganoff on the other. Nevajno, foiled in his attempt to prise Buttonhooke from his seat, had wedged himself into the corner nearest the stage and obstinately closed his eyes. 'It is Petipas,' he explained. In the second row an eager Galybchik perched beside a bored Sadie Souse. The Prince had deserted her for baccarat, and Quill, lounging against the wall, did not seem to be paying her the attention she had every right to expect. The door space which had at first been occupied by the Baron de Rabinovitch was now held by the lavender tie. Muttering that something needed his attention in the office the Baron had left the party. Quill did not like letting him out of his sight, but surely Gustave could not be long now.

The conductor waved his baton. The oboe quaveringly announced the Swan Queen Motif.

'Your orchestra—it play bad—no?' said Stroganoff with much satisfaction.

The curtain went up.

In the wings Ostorojno stood screened behind a batch of friendly skirts. From her position she could just see a few inches of grey leotard belonging to the huntsmen. The purple splendour of the Prince was hidden from her. She giggled in anticipation. What a start David Dovolno was going to get.

Her cue.

A last trial of the foot, a last touch of the hair, and into the white light she ran, achieving a perfectly placed pas de chat. Vaguely she seemed to hear a scream of rage, but one could not be bothered with that. David would be standing against the wings looking at her. A few more bars and they would be face to face.

And now the Prince was hurrying forward. She bowed to him. He bowed back. There was something peculiar about that bow. Olga Ostorojno looked up—straight into the beaming face of Ernest Smithsky. Click went an amateur camera—it was a big moment.

*   *   *

At the Casino Stroganoff, his own secret well kept, a cursing Dovolno was endeavouring to rotate the fat girl.

*   *   *

The playing of the prelude had put Stroganoff into a fine humour. The first fiddle had been noticeably flat and the two harps had both come in two beats late. He discussed the matter fully with Arenskaya just in case Buttonhooke had not noticed it.

The view-hallo of the huntsmen increased his pleasure. He slapped Buttonhooke affably on the back when Ernest Smithsky as the Prince hurried invisibly on.

'You have done well, my friend, to take that one. His technique it is superb—it is a pity only that his personality is imperceptible.'

The jeers seemed to have little effect on Buttonhooke. He chuckled and almost rubbed his hands.

'Wait till you see the Swan Queen.'

Stroganoff was interested. 'You have a new dancer?'

'New to me.'

'She has talent.'

'A very great talent.'

'Poof!' said Stroganoff. 'She cannot compare with my Ostorojno.'

'Hush,' said Buttonhooke, 'here she comes.'

Stroganoff leant forward and nodded approvingly as a perfectly-placed pas de chat landed in its clear-cut fourth position. He leant further forward as the face of the dancer looked at the audience. He almost fell out of the box.

'Thief! Villain! Assassin!' He clutched Buttonhooke's right shoulder and tried to swing him round. He failed, for Arenskaya was pulling at the other.

Prince Artishok, entering the box, raised an enquiring eyebrow. Sadie explained it gleefully.

Lord Buttonhooke, though a little torn, went on chuckling.

'You laugh,' said Stroganoff infuriated. 'You think you spell for me the ruin. But soon you sing the other side of your face. Wait till you see the Giselle that come to me from Paris.'

'What's that?' said Buttonhooke.

' 'Ush,' cautioned Arenskaya. 'The plans of the Ballet—they are for us alone. And also per'aps she do not come.'

'She come,' said Stroganoff, 'she cannot resist me much more.'

Arenskaya changed the subject.

'It is a pity,' she said tactfully to Buttonhooke, 'that your cygnets they are out of step yet again.'

Lord Buttonhooke clapped defiantly as the ballet came to an end.

Ostorojno took her curtains alone. Only Smithsky was with her.

*　　*　　*

'Come, come.' As the contents of the box emptied themselves into the foyer Lord Buttonhooke patted the gloomy Stroganoff on the back. 'Cheer up. It's all in the game. To-day I've put one across you. To-morrow maybe you'll put one across me.'

'Then to-morrow I laugh,' said Stroganoff.

'It's stupid to bear malice,' urged Buttonhooke. 'Look at me. You got me into gaol, but . . .'

'I get you out,' said Stroganoff. 'And to thank me you steal my Ostorojno.'

'Forget it,' said Buttonhooke. 'Let's all go to my office and have a drink.'

'Champagne?' asked Arenskaya.

'Champagne, by all means,' boomed Buttonhooke. 'This way.' And off he marched towards the marble staircase.

'Me—I do not care to drink with the thief,' complained Stroganoff to Quill.

'What matters?' said Arenskaya broadmindedly.

Nevajno nodded agreement. Champagne, he announced with the air of one making a great discovery, was always champagne.

'Come on,' said Quill. He was anxious to get to the office to see if Baron de Rabinovitch was there. Gustave ought to be arriving any minute now.

They moved towards Buttonhooke who was waiting on the marble stairs. A figure catapulted past them. Quill stretched a lightning arm and tweaked it back. Brought to a standstill it turned out to be Kurt Kukumber.

'Just off to meet your uncle?' asked Quill, 'or is the Spanish Prisoner after you?'

Kurt gulped.

'What do you here?' demanded Stroganoff, visibly annoyed. 'Did you not promise me to play only at my Casino?'

'I sought to change my luck,' pleaded Kurt, 'also our arrangement it was to date from the time you bought the shares.'

Stroganoff was a fair-minded man. 'Bon,' he said, 'I overlook it this time. Now go.'

Kurt was quite willing. After a pathetic effort to borrow his cab fare from Nevajno he strode into the night.

'Funny little man,' said Buttonhooke, 'wonder what scared him?'

The cavalcade resumed its marble ascent. A flunkey gravely approached carrying a telegram. Before he could reach Buttonhooke, Stroganoff, who automatically assumed that all telegrams must be for him, had reached over and ripped it open.

He let out a howl of triumph.

'She comes, she comes!' he crowed. 'Dyrakova dances *Giselle* for me on the twenty-eight.'

'Let me see that wire?' said Buttonhooke almost brusquely.

With a flourish Stroganoff handed it across. Prince Artishok moved over and stood behind Buttonhooke's shoulder to help him read it.

'Ah—mon pauvre ami,' said Stroganoff, 'I understand only too well how bitter for you must be this defeat. But it is all—as you say—in the game. So console yourself. You have fought well. It is no dishonour to lose to Vladimir Stroganoff.' He beamed round for applause.

'This wire,' said Prince Artishok coldly, 'is addressed to Lord Buttonhooke.'

Stroganoff stopped beaming and snatched the wire. He read it incredulously.

'It is the mistake,' he declared. 'The post office confuse themselves.'

'There is no mistake,' said Buttonhooke, 'I have been negotiating with Madame Dyrakova for over a month.'

'Me, I have negotiated with Dyra all my life,' retorted Stroganoff. 'It is preposterous that she could come to you. You have but to read the wire to understand this. Listen:

DELIGHTED TO DANCE GISELLE FOR YOU. EXPENSES IN
ADVANCE.   DYRAKOVA

Let us apply to this the logic,' Stroganoff urged his gaping audience. 'First—she is delighted. Now I ask, is it possible that our Dyra should be delighted in a Ballet à la Button'ooke?' He appealed to Arenskaya. 'Is it likely?'

Arenskaya was thoughtful. 'She is a stupid woman. It is well known.'

'Next,' demanded the logician, 'she ask for her train fare. Would she reveal to a stranger her poverty?'

'Never,' said Prince Artishok quickly. 'She has the pride of the devil.'

Stroganoff beamed on this unexpected ally. 'But Dyra and I we have no secrets from each other. I am to her like a father. When she speak I listen.'

The flunkey reappeared with another telegram. This time the lavender tie took no chances and reached for it. But it was addressed to Stroganoff and had been sent on from his Casino. He passed it over.

'Voilà!' said Stroganoff, 'now we will see. She realize her mistake and she hurry to correct.' He extracted the message, glanced at it, crumpled it into a ball, and threw it on the floor. Galybchik picked it up. It read:

'VLADIMIR—SHUT UP. DYRA.'

'A slight hitch?' asked Buttonhooke, as the party resumed its climb.

'Pour le moment peut-être,' admitted Stroganoff, 'but do not yet hatch your chicken,' he added defiantly to Buttonhooke. 'To-morrow she change her mind and she come to me. You will see.'

'I don't care where she goes as long as she brings the Otchi Tchernia with her,' said Sadie to the Prince.

At the door of Buttonhooke's office the party halted.

'This way,' said Buttonhooke and flung open the door.

The next moment he had halted too. 'Good God!' he said. 'What's that?'

They all crowded in and gazed incredulously.

Sprawled over the desk, his head on the blotting-pad, his arms hanging loosely by his side, was the Baron de Rabino-vitch. On the floor beside him lay a broken tumbler. On the table was a decanter of whisky and a syphon.

'Il est malade?' asked Stroganoff.

With a horrible conviction Quill pressed forward and leant over the body.

'He's dead,' said Quill. 'Cyanide, I think.'

'Dead!' said Buttonhooke incredulously.

'Dead?' gasped Galybchik.

The party eyed each other.

'I am unwell,' said Arenskaya suddenly.

Stroganoff supported her to a chair. 'Some brandy.'

His eyes roved the room and alighted on the decanter. He made towards it. Quill interrupted him.

'Do you want to poison her?'

He was thoroughly fed up. It seemed to him that all his life he was to be pursued by the hoodoo of suspects that got them-selves murdered the moment he planned to arrest them.

There was a knock on the door. Quill opened it. A weary Gustave was standing on the threshold.

'Je suis venu,' he announced simply.

CHAPTER XIII

Quill pushed back the shutters. Sunshine streamed into the room.

'Good God!' he said astonished. To think that this could happen in the South of France!

He glanced at his watch. It was eleven o'clock. The hard fried remains of the h'English breakfast leered at him from a bacon-ringed plate. Abandoning all further efforts at waking him up the waiter had left them there in despair.

Quill sighed as the events of last night crowded in. Faced with a second body, Gustave had lost his head entirely. First he had turned on Quill, accusing him of gross carelessness, lack of foresight, and scaring the corpse into committing suicide. Next he reproached himself for releasing the two impresarios, who had misused their liberty to perpetrate a further assassination, and ended with a grand dust-up with Arenskaya, who wanted to go home. It had taken all Quill's resources to steer Gustave safely through the necessary formalities that to the police are the concomitants of death. But he had managed it somehow, and then, with the gallery safely dispersed to their respective homes, Gustave had thrown a *crise de nerfs* and Quill had had to take him home and put him to bed with a cup of cocoa. In bed, Gustave had become calmer. After all, as he pointed out to Quill, even if the Sûreté did come, which now seemed inevitable, they could find no fault with his handling of the case. Considering the way he was overworked, running the gaol single-handed, he had done as well as could be expected. Next week things would be easier. His assistant, who was also his godson, would be back to take charge of the routine work and the weeding, and he would have time to put the finger irrevocable on the murderer himself.

It was five o'clock before Quill got to bed.

As he dressed Quill felt thankful that he was, to all intents and purposes, out of the case. His client was out of gaol, he had solved the chips mystery, and he had nothing to fear from the Sûreté. It was none of his business who murdered Citrolo or Rabinovitch. Even if the Sûreté should decide, as they easily might, that Rabinovitch had committed suicide to avoid arrest there was no reason for him to interfere.

But to his growing irritation his mind refused to abandon its speculations. He could not for a moment accept the suicide theory. Rabinovitch was not the type—he was too much of a coward. No—he was pretty certain that both murders bore the same signature, and it seemed a pity to waste all the work he had put in on the first. He had all his suspects nicely tabulated —including the dead man—it went against the grain to hand it all over to Gustave's assistant. Besides, he was interested in crime. Why should Rabinovitch be murdered? Who was he menacing? Had he seen the murderer in Citrolo's death room? Damn it—this was his holiday!

But as he left his room he had an uneasy conviction that he would not be able to resist going on pottering.

*   *   *

'Bon jour,' said Anatole, the Commissionaire, brightly. 'You have heard the news?'

'I found the body,' said Quill.

'Ah, ça!' said Anatole, 'I do not speak of the Baron. Neither do I weep because he is dead.'

The Baron seemed to have been popular with his staff.

'I speak of the ballet,' explained Anatole. 'The wonderful news—that Dyrakova she dance for us.' A loving look came into his eyes. 'It is ten years since I have seen that développé.'

'I thought,' said Quill, 'that she had agreed to dance for Buttonhooke.'

Anatole smiled knowingly. 'That is but a rumour, spread,

no doubt, by the enemies of our Casino. M'sieur le Directeur
has just assured me of that.'

Quill said nothing.

'If you do not believe me,' said Anatole hotly, 'demand of
him yourself. He is in his office.'

Stroganoff was in a frenzy of activity. The biography had
been abandoned for the long-distance telephone.

'Ah—c'est toi, Dyra. Ici Vladimir. Ecoute, cheri. . . .'

From the doorway Quill heard the clonk that terminated the
Paris end of the conversation.

Stroganoff looked up at Quill like a hurt child. 'As soon as she
hear who I am she do that. It is not fair. How can I persuade
her with my eloquence if she hang herself before I use it?'

'What's this?' said Quill, startled.

'Always she hang herself,' repeated Stroganoff, 'but this
time I will be more cunning.' He returned to the telephone.
'Montparnasse 23-107.'

'Encore?' said the operator.

'Toujours,' said Stroganoff.

'Vous avez tort, mon vieux,' counselled the operator. 'Elle
est de mauvaise humeur. Mieux envoyez un petit cadeau et
essayez encore demain.'

'Mais qu'est-ce que ça vous fait?' howled Stroganoff,
exasperated. 'Je paie chaque fois.'

'Poor darling,' said Galybchik. 'This is the fifth time he's
'phoned this morning.'

'Allo,' said Stroganoff, 'je desire parler à Madame Dyrakova.
C'est urgent. Qui parle?' Stroganoff reflected.

'Bernard Shaw,' suggested Quill.

'Bernard Shaw,' repeated Stroganoff, automatically. 'Mais—
non—non!' he bellowed. He placed a hand over the receiver.
'What is it you make me say?' He removed his hand. 'Ici—
Massine.'

'Vladimir,' said an exasperated voice at the other end. 'I can
stand it no longer. Wherever I go there is the telegram—always
from you. And now the telephone. Will you understand? I
won't dance for you. Never! Never! Never!'

'Entendu,' said Stroganoff, 'mais sans blague I have for you the proposition intéressant. To dance *Giselle*. . . .'

'Plonk.' Dyrakova had hanged herself again.

Stroganoff signalled furiously. 'Montparnasse,' he bellowed. '23-107.'

Quill thought it time to leave.

'You despair too easily, my friend,' reproved Stroganoff. 'Me I do not give in. Dyra she dance *Giselle* and she dance for me. We are confident. Already we design the poster.'

He applied himself to the telephone again.

'Montparnasse,' he said stubbornly. '23-107.'

*   *   *

In his office Lord Buttonhooke was giving the lavender tie his instructions. The death of the Baron, the only man who had ever seemed to like him for himself, had been a real blow to Buttonhooke, but he was not going to let it interfere with his publicity.

'See that it's large,' he ordered. 'Plenty of colour. And see to it that the name hits the eye. I want the whole town plastered with it by to-morrow.' He gloated. 'Dyrakova in *Giselle*. Have I ever seen *Giselle*?' he asked the lavender tie. . . .

*   *   *

Up in the practice-room Madame Ostorojno was not at all pleased. In making the headlines of the local paper, the Baron de Rabinovitch had pushed her daughter right out of the print. On top of that, the little silly was sulking because Dovolno was no longer in the company. She actually wanted to go back to Stroganoff. And as if that were not enough, there was the threat of Dyrakova. True she was only supposed to appear for one performance, but once a retired ballerina started re-emerging. . . . If Dyrakova stayed on with the company, gone was her child's chance of the leading rôles at anything but matinées. And there were no matinées at La Bazouche. Perhaps they would have been better off with Stroganoff, after all, even if he was practically bankrupt. She sighed heavily. What was a mother to do?

At the other Casino, Arenskaya was engaged in her daily tussle with the pianist. Murder, earthquake or flood, the morning classes take place as usual.[1]

'When I say ta-ra-ra——' she was screaming, 'why do you play tootle-ootle-oo?'

The pianist snorted and banged down the loud pedal.

The fat girl led off. But not for long.

'And what,' demanded Arenskaya, 'will Dyrakova say to me when she sees those deboullés of yours?'

'Dyrakova is coming.' The whisper ran round the class.

*　　　*　　　*

'Dyrakova is coming,' jubilated Sadie Souse. 'Prince— you're wonderful!'

The eyebrow very nearly winked.

*　　　*　　　*

With great care Vanilla had enamelled his hair with perfumed brilliantine. He was off to impress Lord Buttonhooke. With the Baron out of the way there seemed no reason why he should not land a job at the Casino Buttonhooke. After all he had a long career as croupier at the back of him, and if it was not all precisely honourable, who was going to bother to tell Buttonhooke now?

His gloves. His walking-stick. His carnations. Tiens! He had almost forgotten his spare pack of cards.

'Have patience,' Kurt Kukumber was pleading with the manager of the *Hotel Moins-Magnifique*. 'My uncle he comes for certain any day now.'

*　　　*　　　*

Gustave looked up wearily from the list of suspects he had arduously compiled. Soon, he reflected thankfully, his nephew would be here to tell him which one to arrest. The Englishman was no good.

[1] 'The ballet it must go on. . . .'—STROGANOFF.

CHAPTER XIV

ON Thursday morning an interested crowd of marketers gathered round an enticing leg, a giddy little wreath and a tu-tu. Underneath it all was the unlikely legend, 'DYRAKOVA in GISELLE.' Above in crimson letters: 'Lord Buttonhooke has the honour to present:'

No sooner had they passed opinion on this work of art than their attention was distracted by Ludwig, the bill-poster, at work on the hoarding opposite. They veered over to watch.

'It is a circus,' hazarded a hopeful.

'Non,' said Ludwig, 'that is not for three months.' He slapped on a wisp of tulle.

Layer by layer, a Wili emerged—a ghostly dancer standing before what appeared to be a graveyard. It was.

The audience shivered deliciously.

'Grand Guignol,' said the hopeful.

Ludwig shook his head regretfully. 'That comes not here again. It was not the success financial.' He slapped on a name:

'DYRAKOVA IN GISELLE.'

'Ah, ça!' The crowd began to melt.

But the bombshell was coming.

'VLADIMIR STROGANOFF has the honour to present:'

'You have mixed up your sheets,' said Madame Bonne-femme, pointing to the poster opposite. 'She dances at the Casino Button'ooke.'

Ludwig went on firmly with his work. Madame Bonnefemme repeated her remark.

'Madame,' said Ludwig coldly, 'I have put up posters in La Bazouche for twenty years and NEVER . . .'

By the afternoon the town was placarded with neutralizing

announcements. Gustave's godson, alighting from his train, stared at the station-yard in some bewilderment. All the time-tables, all the Côte d'Azur, all the Dubonnets, had turned into Dyrakova dancing *Giselle* at different Casinos on the same night. Doubtless his godfather would have much to say on the subject. At this hour he would be in his garden. He hurried to join him.

Mademoiselle Mignon, the postmistress, had never had such a busy day. She could hardly find time to read all the telegrams that arrived and were sent out—let alone scrutinize the post-cards. As the day went on, and his wires increased in pleading, her sympathy for a certain Vladimir grew. Here at last was the persistent lover that every woman dreams of. A man who would not take 'no' for an answer. Not like her own Alphonse, who so many years ago had taken her first hesitating 'no' as final.

Here was another of them.

'DYRUSHKA. DYRUSHKA. What is it you do to me? Vladimir.'

But the creature had no heart it was clear. Here was her response.

'Mille fois—non. Send your next wire reply prepaid. Dyra.'

And the stupid one did. This was no way to win a woman. Mademoiselle Mignon nearly 'phoned up to tell him so.

The telephone girl, too, was having a hard time. There was Buttonhooke getting through to London, the Englishman talking to Paris and Scotland Yard, the Sûreté trying to talk to Gustave, and a Dutchman trying to talk to Kurt Kukumber. And, of course, there was always the Russian with his eternal Montparnasse 23-107.

*　　*　　*

On Friday Lord Buttonhooke's temper was slightly frayed. His liver was no better. His girl-friend would keep harping on one subject.

'But I've never had a real diamond necklace,' she was saying as he shaved.

In town things were no better. It was raining. That clown

Stroganoff had plastered his ridiculous posters everywhere. Some people might even believe him. Fiercely, Lord Button-hooke ordered an addition to his publicity. DEFINITELY AT THIS THEATRE—his posters reassured in purple splashes.

SANS DOUTE ICI—Stroganoff's posters retorted almost immediately, in vivid jade.

In his office Buttonhooke snapped at his assistant manager, snapped at his head croupier, and nearly bit the head off the lavender tie. He was even reckless enough to snap at Prince Artishok, who had dropped in, apparently to stress the immense favour he was doing Lord Buttonhooke by egging him on to purchase a fabulously expensive diamond necklace that he had never seen.

'Nice of you to take so much trouble,' jeered the exasperated Buttonhooke, 'particularly as you're getting nothing out of it yourself.'

The eyebrow worked overtime. 'Are you suggesting that I will profit by the transaction, personally?'

'That's it,' said Buttonhooke. 'Rake-off.'

The eyebrow fell to street level. 'Well, I might be offered a small commission. . . . Why not? Still, if you feel that way about it, I had better wash my hands of the whole affair.' He turned to leave.

Lord Buttonhooke thought of a diamondless Sadie.

'Oie,' he said, 'wait a minute. Have a cigar? You know, I gotta have that necklace now. And I don't mind your rake-off. You know I'm man of the world enough to understand these things. But what gets me is why I can't haggle with the old girl myself? I'd beat her down in no time.'

Up soared the eyebrow.

'I thought,' said Prince Artishok, 'that I had made it clear that Madame Dyrakova has the pride of a Romanoff. It will take all my persuasion to induce her to sell and even then she won't want the sale to be blazoned abroad. She'll know you're the purchaser, of course, but it's my opinion that she won't even mention the subject when she sees you—either before or after the transaction. To her it would be too sordid—too painful.'

'But she'll take my money!'

'She'll take it only if it is offered with delicacy,' said the Prince, 'and only through my mediation. She could never bear the squalor of bartering with—er—a tradesman.'

'What's that?' said Buttonhooke.

Prince Artishok smiled.

By the afternoon, the rain had set in properly. Quill spent a moist four hours dodging from bar to bar, avoiding Gustave's godson, who was panting to swop theories with him. Finally he sought refuge in Stroganoff's office. The impresario had been there all day. 'At any moment she ring me to change her mind,' he announced hopefully.

* * *

On Saturday the Press arrived. It was not the news that Dyrakova was dancing that brought them. It was the two murders at the small plage. They lunched with Gustave and in return printed his views.

Stroganoff was beginning to lose confidence. Gloomily he admitted to Quill that there was just a chance Dyrakova might not dance at all. She was a stupid woman.

Sadie was impressing on Buttonhooke the need for tact. 'Remember what the Prince says,' she kept on repeating. 'Don't go shooting your mouth off to the old lady. I'll die if I don't get those diamonds. The Prince . . .'

'Damn the Prince!' said Lord Buttonhooke.

* * *

On Sunday the Sûreté arrived and reorganized Gustave.

Stroganoff was still telephoning. So was the Dutchman.

By four-thirty the Balleto-Medico could stand things no longer. He, too, telephoned Dyrakova. The number was engaged.

At the post office a great light dawned on Mademoiselle Mignon. 'The poor Vladimir,' she sighed. 'She play him double. Here is a wire for the Buttonhooke.'

'Missed train—coming to-morrow. Dyrakova.'

Two hours later hope was restored. Another wire came.

'Decided train journey too exhausting. Staying in Paris. Regrets. Dyrakova.'

Perhaps she loved Vladimir after all.

But Sir Jasper Buttonhooke went on tempting.

'Yacht will meet you at Marseilles. Wire at once. Buttonhooke.'

No girl can withstand a yacht, thought Mademoiselle Mignon. Poor Vladimir. A sudden resolve was born. She must warn him of his new danger. Putting her shawl about her she went to the telephone.

*   *   *

At six o'clock. Quill entering the Casino found an exhausted Kurt Kukumber recuperating in the bar.

'The Sûreté,' explained Kurt. 'Three hours they question me.'

'Did you tell them about your uncle?'

'Mais non,' said Kurt. 'It was all right. They let me go. And as I leave my luck turns. Picture you, I run into the sucker phenomenal.'

Another Dutchman, thought Quill, and passed on.

'Imagine,' babbled Kurt excitedly. 'He desires to play pinochle with me.'

*   *   *

Stroganoff had almost given up hope when Mademoiselle Mignon took up the telephone. He sat slouched at his desk, his tea unsipped, unhappily doodling all over the opulent box of cigars. It brought tears to Galybchik's eyes to see him so despondent. He would not even work on his biography.

'It is the ruin,' he kept on repeating. 'And what is worse, we lose the face.'

'It is the Casino,' declared Arenskaya. 'Always the Casinos they bring us bad luck. Why you not sell?'

'Jamais!' said Stroganoff, outraged.

'It was at Deauville,' said Arenskaya, 'that the décor fall on Nevajno. It was at San Sebastian that we have the fire without the insurance. It was at Monte Carlo that Palook drop Dyrakova.'

'Is this the moment to remind me of these things?' exploded Stroganoff. 'When my Dyra she goes to dance for a succinsin and I am left here like a stuffed Petroushka.'

Somewhat startlingly Arenskaya burst into tears. 'Is this the moment to remind me of my poor Puthyk—my dear husband— who you never allowed to dance the rôle?'

'Pardon,' said Stroganoff. 'I forget.'

They kissed each other and lapsed into a companionable gloom.

The telephone rang. Stroganoff leapt up.

'Dyra!!!'

But it was a Mademoiselle Mignon.

'What she want?' asked Arenskaya.

'I find out,' said Stroganoff. 'Quoi?' He put his hand over the mouthpiece. 'She is mad,' he explained. 'She try to sell me a yacht.' He turned back. 'Mademoiselle—I am not in the market—not even for the battleship.'

Eloquence poured from the other end. Stroganoff shrugged his shoulders helplessly.

'It is the Buttonhooke yacht that she sell. It is ridicule. Quoi? Qu'est-ce que vous me dites? Mais c'est certain ça? Ah, bon! Merci. Merci—mille fois merci.' He hung up triumphantly.

'We haven't bought it—have we?' asked the apprehensive Galybchik.

'Mais si,' beamed Stroganoff. 'We have bought the whole world and all its diamonds. We have our dear ballerina.' Ecstatically he seized Galybchik and pranced her round the room.

It was at this moment that Quill came in.

'A private lesson?' he asked Arenskaya.

Stroganoff flung an arm round his neck. 'We are saved. Sit down. Wiskyansoda? Listen.'

'What 'as 'appen?' asked Arenskaya, hurt. She, too, wanted to know.

'The victory. Button'ooke we have him by the hair.'

'He has murdered somebody?' asked Arenskaya.

'Better,' said Stroganoff. 'Mooch better. He sent his yacht to meet Dyra at Marseilles.'

Quill gazed blankly at him.

'You do not understand,' burbled Stroganoff. 'Dyra she is the sailor lamentable. I remember well, on the boat from Vladivostok to Yokohama . . .'

'But the sea is beautifully calm here.'

'Calmness to Dyra it is nothing. It is the nerves that is all. She will be unwell—it is certain she will be unwell—it is necessary that she must be unwell. When she arrive she will be fatigué and then. . . . Ah, my friend, never will I be able to thank you for helping me to accomplish this thing!'

'Helping!' said Quill, startled.

'Sit down,' said Stroganoff. 'Listen. I have the idea.'

For half an hour Quill argued, protested, and elaborately washed his hands of the whole project. But it was no use. Stroganoff alone he might have withstood, but when Arenskaya and Galybchik, both of whom seemed to think that the preposterous plan Stroganoff had unfolded was quite sound, joined in the pleadings, he allowed an incautious 'perhaps' to escape him. Stroganoff promptly took this for an unqualified acceptance and bounced him off to a celebration dinner.

In the restaurant, Emilio came hurrying over with his cleanest menu. 'And for the little miss,' he turned to Galybchik and beamed, 'a glass of milk?' Galybchik giggled.

*   *   *

That evening both Casinos were crowded. In search of silence, Quill went to the reading-room. The dinner party had been hilarious and prolonged and Quill needed a quiet spot to meditate.

In the doorway he paused. In the far corner of the room across a card-table a bewildered sickle was facing an upright—and almost regal spear.

Kurt Kukumber was playing his sucker.

The sucker was Prince Artishok. Quill left him to it.

Two hours later Quill returned to the reading-room. The

game was over. The sucker had gone. Kurt Kukumber was still sitting at the card-table making sad additions on the margin of his cheque-book.

'Any luck?' asked Quill.

Kurt shook his head. 'Would you lend me five mille? It is debt of honour.'

Quill whistled. 'That's a hell of a loss.'

'On the contrary,' said Kurt Kukumber, 'it is almost an investment.'

Kurt nodded happily. 'Many have paid far more for a lesson from the great Banco Dacarpo.'

*   *   *

The great Banco Dacarpo. A very thoughtful Quill left the Casino Stroganoff. Surely that was one of the big shots in Citrolo's gallery of untouchables. Curse Gustave for pocketing that diary!

On an impulse Quill turned in his tracks and made for the Casino Buttonhooke. Prince Artishok (or Banco Dacarpo) was helping Sadie to play baccarat. Quill tapped him on the shoulder.

'Could you spare me a moment?'

'Is it essential?' asked the eyebrow coldly.

'Very.' Quill lowered his voice. 'Signor Dacarpo.'

The eyebrow never moved. 'Excuse me,' the Prince apologized to Sadie and made his way regally to a table in a far corner. Then he sat down and relaxed.

'How did you rumble?' said Banco Dacarpo, cheerfully.

'Kurt Kukumber,' said Quill. 'You big bully. Why don't you pick someone your own size?'

Dacarpo laughed. 'He was rather sweet.'

'He's quite proud of himself now that he's found out who you are,' said Quill.

'That's why I told him,' said Dacarpo, 'but I can't understand it—I never thought he'd blab on me.'

'He didn't blab,' said Quill. 'He was boasting. The last thing in his mind was to give you away.'

'But one doesn't boast to policemen.'

'That's where you made your big mistake,' said Quill. 'I'm not a policeman to Kurt. We're practically buddies. He looks on me as quite a promising amateur who's made a good start by getting himself kicked out of Scotland Yard. At any moment now he'll be offering to teach me the finer points of his trade.'

'Weren't you kicked out?' asked Dacarpo.

'That's my affair.'

'And Prince Artishok is mine,' said Dacarpo. 'At least, I hope so. It's taken me years to build him up and I'd hate to lose him.'

'Oh, I shan't interfere,' said Quill. 'It's not my affair.'

'You are wise,' agreed Dacarpo.

'But I can't help being interested in the Otchi Tchernia.'

'A sideline,' said Dacarpo. 'Nice little commission. But, of course, I've got to have Prince Artishok to work it on the old walrus.'

'No swindle?'

'My dear fellow—what a mind you've got! The Otchi Tchernia diamonds are world famous.'

Sadie Souse approached the party. Dacarpo vanished in a twinkling and Prince Artishok stood up to greet her.

'Prince,' urged Sadie, 'come back to the tables. I can't do a thing right since you left.'

CHAPTER XV

'WHEN I say tum-ti-tum, I mean tum-ti-tum, and I do not mean tootle-ootle-ootle-oo. Is that quite clear?'

It seemed to be. The pianist snorted and banged down the loud pedal. Dismally the girls at the *barre* waved their legs—to think that this was Art!

'But this is terrible! Horrible! Stop!'

Everybody shivered. The scene might have been the practice room of the ballet Stroganoff—the culprit, the fat girl—and the shrill scolding voice that of Arenskaya. For that matter much the same scene was even now being enacted at La Bazouche.

But this particular crisis has been brought about in Montparnasse—the cause, a little miss from Sadler's Wells—the outraged teacher, Dyrakova.

Nothing was allowed to interfere with the ballerina's eleven o'clock class. Even the fact that to-day was Monday and she had to catch a train a bare four hours from now, only made Madame twenty minutes late in starting. To-morrow perforce a substitute teacher must be risked, but Dyrakova would be back again on Thursday to give them hell as usual.

Time had dealt lightly with the ballerina. Though nearing forty she had retained her neat, well-controlled figure, her vitality, and her looks. Only her voice had grown shriller—her temper worse—though it would have been difficult to convince Stroganoff that this was possible.[1]

'I am in despair,' declaimed Dyrakova, 'I give it up. I teach no more. My method it will be lost. It is a tragedy, you tell

---

[1] 'She lose the temper—I lose the temper—and poof.—It is terrible.'— STROGANOFF.

me—a calamity—but what avails that I give myself to the last shred, and all for a row of wooden dolls—two rows of wooden dolls?' she demanded. 'You,' she pounced on a pair of terrified blue eyes, 'you have learnt my method three months already, and look at your 'ip—look at your shoulder—look at your over-balance. . . .'

The blue eyes filled.

'The man he comes to put my method on the news-reel,' she continued, 'and what would you have me show? This,' Dyrakova's stick came down on the offending member with a thwack—'and this'—thwack—'and this. . . .'

It was at this moment that she noticed the polo-sweater planted in the doorway. It was accompanied by a movie camera.

The news-reel was taking in the method.

The girls produced their tucked-away radiance. Dyrakova put a hasty hand to her coiffure.

'Eh, bien!' she said, preliminaries over, 'and what would you have us dance?'

'Just proceed with your class usual, Madame—take no notice of us at all.'

'Ah, bon! Back to the barre, my darlings, to-day we make 'istory! Développé à la quatrième en devant—en seconde— passer à la quatrième en derriere. . . .'

The darlings sighed.

'As for you,' she turned on the pianist, 'darling—when I say tum-ti-tum, I mean tum-ti-tum—darling—and I do not mean tootle-ootle-oo—do I make myself clear—darling?'

The pianist bowed, and played three chords tenderly. The darlings applied themselves to the *barre*.

'But this is beautiful . . . lovely . . . exactly my method . . . so . . . and now, we turn, my darlings. . . .'

The darlings turned.

The camera turned.

Dyrakova beamed. 'Ras Dva! . . .' But suddenly the beam hardened. The voice rose. The delicate hands clenched themselves into fists.

'What is this you do?' screamed Dyrakova. 'You!' She pointed to a trembling pink leg. 'But you are 'orrible! You are impossible! Take your wrong-placed 'ips out of my beautiful class at once! And do not bring them in again. Or your knees. Or your thighs. Or your stupid, staring face. . . .'

'Cut!' said the polo-sweater.

The camera looked depressed.

A benevolent white head appeared in the doorway, waiting for the storm to subside. General Dmitri Dumka was used to Dyrakova's eloquence. He had been her business manager for twenty years. He was not a good business manager—this was the reason he had stayed so long with the ballerina.

'Better get ready,' he warned. 'The train it leaves in three hours and five minutes.'

'Mon dieu!' Dyrakova fled. 'Marya,' she called. 'Mes valises . . . my bouillotte . . . un taxi. . . .'

But one taxi was not enough. It took no less than three to take Dyrakova, her baggage, and the little court anxiously waiting to escort her to the station.

As the procession trundled into the yard of the *Gare de Lyon* a porter detached himself from the wall and ambled incuriously over to meet it. It was the last time he was to be incurious that morning.

Before he had time to think, a hat-box whizzed past his ears, three attaché-cases piled themselves in front of him, and two valises and a hot-water bottle were thrust into his defensive arms, while the cabman bellowed for his assistance with a large American trunk.

'Le rapide pour la Côte d'Azur,' instructed the temperamental toque thrusting out of the window. 'Il faut se dépecher —hein?'

'Deux heures d'attente,' said the porter.

Furious the toque turned on the benevolent white head.

'Why do you hurry me like this?'

'Could I foretell that you would leave when I asked?' demanded the white head, not without justice.

By this time the other cabs had disgorged their contents, and a courteous group of Russian *emigrés* disposed itself about the bookstall. With practised ease Dyrakova totted up the pieces.

'Seventeen,' she announced in horror. 'One is missing.'

Little round Marya bustled forward.

'Nothing important, chérie,' she said, 'only the old black trunk with our Press cuttings.'

'Mais vous êtes folle,' screamed Dyrakova. 'Never I travel without this. How else can I entertain the rich dark stranger that my tea-cup tell me I am due to meet?'

'You will be your sweet, gracious self,' said the General, without much hope. 'It will be enough for him to meet the peerless Dyrakova—he will not need her album.'

'Useless to argue,' said the ballerina, with an ominous calm. 'You go back at once and bring it to me.'

'How should I know which trunk it is?'

'There is but one,' said Dyrakova. 'It is in the attic.' 'Good-bye,' she pushed the General into the cab and turned back on the porter.

'Alors! Qu'est que vous attendez, vous?'

*   *   *

The General was a bad manager. He had omitted to reserve a compartment. A twittering of the ballerina's pupils informed the horrified Dyrakova that she was destined to travel with a plaid waistcoat, it's wife, and a large packet of sandwiches.

But this catastrophe was soon averted. . . . An old Etonian tie was discovered with a compartment to itself. A puzzled conductor found himself arranging the transfer for the smallest bribe ever accepted in the annals of the wagon-lits. What had come over him?

A porter came down the platform carrying a slate.

D.Y.R.A.K.O.V.A., danced the white chalk letters. The ballerina hailed him. But it was only a telegram.

'Vladimir again,' hissed Dyrakova, tearing open the wire. She was right.

BON VOYAGE. KEEP CALM. VLADIMIR.

A yelp of helpless fury brought the Old Etonian to his feet.

'Sit down,' said little round Marya. 'Madame s'énerve—c'est tout!'

'Tais toi, Marya—do not mix yourself with my emotions. And you, M'sieur, I thank you for your sympathy.'

The Old Etonian subsided.

With only an hour to go and the General not yet back, Dyrakova could hardly concentrate on her parting presents. She leant out of the window exchanging compliments with her little court, but always her eyes roved to the end of the platform. He was going to be late. She knew it. And the charming man with the pretty tie would be deprived of reading her cuttings.

At last she spotted him. But what was this he was bringing? A perspiring porter trundled up a trolley of luggage.

'There were seven trunks,' panted the General reproachfully, 'four of them black. I've brought the lot. Choose.'

'Celui-ci,' said Marya.

'Mais non—celui-là,' said Dyrakova.

There was nothing for it but to open the lot.

The first contained old ballet-shoes.

So did the second.

So did all the others.

'Mon dieu!' gasped Dyrakova. 'I recollect. Last week I send it to the man who write my memoires. But you,' she turned to the General. 'You go at once and fetch it back. Immediate!'

Obediently the General turned.

The porter arrived with another telegram.

BON APPÉTIT. RELAX. VLADIMIR

*   *   *

'Another cup of Russian tea,' suggested Dyrakova hospitably.

The Old Etonian needed it badly. For the last three hours he had been unable to snatch a wink of sleep. But though it was half-past four in the morning, Dyrakova showed no signs of slowing down. She was still at the dear old Maryinsky and had the whole of her European career in front of her. If only he had known what he was starting up, thought the Old Etonian ruefully, never would he have asked her if she knew Nijinsky.

Nijinsky had lasted till tea-time. And he was followed by Johanssen, Legat, Bolm, and Diaghilev. It was the last time, reflected the Old Etonian, that he would attempt to console a weeping unknown, who, it turned out, was not emigrating from her loving and rather large family for ever, but making a flying visit to some Riviera town for a triumphant appearance in a ballet.

The Old Etonian was not very fond of ballet. Sheer courtesy had prompted him to put the fatal question to the dancer. And Dyrakova had been talking ever since. The only time the monologue varied was when the train stopped at a station, when Dyrakova would temporarily abandon her career in favour of cursing a man called Vladimir who had sent telegrams to all of them. The last one read:

> REPOSEZ VOUS. STOP TALKING. TRY AND SLEEP,
> VLADIMIR.

The Old Etonian wished wholeheartedly that she would take this sound advice.

But there was not a chance. She was still at it when the train puffed its way into Marseilles.

'Here I get out,' said Dyrakova, regretfully. 'You come to my class in Paris and I recount you further triumphs. Tiens! almost I had forgotten—Marushka, my photograph.' But little round Marya had already extracted a photograph from a valise and was sitting with a fountain-pen poised above it.

*   *   *

The train stopped at Marseilles about forty minutes. It was just long enough to marshal the ballerina's luggage.

This accomplished, 'No photographers?' she said, gazing up and down the platform in horror. 'We go back at once.'

'At once!' echoed little round Marya.

An apologetic lavender tie appeared on the scene. The photographers, he explained, were massed on the *quai*. They would take Madame embarking, embarked, and trying on a lifebelt.

'To go on your boat I must be crazy,' declared Dyrakova, 'I will be ill. I know it.'

'The sea is like a mill-pond,' said the lavender tie, reassuringly.

A porter appeared waving a slate. The wire read:

DO NOT FORGET YOUR MOTHERSILL. GO WITH GOD.
VLADIMIR.

Petulantly Dyrakova threw her bottle on the ground and stamped on it.

A monocle picked its way delicately through the valises and stopped within convenient kissing distance of Dyrakova's hand.

'Allow me to present,' murmured the lavender tie. . . .

'It is not necessary,' said Prince Artishok, 'Madame and I have met before.'

Dyrakova had met too many people not to have acquired a technique for glossing over inconvenient gaps in her memory.

'All is well with you, I hope,' she said without committing herself, and held out her hand.

The hand was duly kissed.

'And now,' said Dyrakova, 'the photographers! We must not keep them waiting. My hat—it is becoming?'

'Divinely,' murmured the Prince.

CHAPTER XVI

On Tuesday morning the inevitable happened. Gustave's godson called on Quill. He made certain of his quarry by arriving simultaneously with the h'English breakfast.

Gustave's godson was ambitious, intense, and long-winded. He was not going to spend all his life in a mouldy little village pottering among the vegetable-marrows. He was taking correspondence courses in Economics, International Law and Mass Oratory—all he needed was a jeune fille sérieuse with a nice *dot*, and he was going to end up Chief of the Paris Police. Meanwhile, there was this little mystery to be solved for his godfather. He had to beat the Sûreté to it. Not that this should be difficult. The Sûreté were altogether too laborious. They were still busy with trifling details of the first murder, obscuring the broad sweep of the case with their eternal finger-prints, and inessential details of private lives. All the world knew Citrolo was a blackmailer. All the world knew that the Baron de Rabinovitch was a nasty bit of work. Find someone who disliked them both, and . . .

But just as the much-tried Quill thought he was going to elucidate the 'Means, motive, opportunity' theme Gustave arrived.

'Bon jour, mon ami,' he hailed Quill. 'Bon jour, Gaston. Il fait beau—hein?'

Clearly he was in the best of humours for it was raining.

'By to-morrow,' he announced, seating himself on the edge of Quill's bed and pouring himself out Quill's cup of coffee, 'all will again be peace. The murderer will be arrested. The Sûreté will be gone and at last I will have time to show the man Stroganoff how to grow roses. The first prize in St. Petersburg—pah!'

Clearly the grievance still rankled.

'The Sûreté making an arrest?' asked Quill.

'The Sûreté,' Gustave snorted. 'It is I, Gustave Clemenceau, who pounce.'

'And I,' said the godson.

'Entendu,' agreed Gustave. 'We pounce together. To-night we arrest the criminal.'

'Which one?' asked Quill.

But Gustave was giving away no secrets.

'Mon cher Watson,' he said chaffingly, 'you have all the facts. You have but to draw the inferences. They are irrefutable.

'In that case,' said Quill, 'why wait till to-night?'

'There are reasons,' said Gustave mysteriously.

Quill remembered it was Tuesday. 'You amuse yourself again?'

'Non,' said Gustave, looking apprehensively at his godson.

'Ça serais samedi cette semaine,' said the godson, unmoved.

'Tais-toi,' snapped Gustave. He turned to Quill. 'To complete the case there is still one witness to be seen. We await anxiously the arrival of the widow of Citrolo.'

He was not the only one. The entire town was waiting.

*   *   *

The widow of Citrolo lay in a cabin of *The Ziegfeld Girlie*. The luxury yacht balanced itself precariously on top of a mountain which was soon to subside into a valley.

The lavender tie had stopped telling Prince Artishok what a good sailor he was. He too was prostrate as the boat climbed laboriously up the mountain again.

Prince Artishok sat in the saloon drinking brandy.

The blast concentrated on a mast. It won easily.

'Only once in all my forty years' experience,' began the Captain heavily. . . .

The first officer was damned if he was going to listen all over again. Ever since the Captain had decided to write his memoirs, life was just one long reminiscence.

'C'est le Mistral,' shouted the man at the wheel.

'C'est le Sirrocco,' shouted the man who had come to relieve him. 'Nous serons bien en retard.'

*   *   *

Inside the peaceful harbour of La Bazouche the little launch bobbed comfortably at its anchor. Adjusting its riding-lights was Jean. Jean was an honest man. He had been with Button-hooke for six weeks now, and loathed every one of them. Taxi-ing Sadie Souse to and from the yacht was no occupation for a seaman.

Outside the little port the sea churned blackly. It was past seven o'clock. The yacht should be arriving any minute now.

'She ought to be here soon.' Four mackintoshes battled along the quayside.

'Supposing he won't be bribed,' asked Galybchik, eaten up by last-minute doubts.

'Leave it to me,' promised Stroganoff. 'I am the briber experienced.'

'I will deal with the finance,' contradicted Arenskaya, 'it will be cheaper.'

'Poof!' said Stroganoff, 'you are extravagant. It is well known. Did you not pay the swindle bijoutier. . . .?'

The wind drowned the rest of the reminiscence from Quill's ears.

'Voilà,' said Stroganoff, 'we are arrived.' He gazed doubtfully at the plank that served as gangway. 'You go first,' he suggested to Quill.

But honest Jean had climbed out to meet them.

'Pas à louer,' he said brusquely.

It was very soon evident that honest Jean merited his name. All that Stroganoff wanted was that Jean should risk his job by taking strangers on a joy-ride to the yacht, taking off only one of the three passengers wishing to go ashore, and riding without lights to some strange mooring-place. Practically money for marmalade. Yet it was not till Stroganoff raised his initial offer of two hundred to two thousand francs that honest Jean showed signs of listening. At twenty-two hundred he was willing to consider. At twenty-five the whole thing was off. And at twenty-six hundred they clinched. There was a slight hitch when it transpired that Stroganoff had forgotten to bring his wallet but Quill had incautiously brought his.

'Here she comes now,' said Jean. Nobody could see anything but they took his word for it.

Quill jumped into the boat and helped Galybchik in. Stroganoff put a cautious foot on the plank.

'What you do?' screamed Arenskaya. 'You ruin us. You wish Dryakova to see you?'

'You do not estimate my cunning sufficient,' said Stroganoff, hurt. 'I come prepared. Regardez!' He pulled from his pocket the bright red beard that had been specially dyed for the King in *Coq d'Or* and clamoured for a mirror.

Arenskaya settled the argument by snatching the beard from him and throwing it into the sea.

'Go back,' she commanded, 'and play with your Casino. And do not dare to show your face till Dyra she is on the stage.'

'But it is essential that I go,' argued Stroganoff. 'Without me all is bungle.'

'I go,' decided Arenskaya, picking up her skirts.

Quill hastily ordered Jean to push off.

Out in the choppy seas Quill marvelled at himself. What a holiday this had turned out to be. First he was pitch-forked into a murder case, next he was pitch-forked out of it, and now he was on his way to kidnap a seasick ballerina. If only Scotland Yard could see him now. But then he doubted if Scotland Yard would approve of his growing friendships with card-sharpers and diamond double-dealers.

'Do you think Dyrakova will rumble?' The anxious Galybchik interrupted his thoughts.

To Quill this seemed inevitable but he did not want to sound discouraging. 'Not a chance,' he said reassuringly. 'She's never seen either of us and we'll get her on to the stage so quickly she'll never realize she's in the wrong theatre. That is if Stroganoff has the sense to stay out of sight.'

'He's wonderful,' sighed Galybchik, 'no one else could have thought of such a plan.'

Quill felt inclined to agree.

*   *   *

The Ziegfeld Girlie, staggering slightly, let down a ladder. The passengers were waiting to alight. The one in three overcoats was Dyrakova.

Groggily she allowed Quill's steady arms to lower her into the boat. After her, little round Marya, less groggy, less precious, but stubbornly persistent, awaited assistance. Quill took her too, and her numerous valises.

The lavender tie stepped confidently forward. But the launch had gone. So had his balance.

'How's the water?' asked Prince Artishok blandly, leaning over the rail. There seemed to be a long swim ahead of him.

*   *   *

In the launch a swaying Dyrakova clung to Quill.

'Terrible, terrible,' she sobbed. 'We have been ill. You promise me it will be smooth. You are naughty, Mistaire Buttonhooke, and I not forgive you soon.'

'I am not Buttonhooke,' explained Quill.

Marya bristled immediately. 'Why he come not to meet us? This we do not understand.'

'He's very busy,' said Galybchik.

'I am a busy woman too, but I remember my manners,' declared Dyrakova. 'I regret much that I come. The journey was a nightmare, and the ordeal horrible is in front of me. To dance *Giselle* without the rehearsal and with a musical director I do not know—only Dyrakova would undertake this.'

'Wonderful,' said Galybchik.

'I spoil that Mistaire Button'ooke. De Basil he would have come to Marseille for me. Vladimir he would have come to Paris. Mon pauvre, Vladimir,' she sighed, 'to do what he ask, it was impossible. But my heart it bleed for him.'

To lend plausibility to this statement she rummaged in her

bag for a hanky. It was a large bag—black and forbidding, bristling with odd pockets and substantial locks. Almost a portable safe, thought Quill, examining it with interest.

'The Otchi Tchernia diamonds there?' he asked.

'Once yes,' said Dyrakova sadly, 'but that long time ago. It is five years since I sell them, you silly boy.'

'You've sold them?' With a final click Quill's jig-saw puzzle fell into place. Everything was now so clear that even Gustave could be made to see it.

'But they still live,' continued Dyrakova, 'they are now my studio in Paris, where every day I teach my method.' She turned anxiously to Marya. 'Think you, Anna, she will remember to begin with the *plié?*'

'Who knows?' said Marya darkly.

The launch ran into a choppy passage. With a groan Dyrakova forgot all her other worries and subsided into her seat.

*   *   *

In a deserted cove a powerful car awaited the arrival of the launch. The driver sat jauntily in his seat combing out a moist red beard. One look at it and Quill hastily bundled Dyrakova into the back seat.

The driver experimented with his gears. Dyrakova screamed as the car backed boisterously towards the water. In the nick of time Stroganoff remembered the brake.

*   *   *

Eight o'clock at the Casino Stroganoff. Anatole, the Commissionaire, on duty outside the stage-door is pushing back the whiskered foam of Russian generals. No one is to be allowed back-stage, not even the dancers.

At the Casino Buttonhooke the little Ostorojno is fixing her eyelashes for *Giselle*. Already she has been sick three times. Even though it is by no means certain she will have to go on for Dyrakova in the great dramatic rôle, she is terror-stricken. Even after weeks of preparation *Giselle* supplies a high note in temperamental crises. Though tough ballerinas, bustling on for their three hundred and sixtieth performance in this tinted lithograph, may acquire an outward veneer of nonchalance, the youngsters cannot be expected to achieve these heights. They are going through hell and they show it. Anecdotes of other dancers' failures in similar circumstances for once fail to cheer them up.

And here is the little Ostorojno not really knowing whether she should indulge in nerves or disappointment. No signs of Dyrakova yet. She wished she would come. She wished she wouldn't. If only David were dancing with her. . . .

Eight-fifteen at the Casino Stroganoff. The shining dome of M'sieur le Directeur arrives beaming through the throng. 'But assuredly Dyrakova dances. Have I not promised it?'

Arenakaya is back-stage knocking firmly on Dovolno's door. Dovolno is relieved to hear the news. Nothing would have induced him to go on with the fat girl.

And here is Ernest Smithsky, rapping timidly on the door of Olga's dressing-room at the Casino Buttonhooke. He has come to wish the trembling dancer luck—to reassure her that he will be there on the stage to give her courage. Really it was a shame she did not hear him.

*   *   *

At half-past eight the flowers began to pour in. Yielding though the local soil might be, the town's chief florist found it difficult to cope with all the duplicated orders for bouquets to be delivered to the same person at the two Casinos simultaneously.

*   *   *

Twenty to nine at the Casino Stroganoff. The Balleto-Medico is telling Stroganoff what he will do to him if there is no Dyrakova.

At eighteen minutes to nine there is a familiar pounding down the corridors of the Casino Buttonhooke. Madame Ostorojno arrives to do all a mother can to assure the triumph of a daughter.

'Are your shoes all right? Did they freshen that wreath? Now just relax for five minutes and mother will dress you.'

'Mamushka . . .'

'Of course you'll be all right. I've never known a dress rehearsal go better. Why, do you know what Prince Artishok said to me at the end of your mad scene? . . .'

Mothers have their uses.

At a quarter to nine Bazouche is unable to make up its mind which Casino to patronize. The town has been whipped into one vast purée of excitement. The same star, in the same rôle, in the same ballet at the same hour—in which Casino? The announcements are similar; only the design on the posters differed—and, of course, the Casino. Rumour has been more emphatic, more highly coloured, and more contradictory than ever. The rich, the *chic*, and the near-celebrities invade the Casino Buttonhooke—at least they can be reasonably sure of making the gossip columns of the Continental *Daily Mail*. The ballet-goers plonked heavily for Stroganoff.

But in both factions Dyrakova and her famous *developé* were the common coin of conversation.

At ten to nine the amateur photographer parked himself outside the stage-door of the Casino Buttonhooke—his 'Nose for noos' had twitched him there. The solid phalanx of flash-men already stationed only served to confirm his faith in his *flaire*.

Five minutes to go and no Dyrakova. Already the little Ostorojno was seeing herself on the stage facing a disappointed audience. Dovolno was seeing the fat girl.

At nine o'clock a short huddle of cloak and shawl made its way through the Casino Gardens. It swayed, it lurched, it staggered. Clearly the earth was not its element.

Behind it a shorter, rounder bundle swayed, lurched, and staggered. Clearly the earth was not its element either. Bringing up the rear, cast in the rôle of amateur sheep dog, came Quill.

One look at the figure and Anatole sprang to offer a quivering arm. 'Madame,' he breathed, 'permettez?'

And so Dyrakova—shaken, shrill, and reeling, entered the Casino Stroganoff. The first person to greet her was Arenskaya.

'Ah—c'est toi,' said Arenskaya, with relief.

'Ah—c'est toi,' said Dyrakova, with dislike.

They went through the motions of a warm embrace.

'I am dressed—I am made-up—I am ready—Dyrakova is never late,' she announced—and fainted. . . .

Stroganoff's anxious dome appeared round a piece of scenery. 'She is all right?'

'Perfect,' hissed Arenskaya. 'Get down.' The dome bobbed down.

At the Casino Buttonhooke a sheepish white waistcoat regretted to a sceptical audience the sudden illness of Dyrakova. Her rôle would be taken by that talented dancer . . .

Ostorojno was popular but the audience had come to see Dyrakova. The gallery started to tell the white waistcoat what it thought of Buttonhooke. With great presence of mind the conductor started the overture. The curtains parted to reveal the stage with its lollipop house and blasted oak school of *décor*.

At the Casino Stroganoff the conductor began to beat a vigorous baton. Clearly he was making up for lost time.

The brought-round Dyrakova was calling loudly for Lord Buttonhooke. She'd come all this way to dance for him and he wasn't even here to wish her luck.

'He come,' promised Arenskaya. 'Soon he come racing in (how right she was!) but now he is in his box, waiting.'

'And Vladimir?' asked the fast-recovering Dyrakova. 'You have left him at last, I see. C'était bien le temps. Me, I think that Vladimir is phut!'

An adjacent piece of scenery trembled with emotion.

Arenskaya pushed it upright. 'Vladimir,' she said sharply, 'is the fool.'

This point settled, she escorted the guest artist to her seat in the wings.

'So many of my little ones,' sighed Dyrakova, catching sight of a bunch of *corps-de-ballet*.

'They, too, have follow me to Button'ooke,' said Arenskaya, 'they could not bear to give up my classes.' This explained all, she felt.

But now Dyrakova was about to get going. She tested her shoe, she scolded Marya, she fumed, she fretted, and she ripped off a piece of her fichu. It was too bad that she had not had time to rehearse with Dovolno. But he was an old pupil of hers and she knew him to be reliable. Besides, what did it matter if they did go wrong? The public were the blind ones, and now there was no Pavlo Citrolo to tell on her.

The bunch of ballet-girls flocked into the bright lights. It was at this moment that Dyrakova decided it was high time to remember she was a widow.

'I have had many husbands,' she wept on the unprepared Arenskaya. 'But only one have I ever loved. Pavlo—Pavlo—I am desolate.'

'The stage,' said Arenskaya several bars too soon. 'It waits.'

*   *   *

At the Casino Buttonhooke Ernest Smithsky bounded boyishly on and knocked at the door of the little lollipop house.

At the Casino Stroganoff Dovolno rat-rat-tatted on the door. The Balleto-Medico swallowed.

At the Casino Buttonhooke a roar of welcome greeted the little Ostorojno. The fair-minded gallery had decided that it was not her fault.

'Dyrakova,' breathed a late arrival to the stalls. 'She's very well preserved for her age.'

At the Casino Stroganoff a great ballerina took her stage. She was thirty-eight. She was life-ridden. She was seasick. But she took her stage.

*   *   *

With none of the benevolence of his portrait Lord Button-hooke paced the office door. A fine business this had turned out to be. He was a laughing-stock. All that publicity, and then no Dyrakova. Only a sodden lavender tie.

'So you and the Prince rowed ashore,' he jeered. 'That was resourceful of you.' He turned savagely. 'And where's Dyrakova?'

The lavender tie reeled. 'Isn't she here?'

There was a knock at the door. Prince Artishok came in—every regal hair in place. Lord Buttonhooke veered on him. 'Well?'

'Good news,' said the Prince gravely. 'Dyrakova has practically consented to sell the Otchi Tchernia.'

'Oh, she has—has she?'

'She's weakening,' said the Prince. 'I think perhaps the sight of ready money. . . . Did you,' he asked, 'get that money from the bank as I suggested?'

'It's in the safe,' said Buttonhooke, 'and,' he exploded suddenly, 'it stays in the safe. Just wait till I lay hands on that woman. Making me a laughing-stock—me! Where the hell is she, anyway?'

The lavender tie shrugged. The Prince, who could have made a pretty shrewd guess, remained silent. He was reflecting what a pity it was he did not know the combination of the safe.

'I've got it,' bellowed Buttonhooke. 'She's with that thief Stroganoff. And you—the two of you—stood on that boat and let him get away with it. Pah!'

He tore out of the office. Prince Artishok, after one loving look at the safe, followed.

CHAPTER XVII

Two Giselles had been beautifully laid to rest. Two seducers had staggered their wild despair. The curtains descended and rose again upon two sets of bowing principals. Neither performance had been without its incidents.

The little Ostorojno had all the advantages of youth and endowed her Tess scenes with moving pathos.

But when it came to going mad there was nobody to touch Dyrakova. Naturally.

In the wings little round Marya had gone mad nearly as well.

A mountain of flowers staggered into the star's dressing-room at the Casino Stroganoff. It was Quill. The babble of ecstasy that escorted the ballerina to her door had unanimously picked him for the rôle of porter.

'You were marvellous,' they cooed at the ballerina.

'Superb!'

'Enchanting!'

'Almost I cried myself!'

'Always the great Dyrakova!'

'Tchort vosmi!'[1] cried the great Dyrakova. 'That conductor! He must be dismissed at once. Where's Button'ooke?' she glared.

An uneasy silence settled on the babble. They looked at each other.

A bald dome burst ecstatically into the room and flung both hands firmly round the unsuspecting ballerina.

'Dyrashka, you were superb! Marvellous! Enchanting! Almost I cried myself.'

'Not bad for your age,' observed Arenskaya, who had followed him in.

[1] 'The devil take it.' (Russian).

371

Dyrakova disentangled herself. Gallantly Stroganoff stooped to kiss her hand. It almost slapped his face.

'Vladimir!' screamed Dyrakova. 'What are you doing here?'

'I worship at your feet,' said Stroganoff glibly. 'Ah! You have made me very happy. Never since the night that Benois he nearly come, has the Ballet Stroganoff had such a success. And Button'ooke he bit the dust.'

Dyrakova swallowed. Carried away, Stroganoff shook a playful finger at her.

'Ah, my little one—did you for a moment imagine that I should permit you to dance for a newspaper? No—the *Ballet Russe* it is your home. Your Vladimir has led you back to it.'

A strangled scream tore through the ballerina's throat.

'You are tired,' said Stroganoff, kindly. 'Lie down. Relax while I tell you how clever I arrange it all.'

The ballerina opened and closed her mouth. Still no words came.

'When you step into the launch,' beamed Stroganoff, 'so tired, so ill, so swaying—it was my friends who steady your feet and guide you. And it was I, your Vladimir, who drove you to the hotel. In a beard,' he explained. 'Tiens—I have it somewhere.' He fumbled.

With a suddenness that blew away three carnations Dyrakova's voice came back.

'Aieeeeee. . . .'

A dozen pairs of hands covered a dozen pairs of ears.

'It is the last straw. It is more than too much. You plague me. You beseech me. You trick me. All this I might forgive, for you are mad—it is well known. But is it necessary that you bump me all over the road, that you twist me round corners and that you skid me into traffic lights? . . .'

'Mais soyez raisonnable,' pleaded Stroganoff. 'It is but three weeks since I have my carte rose.'

'Imbécile,' screamed Arenskaya. 'Did I not tell you not to drive? It is the miracle there was no accident.' She sat down, overcome by the shock of the narrow escape.

'Poof!' said Stroganoff, his vanity wounded. 'You excite yourself for nothing. Galybchik she tell me I am the driver superb.'

'And is it nothing,' screamed Dyrakova, 'that my reputation it is ruin? My reliability that has always been a password in the ballet. . . .'

'And our Arabesques,' screamed Marya, 'they are the password, too.'

'And was it in Yokohama that your reliability was so evident?' screamed Arenskaya. 'When you go away for two performances with the Minister of War? Or was it in Buenos Aires when? . . .'

'Aiee,' screamed Dyrakova, 'make way all of you while I scratch the eyes out of this creature.'

'And I,' promised Marya, 'scratch out the eyes of Vladimir.' She advanced relentlessly.

A furious bellow distracted her attention. It was Lord Buttonhooke—his party at his heels.

Buttonhooke glared round, found Dyrakova, and planted himself firmly in front of her.

'So there you are?' he accused. 'You false alarm! You dirty double-crosser!'

'Schwolotz,'[1] screamed Dyrakova, concentrating on this new enemy.

'Schwolotz yourself,' retorted Buttonhooke. He did not know what it meant but it sounded good.

Screaming wildly Arenskaya fell on Lord Buttonhooke and pummelled his bulging shirt into better trim.

'How dare you insult our Dyrashka? How dare you come in here and make the noise? You, bezgramotnie,[2] who do not know a brisé from a battement.'

'You flatter him,' said Dyrakova. 'I doubt if he knows a plié from a pirouette.'

Arm in arm Arenskaya and Dyrakova glared their defiance.

Arm in arm Stroganoff and Marya filled the breach.

Arm in arm Galybchik and Quill collapsed on the sofa.

Lord Buttonhooke took a deep breath.

'After this,' he said, 'you need never hope to dance at any

[1] Schwolotz—swine.
[2] Bezgramotnie—illiterate.

theatre of mine. Neither,' he remembered suddenly, 'need you hope to sell me your Otchi Tchernia diamonds.'

'Diamonds,' said Dyrakova. 'He raves of diamonds. Vladimir, my angel, call me the lunatic asylum. This man thinks I would sell him my diamonds—even if I had them. He must be mad.'

'No diamonds!' Sadie Souse made her first contribution to the conversation.

'No diamonds, my child,' said Dyrakova sadly. 'All that is left of them is a studio in Paris. No diamonds—no cars—no bankers—only a tired old woman, seasick and abused.' She burst into tears. Reaction had set in.

Everyone bustled round with handkerchiefs.

Prince Artishok sighed deeply as he edged past Quill towards the door.

'Bang goes six months build-up,' he complained.

'Hey!' said Quill. 'Wait a minute?'

'Impossible,' said the Prince courteously, and passed on.

Useless to shout when everybody was shouting already. Quill jumped up in pursuit. But the Prince had too great a start. By the time Quill had elbowed his way through the hotly disputing throng the Prince was out of sight. What was worse the doorway was blocked by Gustave. Quill grasped him urgently by the shoulder. Gustave shook him off.

'Everybody quiet,' he shouted. 'Nobody to leave the room. Sit down all.'

Quill took a fresh grip.

'Dacarpo. He's gone—after him.'

'Did you not hear me say—sit down?' asked Gustave, all formal. This was to be his big moment and no one was going to rob him of it. 'Did you not hear me order you to sit down?' he bawled at the throng.

Quill appealed to the severe figure by Gustave's side. 'Let me through, please?'

'Silence!' The Sûreté was solid for Gustave.

By this time some sort of order had been restored. Most of the *corps-de-ballet* sat on the floor—the divan had been collared

by Dyrakova. Arenskaya and Stroganoff inserted themselves
on either side. Buttonhooke paced up and down muttering.

'But you must listen,' Quill argued.

'Make way,' said Gustave, pushing him aside.

Kurt Kukumber strode in. Behind him, far less enthusiastic,
was Vanilla. Gustave's godson brought up the rear.

Gustave ran an eagle eye round the room.

'The fat mother, she is not here.'

'She comes,' said the godson reassuringly.

She came—muttering fiercely of a daughter in hysterics and
a musical director who . . .

Gallantly Stroganoff offered Madame Ostorojno his seat.
Lord Buttonhooke took it.

'Bon,' said Gustave. 'Now we are all here. I commence.'

'Prince Artishok is gone,' said Quill desperately.

'Silence,' said the Sûreté, pained. How right Scotland Yard
had been to get rid of this man!

'You ask yourselves,' began Gustave, 'why are we here? I
tell you. It is to elucidate the assassinations of Pavlo Citrolo
and the Baron de Rabinovitch. In this room there are all the
persons associated with the crime.'

'Hey!' said Lord Buttonhooke.

The Sûreté quelled him with a glance.

'Among them is the guilty one. Let him tremble while I,
Gustave Clemenceau, trace his guilt!'

Galybchik turned pale.

'Mais qu'est ce que c'est que ça,' screamed Dyrakova
suddenly. It had just occurred to her that somebody else was
pinching her floor.

The Sûreté dealt faithfully with her.

Amid a stream of interruptions Gustave began his discourse.
Gradually he got more and more upset. The scene was not
running at all according to script. All day he had been visualizing himself, the centre of an impressed silence, logically
weighing each suspect in the balance, relentlessly sifting the
evidence until at last the stark form of the murderer stood
mercilessly revealed. Instead he was never allowed to complete

a sentence without some interruption. There was the English-man fidgeting to chase some petty thief of his own. There was this Russian dancer who seemed to think—I ask you—that she was the only woman the late Citrolo had ever loved. There was the man Lord Buttonhooke and the man Stroganoff, busily conducting some quarrel of their own and paying no attention to him at all. And there was the fair American who appeared to have lost some diamonds. Only his murderer maintained the proper attitude of decorum.

Tiring of his unappreciative audience Gustave decided to blue-pencil a large chunk of his discourse.

'And so,' he said unexpectedly, 'we are left with only one person who in each case had the motive, the means, and the opportunity.'

Quill swore.

'One who knew the secret passage—who was blackmailed by Citrolo. . . .'

'Not the blackmail,' objected Kurt Kukumber. 'The collaboration.'

'Silence,' said the Sûreté.

'And,' said Gustave, 'one who had good reason to fear the tell-tale tongue of the Baron.' With his grimmest expression he crossed the floor. 'Dino Vanilla, I arrest you for . . .'

'It is a lie,' screamed Vanilla, leaping to his feet.

'It is a lie,' screamed Arenskaya.

'It is a lie,' agreed Quill. 'The actual murderer is by now well on his way across the frontier.'

It seemed to the Sûreté quite time to find out once and for all what this Englishman was babbling about.

Quill told him very quickly.

'Banco Dacarpo,' he said, 'alias Prince Alexis Artishok, left this room just before you came in.'

Banco Dacarpo! That was different.

'Which way?' said the Sûreté and raced out of the room.

*　　*　　*

Enquiry revealed that the Prince had made for the waterfront. Further enquiry found honest Jean ruefully rubbing his head. Something had hit him on it very hard, and the launch had gone without him.

But a speed-boat, the stream-lined property of a Culture King from Kansas, bobbed invitingly at their feet.

'Dacarpo is losing his grip,' commented the Sûreté climbing in. Quill leapt after him. Stroganoff a short head behind. Gustave followed laboriously, most of his mind still on the prisoner he had left in charge of his godson. They all turned to help Buttonhooke.

'I drive,' announced Stroganoff hopefully.

The Sûreté pushed him back.

Quill started the engine. The *Pride of Pittsburg* came to life. Like a greyhound, it nosed round a few boats, brushed against a barge or so, and headed for the straight.

Outside it was still choppy.

'Le voilà!' pointed Stroganoff. In the grey dawn a black blur was riding the waves a mile or so ahead.

Quill opened the throttle. The boat shot forward. Stroganoff shot backwards—on to Buttonhooke's lap.

The *Pride of Pittsburg* ate up the distance wave by wave. The black blur solidified. Almost you could see the Union Jack.

On went the *Pride of Pittsburg*. Now you could see Prince Artishok upright at the helm, as debonair as ever and apparently not at all alarmed at his approaching fate. Easily one of the nicest murderers Quill had ever known.

Another few minutes and they would be alongside.

It seemed almost a shame to catch him.

The *Pride of Pittsburg* seemed to think so too. It spluttered, puffed, and petered out.

'Petrol tank punctured,' announced the Sûreté briefly.

The gap between the two boats was widening again. Soon the Prince would be out of sight. The figure was standing up and semaphoring. Laboriously Quill spelt out the message:

P . A . L . O . O . K . A . S .

Banco Dacarpo had not lost his grip.

CHAPTER XVIII

'I REFUSE to believe he was a card-sharper,' protested Button-hooke, 'why I played pinochle with him every night for three months and never lost.'

'Maybe we have a little game sometime?' asked Stroganoff hopefully.

With Buttonhooke and a downcast Gustave at the oars, the *Pride of Pittsburg* nosed its way slowly towards the harbour. Dacarpo would be well over the frontier before the wires could get busy.

'The capture of a lifetime,' sighed the Sûreté. 'Right through our fingers.'

'Why we chase him?' Gustave asked plaintively. He had not been told.

'It is Banco Dacarpo,' explained the Sûreté, and Gustave was impressed. Even he had heard the name.

'He disguise himself as the Prince,' said Stroganoff. 'This is clever. And Button'ooke he feed him for many months. This is funny.'

Lord Buttonhooke caught a crab.

A sudden apprehension seized Gustave. 'Is it possible that Dacarpo is our assassin?'

'Is it?' asked the Sûreté.

'There's no doubt about it,' said Quill. 'I realized it the moment I heard Dyrakova no longer possessed the Otchi Tchernia diamonds. It made everything clear.'

'Damned if it does,' muttered Buttonhooke. 'What on earth was the fellow up to trying to make me buy a necklace that wasn't there? And all this stuff about not talking to Dyrakova?'

'As pretty a swindle as ever I met,' said Quill. 'And beauti-

fully simple—once he had won your confidence as Prince
Artishok. It was easy for him to persuade Sadie she wanted
the necklace. It was not difficult for Sadie to persuade you to
buy it for her. Insert the story of a Dyrakova, so proud that
she would only discuss money with blue blood—and there he
was—the accredited intermediary. Wasn't it drummed into
you that you were on no account to mention diamonds to
Dyrakova—only to produce the money—ready money?'

Lord Buttonhooke groaned.

'With the vendor and the purchaser not on bartering terms,
the Prince had only to wait a suitable moment to tell Buttonhooke he had clinched the deal, produce some convincing
imitation from his pocket, collect the ready money, ostensibly
to take to Dyrakova, and make his getaway while the ballerina
danced. The Otchi Tchernia are well known and Dyrakova is
above suspicion.'

Lord Buttonhooke groaned again.

'But the murders,' objected the Sûreté, 'Dacarpo has never
been a killer.'

'Dacarpo,' said Quill, 'was a swindler by profession—but a
murderer by accident. A man pierced his disguise. Pavlo
Citrolo, the blackmailer, the man with the uncanny memory
for details, recognized him. It was an unfortunate recognition
for Citrolo, especially as I can prove he had no intention of
blackmailing in such a dangerous quarter. His note-book tells
us that he did not blackmail big shots. It says that he tried it
only once and barely got away with his life. It is probable that
the one attempt was on Dacarpo though we shall never know
for certain.'

'But Dacarpo could not guess Citrolo's prudence. He only
knew that he had been recognized by a blackmailer and he was
worried. I doubt if he decided then and there to murder Citrolo.
But when chance—or rather our friend Stroganoff—put him
in his way, drugged in a deserted room . . .'

'It was the mistake to leave him there,' said Stroganoff
gravely. 'I see now. I should have take him to the hotel.'

'But why,' demanded Gustave, reluctant to relinquish his

Vanilla, 'must it be Dacarpo who murder? There were many others in the office that night.'

'Quite,' said the Sûreté.

'The second murder proves that,' said Quill. 'The Baron was not killed until Dacarpo knew that he had been told of the impending diamond deal. As a matter of fact,' he admitted, 'I told him myself—I did not suspect him at the time. The Baron sent for him while we were all watching the ballet at the Buttonhooke Casino and demanded a show-down. Dacarpo might bluff Lord Buttonhooke that he was on the level but Rabinovitch was too much of a crook himself not to recognize another. I should think that Dacarpo probably offered him a share but the Baron's strange loyalty to Buttonhooke precluded his accepting. So Dacarpo poisoned him. Once you have committed one murder for an object, another murder comes easier.'

Lord Buttonhooke sighed heavily. He grieved for his murdered admirer, he grieved for his reputation as a shrewd business-man, but most of all he grieved because he would now have to give Sadie Souse *carte blanche* at Cartier's.

The *Pride of Pittsburg* nosed its way slowly towards anchorage.

A frustrated sun peered through the clouds. All the really interesting things seemed to happen while it was asleep.

ENVOI

'My marrows,' said Gustave proudly, 'Regardez! Nothing like this at St. Petersburg!'

It was a week since the weary row back. Quill on the point of departure had come to make his farewells.

'I trust,' said the courteous Gustave, 'that you have enjoyed your holiday.' He straightened himself wearily. 'I, too, hope to take a holiday soon. The long holiday.'

'Retiring?' asked Quill.

'Bientôt,' said Gustave. 'I tire of the life of crime. I have ma petite rente and but yesterday I bought the gold-shares that will soon add butter to my petit-pain.'

'Gold shares?' said Quill, startled.

'You have heard?' said Gustave. 'It was the good Kukumber himself who selected them for me. Now I have but to wait for the rise. . . .'

Quill left him waiting and ran back to the *Hôtel Moins-Magnifique*.

But he was too late. Kurt Kukumber had not slept in his bed at the hotel that night.

'The management wait two days,' said the clerk, 'and then we are ruthless. If his uncle do not come by then we open the box.'

*   *   *

The smoking-room of the S.S. *Transatlantic* displayed a notice:

   'Passengers are warned against the menace of professional gamblers making the crossing.'

Feeling vaguely proud, Kurt Kukumber lit a cigar and strode off to make friends on the promenade deck.

*   *   *

'What you think!' Stroganoff pounced on Quill as he entered the office to say good-bye. 'The news stupendous. This morning I receive an offer superb from Bolivia for my ballet.'

'One night stands,' said Galybchik, not too enthusiastically.

'But the money it is good,' said Stroganoff. 'Most of it. Me and my ballet sail immediate. Already I argue with the steamship company for the credit.'

'And the Casino?' asked Quill.

'The Casino—poof!' said Stroganoff. 'For some days already it bore me. We sell—doubtless for the profit immense.'

*   *   *

The newspaper Quill bought at Dover carried an advertisement.

CASINO FOR SALE
The opportunity that tempts
Apply in haste to:
Vladimir Stroganoff
Poste-Restante
Bolivia

Six Curtains

for

Stroganova

"All day long they point the sandal
On the Coast of Coromandel."

OSBERT SITWELL

Chapter One

❦

THE first curtain was all that a curtain should be.

For one thing it came down slowly and gave the company plenty of time to line up, bow radiantly to the audience, and politely to one another. The house rose at them. It cooed, it shouted, it clapped, it waved its programmes.

After all, London had seen worse Coppélias than this—one or two.

The second curtain belonged to Swanhilda. The little Stroganova took it alone, banked in by bouquets, with more arriving. Roses and carnations from Mamoushka, orchids from Stroganoff—which was as it should be—gladioli from the corps-de-ballet (deducted from the salary), rhododendrons from Arenskaya—where had she seen that basket before? Forget-me-nots from the conductor—as though she could! She frowned. She remembered herself. She smiled radiantly and the house roared its approval.

But by the third curtain the going was heavier.

"Assez de chi-chi," said Marie Rambert, and sat firmly down.

The clapping waned. They brought on Franz and Coppelius. They brought on the conductor. He brought on the distinguished oboist. The clapping spurted, but it was only a spurt. They brought on Vladimir Stroganoff. He brought on his banker. It helped a little but not much. Then they panicked, and brought on everything they could think of including a laurel wreath belonging to the imperturbable Ernest Smithsky, who threw a temperament that was nobody's business in the wings. They went on bowing.

In the circle S. J. Simon turned on Caryl Brahms. "You brought me here," he hissed.

By the fourth curtain Arnold Haskell had stopped saying 'Brava.'

The fifth curtain was definitely grim. Little Stroganova still smiled radiantly and bowed herself dizzy but the Duchess was adjusting her furs, Oliver Messel had already reached the pass door and Cecil Beaton was definitely feeling for his hat. Ninette de Valois patted a relaxed Margot Fonteyn on the shoulder and Professor Beaumont, who, it was rumoured, was planning to do for Coppélia what he had already done for Giselle, closed his note-book with a snap.

And still they did not play 'God save the King.'

*   *   *

In the wings chaos had encroached on the congratulations.

"Non! Non! Non!" screamed Arenskaya, the temperamental maîtresse-de-ballet whose slightest shrill was law, "The curtain it stay where it is. Down!" She pointed.

"Levez! Levez!" screamed a little old woman in black, flapping her arms in the air as though willing it to levitate. But as this failed she turned on a stage hand. "Oop! Oop!" she commanded in her fluent English. "All my life I wait for this moment," she appealed to his dazed better nature. Clearly she was a mother.

"Down," commanded Arenskaya.

"Oop," shrieked the mother.

Alone in the centre of the great stage of the Collodeum theatre the little Stroganova looked appealingly at them over a bank of miscellaneous objects.

"Viens! Viens!" Arenskaya was beckoning.

"Stay where you am," the little black woman commanded. "Oop," she jerked the stage hand.

The stage hand disengaged himself. Who did they take him for? Solomon? He made off.

"Ah bon," said the little woman in black. She pounced on the wheel. Arenskaya dragged her from it. They clawed.

A third pair of hands inserted themselves into the struggle and pulled the contestants apart. They were white hands, they were dimpled, and they had a different sort of ring on every finger.

"My darlings," said Vladimir Stroganoff. "Calm yourself immediate—both." He beamed at them. "Is this the moment to dispute yourselves? To-night of all nights, when we are in my dear London again, after the war so black, and make the opening triumphant and nearly enough moneys not to pay everyone. Non, non, non," he insisted. "To-morrow you tear the hair in comfort, but to-night," he patted their shoulders, "we are all the friends inseparable. So you tell Papa Stroganoff what is the matter and rest assured that he will find a way to satisfy you both." And he beamed confidently at the stage hand who had drifted back to watch.

"She demand that the curtain go up," screamed Arenskaya accusingly.

"She demand that the curtain stay doon," accused the small black woman. "You hear, Vladimir! Only five curtains and she demand that it stay doon."

"It is the common sense," screamed Arenskaya.

"It is the treachery," screamed the small black woman.

Out on the stage the little Stroganova was doing fouettés to keep herself warm.

Stroganoff pondered. "My darlings," he began, "soyez raisonable."

"Raisonable!" The small black woman quivered all over. "Moi!"

"A curtain," said Stroganoff, "is not a thing that just go up and down. It has," he pointed out, "to be demanded."

"And I demand that it stay down," said Arenskaya.

"And I," said the little black woman fiercely, "demand that you keep the promise you made to me many years ago in Petersburg in the name of our poor dead Tzar."

"Oh, that old promise," said Arenskaya. "He spit him of his promise."

It was a mistake. Stroganoff drew himself up.

"My word," he said, "is to me my bonds. Much better than

my bonds," he remembered. "Ankara Tramways," he explained sadly.

"Is this the moment to change the subject?" demanded the small black woman. "And anyway, did I not plead with you to buy the British War Loan?"

"Soyez raisonable," said Stroganoff. "What use to me is the three per cent.?"

"And what use to me is the broken promise?" demanded the small black woman. "All my life it bring me bad luck. In Yoko-hama," she said accusingly, "there was the earthquake!"

"And is it my fault?" asked Stroganoff.

"Who else?" said the small black woman. "In Buenos Aires," she went on, "Anton Palook he drop the ballerina in Giselle."

"That was his custom," said Arenskaya.

"Entendu," agreed the small black woman. "But this time," she quivered all over, "it is me! You are laughing, Vladimir?"

"No, no," said Stroganoff quickly. "I am all the sympathy. Continue, my darling." He waved her on.

The small black woman rummaged among her memories. She rejected a defaulting backer, the pearls that were found again—in her dressing-case—and what Massine had said to her at Massa-chusetts. "In Würtemburg," she produced, "I am dancing Lac des Cygnes and the curtain it come down and will not rise again, no—never, though we pull and we pull, and I," her voice rose to a scream, "have done but seventeen fouettés." She rounded on Stroganoff. "You promise me six curtains," she said doggedly, "and until you keep your word there is nothing but the misfortunes for us both."

Stroganoff was visibly impressed. "C'est vrai," he muttered, "did not my company arrive at Yalta au moment précis that Winston Churchill, the President, and One Other they go there too and my publicity," he shook his head sadly, "it go—poof!"

"It was the coincidence," said Arenskaya.

"It was the will of God," said the small black woman. She looked up at the curtain. "Oop," she said.

Stroganoff hesitated.

"Do you wish that history repeat itself," hissed the small black woman. "Was it not because of this that I walk out on you in Petersburg?"

"Only," pointed out Arenskaya, "you have walk back again."

But the small black woman took no notice. She had turned on Stroganoff and was confronting him like an infuriated cottage loaf.

"Nu," she said, "does the curtain go oop, or do I?"

The curtain did.

Out on the stage the little Stroganova, caught unawares, bent herself double as graciously as her hurry would permit. The applause seemed a little thin as she came up to be greeted by wave after wave of an empty crimson sea. The little argument that Mamoushka had waged had taken the best part of a quarter of an hour and the only hands left to applaud belonged to Lord Streatham, press agent to the Company. There was another man with him, but he was only raising a pair of sandy eyebrows.

"Down," said Arenskaya.

This time there was no argument.

Chapter Two

STROGANOFF'S office was the busiest place in the Collodeum Theatre. Accordingly it was situated at the end of a corridor and four flights of stairs, and the lifts had been out of order for years. Once there, however, the climber was amply rewarded. Photographs of Stroganoff festooned the wall space. Here and there a ballerina, poised on the pointes and scrawled all over with affectionate signatures, had somehow inserted herself, but in the main it was Stroganoff on the stage with his company around him, Stroganoff at the station, Stroganoff on the captain's bridge with an infuriated looking Captain, Stroganoff in the sunshine, Stroganoff in the snows, Stroganoff with the Aga Khan, and almost, but never quite, Stroganoff on a hearthrug smiling winningly at his rattle.

But the wall above the desk was reserved for Pavlova. Stroganoff sat below her, for he liked to feel that she was watching and smiling approvingly at the arrangements he made for his company, but there were times when he wondered.

On the desk stood a model of the Gare du Nord, delicately worked in silver and gold. It commemorated the ballet that bore its name and it had been presented to Stroganoff by its grateful choreographer, Nicholas Nevajno, on the opening night. How they had cheered! The bill did not reach Stroganoff till the following week. How his banker had cursed!

Now it was labelled 'Carry with Care. This side Oop.'

This morning Stroganoff was seated at his desk looking over the notices of last night's Coppélia. He read one and frowned. He read another and scowled. He read a third and tore it across.

"Mr. Stroganoff always reads all the notices himself," explained Lord Streatham sunnily.

"In America," said Stroganoff, "I read them too. They are mooch better. There we have the press ecstatic," he explained to the pair of sandy eyebrows, who had been waiting 'un petit moment' quite a long time now.

Lord Streatham, who had been waiting quite a long time with him, smiled uneasily.

"On the whole," he said.

"The *News Chronicle*—poof!" said Stroganoff. "The *Daily Telegraph*—pfui! *The Times*, ça ne compte pas." He threw the lot of them in the waste-paper basket. "Cigar," he offered.

Fortunately the box on the table still contained one. Unfortunately Stroganoff, forgetting his purpose, lit it himself.

"Eh bien?" he turned expansively to the sandy eyebrows. "What can I do for you, my friend? The interview with the little Stroganova?"

"Well . . ." said the sandy eyebrows.

"Bon, it is arrange," said Stroganoff. "You take her to the Savoy. I book the table now." He reached for the telephone. "And if they give me again the one in the corner where I cannot be seen," he thumped his fist, "I kick up the row that is the affair of nobody."

"Don't do that," said Lord Streatham uneasily. "Give the head-waiter a fiver."

Stroganoff pondered this. "It will be better," he decided, "if I give him tenner."

"By all means," said Lord Streatham cordially.

Stroganoff thought of something else. "You lend me?" he demanded confidently.

A shock of black hair slouched elegantly into the room, peered not very hopefully into the empty box of cigars, shook a disappointed head at the sandy eyebrows, frowned at Stroganoff, sighted Lord Streatham reluctantly extracting his wallet and brightened at once.

"Ah," said Nicholas Nevajno, choreographer of the future, "you lend me twenty pounds till next week?"

Lord Streatham looked definitely depressed.

"Or maybe," said Nevajno helpfully, "till the week after."

"Allons, allons," said Stroganoff. "We have not the time now to discuss the finance personal. If anyone borrow money in this office it is me." He stowed away the tenner. "And now you do me the favour and go," he announced, "for soon there comes one from whom I will borrow mooch money. Very mooch." He rubbed his hands.

The man with the sandy eyebrows raised both.

"It is the finance intricate," explained Stroganoff. "My ballet needs money and the man who comes he has too mooch. It is fair that he lose a little."

Lord Streatham winced.

"Lose?" said the man with the sandy eyebrows.

"It is not essential, this," said Stroganoff, "but it is very probable. But we will not weep for the rich one, mon cher, for he will have a wonderful time with my ballerinas while he is losing it and, au fond, it can only be what he expects."

"I see," said the man with the sandy eyebrows.

"Mr. Stroganoff will have his little joke," said Lord Streatham with hollow bonhomie.

"Assez," said Stroganoff. "Back to business. So you interview the little Stroganova at supper, and you remember to congratulate her on her six curtains."

"Ha!" said Nicholas Nevajno darkly. "That is what I come to see you about, Vladimir. If for Coppélia—this old-fashioned children's," his lip curled, "throwaway you have six curtains then for my concept colossal—the new one," he explained to the sandy eyebrows, "I demand twelve."

"Impossible," said Stroganoff promptly. "The stalls will be empty."

"It is not the stalls," said Nevajno, "it is the principle."

But at the word 'principle,' Stroganoff sighed heavily and shook a firm head.

"My friend," he said, "when two Russians discuss a principle it takes all night, and also, which is more important, all day." He looked at his watch. "The rich one is late and it is not good that he should hear too much about principle. So you please me and go. Shoo!" he said to clinch matters.

Lord Streatham went quickly.

"He has not lent me the twenty," said Nevajno. He went after him.

But the man with the sandy eyebrows settled himself more comfortably.

"Now, Mr. Stroganoff," he said.

But Stroganoff was crawling on all fours on the floor. He had unearthed a large poster and was trying to spread it flat.

"This end," he said with considerable exertion, "I fasten under the fender, so. You, mon cher, shall sit on the other so that it does not all the time get up and hit me. Here is a cushion." He flung it.

They arranged themselves, the sandy eyebrows on the poster and Stroganoff standing back to admire.

"It is effective—no?" he asked.

The sandy eyebrows got up to look.

"But non, non," said Stroganoff. "Do not impatient yourself. Presently it will be your turn to admire, and I," he promised, "will sit on the cushion."

"Mr. Stroganoff," said the sandy eyebrows firmly while the poster rolled up over the fender, "I am not here to . . ."

The door opened. Two figures burst in, one a screaming ramrod, the other an offended steam-roller.

"Voilà!" screamed Arenskaya. "Now we shall see what Stroganoff has to say."

"Together," said the steam-roller in the suffocated voice of a mother determined to do battle to the last.

Stroganoff looked steadily out of the window. "I am busy," he said. "Go away."

"*You* are busy," said Arenskaya scornfully. "*You* are busy. I suppose it is you who teach the classes, and see to the dresses, and take the rehearsals, and make love to the electrician . . . the handsome one." She stopped reflectively.

The steam-roller seized her chance.

"If," she said, "that skinny little piece of twopence nothing can take six curtains, then it is an outrage that my daughter, who it is well-known can dance her head off, is not permitted to take even one."

"From the corps-de-ballet?" asked Arenskaya sweetly.

"The corps-de-ballet," said the steam-roller from the depths of her being.

"Mais si," said Arenskaya. "I have put her there. This minute," she explained. "No longer shall she dance the First Friend."

"Ha!" said the steam-roller. "I see! She dances the First Friend too well does my Lulu, is that it? She is getting too much attention. Too much attention and not enough curtains, is that it?"

"That is it," said Stroganoff, weighing in on the side of his lieutenant. "So you go quickly and do not plague me the fuss for I am busy," he held up a hand to silence Arenskaya, "and, later, I will see to it that our good Maîtresse-de-ballet she relent."

"I relent," said Arenskaya. "She shall dance the Second Friend."

"See," said Stroganoff. "So now you go. Shoo!"

It was no doubt a remarkable thing that when Stroganoff said "Shoo!" people should go, but somehow they did.

"These six curtains," said the man with the sandy eyebrows. "They seem to be causing you a certain amount of trouble."

"You tell me," said Stroganoff. He gazed at the portrait of Pavlova. Was there a trace of divine pity in that smile? He stood and gazed and the sandy man watched him in slight wonder.

"My friend," said Stroganoff heavily, "it seems to me at this moment that all my life has been spent with the trouble those six curtains give." He crossed to his desk, opened the cigar-box, shrugged and lit a cigarette.

"Sit down, my good friend," he said, "and I will tell about these six curtains. Make yourself comfortable," he roused himself to remember his duty as host, "for it will take all morning."

"And the rich one?" asked the sandy man.

"He can wait," said Stroganoff. "To-day I must unpack my soul."

*

Chapter Three

*

"IT begins," said Stroganoff, "in St. Petersburg in 1910. . . .

It was Sunday night. It was snowing.

At the Maryinsky Theatre the divine Trefilova was to dance the sugar plum fairy and the Imperial Court, glittering and scandalizing, had assembled to see her do it. Friends bowed cordially, enemies bowed stiffly, and creaky old generals smoked shaky cigarettes in amber holders. Everyone knew everyone else, and had done for generations. A new face was an event, a slightly distressing event—like an uninvited guest at a Christmas party.

And to-night there were two of them sitting in the front row of the dress circle, a bald-headed young man and a girl bending raptly towards each other, an island of mutual admiration in a sea of encrusted hostility.

"Voilà!" said the young man, "everything is as I have promised you. First," he tapped a well-pleased finger, "we are in Petersburg on our honeymoon. Second," he tapped another, "your mamoushka is in Omsk. Third, we are alone together and we are going to have the complete holiday and forget the ballet. And last (which you taunted me I could never achieve), we have the best seats at the Maryinsky!"

"Vladimir, you are wonderful," said the bride. "How did you do it?"

"Ah," said Stroganoff. "That is my secret."

It was no secret to the encrusted nobility around them. Old Godorenko had sold his seats again—though he had promised faithfully not to only five years ago. Old Godorenko would have to be spoken to. Provincials at the Maryinsky! It would be his moneylender next.

The conductor rapped with his baton on the gold stand. The house sprang, rustled and creaked to its feet. The Imperial box had filled with figures as glorious as the suns and moons of the universe, as remote as wax dolls in a shop window. Behind them was Rasputin.

"Vladimir," breathed the young bride, "imagine if it were I who dance to-night. Would I die?"

"A thousand times, my little one," whispered Stroganoff, "and because of this you would dance like all the angels there have ever been."

Light in the myriad chandeliers grew dim. Footlights glowed up, warming the curtain to its exciting crimson life. A voiceless ah! ran through the house, and Tchaikowsky's Christmas music gaily took possession of the auditorium.

The curtain went up.

"Punctual," said Vladimir Stroganoff in awe.

*   *   *

To arrive at the Opera House, Omsk, a dewy choryphée with an anything but dewy mamoushka, to catch the eye of the boss, to dance Raymonda, Coppélia and the Peri within six months, to marry the boss in seven, to come to the capital on your honeymoon, with mamoushka weeping and definitely left behind, and to sit in the front row of the Grand Circle of the Maryinsky, watching Trefilova, of whom one had only dreamed, dancing the familiar and yet so different Sugar Plum—it was altogether too much. Long before the end of the third act Natasha Stroganova was in tears.

She reached for her husband's hand. "Vladimir," she said, "what is the use? I shall never dance better than this."

"Mooch better," said Stroganoff absently. "Mooch, mooch better." He gazed entranced at the stage.

"But I am mad," said Natasha, pulling herself together. "Of course I will dance better. Or at least as well," she amended humbly, gazing in a mixture of joy and sorrow at the perfection of a frozen arabesque.

"Sssh," said the generals on either side of them simultaneously.

On the stage the enchantment continued, glory replaced glory, comical, vigorous, technical and all well-schooled, for were they not specially chosen glories, trained for ten years in a seminary from which a nun would have fled in panic, convinced that her vocation had been nothing but a girlish fancy?

The audience appraised, whispered and applauded.

And now the ballet drew towards its brilliant close. The pas des fleurs disintegrated into separate posies, each tearing off a formidable technical variation with only a slight strain at the edge of the smile to show the concentration that was going into all this floating, and each safely-accomplished passage crowned with applauding hands and knowing nods.

"That one," said Stroganoff as a girl like a frozen flame vanished into the wings, "that one has promise."

In a shower of 'brava! brava! bis!' Pavlova came back to take her bow.

"She is good," said Natasha. She sought for some technical criticism and failed to find it. "But her soul is not yet awake."

"You are wrong, my pigeon," said Stroganoff softly. "The soul of that one will never sleep."

"Sssh," said the generals on either side of them.

"Ssh, ssh," said the general behind.

For now the finale was triumphantly achieved. Everybody on the stage was lighthearted for soon the difficulties of the day would be over and they would be sitting, safe and relaxed, discussing the catastrophies of others over supper and not a thing to worry about till class at 9 a.m. next morning; and everybody in the auditorium a little sad because the ballet had come to an end and there would not be another performance till next Wednesday and not another gathering of such exclusive grandeur till to-day week. After all, what were two seats in the dress circle?

"Brava! brava! Bis!" cried the two seats in unison, as Trefilova took one, two, three, four curtains. And at the fifth Natasha turned to the applauding impresario beside her.

"Five curtains, Vladimir," she said. "Did you count? Five curtains."

"Pourquoi pas," said Stroganoff. He went on clapping.

"I must do better," mused Natasha Stroganova. "Vladimir," she turned starrily, "when I am Assoluta I shall have six."

"A thousand, my darling," said Stroganoff obligingly, the impresario sunk in the adoring husband.

"And that," Stroganoff told the sandy man, "was the beginning of all my troubles. For though I promise without reflecting and forget the next instant, my wife she remind me the next morning. And the morning after. And every day while we are married and long after that." He sighed.

"I made a promise once," said the sandy man reflectively. "In writing." He shook his head.

"Still," said Stroganoff fairly, "if the promise begin my troubles, it also begin my success. For, were it not for that, I would not be the great impresario, famous, powerful and rich." He stopped abruptly. "Sometimes," he added.

"Quite," said the sandy man. He smiled.

"But we are at the Maryinsky," said Stroganoff, "and presently I am arguing with General Dumka—the one who go 'Ssh!' all the time. Poor Dumka," said Stroganoff, "the last time I see him he is serving zakuski in a little Russian restaurant in Paris—but he is still in his uniform of the Russian Imperial Guard."

"Poor old boy," said the sandy man.

"Do not weep for him," said Stroganoff. "He had his memories. You would hardly credit it, my friend," he chuckled suddenly, "but to the last he maintained that Dourakova was a purer Sugar Plum than the divine Trefilova." He kissed his fingers.

"My friend," said General Dumka, "I will not argue with you. Dourakova is far, far purer." In his agitation his cigarette jabbed wide of his amber holder.

"And me, I will not argue either," said Stroganoff hotly. "But I tell you that to demand a greater purity than we have applauded to-night . . ."

"Please," said Natasha, "I would like some supper."

"Trefilova is enchanting," ceded General Dumka. "She is improving all the time," he pointed out generously. "But to compare this with the mastery of the incomparable Dourakova . . ."

"Pardon," said an old lady. Her furs brushed past the passionate little group blocking the exit.

"Please," said Natasha, "I would like some supper."

"Dourakova," said Stroganoff contemptuously. "Where in your

Dourakova do you find the well-placed shoulder, the iron hips, the frozen arabesque. . . .

"And where in Trefilova," interrupted General Dumka, "do you find the fire?"

"Where," said Natasha plaintively, "can I get some supper?"

*   *   *

"To Dourakova," said General Dumka. He raised his glass of Mumm and drank.

"To Trefilova," said Stroganoff. He drank and plonked his glass defiantly on the table.

"To all our dear friends in Omsk," said Natasha and burst into tears.

Almire Cubat, cruising benevolently round his fashionable French-Russian restaurant, condescended to glance at the weeping lady and raised an interested yet slightly puzzled eyebrow. It was not that tears were at all unusual at the Cubat where all the ballerinas came after triumphant and other appearances—ma foi non! but so far he had always known not only the shedder, but also precisely why she was shedding. Everyone knew a ballerina had her sorrows; the fierce rivalries, the broken contracts, the muddled love-life, the papoushka whose pupils were falling off, and the mamoushka who smiled bravely through a trail of dependent aunts—oh, it was simple enough, informed as he was, to keep track of the reasons for a ballerina's tears. But he did not know this pretty little lady, nor the chubby well-waistcoated gentleman patting her. But he knew General Dumka enough and he raised the other eyebrow at him mutely asking for an explanation.

"Madame is a little distressed," said Dumka benevolently. "She weeps because she is not yet Assoluta."

"Ah bon," said Almire Cubat. All was clear. "My best wishes to Madame."

He bowed and drifted off to welcome a bank of roses standing in the entrance, bowed lower, found a white hand among the foliage and kissed it.

"Oh, Almire," said Trefilova, "I am so unhappy." She clutched his hand. "My variation to-night. It was like a circus girl. Oh, how could I dance like that!"

The divine Trefilova winked away a tear.

"Madame is too severe," said Almire Cubat. "The notices will contradict her."

The orchestra burst into Casse-Noisette. Trefilova felt a little sick. She smiled at the leader. She glanced across the room to a table where Valerien Svetlov, the foremost of the critics, was utilizing her twenty minutes' lateness to steep his pen in—what? She felt a little sicker. She would not know until to-morrow though she was supping with him to-night. Probably in vitriol, she reflected, as she smilingly allowed Cubat to lead her to the table, for he had given her charms no chance to soften whatever opinion he might have formed.

"Ah, there you are, my dear," said Svetlov, handing an ominous slip of paper to a courier. "Did the students chair you to the very door?"

No indication. "They did," said Trefilova. She flopped down.

The little bride, her tears dried, had followed every detail of the divine Trefilova's progress with breathless attention. Stroganoff, of course, was too busy arguing the perfections of the dancer to notice that she had arrived.

"How wonderful," thought Natasha, "to enter such a magnificent and crowded restaurant, the greatest of the great, to have the orchestra play your ballet in compliment to your appearance, to take it all so much for granted, and to sail across the room, acknowledging this one, ignoring that one, and so to sup casually with the most dreaded critic in all Russia with never a thought or care of what he might write about you to-morrow."

"You eat nothing, my dear," said Svetlov. "A little caviar."

"I am tired, Valerien," said Trefilova. "I wish to-morrow would never come. Tell me," she nerved herself to ask the impermissible, "was I so very terrible?"

Svetlov patted her shoulder. "A little Mumm, my dear," he said. So she had danced badly. She gulped her champagne.

"I took five curtains," she said defiantly.

"But, of course," said Svetlov. "These Maryinsky audiences . . ."

Through the restaurant progressed a broad-shouldered man. He was tall, but his tread was quiet. He bowed but he did not smile. His hair was black, but there was a white lock in it. He was Serge Diaghilev, bearing the fruits of his first Paris triumph. Already many people in St. Petersburg were afraid of him.

With Diaghilev was a coterie of artists, all young, all enthusiastic, all men of ideas, and all trying to look as inscrutable as he did. Benois, Bakst, Fokine, Stravinsky, Nouvel and P. Puthyk.

But once seated at the table impassivity dissolved into flying hands—hands composing steps, hands executing steps, hands painting scenery, hands playing a hurdy-gurdy, hands describing moods, hands describing characters, and not a single pair of hands concerned with where the money was coming from. Somewhere, well at the back of Diaghilev's mind, was a nasty little nag, but this was not the moment for it. Not with Petroushka beginning at last to take form, a daring, realistic, iconoclastic form that would uproot dead artistic hedges and send every critic in sight doddering to his well-merited grave. They shot a look at Svetlov. Ha! If that one knew what was coming to him!

"Never felt better in my life," Svetlov was boasting, at a happy distance from his doom. "I don't say I like Karlsbad prunes," manfully he swallowed one, "but they do help the digestion."

Trefilova smiled mistily at him over a mountain of meringues. That Conductor! She'd have a word with him to-morrow.

"Your health, Madame," said General Dumka. "And may we see you dancing in our capital soon."

"Oh," said Natasha. The idea planted itself.

"The time will come," said Stroganoff proudly. "For the moment you understand, Omsk has need of her."

"Omsk," said General Dumka. Not for the first time that evening his eyeglass fell out.

"You excuse me!" A young man had slouched over to the recovering General's elbow. "But have you by chance a hundred roubles to lend me till to-morrow?"

The General suffered a relapse.

"Or maybe," said Nicholas Nevajno, for it was none other, "till next month."

"A hundred roubles," said General Dumka weakly.

"You see," Nevajno explained, "I come here to-night and I think I am guest. But alas," he sagged, "it appears that I am host." He looked as though he were about to burst into tears.

General Dumka played for time. "Permit me to present my good friend Nicholas Nevajno," he announced. "A choreographer with a great future."

A Choreographer! Stroganoff leaped to his feet.

"Sit down, my friend," he said. "Champagne," he poured. "One hundred roubles!" he felt for his wallet.

Down the restaurant pranced a dark, petite, heavily perfumed young girl, clearly a dancer, for behind, beside, and in front of her bobbed a foam of balletomane generals of the second rank of discrimination and the last legs of lechery. She was Arenskaya.

Already she was laden with jewels and orchids. Already she was plundering the props baskets. And already she wanted to dance Giselle, but Telyakov preferred Pavlova. Unfair.

She passed by Diaghilev's table. She unleashed her personality on the preoccupied group around him. The group remained preoccupied. Infuriating creatures. All save one, whose entrechatting hand floated static in mid-air as he gazed at her. P. Puthyk.

Maybe that one wouldn't dream of his English Governess to-night!

Arenskaya pranced on. Two generals dead-heated to pull out her chair. Three more reached for her furs. The waiters were nowhere. Arenskaya shook her curls at them and turned her bird-bright attention to the company at large.

There was Trefilova weeping into her coffee. Naturally, after that performance. There was Karsavina drying her eyes—now what had she just heard? Of course—the cancelled matinée. There was Pavlova—crying buckets, that one! And there was Kyasht, blonde, dimpling, and not a tear in sight. Arenskaya pranced over.

"My darling," she said, "but you were divine, and not nearly so fat as all have been whispering. No, no." She pranced back. She stole a glance. Kyasht was weeping all right.

"Champagne," said Arenskaya well pleased.

Nicholas Nevajno had not gone back to his guests. He was drinking Stroganoff's champagne and he was talking. He was talking about his ballet that no one would put on. General Dumka had long since fallen asleep, but Stroganoff was listening entranced. What an attraction for Omsk!

And the little Natasha looked and looked at the glittering, modish, eating, drinking, singing, weeping, laughing company before her. How wonderful it all was. If only she belonged.

She wept.

Chapter Four

"VLADIMIR," said Natasha, "do you love me?"

"My darling," said Stroganoff. He stretched out his night-shirted arms.

"Then," said the bride, dodging nimbly, "you will arrange that I dance in Petersburg."

"We will see," said Stroganoff, side-stepping after her. "We will see," he promised.

But Natasha buttoned up her dressing-gown and crouched over the log fire, her mouth set in a grim little line.

"My darling," said Stroganoff gently, "do not look like that. It reminds me of your mamoushka—God bless her." He put his hands on her shoulders. Natasha shook them off.

Stroganoff gazed wistfully round the bridal suite of the newest hotel in St. Petersburg. It featured red plush curtains with bobbled fringes, two sofas and a footstool, a wardrobe of immense proportions, a double bed with a new spring mattress, a great deal of gold paint almost everywhere, a painting of the Retreat of Napoleon from Moscow,* and a bathroom. There was no hot water, but it had been promised for to-morrow for some days now. In the meantime, if you tugged the bell often enough, old Ivan would stagger in with a couple of cans, steaming—perhaps. Stroganoff fetched a deep sigh. Of what use all this luxury if his little pigeon fastened her dressing-gown.

"My little snowflake," he said. "Sois raisonable. Melt a little."

The snowflake looked reproachful. "Vladimir," she said, "sometimes I marvel at you. How can you refuse me anything at a moment like this?"

She undid a button. It was not a very important button.

"You must understand, my friend," said Stroganoff, "ça, c'etait avant."

The sandy man nodded. His French was not very good, but he could follow that one.

"Vladimir," said his bride, "look at me."

Vladimir threw his hands up to the painted ceiling. "Mais voyons, ma petite," he said, "what else have I been doing for the last hour? And if you take this thing off," he tugged at the dressing-gown, "I could do it better."

"Vladimir, don't be coarse," said the bride. She crossed her arms and shielded her endangered bosom.

"What say you," suggested Stroganoff, playful but diffident,

* We think it was Napoleon. The hat suggested it.

"that I pick you up in my arms like a little feather and carry you to the bed?"

"No," said the bride. "Not till you agree to present me in Petersburg," ultimated the ballerina's firmed mouth.

Stroganoff resigned himself. No fond endearments, however skilfully put, would change this conversation. He too put on his dressing-gown. He crossed to the samovar and brought back two tumblers of tea. He found his amber cigarette-holder and stuck a cigarette in it. Now all was set for reasoned argument.

"My darling," he said. "We are very well in Omsk. We have the Opera with the three performances a week and the many people with the season ticket so we do not care if they come or not. You are famous and my papoushka," he pointed out, "is rich and for the moment can defray the deficit."

How was he doing? But the little mouth had tightened.

"Omsk," said Natasha, "is not Petersburg."

"Bien sûr." A skilled debater, Stroganoff pounced on the point. "In Petersburg there is no new apartment, which you have so tastefully furnished and for which the papoushka does not yet know how much he has to pay. Our Louis Quinze." He kissed his fingers.

"Your papoushka," said Natasha, "is very rich. But also," she added, "he is very rude. He called my mamoushka a cow. My poor mamoushka, who has done everything for me."

"Console yourself, my darling," said Stroganoff. "He meant only that the cow is the mother of the graceful little calf."

"Ha!" said Natasha, "you cannot fool me, Vladimir. I do not believe that you love my mamoushka either."

Stroganoff made to change the subject.

"In Omsk," he said, "we stage all the great ballets and where else can you dance Giselle?"

"In Petersburg," said Natasha.

"Ha," said Stroganoff vexed, "so now she persuades Pavlova to abdicate! Proceed, my pigeon. I will watch you with interest." He folded his arms.

His little pigeon pummelled his chest. "You are a brute, Vladimir Stroganoff," she said, "a tyrant, a boor! And a drunkard," she added for luck. "And why you have not yet beaten me I cannot understand."

"Me neither," said Stroganoff mildly.

"You give me my company, yes. But where? In Omsk!" She shuddered. "In Omsk, where nobody knows anything. Who comes to Omsk?" she demanded.

"Nicholas Nevajno," said Stroganoff. "Already I have pay him the advance in salary. I keep this as a surprise for you, my little pigeon."

Natasha waved the surprise aside.

"Vladimir Stroganoff," she said, "you bring me to Petersburg with my company, and with my mamoushka and," she remembered something, "my six curtains or else . . ."

"My friend," said Stroganoff, "I was very rash. But also," he gazed unseeingly out over Covent Garden, "it was my honeymoon. So I promised."

"Quite," said the sandy man.

"But that night Natasha was tired from her victory," said Stroganoff. "So . . ." He sighed.

Chapter Five

"VLADIMIR," said Natasha, "do you love me?"

"Toujours," said Stroganoff, with wariness.

An unusual emotion for a honeymooning husband when this particular question crops up. But Stroganoff was lying in the upper berth of a railway compartment and Natasha was in the lower berth so the question could not be an overture to a delightful interlude but merely the prelude to some less delightful demand.

"Vladimir," said Natasha, "you have promised to speak to your father."

"As soon as we get to Omsk," said Stroganoff. He dangled his hand into the darkness. A small hand came snuggling into it. One more little hint and he would be clambering down.

"Six curtains," breathed the bride.

"Go to sleep," said the husband, fed up.

The Passenger-Postal Train chugged its way serenely towards Omsk. It had been chugging for four days now and it had still quite a long way to go, and was in no hurry to get there. It stopped for water, it stopped for fuel, it stopped for flowers, and it stopped for luck, it might even stop for a signal if the engine-driver happened to notice it, but in the main it stopped for food. The mail must go through—but in those days, it didn't have to go through so very quickly, the ordinary Russian being only too gratified to receive a letter at all to worry about the time it had taken to reach him. And while the mail progressed, passengers had to eat. All the villagers en route were well aware of this and ran to the station with hopefully-cooked chickens every day in the hope that this would be the one on which the train would arrive. And sometimes it did. It was usually the previous train. But the passengers were always hungry.

In the larger villages they were more ambitious. There would be an inn with hot bortsch and pirojki, great joints and pigs roasted whole. Dining at a stationary table, with the light of a log fire playing over the walls and warding off the home-made baskets the peasants were trying to sell, made a delightful break in the journey. The engine-driver, who liked a good meal himself and a little singing afterwards, thoughtfully allowed plenty of time for it. And his tenor ringing out under the rafters sounded fine and the bass of the liberal gentleman with the looking-down-the-nose bride—what there was of it—blended pleasingly in Gayda Troika if a little less well in the Two Guitars. So pleased had the bass been with their singing that he had promised the engine-driver seats for the ballet whenever he came to Omsk. The engine-driver was wondering if he could hold the train there overnight. He couldn't see why not.

"Vladimir," said the bride into the night, "are you asleep?"

"I was," said Stroganoff.

"I have been thinking," said Natasha. "If I am to have my company in Petersburg this year as you have promised, it is essential that you speak to the Papoushka at once."

"As soon as we get to Omsk," said Stroganoff in his sleep.

For that had been the question which, like the chimes of the churches had punctuated the days and the nights of the honeymoon. The carillon had been heard at all the most expensive places and at the most unexpected moments. At Fabergé, choosing the gold and turquoise tea-set which was to make all Omsk envious so that Papoushka could not afford to send it back. At the Parfumerie and the Pastry Cook's. Crossing the Nevsky Prospekt. In the middle of 'A Life for the Tzar.' First thing in the morning, last thing at night, and twice while cabling Papoushka for more funds. How often was the good old one in the minds of his children and every time his image, usually a wincing one, floated before their eyes, Natasha was reminded of the all-important matter her husband would have to take up with him on their return. For, before Stroganoff could present her in St. Petersburg, the Papoushka would have to find the finance.

"Vladimir," the little voice cooed anxiously into the darkness. "Vladimir," it cooed a little more sharply.

"Yes, my little goose," said Stroganoff, jerked out of Trefilova's triumphant appearance in Omsk with Pavlova begging him to arrange one for her and General Dumka unaccountably asleep in the dress circle. "Yes, my little snowbird—what is it? You would like some water?" And he prepared to heave himself out, if not with alacrity, at least with an appearance of willingness.

"Vladimir," said the bride, "I know you have promised, but promise me that you will speak to the Papoushka as you have promised."

"As soon as we get to Omsk," said Stroganoff and pulled the blankets over his head.

Chapter Six

ℐT was Omsk.

It was four weeks later.

"Vladimir," said Natasha, "promise me something . . ."

She was in her dressing-room, the star's dressing-room, gazing critically into her mirror, while a bent-double black behind, which was all you could see of Mamoushka, stitched the ribbons of her ballet shoes—no chances were to be taken to-night.

For Natasha was dancing Giselle for the first time, and the Opera House was crowded—well, fairly full.

"Now do not unquiet yourself," said Stroganoff. "Relax the nerves, my darling. You will have the success triumphant. At the rehearsal to-day you are unsurpassable," said the impresario. "And also," said the husband, "you are delicious."

He kissed her cheek. The mamoushka unbent herself, put the wreath straight, glared at Stroganoff and returned to her shoes.

"Vladimir," said Giselle, "promise me something . . ."

"Yes, my little angel," said Stroganoff fondly.

"Promise me you will speak to Papoushka. . . ."

Affection vanished.

"As soon as the performance is over," said Stroganoff.

In the auditorium of the Opera House the lights went down. The conductor mounted his rostrum. He bowed to a large watch-chained stomach in the stage-box. The stomach inclined itself.

Aliosha Stroganoff never missed a performance of his ballet. Neither did his banker. But their reasons were different. Stroganoff, merchant, loved art and he loved his son—his only son—and now his dream had come true and the latter was presenting him with the first. But the banker loved Aliosha, and he was there to see his crack-brained young son didn't ruin him.

"Seven hundred roubles in the house," he said. "Hardly enough to cover the salaries."

Aliosha smiled at him. "Abram, Abram," he shook a playful finger and his stomach heaved a little, "here is my daughter-in-law dancing Giselle for the first time and," he pointed out, "my um . . . discovery dancing the Queen of the Wilies and you talk to me about money. No, no, Abram—it is not the moment." And he gazed expectantly at the villagers gathered outside Giselle's cottage.

"It is never the moment not to talk about money," said the banker shocked.

"Sssh—there she is, my Katusha," said Aliosha. He gazed enamoured at the stage. "Third from the left in the back row. Charming—no?" He patted his stomach. "And she dances well too," he said loyally. "In the second act she has her variation. The mother of my daughter-in-law did not wish it, but I was firm."

"Ah, that one," said the banker darkly.

The performance went on. Giselle emerged from her cottage, all blushes and palpitations. In the wings mamoushka was having palpitations too. But the House took kindly to Natasha. She was young, she was pretty to look at, her pointes were not very strong, but what would you, you could not expect an Egorova at Omsk. But as for the Prince! Were there not less knowledgeable cities? Vladivostock, for example. Why didn't he go there?

"That one," said the banker disparagingly as the Prince leapt, but not very high, into the air, "that one," he repeated, "is no Nijinsky."

The dancer who was No Nijinsky came down again. He looked round for the ballerina. He managed to catch up with her.

"He is no Nijinsky," agreed Aliosha, "but he is the second-best Vint player in Omsk." He patted his stomach.

"And that reminds me," said the banker, "must you play so high?"

Vladimir Stroganoff dashed into the box. "She is superb—no? You are happy, yes?" He dashed out again.

"When I was young," said Aliosha fondly, "I too ran about like a zany."

"And now that you are older," said the banker, "you sit still, but you are no wiser. Discovery! At your age!"

"Abram, you are jealous," said Aliosha. "And also you are getting past it. For one thing," he said, gazing critically at the much smaller stomach, "you are too fat." He clasped his hands over his own.

The banker grinned into his beard. That was all Aliosha knew. He thought comfortably of his Saturday nights. Past it—ha!

The ballet creaked on. The Princess arrived with her customary thirst. Giselle's scolding old Mother, not so different from the one in the wings, at the moment rehearsing what she was going to say to the conductor later, helped to slake it. Gratified the Princess bestowed some pearls on Giselle. Overjoyed Giselle danced.

"Oh, my darling," moaned the mamoushka in the wings. She went on crossing herself for the next three minutes.

"She dances like a goddess," said Vladimir Stroganoff, pausing to snatch a peep between his many errands. He rushed away to collect the laurel wreath due to be presented later—it always was—to the man who was No Nijinsky.

It was the interval. The Safety Curtain came trundling down. It was not fireproof, but it carried advertisements. And here were all the advertisers in the stalls gazing raptly at it. The hairdresser, the couturier, the jeweller, the brothel-keeper (Chez Planchette, Massage), and the Best Tailor in Omsk—he said so.

"And he is right," said Aliosha. He patted his waistcoat.

"Rabinovitch," said the banker, "is half the price and just as good." Defiantly he flicked a speck of dust off his sleeve."

"My son," said Aliosha proudly, "had six suits and two overcoats made for him in Petersburg."

"Aie!" said the banker.

"He trembles to tell me," said Aliosha, "and I shall be very angry and nearly ruined when he does. But in the meantime," he grinned,

"I have peered into his cupboard. The cloth." He kissed his fingers.

But not everybody in the house was advertising on the Safety Curtain and not everybody was scrimmaging at the Kvass Counter. Some were returning from it. And in the Foyer the sole topic of conversation was the new Giselle, with Petkov, the local critic, strong on Tannhauser but weak on the Ballet, listening-in to as many places as he could manage.

La Stroganova was bewitching, enchanting, and could have been worse. Her variations had great appeal and not enough strength. Her mad scene was poignant, and enough to make a cow laugh. A finished performance and too immature. What would you—to see Pavlova you had to go to Petersburg, The Management were to be congratulated, and they ought never to have let her go on. A true ballerina in the making, and she would never make a ballerina.

Baffled, the critic withdrew to the Kvass Counter. Oh, for the space to put it all down and let his readers decide for themselves!

But in the wings opinion, dressed in the evanescences of Act II, was more unanimous. A crowd of dancers were warmly surrounding Natasha, a band of good old troopers, long past any hope for themselves save that of getting by, rejoicing in the triumph of a newcomer.

"You were exquisite."

"You were superb."

"You made me cry."

A woodcutter came up. He had been woodcutter to many a Giselle, the Prince's first companion in many a Swan Lake and Burgomaster to countless Coppélias.

"My dear," said Kashkavar Jones, "I am very happy for you." He wept.

"You were better than Preobrajenskaya," said Aliosha's Discovery. "Much," she convinced herself.

"Mind my lilies," said the man who was No Nijinsky.

A little way off a crowd of mamoushkas were surrounding

Natasha's mamoushka, a band of tried old troopers, past any hope
for their daughters save that of getting a rise in salary or promotion
from the third row to the second, and they were rejoicing, after
their manner, in the triumph of a newcomer.

"She looked very pretty—no one can take that from her."

"Her hair was nice—if you like it that way."

"Only five mistakes—I counted them."

"I have seen worse Giselles—I think."

"How clever you were," said a mamoushka, who, though sorely
tried, had been saving this up for weeks, "to marry her to Monsieur
le Directeur."

"I thank you," said Natasha's mamoushka grimly. She could
take a lot of this with her daughter queening it. "And also please
thank from me your own daughters for supporting as best they can
my little genius."

She waddled off with the bridal veil. Honour was satisfied. The
impertinence of these dancers' mothers, she thought, as she placed
the bridal veil over her daughter's tingling head. Their clumsy
daughters would never get to Petersburg. Why, if she'd only had
a mamoushka like herself, she might have danced in Petersburg too
in her time. Nijni-Novgorod! Pfui!

Presently, after the twenty-minute interval had lasted but three-
quarters of an hour, Act II began.

"Now," said Aliosha, as the Queen of the Wilis came plodding
on, "now you will see something." And he leant forward, screening
the stage from the banker. "My Discovery," he gloated, as
Queen of the Wilis distentangled her veil from the grave-
stone.

"She doesn't dance very well," said the banker, peering over
Aliosha's shoulder.

"She is very pretty," said Aliosha sensibly, "no one can take that
from her."

"And," said the banker, nearly nasty, "she has had the sense to
prefer the rich father."

"And why not?" said Aliosha. "At my age I do not expect them to love me. When they did, it was not restful." He patted his stomach.

"Aliosha, you are a wicked old man," said the banker.

"Yes, yes," said Aliosha, delighted.

Nicholas Nevajno, choreographer of the future, came slouching into the box, pushed forward a chair, sat down in front of the banker, and watched the stage critically for some moments.

"Pfui!" he said.

Aliosha bridled. "Sir," he accused, "you spit you of my Discovery?"

"You discover this?" said Nevajno incredulously. "Where?"

Aliosha blushed.

"That is his business," said the banker, quickly.

"Ah, ça," said Nevajno. "As to that I offer no opinion. But for the ballet—pfui!"

Giselle arose from the grave. She floated in the arms of her betrayer. Her partner did his best to float with her, but he was No Nijinsky. The banker wept a little.

"Pfui," said Nevajno, "this is not art. It is but the sticky sentiment. Coralli!" He spat.

The banker blew his nose. He looked at Nevajno with disfavour. He remembered something.

"Young man," he said coldly, "your account at my bank is overdrawn."

Nevajno considered this. "You mean I have no money," he said acutely.

"Not a kopeck," said the banker. "So don't write any more cheques for they won't be met."

Nevajno considered again. He saw an objection.

"But," he pointed out, "the people to whom I give my scheques give me money for them."

"That," said the banker grimly, "is their affair."

"So," said Nevajno. He brightened. "But this is good news," he said. "Then," he sought to get it quite clear. "While I have no money in the bank you pay nothing on my scheques to the people who give me money for them?"

"Not a kopeck," said the banker. "Quite bluntly, Mr. Nevajno, they will bounce."

"You promise," said Nevajno anxiously.

"I promise," said the banker. "They will bounce," he repeated grimly.

"But this is terrific," Nevajno shook him warmly by the hand. "This concept of yours—it is colossal. Never, never will I be able to thank you."

And the banker watched in horror as Nevajno turned to Aliosha, pulled out a cheque book and whispered something. Without taking his eyes off the stage where Katusha was denying the betrayer salvation, Aliosha slid his hand deep into his pocket, pulled out a golden rouble-purse and thumbed out a handful of coins.

"Aie!" said the banker.

Nevajno smiled at him. "It works," he confided. "He has schange me a schmall scheque."

In a dream of bliss he wandered out.

On the stage Giselle was borne back to her grave. . . .

. . . "Ah the emotions of that Giselle," Stroganoff gazed raptly at the ceiling. "The packed house. The cheering audience. The en-thusiastic critics. And me, I am everywhere and my heart is in my mouth, and all the time I am talking, talking, talking."

"Sure," said the sandy man.

"For in those days, you must understand I am young and hoping," said Stroganoff. "Ah, the things that hang on those hopes. I had not then the pessimism that you see with me to-day, my friend." He shook his head and sighed heavily. "For what have I to look for now? Only the worries and the exasperation. If all go well it is the artists' talent, if bad, it is the fault of the management. And also," he faced it, "there is the finance. Always the finance." He sagged.

"There is the rich one," said the sandy man tentatively.

"That one!" said Stroganoff. "He will be fat and bloated and already he will be complaining. Also he will ask me many questions, and all about money. Every time I spend the sou he will look at the books, and," past experience shot up, "complain of the handwriting. You will see, my friend," he prophesied, "the rich one will come into this office as though already it belongs to him, he will ask me why I do not present the comedy musical, he will talk all the time about himself, and also he will have a little friend, whom his wife has not met, and for whom I must find the small solo—say, the Prelude in Sylphides."

The sandy man put his hand over his mouth.

"And even if he give me all the moneys I need," said Stroganoff, "what is there new that I can do with them? I can take a bigger theatre." He dismissed it. "I can engage Markova, Dolin, Danilova and Franklin." He waved them away. "With them, and possibly," he considered, "Robert Helpmann, I could go to Covent Garden and," he brightened, "what is more, I could fill it. And after this triumph," he wagged a finger, "I go straight to the Metropolitan, New York. You shall see I am at the Metropolitan in the Fall." He thought of something else. "Tell me, my friend," he said earnestly, "with what ballet do you think we should open?"

"Er," said the sandy man. . . .

Chapter Seven

"OOF," said Stroganoff. He looked round. His little love-nest bore the air of a room that had held far too many people in it far too long.

Smoke draped the ceiling, deflated cushions littered the floor, the Fabergé tea-set, brought in triumphantly assembled, was now scattered, nicotine ended all over the place—and one less at that (how Little Igor had blushed!), and—Mon Dieu! there was a burn on one of the Louis Quinze fauteuils. Fortunately Natasha had not yet seen.

Stroganoff sat down hurriedly. Maybe with a needle and thread? Or maybe not! He sighed.

Natasha's first-night party was over at last. Stroganoff had invited almost the entire company and the others had come, anyway. Those who could not crowd into the drawing-room had peered round the door of the passage and had vodka and zakuski passed to them in a flurry of 'pardon's.' Anyway, not many of the gowns were permanently ruined.

It had been a triumph and toast after toast had been drunk to the heroine of the occasion. Almost she might have been Kshessinskaya.

"To your four curtains, my darling," said Stroganoff. "No one in Omsk has taken more. Save," he remembered, "the cousin of Chaliapine."

They drank.

"When I am in Petersburg," said Natasha distinctly, "I shall have six."

Aliosha looked up.

"To the papoushka," cried Stroganoff quickly. "Let us drink to the papoushka."

They drank.

Then Kashkavar Jones had made a speech, and though it was inaudible, Little Igor nodded agreement. The man who was No Nijinsky left early, Nevajno did not come at all and the mamoushka had fallen asleep in the kitchen. But the rest had lingered on for two hours after making their final farewells and had started to talk politics, which meant that they would not go at all, and the papoushka was yawning his head off, and Natasha was nudging her husband in the ribs—each time a little more sharply, and something drastic would have to be done.

So Stroganoff said "Shoo!"

Now they were all gone. Stroganoff had seen them into their droshkys and waved them good-bye, and exploded back at the neighbours and come in and closed the door.

o

"Oof," he said, and sat down quickly on the burn.

But Natasha was not noticing. She had savoured her triumph, and now it was time to think of the future.

"Vladimir," she pointed to the stomach rising and falling in front of the fire. "Now is the moment."

Stroganoff backed a little. "But no. Papoushka is tired. See how he slumbers. To-morrow, my little pigeon."

"To-night," said Natasha grimly.

"But my little one," said Stroganoff. "Let us be kind and also tactful. It is not the subject with which to wake the sleeping father."

A log fell out of the fire. The sleeping father blinked awake and heaved himself to his feet.

"It is the time that I was in bed," he said. "And you, too, my children. Where," he demanded, "is my Katusha?" He looked round.

"She has gone home long ago," said Natasha. "And Vladimir wishes to speak to you." She pushed him back into the chair. "Here is a nice glass of tea. Drink it and listen to Vladimir. It is very important."

But Aliosha shook his head. "It is already half-past five," he said. "When I was Vladimir's age and like him married but two months, I did not wish to sit up talking to my papoushka, may he be spared to us for many years yet. Oh, no. A papoushka," said Aliosha, "is all very well in his place, but this is not the love-nest of the new married couple when the dawn is coming. Ah, no." He wagged a finger. "I remember one night on my honeymoon . . ."

"Good night, papa," said Natasha. "Listen to Vladimir." She kissed him and withdrew.

Stroganoff tugged at his tie.

"Papa," he said. He gulped. "I have a little scheme for making the fortune colossal."

"Aie," said the Papa. "And at such an hour."

"Papoushka," said Stroganoff seriously, "you have given me much. You have given me," he started on the lowest rung, "the first-class education. The theatre of my own," he ticked it off. "My wife, my home . . ."

"And the Fabergé tea-set," said Aliosha. "The bill came only yesterday. Aie!"

"I am grateful," said Stroganoff, ignoring this, "and now I wish to pay back all the moneys that you have spent on me."

Late though the hour was, Aliosha looked startled.

"My son," he said, "did I hear you aright?"

"I wish to pay you back," said Stroganoff clearly and loudly. "But this," he made his point, "I cannot do in Omsk."

"Oho!" said Aliosha. He could not see yet where he was being led, but his instinct was warning him that he wouldn't like it.

"In Omsk there is no scope for an artist," said Stroganoff. "The Opera House," he pointed out, "has a deficit."

"This I know," said Aliosha.

"You have given me a splendid company," said Stroganoff. "And a prima ballerina!" He kissed his fingers. "But here in Omsk there is no audience that is worthy of them. So let us, my papoushka, take them to a place where there is one that will be."

"Nijni-Novgorod?" asked Aliosha.

"Nijni-Novgorod, pfui!" said Stroganoff. "There is in all the Russias only one city worthy of my company and my Natasha."

"Nu?" asked Aliosha.

"Petersburg," said Stroganoff.

"Aie!" said Aliosha.

The Stroganoffs mopped their brows.

"Come, my papoushka," pleaded the son. "Let us look at this with logic. We have the company superb on which you have spent much moneys. But we also have the town that cannot give it back to you. What then, is the logic?"

"To disband the company," said the papoushka.

"No," said Stroganoff, "to take it to another town. To Petersburg. Nevajno," he sought to clinch it, "Nevajno is stifled in Omsk."

"Ah bon," said Aliosha.

Stroganoff tried the personal angle. "Natasha," he said, "has too much talent to waste in the Provinces. And also," he admitted, "she gives me no peace."

"Abram gives me no peace either," said Aliosha. "And what would he say if . . ."

"But papoushka," pleaded Stroganoff, "do you not wish to see your son in Petersburg?"

"No," said papoushka.

"The centre of all fashion," said Stroganoff. "My Natasha the Succès fou and Kshessinskaya broken-hearted. Yourself in a box with a duchess—a grand-duchess."

Papoushka tilted his head and pondered the image. He snapped it back into position.

"Do you think," he coined a phrase, "that I am made of roubles? No and no and no!" he thundered.

*   *   *

"Come here, my darling!" A pair of sleepy white arms raised themselves from the depths of the roomy four-poster and definitely beckoned.

Regretting vaguely that he was not already in his night-shirt and pushing to the back of his mind the uncomfortable news he carried, Stroganoff advanced towards the bed, bent his head, and allowed the white arms to twine themselves around it. Tiens! they were not so sleepy after all.

"You are the best husband in the world," said Natasha. "And also the cleverest impresario."

"Entendu," said Stroganoff. "Entendu." He kissed her. Maybe he could turn her mind to something else.

"My darling," said Natasha, "you have spoken to papoushka?"

"Yes, my darling, I have spoken," said Stroganoff. Very tentatively he fondled.

Natasha snuggled up. "Then it is settled?" she asked.

"It is settled," said Stroganoff. "There is no doubt of that."

The white arms tightened their grip. "Petersburg," breathed Natasha. "Six curtains."

Stroganoff snuggled. He had had an idea. Let her be happy this one night—and himself too. To-morrow he would tell her the bad news before the déjeuner—or maybe after.

"But," said Stroganoff to the sandy man, "at the déjeuner my little bride was so happy that I had not the heart to spoil her mood. Besides," he nodded wisely, "it is certain that she would have slapped my face." He looked at Pavlova's portrait. He beamed. "Do you know," he said proudly, "that Pavlova, too, once give me the giffle." He rubbed his cheek tenderly.

"You amaze me," said the sandy man.

"Mon vieux," said Stroganoff with satisfaction, "there is not in the whole of the Ballet an impresario who is more giffled than me. You must understand," he explained, "that I am to the Ballet like a father, always I try that my company are one big happy family. And what happens in a happy family when something goes wrong—poof—the happy family it giffle the papoushka."

The door opened. A small figure strode in. White with rage she stood over Stroganoff.

"Second Friend," she said. "Pfui!" She slapped his face and strode out.

"Voilà," said Stroganoff unmoved. He rubbed his cheek and resumed. "So," he said, "I did not tell my Natasha the bad news at déjeuner. And I did not tell her at tea. And I did not tell her that night. And by next morning it was no longer necessary for my papoushka had gone to see Abram the Banker.

"No and no and no," said Abram the Banker. His firmness was unshakeable. "Aliosha, I cannot permit that you ruin yourself."

Aliosha looked sulky. "It is my money, Abram," he said, "and if I choose to make the legitimate speculation that is my business."

The banker tried a new angle. "Aliosha," he said, "you are getting old. What pleasure is there for you to sit in a grand box with a duchess?"

"A box with a grand-duchess," corrected Aliosha crossly. "Besides, it is not the social angle that counts with me, though, mind you," he admitted, "I have never kissed the hand of a grand-duchess, but the success of my son and his little wife. And also my Katusha," he remembered. "Can I, his father, deny him this chance?"

"I insist on it," said the banker, "if this son of yours cannot make money in Omsk, how can he succeed in Petersburg?"

"Omsk," said Aliosha, "is a small town and has but little culture."

"Omsk," said the banker, "is the most progressive town in all the Russias." He shot his cuffs. "Have we not installed water pumps in all the side streets?" he challenged. "Are we not," he boasted, "to have the tramway soon? And it is even expected that there will be more than one tram!"

The ancient cashier shuffled in, tended a slip to the banker and whispered.

"Bounce it," said the banker tersely.

The ancient cashier shuffled out, shaking his head.

"Nevajno," said Aliosha, as though reminded of something, "is stifled in Omsk."

The banker said he was pleased to hear it.

"Abram," wheedled Aliosha, "relent. Give me back my money."

"No and no and no," said the banker.

Aliosha Stroganoff drew himself up. "Very well then," he said stiffly, "I shall go to my father." He waddled out. He remembered something. He put his head round the door.

"May he live many years yet," he said piously.

Moysha Stroganoff was ninety-one. When you looked at him you realized this at once. He spent his days in an armchair snoozing in front of the fire and his thoughts ranged vaguely round all the people who had owed him money many years ago—for that had been his profession—and had not paid him back—which had still not been his ruin.

For Moysha Stroganoff had been one of the moneylenders at the Court of St. Petersburg and had done so well that practically the whole of it was in his debt. In fact, so many well-bred people were so deeply in his debt that little groups of them might be seen in salons confiding in one another and speculating what to do about it. And when that happens there is only one thing for a money-lender on the fringes of the Court of St. Petersburg to do. It is to go somewhere else. Moysha Stroganoff knew it. He went to Omsk. And there he had lived ever since. He and his son, and his son's son.

A devoted family, the Stroganoffs.

"But, papoushka," said Aliosha pleadingly. "Listen a little. Put aside your knitting and listen."

"My son, I am too old to listen," said Moysha. "And what can you have to say, my son, that I have not already heard many times? Besides, you mutter." He dangled a mass of red wool. "See," he said, "a sock for my son's son's son—when he has one."

Aliosha made the little joke. "Will he then have only one foot?"

"My son, you are a fool," said Moysha. "And also you have too much stomach. When I was but sixty-three I did not have a stomach. Nor have I yet." He rapped shaky fingers on the assortment of bones that were his diaphragm. "And that reminds me," he said, "I am thirsty." He tinkled a bell.

"Papoushka," said Aliosha, "when you were sixty-three you had a young, clever, loving son. Me," he reminded him. "When I came to you for money to begin business you gave it. You grumbled a little, but you gave it. And now," he pointed out, "I am richer than you."

"Ah," said Moysha, "but you have not as much monies as others owe me." He looked wistfully at the files stacked in the corner. "One day," he dreamed, "I will go back to Petersburg and collect."

"Papoushka," said Aliosha, "listen to me."

"No, I am too old to listen," said Moysha firmly. "Besides, I know it already. For was not old Vanka from the bank here last night to play chess? He beat me," he said indignantly. "And that reminds me—why you schange the schmall scheque for the mad artist from Petersburg?"

"But, papa," said Aliosha.

"It is not the action of a son of mine," said Moysha reprovingly. "The bad scheque from the aristocracy—yes, that is the legitimate speculation. But not for the artist. Where," he demanded, "is the screw to turn?"

Aliosha changed the subject. "Then if you know all," he said, "you will approve, and," he raised his voice, "you will help me."

"Speak up," snapped Moysha, "can't hear a word you say."

"You will help me," said Aliosha loudly.

"Out with it, son," said Moysha. "However disgraceful it may be," he brought in an echo from the past.

Aliosha produced a gold pencil. He opened his note-book. He wrote, " Will you find the finance to send Vladimir's ballet to Petersburg and my Katusha." On second thoughts he crossed the second item out.

The old man put on spectacles. He held the note-book upside down.

"Do you think that I am made of roubles," he demanded. "No and no and no," he trebled. "And no,"·he added to clinch it.

"And after this," said Stroganoff to the sandy man, "it will be clear to you, my friend, that now all is agreed and that soon we will be on our way to Petersburg."

The sandy man scratched his head.

Chapter Eight

HE love-nest was a sea of underwear, thick woollen underwear of the finest quality, all of it new. For to-morrow morning Vladimir Stroganoff was leaving for St. Petersburg to make the arrangements for the transfer of his company and when he had finished packing, he was going to have an early night to be fresh for the journey.

Natasha was helping Stroganoff to pack, and Aliosha from an armchair was giving his children moral support, while Nicholas Nevajno, who had dropped in to say good-bye, had been seized with the idea colossal for a ballet in the middle of it, and sat by the fire brooding on the details and speaking from time to time to report his progress.

"Vladimir," reminded Aliosha reprovingly, "the folding photo of your wife. You would not travel without that, my son?"

Stroganoff whipped it up and stowed it in his dressing-case. That made the fifth photograph of Natasha to be transported with him. Packing for the trip should have been a simple affair, for Stroganoff's heavy luggage was to follow with the Company. All that he needed, poof!—it go into a handbag! But somehow the handbag had not been large enough. For one thing it would not hold the spare fur collar that he so clearly required, not his second-best dressing-gown, nor his bath-sheet, nor his bedroom slippers, nor the extra shirts in case the train was late or the laundry slow or the Company delayed or, which was quite probable, all three. This last thought immediately suggested the need for several further articles.

"The brown suit is not enough," said Stroganoff. "Petersburg must not think I have but what I wear. And also for the evenings," he pointed out, "there is the grand tenue—with the carnation." He patted his lapel. "My pigeon, pack me my tails, my smoking, my dark-grey suit with the white stripe, and also my dark-blue suit with the red stripe."

"My son," said Aliosha, "these beautiful new suits for which I have paid many hundreds of roubles, in the valise they will be creased."

"You are silly, my papoushka," said Natasha. "We will put them in the trunk."

"The two trunks," corrected Stroganoff. He trundled them out, opened them, and blew.

Nevajno sneezed.

"And now," said Stroganoff a crowded half hour later, "we come to something very important. What shall I read in the hotel?"

"Read?" said Aliosha suspiciously.

"But voyons," said Stroganoff, "since my little pigeon will not be with me, would you wish that I lie and look at the ceiling?"

"You could think of me," said Natasha petulantly.

"That also," said Stroganoff. "But it is the opportunity unique for me to read my Shakespeare in German." He picked it up, blew on it, and edged it into one of the trunks. He lowered the lid. He pressed. He pressed harder. He sat down on it.

"This ballet," said Nicholas Nevajno into the puffing and blowing, "is called Paradise."

Natasha looked at her ruby-studded watch-brooch.

"It is late," she decided, "we will close the trunks to-morrow."

"How wise you are, my pigeon," said Stroganoff. "For if I closed it now I would surely have to open it to-morrow to put in something I have not yet remembered." He kissed her. "And now, good night, little father. It is but two o'clock," he beamed. "Nice and early."

The door opened. Kashkavar Jones came in.

"I have come to wish you bon voyage, Vladimir," he said. "I had meant to come early, but in the café they were talking of the revolution, and I talk, too."

"For myself I do not believe it will come," said Aliosha. "The rich," he waved his hands largely, "will not hear of it."

"You will hear of it," said Kashkavar Jones cheerfully, "and if not, then your son will hear of it. If you read 'Das Kapital' you will be convinced." He pulled it out.

The apartment panicked. All save Nicholas Nevajno, who went on brooding.

"Put it away," said Aliosha urgently. "Hide it. Tear it up. Do you not know," he said, "that if it is seen with you, you will be sent to Siberia and then you could not come with us to Petersburg. And you want to come to Petersburg," he coaxed.

Natasha and Stroganoff exchanged glances.

Kashkavar Jones looked torn. He muttered something about the glorious revolution.

"Reflect," urged Aliosha. "The revolution will be with us always. It has been with me since I was fifteen. But the chance to go to Petersburg it happen only once."

"The décor," said Nevajno, "is very difficult. For you understand that it must not look like any heaven that anyone has ever seen and yet," he shook his head, "it must look like heaven." He went back to his brooding.

Kashkavar Jones stowed his book away. "Olright," he said, "I will hide it in the cellar until we return." He shook a sorrowful head. "It is a pity, mind you, for all the time that I am in Petersburg, I shall be wondering how it ends."

After he had gone Stroganoff sighed heavily.

"Poor Kashka," he said. "I have not yet had the heart to tell him that he does not come with us."

Aliosha sat up. "Quoi donc!" he said. "Who does not come?"

"Kashkavar Jones!" said Natasha clearly. "His lifts!" She shuddered.

"Kashkavar Jones!" said Aliosha. "Not going! My son, you cannot do this thing."

The son looked sheepish. "But, papa," he said, "he is such a bad dancer."

"What do I care for that!" roared Aliosha. "Was not his mother your English governess?"

"Si," said Natasha, "and it show in his dancing."

"Clouds," said Nicholas Nevajno. "Many clouds. Some of them large." He illustrated. "And some larger."

"In Petersburg," said Natasha, "I must only have the best."

"Entendu," said Stroganoff with dignity. "My company it must be without flaw. And that," he pointed out, "is why we cannot take Kashka. It breaks the heart, but what would you?"

Aliosha shook a sad head. "My son, my son," he sighed, "how little you have lived. Good dancing is not everything—no, not even in the ballet. There is also the affection family. To leave behind our Kashka, who has danced for you since the first performance—we will not dwell on how—is no act of a son of mine. No." He folded his arms.

"It is expensive to take the ballet to Petersburg," argued Natasha, "and our budget it does not include the bad dancers."

"Budget—poof!" said Aliosha. "Have you no heart, woman? Imagine to yourself poor Kashka, who has pulled Vladimir's hair when he was small and whom I have many times chased with a stick from my flower-bed, left here in Omsk without his comrades and with no one from whom to borrow any money to pay his landlady." He blew his nose violently.

"Do not cry, papoushka," said Stroganoff, who was very red himself. "You have convinced me. Kashka comes with us."

"Twelve yards of tissue," said Nevajno. He seemed pleased with this remark.

"It is outrageous, this," said Natasha. "First I have to argue with Vladimir and then I have to argue with his father. Or else I am surrounded in Petersburg by all the bad dancers."

"Only Kashka," said Aliosha. "You do not understand, my daughter. If it were only a matter of dance then our Kashka would not even be in Omsk."

"As I have told you many times, my pigeon," said Vladimir, "his mother was my English governess. That is how I talk it so good." He smirked.

"And his father?" asked Natasha sharply.

"That is not known," said Aliosha. He looked the other way. He blushed.

"No golden gates," said Nevajno firmly.

Natasha threw in her hand. "Very well," she said. "Kashkavar Jones can come."

"Darling," said Vladimir overjoyed. He kissed her.

But Aliosha was still not satisfied. "And who else, Vladimir," he said ominously, "does not come to Petersburg with you?"

Vladimir Stroganoff looked distressed. But Natasha spoke out.

"Alexis," she said, "is no Nijinsky. And what is more he did not grow up in your backyard."

"You cannot blame him for that," said Aliosha. "And you have to admit, my daughter, that he tries very hard. And also," he pointed out, "I have lent him a hundred roubles on the security of his salary. Make a note, Vladimir," he enjoined, "to pay it to me."

"No," said Natasha. She stamped her foot.

The door opened. The man who was No Nijinsky came in. He was wearing a bright mustard overcoat.

"What say you?" he preened himself. "I had it made special for Petersburg."

"A sunset," said Nevajno. "Amber and surprise pink. And after that the deluge." He went back to his brooding.

"My friend," said Stroganoff, "I plan for the early night, and," he pointed out, "it is already three o'clock. Is this the time to ask me to admire overcoats? Mark you," he said judiciously, "it is a pretty colour, but it is too tight round the shoulders."

"I go to the tailor at once," said the man who was No Nijinsky, alarmed. He looked at the clock. "I still go," he said defiantly. "I cannot appear in Petersburg with the too-tight coat."

He went.

Aliosha roared with laughter. "Voilà," he said, "how can you leave this one behind. Poor Yassi the tailor, with his toothache." He roared again. "No, no, my daughter, he has to come."

Stroganoff looked anxiously at Natasha. "What say you, my darling?"

"Oh, very well," said Natasha. "But," her small mouth set, "not Little Igor."

"And why not Little Igor?" said Aliosha really hurt. "What has poor Little Igor done that he should be left behind?"

"He has dropped me," said Natasha. "In class."

"In class," said Aliosha scornfully. "To complain that you are dropped in class!"

"Percussion," said Nevajno.

"Papoushka," said Natasha seriously, "listen to me. Little Igor is not the good dancer, his mother was not an English governess, he did not pull Vladimir's hair in the nursery, nor have you chased him off any flower-beds with a stick. He has only just come to Omsk. Why should Little Igor come with us to Petersburg, tell me that? He has not even bought himself an overcoat."

A giant came into the room. He was effulging with astrakhan. Little Igor had not bought an overcoat, but he had got himself a new collar and cuffs.

"It will be cold in Petersburg," he boomed, "but like this, I shall not feel it." He pulled up a chair beside Nevajno.

"You," said Nevajno, "will be St. Peter. You will play it with your eyebrows. For the rest you just stand still." He went back to his brooding.

"What he talk about?" asked Little Igor.

"We do not know," said Stroganoff. He turned anxiously to Natasha.

"Very well," whispered Natasha. "This one can come. But you-know-who, never, never, never!"

"Then it is settled," said Stroganoff pleased, "and I can get to bed early." He looked at the clock.

The door opened. Old Vanka from the bank, half asleep, came trundling in an invalid chair. In it, very much awake, was grandpère Stroganoff. His cheeks were flushed and his eyes were shining.

"Grandpère," said Vladimir. "You, who have not left your apartment for fifteen years, come here to give me your blessing. I am touched." He knelt.

Moysha patted his grandson's head perfunctorily. "Go with God," he said. He waved him away and addressed the company.

"My children," he said, "I bring you the news that will delight you."

"Aunt Anastasia is dead at last?" asked Aliosha hopefully.

Moysha kept her alive with a shake of his head. "You will not go to Petersburg alone," he proclaimed. "You will not in your youth and inexperience, and," he fixed Aliosha with a bird-like glare, "your stupidity, have to pit yourselves against the sharp wits of the great city. No, my children," he announced, "there will be with you one, older, wiser and much more experienced."

"Nu?" said Stroganoff apprehensively.

"Me," said Moysha, rapping his breast with his bony knuckles. "I will travel there by train," he boasted.

"Aie!" said Aliosha.

Only Natasha retained her presence of mind. She crossed to the old man and kissed him.

"It is noble of you, grandpère," she said, "but we cannot accept this sacrifice. It will be cold in Petersburg," she pointed out, "and the journey will exhaust you. No, mon grandpère," she wheedled, "stay here in little Omsk, in your nice warm apartment, and Vladimir shall write you every day."

"Can't read," said Moysha crossly.

"But, papoushka," said Aliosha.

"Grandpère, listen," said Stroganoff.

"Silence, both of you," said Moysha. "It is decided that I go to Petersburg to see that you do not make fools of yourselves, and also," his face took on the look of a visionary, "to collect the money that many people owe me."

"But, papoushka . . ." said Aliosha.

"Speak when you're spoken to," snapped Moysha. "I have considered this thing in all its bearings and I am decided. I go to Petersburg and Vanka comes with me. Isn't that so, Vanka?"

The old cashier nodded blissfully. "I have always wanted to see the Nevsky Prospekt before I die," he said.

The room at large looked at one another. It shrugged. With fatalistic calm it accepted the position. For was it not Russian? The company embraced the old man. They said how glad they would be to have him with them. They filled hot-water bottles for him, they helped to trundle him into his sleigh, they called "good-bye" as the bells tinkled into the distance and they shouted back at the neighbours. All save Nevajno who sat on brooding into the fire.

"When the Angel of Death it come on, the light it go out," he told the empty room. "It is symbolic," he assured himself.

A quarter to five.

"One last glass of tea," said Stroganoff," and then ho! for my early night."

"Me, too, I wish for the early night," said Little Igor. He passed up his glass.

"My son," said Aliosha, deeming this the perfect moment, "you will do me the little favour. You know my Katusha?"

Vladimir said he knew Katusha. He said it a shade uneasily.

"Katusha lacks the confidence," said Aliosha. "She does not like to demand the parts that her talents merit." He paused. "What say you?" he asked.

Natasha said nothing, but she looked a lot.

"So," said Aliosha, "it is the Papa who must ask the son for her."

The son shivered. As for Natasha her arms were already akimbo.

"When we get to Petersburg," said Aliosha looking carefully at the ceiling, "you will see to it that it is Katusha who dances the Peri at the first performance."

All was silent save for Little Igor drinking tea.

Natasha, arms still akimbo, looked at Aliosha and defied him.

"It is better that you know at once," she said. "Your Katusha is not coming to Petersburg."

This did not register right away. When it did a dull flush diffused papoushka's face. And then he was on his feet, roaring with rage and knocking down the glass Little Igor was passing up.

"My Katusha!" he said. "My Katusha," he repeated. "MY

KATUSHA," he bellowed in capitals. All other words had failed him.

A chair scraped harshly. Nevajno was on his feet.

"It is no use," he said in disgust. "My whole conception it stink."

He strode out. He slammed the front door. He fell down the steps. He shouted back at the neighbours.

"A genius," said Little Igor admiringly.

*   *   *

At last the guests had gone. Stroganoff had taken Nevajno's chair and was brooding into the fire.

He had lost every battle. Kashkavar Jones was going to Petersburg. Little Igor was going, the man who was no Nijinsky was going, that cow Katusha was going. Grandpère was going, Vanka was going, every mediocrity in Omsk was going—except the brothel-keeper. In his hour of bitterness Stroganoff wondered why they had overlooked that one—he'd been in Omsk for years too. What chance would he have to dazzle St. Petersburg with this collection? Might as well stay in Omsk. He kicked moodily at the Louis Quinze.

But this was where Natasha showed her mettle. Young as she was, she realized that, just as there are moments to nag a husband, there are moments not to nag a husband. This was the perfect one.

"Come to bed, my darling," she said. "It will seem much better in the morning." She put an arm on his shoulder. "First things first," she counselled, "and the first thing is that we go to Petersburg. After that we will see."

"Little Igor," said Stroganoff. "The theatre thunders every time he jumps. Kashkavar Jones who cannot point the toe. Katusha!" He kicked the Louis Quinze. "What sort of effect is this we show the Capital?"

Natasha twined the other arm. "Never mind, darling," she said. "I will shine all the more brightly for it."

Stroganoff kissed her arms. He travelled up them, kissing.

"Come to bed," said Natasha.

Stroganoff rose slowly to his feet. He put an arm round Natasha. "To bed," he agreed. He kissed her warmly. He kissed her more warmly.

But as they drew apart a new blow fell. The clock struck. It was clustered with cupids, but it struck.

"Quelle horreur," said Stroganoff in despair. "My train it go in twenty minutes."

He made for the trunk and jumped on it.

Chapter Nine

AS this was a business trip, Stroganoff took the business-man's train—Russia's latest glory, the Trans-Siberian Express—all the way from St. Petersburg to Vladivostok in under ten days. An average speed of thirty miles an hour! No need to bring your own food, for there was a restaurant car. There was also a captain, just as though the train were a ship, and, if you were a personage, he would invite you to his table. No need to leave the train from start to finish, except, of course, at Irkutsk, where you and your luggage and your literature and your relations got into another train with a new set of as yet untipped attendants, and, of course, a new captain.

And the cost of all this luxury was only double the ordinary fare.

Well worth it, as Stroganoff explained to the comfortably-stomached stranger, who had been using the service ever since it started.

"Particularly," he added beaming, "as my *papoushka* pays."

"So you have the rich father," said the stranger. This plausible, bald-headed young man was by no means the first confidence-trickster he had met on the Trans-Siberian Express, though it was the first one who had started babbling at him before his luggage was fairly stowed away.

"Voilà," said Stroganoff, unwrapping a travelling rug and furling it round himself. "We are snug here. My little father," he boasted, "is the richest man in Omsk save one—my little grandfather, may he live many years yet."

"He is then the brothel-keeper?" said the stranger, a man of the world.

"Du tout," said Stroganoff coldly. "We are the ballet."

"Ballet," said the stranger, who had a reason of his own (a plump little reason, at the moment poised rather uncertainly in the first row of the corps-de-ballet at Vladivostok) for being interested in the subject. "You have a ballet in Omsk?"

"Omsk," said Stroganoff, "is a very moral town. There, the brothel-keeper is but the fifth richest citizen, and, since my ballet it come, he is, maybe, only the sixth."

Some of the wariness left the stranger. He opened a basket and passed over the leg of a chicken.

"The food in the restaurant is terrible," he explained, "so I bring the little extra."

Stroganoff produced a hip-flask. They feasted together, penduluming the flask and with every nip Stroganoff owned a slice more of the world.

"In what other Opera in all the Russias," he boasted, "will you find a company like ours. Our conductor!" He kissed his fingers. "Our prima ballerina!" He kissed them twice. "I tell you, my friend, she is the little Pavlova, the Trefilova in miniature, the Kschessinskaya of the East. And also," he remembered, "she is my wife."

"Then you married her," said the stranger. He pondered on this. He shook his head. He was married already.

"Voilà!" said Stroganoff. He whipped out a photograph.

"Oho!" said the stranger.

"But," said Stroganoff, "she has a mamoushka."

The stranger passed back the photograph. "Ah," he said sympathetically. There was a mamoushka in Vladivostok, too. He passed over a wing. The flask pendulumed.

"Mamoushka—poof!" said Stroganoff. He flung her off. "Soon we will be in Petersburg," he glanced at the snow-covered landscape crawling past, "and my little pigeon will be the toast of the town."

The landscape stopped. The locomotive was taking in water, or would be directly they had broken the ice.

"Soon," said Stroganoff, "we shall be in the wonderful theatre of our own, where all is telephone and lifts and even the safety curtain," he said in awe, "they tell me will work. And also," he added, "they tell me it will not burn, though of this I am not yet convinced."

The stranger considered. "It is possible," he said. "In Vladivostok we have the curtain that resists the fire—this has been proved. The theatre, you understand, was built of wood, so it perished, but the safety curtain is still there. They are building a new theatre around it. Of wood," he remembered.

"My theatre in Petersburg will be of marble," said Stroganoff, "with gilt on the domes and angels on the ceiling and red plush fauteuils. Almost one could sleep in them." He seized his chin. "Is this good?" he asked, worried.

"It is as well," said the stranger.

"There will be boxes," said Stroganoff. "Many boxes, for all the world of fashion will wish to subscribe and to be seen. The jewels!" He shielded his eyes.

"H'm," said the stranger. The plump little reason had strong views on jewels.

"The dressing-rooms will be warm, the stage vast, all the fountains, the trap-doors, the transformation scenes—we do them like that." Stroganoff flicked his fingers. "And in the orchestra pit there will be ample space so that," a memory came back, "the trombone does not keep hitting the neck of the double bass. And also," he enlarged, "there will be the foyer luxurious with a ceiling of gold and marble pillars and pictures of my ballerinas on the walls, and maybe," he envisaged, "a picture of myself."

"And where," asked the stranger dazzled, "will you find this—this palace?"

"My friend," said Stroganoff, "I have found it already. My little grandfather has given it to me. A great man, my little grandfather," he said. "The trouble I have had to persuade him to come to Petersburg with us! For days I pleaded. And then he say 'Yes,' and I am happy."

The locomotive hooted.

"Your grandfather has many interests in the capital?" asked the stranger.

"Well," said Stroganoff. He considered. "There are many people there that owe much to him."

"Influential," said the stranger. "I see." His voice took on a note of deep respect.

"Big influence," said Stroganoff. "It is this that get me the theatre. The little grandfather he influence the man who own it."

The stranger looked wise.

"Yes," said Stroganoff. "He demand that he pay back the note of his grandfather's hand or else . . ."

The stranger looked a little less wise. But Stroganoff was rambling on.

"So," he said, "we get the theatre suitable. But the owner does not wish to pay his grandfather's note of hand all at once so, for the moment, we get it for three nights a week and every other Sunday."

"I see," said the stranger. He didn't.

"On the other nights," said Stroganoff, "there is some other company, and that one pays with money to the owner. And this," he admitted, "is right, for he must live too."

"And this other company," said the stranger.

"They are the finest in all Russia," said Stroganoff. "No doubt. I do not yet know what they play," he conceded, "but it is probably the Racine and the Oscar Wilde, or something of that nature. You can assure yourself," he said, "that I will look closely into their repertory and I will not tolerate that they play Chekov or any of these modern comedies."

The stranger rummaged in his metropolitan memories. "I laughed at Dead Souls," he said.

"It is most important," said Stroganoff seriously, "that the company who share my theatre shall also share my high artistic standard. For you understand that I shall assemble around me not only the talent of Omsk but the entire intelligentsia of the capital."

"Oho," said the stranger. "Another Diaghilev."

"Diaghilev—poof!" said Stroganoff. "What to me is Diaghilev? Diaghilev," he pointed out pityingly, "has no little grandfather."

Chapter Ten

ST. PETERSBURG in early spring. General Dumka stopped and bought himself a buttonhole. Who said he was getting old? There was a nip in the air, but it only made his cheeks glow.

The capital, with its domes and spires of snow, was a city in a crystal bowl. Sleighs passed one another, all tinkling bells, cracking whips and puffed-out coachmen. Pedestrians, heavily swathed in furs, waddled along pavements, too wrapped up to bow. The shops were bright avenues of sophisticated Parisian temptation, and here and there a crystal tram clanged angrily at a snow-sweeper to get on with it.

A great city. A proud city. A city to which nothing could ever happen.

General Dumka glowed at it. It was good to be out on this fine spring morning. It was good to be alive. And for the first time since his retirement, it was good to look into the future. For at last he was to take his rightful place in the world of the ballet. No longer would he be just seat number nineteen in the front row of the dress circle—a little too much to the left. When he spoke people would have to listen—even young Diaghilev would have to cock an ear. For was he not about to become the chief patron of a wonderful company from Omsk, and rightly so, for had he not planted the seed that was about to blossom in the great city? Was he not this morning to meet his new bosom-friend, Vladimir Stroganoff, an impresario with vision—even though he might be unsound on Durakova? And was he not to stay at his elbow at every move, like Nouvel with Diaghilev, counselling and suggesting and attending to very detail? Good as the company from Omsk no doubt was, it would need to recruit fresh glory and he, Dumka, only yesterday cut short by Kschessinskaya's mamoushka, would have the final word in the recruiting. What more could a Russian General require?

General Dumka mounted the marble steps of the Hôtel de l'Europe. It had a revolving door and a commissionaire specially engaged to swivel it. What is more he was already there and swivelling.

General Dumka timed it and passed through. A bald dome pounced on him and·swivelled him back into the street again.

"You are retarded my friend," said Stroganoff. "Hurry or we will be late for class at the Maryinsky."

"The Maryinsky," said Dumka. "We cannot go there. They will not let us in."

"Non?" said Stroganoff surprised. "But I am the impresario from Omsk!"

"Omsk is not enough," said General Dumka sadly.

Stroganoff pondered. "And the little bribe," he said. "does it not then work in the Capital?"

St. Petersburg in spring and a lovely morning in Theatre Street. Snow brightened the ledges and crowned the façades of the classical avenue which ended in the State Theatre and flanked and contained all that stood for theatrical tradition in Imperial Russia. Here, cut off from the vulgarity of the city, in rooms of classical proportions, stood the schools, the dormitories, the rehearsal rooms, the wardrobes and the students' theatre.

Here sloe-eyed children of ten came every year to show their paces to an assembly of implacable judges. The more fortunate children were swallowed whole into the mystery; to be fed, clothed and scolded more thoroughly than they would have been at home, to be submitted to a rigorous discipline of muscle, mind and behaviour, and to emerge seven years later, not as full-fledged ballerinas—oh no! but just about fit to be risked in a pas de six on some not too important occasion, and so privileged to carry, in their turn, the flaming torch of the Maryinsky tradition. And such was the strength of the training that, in spite of its weight, few found the torch too heavy, though lately there had been a distressing tendency to abandon it for marriage or for Diaghilev. Telyakov, the State Director, disapproved strongly of both. The first was inevitable more or less, but for the second there could be no excuse. These dancers owed a duty to the State, which had fed, clothed, perfected and helped to keep them safe from the snares of the world and dependent great-aunts. . . .

"The Maryinsky," explained Stroganoff to the sandy man, "might request a dancer to leave, but for a dancer to request to leave the Maryinsky . . ." He threw up his arms. "No," he said, "my good friend Telyakov did not like my good friend Diaghilev."

"Who didn't like what?" asked the sandy man. He blinked.

"Alors," said Stroganoff, "we are in St. Petersburg in the early spring . . ."

A fine morning in Theatre Street.

The sentry on guard outside the seminary was stamping the

blood back into his toes. He wished he were a dancer and could keep his feet warm. But papoushka had been against it. This had been the blow that broke mamoushka's heart, and not the Other Woman, as his grand-mamoushka had always insisted. How had he got into the guards? He couldn't remember.

Telyakov passed through the portals. The sentry clicked his heels and saluted. Diaghilev came through. The sentry saluted. With light steps the ballerinas came hurrying in. The sentry winked at them. Wiry little girls with their hair brushed back, and tough little boys, with their hair unbrushed, raced one another to the doors. The sentry cuffed them. One of the cooks came staggering through laden with two baskets. The sentry gave him a hand. "To-morrow," he said, "we will both be rich." To-morrow was the day of the State Lottery.

General Dumka turned into the avenue. With him was a pair of yellow boots from the provinces. They squeaked. The sentry stopped them.

"Gentlemen," he said, "your carte d'entrée."

They passed it. It was a ten-rouble note.

"Quite in order," said the sentry. "But remember," he warned them, "I have not seen you."

A lovely morning in Theatre Street. The sun came slanting in through the great windows of the practice-room in the State Theatre. It gilded the bare calm wall, it glanced across the barre that had sustained so many sweating featherweights, it reflected from the shiny grand piano (perfectly tuned), and on to the pianist, who was not a beaky old lady with chilblains and a cold. It shone back, a thousand discs of radiance, from the chandeliers and it touched the room warmly to life so that the people moving in the great mirrors seemed as real as the people moving in the great room. It reflected the dancers in practice costumes waiting for the maestro to arrive and limbering up as they waited—and never an odd ballet shoe among them. It reflected a group of intelligent ravens on small gilt chairs lining a corner of the classroom, attendant on a larger raven, with a single white lock, perched on an equally hard chair.

Serge Diaghilev, at the moment not yet edged out of his position as artistic adviser to the Maryinsky, had the right to attend all classes, and, though he generally failed to get up in time, this morning he had done it. He had reasons of his own, which Telyakov, the State Director, would certainly not have approved, for wishing to study this class.

Stroganoff and General Dumka, admitted unobtrusively to a well-bribed recess and told to remain unobserved and act as though they belonged there, had much the same reason for attending class as Diaghilev, though rather worse prospects.

"The maestro," said Stroganoff despondently, "I have to bribe him too?"

"Sssh," said General Dumka horrified.

In the centre of the room a young man was leaping and beating the air.

"Come down, Vatza," called the ballerina Karsavina. "Let us try the lifts in Lac."

But Nijinsky went on jumping as though he had not heard. He was clumsy this morning. He must limber up before the maestro came. Only entre chat-huit so far. Pfui!

The other dancers, too, were working, each after her own fashion. It was as well to be supple before the maestro arrived, for who knew what mood he might arrive in? They went on working like devils possessed.

The door opened. Not a heart but missed a beat. Not a hand but made to cross itself.

The maestro was coming in.

"Non, non, non, non! Aie, aie, aie! You dance like poodles—all of you! And you!" The stick came down on a thigh with a thwack.

It was all right. The maestro was in a good mood on this bright spring day.

The piano tinkled. The stick banged. The maestro moved among his sweating pupils, encouraging them after his own manner.

"And you, Mathilde. What is this effect that you give us? What time were you back from the Cubat last night? No, do not tell me, for you will only lie."

The divine Kschessinskaya, Ballerina Assoluta of the Maryinsky Theatre, the darling of the metropolis, who was to marry a grand duke and who lived in a little palace of her own, the naughty little Mathilde went scarlet.

"But I drink the nothing," she excused herself. "One little glass of Mumm, and that only because of Svetlov entreated me."

The maestro produced a handkerchief. He dried her eyes. He patted her cheek. "Don't do it again, little poodle," he said. He turned on another straining back. "The heel," he rapped, "raised. The 'ip in. The back strong." He stood back and regarded the perfect line. "Ah," he said, "that is better. It begins now to resemble an arabesque."

"But it is not bad—the arabesque," said Stroganoff to General Dumka. He tilted his head. "Ma foi, it is not bad at all."

"It is Karsavina," said Dumka in tones of mingled reproof and prayer.

Anyone else would have hung his head. But not Vladimir.

"And they treat her like this," he said indignantly. "I make her the offer for my company. How much, you think, will she ask?"

"You are too late, my friend," said Dumka. "It is rumoured that she goes again with Diaghilev to Europe."

"Is it signed?" asked Stroganoff keenly.

Diaghilev, too, had been watching the arabesque.

"Exasperating," he said.

"Tatya is being difficult again?" asked Nouvel, sitting next to him.

"If it were only that," said Diaghilev. He sighed. "First she will come to us and then she won't. Then she must dance all the rôles and then not any of them, then it is more money and then it is the guarantee that I will pay it. I tell you that if I did not need her so much I would tell her to go to," he pondered, "Omsk," he substituted.

Nouvel looked at Stroganoff. "Your rival?" He grinned.

Diaghilev did not smile. "Do not underrate the provincial," he said. "If he can get his hand on money he can be a nuisance."

Nouvel eyed Stroganoff again. He noted the bright yellow boots. "What nonsense, Sergei," he said. "Which ballerina would go to him when she could come to us?"

"You can never tell what a ballerina will decide to do," said Diaghilev gravely. Particularly," he added just as gravely, "when she is in a temper."

A small bundle of femininity came into the room, hurried to the barre, lifted a leg, and tried to look as though she had been there all the time. This ballerina was late. So it was the maestro who decided to be in a temper.

"Arenskaya," breathed Dumka devoutly through the falling heavens.

"So, my darling," said the maestro, an adder about to strike, "you have slept deeply—yes?"

Arenskaya clutched the barre. She had to face the cataclysm, she had to survive it, and what is more, she had to survive it without bursting into tears. She threw out her chin.

"The chin—in," said the maestro. He slapped it.

"Did they forget your morning tea, my darling?" he pursued, "or was it that your dear friend was loath to leave you?" He looked at her. "No," he said, "it could not have been that."

Arenskaya breathed in. She clenched her teeth. She shot a look at the maestro containing everything she must not say. But the maestro had turned away. An expert, he knew he could not improve on his last remark.

"Alors," he rapped. "Centre practice, my little darlings."

Wistfully the perfection class of the Maryinsky Theatre abstracted itself from Arenskaya's dilemma and took up positions that were certain to lead to dilemmas of their own.

"Ah—that class of perfection." To the sandy man's horror there were tears in Stroganoff's eyes. "Trefilova, Egorova, Preobrajenskaya, Karsavina, Kyasht, Nijinsky," the names were all part of his personal litany. "And Pavlova," he crowned them, "though, also, she was not at class that day. All young, all ravishing, all with their future before them, all working—all working hard—in that room. And I," he shook his head, "I was young, too, and perhaps a little silly, though you might not guess it. What are they now?" he looked into the present. "They are old ladies and they teach in Paris and they hope to find a talent as great as theirs. And me, the old man with the stomach, I know that it does not exist."

"What about Robert Helpmann?" asked the sandy man.

But Stroganoff had not heard. "Ah, those were the days. All those Goddesses," he mourned, "in one room, and I," he sighed, nostalgia getting the better of truth, "privileged to go and watch them at their practice whenever I wished. To think," he said sorrowfully, "that there were mornings when I did not do it." He paused to regret it. "And to-day," he said, "you have to cross the Atlantic to see Anton Dolin."

The piano tinkled. The stick banged. The maestro sat and gazed non-committally at his pupils.

Egorova, Trefilova, Preobrajenskaya, Karsavina, Kyasht, Kschessinskaya, and the Little Lopokova.

No Pavlova, the maestro noted. Resting! Never heard of such a thing!

"Alors," he said. He waved his hands.

The class stood aside while Egorova, Trefilova and Kschessinskaya watched the old man as he devised a complicated enchainement with his fingers. They sailed through it.

"Disgraceful," said the maestro. "Bad, bad, bad. You dance like a circus."

Egorova, Trefilova and Kschessinskaya went through it again.

"Mon Dieu," said Stroganoff. "And I thought that the class at Omsk was good!" He wept.

Karsavina, Lopokova and Kyasht took the floor, floated flawlessly, and were duly chided by the maestro. They floated again.

"My friend," said Stroganoff. "What am I dreaming of? What use to bring my ballet to St. Petersburg." He got up. "I go back to Omsk," he announced.

The paling Dumka tugged him back. "Courage, Vladimir," he said. "Your troubles but begin."

On the floor someone else's troubles had begun. Arenskaya had overbalanced.

It was too much for the maestro. His gentle irony left him. It left him spitting, clawing and screaming. Terrified, Arenskaya backed. The maestro, bent almost double in a combination of fury and old age, hobbled after her, screaming as he hobbled. Backing and screaming they arrived at the corner of the room where Stroganoff and Dumka were trying to look as though they were not there.

They need not have troubled.

"You," screamed the maestro, "you will get out of my class. You will never come back. You will never let me see your silly face again, nor your deformed développé, nor your bent arabesque, nor," he paused to find the final insult, "nor your big behind."

"It is not big," screamed Arenskaya suddenly. A ballerina can stand just so much. "I take myself from your class. I take me from your stupid teaching. I take me from the whole Maryinsky. I take me from the world." She wept.

"Out!" quivered the maestro. "Out—before my heart it attack me."

"Out," advised the class in an urgent whisper. "Go now and apologize later."

"Apologize, never!" Arenskaya defied them. "You shall all crawl to me. All. You shall eat your word when I get me the other contract. The contract stupendous." She looked straight at Diaghilev.

But Diaghilev, a diplomat if ever there was one, was deep in conversation with Benois.*

"I go," said Arenskaya despairingly. "I go—not to come back no more."

* Footnote to faithful readers: 'E 'ad come–clearly 'e was not yet 'imself.

She waited. Nobody said don't. Blind with rage she made for the door.

A bald dome leapt after her, unfolding a document as he leapt.

"Sign," panted Stroganoff. "Sign quick."

Blind with rage, Arenskaya seized the fountain pen and scribbled. "Voilà!" she said. A thought struck her. "Mon Dieu, what is it that I have signed?" She tried to snatch it back.

But Stroganoff held the document safely behind him.

"It is the contract stupendous," he told her reassuringly.

The maestro marvelled at himself. Why wasn't he having a heart attack?

"Out, out, out, out, out!" he screamed.

He was.

Chapter Eleven

 UNCH.

A quiet little restaurant round the corner.

Everybody went there.

It was the perfect place for confidential conversations. Though everybody could be heard by everybody else, you could be quite confident that not one of them would be listening.

Dancers have themselves to talk about.

"My flowers . . ." said Karsavina, from a table in the corner.

"My public . . ." said Kschessinskaya from a centre table.

"My mamoushka," said Trefilova, Egorova and Preobajenskaya. But they were saying it at different tables.

"Where can I get some ballet shoes?" mused Nijinsky, who wore his out more quickly than the State could supply them.

"My career," said Arenskaya fiercely. "You wish that I bury my whole career in Omsk!"

"Not Omsk, my darling," soothed Dumka for the seventh time. "This is only the town which our dear friend here has left for ever."

The three of them were seated at the draughtiest table in the room. They had come here to cement the contract with the friendly little luncheon. They had ordered champagne, but it had not yet arrived, and the little repast delicious, which would, no doubt, be served in due course. And in the meantime Stroganoff and Dumka were impressing their first ballerina with the opportunities for glory hovering over the contract she had so rashly signed, just before they were thrown out of the Maryinsky.

Arenskaya needed a lot of convincing.

"Me," she said, "the most admired 'ips of all, and you bury them in Omsk."

"Ah—the champagne," said Stroganoff thankfully. It was a little warm, but he poured it out. And as Arenskaya stopped weeping to drink, he seized his chance.

"Not Omsk," he said. "The theatre magnificent in Petersburg—with the name in my valise."

"And you," said Dumka, "shall be the leading ballerina."

"Save, of course," said Stroganoff, "for my wife."

A loyal remark, but tactless.

"In your company," declared Arenskaya, a crouching cat, "I dance as Assoluta or not at all. Is this not in my contract?"

"It is not," said Stroganoff, apprehensively.

At his corner table, Diaghilev began to enjoy himself, though you would never have thought it to look at him. The Provincial was learning. Soon he would begin to understand that it was not so easy to run a ballet company.

"I must go to little Ginsberg again," he told Fokine. "He must get me more money somehow."

The waiter trundled a trolley of zakuski across the floor. Caviar, smoked salmon, foie gras, prawns in aspic—delicious! He pulled up at the table on the far side of Arenskaya and kept an anxious eye on the dishes as he served.

"It will turn to ashes in my mouth," declared Arenskaya, helping herself lavishly.

"And that, my friend," Stroganoff told the sandy man, "was the beginning of the comradeship that has lasted all my life. We have worked together, we have starved together, we have laughed together, and we have wept together. Always, always Arenskaya has been at my side—except for when she walk out on me—advising, helping and encouraging. If she were my darling daughter," he said, "she could not love me more."

The door opened. The loving daughter, an aged crow in a nasty temper, hurried in.

"I spit me of your company," she shrilled. "I leave to-morrow, no—sooner. I go at once." She stayed where she was. "You are the dishonest rogue, the crooked one, the thief of Baghdad." Uplifted by her own rhetoric she turned on the sandy man.

"I do not exaggerate," she assured him. "He is the Prince of Ali Babas and prison is too good for him."

" 'Ush," said Stroganoff. "Less loud. The rich one he comes at any moment." He looked anxiously at the door.

"Bon," said Arenskaya. "I wait for him." She sat down. She glared at Pavlova. "I tell him all—all," she assured the photograph. She fixed Stroganoff with a quivering claw. "I tell him how you stew the books and make the fool of the income tax collector, the poor trusting one, and rob the noble England that has given you so much and also the visa."

" 'Ush," said Stroganoff more loudly. "Shoot oop, or I talk back. I tell the rich one how in your trunk there are two bottles of brandy of which you tell the poor deluded customs nothing. Not one word," he assured the sandy man. "She ogle and she show him the little packet of cigarettes."

"It is you who drink the brandy," screamed Arenskaya. "And also," she remembered, a broken woman, "smoke the cigarettes!

P

Wait," she encouraged herself. "Wait till the rich one comes. Wait till I tell him how you rob everyone, and how," she waved a slit-open pay envelope, "you have just rob me."

"Poof," said Stroganoff uneasily, "it will not be of interest."

"He will put you in prison," said Arenskaya with relish, "and you will eat your English skilly, and me, I shall sit outside the cell and drink the champagne."

The sandy man, an unfledged dove, tried to reconcile the two old friends.

"Poor Mr. Stroganoff," he said. "What has he done? Perhaps he didn't mean it . . ." Before the two-pronged glare that was switched on him by both assailants, he tailed off.

"Done," screamed Arenskaya. "I will tell you what he has done, and you will see for yourself that never has there been such a monster." She took a deep breath. "When we get to London, I need the new dress for the opening night, *his* opening night," she pointed out. "Is it not natural that I wish to do him credit? And he say to me, this monster of perfidity, he say, 'Go and get it, my darling.' And I think he is generous, and I kiss him and go. And now, figurez-vous," she flung out an arm, "he begin to deduct it from my salary. Me—an old woman!"

"And did I tell you, an old woman," thundered Stroganoff, "to spend yourself the fifty pounds so that you look like a schoolgirl who has grown too quick."

Arenskaya's heel tapped. "Now," she said, "now he insult me." She turned on the sandy man. "Why you not knock him down?"

"I defend myself," said Stroganoff. He sprang up and crouched behind his fists.

"Why not split the difference," said the sandy man swiftly.

Arenskaya looked at him with cold contempt. "So you are both against me," she declared. "Very well—I invoke the British justice. We have the court case and the judge make me the compliments on my hat—all feathers. I go to my solicitor to arrange this now."

Full of dignity she made for the door. On the threshold she turned. "If the mirror in the classroom is not mend by to-morrow, I," she paused for the awful threat, "will not take the class."

She swept out.

"It is the third time that the slipper it slip from her hand," confided the suddenly subsided Stroganoff. He shrugged. "What signifies a broken mirror so long as she is happy while she breaks it! Ah, my friend," he said, "the ballet it might go on without Arenskaya, but then it would go on without me." He looked fondly at the photograph on his desk. "I will pay the fifty pounds," he said, "but only after the hard struggle, or else, you understand, she will buy the new dress every day."

"Then this little—er—contretemps," said the sandy man, "was not entirely unexpected?"

Stroganoff beamed. "My friend," he said, "I have been awaiting it all morning."

The friendly little lunch was growing friendlier. The champagne might be warm, but so was the food. Under the influence of both Arenskaya had settled down to make the best of what she had signed, and so, save by wheedling, could not help.

Flushed by his success, Stroganoff had grown more and more ambitious. Not a dancer at the Maryinsky but was visualized, signed up, rehearsed and making the appearance triumphant at the theatre with the name in the valise. He waved away the two obstacles that sprang up monotonously as each name danced across the table—first Arenskaya's dead body, over which it appeared each dancer would have to be dragged, and next Dumka's forebodings that they were signed by Diaghilev already. He gulped more champagne, scribbled down telephone numbers, and urged Dumka to contact them without further waste of time.

"Have in me the confidence," he urged. "I know I come only from Omsk, but," he glowed, "I have the vision."

"You visualize me as the Assoluta," said Arenskaya back to her battements.

"Si, si," said General Dumka. He patted her shoulder.

"Alors," said Stroganoff, "to work, mes amis. You," he told Dumka, "shall speak of our project to the ballerinas. You, my star," he looked thoughtfully at Arenskaya, "shall go and rest yourself after the emotions of the morning. I send you some roses." He made a note. "And I," he gloated, "shall go and look at my beautiful theatre. But first," he remembered, "I must go to my valise."

General Dumka raised his glass. "To our beautiful theatre," he toasted.

Stroganoff raised his. "To our beautiful ballerina," he said.

Arenskaya raised hers. "To our season." She drank. She caught sight of Karsavina and Kyasht, two interested angels at the centre table. They should crawl! Crawl! "To our glorious season," she amended. She drank again.

Chapter Twelve

 EARLY morning in St. Petersburg. The spires and domes of the holy city lay peacefully beneath their eiderdowns of snow waiting for the sun to touch them to life. Even the great railway station looked like the snow queen's palace—from the outside. Inside all was draught and depression.

The booking clerk was wondering why anybody should want to go anywhere and took it as a personal affront that they should disturb him to do it. The porters swore and blew on their fingers and sighed for the revolution—meantime they were determined not to be found anywhere.

But the most depressed figure of all was that of Vladimir Stroganoff, pacing up and down what he hoped was the right platform. Yet this was the hour when his company was to arrive from Omsk, the end of the overture and the curtain going up.

Stroganoff sighed. Two weeks in the capital had wrought a deep change in our optimistic impresario. It had been a terrible two weeks. Getting the company together had proved a nightmare instead of a series of triumphant toasts. Old Dumka had rushed around, promising and pleading, but either the ballerina approached had already signed with Diaghilev or she said 'Omsk' and changed the conversation. Men were easier to find, indeed, a number had been engaged, but they were no Nijinskis, and, as Stroganoff fiercely pointed out, he had one of these already.

One coup they had achieved—Ivan Ivanoff by name, Nevajno's bosom friend, who spat every time the choreographer's name was mentioned. But no doubt this was merely his eccentric way of expressing appreciation.

But for the rest, whether it was dancers or painters or composers or dressmakers, or anything at all of the first excellence, there was always an obstacle and always it turned out to be the same obstacle—Sergei Diaghilev. Either Diaghilev had got in first, which was hopeless, or the party was still waiting to be approached by him, which at the best meant delay, indecision and a long haggle.

For ever since Diaghilev had come back from Paris, where the triumph of his Russian opera and ballet had started a fashion, all St. Petersburg had been dazzled—save the bankers. Last year Diaghilev had conquered Paris, this year it was to be Europe. And everybody wanted to be in on it—save the bankers.

Paris, thought Stroganoff. Poof! What was Paris? What did they know of ballet there? Europe! What was a European tour? What wouldn't he give to have one of his own? Instead of the theatre of his little grandfather!

The theatre magnificent! Ha!

Stroganoff tried to think of something else. Soon he would see his Natasha. He would clasp her in his arms. She would ask him many questions. He grew depressed again.

A certain excitement became noticeable on the platform. Porters, like reluctant rabbits, came out of their burrows and a very old man trundled a samovar on to the platform and fortified himself from it while he waited for the rush.

With a triumphant hoot the engine pulled up. Natasha's little head was bobbing out of a carriage window.

Stroganoff's troubles dropped from him and he sprinted towards it.

"My darling, it is a hundred years," Stroganoff embraced his bride.

"Vladimir, Vladimir," said the smothered Natasha.

"Mind her hat," said mamoushka.

"So this is St. Petersburg," said Kashkavar Jones. He looked round. "Not so big as London," he hazarded a guess.

"My fur collar," mourned Little Igor. "Moth," he pointed.

"Alors, alors, to eat," said papoushka. He linked himself on to Katusha, who was standing in that part of the queue that had not yet kissed Vladimir.

"My native city!" observed Nevajno. "Pfui!"

A warming reunion. But in one more sentence it was over.

"And now," said Natasha on tiptoe with excitement, "take me to see my theatre."

A finger of frost touched Stroganoff's spine. "Presently, my darling," he said. "Presently. But first," he said, "we have the breakfast delicious at the boarding-house." He looked depressed.

"I am too excited to eat," said Natasha. "Let us go now—now!"

"You are tired, my darling," said Stroganoff. "You have been many days on the train. You want the little bath refreshing." He thought of the worn-off enamel. "The little slumber to restore you," he thought of the rattling shutter and the rock-like mattress, "and then," he finished manfully, "I take you to the theatre."

"Come," said Papoushka, "let us eat."

"No," said Natasha firmly. "I must go to my theatre at once." She stamped her foot. "At once, Vladimir."

"At once, Vladimir," said mamoushka. She started.

"We come, too," said the rest of the company. They tugged at their baggage.

"Me," said the Papoushka obstinately, "I go and eat." He stamped off.

Nevajno stamped after him. Somebody might as well pay for his breakfast.

Early as it was, there was a line of droshkis outside the station. The company collared the lot, loaded on their luggage, piled themselves inside, and, a stream of triumph, jingled their way into the heart of the city.

"We must be nearly there," said the man who was No Nijinsky expectantly.

They jingled out again.

"It is very far, this theatre," said mamoushka, suspiciously.

"It is a very slow driver," said Stroganoff quickly. They jingled on.

"Look," said Little Igor, pointing to a poster showing a trainer about to pounce on a lion. "A circus! I must go."

"It will not be as good as the one that came to Omsk," said Katusha loyally.

"In Londres," said Kashkavar Jones, "there is a bigger circus—the biggest circus in the world where everybody goes. It is called," he said, "Pic-a-dolly, I think. Often my mamoushka go there." He sighed.

They jingled on.

"It is very far, this theatre," said Natasha. Her mamoushka nodded grimly.

"It depends from where you start," said Stroganoff firmly.

And they jingled on some more and eventually they reached the Theatre Boris Goudonov and the company stood and admired while Stroganoff paid off the droshkis.

The Theatre Boris Goudonov had been triumphantly constructed many years ago. It combined, in a burst of generosity, the worst features of many types of architecture. This was because so many architects had resigned in rage during its construction and each succeeding architect had had firm ideas of his own, while the owner had been equally firm in refusing to scrap anything already built. But the cluster of golden mushrooms that formed the roof had glistened when the paint was new, and everybody's grandparents on the opening night had marvelled as expected at the enormous shining chandeliers, the drinking fountain in the vestibule and the crimson plush of the fauteuils. How pleased the Official Receiver had been!

But that was nearly a hundred years ago. Now the gold had turned green, the paint was peeling, and St. Petersburg had meanly chosen other spots as its fashionable quarters.

But the company from Omsk was eager to be imptessed. All save the mamoushka.

"Ah," they said. They stood back and looked at their theatre. "Ah," they said again.

"It is very large," said Little Igor loyally.

"But, my friend," Stroganoff shook a remembering head, "it was no use. Already I knew that the goose could not be kept in the bag and that soon my company must know that the debt to my little grandfather had been paid with the pup in the poke. The Theatre Boris Goudonov was . . ." he felt for the word.

"Not good enough," said the sandy man archly.

Stroganoff looked at him gravely. "You are right, my friend," he said. "It was not good enough."

"Shabby old barn! What man of fashion," demanded the mamoushka angrily, "would come to such a circus!"

"Voilà," said Stroganoff quickly.

A fashionable figure was making its way down the unswept stairs. Long-stemmed roses burgeoned from its arms and a ribbon flew out in the wake of its progress.

It was General Dumka.

"Mille pardons," he bowed low to Natasha. "Nothing but business of the most urgent would have kept me from welcoming you at the station." He presented the flowers and while Natasha raved over them and the mamoushka counted the blooms and the other mamoushkas looked enviously on and saw that she didn't cheat, he drew Stroganoff to one side.

"Novikoff," he hissed, "says No."

"He goes to Diaghilev?" hissed Stroganoff.

"It is not yet settled," peeved Dumka. "It is agreed only that he does not come to us.

"Voilà!" said Stroganoff hopefully. "The auditorium."

The company gasped. All those seats to be filled! All that plush!

"The company that play the Racine and the Oscar Wilde," said Little Igor doubtfully, "they draw the town?"

"My friend," said General Dumka, "they pack the house."

The company closed its eyes. For a moment it could not see the red plush for bare shoulders shining with diamonds. For a moment the golden dome was ringing with bravas! The man who was No Nijinsky gave a little skip.

"Vladimir," said the mamoushka, peering keenly along the edge of the stage. "What is this that looks like sawdust?"

"Sawdust," said Stroganoff firmly.

They went backstage.

"Voilà, my darling," said Stroganoff, arriving outside a vermilion door. "Your dressing-room. The star's dressing-room," he added, and flung it open.

Inside was Arenskaya. She was well installed. She must have brought all her possessions, including a baby sea lion that howled immediately.

"Pardon," said Stroganoff. He made to close the door.

But Arenskaya was on her feet and cooing over Natasha. So does a serpent coo at a rabbit.

"Ah," she said, "the little one from Omsk. But your travelling hat is charming—charming. I had one just like this last year! I am sorry now that I have given it to the maid—she does not know how to wear it, that one."

Natasha looked round for her mamoushka. But the mamoushka was in the corridor frowning at what looked exactly like an elephant.

"Pardon," said Stroganoff quickly, "I make the introduce. My little wife," he kissed the no-time-to-snatch-away hand. "Our new friend, Arenskaya, who has come to the company."

"As Assoluta," said Arenskaya sweetly. "We will be the great friends," she followed up her advantage, "see if we are not. Watch me closely and you will learn much, my dear. They tell me," she said kindly, "that already you show much promise."

Once again Natasha looked round for her mamoushka. But mamoushka was still gazing at what still seemed to be an elephant. So Natasha joined battle alone.

"You are very kind," she said, "and I am very cross with Vladimir that he did not tell you this was the dressing-room of the star. Now," she was all sympathy, "you have all the trouble of moving."

But before Arenskaya could reply Stroganoff had intervened.

"Mais non," he said, "it is I who make the mistake. I explain outside," he hissed to Natasha. "Come."

"Vladi-mir!" The voice of the mamoushka floated sharply into the room. Once and for all she meant to decide was this, or was this not an elephant?

"Quick," said Stroganoff. He raced his little bride in the opposite direction and they had mounted a flight of stairs before she had found her breath.

"I take you to your dressing-room," panted Stroganoff. "It is the real star's dressing-room," he assured her, "but do not tell Arenskaya this."

"Above stage level? So?" said Natasha. Her little mouth set.

Stroganoff flew her along a corridor flanked with tanks with fishes in them. At the other end of it was the coming-up mamoushka.

"Vladimir," she pointed to a tank. "Tell me the truth. Is that, or is that not, an octopus?" In a dazed fashion she counted.

"Presently," said Vladimir, and flew his bride down another

flight of stairs. He avoided the elephant and flung open a Prussian blue door.

"Voilà," he said, "the star's dressing-room."

In it was a lion. It was in a wheelable cage and it was asleep, but it was a lion.

Stroganoff gave up the struggle. He stood silent as the rest of the company crowded in and looked at the lion and looked at each other and looked at their mamoushkas and wondered what to say.

"This . . . other company," said Natasha at last. "This company that plays the Racine and the Oscar Wilde, is it by chance," the syllables fell like ice, "a circus?"

The company held its breath.

Stroganoff turned away.

"Oui," he said heavily.

Chapter Thirteen

HE great day had come. It was snowing.

To-night the Ballet Stroganoff from Omsk opened in St. Petersburg.

To-night the Theatre Boris Goudonov would be packed with a critical, appraising, cosmopolitan audience—balletomanes to a brassière.

To-night General Dumka would wear all his medals. To-night Stroganoff would make a speech.

To-night ballerinas would be wildly elated or beating their bosoms. To-night their mamoushkas would be elated with them or beat their bosoms even harder.

To-night was to be a triumph.

To-night Stroganova would take her six curtains.

But at the moment it was the répétition generale. Not, by common consent, sufficiently general to let in the critics, but, by common resignation, insufficiently private to keep out the circus.

Even what had turned out to be definitely an elephant was looking on from the vast recesses of the wings. Whatever this was, it was certainly no circus.

In fact, it was the ballet 'Sylvia,' which had drawn all Paris—for forty years—and which Stroganoff, in a cauldron of seething mamoushkas, had selected for his opening night. For, as sitting alone in the stalls he explained to his stomach-patting papoushka, it contained Sylvia, the part delicious and not too difficult for Natasha, and Cupid, which with a little rearrangement and a seasoning of solos, had been made large enough to satisfy Arenskaya—except, of course, in the billing.

"And my Katusha?" asked Aliosha suspiciously.

"She is the Goddess Diane," said Stroganoff.

Papoushka considered. "Has she got a pas seul?" he asked.

"She dominate the stage," said Stroganoff.

"Ah," said Papoushka. "But has she got a pas seul?"

"She is in her temple," said Stroganoff, "and all kneel to her."

"But has she got a pas seul?" said Papoushka. Almost he might have been a mamoushka.

"You will see," said Stroganoff tactfully. He changed the subject. "We were right," he said, gazing at the fauns and dryads limbering up on the stage, "to choose a ballet Petersburg has not seen for many years. The music is familiar, the story is old, but it is easy to follow and it calls for no one to compare with Nijinsky. Further," he finished in triumph, "no one can say they do it better at the Maryinsky for," he pointed out, "they do not do it all."

A depressed General Dumka wandered in and flopped into the stall beside Stroganoff.

"Kyasht," he said despairingly, "refuses."

"Why you tell me this now," said Stroganoff annoyed. "Have I not enough to despair myself with already?"

And he looked at the side of the stage where a piece of canvas had been spread flat and was being painted in a great hurry by a man who, finished or not, had to leave it that afternoon to add a dado to Carnaval, for Diaghilev.

For St. Petersburg was not Omsk. In Omsk, Stroganoff of the Opera had but to beckon, whether for a dresser or a droshki, to be overwhelmed by a rush of applicants, all eager, all voluble, all proud to be in his employ, all asking to be remembered to the grand-papoushka. But in St. Petersburg, Stroganoff of the Opera was only the man from Omsk, and if anyone listened to him it was a great favour and if they worked for him it was a great expense. He boasted, he begged, he bribed, he beguiled, he sent bouquets and bought bottles of champagne, but always he was confronted by the brick wall of the Maryinsky and, if he scaled that, it was only to meet Diaghilev on the other side. Soon it began to look as though the Man who was No Nijinsky would have to be leading dancer after all. Presently it was a certainty.

"Good God," said the sandy man.
"But it was not so terrible, this," said Stroganoff. "You must understand, my friend, that there was then only one Nijinsky. He stood alone. There were many dancers who," he waved an arm, "did not drop the ballerina, but only one Nijinsky. So whether it is a trusted friend from Omsk, who dance bad, or some grasping newcomer who dance only a little better, who is to support my Natasha—it make small difference. I am clear—yes?"
"Completely," said the sandy man. "I can almost follow you."
"You must understand, my friend," said Stroganoff, "that the technique of the dancers then is not as we know it now. Then all was tradition, the school, the line, the conductor who watch the stage. Then the ballerina took her preparation and went into her two turns and the house applauded. And if she do thirty-two fouettés the house go mad, all save a few die-difficults, who purse their lips and say it is clever but it is the circus. And these ballerinas," said Stroganoff marvelling, "all school, all line, all authority, they

have produce the generation of little spinning tops that you see all over the world to-day. Baronova, Toumanova, Riaboushinska, even the little Fonteyn," he laughed indulgently, "they spin." He waggled his wrist.

"And Natasha?" asked the sandy man.

"She did not spin," said Stroganoff gravely. "She was a flower in porcelain, a china butterfly, when she come on," he raised his arms, "the stage light up, whether it is Omsk, Petersburg, Paris, or any city in the world. C'est une petite ange, my Natasha. She has a charm that none can resist, least of all," he gazed into the past, "me."

The door opened. The Present came in. A woman in black, a cottage loaf in a good humour, waddled across the room and kissed Stroganoff. Stroganoff pinched her cheek.

"So you are happy at last, my pigeon," he asked. "Your little daughter has the six curtains and from now on we have only the good fortune—no?"

The cottage loaf stiffened slightly. "The six curtains and the empty house," she said. "You have kept your word, Vladimir, but do not think that this is enough. To-night we have the six curtains again—and to the house full."

The sandy man looked at the cottage loaf. He took in the bulging legs balanced on high heels, the over-tight black satined behind, the three rows of pearls on the bulging bosom, the hat with the black ostrich feathers, the white face, the eyelashes stiff with mascara. He decided he could resist her quite easily.

But Stroganoff was patting her hand.

"Not to-night," he was saying, "the little one does not dance to-night."

"To-night," said the cottage loaf, "dances the one that stamp out from the Inglesby."

"That is so," said Stroganoff unmoved. "But remember, she stamp out."

"Me, I do not stamp out," declared the cottage loaf. "I stay till you arrange the six curtains for my little one."

Stroganoff considered. "Maybe," he suggested, "on the first night of the new Nevajno."

"That old 'am," said the cottage loaf. This was blasphemy, but fortunately God was not there to hear. "You wish that our curtains be mixed with cat-calls?"

"If there are cat-calls," said Stroganoff, by no means rejecting the possibility, "you are sure at least that the audience is still there." He turned to the sandy man for approval. Certainly he was getting none from the cottage loaf. The fingers were tapping, and so was the toe.

"We do the Sugar Plum here in London, us," she demanded. "Do not forget we do the Sugar Plum."

"I will remember," said Stroganoff. "Rest assured that I will remember . . ."

"You will," said the cottage loaf. "Rest assured that you will— for I will continue to remind you."

She rose. Stroganoff kissed her hand.

"Go to your hotel, my pigeon," he said. "You will find there the little surprise from Bond Street."

"The ruby clip I see in the window!" The cottage loaf was gratified but also surprised. "Vladimir—how you afford this thing for me?"

"I talk a little and they give me the credit," said Stroganoff comfortably. "I tell them that the rich one come soon to pay for my extravagances."

"Vladimir—you are a darling," cried the cottage loaf. Her beam embraced the pensive-looking sandy man. "Always he spoil me." She waddled to the door. "If the rich one make the hully-brou-ha! ha!" she announced, "I give it back." She considered. "But only then," she decided. She walked out.

"So that was Natasha," said the sandy man.

"All gold, my Natasha," said Stroganoff fondly. "And still beautiful," he added firmly.

"And the little dancer with the six curtains is your daughter," said the sandy man.

"Mais non," said Stroganoff astounded. "Why you think that?"

Chapter Fourteen

⁂

T HE opening night.

In ten minutes the curtain would be going up on an evening of all surpassing triumph.

Or would it?

At any rate, most of the costumes had come. And if the audience streaming in lacked the glow of the balletomane entering his taken-for-granted heaven, the Maryinsky, at any rate it was streaming, and, which was curious, bringing its children.

"Can it be," said General Dumka, gazing at the milling foyer, "that they have mistaken the date?"

"Impossible," said Stroganoff. "My friend, you make me laugh. To confuse the circus with the ballet! No, this cannot happen."

He gazed at a group of children, babbling and tugging at the folds of their mother's skirt. Doubt seized him. Soon it became a certainty. The children were howling their heads off and the mother was demanding her money back.

"See," said General Dumka in macabre triumph.

"Poof!" said Stroganoff.

They were fast reaching the stage where their nerves were getting the better of them and making them want to get the better of one another.

Stroganoff proceeded to restore his morale by gazing at the crowded foyer. Why you could not see the marble staircase for medals and sables.

"Look!" said General Dumka. There was awe in his voice.

For the crowd was making way for a well-known black figure with a single lock of white hair and his habitual cortège of lofty followers.

Diaghilev and his disciples had come to the opening.

"It is a great honour," whispered General Dumka, "and also," he admitted, "a big surprise."

"What more natural than that one impresario should come to the opening of another," said Stroganoff casually. But his chest had already swollen out.

The cortège advanced. Stroganoff waited expectantly. The cortège swept by.

"What he say to me?" asked Stroganoff anxiously.

"He nodded," said Dumka. "Be satisfied."

Bowing gravely the cortège kept on its unsmiling way.

*　　　*　　　*

Backstage all was frenzy. Never had so many costumes arrived at the last moment. Never had there been such a last minute of frantic hammering, lost wreaths, mislaid mascots, and nervy mamoushkas commanding maddened daughters to keep calm.

For that matter never before had there been a wedged-into-a-corner elephant.

"Ten minutes," sang the call-boy.

"Mr. Stroganoff!" A strung-up mamoushka planted herself firmly in the bobbing about impresario's path. "In Omsk you promised . . ."

"Later," said Stroganoff. "To-morrow," he soothed her, "I promise you the row colossal."

He hurried on. Dancers plucked at his sleeve, electricians held out appealing hands, Nicholas Nevajno ducked behind him to avoid wishing his best friend luck. But Stroganoff forged purposefully ahead. He was the father of his family and he must bless his children.

First the little wife.

"Ah, c'est toi," said the mamoushka resigned, and she picked up her needle and went on with the ballet-skirt.

"My six curtains?" said Natasha, a porcelain angel in all save voice. . . .

*　　　*　　　*

The conductor rapped his baton. Silence fell on the house. In the background an elephant trumpeted.

A tremor passed down the spine of a pale little boy whose dark brows met. Leonide Massine had been brought to what his mamoushka thought was the circus. But somehow already he wasn't disappointed.

In his box Diaghilev was slightly out of mood. Nijinski at home with a feverish cold and the provincial's curtain about to go up a bare ten minutes late. He hoped his own would be as punctual when he opened in Paris.

"Little Ginsberg," he told Bolm, "has not answered my wire. Bankers are slow, slow, slow."

"Bankers," said the dancer Bolm, not interested.

The house lights went down.

"Sylvia!" said Nicholas Nevajno contemptuously. He sought for further opprobium. "Sylvia!" he found.

The footlights came up bathing the crimson curtains of the great proscenium in their ruby glow. In the dark sea of the auditorium noble bosoms rose a little and military backs stiffened. It was the Ballet. It might be from Omsk, but it was still the Ballet.

The conductor raised his baton. Delibes' beguiling music welled up.

The Company Stroganoff had opened in the capital.

*   *   *

"The orchestra could be worse," said P. Puthyk, always eager to be pleased.

They listened.

"I deny this," said Stravinsky before long.

The curtain became a glade. The glade became infested with nymphs, fauns, and villagers. The statue of love became Arenskaya.

"What a pity she has left the Maryinsky," said Puthyk. "She has," he sought for the word, "personality."

"Personality possibly," said Fokine. He left it at that.

On the stage the simple story leapt, rotated and pattered on its way. The music charmed the house; it was sweet, it was soporific, it was disarming. Dowagers nodded approvingly and Grand Dukes waved cigarette-holders. Stroganoff had chosen wisely after all.

"Who is that?" asked Diaghilev as a Dresden china Sylvia sported by the brook.

"It is the wife of the director," said Nouvel. "Natasha Stroganova."

"The odalisk from Omsk," said Stravinsky.

"She could be better," said Fokine critically.

"But she could be worse," said Diaghilev. He made a note.

In the auditorium old military backs were nodding heads approvingly and young military backs were twirling moustaches.

"Elle est ravissante."

"Delicious."

"A second Trefilova."

The simple story seethed, bounced and overbalanced. The stage was full again of bounding, twirling figures.

"That one," said Diaghilev, gazing at an energetically rotating faun, "that one is no . . ." he paused and corrected himself. "Bolm," he substituted.

The simple story trundled on its complicated way. Presently it was the first interval.

Stroganoff, torn between pride and protest, roamed the crowded foyer, straining and craning to overhear those all-important, lightly-thrown comments that his offering to the capital was bringing out. He was followed by a straining and craning General Dumka.

"I would never have believed it possible," said a Grand Duke with a monocle to a Grand Duke without one.

Stroganoff and Dumka exchanged glances.

"They are in ecstasy," they assured one another.

"The little Sylvia is charming." A young guardsman was twirling his moustache.

"Delicious," agreed his companion. He kissed his fingers.

The husband and impresario glowed.

"I have asked her to supper," said the guardsman.

The husband stopped glowing.

"Come," said General Dumka. "Let us have a drink."

"He has asked my Natasha to supper," said Stroganoff thickly. "I challenge him to a duel."

He took a step forward. Dumka pulled him back.

"Come," he said, "a little drink. What," he soothed, "is an invitation to supper. It does not follow," he argued, "that she will accept."

*   *   *

The Ballet Sylvia. Act II.

The simple story was growing more complicated every moment. In his stage box Aliosha had clasped his hands over his stomach. In spite of this it was still heaving.

"Where," he demanded indignantly as his son's bald dome came bobbing in, "where is my Katusha? Already it is Act II, and I have not seen her yet.

"She is waiting to take the house by storm in her temple," said Stroganoff comfortably. "The rest of the ballet," he waved it away, "is but the build-up."

Aliosha lowered at him. "It is not right that you tuck my Katusha in a temple where she is not seen till," he consulted his programme, "scene eleven."

"Nine," said Stroganoff.

"Now you juggle me the figures," said Aliosha crossly. "Tell me," he became the business man, "how much money you lose this evening?"

"Papoushka," Stroganoff looked hurt. "Soyez raisonable. To-night is the night of my triumph. I have invite all the capital and they have come and," he spread his hands, "they enjoy themselves." He waited hopefully for the roar of applause that should have greeted the end of the Man who was No Nijinsky's solo.

One or two people did clap.

"Voilà," said Stroganoff making the best of it.

"But how much money you lose," asked Aliosha stubbornly.

Stroganoff sighed. "It is not what we lose to-night that matter. It is how much we have left for to-morrow. It is of this that we must talk."

"Very well," said Aliosha. "How much then have we left for to-morrow?"

Stroganoff pondered. "Nothing," he said.

"So," said Aliosha. "So," he said ominously.

"It is not this that worry me," said Stroganoff. "It is the money for the next production, the new creation by Nevajno, that will draw all Petersburg and make me, Vladimir Stroganoff, the most talked-of impresario in," he considered, "the universe," he finished modestly.

"How much it cost?" asked Aliosha.

Stroganoff considered again. "Already it cost twice what we estimate in Omsk," he revealed, "and we only begin. So you see, my papoushka, I must have the finance."

"Nu?" said the papoushka unmoved.

"You must help me," said Stroganoff. "To-morrow," he coaxed, "my little father will write to my little grandfather and ask him for fifty-thousand roubles, or better," he amended, "sixty."

Up went the hands. "Dear God," said Aliosha, "that I should have a son who thinks his little grandfather will risk his own money. Aie! Aie! Aie!" He blew his nose.

"But the little grandfather is rich," said Stroganoff.

"The little grandfather is rich," said Aliosha severely, "because he does not do the good turn with his own money but only the money of others. That is the method practical. He will give you no more—may he live long in this world to bless us."

"May he live long," agreed Stroganoff dully. "Your own investments," he changed the subject, "they do well—no?"

"Sssh!" said Aliosha sternly. He pointed to the stage.

*   *   *

Act III.

The simple rural story had got too complicated to follow. Arenskaya had elbowed in a solo and a pas-de-deux. But at last Katusha was in her temple and Aliosha was leaning forward in his box and wondering if she was going to be allowed to step out of it.

But Vladimir Stroganoff was deep in conversation in the bar. He was talking to the comfortably-stomached stranger of the Trans-Siberian Express.

The first ecstatic greetings were over. The stranger had congratulated Stroganoff on his triumphant opening. Stroganoff had congratulated the stranger on his presence at it. The stranger had sympathized with the absence of the little grandfather. Stroganoff had wished the little grandfather a long life and poofed him away. They had had the little drink, they had had the other little drink, and at the third little drink the conversation had taken a serious turn.

. . . "This little Baskova in Vladivostok," said the stranger, "is— how to put it—my discovery."

"Entendu," said Stroganoff.

"It is not right," said the stranger, "that she should bury her talent there."

"Bien sûr," said Stroganoff, temples in which to tuck her already floating in his mind.

"But," the stranger shook a worried head, "here, in the capital, it is not easy to arrange for the début of a ballerina."

"It is not easy," Stroganoff agreed.

"But it must be arranged," said the stranger warmly. "For if the little Baskova comes to the capital and I have nothing for her, she—how to put it—will have nothing for me."

"It is not impossible to arrange," said Stroganoff. "But it is . . . expensive."

The stranger fiddled with his watch-chain.

"I am not a rich man," he said.

"Me too, I am now poor," said Stroganoff.

They looked at one another. Each understood the other perfectly.

"And so," Stroganoff told the sandy man, "I find my first backer. And as it was in the beginning so it has been ever since."

"Has it?" said the sandy man.

The simple story had come to an end. Or at least it had stopped going on. The artists were lined up to take their curtain.

The first curtain was all that a curtain should be. For one thing it came down slowly and gave the artists plenty of time to bow radiantly to the house and politely to one another. And the house, if it did not rise at them, at least applauded politely. After all, the capital had seen worse companies than this—in the provinces.

The second curtain, according to plan, went to the soloists. The applause was a little warmer—more personal. A great deal of noise came from the stage-box to which the Goddess Diane was bowing.

The third curtain belonged to the delicious Stroganova, to Arenskaya—all personality, and to the Man who was No Nijinsky.

The audience still applauded.

The fourth curtain went to Natasha alone. They brought on her bouquets. They brought on the basket of orchids higher than herself. They placed it in front of her.

Diaghilev went. So did Benois, Fokine, Stravinsky, Bolm and Nouvel; P. Puthyk sat on applauding.

The fifth curtain showed Natasha in front of her company. The applause still survived, but there wasn't much to spare.

As it ended Stroganoff came rushing out of the bar.

"How many curtains?" he panted.

"Five," said a General. He shrugged.

"Ah," said Stroganoff. He fixed his eyes on the tab and held his hands ready.

The curtains were parting. His wife, his little angel, was coming out. What a moment for a husband! Stroganoff closed his eyes.

On the stage, behind the about-to-part curtains, Natasha, flushed and palpitating, listened acutely to what was left of the applause.

"Six curtains for Stroganova," she breathed.

In the wings the mamoushka crossed herself.

The stage director gave the signal. Natasha smoothed her frock, switched on her stage radiance, and moved towards the narrow lane that would bring her out in front of the tabs.

"Six curtains," she breathed, and, stumbling over Arenskaya's outstretched foot, measured her length on the stage.

"Bravo," shouted Stroganoff. "Bravo!" And he stamped and applauded with all his might.

"But, my darling," said Arenskaya. "I am desolated. But what could I do? There were you on the floor, your face all dirty from the dust, your costume—mh, mh, mh! And there was the audience waiting—you could not face them like that. It break my heart, but what could I do? I had to save the day. The public were waiting to applaud. I had to take your curtain for you.

"You showed great presence of mind, darling," said Natasha.

They kissed.

The worried-to-death Stroganoff, hurrying into his wife's dressing-room, blinked.

"You are the friends?" he asked amazed.

"But the friends bosom," said Arenskaya. She blew the purpling mamoushka a kiss and withdrew.

Stroganoff opened his arms. "My darling," he said thankfully.

"Your darling—poof!" said Natasha. "You sack that woman to-morrow or I never speak to you again."

"To-night," said the mamoushka.

"My six curtains," said Natasha. "My six curtains of which I have dreamt, eaten, and slept, my six curtains in the capital—ruined! And," she turned on him, "it is all your fault for bringing that wicked woman to the company."

"My darling infant," said Stroganoff patiently. "Sois raisonable. Is it her fault that you fall down at the moment critical?"

"Yes," said Natasha.

"Yes," said the mamoushka.

They were agreed.

"She trip me up," screamed Natasha. "She stick out her foot as I go forward." She fell upon Stroganoff and pummelled his dress shirt. "Do you hear, Vladimir? She trip me up."

Stroganoff seized the fighting little hands and summoned all his tact as he wrestled.

"She will be put in her place that one," he promised. "To-night I have arranged for a new ballerina to come to the company."

Natasha stopped wrestling. Temperaments could wait. This was serious.

"A new ballerina?" she said.

"A new ballerina!" said the mamoushka sharply.

"The ballerina beauteous from Vladivostok," said Stroganoff. He waited for the chorus of congratulation.

"Villain," said Natasha. "Monster. So already you plan to be unfaithful."

This reminded Stroganoff of something.

"Unfaithful," he said. "Me! What of the invitation to supper that you get from the young guardsman at whom no doubt," he accused, "you make the eyes from the stage or never would he have had the courage to ask."

"One guardsman," said Natasha scornfully. She snatched a batch of visiting cards from her dressing-table and threw them in Stroganoff's face. "I have six invitations from guardsmen. And one from an Admiral." She threw it.

Anger left Stroganoff. He became anxious.

"My darling," he said, "you have not accepted one of them?"

Natasha tossed her head. "On the contrary," she said, "I have accepted them all."

She snatched up her fur coat and strode into the corridor.

The mamoushka ran out after her.

"Natasha," she wailed. "Come back. You are but in your corset."

Chapter Fifteen

❧

CLASS.

But not at the Maryinsky.

There was an assortment of tunics and tights. They did not match. There was a piano. It was not in tune. There was a small group of onlookers. They had no right to be there, and the least they might do was pay attention. There was a lion-tamer. He was watching the teacher. There was a teacher. She was wishing she was a lion-tamer. How to correct the wife of the management without losing her job at once?

"Not like this, chèrie," she said. "So."

She waited anxiously. She relaxed. She was still on the salary list. Natasha had shot her a look, but she had obeyed.

"Beautiful, my darling," said the once divine Korovina. "The head a little higher—so."

"So," said Arenskaya helpfully from a corner. She demonstrated. Natasha refused to look.

Stroganoff came in. He beamed at the teacher who smiled at him. He beamed at Natasha who scowled at him. He ignored Arenskaya who winked at him. He crossed over to General Dumka and embraced him.

"We are the success triumphant," he announced. "For the next performance already two boxes are booked."

"What did I tell you," said Dumka overjoyed. He opened his arms. Now that the first night *crise* was over the desire of the two friends to contradict each other had been replaced by a determination to agree with anything the other might say. "We are the success. Everyone come to us. Except," he remembered, "Trefilova. She admire the turquoise hatpin, but she say 'no.'"

"You take back the hatpin?" asked Stroganoff anxiously.

"Helas!" Dumka shrugged, "it is already in her hat." He turned to brighter topics. "The notices," he said, "could be worse."

They discussed them while Madame Korovina conducted the class gently through little hoops of peril. What would Johansen have said of that pirouette? She shrugged the thought off.

"Concentrate a little, my darling," she said. "Finish in position. You are not," she risked it, "in a circus." She looked at the lion-tamer. She wished she hadn't. "Two turns," she exhorted, "and finish facing M'sieur le Directeur."

Katusha tried again.

But M'sieur le Directeur was juggling with a sheaf of notices.

"Pas mal," he flicked. "Pas mal du tout." He flicked again. His face fell.

Inevitably, irrevocably, irretrievably he had come to the column signed Valerien Svetlov.

"Take no notice of that one," said Dumka consolingly. "It is well known that he likes nothing."

Stroganoff scowled like a disappointed schoolboy. "But he should not raise the hopes," he complained. "To begin with the praise faint. . . . 'Omsk is to be congratulated for one thing!' . . . naturally I think it is my ballet, n'est ce pas?"

"Si, si," said Dumka.

"But it appears later," said Stroganoff moodily, "it is because my ballet has left."

"Poof!" said Dumka.

"Tiens," said Stroganoff. A slight figure stood hesitating in the doorway. "Where have I seen that one before?"

"With Diaghilev," said Dumka impressed.

Smiling politely, P. Puthyk advanced into the room. Arenskaya, who had not been paying much attention to the teacher, stopped attending altogether. She came out to the front of the class and proceeded unasked to do a few solo steps of which she was very sure. The teacher, behind a carefully non-committal face, was wondering whether to say anything. Natasha, behind a china shepherdess smile, was composing sentences to say later.

Puthyk bowed faultlessly to Korovina.

"Mille pardons, Madame," he said, "that I interrupt your class, but I have come with a message for Mademoiselle Stroganova."

"Entendu, M'sieur Puthyk," said Korovina. "Mon ange," she beckoned, "viens ici un moment."

Arenskaya came forward.

"My congratulations," said Puthyk, "on your admirable performance."

Arenskaya bowed low. By the time she came up again Puthyk was whispering with Natasha while an apprehensive Stroganoff had hovered himself as near as he dared which was still not near enough to overhear.

"But at once," said Natasha. She dropped a brief curtsey vaguely in the direction of the teacher and made off.

"Your wife," Puthyk told Stroganoff, "is a very talented dancer. She will go far."

"Yes," said Stroganoff anxiously, "but where?"

But Puthyk must have been deaf, for he had hurried away and already was out of earshot.

"I wonder where I shall lunch to-day," mused Arenskaya audibly.

*   *   *

"Assez de dèsespoir," said Serge Diaghilev. "We have been ruined before. There is no need to be depressed about it."

"But it is getting monotonous," said Stravinsky.

Outside the sun was shining. Inside Diaghilev's apartment the great draperies were drawn and all the lights were on. Diaghilev hated daylight. He admitted its inevitability, but it depressed him. So did little Ginsberg's letter lying on his desk.

"The man is never satisfied," grumbled Benois. "We bring him the success artistic and 'e wants to make the money too,"

"Or at least not lose too much," said Nouvel fairly.

They ignored him.

"He is a business man," said Fokine. "You shouldn't have shown him the figures. It was not the moment."

"It is very important this moment when you wish to raise the hurricane," Stroganoff explained to the sandy man. "You pick it right and—poof! you are the millionaire. You pick it wrong and—biff!" he jabbed his thumb, "you are in the bortsch. So you will understand, my friend, that the choosing of this moment is an art to which an impresario must give much attention."

"I'm beginning to gather that," said the sandy man.

"But, croyez moi," said Stroganoff, "there are many impresarios in London to-day who do not realize this. Because the backer he keep singing that he is a business man, they think it is business that he comes here to do. And they prepare for him the figures elaborate and they talk to him of the house capacity, and the number of matinées, and the get-in and the get-out, and many many things that do not fascinate the business-man at all. And the business-man he see that he can only do in the theatre what he can do with less hazard in the city—mooch less—and he go away. And it serve them right," said Stroganoff severely, "for that is no way to treat a business man."

"H'm," said the sandy man.

"Me," said Stroganoff, "I play the business-man like a fish."

"A poor fish," said the sandy man.

"I cast the bait," said Stroganoff, "I twiddle up and down, I let him run away and I pull him back and presently—poof—he is in the net, and what is more," he waggled a finger, "happy to be in it. For some time at least," he conceded. "But I bore you perhaps?"

"No, no," said the sandy man. "Please go on."

Stroganoff beamed.

"So," he continued, "when I seek to bait my hook I do not dwell on figures for then he would wish to inspect them and it does not do, my friend, to have your backers inspect your figures until too late. But also I am careful to save his pride. Each time he sing he is a business-man, I tell him the figures will be ready to-morrow, and I talk to him of our triumphant season in the Argentine. And it was," he said in awe. "We show a profit." He looked at Pavlova for confirmation. "And then," he said, "I take the rich one to lunch, and I pay for it, for there is nothing pleases the rich one so much as to be given the little lunch by someone else. And I take him to rehearsal but not for too long, and I invite him to my box, and I give for him the little party backstage, where his wife does not come, and where he drink too mooch gin and all the choryphées call him Uncle. And presently, if he can still stand, he make the speech. Ah! those speeches!" Stroganoff shuddered. "And after that," he finished, "he give me the cheque and our season is guarantee."

"As simple as that," said the sandy man.

"It is simple," said Stroganoff. "You must remember only to keep the business-man away from your figures. You must remember it all the time for, if he sees them, he will fear, not the loss, but that you may think he is not a good business-man. Save the backer's pride," pronounced Stroganoff, "and you can ruin him all you wish and he will thank you for doing it. The chi-chi," he summed it up, "it is important. But not to see the figures, that, my friend, it is vital."

"You shouldn't have let him see the figures," said Bolm. "He is a business-man."

Diaghilev swept back his white lock with an abstracted hand. "Where do I go for money now?" he brooded.

"To the State," said Benois.

"It is a pity you were not more polite to Teleyakov," said Nouvel. He shook his head.

"Politeness would not help," said Diaghilev. "The State is jealous of me, do you not understand? They think I take the réclame that is the due of their theatres and that I steal their best dancers and there," he chuckled suddenly, "they are right."

"Money, money," said Benois. "Always it is money that holds us back."

"Where can I get some ballet shoes?" mused Nijinsky. "Teleyakov maybe?" He tasted the idea. "Not Teleyakov," he decided.

"Certainly not Teleyakov," said Fokine. "He is our enemy."

"I will write to little Ginsberg again," decided Diaghilev. "I will tell him," he paused to crystallize the concept, "I will tell him that he must do what he cannot do." He gulped his lemon tea.

"Tell him to find a little grandfather," said Stravinsky.

P. Puthyk hurried in.

"She is here," he announced importantly.

"Who," said the company crossly.

"The porcelain doll from Omsk," said Puthyk. "She ask questions all the way. But I tell her nothing," he assured them.

"I will see her," said Diaghilev.

Fokine looked interested. "You are making her an offer?"

"Why not?" said Diaghilev. "She has chic. She will please Paris."

"But her husband," said Stravinsky. "Will he be pleased?"

"Her husband." Diaghilev went behind his face. "I do not understand you, my friend. I do not understand you at all."

*   *   *

2.15 at the little restaurant round the corner. Russian dancers lunch late.

The room was buzzing with conversation. The usual conversation. "My public."

"In class I . . ."

"That conductor."

"My mamoushka says . . ." floated from the pouting lips of every divinity in the room.

Save one.

This divinity was looking definitely thoughtful. She had to tell her husband something and he wasn't going to like it. The husband was thoughtful, too. He had to tell his wife something and she was going to loathe it.

"The bortsch is cold," said Natasha to pass the time. How to tell him that she had been offered a European tour—with Diaghilev?

"But the champagne is warm," said Stroganoff postponing the inevitable. How to tell her he'd been offered a new ballet with the little Baskova dancing the lead?

The proprietor wandered up. "Everything as you like it?" he enquired.

"Delicious," they assured him vaguely.

Relieved, the proprietor wandered away.

"Vladimir," said Natasha, pushing aside her untouched plate. "What is the dearest thing in the world to you?"

This was easy. "But you, my darling," said Stroganoff. "All day, all night, I plan for you. Everything that I do is for your happiness. I promise you that I will make you the greatest ballerina in the world only . . . only," he hesitated, "not all at once."

"Vladimir," said Natasha. "I have been given a great opportunity."

"But not all at once," repeated Stroganoff, who had not been listening. "Sometimes it is the policy to draw back a little from the public so that they clamour for you all the more. To give the limelight to some," he waved a disparaging hand, "to some lesser dancer so that when you return they realize what they have been missing." He brightened a little. That was well put, he reflected. Tactful.

"He said I had chic," said Natasha, who had not been listening.

"So," said Stroganoff, "I have found the backer with much money with the little protégée with not too much talent."

"Four hundred francs a month," said Natasha. "It is not the money—it is the opportunity."

"And," said Stroganoff, "the little Baskova signs her contract to-morrow."

It was out. Or part of it. And Natasha, who had caught the word 'Contract,' was now all attention.

"Who sign what?" she asked sharply.

"But the little Baskova," said Stroganoff. "I sign her for the new Nevajno, and," he gulped, "she dance the lead."

It was out. All of it.

"So," said Natasha. The mouth tightened.

"It is only so that the public clamour for you the more," Stroganoff hurried on. "And also," he admitted, "because without the backer I have no money to put it on."

"So," said Natasha. "So. The little Baskova is to dance the lead while I . . ." She fought for words to express her indignation. And as she fought she remembered.

"Never mind, my darling," she said with such sweetness that the tensed Stroganoff almost reeled. "No doubt she will do well enough. . . . And also Arenskaya will be livid."

"You are not cross," said Stroganoff dazed. "You do not intend to scratch out my eyes?"

"But why, my darling," said Natasha. "I know that you study only my interests and I know also that money it is important, and if you think that it is right that the little Baskova dance the lead then it must be so."

"But it is an angel," burst out Stroganoff. "A veritable angel." In his relief he drank her champagne. "What other ballerina would be so reasonable? If we were not in public I would embrace you." He tried.

"Then all is well," said Natasha. "You put on the Nevajno with the little Baskova. You have the success—I hope. And when I am back from Europe I lead the company again."

"Si, si," said Stroganoff. "Comment! Quoi donce! What— the 'ell?"

"Europe, my darling," said Natasha. She sighed. "I was worried at leaving you, Vladimir, but now I see that it fits in very well with your plans."

"Comment!" said Stroganoff. "Quoi!"

"I see Diaghilev this morning," said Natasha.

"Diaghilev!" said Stroganoff. "Qu'est ce que tu me chantes?"

"He makes me the offer," said Natasha. "The offer to go to Europe." Now for it. "I accept."

Stroganoff leapt to his feet. "I kill him," he announced. He looked round for an implement and found a fish-knife. Brandishing it wildly, he rushed out.

"Valerien says," said Trefilova.

Q

"The conductor . . ." said Kyasht.

"My mamoushka . . ." said Karsavina.

"My mamoushka!" remembered Natasha. She burst into tears and stumbled out of the restaurant.

They will be back to-morrow, thought the proprietor philosophically.

He put away the bill.

*   *   *

"And so, my dear Ginsberg," the purple ink was spidering its way across the page, "I am in no mood to hear of stock markets, short credits and unfortunate speculations."

Diaghilev passed his hand over his white lock. He crossed out 'unfortunate.'

A bald head hurtled into the room. It was the man from Omsk. He was brandishing a fish-knife. Diaghilev looked up in some annoyance. Had he not told his servant he did not wish to be disturbed.

"Good afternoon," he said to the waving knife. "Your appointment was at . . . ?" He looked at his engagement book where he knew the afternoon would be blank. "I trust I have not kept you waiting."

"Villain," shouted Stroganoff uncrushed. "You wish to steal my wife. Despoiler! Schemer! Cheat!"

"Not despoiler," said Diaghilev.

"I come to demand the explanation." Stroganoff thrust out his chin. "I get it quick or else . . ." Failing to find the threat he brandished the fish-knife.

"Behave yourself," said Diaghilev sharply. "You are not in Omsk. Sit down."

Stroganoff gulped. He decided he could be just as defiant seated. The armchair was vast and deep. He was sunk.

"Sir," said Diaghilev. "To cut this unexpected interview short I propose to answer your questions before you can ask them. Before you can ask them," he repeated sternly and the struggling up Stroganoff sank down again.

"I have made one of your dancers an offer," said Diaghilev. He held up his hand. "One of your dancers," he repeated. "She will accept it." He held up his hand again. "You have made offers to many of my dancers. They have not accepted."

Stroganoff shifted restlessly in the deep armchair. He put the fish-knife in his pocket. He took it out again.

"I have approached Mademoiselle Stroganova." said Diaghilev, "because she has charm and will please Paris, and her dancing is, enfin, not too bad. This to me is a sufficient reason to engage a dancer. Nothing else is my concern.

"But me, it is my concern," burst out the pent-up Stroganoff. "It is my wife that you take to Paris."

"Yes?" said Diaghilev unmoved.

Stroganoff levered himself up. He resolved to speak calmly.

"Voleur!" he shouted. "Tyrant! Monopolist! All, all you want for yourself. You want all the dancers? All the designers, all the musicians . . ."

"That is so," said Diaghilev.

"You want all the Nijinskys . . ."

"That too," said Diaghilev.

"You will not permit anyone to live. Ever since I come from Omsk, every trouble, every crisis—it is you. I approach an artist—you have her. I seek the long-term credit—it is yours. I commission an orchestration and the composer he break off in the middle to orchestrate for you . . ." He ran out of breath.

"If I were in Omsk," said Diaghilev, polite but deadly, "no doubt the process would be reversed."

"You pay with the promises," Stroganoff almost wept. "And me, me—I have to pay with the cash and must plead with my little grandfather to get it."

"The little grandfather," mused Diaghilev. "He is in Petersburg?"

"Non!" said Stroganoff forcibly. "Never, never, shall you get the little grandfather. Never, never shall you lure my Natasha. I will argue with her. I will plead with her. I will promise her all that you can give her." He pointed the fish-knife. "And more!"

"Paris?" asked Diaghilev.

"That, too," said Stroganoff. "I can promise it—yes."

Diaghilev spread his hands. "In that case," he said, "I must not detain you."

Stroganoff brightened. "You withdraw your offer?" He asked hopefully.

"You will have much to do arranging a European tour at such short notice."

"But my wife . . ." said Stroganoff.

Diaghilev shrugged. "The dancer will choose which offer she prefers.

"You wish to separate us?" said Stroganoff passionately, "and we are married but six months—next week."

"You can come with her," said Diaghilev. "I do not refuse to travel the husbands."

"But my company . . ." said Stroganoff.

"Your company?" said Diaghilev. "How can your company possibly concern me?"

He rose. Stroganoff found himself ushered to the door.

"Good day," said Diaghilev. "Should you wish to see me again, please make an appointment. I should be most distressed if I were out."

"That is a lie," said Stroganoff defiantly.

But he said it to the closed door.

It opened.

"Your knife?" said Diaghilev courteously. He bowed. The door closed again.

"Yes, my friend," Stroganoff told the sandy man. "I tell the great Diaghilev what I think of him. I speak freely my mind—never has he been tell off so well. And when I leave he is crush. Crush!" He thumped the desk.

"But all the same," he admitted, "me, I am a little crush too."

*   *   *

"My darling," said the mamoushka, "let us remember we are reasonable women. Six curtains are important. But Paris," she gloated, "Paris is more important."

"He promised them to me," said Natasha mutinously. "At least he said—'all things are possible.' And now he has not put it in the contract. It is no use, mamoushka, I cannot trust Diaghilev."

They were sitting in mamoushka's bedroom and mamoushka was brushing the hair of her daughter. For, naturally, at this crisis in her life, Natasha had gone back to mother, leaving her husband in another bedroom in the same hotel frantic and definitely alone.

"My darling," said mamoushka. "Let us remember we are realists. Let us quietly consider what is the worst that can happen if you sign this contract. We open in Paris and you do not have your six curtains. Hélas! But," she pointed to the bright side, "you have had the success enormous—this is inevitable—and Karsavina she is livid. And after we work on Diaghilev, you and I—but more I than you. We plead, we threaten, we take out our false teeth . . . Diaghilev is but a man like the others. Look," she said, "what we have done with Vladimir."

"Poor Vladimir," said Natasha.

The house 'phone burbled. Natasha crossed to the wall, unhooked the receiver and squeezed.

"My darling," said Stroganoff in an adenoidal croak. "Come back to me, I beseech. Without you I cannot sleep."

"Useless to entreat," said Natasha coldly. "After the things you shout to me through the dressing-room door to-night I have left you for ever."

She stopped squeezing and hung up.

"It is not only the six curtains," she told mamoushka. "But what does Diaghilev offer me in the contract? In Giselle I am a Wili. In Swan Lake I dance the Queen only if Karsavina and Lopokova are ill, and Spessitzeva and Kshessinskaya cannot be there in time— and then only if the programme it is not changed."

"You have a solo," said mamoushka.

"One solo!" said Natasha. "And in what? Les Sylphides. A

novelty that will not last a season! Already they use it as a throw-away to open the performance. No, no," she decided, "I stay where I am."

The house 'phone burbled violently. Natasha advanced on it, unhooked and squeezed.

"Mais, my darling," pleaded Stroganoff. "Is it my fault that I shout?—you would not open the door."

"I will not open the door," said Natasha. "I will not open my arms. I will not dance in your company again—never, never, never."

"But, my darling. Consid . . ."

Natasha had stopped squeezing.

"My darling," said mamoushka. "Remember we are women who do not act on impulse. We know well how to look into the future, us, and how to await our moment. We are newcomers to the company as," she reminded her, "we were newcomers to Omsk. And look what we achieved there."

"Non," said Natasha violently. "I will not marry Diaghilev."

Mamoushka waved the hairbrush.

"Some men," she explained, "it is necessary to marry. Others—no. What is this new ballet they are talking of?"

"Carnaval," said Natasha. "Me, I understudy Papillon."

The house telephone exploded.

"But this is impossible," said the mamoushka as she advanced.

"My darling," groaned Stroganoff. "I cannot sleep."

"Me neither," snapped the mamoushka. She stopped squeezing. "Poor Vladimir." Natasha softened. "He does his best for me. Perhaps I am unkind."

"A daughter of mine unkind!" said the mamoushka incredulously. "The hour is late and I am fatigued. Your career I will discuss, but this nonsense . . ." She waved it away. "To bed," she said briskly.

They settled in side by side.

"The morning brings its own counsel," said mamoushka, "so let us leave our project in God's good hands till then."

"In God's good hands," agreed Natasha piously. "All the same," she plumped her pillow, "if Vladimir had any sense he would come and fetch me."

There was a timid knock at the door. Natasha and mamoushka looked at each other.

The door edged open. A bald dome peered round.

"Ah, my two little pigeons!" said Stroganoff falsely. "In bed already!" He beamed.

They looked at him.

"What a pretty picture you make." Stroganoff took a tentative step forward, making a pretty good picture himself in a plum-coloured dressing-gown on inside out and only one bedroom slipper. He looked anxiously at Natasha's face for the trace of a welcoming smile. It didn't seem to be there. "The pretty picture," he repeated, and took another step.

"Charming," he said, "the conseille de famille. The little daughter who would fly away before the wings are set," he crept forward, "and the little mother who understands where her real future lies." He looked at the unyielding granite face before him and took two more quick steps.

"A conseille de famille," he shook his head, "and the little papoushka excluded. No, no, my children, it is not right—this." In a little rush he sat down on the edge of the bed.

"Go away," said Natasha. "How dare you come here after all the things that you have said to me. I have left you for ever. Go away! Go away!" She threw a pillow at him and burst into tears.

"There," said the mamoushka well pleased. "See what you have done."

Stroganoff clutched the pillow. He looked at mamoushka's night-capped head. If he felt an impulse he restrained it.

"Nu," he said. "I am the clumsy business-man. The wicked ogre. The hard-hearted husband—isn't it?"

"You, you, you," sobbed Natasha. She flung her arms round him.

Stroganoff clutched. "See what I have done," he said triumphantly. "There, there, there."

Mamoushka sniffed. "You are standing in the way of my daughter's career," she said. "That's what you are doing."

"I can give her all Diaghilev can and more," proclaimed Stroganoff aroused. "I will take her to Paris. To London. I will present her at Covent Garden. And she shall not," he made an inspired guess, "have the two small solos and the understudy. She shall have . . ."

"Six curtains," sobbed Natasha.

"Bien sûr," said Stroganoff. "It will be in the contract.

Natasha dried her eyes. "When we go?"

"But at once," said Stroganoff. "Only first we must finish the season and then we are rich."

Mamoushka sniffed.

"Mais si," said Stroganoff. "Did you not count the house to-night. We lose only five hundred roubles—almost the profit," he boasted.

Mamoushka sniffed again.

"The new Nevajno ballet," said Stroganoff undaunted, "it will be the sensation, our prestige it soar, and the Government it give us the backing. Already," he swanked, "I am the comrades bosom with best friend of Teleyakov. Soon all will be arranged."

"My little husband," said Natasha. She climbed out of bed and put on her dressing-gown. She remembered something. "The little Baskova," she said, and climbed back again.

"The little Baskova?" The mamoushka clutched at the new straw. "Who is she?"

"She is from Vladivostok," said Natasha. "Vladimir has rashly promised her the new Nevajno but now," she looked all ready to get out of bed again, "he has changed his mind." She smiled winningly.

"The little Baskova," said Stroganoff, "brings the backing. She rehearses the ballet to-morrow." He raised his hand. "It does not follow my little calf and my little," he looked at the mamoushka, "cow, that she will dance it. It is a long way between the first rehearsal and the opening night, and," he put a finger to his nose, "many things can happen."

"You will sack her," ordered mamoushka.

"Me—no," said Stroganoff, "for if I did the backer will take away his money. But Nevajno," he comforted them, "is very hasty. He has quarrelled," he illustrated, "with his best friend. It is possible that he will quarrel with the little Baskova.

"These things can be arranged," said Natasha.

"Trust me," said Stroganoff. "All will be well."

Natasha considered. "And anyway," she mused, "Arenskaya will be livid."

"Go to bed—both of you," snapped the mamoushka.

She knew when she had lost a battle.

Chapter Sixteen

THREE days later the little Baskova attended her first rehearsal. She was dreadful.

"Picture to yourself my embarrassment," Stroganoff told the sandy man. "On the one hand," he waved it, "I have the new ballet and the money. On the other," he waved that, "there is the little Baskova. It was not that I expected her to be the sensation, but she was . . . a . . . a . . ."

"Little Baskova," supplied the sandy man helpfully.

"She is pretty enough," said Stroganoff. "She has the sex appeal. When she stand still it is not too bad. But when she dance—aie!" He threw up his hands. "It is clear at once that it is impossible she is a soloist in the capital."

"She'd want a solo," mused the sandy man. He was not thinking of the little Baskova.

"What to do?" Stroganoff went on. "I let her dance and my

prestige it is the ruin. I give her sack and my bank balance it is the bust. I puzzle, I think, I argue, I tear my hair, and I am at the end of my wits. Until one day I am lunching with Arenskaya at the little restaurant round the corner . . . we are both a little distrait. . . .

"The Grand Duke . . ." said Kshessinskaya.

"The Director," said Preobrajinska.

"The Wigmaker . . ." said Trefilova.

"My mamoushka . . ." said Karsavina.

"My shoes . . ." mourned Nijinsky.

The babble flowed on.

"Aie me," said Arenskaya.

"Aie me," said Stroganoff.

They put their heads on their elbows and ignored their coffee.

"My bill," called Diaghilev.

The proprietor brought it himself. He waited hopefully. But Diaghilev only signed.

No news from little Ginsberg yet, thought the proprietor stoically.

Stroganoff watched the hated cortège traverse to the door. How to snub sitting down? He turned a scorching glare on Diaghilev's oblivious back.

"The next time I see the villain face to face I tell him something," he assured Arenskaya.

But Arenskaya had not heard. Her eyes were on the cortège. Stravinsky, Benois, Bolm, Nijinsky, Fokine, Bakst, with P. Puthyk prancing importantly in the rear.

"Aie me," said Arenskaya, "I fear I shall marry with that one."

"He is your lover?" asked Stroganoff politely and not very interested.

"As yet he scarcely knows that I exist," said Arenskaya. "But he will marry me all the same. Aie me," she sighed, "it is very sad."

Stroganoff remembered that he was the father of his company. He shook off his own troubles and prepared to listen to Arenskaya's.

"A marriage between artists," he said doubtfully. "M'h. M'h. M'h."

"I know," said Arenskaya. "If I were wise I would marry a Grand Duke." She glanced at Kshessinskaya and raised her voice a little. "It is not too difficult."

"Or at least a banker," said Stroganoff toying with the idea of Abram of Omsk.

"Puthyk cannot help me in my career," said Arenskaya. "He is but the assistant to the assistant of the big Sergei Grigorieff. He is a good dancer and he has great sincerity. But he has no push. He cannot even scheme for himself. How then can he help me?"

"Then why marry him?" asked Stroganoff.

"I love him," said Arenskaya despairingly. "Voilà tout!"

"Poof," said Stroganoff. "The little affaire and all will be well."

"The little affaire I have with others," said Arenskaya. "Puthyk I will marry. You will see. I will be unfaithful to him, bien sûr, but I will never love anyone else. Hélas!" She sipped her coffee and the tears ran down her cheeks. "I am so young," she said, "but my fate is sealed. It would have been nice to have married just one Grand Duke."

Stroganoff looked for the bright side. "Maybe," he said, "Puthyk will not want to marry."

"He will," sobbed Arenskaya. "And it will be the happiest day of my life," she gulped defiantly.

At a corner table Nicolas Nevajno pulled out a pencil.

"I sign the bill," he said loftily.

The proprietor made an effort. "Mais, M'sieur . . ." he began.

"I sign," said Nevajno firmly. He scribbled and strode out.

From a table at the other corner of the room Nevajno's best friend glared after him and gave him a good two minutes' start. Then he beckoned the proprietor.

"My bill," he said. "I sign."

Arenskaya dabbed her eyes. "But enough of my troubles," she said. "Let us talk about yours."

"Me," said Stroganoff, "but I have no troubles at all. I have the new ballet—the money—what could trouble me?" He laughed. It didn't sound so good.

"The little Baskova," said Arenskaya, and Stroganoff was at once plunged in gloom.

"So you notice it too," he despaired.

"Mais voyons, Vladimir," said Arenskaya. "Am I not in class? Do I not watch rehearsals? Is it not evident to the whole world that she would not be there but for her chocolate papoushka?"

"Ah, so," said Stroganoff sadly. "It is as clear as that?"

"Vladimir," said Arenskaya earnestly, "I have all our good at heart. It is not because I want the rôle myself—though it would suit me well—that I tell you the little Baskova must not dance. Let Natasha have it." She waved an arm largely.

"My little pigeon is not as reasonable as usual at the moment," said Stroganoff. "Every day she gets the sweetmeats from Diaghilev and every night she makes me the scene. And there is nothing I can do—nothing! No Baskova," he crystallized it, "no ballet."

"Are there not other rich men in the capital!" asked Arenskaya.

"They have all got little Baskovas," said Stroganoff helplessly. "What will it profit me to change? I tell you, my darling, that I and my brave Dumka are in despair. We cannot plan, we cannot eat, and me, I have not slept for three nights now." He pointed to the circles under his eyes.

Arenskaya was all sympathy. "There I can help you," she said. She took out a golden phial from her bag and passed it across. "My sleeping draught," she said. "I have no need for it now that I get acquainted with Nevajno's best friend, the rascal!"

"It will put me to sleep?" asked Stroganoff.

"One little drop in a glass of milk," said Arenskaya, "and you are asleep immediate for twelve hours. It is very strong," she warned, "so do not take too much."

"Bon," said Stroganoff dutifully. He tucked the phial in his pocket.

"And now," said Arenskaya, "it is time for me to keep the rendezvous with your little wife. We are driving in the Park together . . ."

"You blink, my friend," said Stroganoff to the sandy man. "Arenskaya and my little pigeon the friends bosom in the Park! But in the ballet this is natural."

"Is it indeed?" said the sandy man.

"It needs only a common enemy," said Stroganoff wisely, "for the enemies deadly to become the friends immediate."

"The little Baskova," said the sandy man. "I see."

"But, while to defeat the common enemy they are the friends bosom," said Stroganoff, "there still goes on the rivalry, the look-out and the little schemes for the double cross. It is like," he sought for an example, "the nations united."

"I don't get you," said the sandy man coldly.

★   ★   ★

The little restaurant was empty. Stroganoff sat on thinking, thinking, thinking. Money to get the ballet on. Money to get the little Baskova off. Money to take Natasha to Europe. . . .

The proprietor came over with the bill. Resigned, he extended a pencil.

In his abstraction Stroganoff paid.

★   ★   ★

The new Nevajno creation.

At the moment it consisted of two lines of unsat-upon chairs—the cliffs of Dover. Several chalk marks—footlights, backcloth and wings. A piano—the orchestra. The Conductor—himself. He was waving a conscientious wrist at the ignoring back of the pianist.

Rehearsals held in the classroom are always like this.

The creating genius, clad in a Russian tunic torn under the arms, cotton tights, and dirty white ballet shoes, his black hair escaping from under a cerise bandeau, was working in a glow of satisfaction.

Even his best friend stalking around and sniffing failed to revolt him. His new conception was taking shape, a rather peculiar shape—full of bulges and odd angles. Three people had called him 'Maestro' and two of them had schanged him schmall scheque. He was going to play Baccarat to-night. What more could a choreographer want?

"Mlle. Baskova," he called. "Your entrée, if you would be so kind."

The little Baskova detached herself from her chocolate-papoushka and hipped her way to the wrong chalk mark.

The calm choreographer folded his arms. He resolved to speak gently.

"Little idiot," he hissed. "Do you still not know where to enter?"

The chocolate-papoushka flushed. "She was up late last night," he apologized to Dumka beside him.

"It makes little difference," said General Dumka noncommittally.

They composed themselves to watch the slow birth of the masterpiece.

The piano churned. The conductor waved. The corps-de-ballet went into action—angular action. The chocolate-papoushka stroked his chin dubiously. Nobody *sur les pointes!* No kiss-the-fingers at the audience! No little pirouettes! What was this thing?"

"It is a great conception," said General Dumka. "It is called Boadicea. The umbrella," he explained, "will be a trident."

"Quoi!" said the backer.

"Boadicea," said Dumka. "She was an early British Queen."

"British," said the backer. All was explained. Anything could happen now. . . .

At a table outside a fashionable café, Natasha and Arenskaya were sitting in the sunshine sipping their chocolate. The table beside them was laden with the spring flowers they had bought in the market that morning.

"How nice it is to have the whole day to ourselves," said Natasha luxuriously.

"How nice it is not to have to go rehearsal," agreed Arenskaya.

"I wonder how it is going?" mused Natasha.

"Like 'ell," said Arenskaya. She looked at her watch. Ten to eleven. "The little Baskova will be in tears by now," she said comfortably.

"I hope so," said Natasha.

Natasha was a nice girl when you got to know her, thought Arenskaya. How to make her happy?

"Let us go and watch her weep," she suggested.

. . . "Bring on the chariot," shouted the choreographer.

Little Igor trundled on a wheelbarrow. The backer took it without a blink.

"The true chariot is not ready yet," said Dumka. "The carpenter has trouble with the square wheels. They will not go round," he explained.

"But why are they square?" asked the backer.

"It is the great conception," said Dumka, as one in view of Zion.

Boadicea mounted the wheelbarrow. She brandished her umbrella. The piano galloped. The corps-de-ballet beat its breasts and ran round in circles. The Man who was No Nijinsky came in staggering under Katusha. She was the human sacrifice. Aliosha had yet to hear of this. The Man who was No Nijinsky laid her on three chairs and stabbed her with considerable satisfaction.

The music coagulated.

"Chariot off," shouted Nevajno.

But it was Boadicea who came off.

The calm choreographer clawed the air and screamed.

In the doorway, arms entwined, Natasha and Arenskaya laughed joyously together.

"Come with me to my fitting," said Natasha. "It seems we are not needed here."

"Un petit moment," said Arenskaya. She minced into the room.

"In this company," she announced to the ceiling, "we do not demand much of our ballerinas, but we do prefer that they should at least stand up."

She minced back to the door. She linked arms with Natasha. They smiled joyously at the company. Arenskaya winked. They went.

"It is a plot," screamed the little Baskova at their disappearing backs. "He tilted the wheelbarrow."

The choreographer silenced her. "Back to the beginning," he said with all the dignity of an exiled monarch forecasting his early return.

His best friend sniffed.

They resumed the rehearsal. Stroganoff came heavily in. He stood watching moodily. This time the little Baskova remained on the wheelbarrow, but that was the most that could be said for her.

"Bon jour, mon ami," called the backer, tearing his fascinated gaze away from the little Baskova's precarious balance. "All is well—yes?"

"No," said Stroganoff. The time had come to speak plainly. He drew the backer over to the mantelpiece, tugged his tie three times, blew his nose, and prepared to take the plunge.

"My friend," he said, "let me put to you a hypothetical case."

"She had the night late," said the backer defensively.

"My friend, we must face the facts," said Stroganoff. "Your little friend has the talent—but it is not for the dance."

"That is true," said the backer fairly. "But she is so pretty to look at that who will mind this?"

"Suppose," said Stroganoff, "that, for the sake of argument, I take away the lead from the little Baskova."

"Then," said the backer, "for the sake of argument, I take away my money."

"So," said Stroganoff. He sighed heavily at his entangled corps-de-ballet.

"And now," said Nicolas Nevajno blissfully, "we have the earthquake." . . .

       ★   ★   ★

That afternoon Aliosha Stroganoff decided to take a hand. He had lunched with his son and Vladimir had not touched his roast goose. And when the Stroganoffs refused roast goose, or any other form of food, things were serious. So while the trained seals undulated where ballerinas would later float, he made his way to the wardrobe where the mamoushka was ironing Natasha's tu-tu to the hum of old Medinka's sewing machine.

"Old woman," he said, "I wish to talk to you." He waddled himself to a chair by the mamoushka and folded his hands across his stomach.

The mamoushka went on ironing.

"Your daughter is giving my son no peace," said Aliosha. "He is worn to a shadow."

"I had not noticed this," said the mamoushka. She turned over the tu-tu. She went on ironing.

"He is a wreck," said Aliosha. "There are rings under his eyes and he does not eat his roast goose. It was not for this," he pointed out, "that I bring him to Petersburg."

"And it is not for others to dance the lead that I bring my Natasha," said the mamoushka. She shook out the tu-tu.

"Woman, you are a fool," said Aliosha. "Where the money is—there goes the rôle. It is a law of nature." He replaced his hands across his stomach.

"Why is it not your money, old skin-the-flint?" The mamoushka turned on him. "You grudge to ruin yourself for your only son. You should be ashamed." She took the tu-tu off the board and shook it at him. Aliosha snatched it from her and threw it on the floor.

"When you are dead and buried," he said, "Vladimir will be happy."

"In the meantime, while I am still alive I take my darling to Diaghilev," retorted the mamoushka. "And if Vladimir hang himself, which," she said contemptuously, "he will never do, then it will be your fault." She stamped her foot. "Baskova must go."

"Woman, be silent," thundered Aliosha. "Baskova stays. It is signed, agreed and paid for. It can gain you nothing that my son should lead the life of a dog with a cat," he pointed out. "You have but to speak the word to your daughter and she will be as sweet as the sugar on the Easter cake for, as women go, there is not much harm in her."

"I will speak the word to my daughter," promised the mamoushka. "I will speak the word that will turn her into a wild cat. I will tell her she is too soft with your Vladimir. I will tell her to take his money, to bleed him to death, to drive him into his grave. I will tell her," she finished, "to go to Diaghilev."

Aliosha got up. His stomach heaved.

"Woman," he thundered, "I have heard enough of your non-sense. I will send for my little father. He," he threatened, "will know how to deal with you."

"And I," said the mamoushka unexpectedly, "will send for my old mamoushka."

They shook their fists at each other while old Medinka went on treadling. They would never get the curtain up if she stopped her work for little scenes like this.

*   *   *

The still of the night. The shutters creaked, the blinds swung, outside the-shan't-get-home-till-mornings seemed unlikely to make it even then, but inside the darkened bedroom of the Stroganoffs all was quiet.

But not for long.

"My darling," said Stroganoff, his troubles heavy on him, "I am not happy."

The humped back of Natasha hardly moved. Very tentatively Stroganoff put an arm around it. This time the movement was definite. It was away from him.

"So," said Stroganoff. He unswung his arm, turned himself to the other side, and lay there fuming. Presently he addressed the wall.

"So," he said. "I bring her to Petersburg, I ruin the little grand-father, I am polite to the mamoushka, I owe the fortune for the flowers every time she dances, and what come of all this? The back!"

"The best years of my life," said Natasha to the other wall. "All my charm. All my talent that other managements beg me for. And what do I get? Not even the sleep in peace."

"Sleep!" Stroganoff said to his wall. "I have not closed the eye for three nights."

"It is the lie," said Natasha turning violently. "All last night you snored. Now be silent and let me sleep." She humped back again.

"I have married a witch," said Stroganoff. "A true daughter of a dancer's mother. For you I have made myself into a wreck—even the strangers in the street have pity for me. Even Arenskaya, who should be our enemy, is sorry for me."

"Arenskaya is a very sweet girl," said Natasha. "She is stupid only to bury herself in your silly company." She jerked herself away so violently that she nearly fell out of bed.

"Is it my fault that the Baskova will not do the walk out?" demanded Stroganoff. "Have we not all done our best to insult her? Me, you, Nevajno, even Katusha. Is it my fault that she burst into the tears instead of the fury?"

"The insult to that one is no use," said Natasha. "If she will not give up the rôle you must take it from her."

"But then the backer take away the money!" said Stroganoff. "Have I not told you this a million times!"

"So do not tell me again," said Natasha. "I wish to sleep." She humped.

Stroganoff closed his eyes. The image of the little Baskova floated—well, not exactly floated—before him. He opened them quickly.

The sleeping draught! He would take the sleeping draught. He would sleep like a log and snore like a wild boar and Natasha could shake him till she was tired and he would not hear her. Maybe she'd be sorry then! Or was he muddled?

The sleeping draught was in his waistcoat pocket. It meant

getting out of bed. But it was worth it. Or in his trousers. Or on the shelf. One little drop, Arenskaya had said. He would take two little drops. Three. He would fall asleep at once and remain insensible for twelve hours. Lost to the world. No backer. No Baskova. No business. No performance. . . . Mon Dieu!

Inspiration hit Stroganoff. He sat up in bed. He thought it over. He couldn't see a flaw anywhere. Foolproof! He thumped his wife's back.

"Mama," screamed Natasha waking suddenly, "now he assaults me."

"I embrace you, my darling," crowed Stroganoff. "Our troubles are over. The little Baskova does not dance. We celebrate." He hugged her.

"But what is this?" said Natasha, too overwhelmed to resist. "What good news can have come to you in the middle of the night?"

"It comes from the head," said Stroganoff. "It is my flair as an impresario that has triumphed. So, my darling, it is necessary that from now on you attend all the rehearsals as the understudy so that you know the part well."

"Me, understudy!" said Natasha. "Never!"

"It must be made to appear so," explained Stroganoff. "But you and I will know that at the first performance it is you who will be dancing."

"And the little Baskova?"

"She must suspect nothing," said Stroganoff. "It will be a pact between you and me. You must not even tell your mamoushka."

Natasha thought it over. "Vladimir," she said, "I have in you the confidence complete. But if you fail me again . . ."

"Fail you!" said Stroganoff. "Impossible . . ."

"And if anything goes wrong . . ."

Stroganoff kissed her warmly. "Then," he promised, "I give you to Diaghilev."

Natasha relaxed. She was very young and there was no mamoushka present to sniff cold water on the promises.

"You are the dearest husband in the world," she said for the first time since the Stroganoff company had opened in the capital.

Stroganoff thought happily of his sleeping draught. No need to get out of bed to get it now.

Chapter Seventeen

TO-NIGHT at 9.0 p.m.

But at the moment it was the afternoon.

The capital, if not agog, was quite interested. The publicity for the new Nevajno had worked well; all the newspapers had given space to welcoming if cautiously-worded announcements of the startling experiment at the Boris Goudonov. There was also a certain amount of speculation about the new ballerina from Vladivostok, whom no critic had been permitted to view in class or at rehearsal. 'A second Trefilova,' they said at the Cubat—some of them.

On paper the evening was an assured success.

"Later, they pay," said Stroganoff buoyantly.

"Later they pay," agreed the proprietor of the little restaurant round the corner. He passed a resigned pencil.

But Natasha was pensive.

"It is already two o'clock, Vladimir," she pointed out, "and the little Baskova has not even sprained an ankle."

"Relax, my little pigeon," said Stroganoff. "Have in me the confidence carefree. All goes according to plan."

His hand stole to his waistcoat pocket.

*   *   *

To-night at 9.0 p.m. It was 9.0 p.m

The new Nevajno was preceded by a divertissement from Casse-Noisette.

Natasha danced the Sugar Plum. She danced it beautifully and looked like a thunder cloud.

Backstage Nevajno had dropped into the star's dressing-room for a few last words of encouragement.

"You dance bad and I kill you," he said, and strode out.

The little Baskova turned to her protector.

"Why do they all hate me?" she asked. "What have I done?"

"They are jealous of you," said the backer comfortingly. "But soon," he promised, "they will all love you."

The door kicked open. Stroganoff came in, balancing a tray of glasses with one hand and carrying a bucket in the other. In the bucket surrounded by ice reposed a bottle of champagne.

"A toast to your performance," he said. He arranged the glasses on the table.

"See," said the backer, "here is one who loves you already."

With the air of a celestial maître d'hôtel about to offer the moon, Stroganoff poured out the slightly flat champagne and passed it to the little Baskova.

"Before the performance?" asked the dancer dubiously.

"One little glass," said the maître d'hôtel. "Poof—you will dance all the better for it."

"And me?" said the backer thirstily.

"Bien sûr," said Stroganoff delighted. He poured.

"And you?" said the backer.

Stroganoff nearly dropped the bottle.

"Me—no," he said quickly. "I must keep the head cool for my speech."

"Nonsense," said the backer. "Drink, we insist."

"But it is very important, my speech," said Stroganoff. "Full of the words difficult." He groped for them. "British Constitution," he produced unexpectedly.

"Drink," urged the little Baskova. "I shan't touch a drop until you do."

Stroganoff gazed at her with the hurt reproach of a hooked mackerel betrayed by its favourite sprat. "But it is to pay you the compliment that I carry the heavy bucket up all those stairs," he protested. "Come, my little one," he entreated. "Drink to give me pleasure."

"Not until you do," said the little Baskova mutinously. At any moment she might dash her glass to the floor.

"My darling!" Stroganoff invented wildly. "I would love to drink with you. But I have—I have—the gout terrible," he began to limp, "and my doctor . . ."

"Well, anyway, I'm going to drink," declared the backer. He tossed off his glass.

What use was that, thought Stroganoff crossly.

"If you don't drink," said the little Baskova with a distinct edge in her voice, "I do not go on."

A gleam of hope lit Stroganoff's face only to flicker out again as a thin spatter of applause came floating through the corridor to act as a spur to the little Baskova's ambition.

"Mon Dieu—my make-up!" she said, and fled to her dressing-table.

The applause died away. Casse-Noisette was over. In fifteen minutes Boadicea would be on.

The backer stretched himself. "Aie!" he said, "but I am sleepy." He poured himself a second glass. He poured out for Stroganoff. "Drink," he invited.

Impossible to delay any longer. Stroganoff clutched his glass, chinked with the little Baskova's, raised it and waited. He realized that she was waiting for him. No escape! The things that I do for my darling, he thought.

"God bless us all," he said manfully and drank.

"Amen to that," said the backer. He could hardly keep his eyes open.

"God bless you both," said the little Baskova. She gulped joyously.

The door opened. In it stood Natasha, a pale pink foam of frozen sugar.

"Ah—the little wife," said the backer just managing to recognize her. "Come drink to our success, my darling." He lurched towards the bottle.

"Non!" cried Stroganoff. "Non!" He swayed. "Not before the performance."

"Drink to my success," said the little Baskova. She yawned.

Resolution came to Natasha. "Yes," she hissed, "I will drink. I will drink to," she raised her glass, "Diaghilev."

"Non!" cried Stroganoff. "Non! Non! British Conshtishon-shon."

"To Diaghilev," toasted Natasha. She drank.

*   *   *

Five minutes later Arenskaya peeped in.

Well, well, well, she thought. What was it that Kashkavar Jones always said about the linings of the English clouds?

She set about taking off the sleeping Baskova's costume.

*   *   *

The Cubat restaurant was thronged.

Here, that part of the world of fashion which had not gone to the Boris Goudonov was waiting to meet that segment which had. You could hardly see the trelliswork for roses, and you could not speak for the popping of champagne corks. If you did catch a word it sounded like 'Baskova.'

For everybody who had not been to the Boris Goudonov was waiting anxiously for anybody who had. The new divine dancer from Vladivostok whom nobody had been permitted to glimpse until to-night—was she divine? Not a ballerina in the room who did not cross herself when she thought of her. The rumours were encouraging, but you could never trust a rumour. She might be good after all.

In the centre of the room a table had been laid for twenty-seven covers. It had been ordered by Vladimir Stroganoff to celebrate the triumph of the Nevajno ballet. Twenty-six of them were empty. At the twenty-seventh sat the choreographer stolidly celebrating.

With an impossible-to-awaken host the other guests had tactfully omitted to turn up, but the choreographer did not appear to notice his absence. He ate and he drank and he appeared to be quite happy. From time to time he drew on the tablecloth.

The other tables took him for the first arrival, but as the minutes went by and Nevajno went on eating and drinking and drawing, speculation ran wild.

What had happened at the Boris Goudonov?

The clientele looked reproachfully at Almire Cubat. What was he there for if not to gather gossip for them?

Kshessinskaya pointed imperiously. So did Pavlova and Preobrajenska. Cubat looked towards the preoccupied choreographer. With the cautious air of an ambassador about to scrutinize a peace treaty he negotiated the distance.

"How did the evening go?" he asked. "A triumph, I trust."

The choreographer looked up. "Cabbages," he said curtly.

"Cabbages?"

"They threw them," said Nevajno. He went on eating.

Cubat negotiated his way back.

"Cabbages," he told Kshessinskaya, Preobrajenska and Pavlova.

"But the little Baskova!" clamoured Pavlova, Preobrajenska and Kshessinskaya. "What was she like?"

Cubat spread his hands.

But they had stopped looking at him, anyway. For on the staircase stood a radiant figure, her arms full of flowers and her eyes sparkling with delight. It was Arenskaya.

It was seen at once that she was wearing Natasha's ermine cloak.

With her was General Dumka. He was carrying an enormous basket of orchids. You could not tell that this was meant for the little Baskova until you looked at the writing on the ribbon.

Cubat bowed. "The others will be here soon?" he asked.

"Mais non," said Arenskaya.

She allowed Cubat to lead her to the table, bowing left and right and blowing kisses, and seated, entered immediately into animated conversation, unanswered by the abstracted Dumka on one side and the drawing choreographer on the other.

"The evening was a success?" ventured Cubat.

"For me, yes," said Arenskaya. "Ah, Almire, you should have been there. I dance as I never dance before. The shouting!" She glowed.

Almire bowed low and drifted off. He ignored the uplifted fingers at the other tables. The most sophisticated restaurateur in the world was not going to ask a ballerina to talk of the performance of another while she was talking about her own. The evening lay ahead. Ah—here was M'sieur Svetlov.

But Svetlov was in a hurry. "Appalling, appalling!" he muttered and started to scribble. At his elbow his runner stood waiting and practically peering over his shoulder.

"He gives me hell," said Nevajno, as one who welcomed it. "One sees it in his eye."

"Yes, yes?" said Arenskaya. "But what he give me?"

A handsome guardsman came in. He bent over Arenskaya and kissed her hand. "My princess," he said, "you were divine." He walked away. He was engulfed.

All over the restaurant the news bubbled up between champagne corks.

Arenskaya had danced Boadicea! Arenskaya!

What a relief!

Kshessinskaya, Pavlova and Preobrajenska relaxed.

Karsavina and Kyasht could breathe again.

Trefilova came rushing into the room. She bowed quickly to Cubat. She did not wait for the orchestra to burst into Lac des Cygnes. She hardly paused to exhibit her new bracelet. She rushed over to Svetlov.

"Valerien," she said, "tell me, sans blague, is she a second Trefilova?"

"Tranquilize yourself, my dear," said Svetlov. "She is a little girl who has drunk too much champagne and fallen asleep in her dressing-room."

"Before or after?" breathed Trefilova.

"All through," snarled Svetlov. He ran his pencil viciously over the page.

Down the marble steps, supported on two sticks, his head shaking with ague, his buttonhole sporting a carnation, hobbled a general. Who said he was past it all? Now that his wife was dead at last he was going out again. Every night of his life. Seventeen years since a ballerina had called him Bobka. Soon put that right. . . . Confound that bottom stair!

He crabbed his way across the room and came to a shaky halt beside Arenskaya. He quivered her little hand up to his lips.

"Divine, Baskova," he trebled. "Mademoiselle, you have made me very happy to-night."

Dumka giggled. "It is Arenskaya," he said.

But happily the General had died.

Chapter Eighteen

"AND so," Stroganoff told the sandy man, "you will understand, my friend, that for the next few nights I sleep alone."

The sandy man nodded.

"Only," said Stroganoff, "I do not sleep."

"What about the sleeping draught?" asked the sandy man.

"No more of that," said Stroganoff. "The headache with which I awake in the little Baskova's dressing-room. Aie!" He clasped his head expressively. "I can think of nothing; my plan exploded— what has become of my first night? My Natasha—what she will do to our marriage? Or what the mamoushka who has awaken us is saying? All that I think of is the aspirin. And as for the others, they, too, think only of their heads. But later, when they are recovered, it is different.

"I can imagine it," said the sandy man.

"You cannot imagine it," said Stroganoff firmly. "It takes a Russian impresario with the plan exploded to imagine it. But, in short, my friend, at once everything is the kaput."

The sunlight was bright and spiteful. It flooded the room and meanly lit up an unshaven Stroganoff in his dressing-gown slumped on his bed.

He had a headache. It was not the same headache but a new and worse one. It had been brought on by listening to a succession of people telling him what they thought of him at the top of their voices.

The little Baskova had screamed off the accumulation of her humiliations since her arrival in the capital. The backer had encouraged her, for, if she stopped screaming at Stroganoff, she would start screaming at him. When she had reduced herself to hysterics in a corner, the backer had taken over and removed his backing in a bellow. Hard on the slammed door that signified their departure came the mamoushka, and though she was not so loud, she was twice as shrill. No, he could not see Natasha. He would never see her again.

Natasha came in to confirm this. They wept together, they consoled each other, they pointed out that they had each other left—Natasha and the mamoushka that is. They swore they were going straight to Diaghilev. They swiped Stroganoff's bottle of aspirins and were on their way.

Then Aliosha had come in heaving with indignation.

"My Katusha!" he boomed. "A sacrifice to a plot that not even a schoolboy would stoop to attempt. I find the backer—all right, you find him—who find him make no difference. Now he has gone. And we are left with the bills, and unless I am to pay them myself, which God forbid, I have to appeal to the little grandfather, and what you think he will say to me?"

"What you are saying to me," said Stroganoff. He groaned.

"I am too soft," Aliosha reproached himself. "That is what is the matter with me. If I had any sense I would close your theatre and take you back to Omsk. And if Natasha leaves you that is your business."

"She has left me already," said Stroganoff.

"A nice state of affairs," said Aliosha indignantly. "My son is twenty-seven and he does not yet know how to hold a woman. It seems that I have to teach you that, too." He melted a little. "I will talk with her," he promised.

"She is with the mamoushka," said Stroganoff.

"H'm," said Aliosha. "I will talk with her later."

He waddled out.

Stroganoff pondered his woes as deeply as the continually ringing telephone would allow. No money. No credit. Nobody trusted him any more. Even the proprietor of the little restaurant round the corner had rung up to plead that he was only a poor tradesman.

Nicholas Nevajno came in. He enquired after Stroganoff's head, improved it, and dismissed it.

"Your head is better? Yes. Good. Have you seen the notices?"

Notices! It showed the state he was in that he had not yet given a thought to the papers. The unquenchable optimism that was the soul of Stroganoff soared up. His ballet was a sensation! The day was saved!

"Show me," he demanded.

The ballet was a sensation. The day was not saved.

"It is as I expected," said Nevajno, not at all displeased. "I am in advance of my time." The word "advance" reminded him of something. He asked for it.

"Go away," said Stroganoff. "If I give you a scheque now it will be like one of yours."

"Like mine?" Nevajno rubbed his chin. Depressed, he wandered out.

No marriage. No money. No credit. Back to Omsk.

A bright little head peered round the door.

"Vladimir," cooed Arenskaya. "Here I am. You bless me—no?"

"Me!" said Stroganoff. He looked at the donor of the sleeping draught.

Arenskaya, who had worked out that this must be the perfect moment to ask for a rise, came prancing in and put her arms gently round Vladimir's unshaver. neck.

"I am so happy, Vladimir," she cooed. "So happy to have saved the day for you."

"Did you strangle her?" asked the sandy man. "No," he remembered.

"No," agreed Stroganoff. "But before she go she is another person who tell me what she think of me."

"But at least Diaghilev didn't drop in," said the sandy man consolingly.

"No," said Stroganoff brightening. "For that one had his troubles, too. . . ."

"Sergei," said Karsavina. "Stop shilly-shallying. I tell you I have to know. I tell you I must tell Teleyakov whether I go with you by noon to-day and I cannot put it off till after to-morrow morning at latest. Yes, Sergei, I have the patience, but also I am not the fool. I tell you I must know . . . Sergei . . . Exchange, have you cut me off?"

Or had he hung up? She wondered.

Diaghilev had hung up.

"Women," he said scornfully. "All they can think of is their own affairs. Now I will have to take her sweetmeats and talk for three hours and not commit myself and be charming all the time." He scowled.

A cry of slightly acid mourning arose from the cortège.

"Teleyakov ought to be sacked," said Benois.

"Teleyakov ought to be shot," said Bakst.

"Teleyakov is an ass," said Diaghilev.

For Teleyakov had been working upon the Government to with-draw their backing for Diaghilev's European tour. To-day the news had come through that he had succeeded. If the tour was to take place at all it must do so from private funds and with artists willing to face the displeasure of the State theatres. And, with little Ginsberg stretched to his maximum, the prospects of Diaghilev's getting to Paris seemed about as bright as those of the man from Omsk. And Tatia telephoning every two minutes for her contract. What did that one want with a contract, anyway? Didn't she trust him to pay her? Sometime.

"Ah, if one could only work with men always," said Diaghilev. "A man can see the whole canvas and not be bounded by his own part of it."

"True," said Benois judicially. "Very true. Aie me," he sighed, "that my sets for Petroushka will not be seen in Paris!"

"Paris!" said Stravinsky. "What stimulation can a musician get in Petersburg. Grand Dukes!" He spat.

"What use to show a Russian fair to Russian people!" said Fokine. "They know it," he pointed out.

"In Paris," mourned Nijinsky, "they would give me all the ballet shoes I need.

"Silence," thundered Diaghilev. "I will take you to Paris. Have I not said so? All that I ask is to be left in peace to find out how. Or rather," he decided, "I will leave you." He strode to the door. "With your permission," he remembered.

"Something is worrying Sergei," said P. Puthyk as the door closed, if not with a slam at least sharply.

*　　*　　*

Early summer had descended on St. Petersburg in a shower of sunshades. Sunshades sprouted from Victorias, sunshades burgeoned from the pavements, sunshades bloomed from terraces and café tables. Even if you had come out without your sunshade, you could hardly avoid sitting under someone else's. The sky was blue and the snows had melted and if the church bells weren't ringing in the middle of the afternoon, you knew that they would start at any moment.

Sergei Diaghilev, on his way to reason with the Director of the State Theatres, had decided to walk. Already he was regretting this. From the outset the arguments he had hoped to assemble had been interrupted by a series of beckoning sunshades. All had to be bowed to, some had to be chatted to, and nobody must be told anything.

"Sergei!" A formidable aged Princess, who had known him since he was so high—always a disadvantage—beckoned imperiously to her crested landau. "What is this nonsense I hear, Sergei?"

"It is nonsense," said Diaghilev smoothly. He kissed her hand.

"Now don't lie to me," said the Princess. "I have known you since you were so high," she reminded him.

"Highness, I am taller now," said Diaghilev. He bowed and walked on.

Satisfying, he reflected, but tactless. On the other hand, he cheered himself up, the Princess had never paid for a seat yet. Ah, well!

Outside a fashionable café, St. Petersburg was refreshing itself. Diaghilev bowed to a strawberry ice but looked quickly away from a chocolate angel cake.

A parasol detached itself from an animated group and floated diffidently but definitely towards him. Behind it, like a swollen echo, wafted a slightly larger parasol, less diffident but more definite.

Mon dieu, thought Diaghilev, she has also a mother! "Enchanté," he bowed as Natasha presented her.

"M'sieur Diaghilev," the charming smile of the mamoushka would have deceived anyone but an impresario, "our contract has not yet arrived."

"Tiens, you astonish me," said Diaghilev, who had not yet drawn it up. "You shall get it to-morrow," he promised.

"For Paris?" pursued the mamoushka.

So she had heard too—the hag!

"And six curtains?" asked Natasha.

"Everything is possible," said Diaghilev.

He passed on. He crossed the public gardens, threading his way through the crested carriages. Now all was green and calm with only the shouts of the children to remind him how quiet it was here.

Diaghilev stood and gazed at the swans floating decoratively about the lake.

And not a ballerina among them!

Diaghilev wished he were a farmer. He decided he didn't really. The difficult but rewarding life of the successful impresario, bringing miracles to reality by a commission here, a suggestion there, and a lightning rehearsal lasting twenty-four hours; assembling the groping genius of others into the forcing frame of fashion, filling his theatres with the grace of his dancers and ringing up on them by the grace of God, travelling from capital to capital till the very whisper of Diaghilev stood for excitement and colour and the avant garde—that was the only life for him. But he had to have money to lead it. How much did he owe? What did that matter! How much could he owe? That was important.

He gazed at a drake whose beady eye reminded him of his bank manager.

"Maestro, you waste your time," said a voice at his elbow. "All that can be done with swans has been done already—by Petipa."

Diaghilev turned. It was the choreographer who did the impossible ballets for the provincial from Omsk.

"Young man, you are wrong," said Diaghilev. "There is much to be done with a swan yet. Fokine has a conception but he insists that it needs Pavlova to dance it. And Pavlova will not come to me, though I beg and beg her." He frowned. "It is her one mistake."

"Pavlova—poof!" said Nicholas Nevajno.

"That, too, is a point of view," agreed Diaghilev. He gazed into the green secrets of the lake. Money . . . money . . . money . . . he was thinking.

R

"Excuse me," said Nevajno, "but to-day it happen that by great chance I am out without any money. So," he suggested confidently, "you schange me small scheque."

Diaghilev looked at him. He began to roar with laughter.

* * *

In the director's office at the Maryinsky, Teleyakov looked at the visiting card that his secretary had handed to him.

"Diaghilev," he said. "Well, well, well. Keep him waiting for ten minutes."

He opened a newspaper.

* * *

And how is little Ginsberg?" asked Teleyakov politely. "Flourishing, I trust?"

He was enjoying himself. Diaghilev was here to ask for favours. Diaghilev, who for years had treated him with polite contempt. Diaghilev, who had never sought his opinions and only listened to them because he had to. Diaghilev, who deflowered his theatres of his best dancers. Diaghilev, who produced new-fangled nonsense and discordant music out of the air and sold them to the capital as the last word in art. Diaghilev, who always referred to him as a last-ditch-donkey. Diaghilev was here to ask for favours. And he wasn't going to get them.

"Flourishing, I hope?" he repeated.

Diaghilev did not move a muscle. He was not enjoying himself. To beg for favours from this man, whose life began and ended with Petipa—it almost made you a reactionary.

"Ginsberg is well enough," he said smoothly. Oppressed moujiks! What about oppressed impresarios? "Let us come to the point," he suggested.

"By all means," purred Teleyakov. "Anything I can do." Come, my little Sergei, he was thinking. Plead!

Damned if I'm going to, thought Diaghilev.

"You know why I am here," he said. "You have done me great

harm. Me, Europe and Russia. I would advise you to undo it while you can."

War! Teleyakov almost rubbed his hands.

"My friend," he said, "why should the State Theatre lend you its money, its best dancers, its prestige? In what way does it benefit Russia to have a lot of pretentious nonsense shown abroad? One day," he looked through the wall, "I will persuade the Tzar to let me take the State Theatre abroad and show Europe the true Russian tradition as it has been danced in this establishment for hundreds of years."

"My friend," said Diaghilev, and was he gritting his teeth? "I am not in the mood nor have I the time to argue artistic matters with you now. We have fought over this ground many times in the past—we shall never agree. I am here to ask you to restore the Government backing that you have taken from me," he said bluntly.

"Why should I?" said Teleyakov, suddenly coming out into the open. "Why should I work for a project of which I do not approve?"

"Because Europe approves. Listen, my friend," Diaghilev leant forward, "I only need your dancers for the summer season when the State Theatre is closed and the dancers are resting or on loan to the provinces. Help me in this and it cannot harm you. It may even," he paused meaningly, "benefit you substantially."

The little bribe! Teleyakov had been waiting for it. It only needed this to make his happiness complete. He chose to ignore the implication.

"Why should I?" he repeated. "Why should I foster a project which gives me a lot of trouble and against which my artistic conscience cries out. Why," it burst from him, "should I use my influence to add to your transient glory?"

"Transient!" Diaghilev's deadly politeness disappeared. He rose awfully to his feet. "Let me tell you, my little Government official, that the only reason posterity will hear about you is because of the books they will read about me. So," he demanded with his hands spread flat on the desk, "do I get my backing, or don't I?"

"Damned if you do," said Teleyakov. He thumped the desk.

"That is how the great ones in Russia talk the business." Stroganoff sighed to the sandy man. "Always the politeness, always the manner," he put his hand on his heart, "correct. Not like in your Europe where you shout and you scream and you thump the desk."

The sandy man smiled. "So it was the bottoms for Diaghilev," he said.

"For the moment—yes," agreed Stroganoff. "But if it was the bottoms for Diaghilev," he shrugged, "it was not yet the tops for me."

*   *   *

Thunder in the air. All day long the company had been listless. Only the hardiest dancers had turned up to class, and, as there was no new work being rehearsed, the men had spent the afternoon playing Vint and No Nijinsky had gambled his overcoat away. It was several sizes too small for Little Igor, but at least he could always gamble it back again.

The girls passed the time darning their ballet shoes and washing each other's hair and trying not to spend money for they had been on half wages for weeks. Natasha and Arenskaya went driving in the Park. But not together. Now that the little Baskova had gone there was no longer any reason for it.

Stroganoff had spent the day doing his accounts, but even that optimistic adder-up could not tot them into profit. The only surplus was vegetables. St. Petersburg had taken to dropping into the upper reaches of the Boris Goudonov (25 kopecs) and throwing them at Boadicea.

"But we lose less money this week than last," said Stroganoff, closing the ledger with a defiant bang.

"But we still lose," said Dumka depressed.

Now it was evening and the company was projecting listless Swans on a lackadaisical lake to a half-filled house.

In the wings a flowing moustache was expressing its views to a

bald-headed dome. The Circus Proprietor had tracked down
Stroganoff.

"My friend," he was saying, "let us talk frankly. Your ballet is
not stimulating my business. In fact, it is doing me harm."

Stroganoff gazed at the stage. "Mon dieu!" he said as the Swan
Queen swooned into No Nijinsky's arms, luckily there.

"Before you came," said the Circus Proprietor, "I was playing
every night to capacity—well almost," he admitted. "And now my
houses are but little better than yours."

Stroganoff drew himself up. "And is this my fault?" he demanded,
a truculent camel refusing to break its back with someone else's
last straw.

"I am a man of honour," said the Proprietor. "I pay my wages,
I feed my animals well, and I honour the note of hand of my little
grandfather. But," he pointed out, "it would have been cheaper for
me to have done this with money."

"Money," said Stroganoff bitterly.

"My friend," said the Proprietor, "I have to live. And I cannot
do this while the public comes here to see my circus and finds
instead—this," he waved his arm in the direction of a huddle of
huntsmen, "and so does not come again."

"And what of me?" asked Stroganoff hotly. "The balletomanes
come here to be whisked to dreams of an enchanted land," he waved
his arms towards a wobbly pas-de-bourre, "and when they come
on the wrong night they find instead—this." He pointed to the
wedged-in-the-corner elephant.

"My friend," said the Proprietor. "There is one public for the
circus and one for the ballet, and sooner than confuse themselves
they both stay away. No, no, my friend, one of us must go."

Stroganoff brightened. "When you leave?" he demanded.

Aliosha came wandering up, a sheaf of bills in his hands.

"Vladimir," he announced. "I have decided. On Sunday I go
back to Omsk."

"I shall miss you, papoushka," said Stroganoff relieved.

"You will not miss me," said papoushka. "You will be with me."

"Ah," said the Circus Proprietor.

"But, papoushka!" The camel sagged. "My career! My Natasha's career. Your Katusha's career," he appealed desperately.

"It is no use," said Aliosha. "I and the little father have given you your wish. But if we continue we will soon begin to lose our own money."

"Meanwhile you lose mine," said the Circus Proprietor.

"Is it our fault that your little grandfather ran into debt?" said Aliosha coldly. He turned his back.

The proprietor wandered over and patted the elephant. Would he have to pledge him? Never!

"You are not fair, papoushka," said Stroganoff. "In Petersburg success does not come at once. Already I have moved many mountains. Would you take me away while I am pushing at others?"

Aliosha looked the other way. "Your orchestra is terrible," he said.

"We are losing money, it is true," argued Stroganoff. "But each week we lose less and less. Now I am nearly established. When I go to the Cubat the proprietor bows. I walk in the gardens and I say 'Hallo' all the time. Do not," he appealed, "dash from me the vodka before it flow down my throat."

"Anyone can lose money," said Aliosha, a chip off the old block, "but it takes a wise man to know when to stop. My son—you are not a success in the capital. It is not your fault," he conceded. "The competition is too strong for you. Give in and come home."

"Little father," said Stroganoff. "I am your son. Did you give in when you had the fire before you were insured?"

"No," said Aliosha. "But," he pointed out, "it was my own money that I was losing."

"And me, I will not lose yours," promised Stroganoff. "All that I need now is the little coup. One success and Petersburg is at my feet. If I could get a Pavlova. Just one Pavlova," he emphasized.

Aliosha was silent.

"Papoushka," pleaded Stroganoff. "Write to the little grand-father."

Aliosha fumbled inside his pockets. "It is not necessary," he confessed. "He will be here to-morrow." He pulled out a wire and passed it to his son. It read:

"*Decided to look into things myself. Arriving by train to-morrow, Father.*"

"Voilà!" said Aliosha. He looked a little scared himself.

*   *   *

Conseille de famille.

The Stroganoffs were seated round the table in Aliosha's bed-sitting-room. Hope in adversity had united the family and a photographer, happening to press a bulb at this moment, would have caught Vladimir smiling at his mother-in-law and the daughter smiling at her husband. Also present was General Dumka smiling on all of them.

"We must give the little grandfather the welcome tremendous," Stroganoff was saying. "It must be quite clear that it is for himself alone that we hug and kiss him. You, papoushka," he divided the labours, "shall engage for him the room silent on the south side. You, Natasha, shall select the books that he will not read in it—but they must be there. You, mamoushka, will have ready for him the collation delicious, and I," he took on the hardest labour, "shall go down to the station and listen to how he did not like the journey."

"And me?" said Dumka, left out of it. "What do I do?"

Stroganoff pondered. "You," he decided, "shall push the bath-chair and you must remember to take the corners slowly and also," memory travelled back, "never to leave him in it on top of a hill."

"Aie!" said Aliosha. "What a day that was."

"It is our one chance," said Stroganoff. "We must make the old one so happy that he will not remember to ask for our figures. We must forget our quarrels, we must forget Diaghilev, we must all love one another." He looked at Natasha.

"That is right," said the mamoushka. (No contract from Diaghilev yet.) "That is right, my little one," she said encouragingly.

Natasha coloured.

"And that night," Stroganoff told the sandy man, "Natasha return to my room. And though it is not quite as before it was, enfin, pas mal. Pas mal du tout," he remembered.

Chapter Nineteen

THE great terminus of St. Petersburg was a forcing frame of joined-together black beetles. They chuffed, they shunted, and they let off steam, while all around them on the platforms an army of ants wept, embraced and presented roast chickens.

A bell rang three times. A beetle chuffed bravely out to a trail of waving handkerchiefs, go with Gods, love to Aunt Katyas, and "don't lean out of the windows."

"I wonder why I wanted to be an engine-driver," mused the engine-driver. The stoker went on stoking.

Through the home-going ants and the cries of "you forgot to give her the water melon," two ants were progressing arm in arm. One had white whiskers, the other a bald dome. Between them they carried a huge box of chocolates from which they absently refreshed themselves from time to time.

"See, my friend," said Stroganoff triumphantly. "Did I not tell you we would not be late."

"We would have been late had the train been early," said Dumka stubbornly. "And then your little grandfather would never have forgiven you and the day would have been lost. No, no, my friend," he insisted, "it was not the moment to linger in front of the mirror."

Stroganoff tugged at the effulgent silk on his bosom. "I am not happy about my colour scheme," he fretted. But Dumka was looking at the indicator.

"Tiens," he said in awe, "the train from Vienna is only four hours late."

"What do I care about trains from Vienna," said Stroganoff impatiently. "It is the train from Omsk that is important. Come!" He took a chocolate and forged ahead.

With the Trans-Siberian Express about to arrive two days late and the Vienna Express about to arrive four hours late, the platform was crowded. Stroganoff threaded Dumka to a point of vantage.

"Voilà," he said. "From here we will see the little grandfather leaning out of the window and greet him before he can greet us."

"The old one will be too tired to look out of the window," dampened Dumka.

"We Stroganoffs do not tire easily," boasted Vladimir. "And when the little grandfather sees what I have brought him," he held up the box of chocolates and, as an afterthought, helped himself, "and hears that instead of a droshki he will ride to the hotel in a snow-white landau with the rubber wheels—the years will drop from him and also," he dug Dumka in the ribs, "his money."

"So," said Dumka. He munched. "Next time," he announced, "I pick one with the soft centre." He explored the box.

The ants stirred like a forest in the wind. A beetle chugged triumphantly in.

"The Vienna Express," said Dumka.

"Why you worry me with Vienna," said Stroganoff. He bit into a chocolate and stared down the platform into the empty distance. "Hard," he said disappointed.

But Dumka was looking at a cluster of bouquets gathered in front of a carriage held out in worship to a small dark woman who was descending from it.

"Ciel!" he cried. "It is the divine Dourakova."

"Dourakova!" Stroganoff swung round. "But she is in Vienna," he objected.

"She has come back," breathed Dumka, gazing in worship at a mass of luggage that was piling up and rapidly hiding the ballerina.

A signal fell, but Stroganoff failed to notice. He, too, was gazing at what could still be seen of the sables that dripped from the divine Dourakova. And then he was galvanized.

"My friend," he cried. "We are mad. For what we wait? Come— we approach ourselves."

He dashed down the platform.

"Marya!" screamed Dourakova to her maid. "Hold tight to the jewel case." ˙

"You are holding it yourself," screamed back Marya.

"And count the luggage again," instructed Dourakova, but not trusting her counted herself. "Only thirty-four pieces," she totted up. "This cannot be right," she smiled absently at General Dumka.

Stroganoff caught the recapitulating hand, guided it between a dressing-case and a hat-box and kissed a diamond ring.

"Madame," he said, "this is a great day for me."

A gaunt figure alighted from the carriage and towered over the group.

"I have a headache," it announced starkly.

"Oh, mon dieu!" said Dourakova aghast. "My poor Grisha. We must do something. Do something!" she implored Stroganoff.

Stroganoff extended the chocolates. The gaunt figure munched.

"Soft," it said disgusted. It spat.

"Say nothing," hissed Dumka to the about-to-bridle Stroganoff. "It is Grisha Podushkin."

"I do not care if it is Rasputin," said Stroganoff. "He spit."

"But he is the leader of the claque," urged Dumka. "He organize everything."

"He does not organize this," said Stroganoff. He bowed deeply to Dourakova.

"Madame," he said, "my carriage awaits you. You get in it quick before Diaghilev he pop up. It has rubber wheels," he clinched the matter.

Dourakova hesitated.

"Come," said Stroganoff.

He picked up three valises and swept the ballerina off the platform.

From a window of the Trans-Siberian Express a beady-eyed old man from Omsk glared after him.

*   *   *

"M'sieur," said Dourakova, as the snow-white landau pulled up outside the Hotel Splendide and a swarm of page-boys surrounded the carriage, "it has been most kind of you to escort me to my hotel. And now I will say 'au revoir.'"

"Au revoir," agreed Stroganoff. He followed her in.

The hotel clerk bowed deeply. "Madame, the suite is ready." He stepped into the lift. So did Stroganoff.

"Voilà," said the clerk. "The first suite."

"It faces south?" asked Dourakova.

"But all the way," said the clerk.

"It is silent until noon?" pursued Dourakova. "And at the hour of the siesta?"

"As the tomb," swore the clerk.

"Is the mattress soft?"

"As a snowdrift."

"Bon," said Dourakova. "Then it will do for Grisha. You see," she confided to the clerk, "on the morning of a performance I am up at ten, but my cheer-leader must sleep until lunch. It is so exhausting for his nerves."

Stroganoff nodded profoundly. "Parfaitement," he said.

Dourakova realized him with slight surprise. "M'sieur," she said, "it is very kind of you to escort me to my rooms. But now," she held out her hand, "I will say 'au revoir.'"

Stroganoff kissed it. "Au revoir," he agreed. He stayed where he was.

The clerk led them down the corridor and opened a door.

"The second suite," he announced.

"Is there a house telephone?" asked Dourakova. "Is there a communicating door?"

"Is the water in the bathroom hot?" asked Stroganoff.

Dourakovs realized him again.

"M'sieur," she insisted. "Au revoir."

"Au revoir," said Stroganoff.

"I will send up the luggage," said the clerk. He bowed himself out.

Dourakova turned to the dressing-table. She took out her hat-pins, she puffed up her hair, she allowed her sables to drop from her shoulders. These long journeys were killing her. . . .

"And now," said Stroganoff, bobbing up in the mirror, "for the chat cosy."

"The gentle firmness," Stroganoff told the sandy man, "and not to take hard the snub, always the cheerful, always the hopeful—that is the way to manage the ballerina. Three times she tell me 'au revoir,' and me, I am still there." He glowed.

"And what happened then?" asked the sandy man.

"Oh, she kick me out," said Stroganoff. "But the ground is prepared, and I send round Dumka."

*   *   *

General Dumka stood in front of the mirror and twiddled his carnation.

"What is the time?" he asked.

"Time you went," said Vladimir Stroganoff. He kissed him on both cheeks. "And remember our destiny lies in your hands."

"Go with God," said Aliosha.

"Or we all go back to Omsk," said the little grandfather. He dug his chin in the air.

Vladimir crossed to him.

"Little grandfather," he pleaded, "why are you still angry? Have I not explained to you many times the full reasons why I do not stay to meet you at the station. Why then do you still scowl at your grandson who loves you?"

"And why should I not scowl?" demanded Moisha. "Did not the droshki try to overcharge me—*me*—an old man, who has not been to the capital for forty years but who still remembers how much one should pay a droshki?"

"Little grandfather," pleaded Vladimir. "Give Dumka your blessing. It needs only for him to bring Dourakova to us and all our troubles will be over."

"That's right," said Aliosha encouragingly. "All our troubles will be over."

"Fool," squealed Moisha. "What gives you such confidence in this dancer?"

"She is Dourakova," said Dumka reprovingly.

"The divine Dourakova," said Aliosha.

"Then pay her with your own roubles," snapped the little grandfather, "or hold your tongue."

Aliosha held his tongue.

"Dumka," said Vladimir, patting the General on the shoulder. "My brave Dumka. Be of good courage and do not forget to tell Dourakova what I have told you to say."

"I know well what to say Dourakova," said Dumka testily. "I who have known her since she was a second soloist. Never," he sighed, "shall I forget her début in La Belle au Bois Dormant at the Maryinsky. The Breadcrumb!" he breathed ecstatically.

"Do not remind her of it," urged Vladimir. "Paint instead the picture glowing of our company and offer her the contract fabulous."

"Eh?" said Moisha.

"Tell her," said Vladimir, "that here she will be the Assoluta of Assolutas."

Natasha came in.

"I go now," said Dumka. He picked up his cane and ran.

"He, he," chuckled Moisha. "You forgot to bless him." He waggled a finger at the transfixed Natasha. Old as he was he could recognize a situation when he saw one.

"Who?" asked Natasha ominously. "Who is to be the Assoluta of Assolutas?"

"My child!" The tactful Aliosha heaved himself out of chair and waddled over to wrap his arms around her. "I have for you the surprise that will gladden your heart. Guess who comes to save the day? Guess whom we invite to join our company? Guess?"

"Guess, my darling." Vladimir hovered anxiously.

"The divine Dourakova," said Moisha. He had tired of the build-up.

"So," said Natasha. She wrenched herself out of Aliosha's arms.

"I see you are pleased," said Aliosha gazing at the stony face.

"Say you are pleased, my darling," pleaded Vladimir.

"Pleased!" said Natasha. She took a deep breath. "Pleased—when the Stroganoffs conspire behind my back—all three of them—to bring to my company a ballerina that shall rob me of my rôles." She glared at them. "If she comes I go."

"It is that or Omsk," thundered Aliosha. If tact wouldn't work, he'd show her.

"Not for me," declared Natasha. "For me—Europe. For me—Diaghilev."

"Hoity-toity," said the little grandfather.

"My darling," said Vladimir. "See the reason. With Dourakova we can continue in the capital. Without her we go back to Omsk. Help me, my little wife."

But Natasha did not soften. "I must think of my career," she said.

"You should think of your husband," thundered Aliosha.

"Quite right, my son," said Moisha. "So she should."

Natasha tapped her toe. "If she comes," she said, "I go." She turned on her husband. "Well, Vladimir?"

Vladimir looked round. He saw the heaving stomach of his father, he saw the shocked expression of his little grandfather. He drew comfort from the clan.

"If she comes," he said, "you may go."

Natasha looked at him dazed.

"And that night," Stroganoff told the sandy man, "I sleep alone again. Only this time," he mused, "somehow I sleep."

*   *   *

A quiet night at the Cubat. The table near the service doors was empty. Almire was most upset about this. The beginning of the ruin.

But even as he put a Reserved card on it the divine Dourakova came sweeping in. Straight away there was a fresh complication. How to offer so small a table to so great a ballerina. He would have to expand.

But the divine Dourakova did not even pout. Instead she smiled at him with all the radiance of a dancer returning from a continental tour, intent on giving the impression that it has been triumphant.

"She is with little Dumka," noted Bakst, Bolm, and Benois. "Oho!" they said.

"What do I care," said Diaghilev, gazing gloomily at a sketch Nijinsky had scribbled on the tablecloth.

"Teleyakov," said Nijinsky helpfully. "I hang him." He added a loop.

At the table by the service doors the gay chatter that had started the meal fizzled out.

"So it has been a great success Vienna?" said General Dumka. "Ah, me, that I was not there!"

"A great success," said Dourakova thoughtfully. "Yes, it was a great success. But," she switched on the smile behind which she need not listen, "let us talk about you."

But General Dumka was much too wise for any such thing.

"Oh, no," he said. "I have been supping ballerinas for many years, and when one of them comes back from Vienna it is not about the old General they wish to talk." He poured out the champagne. "Come," he urged, "tell Dumka your troubles. And do not tell me you have no troubles," he said, "for I will believe anything but this."

Dourakova smiled at him—a real smile. "Dear Dumka," she said. "My troubles are not for you."

"And since when?" said Dumka indignantly. "Did I not nurse you through your first Lac des Cygnes? Did I not support you through your first Giselle? Was it not Dumka who stood by your side when you walked out of the Maryinsky?"

"You should have pushed me back," said Dourakova. "You should have pushed me back."

"I tried," said Dumka. "Don't you remember, my darling. All night I push." He mopped his brow.

Dourakova made a great confession. "I was very silly," she said. "And I was very silly, too, to make an enemy of Diaghilev." She looked across to his table. "In fact," she faced it, "I have been a fool."

"Hush," said Dumka horrified.

"It is all right," said Dourakova. "The little table quiet has its compensations. There is no one near enough to overhear."

This, of course, excluded the agog knife boys juggling with the cutlery.

"My darling," said Dumka. "Let us not cry over the broken vodka bottle. Tell me about Vienna. The affairs of the heart, they were amusing—yes?"

Dourakova considered. "Amusing—no," she said. "But I think you will agree that they were sensible. I have," she announced, "married Grisha."

"Grisha!" said Dumka surprised. "But he sleeps all the time," he objected.

"In a husband this is not altogether a disadvantage," said Dourakova. "Else I would not be having supper with you, my darling," she pointed out.

Dumka smoothed out his whiskers.

"And at his work he is a genius," said Dourakova. "Never has my applause been so well organized. Seventeen curtains for Esmeralda and an encore for the thirty-two fouettés in Lac."

"An encore in Lac," said Dumka shocked. "It is not in the tradition."

"It is in Vienna," said Dourakova carelessly. She waved away Austria. "I tell you, my darling, there has never been a leader of the claque like my Grisha. When I marry him and bring him here, Chaliapine is in tears and Caruso come to plead personally with me. And even though he sing Pagliacci, I am adamant. So he has to employ instead Mario, who it is well known has no influence with the upper circle." She laughed merrily.

"A prudent marriage," said Dumka. "My congratulations."

"Prudent!" said Dourakova. "It is sheer genius this marriage. Listen to me, my Dumka," she turned her great eyes on him. "There are some ballerinas who marry their impresarios, there are others who marry their conductors—both of these are good for the career. There are the ballerinas that marry the business men, but soon they cease to be ballerinas. There are the silly ones that marry other dancers, but these we need not discuss. But me," she boasted, "I am the first ballerina who has married her cheer-leader, and now am certain of what, au fond, is the most important thing in a ballerina's life—her applause."

She drank her champagne.

"You are the one ballerina in the world who does not need a claque," said Dumka, "but all the same," he admitted, "it is wise to have it."

He toasted her.

"And now," he said, "when shall we see you dance next?"

Dourakova put down her glass. "It is not when," she said. "It is where." She drooped a little.

"You have no definite plans?" asked Dumka hopefully.

"Oh, yes, I have plans," said Dourakova. "Very definite plans. Odessa, Sevastopol. Kharkov. And," she said with mounting venom, "Omsk."

"The provincial tour!" said Dumka aghast.

"Yes, my darling," said Dourakova sadly. "Your divine Doura is going on a tour of your bug-ridden provinces."

"But, my darling," pleaded Dumka, almost unable to believe his ears. "I cannot let you do this."

"I can do nothing else," said Dourakova. She looked across at Diaghilev. "I have been very silly."

Dumka was nearly in tears. Indeed, it was not until he remembered what he was here for that he brightened.

"My darling," he said, "you shall not dance in these preposterous provinces. I, your Dumka, promise you this. Omsk!" he said scornfully. He remembered something. "Odessa," he substituted.

Dourakova smiled through her tears. "You are very loyal, my Dumka, and I am touched. But do not distress yourself for me. It is not the great tragedy. I will go into exile, but only for a little while, and by the time I return there will have been quarrels at the Maryinsky—new quarrels—and I will allow them to persuade me to take my place again. And what Grisha can do with a claque at the Maryinsky," she saw a vision, "is nobody's business. I will yet," she prophesied, "die twice in Giselle."

"Three times," cried Dumka, carried away.

Caution returned to Dourakova. "Remember," she said, "that what I have told you is for your ears alone. To the world I go to the provinces because the whole of Russia it clamours for me."

"What do you take me for?" said Dumka hurt.

Dourakova patted his sleeve. "There, there," she said, "finish your champagne."

"Doura!" Dumka leant forward. "There is no need for you to go to the provinces. I, too, have had the success. I am now," he announced importantly, "artistic adviser to the Ballet Stroganoff."

Dourakova wrinkled her brow. Stroganoff! Where had she heard that name before.

"But it is the awful man who will not go away all afternoon," she remembered. "He is funny. I like him," she decided.

"He is a great man," said Dumka reverently. "A little obstinate, but a great man. Figure-toi, ma petite, he arrives from Omsk without one friend in the capital—save me. Every door is closed to him and he has no money at all save what his father will not give him. He has an ambitious wife and a nagging mamoushka-in-law, and everywhere they laugh at him, and nowhere will they help him, but his great heart pushes on, and every night his curtain ring up at the Boris Goudonov, and if the audiences are not large they are growing bigger, and if the performance is not perfect it is improving all the time. He will succeed that one, Doura, you will see. And," he finished, "I love him better than my brother. Much," he remembered.

"The Boris Goudonov?" asked Dourakova vaguely. "Where is this?"

"It is not in Sevastopol," said Dumka. "It is not even in Odessa. It is here," he flourished his hand, "in the capital. And, my darling, from the moment that you step on to the platform on the station we all live only that you should come and join us."

He leant back in his chair. He wasn't doing so badly, he thought. Dourakova laughed merrily.

"Oh, my Dumka, always you make the little jokes. Me—join a company from Omsk!"

"It is better than dancing there," said Dumka.

The smile died out. But the laughter continued. With an offer pending this was no time for friendship.

"I think I shall cancel the tour, anyway," said Dourakova. "They want me in Berlin. And I have just had a letter from London for the Coliseum, but I think," she pouted, "it is too small."

"It is also a music hall," said Dumka nastily.

They glared at one another.

"You do not believe me," said Dourakova.

"I do not," said Dumka.

They glared again. Dumka recovered first.

"My darling," he said. "We have been very frank with each other all night. Let it continue so. You," he said, "are in the purée. We are in the bortsch. Come to us," he urged, "and we will all be in the caviar."

Dourakova tasted the idea. "How temptingly you put it," she said.

"Come, my darling," said Dumka. "Come and see our company. Afterwards you shall decide." He glanced at his wrist-watch. "We are still in time for the last ballet. Let us hope," he made the little joke, "that it is not Boadicea."

It was not Boadicea.

As the divine Dourakova and General Dumka took their places in the box, trumpets blared and four elephants stood on their hind-legs and waved their front ones.

The ballerina took her bow. She was a performing seal.

"Dear God," said Dourakova, "are we then at the circus?"

"Oui," said Dumka heavily.

*   *   *

Dourakova was divine, Doura was a veritable angel—but she was not reasonable. No! On the other hand—a circus! Tcha! What a difference did it make to a ballerina what happened at a theatre on the nights she was not dancing in it? A lot of difference, thought Dumka, trudging alone through the night.

He had come so near to success, too. In the droshki driving to the Boris Goudonov the contract was practically signed. Even the two harps for Lac des Cygnes—a permanent clause in any Dourakova contract—had been mooted and agreed. The little grandfather would have to pay for an extra one—that was all there was to it. Practically signed—excepting for her right to dismiss the conductor, if she did not approve of him, and that could have been settled by a little clause obligating her not to exercise this privilege unreasonably and a further little clause calling on her, should she so exercise it, to produce a new conductor mutually acceptable to all parties at a no greater salary. Ballerinas were child's play when you knew how to handle them. But this was an unmanageable child.

Dear Doura! Damn Doura! Where had he walked himself to?

No matter.

How to tell Stroganoff? How to tell the brave Vladimir of the failure of his mission? How to tell the brave little grandfather? If only he, Dumka, were a wealthy man! If only he had not gambled so much when he was young! If only he could win the State lottery! . . .

"Bon soir, mon général. You like the pretty lady?"

General Dumka stared at the mackintoshed figure that had loomed up in the night.

"I loathe the pretty lady," he said. "And," he sighed, "I adore her."

"How you like them?" pursued the mackintosh. "Plump?"

"No," said General Dumka. He shook his head. "I am too old, my friend." He prepared to walk on.

The mackintosh shrugged. "So be it," he said.

A white Homburg hat came sailing up through the night. The mackintosh bent itself double.

"Maestro," it breathed.

The white Homburg nodded vaguely and sailed on.

"That," said the mackintosh gazing after it in awed worship, "is the biggest white-slaver in Petersburg."

His ambitions rekindled. He grasped Dumka by the arm.

"You want the pretty lady," he urged. "Plump," he tempted.

The Wild Strawberry, Dancing and Singing, was one of several dozen similar establishments in the capital but happened to be the best in the neighbourhood. General Dumka furiously waving away the mackintosh whose pretty lady was getting plumper with every step, turned into it thankfully. It would at least serve as a refuge and the little drink would hearten him to break his sad news to the Stroganoffs, at the moment, no doubt, pacing the room—all three of them.

The Wild Strawberry was full of revellers sounding their chest notes, not all of them sober but all of them keeping pretty good time.

Particularly in the left-hand corner, where a bald dome was waving its arms at a gaunt face.

"I cannot live without champagne," it affirmed in a fruity baritone.

One of the Stroganoffs was not pacing the room.

General Dumka threaded his way through the smoke and the Otchi Tchernias.

"Vladimir," he said accusingly, "why are you singing?"

"Dumka!" Stroganoff, a bright pink moon of affability embraced him. "My dear Dumka. Come—sing with us. Two Guitars," he commanded his neighbours.

"Two Guitars," agreed Grisha. He began it.

Dumka chafed impatiently while the Leader of the Claque organized the room through three choruses.

"Vladimir!" He seized on the lull. "I bring bad news."

"To-night no news is bad," said Stroganoff. "Gaida Troika," he suggested.

"As you will," said Grisha. He mounted the table.

"No, no," said Dumka. "Vladimir—listen to me. Dourakova will not come to us."

"Is that all!" Stroganoff thumped Dumka on the back. "My friend, you distress yourself for nothing. She has no choice. To-night," he pointed to the crescendoing Grisha, "I have signed up her cheer-leader."

"Gaida Troika!" roared the swaying, waving, carried-away room.

"See," said Stroganoff, "he is in great form."

General Dumka sat down. He considered the situation.

"Gaida Troika," he joined in, much relieved.

Chapter Twenty

"AND that," Stroganoff told the sandy man, "was the beginning of the turning-tide. From this moment things begin to change for me."

"About time," said the sandy man.

"For," said Stroganoff, "after the argument marital with the Leader of the Claque, the seventeen aspirins, and the little weep on Dumka's shoulder, Dourakova sign with the ballet Stroganoff a contract that run into twenty-four pages, and I am the coming man."

"Hallo, Vladimir. Ça va, mon vieux?"

"Ça va," said the Coming Man, beaming.

Vladimir Stroganoff was taking his morning stroll down the Nevsky Prospekt, though it was not so much a stroll as a royal progress. Ever since Dourakova had signed people had hailed him instead of pointing at him. Invitations to dinner parties, gambling parties, singing parties, which he did not answer, snowed into his letter-box. Photographers offered him free sittings, all of which he accepted. Dukes and Duchesses bowed to him, and only little Ginsberg scurried to the other side of the street at his approach— that one had troubles enough.

"And as things changed for me," Stroganoff told the sandy man, "so they changed for Diaghilev."

"He found money?" asked the sandy man.

"He found courage," said Stroganoff. "He decided to open in Paris without State backing and hope for the best. If I am correctly informed," said Stroganoff, "he did not settle for the scenery till many years later."

Aliosha and the little grandfather, the former pushing the latter, came in for their share of adulation. For the first time Aliosha kissed the hand of a grand-duchess and the little grandfather was called an International Financier, which was not what they had called him in the old days.

"In fact," Stroganoff told the sandy man, "in those days that preceded Dourakova's opening there was but one cloud on the horizon. My wife."

"You sleep alone?" asked the sandy man, smiling indulgently.

"Not always," said Stroganoff. "But I do not sleep with my

Natasha. She is still in my company, but we are not more to one
another than the newest little choryphée. Less," he remembered.

"And the opening was a success then?" asked the sandy man.

"My friend," said Stroganoff irritated. "Who tells this story?
You or me?"

Conseille de Famille—most of it. But instead of Natasha and the
mamoushka, there were Dourakova and the leader of the Claque.

"Stroganoff," said Dourakova. "Listen."

Three heads turned sharply.

"We have been talking delicately long enough," said Dourakova.
"Let us get down to facts." She announced the first one. "Your
company is terrible."

"My company!" Vladimir was on his feet.

"Our company!" Aliosha's stomach heaved.

"Silence—both of you," said the little grandfather. "It is possible
that the woman is talking sense. It is not often that a woman talks
sense, but in this case," he stated, "I have an instinct that she may
be right."

"I am right," said Dourakova. "Mind you," she said fairly,
"every ballet company is terrible, but the difference between the
good and the bad company is that the good has learnt how to
conceal the terrible. You," she denounced, "take all your worst
points and bring them to the front."

"My Katusha," said Aliosha thoughtfully. He dismissed the
dreadful suspicion.

"Consider your leading dancer," said Dourakova. "He is No
Nijinsky, we are agreed. Then why," she demanded, "do you
give him what only Vatza can do?"

"But since we give the ballet," objected Vladimir, "someone has
to dance it."

"Then you do not give that ballet," said Dourakova. "That is the
whole point. You must stay within the limitations of your company. That," she said firmly, "is what I will insist on as long as I am
with it."

"But you have no limitations, my darling," said General Dumka. The Leader of the Claque looked surprised.

"If I could dance all evening I would," said Dourakova. "Believe me I would. But I must have support—every dancer must have support—and," she emphasized, "it must be the right support. So, Vladimir," she turned on him, "you can tear up the ambitious programme you have composed for my opening, for it would take the whole of the Maryinsky and Diaghilev working together and staying like that to achieve it."

"But . . ." said Vladimir.

"Silence," said the little grandfather. "You heard what she told you. Tear it up."

With sulky determination Vladimir ripped.

"I have thought over the programme carefully," said Dourakova. "The opening ballet shall be something slight and it shall be without me. I would suggest Snegourotchka. It is not too difficult and your wife will be very charming in it."

"Not to me," said Vladimir.

"For my first ballet," said Dourakova, "I will do the second act of Lac."

"Lac," said Vladimir unhappily. "Natasha has been dancing Lac."

"Exactly," said Dourakova, "and that is the sort of thing that has got to stop. Also," she discovered, "I shall require Natasha to lead the Swans. With Arenskaya," she added, "they will not be at all bad," she said generously.

"Oh," said Vladimir. He was visualizing himself telling them.

"We will end with Divertissement," said Dourakova. "Here we will give such of your company as merit it a chance."

"Katusha," said Aliosha. But he said it under his breath.

"I," said Dourakova, "will do the Sugar Plum variation, and that conductor will go through it with me and he will get it right or . . . What is the clause, my darling?"

Grisha opened his eyes. "Eleven," he said. He closed them again.

"And so," Stroganoff told the sandy man, "I announce the programme for the opening. And at once all the seats are booked and
I am in the roubles. And then the rehearsals begin and it seems as
if a miracle had happen to my company."

He looked at Pavlova's portrait.

"Yes, my friend, a miracle. The presence of Dourakova acted as
a spur to my loyal little company. For her they could achieve what
before they had never dared to attempt. Figurez vous, mon vieux,
Kashkavar Jones achieve four turns where before he had done but
one and a half and faked. Success," said Stroganoff, "was in the air."

"And your wife?" asked the sandy man.

"My wife," Stroganoff sighed. "She was an aloof stranger. When
I gave her Snegourotchka all she said was 'very well,' and she hold
up her hand to silence the mamoushka."

"And Arenskaya?" asked the sandy man.

Stroganoff smiled. "Doura, she have the little word with
Arenskaya."

"You are the divine Dourakova," shrilled Arenskaya. "Bon.
You have come here to save the company. Bon! You are the
greatest artist the world has ever seen. Bon! But if you criticize my
behind once more," she quivered, "I slap your face."

Dourakova gazed at her serenely. "You should not stick it out,"
she said.

A rattle-snake deciding where to strike next, Arenskaya drew back.

"And it is for this that I walk out of the Maryinsky," she found.
"To have my behind criticized by a ballerina who has only just not
shown her own—much bigger—to Nijni Novgorod."

For a second Dourakova's eyes became slits of ice. She controlled
herself. She could be as shrill as anybody, but this was not the time.

"My little one," she said, "you were rash to leave the Maryinsky
on, shall we say, an impulse. There at least there was no chance that
they would give you to do what you could not do."

"That you should tell me this," said Arenskaya scornfully. "You, who walked out, not on an impulse but after arguing for seven months."

"I am Dourakova," said Dourakova. She looked up as though waiting for the trumpets to sound in heaven.

"And me, I am Arenskaya," said Arenskaya.

No trumpets.

"Not yet," said Dourakova with deadly gentleness. "Though you may well be when I have finished with you. You have temperament," she conceded, "but you must learn to control it. And your behind. You can be Arenskaya when you are older," she smiled, "and can remember your triumphs to pupils too young to have known them."

"Me a teacher!" Arenskaya was aghast.

"In time," said Dourakova. "In time you will almost certainly end up as a teacher. And so," she discovered a little sadly, "will I."

Abashed by this glimpse of the future, Arenskaya's fury ebbed.

"In the meantime," said Dourakova, blinking back her own tears, "control your behind."

"And so," Stroganoff told the sandy man, "to the opening night."

The opening night.

The Boris Goudonov was one vast flutter of programmes. The audience rocked on its feet, glittering, glowing, and acclaiming. Grand Duchesses forgot themselves and not a monocle remained in place.

"Dourakova! Dourakova! Dourakova!"

A great ballerina was restored to her own.

"Dourakova! Dourakova! Dourakova!"

Grisha had done his job well.

In a box Prince Volkonsky tapped Teleyakov on a sulky shoulder.

"You should never have allowed her to leave us," he said for the eleventh time that evening. "After all," he argued, "what are a few insults from a dancer."

Above her flowers Dourakova bowed, smiled, and blinked back her tears. And the house would not let her go.

"Dourakova! Dourakova! Dourakova!"

In the wings Natasha and her mamoushka stood listening.

"Six curtains," said Natasha. "Six curtains."

" . . . Seven," said the mamoushka.

" . . . And eight," said Natasha, " . . . and nine."

" . . . And ten," said the mamoushka.

"I can't bear it," sobbed Natasha. She fled to her dressing-room.

" . . . And eleven," shouted the mamoushka after her.

"And that night the Students carried Dourakova shoulder high all the way to the Cubat," Stroganoff told the sandy man. "And me," he laughed, "I was a student, too." He rubbed his shoulder reminiscently.

The Cubat was crowded out. And when the orchestra played Lac des Cygnes to welcome the ballerina's entrance, the world of fashion stood up to cheer.

And Grisha nowhere in sight.

It took Stroganoff a quarter of an hour to steer his star past the tables insisting on toasting her. And when they reached the forty couverts of their own company, Arenskaya came forward and kissed the great ballerina on the cheek.

"You were right," she said. "You are Dourakova."

"And Natasha?" asked the sandy man.

"Natasha looked radiant," said Stroganoff. "And she presented Dourakova with the diamond bracelet, and she embraced her and she embraced me. Never would you have guessed to look at her that in her bag was a letter to Paris she had written but a few moments ago." Stroganoff looked at the window. "To Diaghilev," he said.

Chapter Twenty-one

𝔄 MADDENING morning at the Maryinsky.

Kchessinskaya had left for Paris to join Diaghilev. Measles had broken out in the school. Once again Pavlova was talking of forming her own company. And now, to crown it all, a crested command from Tzarskoe Selo.

Dourakova! The Emperor would pick this morning to pick Dourakova!

Teleyakov signed to his secretary.

"Send for the man from Omsk," he said distastefully.

      *   *   *

A wonderful morning in Theatre Street. The man from Omsk strolled down it wondering how long it would take him to own the place. The Director of the State Theatres had sent for him—no doubt to ask his advice. Well, he would have plenty of suggestions to make. There was room for improvement at the Maryinsky. That patch on the carpet in the vestibule, for instance. Were they going to offer him a directorate? On the whole he thought he might accept.

"M'sieur, your carte d'entrée?"

Stroganoff flourished it. "See," he said, "to-day I do not have to offer you the little bribe." But all the same, he passed the sentry five roubles.

The sentry stared after him. It was not the same sentry. But Stroganoff was already strolling towards the classroom.

Class at the Maryinsky.

Preobrajenska, Egorova, Trefilova. And a lot of others.

"Pas mal," said Stroganoff indulgently. "Pas mal du tout." He looked around. "No Pavlova! You should not allow her to do

541

this," he told the about-to-overboil maestro. He ran a finger along the mantelpiece. "Clean," he said surprised. He sauntered out.

A secretary hurried up. "Prince Teleyakov is waiting," he murmured behind his hand.

"I will be up in a moment," promised Stroganoff, gazing out of the window at the regimented geraniums beneath. "Ah," he sighed, "if I could but get my girls in line like this. Who is your head gardener, my friend?" he enquired.

*　　*　　*

"Come in," said Teleyakov unnecessarily.

"Bon jour, mon ami," said Stroganoff with warmth. He looked round the walls. Not enough photographs and none of them signed. Yes—plenty of changes to make!

"Sit down," said Teleyakov too late. "Cigarette," he offered only just in time.

"I thank you," said Stroganoff. He inspected it. No monogram!

"Vladimir Alexandrovitch," said Teleyakov, "you are no doubt surprised that I have sent for you."

"Surprised?" Stroganoff tasted the idea. "No," he decided, "I am not saying that I am surprised. Is it not natural that one impresario should seek the advice of another? Now that I am the success all day long, people ask for my advice. And the little loan," he remembered. "The advice I give them."

"Indeed," said Teleyakov.

"Why only yesterday," said Stroganoff, "the Grand Duchess ask me to approve her mayonnaise and poof, suddenly I am in the kitchen and the French chef is very cross. And this morning he leave for Paris." He passed on to happier topics. "You have slept well—no?"

Teleyakov inclined a slightly bewildered head.

"Me, I do not sleep at all," said Stroganoff. "First I am not in bed till five and then I have the troubles marital, and as well as this there are the many problems that the successful impresario must consider each day."

"You're telling me," looked Teleyakov.

"I am the success you assure me," said Stroganoff. "Entendu! But this does not settle everything and my finance," he admitted, "is still the rickets. You like to hear about my overhead?" he offered.

"It is fantastic I am sure," said Teleyakov dryly. Would he never be permitted to come to the point?

"And yet we economize everywhere," said Stroganoff. "The water in the fountain it play in the intervals only."

"Ah," said Teleyakov. He made a note.

"The business is enormous," said Stroganoff, "but so are the debts, and the profits they must go to pay for the lean years."

"Years?" said Teleyakov.

"Months, weeks, days," said Stroganoff. "Why you quibble?"

Teleyakov raised a protesting hand. "M'sieur," he said, "shall we come to business?"

Stroganoff spread himself more comfortably in his armchair. "But it is for this that I am here," he assured Teleyakov. "Time, as my little grandfather says, is money—may he live for ever. And now I am all attention." He sighted a portrait on the wall. "Who is that?" he asked.

"His Imperial Majesty," said Teleyakov coldly.

"Sir," said Teleyakov, "you are a very obstinate man."

It was half an hour later. Teleyakov partly by mesmerism, and partly by lung power, but mainly by Russian tea and pirojki, had got Stroganoff silent for long enough to state his business.

"The Tzar has commanded that the dancer Dourakova appear at Tzarskoe Selo. He has not," said Teleyakov warmly, "commanded your company."

"It is implied," said Stroganoff. He munched. "A ballerina does not appear without a company."

"The Maryinsky theatre can supply all the dancers required," said Teleyakov. "It has done so for more than a century."

"But it cannot supply Dourakova," said Stroganoff unmoved.

"She is under contract to me." He looked at the empty plate. "Finished," he said sorrowfully.

With superb self-control Teleyakov rang for more.

"Vladimir Alexandrovitch," he said. "Think very carefully. It is a great privilege for you, a provincial, with but one season in the capital, to be permitted to present your star at Tzarskoe Selo. Do not be too obstinate or," he lied, "I can easily suggest to the Emperor that he ask someone else."

"If you can do this," said Stroganoff, quaking inwardly but bluffing hard, "then I suggest that you go to work at once, for," he dug his chin in the air, "Dourakova goes to Tzarskoe Selo with my company or she goes not at all. Ah—the pirojki!" He stretched out a hand.

Teleyakov looked at the munching figure. "You are as obstinate as Diaghilev," he declared, "and like Diaghilev you will have to learn your lesson."

Stroganoff shivered.

"But for the moment," said Teleyakov, "you get your own way. Take your confounded company to Tzarskoe Selo." Just in time he snatched the last pirojki.

"Cabbage!" he snorted.

A maddening day.

"And so that night after the performance," Stroganoff told the sandy man, "I call the company on the stage for the announcement tremendous. . . ."

"My children," said Stroganoff. "Have I done well for you?"

A chorus of acclamation arose from the assembled Omskites.

"Papa Stroganoff!" "Papa Stroganoff!" "Well done!"

Stroganoff blushed and beamed and swelled out and blew his nose and opened wide his eyes. To be acclaimed as the father of a ballet company at the age of twenty-seven—this was indeed an achievement!

The meeting was being held on the dismembered vastnesses of

the stage of the Boris Goudonov, with only a very sleepy wedged-in-the-corner elephant and a yawning of stage hands looking on.

"The Tzar!" breathed Katusha.

"Tzarskoe Selo," marvelled Little Igor. "Me—at Tzarskoe Selo."

"It will not be so big as the Palace Buckingham," said Kashkavar Jones, "which," he remembered, "is built of solid gold so the sentries have to guard it day and night."

"The Company Stroganoff at the Emperor's summer palace," gloated Nevajno's best friend. "Hurrah!". He thought of something. "No scheques," he said warningly.

Nevajno stopped beaming.

"A command performance for Dourakova," said Dourakova. "I thank you, Vladimir. It was well arranged."

"The credit, my darling, goes to you," said Stroganoff gallantly. "But me also," he hurried on, "I have done my share. Who was it brought the company from Omsk?" he demanded. "Me! Who was it kept the faith burning bright when all looked dark? Me!" he chanted. "Who was it who beg, who borrow, and who keep the credit good? Me!" He thumped his chest "And when everybody say this man from Omsk is the kaput, who was it persuade you, my darling," he turned and beamed on Dourakova, "to join us?"

"Dumka," said Dourakova.

"Me!" gloried Stroganoff. "And who is now the most successful impresario in the capital with the back salaries nearly paid off? Me!" he triumphed. "Me!"

"Papa Stroganoff. Papa Stronganoff!" cheered the company.

From the dim recesses of his childhood memories Kashkavar Jones burst into song.

"For he's a jolly good sparrow," he carolled.

That night it was Stroganoff who was chaired to the Cubat.

"But before all this happen," Stroganoff told the sandy man, "Natasha comes to see me in my office."

"Stroganoff," said Natasha, "I have something to tell you."

s

With some difficulty Stroganoff prevented himself from embracing her. His little wife and such wonderful news he had to give her! But no, he remembered. An intransigeant member of his company.

"What can I do for you?" he said formally.

Natasha passed him a letter. "It is from Diaghilev," she said. "He has enclosed my fare to Paris."

"So," said Stroganoff. He put on his spectacles.

"It is not that I want to leave you, Vladimir," said Natasha embarrassed. "You do what you can. But my career . . . With you, instead of going forward it is going back."

Stroganoff put away his spectacles. "Little idiot," he said, "is it 'going back' to dance at Tzarskoe Selo before the Tzar?"

"Tzarskoe Selo!" Natasha was confused.

"Oui," said Stroganoff. "The Ballet Stroganoff dances for the Tzar."

The colour came into Natasha's cheeks. "But this is wonderful," she began. "Vladimir . . ." She stopped.

"I congratulate you," she said. "It is a great thing for the Ballet Stroganoff. But what difference can it make to me? It is Dourakova who will dance before the Tzar. Stroganova, she will support Dourakova."

"Bien sûr," said a brisk voice from the doorway.

Dourakova came in. She beamed at Stroganoff and put an arm round Natasha. "And very prettily she will support her, too," she said.

"Mademoiselle Stroganova is leaving the company to join Diaghilev," said Stroganoff in what he hoped was an icy voice.

"What nonsense is this?" said Dourakova. "And at such a moment!" She settled herself comfortably in Stroganoff's chair. "Listen, my child. You have been loyal to the company through the bad times—stay now and enjoy the good."

"Good!" said Natasha. "For whom?"

"But for all of us," said Dourakova. "For me, for you, and for our dear Vladimir, who kills himself for love of you."

Stroganoff tried to look like an impresario. But he only looked like a husband.

"For all of us," he echoed.

"For you, Vladimir, yes," said Natasha. "For Dourakova certainly. Dourakova will get the diamond cipher from the Tzar. But Stroganova," her lips were thin, "Stroganova will not even get her six curtains."

"Curtains?" said Dourakova. "What is this about curtains?"

"My life is a nightmare for her six curtains," exploded Stroganoff. "They break my marriage and they spoil my company—her six curtains. It would take a book to explain about her six curtains. But enfin," he told Dourakova, "she will not be happy until she has her six curtains and at Tzarskoe Selo she sees no hope, so she goes to Diaghilev. Bon," he said exhausted. "So be it. I have wept too much already." He folded his arms.

But Dourakova only smiled. "Then she shall have her six curtains," she said. "Why not?" She patted Natasha's shoulder. "Do not worry, my little one—we will arrange it."

Natasha seemed unable to believe her ears. "Six curtains at Tzarskoe Selo! You are not teasing me?"

"No, no," said Dourakova. "You shall have them."

Six curtains at Tzarshoe Selo. Natasha looked at Dourakova. She looked at her suddenly hopeful husband. She burst into tears.

"There, there," said Dourakova. "You do not have to thank me." She patted the weeping back. "You are very pretty and we will find you a solo not too difficult, and, enfin, six curtains it is not so many. I," she decided, "will have sixteen."

"Sssh," said Stroganoff urgently.

"I am so happy the night my company chair me to the Cubat," Stroganoff told the sandy man. "The Tzar commands my Ballet, my wife does not go to Diaghilev, Almire gives me the best table in the room, Pavlova bows to me," he looked at the portrait with tears in his eyes. "Teleyakov nods. And the band it play 'The Conquering Hero from Omsk' . . .

It was three o'clock in the morning. Someone was tapping at Stroganoff's bedroom door.

"Qui c'est," called Stroganoff urgently.

"It is me," said a diffident little voice. "Natasha. Vladimir—can I come in?"

Stroganoff tumbled out of bed.

"Un petit moment," he called from one side of his mouth. "The other door," he hissed from the other side of his mouth. "Quick! Quick!"

The newest little choryphée scuttled.

"And next morning," Stroganoff told the sandy man, "I have a new pair of cuff links. A present from Natasha. See I wear them still." He shot his cuffs. "And in my ears I hear Diaghilev whistle for his fare all the way from Paris."

Chapter Twenty-two

"AND now," said Stroganoff, "we come to the cornerstone of my career. Pancakes! Delicious!"

The sandy man looked at him.

"Pancakes from the Tzaritza," explained Stroganoff. "Served with her own hands on a gold plate just as though we were the Maryinsky. I have one still," he said reverently.

"What?" exclaimed the sandy man.

"It is the souvenir," said Stroganoff. "Nevajno omit to give his back. The gold plate," he explained.

"Snitched it," said the sandy man.

"Not at all," said Stroganoff warmly. "Nevajno is a genius. He does not snitch, he omits only to give back." He flicked his ash on to the desk. He looked at it. "Where," he demanded, "is my silver ash-tray?"

"Your genius put it in his pocket," said the sandy man.

"Aie! My solid silver presentation in Nevajno's pocket," cried Stroganoff. "I must stop him quick before he take it out by accident at the pawnbrokers."

He lifted the receiver and spoke furiously in Russian. The receiver spoke back.

"It is all right," said Stroganoff, hanging up. "Arenskaya she go chase him. But the trouble I shall have to get it back from Arenskaya. . . . No matter." He dismissed the subject. "Where were we, my friend . . ."

"Pancakes," said the sandy man.

"You smile, my friend," said Stroganoff, "but the pancakes were the most important part of any presentation of the Ballet at the palace. The pancakes and the gold watch for the dancer and the Tzar's initial in a diamond cipher brooch for the ballerina. My friend," Stroganoff sighed, "they say many evil things of our poor dead Tzar, but to the Ballet he was the little father. There is a ballet in Leningrad now and it dances for the people, and it is a very good thing that the people should see the ballet and I would be the last to say anything against it, in fact, I dream that one day my company will dance there, too. But it will not be the same thing, my friend, it will not be the same thing at all." He looked at Pavlova's portrait and it seemed as though she were mourning with him because something had gone from a world where there was no Tzaritza to serve pancakes to the Ballet with her own hands.

"Stalin is a great man," said Stroganoff, "and all of us are learning to love him. It will give me great pleasure that he will come to my box and watch the ballet and maybe send for me. But," he faced it, "I do not see him giving out the pancakes on golden plates."

He blew his nose.

"Yes," he said, "our Tzar was the father of his ballet. And whether he was in his winter palace or his summer palace or at any other palace, he would send for the dancers he wished to see. Sometimes it was the great stars of the State Theatre, sometimes it was the little children studying in the State schools, sometimes it was a foreign ballerina who had come to the capital, and once it was the Ballet Stroganoff. This they cannot take from me." He thumped the desk. "Whatever the critics say of my ballet, they cannot take from me that once I am sent for at Tzarskoe Selo. Me!"

The sandy man maintained a tactful silence.

"My friend," said Stroganoff, "in this country you, too, have the many emotions when your King send for you at the Buckingham Palace or the Castle Windsor. The glory is perhaps the same, but the costume," he raised his hands, "is very different."

"Ah, well," said the sandy man.

"My company at Tzarskoe Selo," transported Stroganoff. "My friend, you have watched your little debutantes going to make their curtseys to your King. The anticipations, the preparations, the palpitations! My friend, I tell you, my whole company it is the little debutante."

The palpitations!

The Company Stroganoff was one mass of curling irons, smoothing irons, goffering irons, and all sorts of other irons—all of them in the fire. Never had there been such a profusion of preparation. Never had so many dancing daughters had their faces slapped by so many *énervés* mamoushkas. Kashkavar Jones, that staunch Anglomane, had dwindled Tzarskoe Selo to a lodge in Windsor Park while madly brushing his tunic, Little Igor had gambled all night to win back his overcoat, only to find that its last winner had cut short the cuffs, and Stroganoff was even now standing in front of a mirror tying and retying his white butterfly in a mounting wail of self-criticism.

"Son of my son," said Moisha, "the Tzar will not be looking at your tie."

"We cannot be certain of this," said Aliosha. He pushed his son to one side, stood in front of the mirror, and twiddled.

"When I used to go to Tzarskoe Selo," said Moisha, "I did not even trouble to change my costume." He shook his head at his carnation.

"Little grandfather," said Vladimir, "this is the first time you go in by the front door."

The little grandfather hobbled to the mirror and pushed his son out of the way. He, too, twiddled.

The carriages of the Tzar await!

They had drawn up outside the Boris Goudonov, the outriders slithering, the coaches clattering, the harness bells ringing—an impressive formation, the horses with the sheen that only a royal stable can give and the uniforms of the postillions glittering in the setting sun.

"They're here!" An excited mamoushka ran out on to the steps and ran in again.

"They're here!" Masses of people ran out on to the steps and ran in again.

And now the Ballet Stroganoff proceeded to transfer itself, encouraged by the advice of every small boy in the neighbourhood. First the heavy baskets of costumes and the harps. Then the choryphées to the rear carriages with here and there a mamoushka, carrying a wicker basket with personal props—tinsel roses, false curls, and every ballet shoe she could lay her hands on. Then the soloists, Arenskaya swinging her hips and Natasha, an angel from an Easter cake. Escorting them No Nijinsky, very pale and quiet, and Kashkavar Jones, talking loudly of King Edward's marriages of gold and rubies, and Little Igor, trying to keep his wrists in his sleeve.

Then Aliosha, Moisha, and Natasha's mamoushka in a state of temporary truce.

"Old woman," trebled Moisha. "If I were a horse I'd eat that hat."

Very temporary.

A carriage for Dourakova and her roses. Somewhere between the blooms the bald dome of Stroganoff, shining as pink as any of them.

If only Diaghilev could see him now his cup would be full and a gold cup at that.

A horseman came jogging into the square. He was covered with medals. On closer inspection he turned out to be General Dumka.

"Courage, mon vieux," he called. "Bonne chance, mes amis. I will be with you in the audience." He reined himself nearer to Dourakova's carriage. "But in order to do this," he explained, "I must start."

His horse nodded, and still together they jogged happily away.

And now the very last straggler clambered into her carriage.

The head coachman waved his whip, the outriders shot away. Chased by the furiously twinkling feet of every small boy in the neighbourhood, the procession moved off.

"My darling," Dourakova's small hand stole into Stroganoff's podgy one. "My darling, you will hardly believe this but," said the great ballerina, "I am feeling very nervous."

"You will hardly believe it," said her impresario, clutching her fingers tightly, "but me, too."

"You will hardly believe it," said the Cheer-Leader to Nicholas Nevajno, who wasn't listening, "but I am very nervous. To lead the cheers when one has no claque to instruct but only generals, who cannot be trusted not to applaud everyone—this is a project very delicate."

"Divertissement!" said Nevajno, which was all he had been allowed to devise. "Pfui!"

"For Doura it is simple," said the Cheer-Leader. "She has but to dance and her responsibility is at an end."

"Divertissement!" said Nevajno. "I offer Vladimir my new

choreographic conception, 'The Revolution,' very realistic—but Vladimir he say 'Wait for it.' "

"And six curtains for Stroganova," said the Cheer-Leader. "It is an order. But how I am to execute it only the good God knows. If He does," he doubted.

"I have brought with me my scheque book," said Nevajno bleakly, "but I do not hope to find the heart to bring it out. . . ."

*   *   *

In the Gold Room at the Summer Palace they had erected a stage. Its crimson curtain bore the Royal cipher and the proscenium arch held the Imperial Eagle's outstretched wings. But what was going on behind it closely resembled what went on behind any other proscenium just before a performance—Catastrophe and confusion. Exhaustion and hopefulness. And worse.

For it is easy enough to chase off an ordinary small boy, who has managed to insert himself into the wings of a theatre and is taking an active interest in the preparations. But it is much less simple when the small boy happens to be the heir to the throne of Russia.

"Shoo, Highness," said Vladimir Stroganoff. "Shoo," he added pleadingly.

"Highness," begged Aliosha. "Where is your nurse?"

"Don't know," said the Tzarevitch. "Don't care." He poised a nail on a plank and reached for a hammer.

"Little boy run away," trebled Moisha. "Highness," he remembered.

A nurse came rushing across the stage, snatched the Tzarevitch from the nail, and held him to her brocaded bosom.

"Highness—thank God I was in time." She turned on the Stroganoffs. "You should be under arrest," she snapped. "The lot of you. Nails indeed! Don't you know what happens if his Highness cuts himself?"

She tucked his Highness under her sturdy arms and waddled off, suffering his kicks with a detachment that could only speak of long practice.

The Stroganoffs groaned. They knew what would happen if his Highness cut himself. The whole of Russia knew that the Tzarevitch would bleed to death, that the doctors could do nothing, that only one man in all the land could master the child and stop the flow of blood with his blessed herbs.

Rasputin.

The Stroganoffs mopped their brows. Practically on their way to Siberia!

*   *   *

The Gold Room at Tzarskoe Selo was gold. So was the throne. Even the chairs were backed by golden eagles. The ceiling was encrusted with semi-precious stones, the pillars were amethyst and amber, and the great candelabras rivalled anything that could be found in Versailles.*

And in this room the guests began to assemble—so much blue blood trapped out in so much bejewelled splendour! Princes and Dukes (for there were none of lower rank save the Foreign Ambassadors and Embassy riff-raff), wearing ceremonial uniforms, and Princesses and Duchesses in the bejewelled brocades of their ancestors with stiff resplendent head-dresses, moving to their inherited places to form two long shining lines, awaiting the entry of the Emperor in a perfection of etiquette on which what sun would ever dare to set? How could anything on the other side of the footlights equal what was going on before them?

" 'Pon my soul," said Bingo Haymarket, the young attaché to the British Ambassador, "and they told me the beggars were savages."

"So they are," said the British Ambassador, his face not moving a muscle.

The lines shivered and glinted like steppe-land corn in the sun and the wind. Princesses and Duchesses sank to the ground. Ambassadors and attachés inclined their heads. The little father of all the Russias was coming in.

Tzar and Tzaritza advanced to the throne. Behind them was

* Now buy the film rights!

Rasputin, with unkempt hair, and food-stained tunic, his hands two dirty claws.

"Well, I'm damned," said Bingo Haymarket under his breath. Suddenly he felt homesick for Sandringham.

*　　*　　*

The lights in the chandeliers faded away. The footlights glowed up. The first bars of Tchaikowsky swept through the room.

It might have been a real theatre.

Behind the curtain the collective stomach of the Stroganoff Ballet Company turned over.

"The rest is with God," said Vladimir Stroganoff. He sat down on a packing-case beside his father and his father's father.

"My son," said Aliosha heavily. "I am wishing I was in Omsk where there is only Abram to say we stink."

"Be silent, both of you," said the little grandfather. He put on his hat and muttered a prayer in Hebrew. If anything went wrong now it would be his fault for sipping that glass of tea on Yom Kippur.

The overture was nearing its end. On the stage a bunch of turning-over stomachs had sorted themselves into a graceful group. How cold they were! How their outstretched arms trembled. If only this were Omsk!

In the wings Natasha's stomach sank into her toes, rose to her throat, then sank again. But the stomach of Arenskaya pulled itself together, though her knees went on shaking.

"Come," she said. "We are not frightened—us! Look at Doura," she exhorted. "See how calm she is!"

The calm Dourakova forced her knocking knees to carry her over to Natasha.

"For once I envy you, my child," she said. "You are dancing first, and it will be the sooner over."

The curtain went up.

On the stage shivering arms stiffened, quaking knees became rocks. Their Tzar was looking at them!

"Bonne chance," whispered Dourakova. "Remember all that you have to do is dance."

Crossing herself furiously, Natasha's mamoushka stumbled over to the Stroganoffs.

"Vladimir," she begged. "Pray with me." She extended her hand. Vladimir grasped it. For the first time they were in complete sympathy.

The difference between a good ballet company and a bad ballet company, Dourakova had said, is that the good has learnt to conceal the terrible.

The Ballet Stroganoff had learned this lesson well. The opening ballet was a dainty affair of buttercups and daisies to the music of Mendelssohn, with Natasha as a butterfly having her day. Dourakova had resuscitated it from an older programme and Nevajno's suggestion of a spider who would eat the butterfly had been firmly waved away.

As a butterfly, Natasha had no limitations. Never a piece of Dresden china that she could not have adorned without comment, a combination of porcelain and purity that none could resist. Crouching in the musician's gallery the Cheer-Leader relaxed; this assignment was not going to be so impossible after all.

In the wings, Dourakova nodded approvingly, the Stroganoffs were swelling every moment, and the mamoushka had decided it was safe to stop praying and had started to weep.

On the stage the butterfly's day was nearly spent. She fluttered weakly but deliciously. She went into a wide spin, not too fast and getting slower and slower until at last she sank to the ground amidst the mourning buttercups and the despairing daisies and to a frightening silence.

"Dear God!" panicked Natasha.

And then the Tzar nodded approvingly and the Tzaritza clapped.

And then the Generals, who had only just managed to wait for it, applauded loudly. And then the whole Court joined in.

Radiant now, Natasha dropped a deep curtsey. The generals went on clapping. Natasha bowed and bowed.

Up in the musicians gallery the Cheer-Leader dropped his unneeded hands.

"Pfui!" he said, "I have been wasting my time."

Six curtains for Stroganova.

The first curtain was all that a curtain should be.

For one thing it came down slowly and gave the company plenty of time to line up, curtsey deeply to the Tzar, bow radiantly to the audience, and politely at one another. And the Court applauded warmly. After all, Tzarskoe Selo had sent for worse companies than this—once or twice.

The second curtain belonged to the butterfly. Natasha took it alone. The Tzaritza was only nodding approvingly, but the Tzar was still clapping.

By the third curtain the Tzar was nodding approvingly. But the generals went on clapping.

As it came down a small boy in an English sailor suit joined the Stroganoffs in the wings.

"I have come back," he announced. "Where is my hammer?" He wandered off looking for it.

"Aie!" said the Stroganoffs.

By the fourth curtain the going was heavier. For one thing the Stroganoffs were too preoccupied to help.

"Highness," pleaded Vladimir. "Not the nail. See—I have the sugar plum!" He fumbled in his pocket. Oh, why had he eaten them all?

The fifth curtain brought out the bouquets. The applause took on a fresh lease of life.

"Pretty lady," said the Tzarevitch, sighting the radiant butterfly. "I will give her some flowers." He pounced on a shield of roses due to be presented to Dourakova, dodged Vladimir's frantic grab at his blouse and ran on to the stage.

The applause stopped dead. The Tzar rose. The Tzaritza put her hand to her heart.

"Flowers for the pretty lady," said the Tzarevitch, struggling to hold up the shield so much larger than himself.

And then he dropped it and was sucking his thumb.

Pandemonium!

Doctors leapt to their feet, niankas streamed on to the stage. Generals turned pale and trembled, the Tzar was shouting and the Tzaritza was beating her breast.

The sleeping Princess wasn't in it!

Bingo Haymarket dropped his monocle. "What's going on?" he asked.

The Tzarevitch looked up. Hundreds of anxious faces swarming round. Clearly a tantrum was in order. He opened his mouth and gave of his best.

And Natasha Stroganova stood unnoticed in the middle of her flowers. Five curtains, and the butterfly's day was spent.

*   *   *

In the end Rasputin consented to attend the child, as he always did when he thought the Tzaritza had wept long enough, and he picked him up in his arms and carried him to his vast uncosy nursery, and he stopped the bleeding with his blessed herbs and he calmed the child—he was the only man in Holy Russia who could.

And after they had sent the Nianka to Siberia, and after she had pleaded herself back, only slightly perturbed, for she knew the Tzarevitch would tolerate no other nurse, and after the Tzaritza had seen her son sleeping for herself, and dried her eyes and taken a sedative, and after the Tzar had taken a little something else, and everybody had given thanks to God, the performance was resumed.

The curtain went up. The ballet went on. The Stroganoffs could breathe again.

*   *   *

The divine Dourakova in Lac des Cygnes. Her legs two tallow candles, her diaphragm a wobble. At least that was how it felt.

"I was wrong," said Vladimir Stroganoff, standing in the wings, "I will apologize to Dumka. Doura is as good as Trefilova. Better," he said magnanimously as the white wings spread, the dark head lifted and the Swan Queen took her stage.

"Doura," breathed General Dumka, transported.

Out in the Gold Room fans forgot to wave and the weight of hereditary jewels lay unnoticed on brow, neck and bosom, and only the Tzaritza thought of the Tzarevitch and wondered when Rasputin would be down again.

On the stage the gathering of swans moved, arched and posed like the drilled swans of the Maryinsky. Never would you have guessed that their lake lay in Omsk. Moonlight persisted. The swans gave way to their Queen, shaking the diamond drops from her feathers—real diamonds. Behind her the watchful richly-encrusted shadow of the Prince. But to-night no one remarked that he was no No Nijinsky. Not that he was for a moment.

And now the four cygnets, pattering and pecking, their pas-de-chats falling on the stage like lightly-shod thistledown. Each dancer out-doing her best, each out to rival Dourakova, straining for a perfection that could never be theirs, but getting nearer to it than they had ever done before. And four mamoushkas were happy women that night.

The fairy tale of tears moved to its tragic end. The curtain came down. The Tzar gave a deep sigh of satisfaction. The Tzaritza sighed, too. What could be keeping the holy little father? The sewing wench?

The music came up and the curtain came down.

Sixteen curtains!

Grisha relaxed.

Seventeen . . . Eighteen . . . Nineteen.

"Dovolno," * said the Tzar to his Generals.

Twenty.

* Enough.

"And they say my word is law," sighed His Imperial Majesty. He looked at General Dumka. "Ah, well." He joined in the clapping.

*   *   *

Divertissement.

Arenskaya was swinging a Spanish hip with verve if not precision.

"I say," said Bingo Haymarket, brought up against a background of 'Pon my souls.' "Now this is something like!"

*   *   *

Pancakes from the Tzaritza. Already they were sizzling.

But before this the presentation of the gold watches for the men and the diamond ciphers for the ballerinas.

First a blush of ballerinas for the ciphers. Then the line-up of the men.

"Nicholas Nevajno," called the Major Domo.*

*   *   *

And now the pancakes sizzling hot and bursting with cream, served by the Tzaritza sitting at the head of her table and carried along it right down to Little Igor by, with any luck, a Grand Duchess—at the worst it would be a Princess.

"At the Palace Sandringham," said Kashkavar Jones, "it is the porridge with the lumps that melt in the mouth."

And the Tzar strolled down the length of the table, talking to this one and that one, making the little jokes that his Court had heard so often. And he accepted a rose from Dourakova and sported it in his tunic, and he recognized Moisha Stroganoff, and he said, "Well, well, well!" and "How much did my little grandfather owe you?" And then he returned to the head of the table beside the Tzaritza, and he spoke to them all, and he thanked them for dancing for him, and he hoped that it would be possible for them to dance for him again, and he hoped that they would work hard and gain lustre for themselves and for Russia. And he sat down.

* But it appeared that that one, having bumped into Rasputin, was under close arrest—Schmall scheque trouble.

And General Dumka nudged the enthralled Vladimir's elbow three times, before the impresario realized he was expected to reply. And he struggled to his feet, and the long table dazzled before him, and brilliant impromptus tumbled over themselves in his mind, mixed with a reproachful incredulity at his failure to foresee this moment and prepare the words appropriate and buoyed up by the determination that his eloquence natural should still bear him creditably through.

Better make a start.

"Little Father of all the Russias," said Vladimir Stroganoff. "Little Mother. . . ." He pulled his voice down. "May you live long in this land to bless us!"

To his own astonishment he found himself sitting down. His natural eloquence had indeed seen him creditably through.

* * *

Nearly time to go home.

The Tzar and the Tzaritza had retired and most of the Court had gone with them. The occasion was over, but the glory still abided. There is nothing so uplifting as glory without tension and the Company Stroganoff was excited and relaxed. And while the mamoushkas packed, the ballerinas flirted and the men swopped little stories, and old generals, who should have been in bed, were growing younger every minute.

But Natasha, though surrounded by Generals, lacked her usual sparkle. She managed to smile and she teased them back and she parried invitations to little suppers all over the place, but underneath her near-radiance those five curtains were nagging at her.

She looked at Dourakova laughing up at Grisha. That one had made certain. She looked at her husband, perched on a piano and beaming at the whole room. Poor Vladimir. . . .

In a corner Bingo Haymarket was taking out his monocle, gazing pinkly at Arenskaya, and putting it in again.

"I say," he said. "Do you really want to go to England with me?"

"But all my life I have dreamed of it," said Arenskaya. "England! London! Piccadilly Square!" she envisaged, entranced.

Bingo blushed. You never knew with Russians.

"You'll come with me to England," he pressed. "With me," he underlined.

If Arenskaya got it, one couldn't see it.

"But, of course," she said. "Are you not a gentleman?"

From his cloud of bliss Bingo remembered. There must be no room for misapprehension anywhere. Only cads took advantage of innocence.

"You realize, my dear," he patted her pearly glove, "that when you come to London with me, I couldn't let you"—how to put it?—"meet the mater?"

"Qui?" asked Arenskaya curious.

*   *   *

Is it permitted to sing in Royal Carriages?

No matter. For on this occasion the ballet sang all the way home.

All save the little grandfather. He sat silent biting his nails.

"Little grandfather," said Vladimir. "What is the matter? Why do you not sing?"

"Son of my son," said Moisha sadly, "I am an old man. I could not remember how much the little grandfather of the Tzar, may his soul rest in peace, owed me."

"You do not remember?" said Aliosha incredulously.

Moisha shook his head. "I will not lie to you," he said. "I remember very well. But," he confessed, "my courage fail, and I say not one word to the Tzar."

"Steppe-land, my steppe-land," sang the carriages on either side.

"I am getting old," said Moisha. "I must go back to Omsk. On the business-man's train," he cheered himself up.

Chapter Twenty-three

"AND that, my friend," Stroganoff told the sandy man, "is how the Ballet Stroganoff danced for the Tzar. And there has been nothing in my triumphant career to equal that glory. And coming at the end of my first season in the capital, it crowned it with the jewel undimable and has set the standard of perfection that my company it maintain ever since." He thought of some of his performances. "Or tried to," he amended.

"You must have felt very proud," said the sandy man.

"And very happy," said Stroganoff. "And all that night my Natasha is very tender and very loving and she listen to everything that I plan for her future, and she do not call me a fool once." He sighed. "And yet, my friend, the next morning she is gone and there is only the letter she has left for me."

' . . . *I know you will think me cruel, Vladimir, but it is better so. . . .*'

A glorious morning. The sun streamed through the window when Stroganoff sat reading his letter.

' . . . *always you have done your best for me and always it has ended in nothing.*'

There was a knock at the office door. "Entrez," called Stroganoff automatically.

It was Dourakova. With her a very worried General Dumka.

"Vladimir," she said, "I must talk to you. They have asked me to return to the Maryinsky."

Stroganoff looked at his ballerina. "And what do you wish to do?"

"But to go back," said Dourakova. "What else could I wish? You understand, Vladimir . . ."

"Mais si," said Stroganoff. "I understand very well."

"I want to thank you, Vladimir," Dourakova extended her hand. "You have been a splendid colleague. You have helped me through a difficult moment." Tears came into her eyes.

"But what is this?" said Stroganoff. "You have helped me, too."

"Without you it would have taken me much longer to get back to the Maryinsky," said Dourakova.

"Without you," said Stroganoff, "I would be back in Omsk. Ah, well," he reflected, "there are worse places."

"Do not think me cruel, Vladimir," said Dourakova, "but I have to think of my career."

"Of course," said Stroganoff. "The career must come first." He nodded to himself. "The career before everything."

"I will always be grateful to you," said Dourakova.

"You can always return to me," said Stroganoff.

He rose. He kissed her hand. The interview was at an end.

But Dumka stayed on.

"You are not vexed, Vladimir?" he asked. "You do not hit the ceiling? My friend," he sat down, "you amaze me."

"What for I hit the ceiling when it fall on me?" demanded Stroganoff. "It is but natural this. When the bird it leave the nest it kick away the stepping stone. The stepping stone," he added, "it must look after itself."

"And it will," said Dumka defiantly. "Dourakova," he voiced a heresy, "is not the only ballerina in Russia."

"No," said Stroganoff.

"Courage," said Dumka. He wandered towards the door.

"Dumka," called Stroganoff. "I think we should make Dourakova the little souvenir. We owe her much. Go to Fabergé for me."

"Vladimir," said Dumka, "I love you."

He kissed him and went.

My husband:
   When you read this I shall be on my way to Paris. I do not think you will be surprised except perhaps that I go so soon.

*I have thought very long, Vladimir, but it is better so. Mamoushka
is right. There is no future for me with you and there is no happiness
for either of us.*

*I know you will think me cruel, Vladimir, but it is better so.
Always you have done your best for me, and always it has ended in
nothing. Always for you I will be the little wife first and the ballerina
afterwards, and that way, Vladimir, it will not work. To Diaghilev
I am a dancer and nothing else. If he did not think so he would not
send for me.*

*This is the end of our marriage and do not think that I do not
care—but my career must come first.*

I do not think you will be unhappy too long. It is better so.

Natasha.

P.S.—It is better so.

Stroganoff held the paper closer. Yes, it was a tear mark.

A pair of arms twined themselves around his neck. Chypre de
Coty! A large red mark planted itself on his bald dome.

"Vladimir," cooed Arenskaya. "You come with me to London?"

Stroganoff wrestled himself free. "Mais voyons," he said crossly,
"is this the moment to make to me the project amorous?"

"Not you," said Arenskaya, "me I am faithful to my Bingo."
She looked thoughtful. "Or will be."

"Bingo, Ringo—poof!" said Stroganoff. "My darling, run away
and leave me to think in peace."

"But what is this?" said Arenskaya astounded. "Do you not wish
to bring your company to London when I take so much," she
coughed, "trouble to arrange it."

"Mais qu'est ce que tu me chantes?" said Stroganoff.

"London," said Arenskaya. "England. Bingo he has ask me to go
with him."

"So you leave me, too," said Stroganoff. "Bon. Now I know."

"Au contraire," said Arenskaya. She stroked the evading bald
dome. "I agree to go, but I tell him that he must take the company
also."

The bald dome stopped evading.

"And he agree?" asked Stroganoff.

"He is very rich," said Arenskaya. "And," she eyelashed, "he can deny me nothing."

"And so, my friend," Stroganoff told the sandy man, "the Ballet Stroganoff came to London. Ah!—that Bingo Haymarket! He is the best backer I ever had. The money it flow like water till the family solicitor he put the foot down. Where," he gazed despairingly around, "shall I find such another?"

The sandy man changed the subject. "And Natasha?" he asked. "What happened to her?"

"What happens to any ballerina?" Stroganoff shrugged. "She dances for this one, and she dances for that one, and presently she has a daughter and then it is the daughter who must have the six curtains. When I meet her in Beirut after thirty-five years, it is the first thing that I hear. After that we remember the old days and we both cry a little." Stroganoff blew his nose. "Pure gold, my Natasha," he said. "I miss her very bad these thirty-five years—when I have time to remember."

Lord Streatham put a winning head into the room.

"Well?" he asked. "Settled your business? What about a drink on it?" he suggested sunnily.

"Business!" Stroganoff remembered something. "But that is what I am here to do. Where," he demanded accusingly, "is the rich one?"

Lord Streatham coughed. Stroganoff rounded on him. "What for I pay you the salary fabulous," he thumped the desk, "if it is not to bring the rich ones to this office when it is arranged?"

The sandy man shook himself into action.

"Well, Mr. Stroganoff," he said, "I've enjoyed our little chat very much. It has been," he searched for the word, "most instructive." He extended his hand.

Something hit Stroganoff. Maybe it was Lord Streatham's expression.

"It is you—the rich one?" he asked.

"Well . . ." said the sandy man.

"Ah," said Stroganoff, beaming vastly. "Why did you not tell me this earlier. Figurez vous," he told Lord Streatham, "I have been telling him all our little secrets."

"Oh, my God!" said Lord Streatham. He sat down.

Stroganoff turned to the sandy man. "You understand, of course, my friend," he said, "that all that I tell you happen long ago when my fortunes sway in the balance and the little push in the wrong direction it is the calamity and me I am at the end of my beam. To lose a backer then was a misfortune. To lose one now—poof!— there are a dozen others."

"I'm glad of that," said the sandy man.

Lord Streatham looked elaborately at the ceiling.

"Yes, my friend," said Stroganoff. "To-day it is very different. My ballet it has the prestige, the renown, the tradition. Everything it run on creased wheels, and if, from time to time, we seek the little capital, what ballet company, I ask you, is any different?"

The door opened. A green baize apron came in. It consulted a slip.

"Seventy-seven pun' ten," it announced and started tugging at the desk.

Stroganoff laughed merrily. "I forget to send the cheque," he explained. He scribbled. "And here," he dug into his pockets, "is the little something for yourself." He inspected his coppers and slid them back. "Give him five shillings," he told Lord Streatham.

"Er," said Lord Streatham.

"Allow me," said the sandy man.

From that moment he was lost.

"My friend, I embrace you," said Stroganoff, rising from his desk as the door closed behind the baize apron. "We are now the partners. The brothers blood." He did.

"Splendid, splendid," said Lord Streatham. "Let's have lunch on it."

"Wait a minute," said the sandy man. "I'm a business man."

He remembered something he had heard this morning on the subject. He blushed.

But Stroganoff had forgotten it long ago. "Even the business-man must eat," he said. "Come. You have the little lunch, with me," he underlined, "and after I take you to meet my company. The little Stroganova!" He kissed his fingers.

"Will she call me uncle?" asked the sandy man sourly.

"They will all call you uncle," promised Stroganoff. "We give for you the little party on the stage—you like that, no? Come," he linked arms.

"Wait a minute," said sandy man. "Don't rush me. Don't rush me."

"Rush you?" said Stroganoff. "Me!" He looked reproachful.

"Rush you?" said Lord Streatham. "Him!" He looked shocked.

"Now see here," said the sandy man. "I don't say I will back your ballet and I don't say I won't, but I do say that I will decide nothing until I've seen the books."

"The figures," said Stroganoff indulgently. "But of course you shall see them. You shall see them any time you ask. But at the moment, my friend," he looked at his watch for the first time that morning, "it is quarter to three et moi, j'ai faim."

"Mwoh ohssee," said Lord Streatham.

"Oh, well," said the sandy man, slipping. "But," he said warn-ingly, "I'll want to see the figures first thing after lunch."

"Bon," said Stroganoff. "After lunch."

He linked his arm. Lord Streatham linked the other arm.

They led him out.